PROLOGUE

A dusty haze hung over the little cluster of mud and brick huts just before dawn, and the smell of cooking fires filtered back to the snipers. A boy with a stick herded a few goats across stony ground to the east, trying to find something on which the animals could graze. The land was barren and bleak, like the lives of the few people who lived here. A single guard with an AK-47 walked about, trying to stay awake.

It had taken Gunnery Sergeant Kyle Swanson and his spotter, Corporal Eric Martinez, seventy-two hours since being dropped by helicopter to reach the hidden over-look position. They had humped through valleys and steep ridges, following faint trails that led them to a rough road running through the no-name village.

They had moved only during darkness, for although they wore the same sort of clothing as the locals, they obviously were quite different. Swanson was a Massa-chusetts Irishman with reddish-blond hair, and Martinez was an olive-skinned Mexican. With such distinctive faces, plus being weaponed up, they could not take the chance of being examined too closely.

They made scheduled radio checks every two hours. Swanson led the way in silence as they closed in on the road until they spotted the lights of the village in the distance. He looked at the map for a final time, smiled, folded it up, and put it into a pocket.

It was still the darkest hours of the night when they discovered the deep cave on the ridge above the village. It had an exit at the far end, which allowed them to crawl in undetected. They gathered weeds and bushes from the rear side of the ridge and stuffed them into the folds of their loose clothing to create crude ghillie suits, and became invisible in the night. They took their positions, set up the rifle and the spotting scope, and lay motionless fifteen yards back in the gloom of the small cavern.

The target was in one of those huts below them on the road that led from Afghanistan into Pakistan.

At 5:00 A.M., Martinez reported on the radio that the hunter-killer team was on station and expected the target to move soon. Swanson gave him some map coordinates, and a routine confirmation was returned. Without contradictory instructions at that final radio check, the mission was to proceed, so the snipers went black. The radio was turned off to save the battery, and the backup satellite phone was also shut down.

They would have preferred to conduct the entire operation at night to help with their escape, but the world isn't perfect in combat. A window of opportunity such as this would be open for a very short time. It had to be done now.

They ran laser ranges on every hut and worked out firing solutions on all of them, including the front door of the target hut, its single window, and the old pickup truck parked out front. There was a scramble of junk in the bed of the pickup to make it appear to be just another vehicle carrying scavenged items for resale at some bazaar.

Kyle Swanson smoothly glassed the area, the huts, and truck. The images jumped in magnification, seeming close enough to reach out and touch. He looked at the guard wandering aimlessly about. Still good.

A light came on in the window, the yellow flicker of a lantern. "We have movement," whispered Martinez.

A big man came through the door. The snipers, working from a picture, examined him closely through their scopes to get positive identification. The bearded face of Ali bin Assam was unmistakable in the brightening morning light. "It's him," said Martinez.

Ali was a top military operative of al Qaeda, one of the operational guys who planned the dirty work, then had others carry out the attacks. He was responsible for a lot of innocent people being dead, and American intel had picked up his scent after a suicide bomb attack in Baghdad had misfired a week earlier. Swanson and Martinez were assigned to hunt him down and kill him.

Now Swanson laid the crosshairs of his rifle on the dark figure.

"I see the target," said Martinez. He quickly glanced at the logbook. "Four hundred eleven meters to the doorway."

"Wind?" Swanson asked softly.

Martinez looked at the smoke drifting over the hut. "Two minutes left."

Swanson fine-tuned until Ali bin Assam filled the scope. "I'm holding center mass."

"Roger. On scope."

The terrorist looked up at the brightening sky and seemed pleased with the coming of morning. The new day held the promise that he would soon be safe in the tunneled sanctuary of Pakistan's forbidding Tora Bora mountains. He raised his big arms and stretched, his back bending.

"On target," said Swanson as he took up the slack on the trigger.

"Fire when ready."

Swanson exhaled and gently pulled straight back on the trigger, and the long rifle fired. The 7.62 mm bullet tore through Ali just left of center, ripped through vital organs and arteries, and took out a chunk of the heart. He staggered back and collapsed against a dirty wall as blood poured out of him.

The guard stared down in surprise at his fallen leader, and Swanson turned the rifle on him, jacked in a new round, and hammered the gunman with a chest shot. The body crumpled to the ground, where it quivered briefly like a piece of Jell-O.

"Two hits," Martinez confirmed. "Two targets down."

To make sure, Kyle Swanson put another round into Ali's head.

The shots echoed across the little valley, but no other fighters emerged from the huts, and no return fire came searching for the snipers. In this harsh land of easy death, no one wanted to get involved in whatever had just happened, and they all stayed inside except for the little boy, who had abandoned his goats and taken off running. They let him go.

Martinez backed out of the rear entrance of the cave

and ran down to the fallen targets while Swanson covered him. He opened a kit containing test tubes, snipped a hair sample from Ali, and shoved a long cotton swab to the back of the dead man's tongue for a saliva sample. He bottled them both and locked them in the small box. The DNA would be used later for positive identification.

When he was clear, they started to hump back to a flat area about 800 meters away, where the daylight extraction could be done by a Black Hawk helicopter accompanied by a pair of Apache gunships. There was no need for secrecy now, just speed. The jig was up and the snipers had to get out of there.

Martinez turned the radio back on and gave the map coordinates to call in the birds, but a raspy and angry voice broke into his transmission. "Where have you been?" the voice demanded. "We've been trying to get you for the last thirty minutes! Abort the mission. Say again, abort the mission!"

Martinez stared in shock, but Swanson winked at him and grabbed the receiver. "Too damned late! Mission accomplished."

"Fuck!" There was panic in the disembodied voice. "You gave us the wrong coordinates on that village. You were on the wrong side of the border. *Fuck!* Choppers are inbound. We'll deal with this when you get back." The transmission was terminated.

Swanson handed the receiver back to Martinez. "Let's go home." They set out in a trot down the ravine toward the landing zone.

"Gunny, we in trouble?"

"Eric, you just remember we took out a real bad

motherfucker today. We may get some shit for it, but when they quit shouting, old Ali's still going to be real dead, and that's a good deal. He was a worthless piece of shit who had a lot of American and Iraqi blood on his hands. Anyway, we can't unshoot him, can we? Can't change a thing. I'll take any blame, but my guess is they will just bury it. The CIA never admits mistakes."

"Did you know we were on the wrong side of the border?" They heard the buzz of the approaching choppers, and Swanson popped a smoke grenade to signal their location.

"I was always lousy at map-reading," Swanson grinned. "That bastard needed killing and now he's dead. That was the job. Fuck the border."

1

The Boatman stood waiting in the cold fog, a ragged apparition resting against a long oar that disappeared into the black water. He smelled of death, and his robe pulsed in the stiff wind. "Do you have another one?"

"No. Not this time." Kyle Swanson recognized the five silent passengers seated in the low craft, for he had brought them all here, one by one. They stared at nothing, with empty and lifeless eyes, and did not know him.

"Then I still have an empty seat," said the Boatman. "Will you furnish someone else soon?"

"I don't know. Probably. Maybe not." Over the Boatman's shoulder, he saw tongues of fire raging along the far shore. "No."

The spectral figure shook its head and exhaled a foul odor. "I cannot leave with an empty seat."

"Yeah. Okay." Swanson looked about, but there was no one else around. He carefully put down his fully loaded M40A1 sniper rifle, unsnapped the web gear, and let the pack fall away. He took off blocks of C-4 explosive and tossed them aside. Two razor-sharp knives, gleaming blades streaked with blood. A silenced 9mm pistol. A sawed-off shotgun. An M-16 and an

AK-47 and a Claymore mine and its clacker. Smoke, fragmentation, and thermite grenades. A small satellite radio. All the tools of the sniper's trade. He wanted to hold onto something. "Can I keep my boots?"

"You will have no need for boots, but it does not matter."

"They're comfortable. I just got them broken in good."

"Keep them." A favor. Bare, cracked teeth showed in the skull. The Boatman usually had little to say, but he and Kyle Swanson had known each other for a very long time.

Swanson took off his boonie cover and put it on top of the stack, tucking it so that the eagle, globe, and anchor emblem of the United States Marine Corps remained visible. Then he removed the plastic-laminated photograph of a beautiful young woman with dark hair and eyes, kissed it, and placed it on the pile.

"Is there anything else?"

"No."

"Very well." The Boatman extended a long, bony hand. Swanson grabbed it for support as he stepped aboard and took a seat among his latest five kills. Ali bin Assam, looking gray and with a big hole through him, was beside him.

Swanson felt the small vessel rock gently as the Boatman shoved off, pushing hard on the oar to begin the passage across that black river to whatever was over there where the flames danced along a brimstone beach.

At least I still have my boots, he thought. At least I still have my soul.

Then the hand grabbed his shoulder.

2

"Kyle! Let's go, lad. Time to do some shooting." Sir Geoffrey Cornwell pushed gently on Swanson's shoulder, awakening him with a start. As a former colonel in the British Special Air Services, Jeff understood that warriors sometimes have dreams, and his keen gray eyes beneath bushy brows studied the sniper, who had been twitching in his sleep.

Swanson blinked in the bright sunshine that made the Aegean Sea glow like burnished copper. The boat was rocking gently, but this was not a death cruise. The fucking Boatman didn't get him this time. Instead, he was safe aboard the *Vagabond*, one of Jeff's favorite toys. One hundred and eighty feet long and twenty-nine feet wide, the yacht was as sleek as a needle and carried five luxurious cabins and a crew of eleven, plus a full-time captain. A pair of 3,240-horsepower engines thrummed quietly somewhere below the polished teak decks.

Swanson yawned. "Okay," he said. "Let me wash up and grab something wet to drink and I'll be ready." His mouth was dry. "Go tend your flock. Five minutes." Jeff smiled and slapped him on the back and returned into the air-conditioned main cabin where three venture capital money men, two Americans and one Brit, were having drinks, and resumed promising them an opportunity to buy into a river of gold. When Jeff retired from the SAS, he had made a quick fortune as a consultant to defense industries, then raked together an even bigger pile of money by designing, producing, and selling high-tech weapons on his own. At the age of sixty, he had a knighthood for his outstanding, although undisclosed, services to the Empire, a Bill Gates-size checkbook, and better hair than Donald Trump.

Kyle Swanson got up, stretched, adjusted his bathing suit, and walked to the hot tub area.

Jeff's wife, Lady Patricia, was in a lounge chair. She wore a big white straw hat that provided a circle of shade that protected her face. She was drinking neat whiskey and smoking a thin cigar as she read a Danielle Steele novel. Her shimmering blue one-piece bathing suit was covered by a gauzy wrap. Lady Pat had put up with being a military wife for years and now openly enjoyed the good life. In Kyle's opinion, she had earned it.

The venture capitalists had brought along the eye candy for the week of cruising among the Greek islands, their stunningly beautiful young trophy wives, who had been topless almost since the yacht left Naples two days ago. Now they lay bronzing on large towels beside the pool, toasting magnificent plastic breasts that gleamed with oil. Kyle wondered if there was a factory somewhere with an assembly line that stamped out these kids for rich old farts.

He sat on the edge of the hot tub, stuck his feet in the warm water, and nodded in their direction. "You ought to do that," he told his girlfriend, Lieutenant Commander Shari Towne. "You know, take off your top for a while. Looks comfortable."

"No," she said, protectively adjusting the top of her red bikini.

"You're already way out of uniform, ma'am." Her long black hair lay wet against her dark shoulders, and just looking into her black eyes made his stomach do flips, because he considered Shari to be the most delectable intelligence officer in the U.S. Navy. She had been born in Jordan to an American father and a Jordanian mother, both of whom worked for their respective governments. Shari was only six years old when her father, a young diplomat based in Amman with the State Department, was killed in a plane crash. Her mother was a public relations and tourism specialist and worked at embassy postings in Cairo, Paris, and Tokyo before her current assignment as head of the public relations department for the Jordanian Embassy in Washington.

Shari was fluent in several languages by the time she entered George Washington University and accepted a U.S. Navy commission upon graduation. It did not take long for her to land in Naval Intelligence, where, after compiling a sterling record, she was snapped up to be an analyst for the National Security Council. Her office was only a desk in a basement cubicle, but the address was still the best in town, 1600 Pennsylvania Avenue: the White House.

"Go away," Shari told Kyle, closing her eyes and leaning against the high-pressure jets that churned the water into frothy bubbles around her. She lifted her face to the sun.

"Hey," Swanson argued. "Your boobs are real! We ought to show them off."

"*We?* You don't get a vote on that. You want tits, go over there and ogle the Desperate Housewives." Her breathing rate had not increased and her eyes remained closed as she insulted him. She added, in Arabic, "Screw you."

"Screw me? Now there's a thought," Kyle replied in the same language. His smooth line wasn't working, but the evening held promise. Swanson splashed water on his face, wiped it with a soft towel, and stole a few sips from the glass of iced tea at Shari's side.

On the deck above, Jeff herded the potential investors to the railing and explained what was going to happen.

Kyle glanced at them. Soft men in shorts and bright shirts. "I gotta go to work now," he said. "Blow up some shit for Jeff's pals."

"So go," Shari ordered. She opened her eyes and gave him a smile.

Lady Pat lowered her steamy novel, peered at him above her sunglasses for a moment, and also got in a barb. "And Kyle, dear, please remember that these ladies and gentlemen are Sir Geoffrey's dear friends, important guests and investors. So do be a good boy and try not to kill anyone, at least until after dinner, would you please?"

"Does that include smartass broads, m'lady?"

3

They were far out in open water, the horizon an unbroken straight line all around. Through an optical illusion, it appeared to be above them, as if they were at the bottom of a saucer.

Swanson made his way to the broad lower aft deck, where he found a tall, thin man working beside three fifty-five-gallon drums. "Hey, Tim," he said, and opened the protective, cushioned box in which a pristine big rifle lay like a jewel. "You ready?"

Timothy Gladden had been a captain with the elite British Parachute Regiment for more than a decade, leaving the Paras only because a broken right leg did not heal properly and doctors would not allow him to continue jumping out of airplanes. He resigned his commission and launched a vigorous new hobby as a triathlete, principally to prove the British Army diagnosis wrong. There was nothing wrong with his leg, nor with his Oxford-trained brain, and Sir Jeff had hired him into the corporate side of his growing weapons development business. Once a poor farm boy in Wales, Tim was now deputy chairman.

"Of course, old boy," he said. "I'll toss in the blue barrel first, then the red and the yellow at fifteen-second intervals, steadily increasing the visibility problem. The blue one is going to present you with a very difficult shot." He thumped one barrel, which gave back a hollow clanging echo. It contained only ten gallons of gasoline, so the remaining space was packed with explosive fumes. "The captain is making a steady twenty knots and will hold her course straight whenever you are ready. Make all three shots from prone, if you will."

A section of the aft railing had been removed, and Swanson slid into the familiar position flat on his stomach and dug the toes of his deck shoes into the rubberized mat. One problem with designing a new generation of sniper rifle was that he had not been allowed to actually shoot an enemy soldier with it in a combat situation, which made all the difference. Range targets cannot think and react or shoot back, while a human being might turn, duck away, trip, or break into a run in a microsecond and spoil an otherwise perfectly good solution. This field test was designed to duplicate those sorts of unexpected movements, as the floating colored barrels would rise, fall, spin, and bounce unpredictably in the waves.

Jeff came down the ladder, his eyes bright with excitement. "The lads upstairs are primed and hungry for adventure, so don't get nervous on me now, Kyle," he said in a tight voice.

Kyle pushed the cool fiberglass stock of Excalibur, the best sniper rifle in the world, hard into his shoulder. It had been molded to fit him like a custom-made Armani suit. "Be quiet, Jeff," he said.

The aristocratic British voice repeated, "Really, there

is no pressure, Kyle. Just take your time, lad, and do it right."

He brought his eye to the scope and clicked a button with his thumb. That activated a BA229 lithium battery and engaged the heads-up display, and the scope came alive with numbers that paraded in a steady, changing readout. The range to the target, measured in meters by an infrared laser, showed in the upper right-hand corner, while digits at the top left gave the wind compensation. Barometric pressure was in the lower right, and the bottom left figures summed up all of that and gave the exact setting to dial in the scope. The weapon was doing the algorithms that he normally would have had to do in his head.

"We will be videotaping this test," Jeff said, rubbing his hands in anticipation.

It had taken a while for Kyle to become familiar with the moving avalanche of numbers, but with practice, they had become part of the background and did not distract from his concentration. He took a deep breath and steadied Excalibur in his left palm, exhaling slightly and tightening his finger on the trigger. He did not want to move in any way that might change his position. "I got it, Jeff. No pressure! Videotape! Now will you please be quiet?"

No pressure. Only that he was being watched by a line of venture capitalist vultures along the stern rail of the yacht with drinks in their hands and fat checkbooks in their pockets. If Swanson could make Excalibur sing today, they would invest millions of dollars and pounds with Jeff to build secret weapons with dream-world technology. Even so, Kyle thought, this was just dollars and cents. Pressure came in battle, when if you missed, your buddies died.

"I can't believe I'm putting the future of my entire corporation in the hands of a bloody Marine," Jeff complained.

"The SAS eats shit for breakfast," Swanson growled. "Now shut the fuck up, get this tub steady, and drop the barrels." He wiped the world from his mind and concentrated on the scope, settling into his personal cone of silence. Things slowed down, his senses increased, and background noises became whispers. He was becoming one with his rifle.

Tim Gladden said, "Trust the numbers, Kyle. Trust the numbers." He felt the big yacht, which handled like a sports car, settle into a smooth glide.

Kyle had gotten to know Jeff Cornwell while running joint special operations, and their friendship had grown tight over the years. When Cornwell had set his engineers and scientists to work designing a state-of-the-art weapon for long-range precision firing, he asked the Pentagon to loan him Kyle Swanson as a consultant periodically when he was not on other assignments, and the generals had agreed.

Swanson had loved the weapon from the moment he saw the raw diagrams, and Jeff knew how to speak sniper talk. Together with the engineers in a span of three years, they built a sniper's wet dream.

It was a very smart weapon, and fired a hand-crafted .50-caliber round that increased the power of a punch over longer distances. Developing experimental material, with Kyle and Jeff insisting on a lightweight weapon that would be easy to carry in the field, the engineers had developed a super epoxy for the stock and a special alloy for the trigger assembly. The rifle was surprisingly light, only 19.9 pounds with a full magazine, a critical factor for the man who would have to lug it around all day in combat. The normal .50-caliber sniper rifle weighs in at 37 pounds unloaded. The free-floating barrel provided space and could whip up and down when fired but not throw off the sight, which was further strengthened with an internal gyrostabilizer. The gyrostabilized infrared laser worked with a small geopositioning satellite transmitter and receiver in the stock to triangulate the precise distance between the rifle and the target. The GPS provided a further element of safety by letting a sniper know his exact position anywhere in the world. When the sniper is out there all alone, that little bit of information can mean a lot. The rifle, therefore, was more than the sum of its mechanical parts. It was an incredibly accurate weapon system that reduced the chance of a miss by at least 75 percent. In many tests, Kyle put a shot group within a half-minute of angle, an eight-inch circle, at up to 1,600 meters in daylight and 1,000 meters at night. The average human head measures ten to twelve inches. If he could see an enemy a mile away, he could kill him with a shot right to the head.

They named it Excalibur, after King Arthur's magical sword, and it was more than strong enough to end any bad guy's day.

Jeff counted down from five and whispered, "Go!" Tim pushed the blue barrel overboard and it hit the water with a loud splash. Twenty knots may not seem fast, but the twisting target rushed away from the boat, tumbling in the wake, already growing smaller. Kyle could not fire until all three were in the water. He heard the red one go over, watched it through the scope as it wiggled into the distance, and the final fifteen seconds seemed like an eternity before the yellow one splashed overboard. "You may fire in five seconds," Jeff said, and did another countdown.

He looked for the yellow barrel, but already the water had snapped it out of the frame of the scope. It was just too close, and he lowered the magnification by fine-tuning the focus ring. As he brought it back into the picture, he punched the laser button once to lock onto the target and a second time to get the range. Exactly 547 meters. That alone was amazing, since he did not have to consult any written tables of mathematics nor wait for a second man, the spotter, to come up with the information. It was all right there in the scope, and the rifle was making its own adjustments. The laser locked on and talked to the GPS system, which had a brief chat with the gyrostabilizer, and it didn't matter what the barrel did now as long as Kyle kept it in view. Excalibur automatically computed any changes and adjusted the firing solution. The barrel squirmed in the water and the rifle tracked it, numbers whirling in the scope.

"You may commence firing," said Jeff. The scope gave a microsecond flash of a bright blue stripe down one edge that meant everything was ready. Kyle gently squeezed the trigger straight back, for to press it even slightly sideways could screw up a shot.

Excalibur barked a sharp, keening sound and the

bullet smashed hot and hard into the yellow barrel, detonating the collected gasoline fumes inside like a small bomb. The container disintegrated in a loud explosion and pieces of shrapnel showered down, some almost reaching the *Vagabond*. Lady Pat was not going to be pleased about that.

Swanson was already looking for the red barrel that was somewhere on the other side of the ball of orange fire and gray smoke. Some movement contrasted with the ordinary motion of the water, and he found it out at 893 meters, about nine football fields behind the boat. This time he didn't wait for the blue stripe, but just locked on the laser and squeezed the trigger. Another explosion shook the water to prove the hit, followed by a ball of fire and more smoke as he jacked in a fresh round.

Jeff was dancing a little jig off to the side. He had stolen a look at the money men and their wives at the rail, and they were pointing and talking excitedly. "They're wetting their knickers up there," he said. Tim Gladden held a pair of big binoculars to his eyes.

But when the smoke cleared, Kyle couldn't see anything but water. The damned barrel seemed to have vanished, but he did not dare remove his eye from the scope. "I don't see it, Kyle," Gladden said.

Swanson slowly glassed the wake directly behind the boat and let the laser scan the surface, looking for something solid. The laser blinked momentarily when it found the steel surface of the bobbing barrel, and Kyle saw a little blue dot that was not much different than the color of the water, ducking and weaving behind low waves.

"There!" said Gladden. "About a thousand meters or so and off to the port side ten degrees."

The laser measured and the computer did its thing. Exactly 966 meters. Tricky-ass shot. *Follow the bouncing ball and trust the numbers.* Swanson exhaled and took up slack on the trigger and the blue stripe flashed in the scope. *Squeeeeze.* Excalibur barked in triumph and he could see the disturbed air trailing the bullet, which ate up the distance in an instant. This time everyone saw the fireball detonate before the sound of the explosion reached the boat.

"Yes!" cheered Tim. "My, what a fine shot!" It was as high a compliment as could be expected from another warrior.

"Beautiful," said a relieved Jeff. "You got them all."

Swanson lowered the rifle to a little stand beside the mat and realized that he was drenched in sweat. "Boys," he pronounced, "this puppy works."

His part of the demonstration was done. Now he and Shari could totally relax for the next ten days. Tim would run things for the next few days while Jeff wrung cash from the impressed investors. The rest of the cruise would be a treat, with opportunities to sample the local wines, food and grapes and cheese, and fire-breathing ouzo in places like Piraeus, Monemvasia, and Mykonos. The two of them planned to spend a few days alone in Venice, walk over the Bridge of Sighs, visit the Doge's Palace, slip through the canals in one of those big canoes called gondolas, and dance in the moonlight on the wet stones of St. Mark's Square. Time for fun.

4

Two mercenaries rested their elbows in pockets of loose sand and held large binoculars steady as they watched the oncoming Thursday morning traffic. Only their hands and heads, covered by desert-brown camouflage, were visible above a small hill crowned by scrub brush about ten meters from the highway between Riyadh and Dhahran in Saudi Arabia. AK-47 assault rifles were strapped across their backs and rocket-propelled grenade launchers were at their sides. Between them, a radio transmitter lay sealed in a plastic bag that protected it from sand. Everything was in place for the snatch-and-pull ambush.

They had worked through the night, digging into the gravel beside the highway. By dawn, passing vehicles had whipped up enough dirt and debris to erase almost all traces of their work. The only evidence that a bomb had been planted was a needle-thin wire antenna that stuck up six inches above the dirt.

The night had ended suddenly, and the brilliant summer sun rising behind them punished the eyes of oncoming drivers. It was hot, already in the low nineties, and sweat trickled down their faces, but they would not lower their binoculars.

"Gettin' hot, Vic," observed former U.S. Army Ranger Jim Collins. He stood six feet tall but was the smaller of the two.

"No shit, Jimbo? Hot in Saudi Arabia? You're fuckin' brilliant." Victor Logan's rumbling voice was more like a low growl. The former chief petty officer in the U.S. Navy SEALs never let Collins forget who was in charge of this Shark Team.

"Just sayin'," Collins replied, then shut his mouth and thought about the money instead. They were getting fifty thousand dollars each for this job. He wanted to talk about what he planned to do with the cash. Definitely a new truck. When they got back to the house, he would log onto eBay Motors and shop for a while.

Vic Logan and Jimbo Collins were part of an elite group of hand-picked former special ops warriors who were used only for high-risk, off-the-books jobs by a multinational private security company. Logan grinned. *If we're Sharks, then I'm a Great White and this dumbass is a fucking Hammerhead.*

The big American was pissed at everyone, including himself. He had been less than six months from retirement, with twenty years in the navy, when his career went down the toilet. The body of a badly beaten young prostitute was discovered in an alley in Naples, and the shore patrol found him passed out a block away, drunk as a skunk. Since the only witness was dead and no evidence tied him to the girl, the cops had to cut him free, but Vic Logan was through as a SEAL. They had kicked him off the teams so fast it had made his head spin. *And I hadn't done anything all that wrong!* There was not enough evidence for a court-martial, but some sea lawyers picked through his records and found enough dirty laundry for fighting, drunkenness, assault on an officer, and suspicions concerning another dead whore in Olongapo, that dirtbag town right outside of Subic Bay, to lay an Administrative Separation hearing on his ass. The AdSep ruled Logan to be morally unfit for service, which was the navy's chickenshit way to get rid of him. It took everything—rank, loss of pay, benefits, and retirement—and he was told to consider himself lucky that there was no jail time and no federal conviction.

Fuck the navy, the SEALs, and the whores, including the ones they never found. In his view, the AdSep was trumped-up bullshit. If he killed enemies of his country, he got medals. Stop a couple of whores trying to rip him off and he was framed. Within six months he hired on as a merc. This was payback.

The most difficult part of the job was waiting, and their patience was rewarded when three boxy, shiny black Hummers came into view, heading toward them like a line of big beetles.

They knew exactly who was in each vehicle. A radio update had come in moments after the convoy had departed the U.S. Embassy compound in Riyadh. Brigadier General Bradley Middleton of the U.S. Marine Corps was alone in the back of the big vehicle in the middle of the small convoy. A Marine guard was in the front seat, along with the Saudi driver.

Another armed Marine rode shotgun beside the driver of the lead Hummer, with two Saudi security troopers in the rear. The trailing vehicle had a driver and another

Saudi guard, and its passengers were a young woman Marine captain who was the general's aide, and a civilian escort from the foreign ministry.

On they came, arrow-straight along the broad road. A mile. Half a mile and coming fast. On the ridge, Vic Logan readied the little radio transmitter.

In the lead car, Staff Sergeant Norman Burroughs was glad the trip was almost done. He felt naked in the unarmored, civilian-style Hummer. Cool air-conditioning blew on his face, but he would have preferred to be sweating and uncomfortable inside a Marine armored vehicle with a .50-caliber machine gun up top. Burroughs did not like this place. Trouble just seemed to ooze from the desert sands. The Saudi guards and the driver were joking and smoking cigarettes instead of paying attention. Security was for shit. The staff sergeant tugged the brim of his hat lower, adjusted his sunglasses, and continued to stare into the morning sun as he counted off the miles back to the real world, which for him was the Marine Expeditionary Unit aboard the task force cruising in the Persian Gulf. His fingers unconsciously traced the trigger guard of the M-16 rifle propped between his knees, locked and loaded.

The driver smirked at the nervous American. Dhahran and Riyadh were the two safest places in the kingdom, and the long road between them was smooth as glass and totally safe. He had driven it a hundred times or more just in the past year, and knew that he would soon be away from this unpleasant heat, spending the day at a villa in the cooler Dhahran Hills, waiting to pick up a government official for the return trip to Riyadh in the evening.

Burroughs kept his eyes moving, looking for possible threats, but by the time he saw a glitter of sunlight bouncing off the thin wire antenna, the speed of the Hummer had taken them into the kill zone. The staff sergeant started to yell a warning, but didn't make it.

The bomb detonated with a horrendous roar, and the first Hummer catapulted into the air, flipped twice, and crashed down on its roof. The fiery wreckage skidded and ground forward on the pavement, bathed in churning smoke and flame.

When the blast wave rolled over them, Logan and Collins moved smoothly into kneeling positions with the rocket-propelled grenade launchers on their shoulders. They triggered a pair of missiles that rushed with low hissing sounds toward the last Hummer, and the car exploded in a ball of fire.

They tossed the launchers aside and ran down the slope with AK-47s in hand. Collins broke away to check the rear vehicle, while Logan opened fire on the middle Hummer, a careful fusillade that destroyed the tires, crashed into the engine, shot out the front windshield, and killed the driver and the guard in the front seat. Bullets sang in ricochets, glass shattered, and a smell of burning rubber and oily smoke oozed from the destroyed vehicle.

Jimbo Collins returned from the rear vehicle dragging the general's aide, Captain Linda Hurst, by her arm. She was dazed. Her face and short blond hair were caked with sticky blood, her ribs ached, and a leg was broken. She had barely been able to focus when she was pulled from the wreckage, and thought for a moment that she was being rescued. Instead she was jerked from the car and pulled down the road, the pavement peeling away bloody strips of skin from her legs. She was dropped at the feet of a large man wearing old blue jeans, a brown T-shirt, tan desert combat boots, and a brown scarf that masked his face. Captain Hurst could not hear her own screams, because the RPG blast had destroyed her eardrums.

"General Middleton! Get out of the vehicle right now, or I kill this bitch!" Logan pointed his rifle at the wounded and bleeding woman.

Middleton, gasping for breath in the smoke, had his pistol out, but recognized the situation as hopeless. He had seen the lead Humvee evaporate in the explosion, and when the RPGs took out the car in back, he dove to the floor for safety as his own vehicle was shot to pieces. His entire security detail was dead and all he had left was his Colt .45 pistol, while the attackers had automatic weapons, RPGs, and a hostage. Although he knew all of this, he still hesitated, because Marines don't surrender. Why hadn't they killed him, too?

A few seconds later, another burst of AK-47 fire tore into Captain Hurst's right arm and her screaming rose. Several cars that had slowed on the far side of the highway scurried away when the drivers saw what was happening.

"I SAID GET OUT OF THAT DAMNED CAR!" Vic Logan roared again.

Middleton hardly knew the young officer who lay out

there. She had been assigned as a temporary aide at the start of the trip, and had done little more than carry his briefcase in Riyadh while he talked with the Saudis. Had he been alone, he might have chosen to fight, but he could not let the kid be murdered. "All right! I'm getting out!" he called, and dropped the pistol. He opened the car door, raised both hands above his head, and stepped into the bright sun.

Jimbo Collins jerked the general's arms behind his back and expertly slapped on steel Smith & Wesson handcuffs. Once he was secured, Vic Logan casually double-tapped Captain Hurst. Two 7.62mm bullets blew off the back of her head.

The Shark Team pushed and hauled the general away from the burning pyre of the highway, over the sandy ridge, and down to where a dark green Land Rover was parked in the dry gulch. They threw him into the back seat and Logan got in beside him. Collins slid behind the steering wheel and started the engine, and the strong Land Rover surged forward in four-wheel drive.

Middleton flinched when a hypodermic needle plunged into his arm. He felt the morphine circulate through his system, and hissed through gritted teeth: "I'll kill you both."

"Shut up," said Logan. "You ain't gonna be killing nobody." He tossed the needle out of the window.

As he collapsed, Middleton's mind finally registered what he had been too busy to comprehend. The general's last thought before the morphine swept him into blackness was, *My God, these are Americans!*

5

"You are a very troubled person," said the sniper to the knight, pointing at a beautifully presented Hearts of Palm salad that was the first course of a fantastic lunch aboard the *Vagabond*. It was an old Special Forces thing. In desert survival training, with no food, you could chop down a palm tree to get at the tasty, edible centers. Anyone who endured the experience would have done it so many times that they would swear never to eat another Hearts of Palm salad as long as they lived.

"You ungrateful American! My chef will be crushed," said Jeff with an easy laugh as he pushed away his own salad. "Perhaps you would prefer a peanut butter and jelly sandwich?" Tim Gladden also passed on the salad.

The others at the table had no idea what the three military men were talking about, so Jeff steered the conversation into areas in which his business guests could glitter and glow. As if wound up mechanically, they soon were rattling on about new companies preparing IPOs, who got how much of a bonus for leading a company into bankruptcy, and who had been indicted. It was too easy to get those guys to talk about themselves. They did not include or need anyone else in their conversation about finances and the venture capital world. The ladies switched to serious relationship chatter about the breakups and marriages of supermarket tabloid celebrities, and when Lady Pat and Shari tuned in to the gossip, Jeff hauled Tim Gladden and Kyle Swanson out on deck.

They toasted with cold green bottles of Heineken beer and lit fresh cigars that Jeff vowed had been rolled on the thighs of Cuban virgins who afterward were personally deflowered by Castro himself.

Kyle said, "You know, I swear that little blonde was giving her husband a hand job beneath the tablecloth. His eyes were crossing."

"Gawd. How does one control newlyweds? She's thirty years younger than he. I hope she doesn't give him a heart attack before we can cash his Excalibur check," said Tim.

"Our bank already confirmed it," said Jeff. "If he dies, he dies with a smile, we bury him at sea and console the grieving widow." He turned to Swanson and put on his serious face. "So, what's your answer?"

"Same as always. Thanks but no thanks." The wind pulled the smoke away, toward the distant lights that marked towns along the heel of the Italian boot.

"Kyle, you are not getting any younger. You cannot do your sort of work forever."

"I like what I do, Jeff. I'm a pretty fair sniper, and somebody has to do it."

Tim spoke up. "I have news for you, old man. You are not indispensable. When you leave, another Marine will step into your place. I didn't see how Ten Para could possibly get along without me, either, but somehow they did just fine."

Jeff agreed. "The biggest hurdle is the first one, hanging up the uniform. You know it's going to happen sooner or later."

"The time isn't right. I'll know when. Not yet."

"Don't wait too long," said Gladden. "Thanks to this grumpy old man, I found a new and worthwhile career. I used to think a hundred thousand dollars was a lot of money, but with the patents and proprietary interests the company has developed, there is much, much more available. And we desperately need your help on new projects."

Jeff emptied his beer, tossed the bottle overboard, and uncapped a new one. "You and Tim and I are the only people who know everything about the Excalibur project. We had the engineers work only on specific sections. Once we finish the field trials, those guns are gold, Kyle. After that show you put on yesterday, those investors couldn't write checks fast enough. You have more than earned a share."

"I worked on it as part of my job, guys," Swanson replied. "The Marine Crotch would throw my ass in the brig if I got paid extra for it." The sideways offer had caught him off guard. They were willing to put up part of the action on the future licensing and sales of Excalibur. A fortune.

"We only bribe politicians," Gladden said. "We are just pointing out that you would be an extremely valuable asset to our company, and also that we could make it worth your while financially."

Jeff looked at Swanson like a priest at a sinner and abruptly changed the subject. "Damn it all, man, why don't you and Shari *both* just get out of the military business? I know you want to get married, but you're wedded to your jobs instead of each other. That is not good at all, lad. You must grab time before it passes you by. Anyway, I want a grandson."

"Been talking to her, have you? And you can't have a grandson by us because we're not related."

"I was speaking in general terms. A granddaughter would be just as welcome. No, we haven't spoken with her about it, although Pat has been planning the wedding for some time, something terribly romantic and worthy of a pop diva. You may not have reached the point yet where you want to make the change to private enterprise, but you will, my friend. When you do, I promise you a soft landing. We just want you to hurry up."

"You'll be the first to know."

Tim gave him his unsmiling commando look. "Maybe we have a competitor for your highly marketable skill? Has one of those dreadful PSCs come a-knocking on your door, offering some big money to the super sniper?" He was talking about private security companies, the modern mercenaries.

"Oh, hell, no. I would never be a merc. There are a ton of those jobs out there, but you can never trust them because you don't know where their loyalties really lie. They're like Doctor Frankenstein's monster, and could just as easily spin out of control. Anyway, if I kill somebody while I wear the uniform, it's okay. I don't know how that would play out if the mercs take part in combat ops."

Gladden laughed. "Oh, Kyle, you are so naïve. They're already running combat missions. Have been for years. Some PSCs have armored vehicles, choppers, and even some old jet fighters now. Bleedin' private armies, they are, for sale to the highest bidder. And with the U.S. military heading toward privatization, it's only a matter of time before they are authorized and paid to fight an entire war by themselves. It just plays better to the public if some South African merc is lost in action for a noble cause rather than the boy next door."

"If it's so great, why aren't you two in on it?" It wasn't like Jeff to pass up a good business opportunity. There were hundreds of millions of dollars in the PSC game.

Jeff shrugged. "Like you, chum. We were professional soldiers for much too long. I'm more than satisfied with my company and its products, and I'm old-fashioned enough to enjoy being in the service of my queen and country."

"So, as you Marines would say, 'Fuck the Frankensteins,'" said Tim Gladden, holding his beer aloft.

Jeff raised his bottle, too. "Fuck the Frankensteins."

Kyle Swanson touched theirs with his own. "Fuck the Frankensteins."

6

The immaculate Pilates, a Swiss single-engine private aircraft painted midnight blue with gold trim, lifted smoothly away from a dry riverbed, its powerful turbo-prop engine leaving a triangle of sand hovering momentarily in the air behind it. By the time the dust settled back onto the desert, the beautiful plane was gone, building to a cruising speed of two hundred knots while skimming no more than two hundred feet above the sand to avoid radar. In the two and a half hours since taking off from a crude airstrip, it had flown northeast from Dhahran, and then dashed out of Saudi Arabia and into Jordanian airspace without being spotted by the air defense commands of either country. It was just another private executive plane in a region that had fleets of them belonging to rich and powerful princes and sheikhs. Even if it had been seen, no one would have questioned it, nor paid it any mind. The color scheme was recognized as that of a powerful Iraqi, Ali Shalal Rassad, the Rebel Sheikh of Basra, and it was best not to be too curious about him.

A dirty truck was waiting when the Pilates landed on a macadam road outside a village, and the unconscious General Bradley Middleton was carried off the plane by his two American captors and stuffed into the rear seat of a waiting car for a ten-minute drive to a specific address. Vic Logan pulled another hypodermic needle from his kit and injected Middleton to start bringing him up from the blackness.

Dull colors, garbled words, and a sense of awkward, jerking motions blended in Middleton's drug-muddled mind. His brain could not separate the individual things happening around him, nor grasp any meaning. The only thing he felt was a pounding headache. Pain got through. Strong hands held his arms and propelled him forward. His feet would not respond; his legs were rubbery. The dragging stopped, and he was forced to sit in a chair. More words he did not understand, and a sensation of something wet cooling his face. Scrubbing hard. Words. He shook his head to clear the cobwebs of scrambled thought, with no result. Laughter. Hands worked with his clothing, tucking in his khaki shirt, smoothing his collar, straightening his tie, and adjusting the shining single star on each collar point, half-inch and centered.

Pinpoint flashes of shifting light danced at the edge of his consciousness, blinking like a field of fireflies. Then they were gone. The fireflies had flown. A smell of something rotten rose in his nostrils. Camels or goats close by.

A soothing female voice spoke English words with a lilting accent, and a gentle hand tilted his chin back. *"Here, General. Drink this. All is well. Just drink this."* A cool stream of water went across his tongue and down his throat. He gulped it in relief. Thirst. *"That's enough*

*for right now, because we don't want to make you sick.
You can drink more in a few minutes."*

His arms were tied around the back of a small chair
to keep him from falling. He sensed other people.

A moment of total silence was followed by the blazing
lights of a dozen suns, strong enough to make him
wince. He began to breathe fast, and unreasoning panic
set in, bringing a childhood nightmare of a monster,
frothing at the mouth, that chased him. He struggled
momentarily, and then settled.

When he was calm, a soft command was given and a
video camera began to record the image of the Marine
general bound to the chair, the shining single star of his
rank leaving no doubt as to his identity. A man's voice
read a statement in Arabic. The camera caught it all the
first time, but the statement was repeated just in case.
The lights went out.

Middleton felt a tiny prick in his arm as another
needle went in to return him to the dark world, then
strong hands lifted him. A fist slammed into his stomach,
doubling him over. He gasped for air, then vomited.
Another blow, and he was on his knees, being kicked to
the floor. Laughter, fading. Blackness. Pain still got
through.

The cameraman reviewed the scene to be sure his Pana-
sonic PV GS250 had done its job, and nodded in
approval. The low-light problem had been solved by
stealing a rack of huge bulbs that a road crew had been
using for night work. He plugged a USB cord between
the camera and a Dell computer and downloaded the
images and soundtrack onto a small disc, which he slid

into a protective hard plastic case and handed to the woman. She folded a written copy of the statement and dropped it and the videodisc into a common brown envelope that she taped closed. Licking it would have left traces of her DNA. In an hour, she was in Amman, Jordan, where she handed the package to the front desk clerk of the hotel that was the residence of the local correspondent for the al Jazeera television network. She walked two blocks, paused beneath a tree, and called the correspondent on a cell phone. "This is the Foreign Ministry's press office, sir. We have delivered a news release to your hotel," she said in French, cut the connection, and tossed the phone into a trash bin.

The correspondent recognized her voice, and knew this had nothing to do with the Jordanian Foreign Ministry. A confidential contact had resurfaced, one who had never given him a bad story. He hurried downstairs, retrieved the envelope, returned to his room, and dumped the contents onto his desk. After reading the statement, he watched the video. *Unbelievable!* He pulled a bottle of Jack Daniel's bourbon from a suitcase, and only after two stiff shots of whiskey did he call the busy al Jazeera newsroom in Doha, Qatar. It was two o'clock, plenty of time for the evening newscast, but he knew they would not hold the story until then. It was too important.

When it was broadcast, the sedated General Middleton was finishing a smooth hop aboard a twin-engine Cessna 421 into Syria. A Land Rover hauled him on the last leg of his journey, and he slept for fourteen hours.

7

"Good day, ladies and gentlemen. I have to brief the President in a few minutes, so let us get right to it. What's happening with this kidnapped general?" National Security Advisor Gerald Buchanan swept his gray eyes around the White House Situation Room at nine o'clock in the morning. Every chair was occupied and staff members hovered nearby. "CIA. You start."

John Mueller, the deputy director of operations for the Central Intelligence Agency, flipped open a folder branded with a diagonal Top Secret red stripe, hunched forward in his chair, and read the cover sheet that distilled the basics. "General Bradley Middleton of the Marine Corps was abducted just outside of Dhahran, Saudi Arabia, about 0300 hours this morning, Washington time. His two Marine bodyguards, his aide, and the Saudi security team were all either killed in the explosion of the roadside bomb or executed during a follow-up attack. Witnesses saw two men take the general away over a ridge beside the highway. Tire tracks led to a nearby paved road, where they could have gone either way. Al Jazeera was broadcasting the story only a few hours later. An anonymous caller to al Jazeera, after the broadcast, claimed credit on behalf of the Holy Scimitar of Allah. The Holy Scimitar, of course, is the name of the militia of the Rebel Sheikh in Iraq. The caller said the kidnappers would cut off the general's head unless all U.S., British, and NATO troops and citizens leave the Arabian Peninsula." The CIA man closed the folder and pushed it away. "The demand is obviously ridiculous, so we conclude there must be some other reason or reasons." Mueller quit speaking and crossed his arms on the big table. He had learned to keep his mouth shut when he didn't know anything.

Buchanan glared at him and swore. "Holy Jesus Christ! I heard the same thing on CNN and Fox before I came in here. Does anyone have something that hasn't been on live television? FBI? Talk to me."

"We have a team working with the Saudis on forensics. Nothing conclusive yet. It's just too early." The FBI director also knew not to go too far with Buchanan. Answer the question and shut the hell up.

The National Security Advisor ran a palm across his neatly trimmed hair and sighed. Then he removed his rimless glasses and wiped them with a handkerchief. He wanted these people to stew for a while.

"Anybody?" Buchanan snapped. "How about you, Homeland Security? NSA? DIA? Pentagon? State Department? Anything other than what al Jazeera has been showing to more than fifty million people in their part of the world? The domestic networks and cable over here are going to run it forever."

No one wanted to challenge him. Gerald Buchanan would end a career without a second thought if he detected weakness or a lack of political loyalty, and the fuse was burning on his infamous Irish temper. He unscrewed a fountain pen with a gold nib and scribbled a note to himself, closed the pen, and folded the piece of paper. Everyone wondered if their name was on it. "Ladies and gentlemen, I am not pleased. The President will not be pleased, and our countrymen will not be pleased that after spending billions of dollars to build a global intelligence apparatus, you have once again failed. I would strongly suggest that when we gather again later today, you have some facts for me. Is that clear?"

"Excuse me, Mr. Buchanan. May I?" General Henry Turner, the four-star Marine general who was chairman of the Joint Chiefs of Staff, was not afraid of Buchanan's bluster. He had seen civilians come and go through many administrations and had served them all to the best of his ability. Hank Turner was as close to untouchable as anyone in the room.

Gerald Buchanan detested him. Turner had almost as many advanced degrees as he, plus the general had a heroic reputation, could do more push-ups than a boot camp private, and had even penned a volume of poetry. Still, Buchanan enjoyed recalling that Turner had stood third when he graduated from Annapolis while Buchanan was first in his class at Yale the same year. And his poetry was not all that good.

It was personally satisfying to Buchanan that the highest-ranking officer in all of the military services could speak only with permission in this room. He said, "Go ahead, General. Please. I grow weary of this silence."

"Sir, it is frankly too early for anyone to know much about what has happened to General Middleton. It will all be discovered, but it's going to take some effort and some time. My point is that I really don't care much about what happened *before* Middleton was snatched. I am confident that the intelligence agencies represented around this table will discover that. I want to focus on getting him back as soon as possible."

To Buchanan, the military mindset had always seemed very limiting. Good to have the uniforms around to carry out policy, but original thought was not their strong point. All those badges and ribbons meant little in the halls of real power. "And how is that going to happen? Do you have a plan?"

"With all respect, sir, at the Pentagon, we plan for almost everything, all the time. As soon as we find out where Middleton is being held, we will pull out something suitable and adjust it according to present conditions, and when we receive the authority of our civilian leadership, we will execute it."

"So you don't have a plan."

"Not a detailed one, no. Of course not. But preparations are in motion. The air force has offered its assets, the navy SEAL teams are on alert, the army is spooling up Delta, and the Joint Special Operations Command is on board. We all want the same thing."

"Well, at least that's something that I can take into the Oval Office," said Buchanan. "Thank you, General." He inwardly recorded Turner's condescending *Of course not* as a debt of rudeness to be repaid later.

But Turner was not quite through. "Only this, sir. General Middleton is a Marine. He's one of us. We welcome the support of all branches of service, but we will be the ones to bring him home. I have issued an alert to MARCOM, the Marine Forces Special Operations Command at Camp Lejeune in North Carolina. They are passing the word to the Marine Expeditionary Units in both the Arabian Sea and the Mediterranean. The MEUs are always on a short leash, ready to go."

"You really believe you will be able to do it?" Buchanan raised an eyebrow. "Pull him out of hostile territory?"

"We don't just believe it. We *know* we can." The chairman did not wilt before Buchanan's stare.

"Very well, then. We meet again at noon." Buchanan rose and left the room, annoyed with the arrogance of the Marine. Once back in his office, he dialed the number of Samuel Shafer, his deputy, whose office was across the street in the Old Executive Office Building, and asked if everyone in their shop was present for this emergency. There must be no holes in his own operation that some rival might exploit. He was told that five staff members were absent, for reasons ranging from maternity leave to scheduled days off, but the only one who was really needed was their top Middle East analyst, Lieutenant Commander Shari Towne.

"Then get her in here," Buchanan ordered.

"Sir, she's vacationing on a boat somewhere! Greece, I think. Maybe Italy," exclaimed Shafer.

"I did not ask where she was! Just get her!" He slammed down the telephone, then exhaled slowly and rested both palms on his polished desk. He rubbed it, the smoothness of the shimmering old oak grain almost sensual to his touch. It had been built from the timbers of one of the navy's first warships, and had been used in the Oval Office by President Lyndon Johnson. Buchanan allowed himself a private smile. Old LBJ. Now there was someone who was never afraid to exercise power. He would thump men on the chest when he was talking to them to make sure they got the message, personally telephone reporters in the middle of the night to harass them, and when a Marine guard once advised Johnson that his helicopter was waiting, the President replied, "Son, they're *all* my helicopters." Maybe, Buchanan thought, some of Lyndon's magic was still in the wood of the ancient sailing ship.

He savored the moment. There was nothing better than this, not even sex. Buchanan had controlled the emergency conference on an international crisis and, with a simple instruction, had set in motion a scramble that would ricochet throughout the U.S. government until a low-ranking naval officer was found on a boat and fetched back from half a world away. He gathered his briefing book and headed toward the Oval Office. Power. Delicious.

8

Senator Thomas Graham Miller, chairman of the Senate Armed Services Committee, pushed away the remains of a seafood dinner, stood, and gave a crisp salute to the three hundred cheering veterans who had paid $1,000 each to be with him tonight, paratroopers all. He was proud to be one of them, for when he was young, he, too, had worn the distinctive shoulder patch of the 82nd Airborne Division. He could always count on his fellow vets to help fill the election coffers, but they were more than cash cows to him, just as Miller was more than just another politician to them. This was his Band of Brothers. It irritated him that the Screaming Eagles of the 101st always got the good publicity.

Miller had used his military benefits to get his college education, then a law degree, and became an aggressive prosecutor. He rode a record of achievement, impeccable behavior, and honesty to a seat in the House of Representatives for six years before he was fifty years old, then vaulted to the Senate, where he was in the middle of his third term. He still had the build of an airborne trooper, ran every morning, and was a widower. His wife and infant daughter had died when the birth went horribly wrong twenty years ago, and he never remarried. The image of such a strong and handsome man also being a brokenhearted husband and father made the ladies wilt. Instead of family, Miller devoted himself to the men and women of the armed forces of the United States, even the damned 101st.

He had begun this long day in Washington, and after lunch he went down to Fort Campbell to view an afternoon jump, some five hundred troopers pouring out of the fat bellies of transport planes from five thousand feet. Miller could almost feel the familiar jerk of the parachute harness as the chutes blossomed like sky flowers and the soldiers drifted to earth. When they landed, formed up, and conducted a maneuver, he felt a tear in his eye, as if he saw himself as one of those strong youngsters who could leap out of a plane, fight, and have energy left over.

After the drop, Miller had scheduled three "political events" across the state, which meant he was grazing for campaign money, and was ending the day at this fine dinner in Louisville. He rolled out his tried-and-true stump speech for a friendly audience, bounding to the podium with gusto, smiling and saluting and waving and pointing to individuals. The senator squinted into the bright lights and made a slightly off-color soldiers' joke to put everyone at ease. The lapel bar of a Silver Star flashed in the light, and the slight limp in his right leg silently proved that he also had been awarded a Purple Heart. He did not need notes, for he knew this speech cold.

"The armed forces of the United States are the finest the world has ever seen, just as they were when you and I wore the uniform," he declared, and leaned close to the microphone and gave the guttural fighting call of the clan: *"HOOO-AH!"* Although the audience had just resumed their seats after his introduction, they leaped up again in a standing ovation. It worked every time. He could have filled a bucket with checks after just that opening. But Miller had more to say, and launched into firming up their important support for his current battle.

"The biggest threat we face is not an external enemy. None at all. There is no one, and I mean no one, out there today who can match our planes, our ships, our technology, and the spirit of our fighting men and women. We own the sky, and the space above it. We own the top of the seas, and the waters beneath the waves. When our soldiers put their boots on the ground somewhere, well, we own that, too. Yes, we have a huge budget, one worthy of a superpower, but we spend it wisely, from communications satellites to bullets and beans, and we can take pride in what we have bought. Have no doubt, my friends, that we are still number one. Anyone who messes with us is going to lose.

"But we don't have time to relax and go to Disneyland. Our biggest threat is not from terrorism. We will do our part, and the intelligence and law enforcement agencies of this great land will do their part, and we can keep control of those maniacs. They will occasionally make a splash and create terrible headlines, but they cannot even hope to shake our government or our will. The United States of America and our allies will root out these cockroaches and squelch their evil. That job will take years to complete. It will be done.

"No, my brothers, we face a much more serious threat today, and it comes from inside the Beltway.

That's right, in Washington, D.C. There is a crisis facing our military that could be the equivalent of another tsunami or 9/11 or Hurricane Katrina in the danger it poses. I tell you this both because it is true, and because you, as veterans, can see it better than anyone.

"Private security companies threaten our base of funding. In fiscal 2003 alone, the United States spent twenty billion—BILLION!—on contracts with PSCs, which back then were called PMCs, or private military companies. They changed the name from 'military' to 'security' companies to polish their image, but no matter what name they are called for public relations purposes, they are still mercenaries, soldiers of fortune, and professional adventurers. That is our money, dollars that should be going to support and protect our troops. The glossy literature and the K Street lobbyists have found friendly ears, and have changed the debate. Mercenaries have been around for centuries, fighting for whoever paid them the highest dollar, and their reputation was that of guns for hire. Now private enterprise has put the old merc into a clean shirt and tie, scrubbed his face and reputation, and, behold, we have the private security company.

"They started small, just supplying minor logistical support, and we let them take over the preparation and serving of meals in mess halls. They said they could do it cheaper and free up soldiers for more duties. Step by step, as our money flowed their way, they expanded into everything from transportation to ferrying aircraft to providing personal security to VIPs in hot zones. You see that merc in the news pictures all the time—the beefy and bald guy with the Fu Manchu mustache, wearing dark sunglasses, jeans, and an armored vest, and carrying an assault rifle as he escorts some civilian to a meeting. Again, the arguments were cost-effectiveness and not having to assign troops to those duties.

"Now, my friends, the PSCs are taking the next step. The same companies are now running private combat teams, some in the pay of small countries with lots of money but little military expertise. Other units are being inserted into our own areas of operations. The PSCs are back to their basic tricks of being the gunslingers who fight for hire and give short-term loyalty to whoever pays them."

Miller paused for dramatic effect and let his eyes sweep his audience as he took a sip of water. The room was silent, and the audience knew what was coming. He made the same speech almost every day, and it was often shown on television.

"As you have read in the newspapers and seen on the talk shows, I have been making a big deal with the Senate Armed Services Committee, for we are being pummeled to further loosen the rules on the use of mercenary fighters. I have been shown proposals that would make any professional soldier tremble in anger. The Pentagon would turn over entire sectors of our fighting force to the private sector, and give them the most modern equipment to meet today's battlefield challenges. Some argue that these men are also professional soldiers, trained former members of the SEALs and Marines and Rangers and other elite units such as our own 82nd Airborne, and that they are volunteering for hazardous duty. The wage and benefit packages are attractive to a soldier on active duty.

"By hiring these people, the United States would not have to put as many of our soldiers in harm's way. In other words, they are making a play to take over the armed services. If we surrender in this fight, they will grow stronger while our uniformed services would grow weaker, because all of that money comes out of the same budget. And when the crunch comes, my friends, we won't have soldiers like you out there defending America. Instead, there will be a line of mercs who look tough on film but answer to the call of their paymaster, not to any flag, not even the Stars and Stripes. Some PSCs already hire foreign soldiers whose own armies no longer exist. To whom are they loyal? Would a merc from South Africa or Ukraine or Libya really lay down his life for the USA? Are you willing to bet the lives of your family on them?"

Now he gripped the podium so tightly that his knuckles whitened. The friendly, famous smile was replaced by a grim face that had seen battle. Everyone in the audience detected the change and responded with hushed attention.

"In two weeks, my committee will vote on the first important set of these privatization proposals, and rich lobbyists are swarming around us like sharks. Billions and billions of taxpayer dollars are at stake, but so is the safety of our country. I want you to pull every string you can, call your congressman, wave the flag, write letters to the editors, call up talk shows, chat with your neighbors. I am traveling the country to alert Americans to this new and unique danger, and I need your help. I am counting on it. We must not allow that bill to pass."

He leaned forward again. "Stand up and hook up,

troopers. Stand in the door. Your country needs you to make one more jump."

Tom Miller was exhausted. His press secretary had been dismissed after handing him the typed itinerary for tomorrow's activities during the elevator ride up to the top floor. He closed the door, clicked the television set to CNN, and neatly hung his coat and tie in the closet. He undid his collar and washed his face in the bathroom, letting the cold water rinse away the fatigue. Long days like this made him feel his age.

He groaned when there was a knock on the door. This was supposed to be *alone* time. "Who is it?"

"Trish Campbell, Senator. I'm the night concierge and the hotel manager asked me to be sure you had everything you need for tonight and tomorrow morning." The voice was pleasant.

The senator peered through the viewing glass in the door. A pretty young woman was smiling, knowing she was being inspected. Her dark hair was in a ponytail, and she wore wire-rimmed glasses and a blue blazer buttoned at the waist. She held a clipboard against her chest. "I'm fine, Ms. Campbell. Just a moment." He opened the door.

Trish Campbell shoved him backward, hard, and a huge man hiding beside the wall spun into the room and immobilized Miller, slapping a big hand across his mouth. Miller tasted rubber and realized the man was wearing latex gloves.

Trish closed the door. "Sorry for the intrusion, Senator. This is Big Lenny," she said. "We will be brief." She also pulled on a pair of gloves and removed from her pocket a plastic bag containing a syringe with a long tube on it instead of a needle. Trish clicked the stopwatch function knob on her big wristwatch, then fed the tube into Miller's mouth between Lenny's fingers and pushed the plunger.

Miller tried to struggle as liquid flowed over his tongue and down his throat. Big Lenny held him like a steel clamp.

Trish Campbell returned the syringe to its sealed bag, which went back into her pocket. She watched him closely with intelligent eyes. "If you're wondering what is killing you, it's a particularly bitchy little strain of shellfish toxia along the lines of a solvent-based tropo-dotoxin and ricin. I don't know the details because I'm not a scientist. Big Lenny and I are just the messengers. In addition to poisoning you, I am to bid you a fond farewell from Mr. Gordon Gates."

Senator Miller struggled as fire spread through his veins, the heart pumping hard. *Gates!*

"The short version, as I understand it, is that chemical agents are busy shutting down your central nervous system right about now and that is going to cause your heart to fail." She looked at her watch. "You will be dead in a couple of seconds. By the time your body is found tomorrow morning, the toxins will have evaporated and you will be ruled to have croaked from a simple old heart attack." She leaned close and peered hard at his eyes, which were rolling back. "Let him go, Lenny."

Senator Miller fell to the floor and went into convulsions. A vicious spasm arched his back at an impossible angle, he gargled, and his hands flailed at his chest. A final breath was exhaled. Trish Campbell felt for a pulse. There was none. She clicked the stopwatch. Thirty-two seconds, start to finish.

She took a hotel vacuum cleaner from the closet and ran it over the area of carpet that she and Lenny had occupied, returned it to the closet, then opened the door and checked the hallway. It was empty. Lenny went out first and Trish pulled the door closed. When it locked, she hung a plastic white-and-blue DO NOT DISTURB sign on the handle and the Shark Team left the hotel.

9

Sir Jeff was in a good mood. To mark the success of the Excalibur demonstration, which had won over the investors, he decided a celebration ashore was in order on the bright afternoon. His captain found a quiet, rocky cove on the northeastern coast of the Greek island of Corfu and dropped anchor into perfectly green water. The ladies and the venture capital guys went ashore in the runabout first, and Jeff promised that he, Kyle, and Tim would be right along when the inflatable motorboat made a return trip. The sneaky Brit had a surprise for the money men, who planned to leave soon and make their way up through Italy to Florence before returning home.

When the little boat sped away, Jeff ducked into his cabin and returned with three bell-shaped bottles of thick glass containing a dark amber liquid. "Gifts for our departing friends," he said. "Two-hundred-year-old Hennessy Richard Cognac. I picked it up from a wine merchant in Paris just for this occasion." He handed one of the heavy bottles each to both Tim and Kyle, with a stern warning to handle them gently. Each cost $2,000. He liked to keep his business associates happy.

The sheer green beauty of the island was stunning as

they approached in the little runabout that bounced fast over the water. Olive trees were everywhere, millions of them, from the heights of Mount Pantocrator down to the white sandy beaches. Kyle was looking forward to a fresh salad with cheese from the local goats as Gladden swung to a smooth stop at a narrow pier. They tied up, grabbed the cognac, and headed ashore to where their group was seated on an odd collection of stools and wooden chairs around little tables at a *psaro taverna*, a fish restaurant. Like most eating establishments in Greece, this one was called the Café Olympia. Irregular weathered stones spread along the front, and tan walls were shaded by the spreading olive branches.

There was a problem with the idyllic scene. Four rough-looking men also were at the tavern, obviously drunk and taunting the guys and making lewd passes at the women. The money men were sitting there, embarrassed, while the girls were trying, without success, to ignore the drunks.

"Oh, my," said Jeff, who wore cream-colored linen trousers, a soft blue shirt, and leather sandals. Tim Gladden had on a lightweight white short-sleeved shirt, creased white pants, and Converse sneakers. Swanson was barefoot, in wrinkled khaki cargo shorts and a brilliant blue Hawaiian shirt with orange palm trees. They looked as threatening as three lost missionaries.

"I say, chaps," Jeff pleasantly addressed the men as he carefully placed his precious cognac bottle on a table. "Would you please be off now? We are just here for a quick and a pleasant lunch and then will be on our way."

The four Greeks stopped pestering the visitors and

stared at the newcomers, knowing that playtime was over. Kyle shifted his weight a bit as the drunks rose from their table, pushed aside the chairs, and formed a line, one-two-three-four. In any street fight, the tough guys lead, and the biggest of the bunch was slightly forward in the two position, shoulder-to-shoulder with number three, a husky man with a face scarred like an Ultimate Fighter. The remaining two flanked them. Kyle glanced at Shari and winked. Lady Pat sat back, took another sip of ouzo, and lit a thin cigar.

The largest guy, around six-two, spoke. "You will fuck off now, you rich bastards, and take these three other queers with you. The women can go back to your big boat when we are done."

"Ah, I see," said Jeff. "Well then, lads, I guess we are for it. I'll take this big fellow, if you don't mind."

"No," Tim disagreed. To free his hands, he also put his bottle on a table and moved to a fighting stance. "I want Mr. Big. You can have that ugly one. Scarface."

Kyle smashed his heavy bottle over Big's head, catching him on the left side of the forehead, and raked the jagged edge down across the eye, cheek, and mouth for a maximum cutting effect. Deep inside Swanson, the switch had clicked into combat mode and he was running on automatic. Speed and surprise. Don't let them regroup. Eliminate the threats in descending order of importance.

The first guy collapsed to his knees with a scream, the strong alcohol biting into the deep and bleeding cuts. Kyle already had spun away to his left and slammed his left elbow into the nose of Scarface, knocking him backward across a table. Blood spurted from the fractured nose, and the man's head cracked against the paving stones.

"He is going to be even uglier when he wakes up," Shari said to Pat.

Kyle's momentum was still at work and he finished the spin facing number four. He locked Four in a bear hug, slid his clasped hands up behind the man's head, and pulled the body weight toward him. When the man leaned back, thinking Swanson was going after his face, Kyle drove his right knee deep and hard into the crotch, sending the ruptured balls somewhere up between the eyes. The man gasped for breath and crashed over a chair.

"An emergency surgical suite for that one," Pat commented. "Kyle is very messy today."

Number one, who had been at the far end, came on fast as Kyle came to rest in a squared position, perfectly balanced. The man's right leg locked as he ran forward, and Swanson leaned back, lifted his own left foot, and came straight down with a kick on the knee. The leg snapped sharply, with a sound like breaking wood.

"*Kyle! My God, man!*" Sir Jeff screamed in anguish. "*You broke a bloody two-thousand-dollar bottle of cognac!*" He gathered the two remaining bottles, looking at Swanson with horror in his eyes.

"Sorry," Kyle said. The whole thing had taken about ten seconds.

Tim walked to the stunned guests. Lady Pat and Shari were already standing and stepping over the bleeding debris on the stone slabs. "I think we had all best be leaving now," said Gladden. "We will finish lunch aboard the *Vagabond*, all right?" He escorted them to the waiting small boat.

The owner of the taverna was standing in his doorway like a statue, with fresh bowls of salad in each hand. Kyle took one, gave him more than enough money to cover the damage, and walked away. The big guy, number one, stirred and looked up with his bloodied face as if he was determined to rise. Since the man was no longer a threat, Kyle felt there was no need for a lethal blow and settled for kicking him in the sternum to take away his air. The large man passed out, gasping for breath. Kyle thought the goat cheese was delicious. He wished he had not had to eat it with his fingers.

One of the Desperate Housewives looked back over her shoulder as she walked down the pier, her blue eyes wide in shock. She could not believe what she had just seen. "How did he do that? He was like a crazy man," she asked Shari.

"It's the way he is trained," Shari replied. "He doesn't think, just reacts on instinct. Believe me, those guys got off easy."

"Do you mean he might have killed someone? There were four of them. Wasn't he afraid?"

"This is what he does," she said, stepping into the runabout. As she took a seat, she gave a tight smile to the woman, who lived in pretty places far from the dirt of the real world. "Kyle is not afraid of anyone . . . but me."

Late that night, the *Vagabond* cruised through the narrow Strait of Messina. Since the dawn of written history, those waters had gobbled up ships, with the deadly whirlpool Charybdis at the edge of Sicily forcing captains to sail close to the very toe of the Italian boot, where the mythological monster Scylla prowled the rocks. Now the electronic eyes of radar and satellite navigation systems defeated the dangers of superstition.

Shari leaned against Kyle's chest as they stood at the port rail, and he buried his nose in her silky hair. It carried the gentle scent of an English flower garden. He wrapped his arms around her and she covered his hands with hers as they watched the boiling bowl of the distant volcano, Stromboli, erupt in flashes of bright orange, with red flame illuminating the underside of passing clouds.

"I love this," she said. "My favorite guy, a luxury yacht, a beautiful night, and an exploding volcano. What could be better?"

He squeezed gently and she turned her head enough to give him a kiss. They were alone on the deck at two o'clock in the morning and the churning fire on the distant island made it seem that they might be the only people left at the end of the world. "Being able to stay out here with you a while longer would be better."

"Did Jeff offer you a job again?"

"Yup. Says we ought to get married and make a lot of money and beget him and Pat some godchildren they can spoil rotten."

"Sounds like a plan. You turn him down again?"

"I told him it was all your fault, because you make that white uniform with all the gold stripes look so good and you like people to salute you."

She sighed. "I make anything look good. Really, does he understand that we're just not quite there yet?"

"He understands. Both he and Tim put the full-court press on me tonight and threw in the promise of a share of Excalibur sales."

Shari turned in his arms, and the glow of the volcano reflecting off the water seemed like a halo around her. "Maybe we should reconsider, Kyle. I've had the strangest feeling that something bad is going to happen. And that I won't see you again."

Sixth sense, witchery, hunches, woman's intuition, or whatever, she had it in spades. Her ability to not only connect the dots, but the spaces between the dots, was what made her such a great intelligence analyst. Shari's brain dwelled in a place where one and one did not necessary always equal two, and Kyle always paid attention when she got one of her feelings. This time, he downplayed it. "Fat chance. I'm like a boomerang. I always come back to you."

"Yes. But after that last mission, the cross-border incident, you caught a lot of flak and they tried to make you the scapegoat. A lot of people would just like for you to go away, Kyle. Who knows what they may hand you next time? Maybe something where you're not supposed to come back."

"Never gonna happen, Shari. I know how to play their game too well."

She kissed him, pulled away, and looked around. The deck was empty. "Then maybe I should give you even more reason to come home." She slipped the straps of her black dress from her shoulders. "So look at me, I'm Sandra Dee!"

"Who the hell is Sandra Dee?"

"You know. *Gidget*?"

"What's a *Gidget*?"

"Shut up before you ruin the moment," she said, and slid the loose folds of her dress down to her waist. Her breasts gleamed gold in the volcano firelight. Kyle brought her close and lowered his lips to her nipples. Shari moaned softly, and he ran his hands over her soft skin. Then her hand moved along his leg.

"Unless you want to be screwed right here on this expensive teakwood deck, young lady, I suggest we retire in great haste to our suite," he whispered. Kyle saw a familiar impish look come into those dark eyes.

"In a minute, Marine. In a minute." Shari pushed him against the chill steel of the bulkhead and dropped to her knees, reaching for his zipper while Stromboli painted the night. In a few moments, Kyle thought that the volcano was not the only thing erupting that night. When he finished panting, they rushed off to wrestle between white silk sheets.

There was a loud pounding on the door, and Kyle heard Tim Gladden calling loudly from the passageway. "Kyle! Shari! Geoffrey wants you in the main cabin right away to see this incredible news report on television! A Marine general has been kidnapped!"

10

United States Senator Ruth Hazel Reed of California—called Ruth Hazel by her friends and Rambo by her enemies—would replace her very dear colleague, the late Senator Graham Thomas Miller of Kentucky, as chair of the Senate Armed Services Committee. She was an attractive woman with blond-going-gray hair that was as stylish as her tailored wardrobe. The slender body was kept under strict control through rigorous exercise three times a week and a delicious diet provided by her private chef.

"Congratulations, Madam Chairwoman," said National Security Advisor Gerald Buchanan, lifting a glass of seventy-five-year-old scotch in a toast. They were standing before a warm fireplace at the mansion of Gordon Gates, deep in the fox country outside Culpeper, Virginia. The huge room had thick wooden ceiling beams. Old furniture, old staircases, old books, old money. Lots of it.

"A bit premature, Gerald, but thank you." She clicked her glass against his. "The Senate president will make his decision in a few days."

"Oh, that's just a technicality. I've already told him that the White House will be pleased to work with you."

Buchanan had reviewed her file again before coming out here tonight for the meeting. So much depended on this woman! Was she really up to it?

She had graduated from Stanford and married a helicopter pilot who was killed in Vietnam. Ruth Hazel buried her grief along with her pilot, obtained her real estate license, and opened an agency in Del Mar just as the sunny coast of San Diego County became the hottest housing market in the nation. She made a fortune before turning her boundless ambition and energy to politics. A single term on the Del Mar City Council led to a big leap into the House of Representatives for two terms. Reed had been in the Senate for the past eleven years.

Land speculation and the military, the twin engines of the dynamic San Diego economy, formed her primary political base. The senator was adamant in getting tax breaks for land developers and big business and voted for any military spending proposal. Nobody gobbled up more taxpayer dollars for the Pentagon than Rambo Reed of California. The defense contractors and housing industry tycoons at the receiving end of the money pipeline showed their gratitude with campaign contributions.

Despite all of her money, power, good looks, and adroit phrasing, Buchanan considered Reed to be just another politician to be used like a sweet-smelling bar of soap until there was nothing worthwhile left to be used. There was always another Ruth Hazel Reed out there waiting to be groomed like a colt in training for the Kentucky Derby. This filly might break out and actually win the race for the roses, but a wise owner would have a lot of colts. She had been carefully selected for the role she was to play.

Senator Reed moved to a soft chair and sat down, putting her drink on a small Chinese-style table with a polished marble top inlaid with intricate stonework of precious gems. She considered Buchanan to be a competent number-cruncher and an above-average strategist. It was quite helpful to have him around, and he could be discarded the minute he did not deliver the goods. Headlines hailed him as a genius, but these guys were plentiful in Washington. Arrogant, too. She hoped that Buchanan did not let his pride get in the way of the job he had to perform. Was he up to it? The senator wondered how much the table was worth.

Reed had also spoken with the Senate president, and knew her appointment to succeed Miller was a done deal. Buchanan had to make a big show of everything. To chair that committee was definitely another rung up the ladder, but it should be only temporary. Reed had no plans to run for reelection. By this time next year, she planned to be President of the United States.

"As they say, Ruth Hazel, we live in interesting times," mused Buchanan.

"True enough. And during such difficult times, our country needs very careful guidance. Not knee-jerk action based on snapshot poll numbers."

Buchanan caught the insult. He was the most famous consumer of polls in Washington. "Indeed. That is precisely why you will be so valuable in your new position. From the untimely death of one senator can come progress for all." Unspoken was the barb that Reed was also just one senator of fifty. Only one-fiftieth of one-half of one-third of the United States government. They were even.

Buchanan poured himself a refill and offered her one with a smile. A peace offering. He found politics rather loathsome and did not want public office of any sort. He was a scholar and much too good, too intelligent, to have to explain himself to common voters and fools. Nothing lasted forever, including what he viewed as the American Empire. Buchanan believed that it was his destiny to shepherd the troubled nation to a new level of political evolution, which included writing a new Constitution. *His* Constitution would replace that antique Jeffersonian piece of parchment displayed under glass in the National Archives. What had been unique and powerful ideas for a democratic republic in the eighteenth century simply did not apply in today's complex world. It would be even less relevant in tomorrow's. Thomas Jefferson had been dead for a long, long time.

Rambo Reed could sit in that big chair in the Oval Office, but Gerald Buchanan would run the government.

"You two should hear yourselves talk! What total bullshit!" A slight, whippy man with the build of a marathon runner came into the big hall, walked over, and gripped their hands with the enthusiasm of someone who relished life. "We're the first of a new generation of leaders, my friends, and we are going to kick a lot of ass and make a ton of money while we save our country."

Gordon Gates IV had an easy, confident smile that indicated he did not have a care in the world. He wore a loose white shirt of Chinese silk, dark Armani trousers, and soft black Prada boots. A slim, clean Louis Vuitton Tambour chronograph was on his left wrist, and thick sandy-blond hair swept down over his forehead. He was fifty-five years old and looked ten years younger. The intelligent green eyes missed nothing.

He was very rich. His great-grandfather, the original Gordon Gates, was a grease-stained machinist who had invented a tiny part for aircraft engines before World War II, built on that modest success as aviation grew, and within five years owned a giant corporation. America's fighter planes and bombers could not stay in the sky without Gates equipment. Gordon Gates Jr. expanded military production when jet propulsion came along, established offices abroad, bought a shipbuilding company to make nuclear-powered submarines, and renamed the international company Gates Global. When "GG III" came along, a brilliant engineer in his own right, he seized the early days of the rocket age. Gates Global helped man walk on the moon, provided the electronic brains for missiles that could reach anywhere on the globe, then got into Area 51 secret weapons development with lasers and sound. Markets were locked up and money poured in. When politicians spoke of the military-industrial complex, they were talking about Gates Global. The company always rewarded its friends on Capitol Hill, and its executive ranks were loaded with former generals and admirals, and ex-members of Congress.

The family groomed Gordon Gates IV to carry on the torch. He was a very bright kid when he was attending an elite prep school, but he had a vision of his own. All he had to do was say the word and he could step out of prep school and into Harvard, Yale, or Stanford, and then be prepared to take over Gates Global when his flashy playboy father was ready to pass the baton. But with the added bonus of aggravating his old man, young Gordon joined the U.S. Army as a private, determined to start at the bottom and get the kind of on-the-ground experience that would help him know what the hell he was talking about when he finally joined the family business. He still planned to run it someday, but Dear Old Dad wasn't anywhere near ready to voluntarily give up the throne. GG IV detested GG III, who felt the same about his only son and heir.

The smart kid from the mansion in Mission Hills, Kansas, enlisted in the U.S. Army as a grunt soldier, became a Ranger, and was a sergeant in the 101st Airborne when he was qualified for Delta Force. After two years as a Delta operator, he allowed the Army to pay for his higher education and was scooped from the ranks to attend West Point. Once commissioned, he took a Rhodes Scholarship at Oxford and then got back into the mud with a year's secondment to the British SAS.

He returned to Delta deep-selected as a major, and served three more years on special missions to the dark holes of the world. The Pentagon loved having Gordon Gates on the payroll, brought him to Washington, made him a light colonel, and buried him deep undercover to plan and implement black operations. It was said around the E-Ring that Gates was a slam-dunk for his first star.

Then Daddy GG III wrapped his Ferrari 512 Berlinetta Boxer and his mistress around an oak tree alongside a curving, wet road.

And he was always bitching at me about taking risks in the army! Gordon thought as the casket of Dear Old Dad was lowered into the grave in the family plot in Kansas. It was his turn to take over Gates Global, and he came to the job totally ready as a dues-paid-in-full member of the Pentagon Gun Club.

He established his supreme authority by bringing a squad of lawyers to his first meeting with the board of directors, and fired most of the men and women who had been his father's staunchest friends and allies. He told the survivors what was coming. The Berlin Wall is a pile of old rocks: there was never going to be a battle between Soviet and American tanks for the Fulda Gap. Continuing to manufacture thousands of new tanks was stupid. Nuclear-powered aircraft carriers were sailing toward a horizon of obsolescence and the giant submarines crammed with world-crunching missiles were outdated. Whole generations of fighter planes had nobody to fight. That really didn't matter, he said. Gates Global would continue to build the steel and titanium dinosaurs as long as the profit margin remained solid.

Gates would leave a hand-picked CEO in place to run the public face of Gates Global. That person would be a technocrat and use terms like "littoral battle space" and "netcentric communications" and "transformational combat force projection" to lasso contracts for new ships and planes and weapons systems. "Build whatever the fuckers want," Gates said. He would have nothing to do with that side of the company, as long as it made a lot of money.

In return, he demanded an unlimited budget that would not be answerable to them. Let the lawyers and accountants figure out how to hide it from the IRS, but it had to be a totally black account and available when he wanted. "Gates Global is expanding and you don't need to know the details," he told them. "Stop thinking in millions and start thinking in billions. You all will make a lot of money and nobody will ever be indicted for anything if you keep your mouths shut and stay out of my way." He stared around the room and then abruptly walked out, leaving no doubt about who was the company's new leader.

Gates's vision was that the United States military was going right back to where wars are always won, with boots on the ground. It was the topic he knew best, because he had walked many miles in those boots, humping a pack and carrying an automatic rifle. Teams of highly trained Special Operations soldiers would fight the country's future conflicts because the national defense could not be entrusted to acne-pimpled National Guard soldiers or fat-ass regular army colonels. In his plan, the private units could be combined in any size, from the lethal two-man Shark Teams that did special jobs all the way up to battalion size or even bigger. Gates was building the preeminent private security company in the world, and that was only the first step.

Gates, Buchanan, Reed. The three people standing before the fireplace, holding crystal glasses of scotch, would redirect the enormous and ever-growing Pentagon budget to fund private armies, with Gates Global positioned to provide everything from bullets to beans, transportation to firepower, for a nice price. Other major corporations could handle infrastructure needs or be front companies to keep the Gates name out of tricky situations. PSCs were the future. American soldiers did not need to spill their blood abroad when mercenaries could do the same job better, faster, cheaper, under no political restraints, and without press coverage. He would draw upon the Pentagon's resources as needed for the big stuff like close air support and satellites and aircraft carriers, but all of that eventually would come under his umbrella, too.

Just a little tinkering was needed to get the plan past the Democrat and Republican politicians and the media howlers. That should be simple enough when America endured the worst siege of terrorist attacks in its history and thousands of U.S. citizens were slaughtered in shopping malls and hospitals and homes. Enraged and frightened citizens would demand that they be kept safe!

Civilian police were not up to the task. American troops would be needed to protect American shores and borders and cities and towns when martial law was imposed. To fill the vacuum abroad, Gates Global would be given the grateful appreciation of the nation to fight Washington's foreign battles. After a few years, the door would open wider for stateside operations as well. Martial law would morph into a new, firmer way of running the country under a banner of national security.

It was time to implement Operation Premier while Senator Reed had the legislative clout and Buchanan could deliver the executive branch.

"So, Ruth Hazel, now that Senator Miller is out of the way, where does it leave our privatization bill?" Gates brought those harsh eyes to her.

"I will bring the American Defense Act before the subcommittee next week and fast-track it through the full committee, both in closed sessions. When Operation Premier creates a significant domestic terrorist strike just before the vote, the House of Representatives will respond with a similar bill and a conference committee will rubber-stamp it. It will be political suicide for any of them to oppose defending America while the blood of innocents is in the streets. Gerald should see the bill come down to the White House in no more than thirty days."

Buchanan nodded. "I will brief the President and endorse the act. That crap in the Middle East has tortured him enough, the media is always bitching about it, and he's anxious to get out of there. There are a lot of fronts in the war on terror, and something decisive hitting in the American heartland will give him the political cover to readjust his sights and bring our troops home."

"You're sure that he will sign the privatization bill?"

"Absolutely." Buchanan lifted his own eyes and looked at his comrade's. "If we wrap up the one remaining loose end."

Gates laughed out loud. "You mean with General Middleton?"

"Middleton cannot be allowed to testify before my committee!" Senator Reed said firmly, putting down her glass and crossing her arms. "He's only a one-star, but he is influential as hell with his books and lectures about the value of a professional military that answers to elected civilian officials. Together, he and Miller would have stopped us cold. They were planning a public relations offensive on this, including getting television networks to cover the hearings. Open hearings!"

"Which is exactly why they are not in Washington today," said Gates. "We have gotten rid of Miller with the heart attack, and the general has been kidnapped and will not survive the adventure. Neither can be traced to us."

Buchanan shuffled a toe of his tassled loafer into the thick carpet. "I have been riding the Pentagon and the intel services hard. When your people reveal the location, the Marines will launch a rescue operation, just as you predicted, Gordon. I will let them do it, of course, reporting the plans directly to me."

Gates nodded. "The Sharks and some of the Rebel Sheikh's militia boys will be ready when Force Recon guys arrive in Syria. Cameras will record the destruction of most of the assault force, but a few Marines will be allowed to fight their way into the house where Middleton is being held."

"And they will all be killed together in the shootout, on video," Reed said. "Another military debacle."

Gordon Gates smiled. "I want to add one last piece to the scenario, Gerald. Just imagine that in the middle of the shootout, a U.S. Marine is actually shown to be the one who kills General Middleton."

"How could we possibly arrange that?"

"Simple. You, my friend, take one of the best snipers on the CIA roster and order it done. Remove him from the chain of command. When the rescue fails, the sniper is to make certain that the general's vast knowledge of homeland security information does not fall into enemy hands."

"How does he survive that initial ambush?" Buchanan scratched his ear.

Gates knew the capabilities of a good operator and waved away the question. "The firing will not be very heavy, and if he is any good at his job, he won't have much trouble being among those getting to the right house."

"Would he actually do it? Shoot the general?" asked Senator Reed.

"Only if it was a direct order from his commander-in-chief in the White House," said Buchanan. "When the last members of the rescue team are being wiped out, the sniper becomes both our insurance policy and a fall guy for any blame. Then he is also taken out. End of a tragic fiasco."

"You boys can take care of that, Gordon. All I care about is that Middleton not show up before my committee." The senator brought the conversation back to center point. "He could wreck everything."

"Excellent. Excellent," said Gates. "So that brings us to decision time on Operation Premier. Senator?"

"It has to be done," said Reed.

"Don't go vague on us, Ruth Hazel. Say exactly what you mean, not some political bullshit. You agree that we will prepare the Shark Teams for the theater attacks. We must be absolutely plain with each other. After all, the three of us essentially are staging a coup."

"Yes," she replied.

"Gerald?"

"Yes. Do it."

"Me, too. Yes. It's unanimous." He flashed that enigmatic smile again. "Now let's have a nice dinner and a good bottle of wine to salute this historic creation of New America."

11

Kyle Swanson watched the television report silently, his arms crossed. Bradley Fucking Middleton! The general's picture came on the screen, a stock photo of him in full dress uniform and an American flag in the background. It was not a face that Kyle ever enjoyed seeing. Every time they met, something bad seemed to happen, until finally Middleton had tried to cashier Swanson out of the Marines. As the newsreader droned on, Kyle's mind rolled back to his first clash with Middleton years ago during Desert Shield, in the abandoned town of Khafji, on the border between Saudi Arabia and Iraq.

It had been two days into the new year of 1991, and there was something happening in the black desert night. The growl of engines and the clank of tank treads, out where there was supposed to be nothing but sand. "Multiple heat signatures, Sergeant. More than ten vehicles. Hard to say with this piece-of-shit night vision gear," the spotter said quietly after looking hard and long through his thermal imaging glasses. "Lots of movement, though."

Kyle Swanson pulled the ten-power Unertl scope of his M40A1 sniper rifle to his eye. Nothing but darkness across the border between Saudi Arabia and Kuwait. "Call it in. Tell 'em it sounds like more than just a recon."

Iraq had overrun Kuwait, and the Iraqis were not sitting still while an American and international coalition of forces was building up to take it back. Kyle had been a scout-sniper sergeant at the time, heading a two-man observation team hidden between the floorboards of a building at the edge of town. Several other OPs were scattered throughout other buildings, but until now, Saddam Hussein had kept his people out of the area. Boredom had been the biggest enemy.

A chill crawled up the back of his neck that had nothing to do with the cold temperature. All that noise meant armor. Saddam was about to expand the playing field, and the OPs were right in the path, with the closest friendlies about thirty minutes away, a very long time in a firefight.

They remained motionless as the mumble of impending battle moved closer, and the first light of dawn brought the startling truth. The sun outlined Iraqi T-62 tanks and a herd of other alphabet armor—MBLTs, tracked personnel carriers on the main chassis of a battle tank; BDRM recon scout vehicles, and the BMPs with anti-armor cannon. A bit of everything. This was no probe, but the advance guard for an entire armored division, and they were already on the outskirts of town, moving closer by the minute. Dismounted Iraqi troops hustled around the vehicles, darting like a swarm of ants going after a picnic basket as they cleared the abandoned houses. The spotter called in radio reports while Swanson ran a final check of his rifle, ammo clips, the clackers for the Claymore mines, and grenades.

To try to leave would be suicide; a tank and the supporting infantry would make quick work of anyone they saw. Swanson glassed potential targets with his scope, and his mouth watered with anticipation. Behind the troops coming into the town there were guys riding atop the vehicles, talking in groups and moving in the open, lacking discipline as they pressed forward, for they expected no opposition. Careless ants. He put the cross-hairs on an officer wearing a red beret and standing in the turret of a tank, gripping a handle so he could get a better view of Khafji. He had a big thick mustache, a pressed uniform, and a pistol on a polished belt of brown leather. Kyle thought: *He's mine.*

"Mike Tango three niner, this is Hunter One. Fire mission. Over." The spotter had headquarters on the net and was quietly lining up an artillery strike. He pinned his finger on an exact spot on the plastic-covered map folded before him. "Grid. Six two niner four. Niner eight seven six. Direction: five niner one one. Twenty to thirty Iraqi tanks and APCs in the open. Fire for effect."

Swanson tracked the officer, waiting for a sound louder than that of his rifle. The first 155mm artillery rounds came in like loud zippers in the sky, and when they exploded, throwing dirt and debris into big mush-rooms of destruction, he finished squeezing the trigger. His bullet took the Iraqi officer in the throat and knocked him from the tank. Soldiers were scrambling for cover and paid no attention to the fallen officer, thinking he had been hit by the artillery. Kyle fed a fresh round into his rifle and looked for a new target, found one, and waited for another big round to explode and mask his shot.

The Iraqis opened up with everything they had, shooting wild. There was no enemy visible, but the artillery salvo had been so precise, it was obvious that someone was watching them. Their entire line surged forward, firing as they came, and violent explosions blew walls apart. The soldiers rushed to find shelter from the artillery, and Swanson and his spotter shrank back into the shadowy hide. A squad of Iraqi infantrymen ran into the main floor of the small building for cover. One came up to the second floor but could not see them between the floorboards, and stomped back downstairs to the rest of the squad, which moved on to clear another building. "Sloppy," Kyle whispered.

The Iraqi tanks and armored personnel carriers prowled the streets, unleashing cannon and machine-gun fire on anything suspicious, and small-arms fire rattled on both sides and to the rear of the observation team. The bad guys had the town, and Kyle, his spotter, and the other Marines were trapped inside it.

The situation was beyond serious, and Swanson made the decision without conscious thought. If they were going to survive, they needed help in a hurry, because those enemy soldiers soon would be prowling about in a more thorough search for the observation teams. He grabbed his spotter by the shoulder. "Call Broken Arrow!"

The emergency signal meant that U.S. forces were being overrun. Every warplane in the sky that morning diverted immediately from its mission and accelerated toward Khafji, afterburners thundering to pour on more speed. The spotter started guiding them in, while other OP lookouts adjusted the artillery strikes. Nearby buildings vaporized with concussion blasts that shook them like a couple of gerbils in a cage.

Swanson cleared away debris that fell in front of their hide and got back to work, taking targets of opportunity whenever an artillery round came in or a plane made a bombing run.

It was all now in slow motion. The chaotic sounds and sights passed through his mind only as parts of the mathematical equations he needed to figure out the next shot. He was an emotionally empty vessel, without fear, mentally shutting out any personal feelings for the targets—not men, but targets—and became an extension of the rifle. He wasn't counting, he was killing, and hoping to avoid getting killed in turn.

The morning grew brighter and the allied planes circled like fast vultures to pounce on the exposed Iraqis. Kyle's world shook and burned as bombs rocked the city, and the artillery punished the Iraqi infantry troops who had taken cover in some of the same buildings in which the Marine observers were hidden.

Finally, U.S. and coalition ground troops and armor showed up. A Saudi National Guard unit was allowed to roll into the town first, for symbolic reasons, but the big chase was conducted by a Marine light recon battalion that roared through the broken town like it was Saturday afternoon at the Daytona Speedway. TOW missiles and 25mm Bushmaster cannons obliterated any Iraqi vehicles that were too slow.

Kyle and his spotter climbed from their hide like filthy

moles, covered with dirt and debris. Only then did he realize that a big splinter had punched into his left bicep. Blood stained his uniform. He had been too busy, and the adrenalin was pumping too hard, to notice when it happened.

A medic yanked out the splinter, cleaned the puncture, and tied on a quick bandage. "You'll get another Purple Heart for that one, Sar'nt," the medic said.

"Forget it," Kyle responded, rubbing the sharp piece of wood, about three inches long, between his fingers, then tossing it away. "Ain't worth nothing."

As the other teams emerged, similarly battered and bruised, Kyle walked off to get some water and find a quiet place to be alone.

It was part of his routine that let his mind disengage from the combat mode and come back into the real world. He found a cool, dark room in one of the empty houses and sat down as his body began to quiver. He thought of that big gaping hole he had blown in the throat of the first officer. Of the infantryman who believed he was safe behind a wall until Kyle shot out his liver in a splash of blood. Of the driver of the armored personnel carrier who popped out of his hatch and caught Kyle's bullet through the left eye. Sights of inflicted death paraded before him, and he knew that in future months, those Iraqis would visit in his dreams. Kyle Swanson, exhausted, curled into a fetal position and grabbed his knees tightly while his mind dealt with the carnage of his trigger finger. Tears streaked the dirt on his cheeks.

A hand touched him on the back. "S'arnt Swanson?

You hit?" A Marine major had found him, saw the bloody shirt, and thought he was wounded.

Kyle relaxed. His eyes were still unfocused. "No, sir. I'm okay." He swiped a hand across his dirty face, the sweat and tears leaving muddy tracks. "Just catching my breath. It got kinda intense out there."

It took a few moments for Kyle to recognize the face of Major Bradley Middleton, the executive officer of the Force Recon battalion. The major was a veteran but had little experience with snipers, and had never seen one personally deal with the aftermath of a day of battle. Ordinary soldiers shoot almost anonymously and seldom see what they hit. Pilots never view the bodies blown away by their bombs, and tankers have limited visibility. But with a powerful scope, a sniper sees every strand of hair in an enemy mustache, the color of an eye and the movement of a finger. They also see the gory holes they make in a man, and after the battle is over, that has to be dealt with. Every sniper has his own way of adjusting.

Kyle told his shooters when they were in training, "We have to be peculiar, or we wouldn't be snipers in the first place. None of us do what we have to do simply because we enjoy killing people. That would be crazy." Some, the lucky ones, would just get drunk and wash away the images with beer and whiskey. Nightmares and divorces were common. Others would be gripped by unreasoning anger and fight whoever came along and end up in the brig. Kyle's own habit was to shake and bake a little bit and be done with it.

Middleton just squatted there beside him, mystified at

the quaking Marine sniper. He had invaded Kyle Swanson's private world uninvited, and after a minute he rose and walked back into the sunshine and left Swanson alone.

Neither of them forgot the incident. Then Middleton saw him do it again after a brawl in Somalia, by which time Swanson was a staff sergeant and Middleton had risen to light colonel. Middleton considered the continued strange behavior to be important and gave Kyle a negative evaluation report. "Shaky," he wrote of Swanson in an evaluation report, by which he meant undependable, unworthy, and unreliable. He recommended that Swanson undergo psychiatric evaluation and be retired from the Marine Corps because he was a walking time bomb. Who in their right mind would want a shaky sniper around?

Kyle had come within an inch of being ruined until other officers and senior enlisted types jumped to his defense and forced the potentially career-ending piece of paper to be withdrawn. But the term "shaky" leaked out and his fellow snipers loved it, for they gave no quarter in busting balls. "Shake" stuck, an unwanted nickname.

As he watched the news report aboard the *Vagabond* that Brigadier General Middleton had been taken hostage, Kyle felt conflicting emotions. It made him angry because he hated that kidnapping shit. Terrorist assholes could not just go around snatching American generals or anyone else without consequences. That anger was on principle alone.

Personally, the moment also made him proud to be an American, because he knew the United States had a firm policy of never bargaining with terrorists. Well, almost never. So there would be no deals made to get the general back. Kyle believed that the unwritten rule book on international terrorism was very clear on that point.

Therefore, now that terrorists actually had taken Middleton, Kyle reasoned that they had to keep him. That was just fine with the sniper.

12

Two old men leaned upon the railing of the bridge on which the Boulevard de la Gare crossed the Seine. Clouds had rolled in to chase the sun and a chilly afternoon breeze swept up the river, warning of coming rain. Sweaters protected their shoulders. Automobiles swarmed behind them on the roadway, and trains clattered into and out of the Gare de Lyon and the Gare d'Austerlitz stations on either side of the river. It would have been impossible for either to have been followed by someone without being seen, and the noise drowned out their soft voices.

They had been competitors, enemies, partners, allies, and opposing spies in their younger years. After retirement, both stayed in Paris and a friendship followed. It was enjoyable to pass the time talking about the good old days of the Cold War over cups of hot café, particularly since they could now laugh at the absurdity of six decades of spying for the United States and France.

Buzz Higbee had grown up in the Minnesota woods and could have returned to the U.S. of A., but found the thought of retiring to a cabin beside a lonely lake that was frozen half the year to be unattractive. He had lived most of his adult life in Paris, and his wife, children, and grandchildren were all French. Minnesota had become

82

the foreign land. He was a healthy eighty-two years old, with white hair, weak blue eyes, high blood pressure, and a hearing aid.

Higbee had ventured out today to meet Jean-Paul Delmas, who was only eighty. Delmas walked with the help of a cane, but his intellect remained sharp and since his spy days he had devoted himself to an extensive collection of rare stamps. Buzz called him "the Kid."

"This is rather delicate," Delmas told Higbee.

"*Merde*, Jean-Paul. Where our two countries are involved, what is not rather delicate?"

"It is true. But I was quite pleased when your people in Washington changed the name of French Fries to Freedom Fries. What awful things you Americans have done to food."

"I'm glad that we were able to please the republic in our own little way, Kid, but that was bullshit and anyway, they changed the name back. You eat them, too, but with a Frenchified name. *Pommes frites*."

"Entirely different."

"Same thing. Now why are two over-the-hill spooks like us meeting clandestinely? Everybody knows who we are, what we were, and that we hang out together. My landlady calls me the 'old American spy who lives upstairs in 2B.'"

Delmas laughed and looked down at the fast-moving dark water. "Which is why we have such excellent cover, no? No one would suspect that we had any worthwhile missions left in us."

"They may be right. How are you doing?" Higbee knew that Delmas had undergone chemotherapy for lung cancer.

"It may be coming back."

"Jesus. Sorry to hear that, my friend."

Delmas shrugged. "Life. Death." His wife had died twelve years ago, and the way he spoke those words showed that he no longer cared about living or dying, and probably would choose death if it meant a chance to reunite with his love. He turned in a circle, as if watching a passing pigeon, but checking to be sure no one was loitering nearby. "I have been asked to give you something to relay to your former masters at Langley. My people wanted to keep this affair as back-channel as possible, and nothing can possibly be any more back-channel than you and me."

Even when governments are locked in extreme disagreements over international policy, sometimes even while at war, their intelligence services maintain unofficial contacts. Such was the case with the current strain between Paris and Washington. The French could not afford to be seen as helping the Americans in the Middle East, so passing an urgent and sensitive message was better done through very unofficial means.

Buzz put on his CIA game face for the first time in many years. It felt good. Jean-Paul had been an agent with Le Service de Documentation Extérieure et de Contre-Espionnage (SDECE) back in the dirty days of Algeria, and since 1982 with its successor, the Directorate of External Security. He was retired over his protests.

A crash of thunder rolled over the city, and raindrops began to fall from the churning, slate gray sky, speckling the bridge. In unison, they raised black umbrellas.

"It is your missing general. You heard about him? This Middleton?"

"Been all over the television. Yeah. What about him?"

"As you know, we depend heavily upon human intelligence sources, where you Americans rely more on technology. We don't have your capability in that field, but we have been growing agents in Africa and the Middle East for better than a century."

"Tell me about it. If somebody was about to fuck a sheep in Algiers, you knew about it before the sheep did." They both laughed. The rain fell steadily, lightly.

"Buzz, the Directorate has been contacted by one of our people, a former soldier in the Foreign Legion. He now lives in southern Syria, travels all around the area for us, and he saw your general being taken into a house in a village called Sa'ahn. The general appeared unconscious, but our man recognized that distinctive Marine uniform."

"Whoa, partner. You have a man on the fucking scene?"

Jean-Paul reached into the pocket of his sweater and pulled out an envelope. "*Oui*. Here is his name, photograph, and the location of the village and the house he maintains there. I am authorized to tell you that the Directorate persuaded him to stay where he is to help guide any rescue effort, and to point out the house where the general is being held. You'll have to pay him some money, of course. Probably a lot of money. He wants a million dollars, U.S."

"Damn. Just a mil? He'll have to buy a couple of new camels to carry all the gold they will give him to get Middleton back safe." Buzz Higbee put the envelope in a deep sweater pocket. "How does Washington contact this asset if they want to do something?"

"Get a quiet message to our military attaché in Washington. Paris will pass it on through a coded microburst transmission to the asset."

"Sounds almost too good to be true, Jean-Paul, which means it probably isn't. What's the catch?"

"I considered that and asked about it. There is nothing that we know of," the Frenchman said. "Nobody wants to see still another flareup in that region. This isn't Iraq, and Paris is more than willing to work with Washington on the problem. So I believe the only downside, as you say, is that you are now in my personal debt. I demand a lunch."

"Anywhere you want, and make it somewhere expensive. CIA is buying."

Jean-Paul smiled. "I was hoping you would say that. I will call you in the morning to name a place. Tell Marie that I send my love."

They shook hands and parted, heading toward opposite ends of the bridge, hurrying to reach shelter before the storm broke.

13

The CIA representative at the meeting of the National Security Council wore a private, satisfied smile. He had something that would get Buchanan off his ass. CIA tapped the keys on a laptop computer and the photograph of a middle-aged man with dark hair and a thick brushy mustache flashed onto one of the wall screens. "His name was Pierre Falais when he served in the Foreign Legion. He became a Muslim after his enlistment was up and took the name of Abu Mohammed. Father was French, mother Algerian. Studied to be an engineer in France, but gave it up, did the military stint, and then moved to Syria in about 1985 and worked as a skilled carpenter. Injured in a fall from a ladder and couldn't do the high work anymore, so he moved to this village and set up shop. Does a little carpentry, a little farming, and a lot of spying for the French."

"Why should we trust the French on this?" asked National Security Advisor Gerald Buchanan.

"They controlled the area for years in the colonial times, and French roots run deep there. The information was given to us through a totally reliable channel, Mr. Buchanan. Our own contact agent is retired, but has known his French counterpart for many years. He believes the information is valid." CIA stopped briefly to consider his next words. "Paris has done an extremely rare, timely, and thorough breakout on this guy for us."

"So this Abu Mohammed actually saw General Middleton and knows precisely where he is being held?"

"We consider the information to be accurate as of this moment. It could change at any time." CIA replaced the large photograph with a map, satellite imagery of a small town just to the east of the rugged Mount Druz. It was only a couple of streets and blocky buildings. "This is where the informant claims Middleton is being held . . . right . . . here." He tapped a key and a red circle blinked around one of the small buildings near the edge of town.

Buchanan tapped his fingers against his pursed lips. "Anyone care to comment?"

The table remained silent for a few moments as he watched them all carefully. Finally, the woman from State gathered her nerve. "I'm uncomfortable with it."

"Why?" Buchanan had never liked her. One of those faceless drones who had lived overseas too long, enjoying the good life and throwing embassy parties. She had been in Rio until she came back home to that roost of diplomatic vipers over on C Street, for God's sake. What would she know about the Middle East? "What troubles you?"

"It all seems too easy. Too convenient," State said, keeping her voice quiet and level. Buchanan was trying to move too fast, she thought, and nobody was willing to buck him. "Anytime there is a major incident, we start getting walk-ins to embassies, our intel communities see their switchboards light up, and the FBI has to beat informants away with a stick. These potential informants all smell money and want to swap information for cash. On the Middleton kidnap, however, the secret world has gone quiet. Nobody got anything until this retired old CIA guy is contacted by his buddy, a retired senior French intelligence officer, and the whole thing falls into our laps. We get a local guide, his picture and history, and the address where the victim is being kept."

"So you think they are lying?" Let her dig her own grave.

"No. But it's possible that both Washington and Paris are being used. I have been in government service more than twenty years, Mr. Buchanan, and it has never been this easy. Problems of this magnitude do not just resolve themselves."

"Your concern is duly noted," Buchanan said, knowing her comments were true. The contact in Syria was working with the Shark Team there and the information was intentionally being fed in from the field. He had to sidetrack her. The others at the table remained silent as Buchanan smirked. "This one indeed has come out of the blue. I think Paris realizes just how deep in the crapper they are with us on other things, particularly Iraq, and are offering this up as a goodwill gesture without having to do so publicly. That's why they used the old boys. Okay, so everybody knows where we are. What's the next step?"

General Henry Turner, chairman of the Joint Chiefs, leaned into his microphone. "We want to go in and get him as soon as possible. The navy is moving a task force into position in the eastern Med, and we can fly a Force

Recon rescue team in over Israel and plop right down on these people. Thirty minutes on the ground and we bring out both Middleton and the informant. All we need to green-light the mission is the President's authorization."

Buchanan nodded once. Good, the general had shifted the attention of the group from questioning the "how" to the "what next." He stood abruptly. "Sounds good. Make your final plans and prepare a briefing for the President."

"Yes, sir. We will get him everything he needs to know."

"Then let's go and get your general," said Buchanan. He turned and left the room.

State caught up with CIA on the way out. "This is too damned easy," she repeated.

CIA shook his head almost imperceptibly in agreement. "I just work here," he said. They left the White House together.

Gerald Buchanan stood at the window of his office with the door closed, ready to sign the death warrant. A high position carried burdens. He, and he alone in this building, including the fool who sat in the Oval Office, had the guts to sign an order of the sort he contemplated. Few men in the entire city would be willing to sign it. That bitch from State certainly could never do it. They were weaklings who did not understand putting higher needs over the survival of one man. For the good of the United States of America, General Bradley Middleton had to die.

General Turner had made a tactical verbal mistake in

his eagerness to rescue Middleton by unveiling his determination to use only Marines. Buchanan had captured
one of Turner's pawns in that move, because he would
now be able to confine his search for just the right man,
someone qualified to carry out the order, to a handful of
Marines, to put U.S. military fingerprints on this assassination.

He moved to his wall safe, placed his right palm
against the biometric reader, and dialed a combination.
When the heavy door swung open, he pulled out a file
that had been secretly ordered from the CIA on a dozen
Special Forces operatives who were occasionally used
for unique missions. "The wet stuff," CIA had explained.

Taking it to his desk, sitting in the black high-backed
chair and studying the papers under the bright light, he
flipped to a section that identified three Marines who
were employed for such work, and saw that two of them
were already on other assignments.

The remaining candidate was an expert scout sniper
and gunnery sergeant. The statistics and the photograph
showed that he was five-nine, 160 pounds, with gray
eyes and short brown hair; a combat veteran; age thirty-
four; single; and numerous decorations including awards
from foreign governments and letters of commendation
that were marked top secret. Buchanan read the biog-
raphy with some interest, for it seemed that the man had
been in almost every hot spot around the world for the
past ten years, including special missions with the Israelis, the British, and the Russians. He was officially
credited with eighty-one confirmed kills, but the real
figure was much higher, for the number included only

his victims who had been confirmed, and not any killed in special secret operations. Interestingly, the file also had a couple of letters of reprimand that indicated problems with authority. His last mission had involved a questionable kill on the wrong side of the Pakistani border, which had caused a serious diplomatic incident. The shooter was reprimanded and temporarily banished from the active list of covert agents. This would be a good time to bring him back. Not only was he finishing a contract job with some weapons company and was free for new orders, but he also might be wanting to prove that he was still up to doing clandestine work. Buchanan underlined the name: last name Swanson; first name Kyle.

The National Security Advisor possessed one of the most secure computers in the entire U.S. government, but Buchanan refused to believe it could not be hacked. All of those whirring and clicking sounds only meant that the hard drive was storing and shuffling information. There was no such thing as a really secure computer. He did not want anyone to someday unveil his secret correspondence to a Senate investigating committee or have it become a headline in *The Washington Post*. He would not even trust his secretary on this one.

From his middle desk drawer, Buchanan slid out a single sheet of expensive stationery that bore THE WHITE HOUSE across the top in simple blue letters, and began to write in a neat, precise longhand. There would be only this one original, and it would rest in a briefcase locked to the wrist of a special courier. Once the instruction was read by the Marine sniper, the courier would destroy the document. No copies, no paper trail.

Buchanan finished the note, sealed it in an official envelope, and put it into a light blue file folder with a red stripe diagonally across the front and WHITE HOUSE TOP SECRET stenciled in big black letters. He sealed that, too.

Then he told his aide Sam Shafer to locate this Gunnery Sergeant Swanson and get him to that fleet Marine unit in the Mediterranean as soon as possible. Shafer would also fly out to the task force, carrying the letter in a burnished aluminum briefcase handcuffed to his wrist, to personally deliver it. By using his private staff and a CIA cover, Buchanan would bypass General Turner and the others in their fancy uniforms.

As he worked, Buchanan once again had to grudgingly approve of Gordon Gates's enterprising and far-sighted ideas. Sending in a bloodthirsty robot like Swanson was indeed a good insurance policy.

14

Ali Shalal Rassad knew that sometimes just a little shove was all that was needed to force friends and enemies alike to do something they would later regret. He was a master of that quiet tactic, and was about to employ it against the United States of America. Rassad was known as the Rebel Sheikh not so much for being a great fighter, although he was, but because he refused to be consumed by any higher political power. His streak of stubborn independence made him an ally of convenience from Baghdad to Tehran to Washington. He worked with all, trusted none, and worked only for himself.

He had agreed to perform a very precise role in the drama involving the American general, the sort of multi-layered deception that he most enjoyed. He was being paid well to lend some of his militiamen to the mission, then to hold a single brief meeting with the Pentagon correspondent from a major American television net-work. The reporter had been in Iraq many times and had great credibility within the United States. His story would be accepted as fact.

Rassad sipped a cup of strong tea as he scanned the *International Herald Tribune* and other newspapers and magazines that were brought daily to his office in Basra.

A staff that monitored the Internet furnished its hourly report: the blogs were busy, but had nothing significant. Just braying opinions of people who didn't really know anything. Three television sets ran CNN, al Jazeera, and Sky News, and stories about the disappearance of General Middleton and the peculiar demands made by the Holy Scimitar of Allah dominated the news.

There was nothing in the papers or on television to match the fresh information on a decoded message that was also on his desk. Task Force 32-A of the U.S. Navy's Seventh Fleet was moving into position in the western Mediterranean. Israel had granted flyover permission for the Americans. The Marines were coming. Rassad intended to spur everyone along with a renewed sense of urgency to prevent them from having second thoughts that might breed caution.

Rassad loved the game. He pushed aside the papers, finished the tea, and snapped his fingers for an assistant to clear the desk and incinerate all of the papers. Some posturing politician someday might send a raiding party to his palace in an attempt to find and seize incrimination information. That would fail, of course, and the politician would soon be assassinated, but Rassad kept his most important information in his head. Everything else was consigned to ashes.

He returned to his living suite, where a barber waited to trim his beard, eyebrows, nose, and ears. The valet had laid out clothing chosen for the interview, a dark gray suit from London, an off-white dress shirt with a muted silk tie, and highly polished Italian shoes. The trousers were tailored to help offset the fact that his left leg was an inch shorter than his right, a reminder of the year and a half he had spent in Abu Ghraib prison for the crime of defending his beautiful girlfriend when Uday Hussein's thugs had come for her. Uday himself, laughing, had wielded the long steel crowbar that smashed Rassad's bones while telling in great detail how the girl, a virgin, had been fucked and how she screamed and how when Uday tired of her, he tossed her to the guards in a rape room, where she died. Rassad would be allowed to heal for a while after one of the torture sessions, only to undergo a repeat performance with the crowbar when he had recovered enough. He was not beaten to get a confession, for he had nothing to confess. Uday just enjoyed beating him. In the end, when the Americans had released him, Rassad could not walk on the mutilated leg.

The limp became a badge of honor for his new life as it healed, an unspoken reminder that he had paid dearly for opposing the dictator Saddam Hussein. When he was taken to prison, he had been just another bureaucrat in the Ministry of the Interior, but he emerged as a new political force, for he had channeled his powerful mind away from the pain and into how he could capitalize on his experiences. There were days now when he could almost thank Uday for the cruelty, because no one ever questioned Rassad's loyalty to his country. It was a wonderful political bargaining chip. In the end, Rassad had the final laugh on Uday by directing the Americans to the location of the Hussein brothers, where they were killed. He kept a picture of Uday's misshapen dead body in a folder in a desk drawer, and he looked at it often.

Today, Rassad would wear the fine suit instead of the comfortable robes in order to appear as a reasonable, moderate, westernized Iraqi leader. He did not want the American television audience to equate him with some ordinary Koran-thumping radical mullah. He had graduated from MIT, for Christ's sake.

A sleek Bell helicopter, ornate in its coat of glistening midnight blue with gold trim, skimmed in to land at the palace after a smooth trip from the big American base in Doha, Kuwait. Jack Shepherd unfolded his lanky frame from the comfortable seat and stepped out, shielding his eyes against the rotor blast. He was disoriented. Something was missing. Something was wrong, a sense of incompleteness. It wasn't until an escort shook his hand and helped his television crew load their gear into an air-conditioned limo that Shepherd could put his finger on what was different. It was quiet! He had heard others speak about the eerie feeling in the broad neighborhoods around the Rebel Sheikh's palace, but he had not been here for at least a year. In Iraq, he usually came in tense and expecting danger, with bomb blasts echoing throughout the countryside, something somewhere always blowing up with the erratic constancy of a popcorn machine, but this area of Basra was an oasis of calm.

The escort gave them a quick tour before going to the palace. Shops were open, private cars jammed the clean streets, children played soccer on neat green fields, and women walked freely in the street markets, some with heads uncovered, with bags of goods on their arms. Police without sidearms directed traffic, and men in robes or open-necked shirts and trousers sat around the tables of sidewalk cafés. There was laughter.

Shepherd saw a sign giving directions to the new Toyota plant, and passed other signs of German, French, British, Japanese, and Russian companies. Foreign investment was flowing in. The new buildings being erected were not slapdash brick-and-mortar jobs, but well-engineered concrete and steel. Shepherd flipped through his mental index cards until he found the comparison—Beirut, and how the older correspondents described it back when it was a pearl of a city and not a terrorist hellhole. Military units stayed outside Basra, and some of the Rebel Sheikh's feared private militia had been transformed into civilian police. This area of the city had been good last year when he visited, and was better today. Whatever the sheikh was doing was working.

"Jack Shepherd! It is good to see you again." Ali Shalal Rassad stepped from the shade of an arbor of trees beside a fountain in the courtyard of the palace and extended his hand. "Thank you for coming on such short notice."

"Thank you for the invitation," Shepherd replied. "This is a big story and I appreciate getting your comment."

Rassad nodded and led the correspondent into the coolness of the palace. "Indeed. Please have your crew set up right away. I fear that time is not on our side. After the interview, you can use my press office to feed your story back to your editors. My technicians will help in any way they can."

As they took their places and were miked up and lights were arranged and tested and the camera was prepared, Rassad steered the off-camera conversation toward what Shepherd had observed on the way in.

"I must say I was quite impressed," the reporter answered. "Everywhere else this country is torn by violence, but your zone shows none of those signs. Why is that?"

"Many reasons, my friend, and I will be happy to discuss them when we have lunch after the interview. The easy answer is that we just want to live in peace, and the Prophet, may his name be praised, is leading us in that direction. Foreign armies have invaded our country over the centuries, and we know how to rebuild," he said as a technician adjusted his suit and tie and a makeup artist applied a little powder to a bright spot on his forehead. "The problem this time was that the Americans wanted to do everything their way, and not our way. Luckily, we drew the British as occupiers, and they were more understanding. Once we endured the violent time and proved we could provide our own security and were no danger to others, London was glad to allow us room to grow and so withdraw some of their troops."

Rassad suddenly looked grim. "No American contractors are allowed to come in and pay fantastic sums to their U.S. employees while giving our people slave wages, and making decisions in Dallas that should have been made in Iraq. We wanted equal pay for equal work. If they didn't want to oblige, they would learn that they were not the only outside nation on this earth that had contractors wanting to help us. The hubris of the American administrators was their downfall. We were building an entire nation, not some shopping mall. The result was that we were able to establish security, clean water, adequate food, electricity, and a civil government that is quite secular and that emphasizes fairness and tolerance. There is no reason that the rest of our nation cannot be the same way, if the foreigners— all of them, including our fellow Muslims from other countries—will simply go home."

He did not mention his personal militia, the feared Holy Scimitar of Allah. They were kept out of sight at distant bases and trained daily with the deadly specialists from Gates Global, one of the world's best private security companies. One reason things were so quiet in Basra was that everyone in town knew that stepping out of line would result in a quick trip into the desert, never to be seen again.

Shepherd made notes. "That sounds rather like a threat," he observed.

"Not at all. They will leave sometime anyway, for they have done so throughout our history. The sooner the better. Let us get on with our lives."

Shepherd got a nod from his cameraman. "Okay, we're ready to roll if you are."

Rassad's manner changed dramatically, the facial expression eased, and he became a quiet diplomat. "I will make a brief statement, then you can ask questions."

The cameraman pointed and Rassad began. "The people of Iraq have been greatly shocked by the news that Brigadier General Bradley Middleton of the United States Marine Corps has been kidnapped. We also have been shamed by the outrageous claim that this crime was committed by the Holy Scimitar of Allah. As a humble representative of the Holy Scimitar, I want to denounce that falsehood in the strongest way possible. As everyone knows, the Holy Scimitar is a benevolent society, much like the American Red Cross, and is dedicated to the health and welfare of the Iraqi people. It has no connection whatsoever with any terrorists. We were not involved with the kidnapping of General Middleton and we reject those who have tarnished our good name. They are thugs and beyond the protection of the Koran's teachings." The sheikh paused and stared into the camera. "We had no hand in this."

Shepherd had a hard time keeping his face straight and professional. Great stuff, and the sheikh had adroitly danced around the Holy Scimitar's violent history. "Do you know who did it?"

"Unfortunately, no, we do not. But our security people have uncovered something which we feel we must convey publicly to your government. We did not contact them directly because while we wish the general no harm, we do not work for the Americans. I contacted you, Mr. Shepherd, because I consider you to be an honest broker of this information."

"What is the message?" Shepherd was glowing inside. That unsolicited compliment, plus this invitation to interview the sheikh, would play well in the upcoming negotiations to renew his contract. He damned sure was not going to screw this up now by challenging the sheikh about the real reputation of the vicious militia.

"Evil men are planning to execute General Middleton before a television camera at noon on Tuesday. He is to be stoned to death in symbolic retribution for the destruction American forces have wrought. The true villain in this horrible episode is al Qaeda."

Shepherd was shocked. "Can you prove that, Sheikh Rassad?"

"Yes." He removed a white envelope from the inside pocket of his jacket. "After we finish speaking, the Holy Scimitar will turn over to a Swiss diplomat this written message that was delivered from an al Qaeda messenger only a few hours ago. It claims to contain details known only to someone who participated in the kidnapping. Beyond that, it gives only the time of the execution and says there will be no negotiations."

Rassad eased back into his chair as Shepherd said something inane to close the interview. As the lights went off, both men unclipped their mikes and Rassad took him by the elbow, steering him away. "Now you must go to our press center and file your report, John. Please hurry, for I consider this to be extremely important, and perhaps you can save the life of General Middleton. When Washington calls, as I am sure they will, you can tell them from me personally that we are digging hard for any information that could be helpful and will pass along anything we find immediately. Now go, go! When you are done, we will have lunch. I want to talk about the coming football season."

Sheikh Ali Shalal Rassad was satisfied. This was Arab politics at its best, built on shifting sands, bargaining in which something could be nothing, or anything. Gordon Gates had paid him a hundred thousand dollars for assisting in the capture of General Middleton and meeting with the reporter. Buying Rassad's help was not the same as getting his allegiance. Gates was a comrade of convenience. Rassad was now moving to convince Washington that the danger to the general was great, but that he wasn't involved at all. They were always ready to believe that al Qaeda was at fault, which meant that those radical fools who were trying to weaken his hold on Basra would be hit hard again by the Americans. As a further goodwill gesture, he would have the Holy Scimitar sweep up a couple of al Qaeda operatives tonight and turn them over to the CIA and further rid him of that nuisance.

Ali Shalal Rassad walked down a cool, tiled hallway toward his living quarters, pulling at the confining necktie. He had time for a nap before the reporter finished filing and joined him for a late lunch.

15

"Prepare for landing." The anonymous voice on the public address system woke him up, and Swanson tightened the belts holding him in the uncomfortable seat. He was aboard a twin-engine Grumman C-1A, technically called a Carrier On-board Delivery System, but familiarly known to all as a COD. Many of the twenty-eight passenger seats were occupied by young sailors and Marines returning to the huge CVN-71 after spending a shore leave as drunk as skunks. The seats faced the rear of the plane, which created a disoriented feeling of flying backward and severe cases of motion sickness and a need for extra barf bags. A hangover combined with a COD ride is just too much for most human stomachs to handle at dawn on Sunday morning.

The pilot lowered his flaps and gunned the twin Allison engines, and the COD fell out of the sky, the tailhook catching the three-wire across the deck of the USS *Theodore Roosevelt*. Swanson was jerked hard against the seatbelts as the plane went from 120 knots to flat zero in only 60 feet. Since the insides of the passengers underwent the same rate of instant deceleration, it felt like the stomach was coming out of the mouth, and a young sailor down the aisle puked noisily, starting a chain reaction.

It took a few minutes for the COD to be released from the wire and taxi to a parking place on the broad deck; then the side door opened and sea air poured inside to remove the stench of fresh vomit. The awkward-looking CODs ran regular missions out to the carriers to deliver personnel and supplies, and Swanson was just part of the day's cargo being hauled from the U.S. Air Force Base at Injerlek, Turkey, out to the carrier battle group steaming in the western Mediterranean Sea.

Shari had received her summons to return to Washington two hours before a duty officer called on Kyle on his cell phone, ordering him to return to the fleet as soon as possible. All leaves were cancelled. Shari pointed out that she was called first because she was much more important to world peace and protecting the nation. Sir Jeff had directed the *Vagabond* to Naples at a speed that would allow Shari and Kyle to catch flights out first thing Saturday morning, yet slow enough to make time for a final fantastic dinner aboard and a night together. The yacht trip had been a balm for both of them, a rare occasion that stitched their relationship even tighter, and leaving her in Naples had been difficult, but they parted knowing they would have plenty of tomorrows. For now, it was time to get into a warrior frame of mind and concentrate on business.

He waited until everyone else was off the COD before waddling down the aisle, carrying Excalibur in a gun case in one hand and a Val Pak suitcase in the other. Swanson stepped out through the hatch and down the small metal stairway. Wind howled across the flight deck, which was busier than a Wal-Mart at Christmas and smelled of jet fuel and oil.

"Are you one Gunnery Sergeant Kyle Swanson?" The question was yelled in a deep voice that pierced the chaos of the flight deck by a Marine top sergeant whose head was scraped clean of hair.

"Who the fuck is asking?"

"I am God Almighty as far as you are concerned, you piece of pond scum. Fear me!"

"Fear. Right. Here, Double-Oh, catch." He tossed him the Val Pak. The other Marine grabbed it with one big paw, laughed, and clapped Kyle on the shoulder.

"Come on. We ain't waiting around on this barge. They sent me over from the *Wasp* to fetch you, and our chariot awaits over yonder." Master Sergeant Orville Oliver Dawkins of Pratt, Kansas, pointed across the deck to where a boxy UN-1H helicopter was warming up, the big rotor whomping the air around it. They went over to the port edge and down a couple of ladders and entered the subterranean, pipe-laced caverns that were filled with planes and busy crew members in different-colored jerseys. Mechanics and technicians burrowed into the parked aircraft.

The two Marines did not speak openly with so many people about, but Kyle's curiosity was running away with him. He had learned in Turkey that for some reason he was a high-priority item, and now he had been met personally by a top sergeant with a private helo. Kyle thought for a moment that maybe he was as important as Shari after all.

"So what's this all about, Double-Oh?" Their boots thudded on the steel deck.

"I didn't catch the whole conversation, but the colonel said something about either giving you another

Navy Cross or finally kicking your skinny little ass out of my beloved Corps. I forgot which."

"Some god you are. A top who doesn't know what's going on? What is our world coming to?" Swanson said.

"I know all. The beasts of the field and fishies in the ocean do not move without my knowing."

"It's just 'fish,' not 'fishies.' Fish is both singular and plural."

" 'Fishies' sounds better, and since I am God, I can say it however the fuck I want to." They stepped out of the way of a little yellow tractor that crawled toward them, pulling a wings-folded F-14 Tomcat.

"So you really have no idea what's going on, do you?"

"Not a clue, Kyle. Just bet your ass something big league is coming down involving your old pal General Middleton. Why else would you get a private whirlybird ride?"

Dawkins looked back over his shoulder long enough to give me a smile that contained no warmth whatsoever. "And a 'special guest' is waiting for you."

They started up the stairs and ladders to the main deck. "Shit. A spook?"

"Spooky as Freddy Krueger on Halloween. As Jason with a chainsaw. As *Scary Movie 3*. CIA dude straight from Langley. Got here last night."

By the time they reached the deck, the Huey was ready to go. The bird was primarily used as a command-and-control platform, which meant it had cushioned seats. Neither Double-Oh nor Swanson buckled in, because they made a living jumping out of helicopters and hated being confined inside one. The Huey smoothly lifted away, the open doors letting the fresh morning air swoosh through the cabin. The giant *Roosevelt* grew small in size, and then disappeared behind them as the green Med rolled gently underneath, five hundred feet below.

On the way over to the *Wasp*, Kyle considered the unexpected appearance of the "special guest." Last he had heard from the CIA, he was standing at attention in front of some civilian and a bird colonel and being told that he had fucked up the border mission, that he was more trouble than he was worth, and that he would never get to play with them again.

"What?" he had asked the spooks. "Did that asshole Ali bin Assam come back to life or something? You wanted him dead. He's dead."

He was then chewed on for a while for constantly violating accepted doctrine in the field, and told that the agency had no room for renegades. Kyle shrugged it off. He had heard it all before, just the usual complaints made by the office weenies when they had given him their unspoken blessing before the black mission began to do whatever was required. They were just covering their asses for the files, and he knew those loud threats to absolutely, positively, never, ever use him again would last only until the next time he was needed.

Now it seemed that time had arrived. Something had changed their little bureaucratic minds, which probably meant he was going to get shot at and that a snatch raid was planned to get Middleton back. Kyle reached between his boots and gave the gun case an affectionate pat, quite happy that Sir Jeff and Tim insisted that he take Excalibur along and give it a real field test. Somebody shot at him, he was going to shoot back.

16

Swanson knocked on the hatch and heard a sharp command from within the VIP cabin: "Enter." His boots made impressions on the soft carpet covering the steel deck of the well-decorated room. Prints of sailing ships, old admirals, and sea battles hung on the walls, flags stood in the corners, and the curtains were pulled away from a large porthole that lit the room with sunshine. A civilian with an astonishing helmet of black hair slicked straight back stood to meet him. He wore a moderately expensive dark suit with a white shirt so starched that he probably stood it up in a corner at night. The guy reeked of ego.

"Gunny Swanson, I'm John Smith," he said with an easy smile that showed a lot of even teeth. "Please feel free to call me John."

How original, Swanson thought. "I'm not working for the CIA anymore, Mr. Smith. I've been back with the MEU for about a year, after a, uh, dispute about my last mission."

Smith sat down on the large sofa and crossed his legs carefully. "I flew all the way out here from Washington to personally hand you some new orders. You stay with the Marines on paper, but there will be a temporary and a simultaneous mission for the CIA."

Swanson went silent, considering the situation. The squeaks and thumps of an aircraft carrier under way filtered into the quiet. "Who knows about this?"

Sam Shafer lied. "Myself and my boss, the National Security Advisor, Gerald Buchanan. The commandant of the Marine Corps and the President of the United States." Actually, Shafer did not know, but admitting that would lower his sense of importance. Neither did the President or the commandant know, because Buchanan was running this on his own. Shafer was itching to get a look at the letter. Buchanan had only given him crumbs of information and terse instructions about how to handle this interview.

"What about my MEU commander?"

"This is a *need* to know situation, Gunny. Not a *want* to know."

"That sort of complicates the hell out of things right out of the box, Mr. Jones."

"Smith."

"Smith. Jones. Who the fuck cares? It's not your real name anyway. So this is a black job that even my commanding officer will not know about? That sucks big-time. How can it work if he doesn't know what I'm doing?" Clearly the mission had been dreamed up by people who had never served in a combat role. That made Kyle suspicious about whether the Marine commandant was really in the loop.

"As far as your commanding officer is concerned, you are going along on the mission to rescue General Middleton as a sniper for extra firepower. If everything goes smoothly, this other order is to be disregarded."

"So what's the job?"

Sam Shafer walked to a small desk on which lay his aluminum briefcase, and dialed the combination to open it. He handed Kyle a sealed white envelope. Swanson took it over to the porthole and read it in the bright light. The first thing he noticed was small blue printing across the top: the white house. The order took his breath away. He read it a second time. Same result. "Shit," he said. "You're out of your fuckin' mind."

"I assure you, Gunny Swanson, this is as serious as a dozen heart attacks." Shafer was bluffing, but he knew Buchanan was not playing a game. The instructions, whatever they were, meant what they said.

"And if I refuse to carry out this order?"

"Then you will be held in isolation in the brig aboard this ship and we get somebody else to do the job. You are forbidden to discuss it with anyone. After the mission is over, you would be thrown out of the Marine Corps."

"And if I do it, not only do I probably still get run out of the Marines, but maybe I also face a firing squad for having done such good work for the CIA. Fuck this."

"Are you refusing the mission?"

"Let's just say I have some big questions. For starters, I don't know you. You haven't shown me any identification, which leads me to believe you're not CIA at all. So let's start at the beginning, Mr. Smith. Who the hell are you?"

The civilian's brown eyes went cold as he reached for his wallet and pulled out a laminated government identification card. His real name was Samuel Shafer and he worked at the White House as assistant to the National Security Advisor. That clicked, for the mission order was signed by Gerald Buchanan. Shafer was a messenger boy.

Kyle handed the order back to him. "Now I want you to tell me face-to-face, so there is no misunderstanding. What are my orders, Mr. Shafer?"

Shafer had a difficult time keeping a stone face and maintaining his glee. At last he got to see the order. When he read it, he was shocked, too, but buried the reaction to pretend he knew what was going on.

"Just what it says, Gunny. If things go wrong on this mission to rescue the general, you are instructed by the White House to shoot him dead."

"And why would we want to do that?"

"We don't *want* to do it at all." Shafer was thinking on his feet. "Middleton is too valuable to stay in enemy hands. He knows too much about certain highly classified projects that are time-sensitive. We cannot risk him being made to talk. Too much is at stake to take the chance that the torturers may pull the information out of him. He knows that, too."

"They wouldn't get anything from Middleton," Kyle said. "I hate his guts, but he's a tough bird. He would die before giving up a secret."

"Drugs and torture could leave him no choice. He would be interrogated in a hospital somewhere, with an IV drip in his arm and his mouth running like a motor. If we can't bring him back, they cannot have him, either. Simple as that." Shafer handed the letter back to Swanson. "Gunny, this is obviously a difficult assignment, but we have to put our country's security first. It is a national security emergency."

Swanson studied the authorization letter again. "If

that's so, why is the order signed by this guy Buchanan and not the President himself? You said he knows about it."

"Are you being intentionally naïve? Deniability. The President's name can't be on anything like this, even though this is the only copy and I'm going to destroy it right after you tell me whether you are taking the job or not. So, Gunny, time's up. Consider that to be an order to you directly from your commander-in-chief. You in or out?"

Kyle paused, then walked away from Shafer, folding the letter and buying moments to think. *Since there was no way the Marine commandant would be in on this, was the President's involvement also a lie?* Murdering a general was huge! But the order came straight from the White House. Swanson made a decision.

"Okay. I'll do it, Mr. Shafer. But you're not going to destroy this letter. We'll have the captain put it in the ship's safe until the mission is complete. If I have to pull the trigger, the order is transferred into a secure safe under the control of the CIA director of operations. I won't be left hanging out to dry with no way to prove I was following orders."

Shafer reared. "Out of the question! Give me the letter, Gunny. I will burn it and then you go off and do your goddam job as you have been ordered to do." He put on his angry face, raised his voice, and pissed Swanson off.

"No. The letter goes in the safe."

They stared at each other for fifteen silent seconds and Shafer spun on the heel of a highly polished shoe. "I'm going to get a secure radio link back to the White

House, and you will be ordered directly by senior civilian authority to surrender the letter to me. Take it from me, Gunny Swanson, you do *NOT* want to have that kind of conversation with Gerald Buchanan."

Kyle moved to the desk and plopped into the seat. He shoved the telephone toward the visitor. "I'll wait here for you, Mr. Smith. Patch the call to this extension."

Shafer went through the hatchway and stormed down the corridor.

Swanson jumped up and found Double-Oh waiting outside. "Problem, Double-Oh. Catch up with that dude and lead him around for about ten minutes. He's looking for the comm center, so steer him through the berthing areas or engineering spaces or whatever, then bring him back here. I'll explain later." The big guy took off after the angry civilian.

Kyle went the other way, down a ladder, and made his way aft to the little shop where the ship's daily newsletter was printed. A yeoman was clicking the keyboard of a computer.

"You got a copying machine?" Swanson waved the folded letter.

The sailor didn't reply, just pointed to a big beige box in a corner, a Xerox that would have been at home in any civilian business office. Kyle peeled back the flexible lid, pressed the letter flat, lowered the lid, and hit the green copy button. After a brief hum and a flash of rolling light, the machine spit into a side tray a copy that was indistinguishable from the original. "Thanks," he told the swabbie, who had not looked up from his computer. Back in the VIP suite, Swanson found an envelope in the center drawer of the desk, put in the original letter, and sealed it. The envelope went back into the drawer. He folded the copy just as the original had been folded, and laid it on the desk.

Within two minutes, Double-Oh delivered the exasperated Sam Shafer back into the room, where Gunnery Sergeant Kyle Swanson was standing at a sharp parade rest position. Shafer closed the door, his face red with anger, but before he could speak, Kyle did, very formally.

"Sir. I have reconsidered my position. I was confused about the chain of command, but if you were willing to get Mr. Buchanan on the horn, then this order is obviously valid. Therefore, I apologize and accept the mission, although with reluctance."

Shafer, having won the point, calmed down. He was back in control and oozed White House power. "And the order?"

Swanson pointed to the paper. He did not want to allow Shafer too much time to examine it. "Right here, sir. Burn it and get it over with. It would be best for me that it is never seen again."

Shafer placed the paper in a large ashtray and took out a cigarette lighter, and a quick flame nibbled the corner, then fire ate the entire page. Shafer took the ashes into the bathroom and flushed them down the toilet.

"When will you be returning to Washington, sir?" Kyle asked.

"As soon as they can launch me. I've been assigned a two-seat F-16 for this trip," he said.

Swanson gave him a sharp salute. "Yes, sir. Have a good trip back, sir."

"And good luck to you, Gunny. I know this is a tough one." He extended his hand and Swanson shook it, then stepped outside as Shafer left. Double-Oh had been waiting, and after Kyle retrieved the letter, they went to get some coffee and find a quiet corner.

"You ain't going to believe this shit," Swanson told his friend, and Double-Oh didn't, until Kyle gave him the envelope for safekeeping. "Now I have you as a witness *and* the original letter, and Mr. Shafer from the CIA or White House or wherever he works can go fuck himself and the F-16 he rode in on."

17

In the middle of the night, Kyle Swanson stood in the well of a portside gun turret next to the flight deck and let his thoughts roam away from the mission at hand. The irony of the job struck him. He was aboard the USS *Wasp*, a small aircraft carrier designed for special operations, sailing in the eastern Med beneath a massive umbrella of protection. It was part of an entire battle group that spread around the nuclear-powered carrier USS *Theodore Roosevelt*, about hundred thousand tons of steel and one of the biggest ships ever to sail the seas. Needle-nosed destroyers, daunting cruisers, and big submarines also were slicing the waters, and there were enough missiles, planes, bullets, torpedoes, and sailors on hand to take care of anything that any enemy could throw at them at sea, and also to strike deep into hostile nations. So if this mighty task force, the best the squids had, was so tough, why was he standing here, dressed all in black, his face smeared with grease, and decked out with his personal firepower, getting ready to head out once again on a raid against some low-tech ragheads not all that far from the shores of Tripoli? The Marines seemed to keep coming back to this part of the world that was part of their hymn, as if there was some magnet for them in the desert sands.

Swanson felt rested. He had caught a couple of hours of sleep following a late operational briefing, and then test-firing and cleaning his weapons for a final time. He rolled out of his rack at oh-dark-thirty and joined up with the Force Recon team that would be the assault force on the TRAP, the initialized way of saying "Tactical Recovery of Air Personnel." A longer acronym labeled them as part of the Marine Expeditionary Unit, Special Operations Capable, or MEU-SOC. The mission was a frequently practiced operation designed to rescue a pilot downed in enemy territory and had therefore been easily adapted to pull out a hostage. Two helicopters would go in, and the first to land would have the mortar platoon aboard, which would spread out and secure the landing zone. A TRAP moved so fast that heavy mortar tubes were not part of the attack, so the Marines normally assigned to them were free for other jobs like protecting the LZ. The second helo carried the attack force. This package was built for speed, not total firepower.

The mess table was crowded with young Marines packing in big, greasy breakfasts of eggs and sausage, biscuits and bacon, and bragging and shouting insults and curses to cover their prebattle jitters. Kyle found a place on a bench and satisfied himself with cereal and hash browns to load up on carbohydrates, and some fruit. Juice instead of coffee, to avoid the caffeine. Then he went to the war room on the second-level hangar deck of the *Wasp*, found a soft chair, and fell asleep while the younger dudes, eager to rock and roll, continued their grabass. When the noise abruptly stopped,

Swanson awoke and saw a cluster of officers filing in to conduct the confirmation briefing.

In moments the room was totally silent, and the briefing officers began flashing photo recon pictures on the screen and putting up transparent overlays of maps. Swanson perched on the edge of his seat, watching closely. Only a few hours ago, the mission had still been vague on many points, but now it had slammed together like the hatch of a tank. Kyle had been through many briefings, but never had heard such a rapid-fire discussion of precise targets, operations, and methodology for exactly who was to do precisely what. No significant opposition was expected, since surprise would be total and only two guards were with General Middleton. *How the hell do they know that?*

The intel geeks claimed to have pinpointed the exact location where Middleton was being held, right down to the specific house, had downloaded satellite pictures and maps, and even had a photograph of a local guide, some French Arab who was a veteran of the Foreign Legion. Small pictures of the man were distributed with both of his names, Pierre Falais and Abu Mohammed, printed on the back. Having an inside operator should certainly make the mission a lot easier. The briefer predicted a smooth snatch-and-grab with little action, if any.

Kyle never liked planning for the easy scenario. There were always sudden twists and turns in combat, the enemy never reacted exactly as predicted, and really good intelligence was usually bad. To top it off, Murphy's Law always clicked in: If something can go wrong, it will, and at the worst possible time. A damned goat wanders into the wrong place, or a woman decides to string a laundry line across the landing zone, or somebody breaks a leg. He settled back into the chair. Sometimes it is best not to look a gift horse in the mouth and just accept what the man says. Occasionally, the bullshit works.

There was a stir among the senior combat-seasoned guys in the room, and Kyle exchanged a quick glance with the major who would lead the assault force and received a nod of silent agreement. *Here we go again. No enemy on the ground. Don't worry about it. Yeah, right. In the Middle East, land of fairy tales and mirages.*

Judging by the briefers who were taking turns at the podium, every government and spy in the Middle East had been working to find General Bradley Middleton, because his death would bring down the wrath of this big task force on somebody's head. For him to be executed in a television spectacular would make all Muslims appear to be savage maniacs before an unsympathetic world audience. Maybe some king or prince had dropped the dime on the bad guys, Kyle thought. Middleton was being held in Syria, and the leaders in Damascus well remembered the shock-and-awe campaign that opened the war with Iraq. Whoever these kidnappers were, their security sucked.

Still, this was a hell of a lot of information to have been gathered in such a short time in a part of the world where hostages and kidnap victims regularly were missing for weeks before any word surfaced about them.

The briefing done, Kyle slung Excalibur over his shoulder in a zippered drag bag and wandered up to the gun turret to find some privacy. Noise and movement assaulted him as soon as he stepped through the hatch, for it is never quiet on a ship. The pungent smell of oil, grease, and jet fuel hung over the carrier despite the stiff wind, and grease-stained sailors looking as dirty as coal miners were working everywhere. He punched the button on his cell phone for frequently dialed numbers, hit the send button, and listened as the *beep-beep-beep* sounded on the East Coast of the United States.

"Hey, you." Shari Towne usually was annoyed if she received a personal call during working hours, but the incoming number showed it was Kyle.

"Hey," Swanson said. His voice was soft, distant, concerned.

"You okay?"

"Yeah. I'm good. How was your trip home?"

"Quick and comfortable, but boring. Some kind soul laid on a little jet plane just for me. The movie was a chick flick that you would have hated."

Kyle paused, visualizing her sitting in her tiny office, surrounded by papers while intel reports pumped out of the computers. She would speed-read them, unconsciously translating as she went, remembering almost everything. "What are you wearing?" Swanson asked.

"The shoulder boards of a lieutenant commander in the United States Navy, you horny jarhead." She laughed.

"I just needed to hear you," Kyle said, turning serious. "I'm going to be gone for a little while." The conversation was a struggle. They wanted to be intimate, but professionalism and the need for security would not let them. Just hearing her voice was the best he could hope for.

"I know." Her mood shifted, too.

"You do?"

"Umm. Been working on it at this end. It's a strange one."

"You don't know the half of it."

"I don't? I'm supposed to know it all."

"Well, you don't. Trust me."

"Kyle? What's wrong?" Her voice was tinged with genuine concern. "Should I get involved here?"

Swanson caught himself. He had said too much, and telling her more might put her in jeopardy, since the letter containing what he considered an illegal order had come from her boss. "No, no. Absolutely not. Forget it, and please don't say anything to anyone about my bitching. It's just some Pentagon backseat driving, and nothing I can't handle. That's why I get the big bucks."

"But you're okay?" she asked.

"Oh, yeah. All dressed up for the prom, and the limo is waiting."

He ducked below the level of the flight deck as the launch crews moved an AV-8B Harrier II Plus attack jet into launch position, their purposeful ballet underscored by the plane's two screaming engines. Tongues of blue-white fire spit back from the exhausts and illuminated the darkness. Kyle told Shari to wait a moment while the plane built to a thunderous roar and lifted straight up from the deck, its exhaust rolling out in an engulfing cloud of heat. The plane hovered and changed the position of its wings and engines, then thundered away. Two Harriers, loaded with everything from iron bombs to cannons and missiles, would orbit near the target zone as part of the TRAP package, ready to zoom in if things started going to hell.

"I love you, girl," he shouted into the phone as a second Harrier was rolled into place. "I gotta go now."

"I love you, too. Call me when you get back. The very instant, you hear me? You understand?"

"Yes, ma'am."

"And be care . . ." She stopped talking. "We better stop."

"Yep. I'll call you in a while. Love ya." He thumbed the off button and the connection was broken, leaving Kyle feeling empty and alone as the plane wound up its roar to launch. Shari knew more about this rescue mission than she was able to say on an open line, which meant that one hell of a lot of people were involved, from the guys putting the Harriers in the air all the way up the ladder to the White House. The more people who know, the bigger the chance for a fuckup, the bigger chance of losing the cloak of secrecy.

He came up the ramp and walked onto the deck after the second Harrier had cleared out. The hostage rescue raiders were gathering near a pair of giant CH-53E Super Stallion heavy transport helicopters that were waiting with the rear ramps down and the big rotors starting to turn.

Twenty-four Marines were split into two groups, with a lieutenant already leading his stick of men up the ramp of one chopper. Kyle checked in with the major leading the assault force as it also moved to load. Double-Oh appeared at his elbow.

"Fuck if I shouldn't be going on this job," he told Kyle. "You get all the fun."

"Piece of cake, man. Didn't you pay attention to the briefing?" Kyle had a small bag of personal items in his hand, including his watch, cell phone, and wallet. He handed it to the big master sergeant. "Instead of all of us, maybe they should send a taxi to pick him up, huh?"

"Or maybe the briefers should go." He accepted the personal items, to hold until Kyle returned.

"An officer would never lie. You still got the letter I gave you, right?"

Dawkins tapped the chest pocket of his battle dress uniform and said, "I'll keep it right here until you get back." Kyle noticed that his friend had also put on a shoulder holster rig with the butt of a pistol in easy reach. Nobody was taking that letter.

The last Marines were stepping onto the ramp, and it was his time to board. "Look, Double-Oh, I just talked to Shari. If you need to show that note to someone later, bring her into the loop. Just remember, she works for the asshole who signed it."

"You're going to disobey a direct order from Washington, aren't you?"

"I'm not going to murder a Marine, even an asshole like Middleton," Kyle said. "I'm going to bring him back alive, just to piss everyone off." He tapped fists with Double-Oh and vanished into the dark cavern of the big helo.

"Hey, Swanson!" Master Sergeant O. O. Dawkins bellowed, his best parade ground voice cutting through the racket as the ramp began to close. "If you die, can I have your girl?"

18

"Five minutes out." The pilot's scratchy voice came into Kyle Swanson's ears through the internal radio net as the two CH-53E helicopters lurched through the night sky. The interior of the birds was deafening because each had three powerful GE engines and little insulation. Everyone wore special flight helmets fitted with thick earmuffs that contained radio receivers. The team was all on a single frequency, but the assault leader and Swanson could also communicate with the aircrew.

It was uncomfortable and cold in the narrow compartment where he sat scrunched among a dozen Marines, for although the huge helicopters were almost a hundred feet long, the cabin was thirty feet long, less than eight feet wide, and not even seven feet high. Looking around, the scene of the young warriors with painted faces and weighted with gear reminded Swanson of the old pictures of American paratroopers jammed aboard ancient C-47s going into the D-Day invasion.

The helicopters had flown an impeccable mission, and had gone "feet dry" over Israel right on schedule. From that point, they were wrapped in a protective embrace by Israeli jet fighters that just happened to be conducting a night exercise along the same path. Any hostile radar would have a hard time picking the two helicopters out of the clutter on their computer screens.

The assault force members had gone silent, each man alone with his thoughts, when they flew out of Israel, moved into unguarded airspace over Jordan, and finally reached the edge of Syria. They spent the long passing minutes checking their equipment or leaning back against the vibrating bulkhead, eyes closed and lost in thought. The first CH-53E would land about two kilometers from the village and the mortar platoon Marines would pour from it to form a protective cordon for the landing zone. The second one, which Swanson was aboard, would come in simultaneously and the raiders would hustle off, conduct the rescue, and bring the general back to the safe LZ and they would all be away.

The choppers hurtled along at their cruising speed of 175 miles per hour, the pilots handling the huge machines as surely as if they were driving their own cars, with hardly a wiggle in the flight path. The change in the pitch of the rotors, the sinking feeling in Swanson's stomach, and the pressure in his ears confirmed the beginning of the approach run, and he unbuckled his seatbelt. "Four minutes," came the warning call from the cockpit.

There were two open hatches near the front of the cabin, and a crew member was at one, perched behind a .50-caliber machine gun. At the three-minute alert, Swanson unplugged his commo line from the net and made his way forward to the second hatch, trying not to step on anyone as he sidled past the small motorcycle lashed in the aisle. The dirt bike was to be used by a scout if the mission commander wanted extended reconnaissance.

A typhoon of wind rushed through the open hatches, blowing hard when he reached the opening and looked out. The darkness had a deep vastness, and a little slice of moon provided the only glimmer of light. He adjusted his night vision goggles and watched the green world pass below him. Swanson was to be the last man to leave the helicopter, remaining out of the way while the other Marines charged out. Positioned in the open hatch, he could provide extra firepower until it was time for him to join them. He plugged the commo line in at the new position in time to hear the pilot say, "One minute."

Swanson put his hands against the sides of the hatch and shifted his fifty-pound pack and other equipment to be able to sit down. His stubby M-4 assault rifle hung across his chest, and Excalibur crossed his back, safe in its padded bag. With thirty seconds to go, the major ordered, "Stand up! Lock and load!" and the other Marines unbuckled, exchanged their flight helmets for real ones, and formed rows in the narrow aisles.

Kyle removed the night vision goggles, pulled the M-4 into firing position, and put his eye to the scope, which could penetrate the darkness. He could engage with precision shots at up to eight hundred meters and switch to rapid fire if necessary, but he saw nothing of interest. He kept the sight moving, searching for threats as the two aircraft jockeyed for the final descent, sharply reducing their altitude and bleeding off speed.

The rear ramp began to lower and the wind through

the chopper increased to gale-force proportions. The tail dipped as the helicopter flared to almost a complete stop in the air, braking its forward momentum less than twenty feet off the ground and barely moving forward. With the more stable platform, Swanson stood and continued parsing the LZ with his rifle and night scope. Nothing out there.

A loud scream erupted over the crew net. The two helicopters were hanging almost motionless in the air when a freak wall of wind that had swept unimpeded across a hundred miles of desert tore through the LZ and threw the birds together with train-wreck violence. The churning seventy-nine-foot-long rotors chopped like long swords, and both aircraft were instantly out of control, tangling with each other.

The standing Marines went flying and crashing about the spinning cabin like dolls, breaking necks and spines and limbs as the helicopter blades dug through the thin metal sides of the helicopters and went after the men like sharp knives. When his helicopter lurched onto its left side, Swanson was propelled straight out of the open hatch by the centrifugal force, like a piece of trash thrown from a car on a highway. The force of the ejection tore the helmet commo line free to prevent him from being lynched. The M-4 assault rifle snapped from its strap and flew away. His last sensation as his body was pulled into the void was of the cold wind caressing his face. He tumbled toward the desert floor.

19

Swanson slammed belly first onto the downward sloping side of a small sand dune and skidded, rolled, and bounced over and over before his tumbling body came to a stop at the bottom of the wadi. An explosion that would be heard for miles detonated behind him, and pieces of the disintegrating helicopters whizzed overhead and whiplashed the sands. He lay dazed, almost unconscious, trying to get some air into his lungs.

He lay motionless for about thirty seconds before coming out of his stupor, choking and gasping while his brain reeled and his face felt as if he had been punched by a young Mike Tyson on his best day. He pushed into a sitting position and used two fingers to dig gobs of sand out of his cheeks, then found his canteen and poured water over his face, sluicing it in his mouth and spitting it out. He doused his bandanna with water and rubbed his aching eyes. Blood came away on the cloth, and he explored his face until he found the gash across the bridge of his nose where the helmet had cracked him. In times of dire emergency, he knew, it was best to take a moment to gather his wits before doing anything at all, so he pressed the bandanna against the cut, flopped back against the sand, and took deep breaths, repeating his personal mantra softly: *Slow is smooth; smooth is fast.*

When he felt able to move, he crawled to the top of the dune and looked in horrible fascination at the wreckage that only moments before had been two powerful transport helicopters loaded with combat-ready Marines. It was hard to tell one of the birds from the other now because they had come down in a heap, cutting each other into chunks and merging into a single pile of smoldering wreckage. Twisting columns of red and yellow and orange flames spun into the dark sky.

Swanson dropped his gear and ran to the wreckage, stepping through the hot, sharp metal and pockets of burning debris to check for signs of life and finding only bodies and parts of bodies. There were no moans, no cries for help. Had the Marines been seated and strapped in, some might have survived, but he found nothing but carnage. The machines had slaughtered each other as well as every human being aboard except him.

Almost thirty men had been killed, and the scene sickened him. "Fuck me," Swanson said. He turned away, took a few steps, and threw up.

It was a fiery end for the ambitious plan that the briefers had predicted would be a cakewalk. Motherfucking Mr. Murphy and his bad-luck law had showed up early on this one, and Kyle, breathing deeply, forced himself back into the cold reality of the moment. *Get your shit together!*

He could see if there was a workable radio and call the Fleet, where everyone would be listening to the net. But Washington probably was also plugged into the radio chatter, and the White House would simply hand the assassination job to someone else. If Swanson called for help, General Middleton would surely die.

Think, damn it, think! If he didn't call, everyone would think that he was dead, too. But that would allow him to work alone, and although Buchanan would probably still assign another assassin, Kyle stood a good chance of reaching the general first because he was already on the ground.

Hell, he should be dead anyway, so why not continue the mission by himself, in total secrecy? The odds were astronomical, but Kyle would not allow himself to think of it as a suicide trip. *That's it, then. Just get on with it! Go!* New confidence surged through him like electricity.

He looked toward the village, which was about fifteen hundred meters away. That distance had not been changed by the crash. The helicopters had come down right where they were supposed to, just in a terribly wrong way. With the crash, the jig was up as far as surprise went, and everybody in the village might be temporarily stunned by what happened, but they would be coming his way in a hurry. Time was not his friend.

He went back into the wreckage and gathered canteens of water, more ammo, plenty of blocks of C-4 explosive, a couple of Claymore mines, a portable satellite telephone that still had power, and a survival radio from one of the pilots. He snapped them both off. Even when not in active use they would still send electronic signals, and when the little green power lights vanished, Swanson could no longer be tracked. On the screens, he was dead. He found an M-16 rifle, locked and loaded.

A glance at his watch showed him that three minutes had flown by, and he still had two more important chores.

Kyle stepped over bodies and debris until he was beside the little Kawasaki motorcycle. He gave it a quick check and it seemed undamaged, having been held tight on the deck throughout the disaster. Unlike the Marines, it had been professionally secured, and Kyle unsheathed his big knife, cut away the loading bands, and pushed it out. He loaded everything he had on it and rested it on the kickstand.

Now came the hard part, leaving a clue for Shari, something only she would recognize. She was in the informational loop about the mission, and would assume that he had died in the crash. He wanted to let her know he had survived, but also to provide some misdirection for anyone else.

He scanned the dead Marines and found one in the jumble of corpses, someone whose face could not be recognized but was about Kyle's size. The rubber-rimmed dog tag identified the man as Lance Corporal Harold McDowell, and his neck had been snapped when he was thrown against the bulkhead. A Marine Corps tattoo was inked on his right forearm. The kid had been proud to be a warrior and would not object to doing one more job.

Kyle exchanged the neck dog tag with his own. "It's this way, McDowell," Swanson whispered while he untied the kid's left boot, then his own, speaking to the pale face. "I need your help here. The bad guys are going to be looking for survivors. If they figure out some crazy sniper is missing, they'll really start hunting. If a radioman is missing, no offense, they won't give a rat's ass and think you will holler for help and get picked up sooner or later. You would pose no threat to them."

Kyle unbuckled the big radio from the dead man's shoulders. He would dispose of it later, but he needed to take it along to complete the disguise and misdirection play. The pursuers would logically believe that a missing radioman would have kept his radio. "And for the good guys, well, Harold, some of them ain't so good. For this plan to have any chance of working, we need those assholes to also think I'm dead. That's where you come in, Harold. What did they call you: Hal? Mac? So convince them that you are me, okay, Lance Corporal McDowell?" Swanson stood and threw the youngster a quick salute. "Semper fi."

He hustled over to the bike, hooked the radio pack over the handlebars, straddled the motorcycle, and, with a prayer, pushed the starter button. The little engine coughed once, then kicked to life, ready to run. His wristwatch showed that he had used up his time cushion, about six minutes since the helos went down.

He adjusted his night-vision goggles and drove away from the wreckage, the muffled exhaust helping avoid making any more noise than necessary. In the unlikely case that someone from the village figured out there was a survivor, Swanson steered the motorcycle to the east, leaving clear tracks that would indicate he was running to the Israeli border.

A minute later, he was on the paved road that ran through the village behind him, and far enough away from the wreckage to pile on a little more speed with the 1,200-cc engine. Dawn was coming, and he had to be invisible by then.

When radio contact was broken between the operations center aboard the USS *Wasp* and the TRAP team helos, several minutes elapsed while the sailors at the consoles tried to reestablish a voice link. A download from a stationary satellite watching the area showed a flash in the darkness and the lingering bloom of immense heat at the landing zone.

Colonel Ralph Sims, commander of the 33rd Marine Expeditionary Unit, chewed a fingernail. "Get the Harriers in there to take a look," he ordered, and the pair of fighter jets broke out of their orbit over Israel, heeled over from 40,000 feet, dropped to the ground, and sped into Syrian airspace riding their afterburners. Nearing the scene, they saw the fire, cut their speed, coasted over the wreckage, banked into a sharp turn, and ran past it again.

Aboard the *Wasp*, the speakers crackled in the quiet commo room. "Henhouse, this is Rooster One. They're down and burning," a pilot reported.

"Survivors?" Sims asked. The radioman relayed the question.

"Negative. No sign of life or movement at the scene, but there are bad guys coming out from the target zone. Request permission to engage."

Sims wanted to say, "Hell, yes," but could not. An attack run by the Harriers would probably result in casualties among Syrian civilians, which would make a bad situation a lot worse. It was time to call it a day. "Negative," he barked, and turned to the commander of the ship's Marine Air Wing. "Get those planes back home."

The Tactical Air Center sent the order. "Egress! Egress! Egress!"

The pilot hesitated. "Henhouse, Rooster One. What about a bombing run on the wreckage? I can torch the scene."

"Negative," came the immediate reply from Colonel Sims. He needed higher authority for that, and didn't have time to get it. He would message Washington for permission to send in a Cruise missile for that demolition job. "Repeat. Negative. Return to base."

"Rooster One. Roger that. I copy egress, return to base." The Rooster Flight headed home.

He heard his wingman come on the air. "Rooster Two to Rooster One, push to Rooster freak." Both pilots switched to another frequency so they could talk without being overheard.

"Go ahead, Two, this is Rooster One."

"Boss, did I copy that last right? We really leaving these guys behind?"

"You heard the same thing I did."

"I know, but what about 'Marines don't leave their own'?"

The flight leader's temper was simmering. He felt the same way, but because he was in command, he could not agree with his friend over an open radio channel. "One to Two. You saw it as good as I did. They're all dead!"

"Well, if they weren't then, they are now. Or worse."

"That's enough, Rooster Two. Follow your orders. Rooster One out."

The Harriers hugged the ground as they dashed back to Israeli airspace, where they would climb high for the rest of the return flight to the *Wasp*. The pilots remained silent, lost in thought about a rescue raid that had flipped into total disaster. Rooster One knew that by flying away, they were erasing any chance American survivors might escape captivity, torture, or death. "Please, God, don't let me see one of those kids show up on Al Jazeera," he said in a soft prayer, words that would never leave his cockpit.

Aboard the *Wasp*, Colonel Ralph Sims sent the message about the Cruise missile to Washington, then walked rigidly out of the command center, seeking fresh air and a moment of privacy. He lit a cigarette and thought about his Marines lying entombed in the helicopters in Syria. There would be a lot of investigations, and people, including him, would probably lose their jobs. At the moment, he didn't really care, for he had a bigger worry, one that was much more personal. *What the hell am I supposed to tell their families?*

The sky was losing its blackness, and the first rays of the new day crawled across the Middle East.

20

"Rooster One. Roger that. I copy egress, return to base."

The Harrier flight leader sounded calm and professional as he was heard in real time over a satellite linkup straight into the Situation Room of the White House. Members of the National Security Council had been there for an hour, monitoring the Middleton rescue raid. Now they were immobilized in shock.

Lieutenant Commander Shari Towne brought both hands to her mouth, fighting not to cry out in anguish at what she heard. Both helicopters down. No signs of life. Unknown people moving in fast. *KYLE! NO!*

National Security Advisor Gerald Buchanan was at the head of the long table in his big chair, tapping a yellow pencil against a legal pad as he listened to the disembodied voice. This was something he had not counted on, and he was busy weighing the up sides and the down sides. He looked around at the military people and detected an advantage. Make it their fault.

The chairman of the Joint Chiefs of Staff, General Turner, was chewing a knuckle, and lines of thought creased his forehead. He was, after all, a Marine, although he represented all of the military services. He had previously been the Marine Corps commandant, so those were *his* men who had lost their lives. He was emotionally involved.

A definite advantage! Grab it! Buchanan, however, spoke quietly. "Your Marines failed, General, so we now have a situation."

Turner had to agree. He had watched the crash via the satellite feed and had heard what the pilots had to say. "Yes, sir. It does appear the mission was unsuccessful."

Buchanan did not follow up his first jab. He stared at the satellite picture of a glowing hot spot in the Syrian desert. He could remain the consummate professional. "A tragedy, but we must move ahead. I need to hear options. Right now."

An admiral joined the conversation. "It's too late for an emergency rescue extraction. A team of Special Forces would not be enough at this point, with the Syrian military obviously going on alert. I would expect the Syrians to be controlling the scene within hours. We would have to insert nothing less than an airborne battalion, and that probably would not be enough. They would soon be surrounded and chopped up without massive air cover, and that would really up the stakes." He paused. Looked directly at General Turner, then Buchanan. "No further troop deployment is advisable."

"You can't just leave them there!" Shari Towne exclaimed, and all eyes in the room were drawn to her. She was the lowest-ranking officer present, in charge of nothing.

"Stay out of this, Lieutenant Commander," the admiral, her immediate boss, growled impatiently.

Shari caught the warning and flipped the pages of a red three-ring binder. "Yes, sir." She stopped at a page. "I was referring to the protocol in the operations manual."

Nice recovery, girl, the admiral thought. He knew of her personal relationship with Kyle Swanson and that Swanson was on the mission, but he wanted her to shut up before she went too far. The admiral liked them both and believed that their personal life was no business of anyone else at the table.

"What would that be, Lieutenant Commander" asked Buchanan. Had he caught some distress in her voice? More than normal? *Why?*

"Standard operating procedures instruct the incineration of wreckage, just as the pilot suggested."

"And how would that be accomplished?"

The air force general at the long table answered. "We can get some fast movers in there, either from the carrier in the Med or up out of Iraq, sterilize the area with napalm before the Syrians can plant ground-to-air missile batteries around it. We would have to move pronto."

The admiral interrupted. "No use putting more of our people in jeopardy. We can spin up a Tomahawk on a ship in the Med and get it in there even faster, and the missile would have a bigger clout. That's what the Marine mission commander recommends. He's waiting for a decision."

Buchanan kept tapping his pencil like a little metronome of menace, seconds ticking away in a crisis. "Why do we need to do that? What is the benefit?" he asked.

"There is a lot of sophisticated equipment and

material aboard those helicopters, sir. Everything from secret commo gear to night-vision goggles. Crypto. Maps. Weapons. Even avionics. Maybe some classified papers. We have no way of knowing if it all was destroyed," Hank Turner replied. "The Syrians will strip them bare, and we cannot take the chance of all that material falling into their hands."

"So you people are telling me that now that rescuing General Middleton is beyond your reach, that disaster may be compounded by still yet a bigger disaster? Jesus Christ."

Everyone noted that Buchanan had stopped tapping the pencil and had used the phrase "*your* reach," not "*our* reach."

"That sort of criticism is beside the point, Mr. Buchanan," Turner responded, his voice terse, growing angry with the man he considered nothing more than a political predator. "Right now, we have to decide between a missile and a bombing run, and there's not a minute to lose."

Buchanan abruptly stood and buttoned his coat. "Very well. Then my decision is the *third* option, something that none of you suggested, I might add. We do nothing. We will not, repeat not, strike the wreckage with either the bombers or a missile." He looked directly at Shari. "What was the protocol term that you used, Lieutenant Commander Towne? Incinerate? No, absolutely not. Sending a rescue attempt into Syria was one thing, but conducting an air strike on a sovereign nation that has not attacked us could be considered an act of war. God knows whether it could be contained."

He gave a little bow to the woman from the State Department. "We have to go the diplomatic route now, ladies and gentlemen, and hope that State can pull the Pentagon's nuts out of the fire."

Shari's last wall of reserve was cracking. She had to get back to her office before she broke into tears, and it would take every ounce of strength to make that short walk. But the professional side of her mind kept turning over her intuition. Something was not right. Buchanan had driven the point home hard that the military efforts had failed, but he had hardly mentioned the deaths of American Marines. There was no anger or sorrow. *Why?* She put the thought aside as the admiral stepped beside her and whispered, "Get out of here, Shari. Take the rest of the day off. We'll let you know if we hear anything about Kyle."

Buchanan walked back to his office mentally chalking up a most beneficial outcome. He had put those military morons in their places again, particularly the crew-cut, spit-and-polish General Turner. The raid had not gone as planned, but the unexpected crash of the helicopters had resulted in a total, dreadful, and irreversible failure that would be shown in the starkest light all over every news program in the world within a few hours. The world's most professional and powerful military establishment had failed. Shades of the mess in the desert of Iran back in 1979.

This could definitely help the privatization act. With his office door closed, Gerald Buchanan rocked back in his chair and propped his feet on his desk. There was a broad smile on his face as he picked up his secure telephone to brief Gordon and Ruth Hazel that he had sidetracked the bombing run or any further rescue attempt. Those bodies would be coming home in flag-draped coffins. It would make great television.

21

Victor Logan pressed his face hard against the cheek pad of a Russian-made Dragunov SVD sniper rifle to steady the four-power telescopic sight on the place where the helicopters had crashed. His partner, Jimbo Collins, scanned the rest of the area with night-vision goggles, looking for infrared heat emitters. Since kidnapping General Middleton, they had been waiting for the rescue attempt that was sure to come, ready to ambush the Marines, only to have it all go to hell right in front of them.

"Nothing but the wreckage," said Collins as he put the goggles away. "The fire and the hot metal just kills this heat-sensitive imagery. All I can pick up are those damned ragheads running around." He glanced at the brightening sky. "Think the Harriers will be back to burn it?" Collins had a shoulder-fired Stinger ground-to-air missile beside him. Other Stingers lay scattered in the other trenches.

"That's the SOP. Makes no sense to leave all that gear for the sand monkeys to pick over, but the Harriers seemed to be getting out of here in a hurry." Vic Logan had been in too many emergencies, in too many places, too many times, to let shit like this bother him. "Let's go see who's what. Big fuckup, this."

The American mercenaries moved from the sand-bagged trench and walked around a large ZSU-23-4 antiaircraft weapon. The gunner had abandoned his position behind the ammunition feed trays immediately after the helos went down, leaving the powerful radar-guided gun useless in his run to get to whatever booty he might steal from the helicopters. The quad rack of 23 mm cannons was still locked into position, useless if the Harriers returned.

Logan and Collins walked easily, not bothering to keep distance between them, because they were in no danger. "Too damned bad, Vic," said Collins. "This was a good ambush configuration."

Logan's big strides ate up the ground. His head was on a swivel and his hard eyes captured the tactical situation. The ragheads from the trench to the right, which would have supplied a cross-fire, were also out of their holes and heading toward the wreckage, along with women and children from the village. From soldiers and civilians to scavengers in the blink of an eye. A verse of Kipling came to him: *"When you're wounded and left on Afghanistan's plains, And the women come out to cut up what remains, jest roll to your rifle and blow out your brains An' go to your Gawd like a soldier."* Afghanistan then, Iraq yesterday, Syria today, who knows where tomorrow? These people were going out to the crash site to do what they had been doing to foreign soldiers for centuries. *Fuckin' vultures.*

Logan sort of hoped none of those jarheads were still alive, although the idea of killing Americans had not cost him a moment of sleep. It was a business deal, sweet payback for being screwed over by the navy, and

Logan was determined to come out of all this rich. He had shopped his services around until he discovered that being part of a Shark Team paid better than any of the other private billets. He was pulling in ten thousand dollars U.S. a month, and complicated things like this brought more. For these big bucks, he didn't give a fuck if he had to kill the pope.

The fact that the birds went down by themselves made no difference to Logan, because the result was the same. He got fifty thousand for snatching the general and now the rescue mission had failed, which meant still another fifty would flow into his bank account. He figured to retire when he topped two million.

He clicked his AK-47 to full automatic and fired an entire clip into the air while shouting in Arabic for the ragheads to clear out until he and Collins were done searching the area. Reluctantly, the crowd pulled back away from their looting and stood in sullen groups while the two American mercenaries got to work.

"Get the camera going," Logan said as they approached the twisted wreckage. "I'll look around the perimeter. You take pictures of every one of those Marines, get the dog tags, and read off the names loud enough to be recorded, clear enough to be understood. Any funny names, spell them out. I want a stone-cold positive ID on every one of those dudes."

"Got it." Collins stepped into the wreckage. It was a mess in there. He started photographing.

"And make sure all the arms and legs add up!" Logan called, then began a slow walk around the site, circling from the nose of one of the choppers out to about a hundred meters. That put the helicopter in the center of an imaginary clock, with the nose pointed to twelve o'clock, and Logan switched on a powerful flashlight as he worked back and forth in pie-shaped segments. One o'clock. Two o'clock. Raghead footprints and chunks of debris from the aircraft reached out in all directions. He would have missed the puddle of vomit near the seven o'clock position had he not smelled it before locating it with the bright beam of his flashlight. Nothing much more than some discolored yellow bile. A raghead sickened by the sights and smell of new death? Not likely, but possible. He walked on, and two slices of the clock later, almost obscured by the scuffed footprints of the scavengers, he found the unmistakable tire tracks of a motorcycle. He did not recall hearing any. How old was the track? Some civilian ride through yesterday? It led toward the road, east.

"Hey, Vic!" Collins hollered from the ruptured end of one of the helicopters. "Take a look."

Logan was there in a couple of big strides. "What?"

Collins was squatting down and had the loose end of a big strap in one hand. He tugged on it to show that the other end was secured to the deck of the fuselage. "Three more of these straps. There, there . . . and there."

All four ends had been sliced clean. Something had been secured here. Had the ragheads already stolen it? Something large? No, he would have noticed. Logan backed out of the wrecked bird and Collins followed, putting away his camera after photographing and identifying the final two bodies. They went to the fuselage of the other helicopter. A little Kawasaki dirt bike, badly damaged, was still lashed to the deck with straps like the ones that had been cut on the first helo.

Logan scratched his neck, came to a conclusion. He waved to the onlookers and they poured back into the wreckage like honeybees after a lump of sugar.

"Somebody survived that mess," he told Jimbo as they returned to the village and their satellite radio. "We got a runner."

22

He hated noise. Kyle Swanson valued silence, for stealth was his cloak of protective comfort. On a wide battle-field, there was so much racket in a raging shootout of tank cannons, masses of small arms, machine guns, grenades, and artillery that soldiers talked in shouts for a week afterward, long after the fighting stopped. As a sniper, he preferred to be far from that chaos, out on his own, where making sounds could spell doom. Swanson was the ghost at the party, able to move unseen and unheard. Noise weakened snipers and made them vul-nerable, almost like normal human beings. The only noise he liked to hear in combat was the single *POP* of his silenced rifle being fired.

So although the dirt bike had a silenced muffler, the steady throbs of the engine still reverberated in the desert night. Kyle believed any fool with ears could hear him. Combined with the coming dawn, that would leave him exposed and vulnerable. He weaved slowly, deliberately along the pavement, steering through patches of loose gravel normally avoided by motorcyclists because bikes have a tendency to skid. A mistake could dump him in a heartbeat, but he wanted those tracks to be found.

His mind was also busy on another level, thinking

about possible places where he might hunker down for the day, when people would be everywhere. Being caught near a population center, even a small village like this one, was never good, plus people were probably going to be out searching for him when they figured out someone had lived through the crash. The flare of a match straight ahead snapped him back to reality.

Someone had lit a cigarette. Swanson took his hand from the throttle and coasted the motorcycle to a halt. He turned off the engine and sat balanced on the dirt bike with a boot down on each side. Focusing his night-vision goggles, he saw two men about two hundred meters ahead, a pair of careless Syrian soldiers at a road checkpoint. Both were watching the area where the helicopters went down instead of paying attention to their jobs.

Kyle laid the bike down along the hardball highway and carefully dropped his gear, except for the M-16 and a couple of hand grenades. On his arms and knees, he low-crawled until he was within twenty feet of the guards. They were cooking something in the guard shack. Smelled like rice and lamb. The guards were jabbering like tourists about the crash and had stacked their rifles against a wall when they climbed onto the flat roof of the shack for a better view. Controlling his breathing, Kyle circled behind them, moved in close, rose to a sitting position against the wall, and pulled the pin on a hand grenade. He let the spoon flip away, held it for a count of two, and then tossed it onto the roof and sprawled to the ground next to the structure.

The explosion blew both of them from their perch, and Kyle quickly checked the bodies, which were riddled with shrapnel. Not good enough. The people back at the crash site were more than a mile away and probably would not have heard this small explosion, so he had to leave enough information to convince whoever eventually investigated the deaths that the work was sloppy enough to have been done by a rookie Marine. A young radioman would have done the easiest thing available and smashed right through the checkpoint, using the basic weapons at hand, in his haste to escape. Kyle wanted to leave this scene as American as possible. He clicked his M-16 to full automatic and raked an entire magazine of bullets across the chests and stomachs of the dead men, and the bullets dug through the bodies and into the hardpan pavement beneath them. Shiny brass cartridges flipped and bounced wildly everywhere. He walked in the sand to leave bootprints. Window dressing. He could easily have taken them both out with Excalibur, or up close with his knife, but this was a stage show. As a final touch, he ducked inside the small bunker and gobbled down some of the meal the men had been preparing. He was right. Spicy lamb and rice.

He reassembled his gear, remounted the bike, and rode past the checkpoint, spiking a piece of cloth torn from his camouflage uniform on the barbed wire. The track of the dirt bike then continued west, again toward the border.

A hundred meters later, he made sure he was on clean pavement, stopped the bike, got off, picked up the bike, and turned it around 180 degrees. Now he would disappear and leave no tracks at all. He pushed the motorcycle through the roadblock, past the dead men. Swanson propped the bike on the kickstand long enough to pull up some bushes and sweep away any prints that might give away his direction change, and then headed back toward the village.

When he entered the vicinity of the crash, people were milling around the wrecked choppers. Kyle knew that meant they might see him, too, but he knew human nature had them in a near frenzy. They were only looking for booty. A lone man in the distance was of no interest. Still, every moment he was out there was a risk because the first hot curve of the rising sun had crested the eastern horizon and painted the underside of the morning clouds in a sheet of shining gold. When Swanson was working, he hated the arrival of daylight as much as a vampire like Count Dracula, for he, too, was a creature of the night.

Swanson went off-road and skirted about a kilometer to the right of the scene, keeping low in the wadis to avoid being spotted. Within a mile, the country flattened again.

The village of Sa'ahn had the familiar, compact look of any other desert town he had ever seen, houses and shops that had grown up over the centuries around a water source. Rainfall in this section of Syria was adequate to feed fields of sugar beets that were bordered by tight patterns of apricot trees in the east. North of town, he could smell as well as see and hear the feed lots where sheep and goats were being fattened for market. Irrigated rows of ragged cotton were planted on the western side. Mount Druz dominated the land, and a carpet of desert stretched to all horizons.

The homes all looked alike, squat and square, with low walls that corralled the family's chickens and goats.

Drooping lines between poles carried telephone lines and delivered electricity from a dam about twenty miles away. One large building near the center appeared to be the town's administrative center. Lights were on in a few windows of the private homes, brightening colorful small curtains of green and red, so people in those homes were already moving about. He had to hide.

Kyle stopped the bike about three hundred meters from the nearest building. He had run out of darkness and did not have time to bury the motorcycle, which he preferred to do. So he hid it in a deep wadi and covered it with bushes, hoping that the obscure location, the crude disguise of weeds, and the camo paint job would keep it hidden.

With the M-16 locked and loaded and his finger resting on the trigger housing, Swanson moved closer to the village until he found a forlorn and bare hillside that overlooked the approach road. A berm lined with thick brush rose like a dirty pimple near the top, and he ducked down to keep it between himself and the town. This was it.

He circled to the back side and dug a shallow trench straight up to the rim of the berm. The rising sun was already heating the dirt, and Kyle sweated the last few meters, but when he came up in the middle of the bushes, he had a clear view from the high ground.

Dumping his gear, he wiggled back down, gathered more brush from random spots in a radius of about twenty meters, and swept his tracks, then planted the foliage around his new hide until he was sure that it would look to a passerby like a single big bush. Time would slow down for him now, so he arranged things in his shady nook to get some rest. Real sleep was not an option, not alone in hostile territory, but he could allow himself a light doze, just under the edge of total awareness, with his hand always on a weapon.

As the sun cleared the horizon and full daylight arrived, he drank some water and took out the binocs again for a last look at the village before settling down. The homes, the goats, the women and children moving about. Normal tempo. Most of the men were probably still busy stripping the helos. He stopped his sweep with his glasses abruptly when he got to the area where the major road entered the town. Sandbags were stacked along a trench line, and just to his side of the road was another deep trench. AK-47 rifles were laid carelessly over its sandbags, and missile tubes leaned against the sides. Sticking out of a protected hole where the trenches came together were the snouts of the four barrels of a ZSU-23-4.

"Well, now, ain't this a bitch?" he asked himself. "A Zeus, fighting holes with AKs, and lots of guys. We were flying into a fucking ambush."

Kyle put away the glasses, took another drink of water, and let the adrenaline and excitement leave his body. He shifted his shoulders to get comfortable, laid the M-16 across his chest, and felt the heavy exhaustion from the past few hours pull hard on him. His last conscious thought before he passed out was, "They knew we were coming."

23

Victor Logan sat at a small table, pecking at a laptop computer to input the names of the Marines killed in the crash. His big, thick fingers were blunt instruments, meant for things much more coarse than dainty taps on a keyboard, and he found this work both laborious and somewhat insulting. Clerks did this kind of shit, not warriors. He detested having to wear reading glasses when he worked on this machine. They were a sign of weakness, of getting old, past the prime, but Logan had decided to adopt the modern age to get the technological edge. Just because a gorilla eats leaves does not mean he is any less of a mean son of a bitch.

He could tell the sun was up by the steady increase of the temperature in the room. Finally, he finished copying the names that Jimbo Collins had culled from the dog tags and clicked the key to save the file to a directory. He called up another list that had been downloaded from Washington several hours earlier, did a cut-and-paste job with the one he had just written, and compared the two. He highlighted one name in bright red, increased the font size to make it bold, then pushed away from the screen and studied it. "I was right, Collins. Somebody's missing. The Washington list has one name more than the dog tags on the kill list. You damned sure you got them all?"

"All of 'em, Vic. I pulled the tags off every one of those crispy critters." He held up a plastic bag filled with dog tags and shook it with a definitive rattle of metal against metal. Collins was at his own computer, working with his camera to freeze-frame individual images of each of the dead Marines, inject them into a folder, and adjust the color and clarity.

There was a knock and a shout at the door, and both men grabbed weapons. Security was always on their minds, and they kept an extra AK-47, locked and loaded, on two pegs directly above the front door for emergencies. "What?" called Collins. He went to the front wall and put his back to it.

"Open up! Something else has happened!" The English came in a familiar French accent.

Collins held a mirror to the window and angled it to confirm who was there. "It's the frog. He's alone." Logan nodded, and Collins opened the door.

A small man, thin but muscular, came in. He had a sharp face with prominent cheekbones, dark eyes, and a slit of a mouth that never smiled and was almost invisible in a long, thick black beard. Pierre Dominique Falais was a familiar figure in Sa'ahn, where he had settled after getting out of the Foreign Legion. As a converted Muslim, he was welcome everywhere, despite his European background, and he would drive to other towns and villages to buy crafts, wool, and rugs and load them into his white Toyota truck, then usually find a reason to stay overnight in order to smoke and eat and talk with the locals. The Syrian villagers considered Abu

Mohammed to be a most generous man and an honest trader. Success in the little trading enterprise and some carpentry meant nothing to him, for his real money came not from peddling items to stores and bazaars, but by selling his intelligence services to the governments of Syria, France, and Russia. He was able to work openly with all three countries because their policies were seldom in conflict.

For the time being, however, these two large American mercenary soldiers, who had deposited five thousand dollars into his bank account in Damascus, had his total cooperation. A similar amount would come in when the task was completed.

"The fuck you want, Pierre?" snapped Logan, turning back to the name on the laptop screen. *A radioman lived through that and escaped?*

The Frenchman stepped inside and closed the door. The place stank. These little homes were usually kept very clean by the women, with the pungent aromas of hard tobacco and cooking food welcoming visitors like a pleasant cloud. In here, the smell of human waste, sweat, and filth offended him. He shrugged it off. They were, after all, Americans, a disgusting people. "Two guards at that checkpoint a few klicks to the west have been killed. Bullet holes all over the bodies, and a villager described some open wounds that sound to me like they may have been made by grenades. I'm going out there."

"Sounds like our runner, Vic. Somebody had to have some firepower to do that," said Collins. "Want me to check it out?"

Logan grunted and waved them both away, absorbed by his work. *A radioman fought his way through two armed sentries? Yeah, he was a Marine, but that was a good piece of work.*

"Okay, Pierre. Lead on." Collins followed the Frenchman into the light and over to the pickup truck, a well-maintained vehicle with extra suspension and wide desert-quality tires with deep treads. The custom heavy-duty engine turned over on the first try and the straight exhaust pipes rumbled low. Falais wheeled the Toyota onto the road and sped away. Jimbo Collins immediately started talking to him about different kinds of shock absorbers.

Vic Logan kept staring at the name in red and studying the kill list: McDowell, Harold. Lance corporal. Radio operator. Twenty years old. He had heard lots of stories about people walking away from a plane crash or an automobile pileup that killed everyone else. It was possible. So the kid grabs the bike and takes off for Israel and just surprised the lazy guys at the checkpoint. It was the logical play. "Fucking Syrians can't even stop a damned radio operator," he grunted. The Marine would be picked up soon. He probably had a little spec ops training in escape and evasion, but it was a long way to the border, and most of it was either over open territory or on busy roads. He was good as caught and just didn't know it yet.

Logan opened an encrypted file to transmit to Washington. Collins could send the pictures later. It took him only fifteen more minutes at the keyboard to finish his report, and he saved the work, leaving space at the bottom to add whatever details Collins picked up at the roadblock.

There was nothing more he could do now. Logan felt he had earned some relaxation. He rose, stretched his six-foot-five frame, and peeled off his clothes as he went into the small bedroom. It was a little cooler there.

On the bed lay a terrified, wide-eyed girl, tied to the four corners, spread-eagled and naked. A piece of gray duct tape was across her mouth, and although she could not scream, she wiggled in terror when she saw the huge American approach. He had first spotted her at the local store, where the fourteen-year-old beauty worked with her mother and father, and had checked her out as best he could while he bought a few items. Not really much to see, since the small girl wore one of those damned black bedsheets. But the flashing eyes were unafraid of the foreigner, and Vic imagined there was a flawless body with long, coltlike legs and budding breasts under all that cloth. He snatched her the first night he was here. Knowing the ragheads really thought their women were something special, he went to great lengths to keep her out of sight and quiet. She was tight that first time, struggling, fighting hard, just like he enjoyed his women. A little tiger. Lots of blood. When he was through, the young body was no longer virginal and wore a number of ugly bruises, varying shades of green and purple and yellow. The eyes were no longer unafraid. She had been taught respect.

The only question for Logan at present was whether to feed her or give her a chance to pee before he raped her again. The hell with it. Those helos going down had changed everything and he would be out of here as soon as Gates decided what he wanted done with the general, who lay trussed up in the next room.

Just thinking about the general pissed Logan off. The mercenary was angry that he couldn't hit that one-star asshole in the face or anywhere that would show a bruise, because they were going to need him looking good for another television show. So he turned his frustrations on the girl instead, and went to her again, his hand moving to his penis. He wasn't hard yet. This dirty whore was going to have to work to get him aroused.

He struck her hard across the face with his right hand, just to make sure she was paying attention. Her head snapped to the side like that of a doll, and the tears began to roll. Too bad he had to leave the gag on, he thought as he rolled his belt around his fist, leaving the sharp brass buckle dangling free. He slapped it on her thigh and a bloody gash opened in the smooth olive skin. Again, and a crimson streak flowed down the ribs as her body arced in pain. Again, clicking the metal buckle across both nipples. The screams would have been nice.

He looked down at himself with growing frustration. He still wasn't hard, because she wasn't working to satisfy him. "Bitch!" he yelled, and the belt came down again, on the side of her head, and dark blood oozed through the tangle of black hair. "Move it, damn you!" Logan's fury grew like the heat that cooked the room, and he beat the girl without pity. No matter how hard he struck her, no matter how much he made her bleed, his goddam dick would NOT get hard.

A pounding sound drew his attention. The damned general was kicking the wall. Tied up like a turkey and still a pain in the ass. Logan shouted, "Shut the fuck up! I'll be in there and beat your ass soon as I'm through with this little bitch!" The pounding continued, even harder.

And still the girl just lay there, moaning, refusing to help even though he had total control over her worthless body! *Little whore! It was her fault!* He had taught others, and he would teach her, too. With his free hand, he balled up his big fist and slammed her in the mouth. *Her fault!* Finally, he got hard, grabbed his penis, and ejaculated on the small breasts before falling across her, exhausted, into the pool of blood and semen.

Then Logan, still naked, went into the other room, where the general was handcuffed to the steel frame of a cot. Middleton's eyes were filled with fury at having to sit there helplessly while a young woman was torn apart.

"You got a problem? Kickin' on the wall like that?" Logan asked with a sneer.

"You sick shit." Middleton spat on the floor in disgust. "You're going to die under my knife!" He wore a loose and dirty Arab robe, was totally under Logan's control, and yet still was making threats.

"Assholes like you got me kicked out of the Teams," Logan said, squatting down beside Middleton. "I expect that we are going to get permission soon to blow your ass away. I'll enjoy it." He rolled Middleton over, grabbed the little finger of his left hand, and bent it back until it broke.

The general exhaled a sharp groan, then sucked up the rest of the pain, refusing to give Logan the satisfaction of hearing him cry out. When the sharp wave of having a bone snapped ebbed, he glared at the big man. "That changes nothing, you psycho."

"Don't judge me, dickhead. You've got nine more fingers I can break before I start on the toes." He left the room, slamming the door behind him.

Logan was washing up in the small, stinking bathroom when Jimbo Collins returned. The water had cooled his body and the demons within.

Collins called out, "Vic? You in there?"

Logan walked back into the main room. "Well?" He was wiping himself with a towel.

"The frog had it right. A grenade apparently was used first, and there was a bunch of brass all over the place. M-16 cartridges. I found tracks of the motorcycle for about a hundred meters on the other side of the checkpoint. The runner took those Syrian dudes out without hardly slowing down."

"Okay." Logan sat down and added the checkpoint incident to his report, then hit the transmit button. The names and the details of what happened before dawn near the little town of Sa'ahn zipped into the morning sky and were relayed by satellite to a computer that was waiting far, far away.

Collins tossed his weapon aside and kicked off his boots. "Say, Vic. It's gonna take some time for me to finish the video. How 'bout you let me have another piece of that kid first? We'll probably be leaving soon anyway."

"Be my guest, Collins," Logan replied with a sweep of his arm toward the bedroom door and a dark laugh.

"And when you finish screwing that dead pussy, you can feed and water the general."

"She's dead?"

Logan grinned, his eyes almost sparkling. "Little whore just laid there like a pillow. No enthusiasm at all. The scrawny bitch didn't earn her life."

Jimbo Collins looked into the bedroom. The girl and the bed were covered in blood. This was not the first time that he had thought there was something really wrong with Logan, but it was wise to keep that thought to himself. A few more hours and he probably would never see the asshole again. Concentrate on the money, not the corpse. "Good thing we got dirt floors," Collins remarked as he turned to his camera equipment. "We can bury her right here, then burn this shithole to the ground."

24

The Asshole of the World sounded like a pig going after slops, snorting in his pleasure, so she just let her mind drift that way. Sprawled in the pigpen, down in the muck, a worthless piece of pork wallowing in a place where feelings were meaningless and the next "oink" meant only that she was still alive to hear it. A surge, heat, a final groan, and her father released her wrists and rolled off, spent. "I'm going downtown," the Asshole muttered, wiping himself on her bunny sheets. *Like I even care.* Ruth Hazel Pierce blinked her blue eyes and came out of the pigpen stench enough to hear that. On this night the fourteen-year-old girl decided to care very much, a moment of decision that changed her life and ended his.

Usually she curled into a fetal position for a while, safe in her happy place, a pretend enchanted castle, surrounded by good friends and fire-breathing dragons that protected her. Only after an hour or so would she return to the real world of fear and shame and hate and get cleaned up before her mother came home from her late shift as a waitress. On that final night, however, Ruth Hazel exhaled a big sigh and headed for the hot shower and sweet bath soaps and freedom. From her dresser, she removed the tight one-piece black swim team suit she wore for school meets, stretched into it, and then put on old jeans with torn knees, a bulky San Diego State University sweatshirt, and jogging shoes. Out the door and down the hall to her parents' room, where the Asshole of the World, the gun nut, kept all those weapons loose in the closet. When she was small, before the molestation got really serious, he had taught her how to shoot, thinking that a girl enjoyed the explosions. Respect a weapon, he said. Guns can hurt you if you're not careful. No shit, Pops. She grabbed the Ruger .22, made sure it had a full ten-round magazine, tucked it into her waistband, and walked out of the house to change her future. One of them, either herself or the Asshole of the World, would not be coming back.

She walked along the beach from the trailer park to Oceanside in the early darkness, thinking she could see his footprints, since he always came this way. He walked because he had been picked up too many times for driving drunk. On the edge of the seedy downtown area, Ruth Hazel found a dumpster in an alley directly across the street from the Asshole's favorite bar, a rundown strip joint, and she sat on the concrete in the shadows, crossing her legs and listening to the traffic on the street and the rumble of the surf. He staggered out two hours later, alone. Either he had run out of money or had been thrown out again. She didn't care. It didn't matter. Oink.

He ambled down the sidewalk and cut through a vacant lot to the high, dry ground of the beach. She followed his wavering silhouette against the starry night as the waves nibbled and sloshed at the sand about forty yards away. The tide was coming in. Not a soul in sight.

Ruth Hazel pulled out the Ruger and began a little jog that closed the space between them in only a few steps. She stopped and took a firing stance, both palms around the grip like he had taught her. "Daddy?" she called in her little-girl voice as she snapped off the safety.

The Asshole of the World turned. The first bullet caught him in the stomach, but he was a big man and a single .22 shot was not much more than a hard punch to the gut, not enough to put him down. The other six shots went into the chest, careful shots, one after another, and sprawled him on the sand like a beached porpoise. Ruth Hazel stepped closer. She saw recognition in his eyes, then horror as she deliberately aimed the Ruger at his crotch and fired. He screamed. She put the last two bullets into his eyes.

She rolled him onto his side and snatched the wallet from his back pocket, put the pistol back into her waistband, and jogged smoothly away down the beach. About a mile later, she shucked off her bloody clothes and swam through the surf, fighting stroke after stroke to get past the steep slant where the water went deep and the currents were crazy. Treading water, she pulled the pistol and the wallet from within her stretchy bathing suit and dropped them. As the items settled to the bottom of shifting sand, Ruth Hazel went into an easy butterfly kick and let the waves carry her to the beach. She walked home, her feet light on the sand. Another hot shower, stain remover on the blood spots on the jeans and sweatshirt, and those went into the washing machine. Ruth Hazel was drying her hair with a big blue towel, watching TV and eating popcorn, when her mother came home. "Hi, Mom!" she called.

The small woman who had lived with the beatings for years cast her worried eyes around the mobile home, puzzled as to why Ruth Hazel was in such a good mood. "Is your father here?"

"No. He was in for a little while after work but then went out again a few hours ago. Come on and sit with me, Mom. This is a hilarious movie. Have some popcorn."

"Have you done your homework?" Doris Reed put down her purse and went to the sofa and smiled at her daughter. So much happiness! She seemed to glow.

"Yes, Mom. I did everything I had to do."

Senator Ruth Hazel Reed kept two framed photographs on the long polished credenza behind the desk in her office in the Russell Senate Office Building off of C Street. One was of her handsome young army Warrant Officer Chuck Reed, lounging against a helicopter in Vietnam, the black-and-white picture taken four weeks before he was killed in action. The other was a family photo of ten-year-old Ruth Hazel snuggled between her smiling mother and father during a vacation to Sea World in San Diego. All of them were gone now. The Viet Cong had killed Chuck, cancer had taken her mom, and Ruth Hazel had murdered her father. Ancient history.

She never told anyone about the shooting; not her mother, not her husband, not even her hairdresser. The cops did a brief investigation and decided it was a robbery by some Mexicans coming up from the border, although the savagery of the attack, the clear rage, made them suspect a family member had done it. But they had alibis, sitting at home watching TV and eating popcorn together. Had to be Mexicans.

Ruth Hazel had absorbed the lesson that her rapes had not been about sex as much as about her father exerting power over her until she became more powerful than he. Since then, the search for power was her fuel in everything from sex to academics to business to politics. She might allow a man equality, as she had with Chuck, but she would yield to no one, ever again.

That included Gordon Gates and Gerald Buchanan. When she became President of the United States, she would be the most powerful person not only in New America, but in the world. Privatizing the military would give her off-the-books strength that no other President had ever possessed because she would not have to bring politics into play to assassinate a foreign dictator or sink a ship bringing in drugs or make some terrorists disappear. Just a phone call to Gordon would do the job. Under her reign, New America would be secure.

Now discomforting news had come from Syria, and the three powerful people were alone in a long black limousine parked near the Lincoln Memorial. Gates had told his chauffeur to come back when he called on the cell phone.

"Is our plan in trouble, Gerald?" asked Ruth Hazel. "You said it was foolproof." Idiot.

"No, Ruth Hazel, the plan is not in trouble. The Marine rescue fiasco actually plays into our hands," Buchanan responded in a smooth tone, holding his tongue so as not to respond with an insult. "I've been riding the Pentagon and intel services hard. There won't be another rescue attempt, and the Syrian government is in an uproar."

"Middleton is still alive, Gerald. He was supposed to be killed in the rescue attempt. You even sent in that sniper as a backup. But they are all dead and yet the general lives. Hardly a success so far."

"Easy, Senator," said Gates. "I also think it may turn out to be fortunate for us that the Marines screwed up on their own and did not have to be ambushed." He took a folded piece of paper from his briefcase and handed it to Buchanan. "Look at this. My Shark Team over there just sent this list of all of the Marines who were killed in the crash, verified by their dog tags. I expect to have pictures soon to help with the identifications."

"So what am I missing here, Gordon?" Senator Reed asked.

"Look, Ruth Hazel. We wanted to show your committee and anyone else we could get to listen that while the U.S. Marines created a disaster, two special operators from Gates Global had infiltrated the village so deeply that they were able to go in and get these identifications and even make contact with the French guide. We can now say that if the Pentagon had not intervened and screwed up, my people would already have brought General Middleton out of there, safe and sound."

"Not really."

"Of course not. The only difference is that instead of the ideal of having the Marine sniper shoot him while we take pictures, or having our Shark Team finish the job, we let the jihadists kill him."

"I don't care who shoots him or if he steps on a scorpion. I just do not want him coming back to testify before my committee next week." She pushed back in the soft seat and folded her arms.

Buchanan finished reading the list and handed it to the senator. It didn't add up. "Somebody got out?"

"Apparently," Gates responded with a slight wave. "Some kid who is only a radio operator took off on a dirt bike that was on one of the helicopters. I know that country, and he won't get far. The Syrians will pick him up before he can reach the border, and I predict that we will be seeing him on television soon. We can exploit that when it happens. Not really a bad thing, when you think of it, because his comments will show even further how fucked up the mission was."

Buchanan nodded in approval, pleased that Rambo Reed had been slow to understand how any situation such as this was fluid and one had to adapt to change. "So the senator and I can use the identifications as additional proof of how efficient private contractors can be, and how we can accomplish missions better than rote-memory military teams that court an international incident every time they get involved."

Ruth Hazel read the list without changing her expression and handed it back to Gates. "I don't like it when plans fall apart, but I agree that this problem can be turned to our favor."

Gates switched on his cold voice, totally unemotional. "Good. We're back on the same page. If you two approve, I'll fire off a signal to the sheikh in Basra to have his men execute the general in some interesting and public manner as soon as possible."

"And your team on the ground?" Buchanan raised an eyebrow.

"They will not be seen, nor will they interfere. They will simply hand Middleton over to the sheikh's people and get out. So I expect Middleton will be dead within a few hours, and we can get on with Operation Premier."

25

He awoke with a start. The tinny recorded voice of a muezzin was being broadcast from a loudspeaker attached to the minaret of the little town's mosque, the summons to morning prayer. Gritty crumbs of sand had fallen into his mouth, and every one of the over two hundred bones in his body felt broken. The fear of falling completely asleep had kept Kyle hovering near the surface until he heard the familiar call: "Hasten to prayer!" Over and over and over, broadcast five times every day. It reminded him of Somalia, where he occasionally would shoot the broadcasting loudspeakers in revenge for the annoyance.

He looked at his watch and cursed. He had been out for almost an hour, much too long, and wondered what he had missed. There was no way to recover anything that might have happened during that time.

Swanson fumbled for a packet of MRE crackers, popped all eight out of the vacuum-packed seal, lumped peanut butter on them, and started chewing. Tasteless, but it would keep the digestive tract well plugged during the coming hours. Dessert was two Motrin tablets for his aches and pains, and some water, and then he exercised with some isometric stretches and told his body to stop bitching about being so thrashed. Swanson never liked that macho line about pain being a friend. He hurt like hell, but nothing was broken, and he would make time to moan later, with a pretty nurse in attendance. Right now, he had to get back to work.

He pulled out the powerful spotting scope that had been on his gear list, only to find it had broken in the crash and was useless. But the Steiner binos had survived, and their 10×32 viewing field would serve him almost as well. At five hundred meters, objects would appear about twenty times their normal size. He removed the lens caps, gave the glasses a quick wipe, rolled onto his stomach, and slowly raised his eyes above the edge of the hide.

He had no specific plan other than to observe for a while and, after that, play things by ear, with the big advantage of the enemy not knowing he was in their backyard. First he would conduct the basic recon to determine the security posted by the bad guys, what kind of patterns the guards had, and determine the weakest point and how to exploit it. After that, he would be able to make realistic, systematic decisions to set conditions of battle in his favor. What he saw through the binos made him smile.

People were going about their business. Shops were opening, goats were in the streets, women were cleaning around their homes, farmers moved to the fields, some dude was selling bread from a cart, and other men were settling down for some early-morning smoking and coffee. It was the normal tempo of a village. The big four-barreled Zeus still sat brooding beside the road, but there was no gunner in the seat. The fighting holes and trench lines were empty, and the guys with the guns were gone, except for two lazy guards sitting on the ground in a patch of shade beside the Zeus.

There was nothing Swanson could do until dark other than gather information, so he took out his logbook and started a detailed sketch of the village. He started with the building to his far left, where a woman swept her front stoop with an old broom, and slowly examined the small house with a left-to-right, up-and-down grid. Then he checked the surrounding streets and pathways.

He laid the M-16 aside and unsheathed Excalibur. After giving the sniper rifle a quick once-over, he brought the scope to his eye and touched the button to turn on the laser rangefinder. The numbers stopped scrolling when he clicked on the doorway of the woman's house: exactly 680 yards. He jotted the figure on one of the logbook's green range sheets as the woman finished her sweeping and propped her broom against a side wall. He shifted his attention to the next building.

Someone cursed in Arabic and the two Zeus guards scrambled to their feet. A chubby little man in civilian clothes with an AK-47 slung across his back had emerged from a doorway and moved toward them, shouting that they were worthless pigs and gesturing at them to stand up. Kyle examined him closely. *Who are you, Pudgy? No uniform, but obviously in some kind of command.* Another man, tall and bearded, also with a rifle on his shoulder, came from the same house and stood idly while the sentries were chewed out. *Okay. You're Beanpole.* Assigning nicknames helped Kyle sort out the various players.

They laughed at the young guards, then crossed the

street to a café and disappeared inside through a front door shaded by a small cloth awning. Fifteen minutes later they came back out, carrying stacked boxes of food. Pudgy and Beanpole had not had time to have eaten at the little store, so they obviously were taking meals back to the house. Judging by the number of boxes, it was a hell of a lot more food than for just the two of them. Kyle's interest had perked up at the appearance of the Arab fighters, and he sketched their house, did the ranges to the door and windows, and marked it as a probable target.

Beanpole came back out with a couple of the meal boxes and walked casually to another house nearby, where the door was closed and the curtains were drawn. He leaned toward the door, and his lips moved as he spoke to somebody inside. More than a minute passed before the door opened quickly and from the shadows, two arms reached out, grabbed the food, and vanished back inside. The door was shut again. Beanpole walked away, and Kyle saw the man's lips moving, probably in a soft curse at the rudeness of whoever snatched the food. It had only been a momentary glance and at an awkward angle, but Swanson could have sworn that the skin of whoever took the food was light-colored, possibly even white.

He resumed studying each house in the village, taking time out periodically to check around his hide and make sure he was not under observation himself. Not having someone covering his back left him feeling naked and completely alone. Staying busy by building the range card kept his mind off his vulnerability.

Over the passing hours, the normal life of the village became his private reality television show, and he noted the times of all significant movement in the area, looking for patterns, sketching and lasering ranges to important aiming points. Seventy-forty-three to the major intersection. Six-twelve to the right edge of the restaurant. Left, right, and middle distances to suspicious houses. He mapped it all out systematically as time ticked by, and tried to commit as much as possible to memory. There was no such thing as too much information.

"Hasten to prayer!" The noon call of the muezzin surprised him because he had been so busy that hours had slipped away. Then he got an unexpected break. A group of armed men came from the house used by Pudgy and Beanpole. While most residents simply worshipped within their homes or workplaces, or went to the small mosque in the center of the village, these men wanted to make a public show of their fervent devotion. Each unrolled a small rug or a straw mat in the street, knelt, and performed the rituals of prayer. Kyle got an accurate head count: eight men, all with their weapons. Nobody had come from the other suspicious house, where the door remained closed.

Prayers done, two of the men repeated the breakfast run and went to the store for the group. A small, wiry man tagged along behind a large character with a square head and big shoulders. *SpongeBob and Pee-Wee.* Back to their house with arms overflowing with boxes and bottles, and then SpongeBob made the delivery run of three boxes and six water bottles over to the second house. This time Swanson was ready when the door opened, and was looking only for the hands that reached for the boxes and bottles. *White!* No damned doubt. Not a damned doubt in the world.

I'm starving out here on crackers and peanut butter while you assholes are having meals delivered.

Swanson turned over to rest. Seeing all those clowns down there made him start to think that he might have bitten off more than he could chew with this. He considered that the eight in the house were probably hardcore fighters, but how many else were down there? Enough to keep shifts of guards around the Zeus. Add whoever was in the mystery house. Round it off to at least a dozen, probably more. Clowns with guns could still shoot. He was strongly tempted to break radio silence and call for help.

It was not fear, for he was not afraid to die. He was just afraid to fail. But if he could get the general, it would take only a moment to light up his phone and get an air strike to take out the main group with a single smart bomb. He could pull Middleton out during the confusion and evade to a landing zone where a chopper could come in under air cover and pick them up. He almost convinced himself that was the way to go.

Then he weighed the down side. His people would be monitoring the cell phones of the members of the TRAP team to see if they had been put into use by the enemy. Using his own would announce his existence. The element of surprise would be gone, and the tactical situation would tilt back to favor the bad guys. Better that they continue to think he was a lone radio operator running for his life. Same thing with the pack radio he had taken from the dead Marine.

He rubbed water over his face to cool it. This whole

deal smelled as rotten as a month-old banana. Those people down there had known exactly when, where, and how the Force Recon choppers would arrive, and that meant there was a leak somewhere. Not a leak. A flood! The person responsible had to be high enough up the food chain to have been trusted with details of the plan. *Who?* Kyle dug out another bottle of water. Sweat was pouring from him, even lying motionless in the little bit of shade provided by the bushes roofing his hide. It was probably 120 degrees at midday.

A call to alert the Marines that he was alive would risk that the traitor would also find out and block any new rescue attempt.

How high up the food chain was the leak? The mission had been put together in a hurry, but a lot of people knew about it, both civilian and military. But only one person had done something truly unusual: Gerald Buchanan, the man who wrote out in his own hand the order for Kyle to assassinate the general if things went haywire. Why even issue such an order unless he anticipated that something was going to go wrong? As far as the Marines were concerned, it was supposed to be a rather ordinary in-and-out mission with sufficient speed, troops, and firepower to get the job done. The commandant of Marines would never have approved such a plan. The President of the United States knew? Impossible. The man was a decorated veteran himself. The guy who came to the carrier, Shafer, was just the messenger boy. The circle led back to Buchanan.

He thought about why a man like Buchanan would betray his country, and then he considered what would be a suitable punishment. What would be worse for a deskbound political animal than having to spend the rest of his life cramped in a supermax cell in Colorado alongside big-league terrorists? A bullet in the ear would work, but Kyle felt Buchanan should be brought into public shame and disgrace. Like that Enron guy, he could always have a heart attack after being convicted. Swanson shook his head to clear the cobwebs. The whole thing was irrelevant and had nothing to do with his job at the moment.

He would trust Double-Oh to get that letter into the hands of the right people and that they would take care of the problem. Isn't that what the FBI does? He was a sniper, not a cop, and all he could deal with at the moment was whether to make this fight all alone, or risk using the damned telephone. He was fucked either way. He would not make the call yet. Anonymity was his friend, and the best route, the only route, was straight ahead. He kept the sat phone and buried the pack radio. No use lugging it along, since it had only been taken as a diversion in the first place.

He rubbed his eyes, picked up the binos, and got back to sketching the village.

Boredom set in as the sun baked the town and the lone man watching it, but Swanson would not let himself fall asleep. There would be no more sleep until this job was done, for to sleep would be to yield awareness of the situation, and that could be the end of everything. He began arranging what he knew, planning his attack. He studied the little grocery, putting it on his mental list of places to visit after dark.

About four o'clock, a dirty white Toyota pickup truck came down the shady side of the main street with a throaty rumble and stopped in front of the suspicious place Kyle now called the House of White Hands. Although he had a beard, the driver was not an Arab, but he moved with the loose gait of someone comfortable in the surroundings. He wore lightweight slacks and a long-sleeved blue cotton shirt rolled up at the wrists, with sunglasses pushed up on top of his head. He greeted a few men seated on stools in some nearby shade. *Damn!* Kyle kept his right hand on the binos while his left dug into a thigh pocket and grabbed a plastic envelope. It contained the small photograph of the Frenchman who was to be the contact for the Marine raiders, and he looked at the picture, then back at the man. Pierre Falais. The Frenchman knocked on the door, said something, and was allowed inside. Fifteen minutes later he was out again, and his truck roared to life. Toyotas don't roar, Kyle noted, and they don't wear big desert tires. This was a custom job. He watched it drive to the gate in a low wall that surrounded another flat-roofed house three blocks down the main street, and then he lasered the hell out of the place.

It was finally time to move. Swanson spent two hours backing out of his hide and working his way down the wadi to a new spot a hundred meters to the right to get a better view of the mysterious door before the dinnertime delivery at the House of White Hands. This time, when the door opened, he had a plain view of a big man wearing desert cammie pants and an olive drab tank top. Not only was he white, but he had a line of tattoos

179

on his right arm from shoulder to wrist. He took the food and shut the door.

Swanson was stunned. Who the hell was that and what did he have to do with the situation? The white skin meant westernized: Eurotrash or Aussie or Kiwi or Canadian or Scottish or whatever. Maybe even American. The tattoos helped narrow the field because they indicated a military background. That meant a spook of some sort, or a mercenary, and so much food being delivered indicated more than one in the house. A couple of Frankensteins just happen to be in the neighborhood during a Marine raid? No chance that could be just a coincidence, and it sure as hell didn't help the odds against him.

Kyle crawled back to his hide, ate some more crackers, and checked his water supply before taking a sip. He had taken two one-quart and four two-quart canteens from the other Marines so that he could be liberal in staying hydrated, because he planned to resupply after dark. But he never drank more than half of the water on hand. Water was life in the Middle East, and he judged that he still had plenty. As he ate, he considered his list—the Zeus and its guards; the house with Pudgy, Beanpole, SpongeBob and Pee-Wee, and a minimum of four other Arab fighters; the frog and his souped-up Toyota; and finally the House of White Hands, which contained at least one non-Arab guy who was most likely a merc.

Places to go and things to do, and Middleton was down there somewhere. *The frog will tell me.* Lots to do. He cut chunks of C-4, rolled them into tiny balls and put them in an arm pocket. A handful of pencil-sized detonators went into another pocket. From a full roll of black duct tape in his pack, he ripped off a half-dozen long strips and stuck them along the legs of his pants. He cleaned his weapons. He waited for darkness.

26

"News from the front, General! Guess what? You're gonna be a fuckin' TV star again!" Victor Logan squatted before his captive, grabbed Brad Middleton hard by the jaw, and turned him so the prisoner had to look into his eyes. Logan laughed, a mirthless sound that echoed in the small room, and he wore a smile of triumph.

As the heat of the day was easing, Middleton, prone on the bunk, was able to breathe a bit easier, pulling air into his lungs despite the aching rib that had been broken in one of the beatings. The broken finger was useless. He had ripped a strip of cloth from his robe and tied it to the next finger to immobilize it. The room stank so badly it had become part of him. His guts were sore, and he had neither bathed nor shaved since they had used him in that earlier rigged media show.

Middleton's right wrist was chained to the metal cot, giving him only enough movement to reach two buckets, one about a third full of fresh water and the other a stinking one that he used as a toilet. The loose full-length cotton robe was filthy.

"We just got some new instructions," Logan said, letting go of the jaw but giving Middleton a medium-strength slap on the side of his head, enough to make the general's ears ring. "I guess you might consider the good news is that this is going to be our last day in this shithole. The bad news, for you that is, comes tomorrow morning. Jimbo and I are going to clean you up, get you all dressed in that spiffy uniform hanging on the door over there, and hand you to the raggedy-heads. The jihadists plan a big show. Might call it the local version of *American Idol*."

Middleton ignored the flash of pain, slowly swung his feet to the floor, and spat on the floor to disrespect Logan. He wasn't afraid of the giant, because almost by definition a Marine Corps general has a streak of arrogance. His mind had cleared as the drugs wore off and he had thought long and hard about why he had been taken hostage, adding in the snippets of information he overheard through the door as his captors talked. He knew that he would never be released, so damned if he would go down sniveling. Middleton decided to interrogate the big man.

"If you have something to tell me, Logan, just say it. You and your partner: Dumber and Dumbest," the general said with a condescending sneer. "I can't understand why a company as big as Gates Global, with hundreds of pretty good people on the payroll, would stoop so low as to bring a couple of losers like you aboard."

Logan reacted sharply and stood to his full height, glaring down at Middleton. "They came recruiting me, not the other way around! The company uses Shark Teams to handle the uncomfortable side of things."

Middleton gave a wry smile. "And you were stupid

enough to sign on. Look. I know Gordon Gates personally. He eats guys like you and Dumbo for breakfast.
Sharks. Jesus."

"Jimbo, not Dumbo."

"Right. So Gordon waved his checkbook and you
fools jumped on board." With a couple of oblique
probes, Middleton had gotten Logan to admit that Gates
was behind the kidnapping. He decided to push harder.

"He's paying me a hell of a lot better than the military
ever did. Way better. I got more money in the bank than
you ever dreamed of."

"Good for you. I hope your 401(k) brings you peace
and comfort for the next few hours, because you're
already a corpse, too, and just don't know it yet."

"Bullshit."

The general stretched to loosen his muscles. "You are
not going to live long enough to spend it, Logan. I
guarantee that a big reward has been put on the street,
and your best friends are already looking at you as a
piece of meat that is worth about a half-million American dollars, dead or alive." Middleton tugged at the
handcuff chain, let it drop, and faced Logan again.

"Also, you and Dumbo are the only links to my
actual kidnapping, and Gates Global is going to cover
its own ass. You are loose ends. Another one of your
gear-queer Shark Teams probably will be sent out to
gobble you up. You may be King Kong today, but
between the tickle of a big reward among the ragheads
and the double-cross coming from your boss, you're
going to be just another dead monkey."

DAMN. Logan wanted to hit the general, beat the
crap out of him, cut him, make him bleed. That was not

allowed. "Shut your damned mouth, Middleton, or I'll shut it for you. You don't know nothing."

"I know it all, Logan," Middleton said, staring at the merc. "It's so quiet around here that I can hear the rats fart, and I've been listening every time you guys talk. You're going to have me killed on TV. Big deal. The Marine Corps is a big organization, and six colonels are probably already fighting for my desk. I'll be missed at the Pentagon about as much as you have been by those wussy SEALs. Let's make a bet: I say your freedom fighter buddies will bury all three of us in the desert tomorrow: you and me and Dumbo together through eternity." The general lay back down as if he did not have a care in the world, but continued the questioning. "No wonder they kicked you out of the shitbird SEALs. You weren't even good enough to meet their low standards."

Logan snapped at the bait. "Yeah? You think your Marines are such hot shit?" He was pissed that Middleton was ridiculing the Teams. SEALs were the best! "Your Spec Op boys couldn't even fly two helicopters without running into each other out here. Wouldn't have mattered if they landed, neither, because we had them in a kill zone even before they fucked up."

Middleton made a point of grimacing as if disappointed and said nothing while he made another mental note. Confirmation that this whole thing was a setup for an ambush. Blabbermouth.

"You think I ain't already got my own escape covered? You may be a general, but I'm as smart as you."

"Sure. That's why we're in here together in this smelly

185

house. Couple of Einsteins, we are. E equals MC squared."

Logan had never liked really intelligent people. He didn't get that part about EMC. "You know why you're really here? Think you figured it all out?"

"Yeah. It's not all that hard. Real terrorists would have gone after an easier target, not a moving convoy with armed Marine and Saudi guards. That's why they snatch schoolteachers, not soldiers. So who would consider me important enough to risk an ambush that would certainly result in casualties and guarantee media coverage and a manhunt? Who profits?"

"What's your answer?"

"Simple. Gates Global. Your job was to put me on the sidelines. The only thing worthwhile on my schedule is testifying next week in Washington before the Senate Armed Services Committee. That is where I intend to stop this nutty privatization of the United States military and keep disgraceful incompetents like you from sneaking back into the tent. Shit, Logan, I wrote the book on privatization while I was at the Naval War College. The PSC concept is long on cost and short on loyalty. The Naval Institute Press published it and we even got some good ink in *The New York Times Book Review*." Middleton laughed derisively and glanced at Logan. "It helped me get my star. I'm sure you read it."

"Big fuckin' deal."

"You're working for a private security company, but any way you cut it, you're nothing but a mercenary. A gun for hire. You work for Gates Global, which ordered you to kidnap me. Now, for some reason, which I assume is related to the helo crash, the original plan has changed. You never planned to let me live anyway, but Gates was just trying to figure out how he could benefit the most by my death. So it turns out the jihadists will do the honors. Once that is done, you are no longer needed either. Probably just one hole will be big enough for the three of us."

"Not gonna happen, Middleton." Logan moved to the door. "I've listened to enough of your shit. Anyway, let me tell you how it's going to come down tomorrow. Once we get you all pretty again and give you to those Iraqis . . ."

Middleton snorted, a bark of a laugh. "See? You just did it again!"

"Did what?"

"Gave me information I did not need to know. I had no idea those guys were Iraqis. You furnished another piece of the puzzle, you shitbird."

"Fuck you. I'll tell you something else, because you're going to be dead real soon. Not only are they Iraqis, but they work for that badass Rebel Sheikh down in Basra. At eight o'clock tomorrow morning, they are going to prop you up in a chair and cut off your fucking head!" He let the big cocky grin creep back across his face. "And I'm going to be standing there to watch. Gonna really enjoy the show."

Middleton closed his eyes as if bored. "Okay, Logan. See you in the hole." The general turned his back to the mercenary and did not move again until the door closed. Even then he did not move, thinking about beheadings and the alliance between Gordon Gates and the Rebel Sheikh.

27

Master Sergeant O. O. Dawkins had not slept since the choppers had lifted off earlier that morning from the *Wasp*, and had smoked a whole pack of cigarettes. What a cluster fuck. He leaned on a railing of the USS *Blue Ridge*, flagship of the Joint Amphibious Task Force commander, and watched the water churning past far below. The entire TRAP team and two helo crews down in the desert, probably dead in the smoking ruins, and then abandoned. Just like that hostage mess back in 1979 with the Rangers and Delta operators in Iran. All of the high-tech toys in the world were bound to screw up sooner or later, and when Marines ride on the razor's edge, Mother Nature gives no second chances. He flipped his cigarette butt overboard and made his way through the chutes and ladders up to Flag Country.

His boss, Colonel Ralph Sims, looked like he had been punched in the gut, and waved Dawkins to a chair in his small but private stateroom. Sims was commander of the 33rd Marine Expeditionary Unit, the first one to work under the banner of the Joint Special Operations Command. Dawkins, an ex-Force Recon platoon sergeant, normally would have been the MEU operations chief, but under the realignment into special forces, he was called the MARSOC team sergeant. He was an operator, not an administrative type. New generation of titles, same jobs.

Sims and Dawkins had been friends for more years than they cared to think about, and just sat there staring at each other in silence for a time across the desktop that held a small computer, a cup filled with pens, scissors, and a small ruler, and a little nameplate sign carved in the Philippines. They felt helpless, and could do nothing more to either save their men or bring the bodies home for honorable burials. Marines had left Marines behind. Sims opened a locked drawer and pulled out a bottle of Jack Daniel's Black Label bourbon. He poured shots for each of them into black coffee mugs emblazoned with the scarlet and gold crest of the 33rd MEU, and they drank the whiskey in quick gulps.

Outside sounds seeped dully into the quiet room. Ship noises. The creaking and groaning metal, the whines and whops of Harriers and helicopters, water moving through exposed pipes along the ceiling and around the red emergency lighting fixtures. The wall intercom, volume turned low, muttered just at the level of hearing. The stateroom, painted navy gray, was a combination work space and living quarters, so Sims could dash to his station in the Tactical Center only one deck up in an emergency. There was no porthole for outside light, but a small refrigerator worth its weight in gold was wedged into a corner.

"Anything new?" Dawkins asked.

Sims shook his head. "The Harrier pilots were thoroughly debriefed, Double-Oh, and their stories match. All they really saw was a big fireball when the choppers went down and no signs of life afterward when they flew over at low altitude, other than people coming out from the village. We lost 'em all."

"No chance, I suppose, of sending in another mission for the boys and the general?"

The colonel turned around and looked at a map taped to the bulkhead that showed the route. "Washington says it's out of the question. They won't even authorize a missile strike to eradicate the wreckage, and a diplomatic shitstorm is on the way. Syria is yelling 'Invasion!' and our State Department is trying to explain, 'Well, not really. It's this way . . .'"

"Then the fuckin' media and the United Nations will get involved."

"Yup. Too big a development to keep secret. The Muslim world is going to go nuts with demonstrations." The colonel poured more bourbon into the mugs. "We're going to get hammered."

Dawkins nodded his big, crew-cut head. "Not our best day, sir. Looked easy on paper."

"Always does, Master Sergeant. Always does."

"So you think it is a safe bet that Gunny Swanson is dead?"

Sims nodded. "Pilots said no signs of life. With daylight, we got better satellite imagery, but it still shows nothing useful. I don't see how anyone got out of that mess in one piece, even a ghost like Swanson."

A small speaker on the bulkhead crackled, and a quiet voice announced: "Attention all hands. A sunset memorial service will be held on the flight deck at eighteen hundred hours for the men who died on today's mission."

They raised the cups in salute. "To those who won't return. May they rest in peace," said the colonel.

"And to Kyle," responded Double-Oh.

"To Kyle."

"Semper fi."

They downed the smooth whiskey.

"Hard to imagine him gone." Dawkins settled back into the chair.

"What are you trying to tell me, Double-Oh? You didn't ask for a private meeting just to talk about old times."

Dawkins took a deep breath. The colonel had the uncanny knack of reading right through people. "No, sir. Well, since there is always room for more bad news, I guess I need to give you some."

"This has something to do, I assume, with why you have been wandering around the ship wearing a locked and loaded .45?"

"Yes, sir."

"So you weren't really expecting pirates to come charging over the starboard bow shooting RPGs?"

"No, sir. This is for real." Dawkins undid a Velcro snap on the sleeve of his flight suit and retrieved the envelope. "You remember when that spook from Washington came aboard to meet privately with Gunny Swanson?"

"Ummm. Figured he was getting tagged for a special mission when this was over."

"Sir, this *was* the special mission. Kyle was put under some top-secret orders, and his death leaves us with a situation."

"A situation." Sims put his forearms on the desk and

leaned forward. He was tall and lean, with dark brows and a beaked nose that gave him the look of a pissed-off eagle like the ones he wore on his collar.

"Yessir. Maybe more a major league fuckup that will make people look back fondly on Richard Nixon after Watergate and Bill Clinton's blow job." He slid the letter across the smooth desktop with his fingertips. "It's all in there, sir."

"Swanson told you about this?"

"He refused to carry out the order until the spook threatened to get the White House to verify it. Then Kyle somehow snuck a copy without that Washington fuck realizing it, and the fool burned the copy, thinking it was the real thing. Gunny gave me the original in case he got whacked. He got whacked. So here it is."

"I don't think I really want to open that."

"No. Probably not, and I don't blame you one bit. But that's why you're a full bird colonel with a bunch of college degrees and I'm just a master sergeant. You decide where it goes from here."

"What's it say?" The colonel held the envelope as if it were scalding hot, turning it over and over in his hands.

"If it looked like the rescue attempt was going to fail, Gunnery Sergeant Kyle Swanson was under orders to execute Brigadier General Middleton."

"The hell you say," said Sims, running a thumbnail under the envelope flap. His eyes gave away nothing as he read the handwritten note.

"The hell I do say, sir. The reason I went around the chain of command to get straight to you is that we don't know who may be involved in this thing. I guess it is going to be a very special need-to-know category."

Sims dug out some thin plastic map overlay sheets from his desk, folded them around the letter and envelope, and carried them to his private safe to lock them away. "You're right, Double-Oh. In fact, you're so damned right that I'm going to have to think about our next step. A wrong move and we both end up at Gitmo with German shepherds chomping at our balls. You got a suggestion?"

As the colonel resumed his seat, Dawkins stood. His leathery face actually wore a smile. "Yeah, Skipper, I do. The Thirty-Third MEU is an independent Special Ops unit, and as its commanding officer, you report straight to Central Command. I suggest you pack your bags for a routine trip back to Tampa to give the boys at MacDill a 'special briefing' about why the helicopters crashed. Have your staff type up a bunch of papers and make a PowerPoint show for cover."

Sims rubbed his thumb across his lips, which had gone dry. "And while I'm there, I get some private face time with CENTCOM?"

"No, sir. Halfway across the Atlantic, your flight will be diverted because the Pentagon will decide it wants to hear your lame-ass excuses in person. I can cash in some favors and get the Sergeants' Network to cut orders that far and keep you below the official radar. Once in Washington, it will be up to you to snag a meeting with General Hank Turner, our old boss from the First MARDIV. Although he happens to wear four stars and be chairman of the Joint Chiefs of Staff now, he's still an old Force Recon operator at heart. Him we can trust."

Sims agreed. "You're right. Turner will kick in the

doors to find out what is going on." The colonel folded his hands behind his head. "Make it happen, Master Sergeant."

"Semper fuckin' fi, Colonel."

28

Ali Shalal Rassad made his afternoon prayers in one of Basra's crowded mosques, in the midst of a crowd of kneeling, praying men. Afterward, he smiled his way to the door, hugging fellow worshippers along the way and dispensing words of encouragement, a whispered promise of help, a handful of coins. He was a leader because the people considered him to be one of their own, a warrior and a dutiful, humble servant of Allah, whose name be praised. The prayers provided quiet moments during which he often thought about how much he owed to the dictator Saddam Hussein. Without pure evil, how would people recognize good?

Like so many Iraqis, Rassad had grown up in poverty, a product of the Baghdad slums. He caught the attention of his teachers at the religious *madrassa* schools because he possessed an intellectual curiosity and showed a natural leadership ability. They decided he was worthy of more education, with the idea that he might become an Islamic scholar and religious leader. They misjudged the boy. During the day, he piously studied the Koran, but at night he read other books, and led a small gang of thieves through the alleyways of Baghdad. Death was never far away in the slums, and Rassad had gutted several men before his fifteenth birthday. He was a realist instead of a zealot, interested in obtaining his own goals and not simply obeying the rules of any book, not even the Koran.

No one was surprised when Rassad passed the exams to qualify for university study abroad as an engineer, nor that the government let him go to school in the United States. His family would remain in Baghdad as hostage until he returned to take a job with one of Hussein's ministries.

Rassad studied electrical engineering at the Massachusetts Institute of Technology, and also studied the complex organism that was America. He traveled to the oil fields in Louisiana and the West, to Silicon Valley in California, and to the vast farmlands of Kansas in search of understanding how and why democracy worked in Washington, D.C.

The individual experiences started coming together during his junior year, when he drove from Boston to Florida to participate in the annual ritual among students known as spring break. The all-night parties had been quite educational, and several pretty girls had found his dark eyes irresistible. The important lesson came late on a Monday night as he grew tired while driving back from Daytona Beach. A green neon sign of a little diner beckoned near Brunswick, Georgia, and Rassad followed a side road north for two miles. There was only a weathered pickup truck and a little Honda parked in the lot, which was illuminated dully by the ragged circles cast by three lights attached to the eaves of the building. He parked his new BMW 735i SE, went inside, and took a stool at the counter. A disinterested waitress took his order for a glass of water with ice and a piece of the fresh pecan pie that sat in a plastic case.

"Looky here," Myron Hix muttered. He was seated at a table crowded with empty beer bottles. A younger man, small, thin, and unshaven, was pushed back in another chair, a grimy Atlanta Braves baseball cap on his head. Rassad ignored them.

"Give that boy a beer!" Hix bellowed. A thick man of middle age with close-cut hair over a red, round face, he lifted a bottle of Budweiser in a toast. "You look like a man who needs a drink."

Rassad raised his hand to the waitress to signify he did not want a beer. "Thank you, but I do not drink alcohol," he said to the man.

"He 'do not drink alcohol.'" The man laughed, and so did his friend. Both wore dark blue shirts with open collars and name patches sewn above the pockets, the uniforms of a local garage. Scarlet script spelled that the big man's name was "Myron." The other man was "Robert."

The waitress slid the saucer with the pie and the glass of water before Rassad with the clatter of cheap china on thin Formica. Georgia was famed for its pecan pie. He took a bite. Delicious. The waitress, a bored woman with dyed blond hair, vanished into the kitchen through a swinging door.

The man approached him and perched uninvited on the torn leatherette stool. "Name's Myron Hix, boy. You a stranger in this neck of the woods and I wanna buy you a drink. So what'll it be?"

"Just water." Rassad faced the man. Bright eyes and

beer breath. Glancing at the table, Rassad saw a stack of empty bottles.

"Ain't polite to refuse a man's offer," said Hix. "Not down 'round here."

"I do not wish to be impolite. My religion forbids alcohol."

"Where is it you from, then? Me and Robert are Baptists. Our preacher don't like us to drink neither, but the Bible says wine is okay. If wine is okay, then ain't beer and whiskey?"

"I am Muslim." He finished the pie, drank the water. "Thank you for your kindness." He fished a ten-dollar bill from his wallet and put it on the counter.

Hix slapped his hand down on the green face of President Andrew Jackson. "Moos-lim? I thought so." He spun on the stool to face Robert. "I tole you he was some kinda sand nigger, din't I?"

Rassad tensed. "Please. I wish no trouble. I will just get in my car and go."

"You damn sure will. And you don't come back. Hear? Go on back to Egypt and fuck your camel." Both of the men laughed.

He had just unlocked his sleek gray sedan when he heard the screen door of the diner slam shut, and tensed just as beefy hands shoved him against the vehicle. Rassad smelled the dirty breath of Myron Hix. Two miles away, a stream of headlights moved north, kids going back to school after the holiday. The lighter steps of Robert approached. "We ain't through with you yet, boy," said Hix. "You need a good lesson in 'firmative action so you don't forget who you are." Hix spun Rassad around and loomed over him like a bad dream.

The Iraqi looked steadily at the bigger man. "I believe that you are what people call a roughneck?" he asked mildly. "No. My English is poor. The term is stupid fucking redneck. Is that correct?"

As he was being turned, Rassad's right hand was hidden long enough for him to pull a sharply honed knife with a three-inch blade from the leather sheath clipped to the back of his belt. He had worn such a knife since he was a boy, and it almost jumped into his hand, like an old friend. He knew exactly what he was going to do with Myron Hix.

Rassad kept the knife shielded just behind his right ass cheek while he rotated the blade into position, then he struck upward in a quick, smooth motion with all the force he could muster.

The tip of the blade slid into the soft flesh under Hix's chin and Rassad shoved it in all the way, up behind the nose until the butt of the knife came to a stop. He ripped to the right and down, hard, cutting the jugular vein before jerking the knife out with the sharp edge toward him in order to cause a maximum of damage. One of the most valuable lessons of his brutal childhood was that once you start an attack, never pause until it is done, and be utterly ruthless.

He held Hix steady and watched the eyes go wide in anger, then surprise, then fade to dimness. Rassad let the body fall, stepped over, it and took three long strides to close on Robert, whose last word was, "Myron?" Rassad plunged the knife in at the belly button, careful to avoid the big metal belt buckle, got his left hand into Robert's hair, and pulled him forward while he stabbed three more times in the midsection. As Robert fell, the blade stabbed into the neck on the right side and was raked across the throat, opening a deep and bloody track.

Rassad wiped the knife on Robert's jeans, returned it to the sheath, got into his car, and started the engine. He wasn't even breathing hard. His clothes were soaked in blood, and he wiped his face clean with a hand-kerchief.

All the way back to Massachusetts, he drove safely among the hundreds of honking cars of other students, avoiding police attention and notorious speed-trap towns by just being one of the crowd. Friends at his local mosque arranged for the car to be stolen, and for the knife and clothing to disappear. Rassad replaced the Beemer with the insurance settlement. The *Boston Globe* reported a violent double killing at a roadside café in Georgia, identified the victims, and quoted a Georgia state patrolman as saying, "It was the most terrible thing I ever saw, even better than when that truck full of Vidalia onions squashed the Volkswagen crammed with drunk Florida Gator football fans."

Rassad now considered that Myron Hix had been sent by the Prophet to point out the darker side of American political history. More than twenty years later, Ali Shalal Rassad, the Rebel Sheikh, still savored that delicious moment when Myron—he liked to refer to him by his first name—called him a sand nigger to his face.

In his senior year at MIT, he expanded his explora-tion of United States history to include racial hatred. Signs in Texas restaurants once decreed, no dogs or mexicans allowed inside. Native Americans had been slaughtered for their land. Railroad builders hung Chinese workers over the sides of mountains in baskets to blow away chunks of rock with dynamite and created the saying that an unfortunate person might not have "a Chinaman's chance." Japanese citizens were thrown in huge camps during World War II, but German citizens were not. The South was still dealing with the aftermath of slavery. Mexican immigration was a burning issue. The color of a person's skin seemed very important in America.

Rassad was fascinated by the political demagogues. Each brimmed with vices, but rose to political prominence by painting themselves as ordinary men of the people. It was called populism, but extended only to those of their own kind: white voters who were extremely religious. When Rassad attended their churches, the congregation stared. Americans taught him racial intolerance.

His professional degree was as an engineer, but his life was about politics, a thirst for power that increased when Saddam's son threw him in prison, where he somehow endured until the Americans came. Prison always seemed to be a good place for visionaries, and torture was excellent fuel for serious thinking.

When he was released during the first weeks of the American occupation, Rassad set out to perform political magic in Basra because he knew that populism would work as well in Iraq as it ever had in the Southern boondocks. Tribal strength, blind hatred, and fervent religious beliefs inherited over generations proved to be a potent combination. All that was needed was a leader to focus it all, someone to unite the factions.

Within a few years of the occupation, the people of Basra thought they had chosen him for that task, when in reality he had created a political vacuum by getting rid of his enemies. He was trusted by other Iraqis and bridged the gap between the religious factions by showing them there was more to be gained by working together. Peace got the oil flowing, and the oil brought in money enough for everybody. His private militia kept the peace by frequently reminding citizens about the horrors of war.

He had recognized the precise moment to shed his old skin as the leader of violent opposition and be reborn as a strong political savior, the man of peace. Rassad had the grace and intelligence to win the confidence of other foreign leaders, and the Americans were desperately begging for someone, anyone, to step forward and become the Iraqi George Washington. Rigorously managed, democracy could be just the springboard he wanted to expand beyond Basra and take over the government in Baghdad, with all of the levers of power and a treasury that King Midas would have envied.

In the coolness of his air-conditioned office, Rassad again read the urgent coded message he had received from America. It was an instruction to kill the American general Middleton immediately, but gave no details.

He let out a soft, tuneless whistle and smoothed the note on his desk as he let his mind roam free. This was tantamount to an order! Something had changed in his arrangement with Gordon Gates, and he had not been informed in advance for approval. It was irritating.

Therefore he had to examine the entire plan again.

The game obviously had entered a new stage, and he would not risk losing all of those lucrative U.S. contacts because of a plot in Washington to change the way their military establishment was funded. Old alliances had to be constantly weighed on the scales of current and future value. Gates would be angry, but they would still work together in the future no matter how this single incident turned out. Gates would have no choice. There was a bigger game. Rassad could not allow the kidnapping to convince the American government to pick someone else to be George Washington.

Rassad asked his aide, "Have you acted on this instruction from the Americans to have our friends in Syria execute the Marine general?"

"Yes. I made the contact within this past hour. They will gather the needed video equipment overnight and record his beheading tomorrow morning." He bowed slightly, expecting praise for a well-done job.

The Rebel Sheikh puffed out his cheeks, then ran a finger across his dry lips. "Send this new order. Do *not* kill him. Dispatch my plane to Syria at first light and fetch the general down here to me. Dispose of the two American mercenaries who deliver him."

"As you direct." The assistant bowed and left the office.

Rassad had not decided what to do with Middleton. He might yet kill him, or give him back to the Americans and appear to have negotiated his release. What had hardened in his thinking was that he would be the one to make the decision, not the American power brokers.

29

The small U.S. Air Force C-20 executive jet sped across the Atlantic, bucking through pockets of rough air that were being pushed east by a storm front. Colonel Ralph Sims, the only passenger aboard, was strapped tightly into a wide, comfortable seat. This rough, bucking ride might be a mild flight compared to what awaited him when he landed.

An Air Force staff sergeant came back to check on Sims, and perched on the armrest of the seat across from him. She was an attractive brunette, with her hair cut short to frame her face and flawless makeup. Slender and with long legs that were close enough for him to touch when she crossed them. She was barefoot, and had replaced her uniform jacket with a small dark blue apron. Her perfect breasts swayed with the motion of the aircraft, threatening to break free of the little buttons on her shirt. The staff sergeant obviously had been chosen as a hostess for VIP flights because of the sum total of all of her assets, and she was given custom-tailored uniforms and had her hair done professionally at a pricy salon, courtesy of Uncle Sam.

"How are things back here, Colonel?" she asked. The

accent was uniquely regional to her native West Virginia, and added to the package of charm.

"Bumpy." Sims had larger things on his mind than this girl's sexuality, but damn, she looked good.

"It does get that way sometimes, but the pilot is going to take us up higher and bend a little to the south to pick our way through this muck." She waggled her foot up and down.

"No shoes today, Staff Sergeant?"

"I'm from the coal fields, sir. Didn't even *have* shoes until I joined the Air Force and the government gave me some," she laughed. "That's a lie, but unlike most women, I hate shoes, and kick 'em off after everyone is aboard and we're off the ground. Easier to work barefoot." She waved her right arm at the otherwise empty cabin. "Can you imagine trying to carry a tray while walking on high heels during a storm like this? Some gay designer who hates women created high heels, that's what I think."

Sims smiled. "Well, I guess none of your passengers tonight will complain."

"Nobody has yet, sir. We were going to be flying back empty tonight, but got a last-minute call to hold and wait for you." She enjoyed only having to deal with just one person. "It's dark outside and we're flying into time, so maybe you want to get some rest? Nothing you can do to hurry us along."

He thought about the valuable hours that were falling from the clock, never to be recovered. Double-Oh and the Sergeants' Network had done a great job on logistics, for his departure had to look normal, which meant the staff had to be given an opportunity to prepare the

PowerPoint slide show and a set of briefing papers. He spent the interval finishing the hardest part of his job as the commander of an elite unit, writing letters to the families of the Marines who were killed on the raid, personal notes that said how proud he was to have served with them. The letters would console some of the heartbroken recipients who would cherish the letter and read it out loud on birthdays, holidays, and special occasions. For others, his message would only fuel the deep personal hurt of losing a loved one, and he would be blamed. He had finished the last one just before going on deck for the evening memorial service for the fallen Marines, HIS Marines!

A helo carted him from the *Blue Ridge* to the battle group carrier in time for the last COD run of the day to Aviano. He boarded the awkward plane carrying a large briefcase that contained the mystery letter amid the other papers, and wore the grim look of a dejected officer going to a balls-cutting session. Rumor spread that he was being called back to CENTCOM to explain the fuckup in the desert. At Aviano, the sleek C-20 had been waiting with its engines buzzing quietly and the beautiful staff sergeant at the bottom of the small, carpeted staircase.

"What time is it?" he asked. He had crossed several time zones since leaving the boat.

She turned and looked at three small clocks in gleaming brass holders on the rear bulkhead. One gave Greenwich Mean Time, one read Washington time, and one was set to the aircraft's current zone. "Right now, in our itty-bitty piece of sky, it is exactly twenty-two hundred hours and, uh, forty-three minutes and, uh, fifty-eight seconds. We are right in the Greenwich zone."

He had not realized the clocks were right behind him. Almost 2300 GMT, an hour before midnight. Subtracting five hours meant it was 1800 at both CENTCOM in Tampa and the Pentagon in Washington. No matter how fast the little bird flew, it was unlikely that there would be any meeting with General Turner today.

"Tell you what, Sergeant. I'm a bit wound up, but maybe if you bring me a Jack Daniel's Black, ice, no water, it will help. After I work on these papers a little longer, I'll try to get some shuteye."

She smiled again. White, white teeth. "Yes, sir. One Black Jack coming up. How about I make that a double, and then tuck you in beddy-bye. You could get shitfaced, knee-walking drunk tonight and still be sober enough to finish your papers by the time we get to Tampa."

The telephone beside him buzzed. "Your language needs work, Staff Sergeant."

"Yes, sir! That's what they tell me." The girl laughed and padded away to the forward galley. She had long ago become a member of the Mile High club, and this colonel was sort of cute, in a dumb brute kind of way, kind of like a big German shepherd that needed to be cuddled. Possibilities loomed.

The colonel answered his encrypted STU-III satellite telephone. "Sims."

"Double-Oh here, sir. Your pilot is going to be getting the course-change message from Tampa to Andrews in about an hour, but there's a problem."

Sims gripped the telephone tightly. "What?"

"General Turner has left the Pentagon. He won't be there when you get to Washington."

"Damn, Double-Oh. Where is he?"

"The general is on his way to China, sir, some kind of emergency defense committee meeting about the new round of North Korean missile tests."

"Oh, fuck me," said Sims, closing his eyes.

"Not to worry, colonel. I got the Network on it. His plane lands at Elmendorf in Alaska to refuel before jumping the Pacific by the polar route. A mechanical problem will keep him on the ground until you get there."

"He will just take another plane."

"Yessir, that's probably exactly what he will try to do. Then that one will also have a malfunction. Airplanes are tricky things, particularly up there in all that extremely cold weather. You just keep going, colonel. We will have another C-20 waiting at Andrews. Keep closing the gap, sir. He's got to stop. You don't."

"But he's got a half-a-world head start!" Sims replied. "Okay. Do your thing. Keep me posted." He turned off the phone, tossed it onto the seat beside the briefcase, and shook his head. "China. Oh, fuck me, fuck me, fuck me," he whispered.

"Ooooh, high-altitude sex. I think that can be arranged, Colonel Sims," the soft voice with a West Virginia twang purred. The staff sergeant was kneeling at his side with a glass of whiskey and two buttons undone on her blouse. "Drink up while I lock the door, turn on some music, and dim the lights. By the way, my name isn't Staff Sergeant, it's Mandi."

30

Darkness came slowly, a gauzy haze of dust-laden, fading light streaks. Even when the final fiery edge of the sun disappeared, the temperatures stayed stuck in the nineties. Within a few hours, Swanson would be freezing his butt off. It would not really be cold by the thermometer, but a thirty-degree drop after sweltering in 110-plus heat would bring a good dose of the chills. When the sun took away its warmth, the sweat that had oozed from him all day and drenched his clothes would feel like ice when the nightly winds blew. The mission was to have been a quick in-and-out, so he had only the clothes on his back. Fuck it. Nothing he could do, and that missing sun was his clock.

It had to shift away and benignly bathe places like the south of France and Miami Beach and Waikiki and Bondi Beach before returning to Syria, but it would not really be gone very long. The sniper had to be out of the hide, do his job, and be long gone before that orange beast once again started to eat this chunk of sky.

He had finished the logbook, done the surveillance, eaten some more crackers and water, and pissed into a hole in the dirt beneath him. A Syrian army contingent had shown up at the helo crash site, done some cursory investigation, loaded up the bodies, and taken them away. Swanson felt pangs of guilt while he watched. What were they going to do with the bodies? Give them back? Deep in his gut, he had a sense of failure and was angry with himself. The saying that Marines don't leave their own casualties behind was not just a catchphrase. Dead or alive, everybody comes home.

Then reason took over. He did not have the resources to change this situation, and if he survived, he could report what had happened. And importantly, there was still one Marine who was alive and needed his attention, so all Swanson could do was bid a silent goodbye to the dead rescue team of Marines and hope the pinheads in Washington fought to bring them back.

The wrecked helicopters, stripped of all value, were left where they fell, just more bones in the desert, a macabre tourist attraction for snooping American satellites to photograph from space. Two new soldiers were dropped off to replace the guard post sentries Swanson had killed, and the army convoy left.

Swanson waited without anxiety as life began to slow down with the approach of action. His focus would narrow and he would see things differently, at a slower speed, more of a black-and-white film in a neighborhood theater than as a jerky, quick-cut television story. The metamorphosis would continue, like he was changing into someone new, and the sounds would amplify, the smells would become more intense, his eyesight would sharpen, and his reactions would quicken. Each breath would be slow. He had been an observer all day. Now he was becoming a sniper.

The village activity settled into an easier pace for the

evening prayers and meal. Stores closed and the streets emptied. One by one the lights blinked out in the little windows because after a hard day of toil, working people wanted their rest. Some would make love, some would smoke a cigarette, some would dream of better times, and some were going to die by Kyle Swanson's hand. That was a fact.

He used the final hour to finish settling into his zone, almost physically filing things away in mental drawers and cabinets and closing them tight. Shari was in a special compartment, with a tight lock on it. Whoever started all this mess back in Washington was in another. His family, friends, even the Marine Corps were banished from his thoughts, and as time slowed down, Swanson felt that familiar presence of another Kyle Swanson, someone outside himself who would help him through the night, guiding and watching and planning and whispering in his head. Kyle knew a psychiatrist would love to get hold of him someday, at first for a long talk, and then maybe to saw open his skull, shake out his brain, and try to find what made it work. Swanson was curious about that, too, but did not question that other voice in his head. It was part of his natural progression into his lone gunman battle mode, and he trusted it. The voice had been a big help in other tight places, when he was kicking in doors and crawling through swamps. A bit of paranoia was a good thing when you were really in danger. It was not fright, just instinct, a sixth sense sharpened over the years, a total awareness of his environment that almost let him know what was around a corner.

Turning to Excalibur, he checked the ammo load. He

pulled the bolt back enough to slide a fingertip into the raceway and tap the brass bottom of the big .50-caliber round seated in the chamber, then pushed the bolt home again. Four more rounds rested in the magazine below.

Another hour passed and he hardly moved at all, just waiting. Black dark now. Dark as sin. It was time to roll.

The first thing he planned to do was tweak the single guard on the Zeus, apparently the only person still awake in the entire village. Swanson checked the logbook for the range, 547 yards, then brought Excalibur's cool epoxy stock to his cheek, stared down the scope, and saw the figure standing motionless, probably leaning against a tire, with an AK-47 drooped across a shoulder. He was obviously having a hard time staying awake at one o'clock in the morning. The advanced night-vision ability of Excalibur showed every possible detail, not just a green shape, and Swanson fine-tuned the focus ring. He clicked the button to lock onto the target, and again to confirm the range. The GPS, the gyrostabilizer, and the laser communicated, and numbers flashed in the scope as the built-in computer continued to enhance and clear the picture and figure out the range, windage, and barometric pressure. When all was ready, the azure stripe flashed on the edge of the scope. It could just as well have been a neon sign spelling out, "This dude is history." This was just target shooting and almost unfair. Almost.

The guard's figure almost filled the scope and Kyle could see the young, bored, sleepy face. Adjusting to the final numbers, he dropped the sight to an inch above the center of the chest. Roy Rogers and John Wayne might shoot guns out of a bad guy's hand, but professionals went for center mass, the sure hit. Swanson slowed his breathing even more, and the heartbeat followed suit, and the crosshairs of Excalibur did not wiggle.

It was unfortunate that this young man had been so low on the totem pole that he drew the midwatch guard duty. He had been on post for only ten minutes, since one o'clock, and Kyle had watched as the boy relieved the earlier guard. They stood four-hour shifts. Nobody would miss this fellow until at least 0500. Swanson exhaled a half-breath and started the easy trigger pull as his muscle memory kicked in—time to work—slow and smooth and straight and steady and squeeze. The rifle seemed to fire on its own, and although Kyle felt the recoil buck against his shoulder, there was no sound other than a quiet cough as the silencer killed the noise. In the scope, Swanson watched the big bullet slam into the guy's chest and explode inside him, ripping his muscles and guts to pieces. The location, speed, and power of the shot did not give the guard time to cry out or even look surprised. He crumbled to the dirt beside the big antiaircraft gun, dead before he hit the ground. The front of his shirt was soaked in blood. Swanson used his thumb and two fingers to jack a fresh round into the chamber and swept the scope around the village. He heard a goat bawl and a dog bark twice, but nothing indicated anyone had heard his shot.

He moved from the hide on his elbows and knees, the other voice talking now, whispering, *Slow is smooth, smooth is fast.* He squelched the natural urge to get up and run to the downed soldier, and instead began crawling, fast but quietly, with the easy grace of a night predator.

31

Search. Evaluate. Listen. The game had begun. Swanson had to cover about the length of one and a half football fields, and while speed was important, doing it right was more important. He was out in the open for God and everybody to see, slithering forward, his heartbeat slow and his eyes constantly moving.

Just because the village was quiet did not mean that no one would be up and around. It could all change in an instant, but for now the only sounds were the scuffling of animals within the walls around the houses. Rocks slid beneath him as he crawled, and the weight of his pack pressed him down. The M-16 was cradled in his arms, and Excalibur was in its drag bag, sliding along behind him, attached to a D-ring on his web gear.

It took twelve minutes to cross the open space and reach the body, where he stopped to take a careful look around, checking likely places where danger might hide, points from which a threat might emerge. He had to be lucky every time he moved. The enemy only had to be lucky once to detect him. He was burning minutes, but not wasting them.

The glazed eyes of the guard pointed up at the night

sky, but Swanson checked the pulse anyway and found none. It was a boy, no more than sixteen, probably a product of the radical religious schools who had joined the war for his true faith and paid with his short life, the end coming so fast that he had not even felt the shock. *Tough shit, kid.* Kyle jerked the corpse into a sitting position, stood, and pulled the guard upright against the side of the Zeus.

Propping him up with one hand, he peeled off the long strips of duct tape pressed along his uniform and secured the body to the hooks, rails, and protrusions on the big weapon. A belt of tape went around the waist and was tied to a heavy ammunition box. With the tape taking the weight, he crossed the ankles and taped them in place, crossed the dangling arms, and tied them at the wrists. Swanson draped the AK-47 over the boy's shoulders. The head lolled forward, which was fine, and he made a few adjustments to the clothes so as to obscure the bloodstains. Swanson took two steps back. To any distant passerby, the kid would appear to be dozing on the job, standing but sleeping.

The sniper checked the area again. Still cool. He knelt on the ground, reached into his pack, and pulled out a claymore mine, then carefully broke it open to get at the small ball bearings packed inside. He gathered a handful and rolled them, one by one, down a barrel of the Zeus, repeating the procedure until all four barrels were packed with dozens of tiny steel balls. Then he inserted the little rolls of C-4 explosive he had molded earlier. Each roll had a detonator. He opened the butt of his M-16 and took out the four-piece cleaning rod, which he twisted together into a single long, thin shaft that he thrust into each barrel to compact the mixture.

Time. Time. Tick-tock. Keep going. The voice was insistent. Swanson's senses were honed to the rhythms of the sleeping village. This was their everyday life. Nothing was supposed to happen here, particularly at night. It was like a base camp for the jihad fighters, and routine gave them an illusion of safety. Many people had washed their clothes to get rid of the day's dirt, and now the various shapes of cloth hung on lines behind the houses to dry overnight, shifting slowly in the low breeze and providing Swanson with an extra shield from sight.

He moved into the village, to the little store he had watched throughout the day. A low wall surrounded most of the two-story building, with a rollaway gate locked across the front. When open for business, the gate was pushed back to allow customers to wander in and out. The owners lived upstairs.

Kyle went over the rear wall and dropped into a crouch, pausing long enough to drop his pack and rifles inside the yard. From a lightweight vinyl holster near his left shoulder, he pulled a silenced match-grade .45-caliber pistol with an infrared laser scope, a competition-class weapon that carried an expanded magazine of fifteen rounds.

The front door of the store was locked, but a side window stood open to catch the night coolness. Swanson looked inside with his night vision goggles to avoid kicking anything, and then went over the windowsill. The pungent smell of spices was overwhelming. He did a 360-degree check of the room, holding his pistol in a firing position. Shelves, crates, a table with two chairs, a cooler in the corner, where an electric motor hummed. A stove was along the back wall beside a big cutting board on some cabinets. A carcass hung from a hook, waiting to be butchered. Cans were stacked in neat rows.

A plate of small cakes sat in a bowl on the main counter and Swanson wolfed some down, and it was the best food in the world, although he had no idea what it was. Taking a chance, he moved to the cooler and lifted the lid only a millimeter at a time to avoid making it creak, and a wave of chilly air rose into his face. Bottles of juice, water, and soft drinks were lined up like little soldiers and he pulled one out. The cold water went down better than the cakes, and he drank until he was ready to puke. After hydrating himself, he topped off his canteens. Water came first. He could not live without it. Then he grabbed an orange juice drink and gulped it down for the electrolytes, vitamins, and nutrients. *It ain't Florida OJ, but it's better than nothing.*

With his thirst slaked, he checked the available food, still able to read labels in the crisp green light of the night vision glasses. The shopping list was short but definite, and he fought the urge to belly-up on food. He had a roll of Ziploc bags in a pocket and loaded them with things that were small, easy to carry, and required no preparation. Dried figs and dates were in trays, in measured little plastic bags with twist ties, and he stuffed some into his Ziplocs, the sides of which had been strengthened with duct tape. He hated dates, but fruit was fuel. Flat cakes of day-old pita bread were taken for their starch, along with the peculiarly Middle East favorite, the ever-present Mars bars, with chocolate to provide sugar and energy. Finally, he grabbed a few boxes of unscented Baby Wipe tissues, one of the best things going for desert hygiene. One more look around and he decided that was enough. *I'm not packing for a vacation, for cryin' out loud.*

The luminous dial of his watch showed that eleven more minutes had elapsed, so he packed his goodies and went back out through the window. He gathered the rest of his gear and scaled the wall. *Slow*, warned the voice. *But go!*

Swanson reassembled everything, took some deep breaths, and turned the NVGs to his next target, the house where the fighters nested. Nothing stirred, not even a fucking mouse.

He crossed the street and stalked completely around the wall of the house, peering over the wall and into the shadows. Nothing. He hoisted himself onto the barrier and spider-dropped down the other side into the space between the wall and the right side of the house. A window was open, and he could hear the grunts of sleeping men. At least two were snoring. He had counted at least eight men going into the house, and guessed there were probably a few more, each having a gun within reach, and he planned to kill them all.

His first move was to check the inner perimeter, and he again stashed the pack and took out the pistol. Holding it in his right hand, Swanson flattened against the wall of the house and slid in a sidestep to the first corner on his right. He did a quick peek around and saw the dark backyard, crisscrossed by clotheslines laden with tunics and robes. With careful strides, he turned that corner and stepped along the rear wall to the next one, where he again stopped and slowly leaned his face around the edge.

A guard with an AK-47 on a shoulder strap, who had been obscured by the drying clothes when Kyle had studied the place, was staring straight back at him, face-to-face, within a foot of each other. The guard's eyes went wide with surprise at the goggle-eyed creature that had appeared before him out of the night. He had one hand on the stock of his AK-47 and started to raise it at the same time Kyle brought up his pistol and pulled the trigger. The gunfire sounded like the explosion of an ammunition dump to Swanson, and he felt and smelled the heavy warmth of blood wash on his head and chest, and pieces of flesh and bone plaster his arms and face. *I'm hit! It's over! I failed!* Kyle Swanson staggered backward and fell to the ground.

32

Lieutenant Commander Shari Towne spent a long time in the restroom preparing for the afternoon meeting of the National Security Council. She peered into the mirror and thought she looked horrible, but her magic bag of makeup, with careful application, helped hide the lines of worry and the darkness beneath her eyes. She put on a fresh white uniform and brushed her short hair one final time. Still horrible, but it would get her through the meeting. Through every source of effort she could summon, she donned the professional, no-nonsense mask of a neutral expert.

She just wanted this over with, and to go home to her little brick condo in Alexandria, pour a stiff shot of ice-cold Boodles gin with a lemon twist, follow that with a scalding shower, a warm cup of Celestial Seasonings tension-tamer tea, and a little oval white tablet, 10 milligrams of Ambien. That combination cocktail would go a long way toward putting her down for the night, and at least allow her body to get some rest, but she did not expect much sleep. Her mind was still on Kyle, and tears were only a couple of blinks away.

Doing her duty, making automatic responses to familiar sights and sounds and questions, had propelled her through the personal sorrow so far, and she would be back on the job tomorrow, because what was happening in Syria was much bigger than any one individual, even bigger than two people in love. When it was all done, she intended to call Jeff and Pat and get back out on that yacht and forget everything, particularly this job. The damned Middle East was her desk, and bad things were always happening there. There would be another crisis next week, and the week after that, and the week after that, and plenty of work would always be coming her way. She knew from watching other people go through grief that the mind-numbing work would help her start getting over what had happened to Kyle, one day at a time, never forgetting the death, but learning to accept it. She already missed his crooked grin, and longed to be able to go home tonight and find shelter in his strong arms.

Shari made a final mirror check and grimaced at what she saw, and five minutes later she entered the Situation Room to take her seat along the wall behind Gerald Buchanan, beside Sam Shafer.

She neither liked nor trusted Shafer, who was smart, slim, and handsome, with thick black hair slicked straight back. He was nothing more than Buchanan's slavish go-to guy for shortcuts on things that might stray over the foul line. Shafer was always flirting with her, eyeing her with open desire and working sexual innuendoes into almost every conversation.

He turned as she sat down and handed her a brown folder with a red stripe running diagonally across the front. "Here's a new file on the helo crash. Crazy stuff. Turns out that Gates Global had a couple of operators near the village, looking for the general on their own. They made it to the crash site and brought back these images of the victims."

Shari looked at him. "Gates Global? The private security company? What were they doing there?"

"God knows how they did it. It's really making us look bad—not only did the rescue mission fail, but a PSC team infiltrated and got these photos. Buchanan received the file from Gates himself. Now the boss wants somebody in this meeting to explain how a private company could do something we could not."

"Good question." Shari hesitated before accepting the folder. If these were the dead Marines, then she surely would see Kyle's body. But she wanted to do it, for maybe photographic proof would finally erase any lingering hope that somehow the man she loved actually had survived.

"I've got to back up Buchanan during the meeting, so could you take a look at it and let us know if everything is in order? Brace yourself, because it's awfully graphic, Shari, but you have the best eyes for detail of anyone at this table. We need to match up the Gates Global data with the names of those actually on the mission. The roster is in there."

She nodded and put the folder in her lap, then looked around the table. So much power. The Vice-President. The Attorney General, the Secretary of State and several cabinet members, the American representative to the United Nations, and military leaders. Buchanan, quiet and arrogant, sat directly across the table from the President. Many considered him a peculiar hybrid of Henry Kissinger's showboating, Colin Powell's confident manner, and John Poindexter's sneakiness, a man who placed himself above his position and somehow got other powerful people to recognize that self-created authority. Shari was part of his staff, but she wouldn't trust Gerald Buchanan to paint a fencepost. It was impossible to ever determine what the man ever really wanted.

She tuned one ear to the conversation and reluctantly opened the folder, then snapped it closed again, her heart beating hard. The first photo was of a charred corpse, the skin of a blackened skull dried out and pulled back so tight by the heat that it was set into a horrible grin. Shari felt a nudge from Shafer, who whispered, "You okay?"

She nodded again, and listened for a few minutes to comments of the NSC principals. Buchanan railed about the Gates Global identifications, letting unspoken accusations of Pentagon incompetence hang in the air like invisible vultures. The Syrian government was outraged, but there had been no major troop movements. U.N. and SecState both believed the biggest danger now was a possible Syrian or Hezbollah missile strike against Israel for allowing the Americans to fly through Israeli airspace. The Israelis were saying they would respond to any rocket attack. Shari tuned them out. The eternal Middle East waltz. *So what's new?*

With a deep breath, she turned her attention to the folder again and steeled herself against the ghastly images. The names of the dead Marines were on a separate page that she removed, and found "Swanson, Kyle M., Gunnery Sergeant" listed close to the alphabetical bottom. An asterisk beside the name of "McDowell,

Harold, H., Lance Corporal," indicated that he was missing.

She turned the pages slowly, one by one. Each photo had the matching dog tag image superimposed in the lower left-hand corner. Shari mentally checked off the names against the complete flight manifest. The names were seared into her brain. Three-quarters of the way through, she paused, knowing the next photo in alphabetical order would be that of Kyle. She bit her lower lip and turned to the picture, keeping her mental defenses firm and letting her analyst training guide her eyes and thoughts.

Her fingers grew white with a tight grip at the sight of the broken and burned body. No facial identification was possible because of the fire, but the size and shape of the torso seemed about right for Kyle's dimensions. She felt wetness at the edges of her eyes as she studied the picture, read the dog tag, and examined the photo in detail. *Something isn't right.* The dog tags were authentic and accurate, but an anomaly she could not pinpoint chewed at her. Instead of looking at the grisly picture as an entirety, she studied it a square inch at a time. Left to right. Top to bottom. Shadows and light. Pixels. Uniform and flesh. A dead Marine. A destroyed human body. *There!* She stared in disbelief, trying to persuade herself that she was wrong while knowing she was not.

"Oh my God!" she whispered loud enough for Shafer to hear. The folder spilled from her lap and onto the carpeted floor of the Situation Room as she grabbed the single picture with both hands and stared at it. Buchanan spun in his chair and gave her an angry stare as the most powerful people in the United States government turned to watch her gather the papers.

"Sorry," she said, shuffling the papers and photos back into the folder. Using every ounce of her considerable willpower, she sat motionless through the rest of the meeting, letting her mind work the problem. A slight smile played over her lips and a new brightness shone in her eyes.

33

Kyle snapped back into consciousness, flat on his back. He took a deep breath, surprised that he wasn't dead. The air he pulled into his lungs was fresh and cool and reviving, and he lay still as his brain stitched together wisps of memories about what the hell had just happened. Being right-handed saved his life.

The brief, deadly confrontation was nothing but a quick-draw contest. The guard had been holding the stock of the AK-47, but not with his finger on the trigger, and hesitated for a heartbeat before trying to bring it to bear on Swanson. Professionals do not hesitate, and Kyle put the barrel of his pistol right against the man's eye and double-tapped him. Two big bullets at point-blank range totally destroyed the head.

Swanson roamed his hands across his own body and felt no pain, no wounds. The gore covering his face and chest was the blood, brains, and bone fragments of the other man, whose skull had exploded, and the unexpected concussion had scrambled Kyle's senses for a few seconds. He pushed onto his elbows and wiped his face. The guard lay dead at his feet.

Where are the others? The whole village had to be awakened by those explosions! He grabbed the pistol that had fallen by his side while his befuddled mind realized the guard had not shouted, had not fired his rifle, and Kyle's own silenced pistol had spoken with only two burps, quick and quiet except for the weapon recycling. There had been no detonations at all, and the great sounds he imagined that had been heard by everyone were only his gun firing almost next to his ear. He and the guard had both fallen where they stood, but everyone else slept on. He wiped his eyes with his sleeve, and poured water from a canteen over his face for a quick cleaning while he caught his breath.

Enough of this recovering shit! Get back to work! The inner voice, immune from physical hurt, was pissed, and the minutes were slipping by like desert sand.

The shadow of the house loomed like a big castle, and Swanson dropped the pack and stuffed eight blocks of C-4 into his pockets. He had guessed right back at the helicopter crash by topping off with C-4. Before the night was over, he would need a lot of explosives to help him survive.

He found a handful of pencil-thin detonators that had small timers like a digital watch and spent a moment activating them all to blow at exactly the same time. He needed at least an hour, with extra time for unforeseen circumstances, but he wanted to keep as much darkness as possible to help his escape. He set all of the timers to go off at exactly 0300.

He attached the first of the six–inch-long blocks of gummy explosive to the corner of the house where he had had the shootout, pushing the clay tight, like a kid playing with Silly Putty, and sticking in two of the detonators, just to be sure. The second block was placed just below the single window on the left side of the house, and he repeated the pattern all the way around until C-4 was in place on each corner and in the middle of each wall, all molded to force the explosions inward. The detonators blinked silently, and Kyle was sweating hard by the time he was finished, drops of water falling into his eyes. He struggled back into his pack, gathered his weapons, and stole enough laundry from the clothesline to outfit himself and the general.

This was going to be overkill. The simultaneous explosions would destroy the supports of the house and collapse it on the sleeping men, then the surrounding outer wall would bounce the concussion wave right back toward the house instead of letting the blast effect roll away. It was time-consuming, but the house was the roost of his biggest source of potential opposition, the jihadists, and to wipe them out in a single attack was worth the risk of time.

It would also be a hell of a diversion, and Swanson had to be gone before the place lit up like a space shuttle launch.

It had taken him another eight minutes to plant the C-4, and he was at the wall at 0153. That left only another hour and seven minutes to do what he had to do and get the hell out of Dodge, including the ten minutes he had built into the timetable for the inevitable visit by that black cloud asshole Mr. Murphy. He ran through a mental checklist: *The guard. The Zeus. The groceries. The fighters. Time to go.*

He pulled himself onto the wall, rolled over, and almost landed on a goat. It jumped back, then stood facing him, shaggy and white, big ears, the lower jaw chewing something and the dark eyes staring without curiosity or fright. Two stubby horns had been cut off. Behind it was another goat that looked exactly the same. If they panicked, they might awaken somebody, and he couldn't shoot both of them at the same time. Swanson stood stone still and let the animals take a good look at him. They walked away.

Kyle headed the other way, down the street, sticking close to the walls. Time to *parlez-vous* with a Frenchman.

34

Double-Oh was emotionally exhausted after working the Sergeants' Network most of the night and stood at a rail of the USS *Blue Ridge*, letting the sea wind revive him with its chill. His Air Force and Marine contacts in Washington were unable to rustle up another spare C-20 for him, and even the Army guys down at CENT-COM couldn't find anything appropriate that they could spring loose. So as far as he knew, Colonel Sims would be landing on a bare runway at Andrews, but he was confident that the sergeants would turn up at least some sort of rust bucket with wings so Sims could continue chasing the chairman of the Joint Chiefs.

"Since this is about those boys who died out yonder in the desert, we'll come up with somethin'," promised a flyboy master sergeant who had a thick Southern drawl. "Just won't be no C-20. But I got me an idea. Lemme make a couple of calls." It was, Double-Oh thought, a hell of a way to run an airline.

Weariness and tension had crept into his bones, and he was ready to go below to his quarters, one of the six racks in a small squad bay reserved for chief petty officer ranks. Privacy was not a high priority on a ship, and the bunks were arranged in two stacks of three each. With the combined farts, snoring, and belching of six middle-aged men at night, sometimes the flight deck was more quiet, and never mind the smell.

Once he entered that steel-walled room, there would be no cell phone reception, so he made one last check of his messages before putting the phone away until morning. He would be able to catch an hour or so of sleep before Sims changed planes at Andrews, if the Air Force types came through. He pressed a button on his Nokia and the screen showed that two calls had come in while he was busy, both from the same number in Washington, both from Shari Towne. Each flashed a red exclamation point icon that meant "urgent." He hit the automatic dial and heard the beeps and squawks of an international commercial call, then the phone was answered after the first ring.

"Shari? What's happening?"

"Thank God you called back, Orville. Something is going on here that I don't understand . . . about the mission." Her voice was agitated, unusual for Shari. "Have you heard anymore about Kyle?"

Double-Oh's thoughts began to race. She worked for Buchanan at the NSC. Had she found out about the letter? "No, we haven't. It's tough to accept, Shari, but he probably died in the crash. I know you're hurting, girl. Me, too."

"No, no, no. Listen," she said rapidly. "I apologize for bringing you into this, but just listen. I've got what may sound like a silly question, but it's very important."

"Okay. Shoot."

"Did Kyle get a tattoo before he left the boat?"

"What?" Double-Oh was rocked by the question.

"Hell, no. First, there is no place to get a tattoo around here because we are at sea. Anyway, you know how he feels about that stuff. No markings for a sniper. Ever. No way would he put any distinguishing marks on his body." If a sniper was captured, he did not want the enemy to know his job.

Shari exhaled, and Double-Oh heard the breath from thousands of miles away. "Well, then. He's alive."

There was silence for a moment. "What makes you think that?" Double-Oh was suddenly wide awake again.

"They gave me the official file on the crash to examine, and it contained horrible photographs of each of the Marines who were killed."

"Photographs? How the hell did you get individual pictures?"

"That's just one of several weird things. They came to Buchanan through Gordon Gates. Seems a couple of his PSC guys were near the village and able to get into the crash site. We have no idea how. Anyway, each photo included a close-up of the dog tags for identification. Double-Oh, the picture that was supposed to be of Kyle was of someone burned beyond recognition about the face, but the dog tags were clearly readable. They had not even been charred and the rubber ring was still intact. How can a torso and face be destroyed by fire, but the dog tags around the neck remain untouched by heat? The tag laced into his boot was identical. No doubt that those were Kyle's tags."

The big sergeant was holding tight control of his voice. He was not going to jump to conclusions. A couple of mercs were at the scene? "Maybe they made a mistake, screwed up with the wrong dog tags."

"Doesn't matter, Orville. It was the left forearm that really caught my attention. It was visible and in pretty good shape, with death before dishonor lettering around a good-size USMC tattoo of the eagle, globe, and anchor. I think Kyle was betting that you or I would see the report, and would pick up on it."

Double-Oh rubbed his face. *Good God!* "I don't know, Shari. Maybe he got a tattoo somehow that I just didn't notice because I wasn't looking for one. Anyway, he was sleeves-down when he left the boat. We can't get into wishful thinking."

Shari paused, then said, "Okay. Try this. They report one Marine is missing and presumed alive; a young radioman with no combat experience. So far, this kid is out there on his own and has not only managed to escape the crash site without being spotted, but has evaded the Syrian army, dodged all of the civilians and any Bedouins in the area, and has not even been spotted by our own satellites. You tell me, Double-Oh. How many men on the mission could do that? Not some dial-spinner, that's for sure. So who would it be?"

"Jesus." There was a moment of silence, then Double-Oh agreed softly. "Gotta be Kyle. He's alive."

"Yes. He is. I just needed to confirm my conclusions with you before I did anything. We have to go get him. I'm going to talk to my boss and get things moving from this end right away."

"No!" Double-Oh's voice changed from wavering uncertainty to parade-ground intensity. "You can't do that, Shari."

"Why?"

"Are you calling from your office?"

Jack Coughlin with Donald A. Davis

"Unh-uh. I'm on my cell outside of Starbucks. I took a walk after the meeting to clear my mind and call you to confirm my thoughts about the tattoo."

"Okay. Listen up. I've got to bring you up to speed on something that's going on. My boss, Colonel Sims of the Thirty-Third MEU, is heading your way." He outlined the letter Kyle had received from Gerald Buchanan's courier, how Kyle had refused the assassination order, and that Sims was flying under covert conditions to deliver the letter to someone higher up. "It seems like Buchanan is involved in some borderline treason, Shari," he said. "If Kyle brings General Middleton out safe, there is going to be some big trouble when this thing blows up in public."

"Tell me about the courier." She dropped the cardboard cup of coffee in a trash can. Down the street she could see the White House, the black fence in front of it, and the broad open plaza. Protesters, cops, and tourists mingled. Buchanan secretly sending a Marine sniper in to kill the general instead of rescuing him was illegal. No wonder there had been no memo about it, not even Top Secret. "The man who came out there to meet with Kyle. What did he look like?"

"Civilian dude, playing at being a spook. He admitted later being from the White House. He was slim and tall, with a big mop of black hair that was slicked back like he was a singer for some doo-wop quartet. I never caught his real name, but he was a real cocky asshole."

Shari sighed. "That's Sam Shafer. He's Buchanan's right-hand man."

Double-Oh said, "Look, Shari. This is spinning off

the deep end fast. Did you tell Buchanan and Shafer what you were thinking about Kyle?"

"Not yet. Like I said, I wanted to call you first and make sure."

"You can't trust those two. If they are suspicious about why you acted strangely at the meeting, they are going to force you to give up the information."

"What do you want me to do, Double-Oh? I can't just sit here while Kyle is in big trouble!"

"Don't worry about Kyle right now. He can take care of himself. I'm more worried about you calling me on an open circuit. Shari, my special ops nerves are shaking like leaves on this. Those two guys will do anything they have to in order to keep that letter secret, because if they don't, it will mean prison for them." His voice went softer. "That includes getting rid of everybody who may know about it. That means Kyle. It means me. Now it means you, too."

"Me?"

"Yes. You can't go back to work until this thing is settled. And when you don't show up, they are going to pull out all stops to find you and get what you know. Guaranteed they will discover your relationship with Kyle. We have to assume that Buchanan, with all of his intel assets, will have the NSA recording this call."

"They won't bother me. I'm a serving naval officer."

"That will be no protection whatsoever. Trust me on that. You and I both have to disappear before Buchanan can get his hands on us, Shari. Hang up this phone and dump it, then get to somewhere safe. Not your apartment."

"Orville, I can't just leave! If I don't show up for work, it will be an unauthorized absence."

"Take it from me, honey," said Double-Oh. "Right now, that is the least of your worries. When the house is burning down, your first job is to save yourself, then worry about the house. You get out to Quantico right now and contact the duty NCO, and he will stash you in the VIP lodgings . . . until I can contact you on an *encrypted* line." He emphasized the word.

Shari almost dropped the phone when she realized that Dawkins was right. The NSA would be listening to her call, particularly since it was being made within an invisible listening cone that surrounded the White House. "Right. The duty NCO at Quantico will be expecting me."

"We'll talk soon." Double-Oh broke the connection and threw his cell phone overboard, watching until it splashed into the Mediterranean Sea. There would be no sleep for him tonight.

In Washington, Shari Towne moved quickly. She put her phone into the same trash can as her coffee, stepped to the curb, and hailed a taxi.

By the time the cab drove away, a supercomputer at the National Security Agency had recorded the call and traced it from Lieutenant Commander Towne to a number assigned to Marine Master Sergeant Orville Oliver Dawkins.

Instead of racing down to Quantico, Shari Towne had the cab driver turn right and head toward the Hashemite Kingdom.

35

Gerald Buchanan and the secretary of state had a private meeting with the President following the NSC session, but as soon as he returned to his office, he called for Sam Shafer. "What the HELL was that all about with Towne? The world is coming apart and one of my staff members interrupts an important meeting by dropping her schoolbooks? In front of the President of the United States? For God's sake!"

"Commander Towne has been under a lot of pressure, sir. She was the one we brought back from leave to work on the crisis."

"The woman is supposed to be a professional!" He spun his chair around to stare out the window. "Her action today reflected directly on me. Everybody will think I hire morons who can't take the pressure."

Shafer ran a hand through his hair, a finger comb. "I don't think that's what happened."

Buchanan turned back around, his anger replaced by curiosity. "Talk to me, Sam."

"I've worked with Shari Towne for a long time, sir, and nobody has a cooler head in a crisis. That damned brain of hers goes so fast it throws off sparks, and I have never seen her rattled. If a situation is really going to hell, she might squint an eye in thought. Nothing more."

"So why was she dropping Top Secret files all over the President's expensive rug?"

"She saw something in that folder of the dead Marines, sir. I gave it to her to review while I took notes on the meeting. She was going through the meat shots when it happened. I thought at first that it might be because the pictures are pretty gruesome."

"So what? Pictures of dead people usually are."

"I agree. She had not yet reached the pages of text, so all she had seen were the photographs. Right before she dropped the file, she was looking at the picture of one of those poor faceless bastards. More than looking at it, she was studying it hard, almost breaking it down into pixels. When everything else hit the floor, she held that picture so tightly her knuckles were turning white."

Buchanan shook his head. *So what?* "Several people, including me, have looked at the file and none of us had that kind of reaction."

"That's just my point, sir. But how many of us who examined it were trained intelligence eyes? Shari Towne is one of the best analysts in the building, and she doesn't work here because she misses things. No one else apparently picked up on whatever it was she spotted. It's not the first time she's done that. Remember how she pegged the Libyan missiles that Gadhafi claimed he had destroyed?"

"So she saw something." Buchanan had found the file to be exactly what he had expected. Bunch of dead guys. It was supposed to be nothing more than an impressive visual prop to demonstrate the abilities of the Gates

Global operators. He did not like the idea that Towne had picked up a detail he had missed, something that might be important.

Shafer crossed his arms. "Whatever was in there made the stone-cold lieutenant commander lose her cool, for maybe the first time in her life, outside of an orgasm."

"Wait a minute, Sam. She didn't tell you what it was after the meeting?" Buchanan leaned forward, elbows on the desk blotter. "Get her ass in here. Right now!"

"Can't do it, sir. She grabbed her purse and left the building. Told a secretary she was going for a walk and hasn't come back." Shafer glanced at his watch. Seven o'clock. "She left about thirty minutes ago. I called her cell phone. No answer."

"The bitch is keeping a secret from me?" Buchanan's anger flared so hard that he broke his pencil.

"It gets worse, sir. I had the White House operator call Towne's secure beeper ten minutes ago. All White House staff must answer such a page immediately, without exception. Nothing. For whatever reason, the commander is choosing not to communicate."

"Damn! We have to find her, Sam." Buchanan's mind churned. "Meanwhile, put some of our other intel people on the file and see what they can get. And I want to know more about Miz Towne. Put the bitch under a microscope."

"Just here in the office?"

"No. I don't think she's coming back," said Buchanan, making a guess, then a decision. "Do the full package. FBI, CIA, Homeland Security, and the National Intelligence Center. Pull her Secret Service background check. Yank the computer hard drive from her office and have the NSA crack it. Wiretaps, computer scans, the full audio-video surveillance package, pictures, financial information, the whole nine yards, including interviews with people who know her. I want to know everything she does, everybody she knows, where she buys her damned groceries, who she is screwing, and the name of her third-grade teacher's pet canary. Everything!"

"Warrants?"

The National Security Advisor leaned back and dodged the question. It had been proven too many times that White House walls have ears. "Sam, as I recall, isn't Lieutenant Commander Towne of Middle Eastern extraction?"

"Her mother is Jordanian, father was an American diplomat. He died in a plane crash when she was a child."

"An Arab, then. So considering the seriousness of her withholding vital security information during an international crisis, I must direct that Lieutenant Commander Towne be considered a terrorist mole who somehow infiltrated the White House. She may be aiding our enemies."

Shafer broke into a big grin. Buchanan amazed him. Nothing was beyond the man. "Yes, sir. A possible al Qaeda connection would be a very serious matter. I'll get the file."

"And Sam?"

"Sir?"

"Have Towne in custody before dawn."

36

Colonel Ralph Sims deplaned from the luxurious C-20 executive jet at Andrews Air Force Base in Maryland with some reluctance. He was freshly shaved, in a pressed uniform with shined shoes, and although somewhat tired from the long journey, he felt like a million bucks. Staff Sergeant Foster, Marcia L., who had turned the routine puddle-jump flight into a cruise among the stars for him, stood at attention at the foot of the small stairs, saluting smartly as Sims stepped to the ground.

"Call me," she said with a wink, passing a card with her telephone number to him. She hurried back into the plane, pulled up the stairs, and closed the door, and the sleek C-20 followed a Jeep with a rack of lights down a long, empty approach runway.

Sims had expected to be deposited in front of a terminal, with another C-20 waiting for him, but instead there was nothing around but darkness. A tall cyclone fence was set back at the edge of the field, and no blue lights marking the runway reached into this far corner. Low bushes and scrubland fell away from the tarmac and into the field bordering the fence, and he could barely make out the big control tower outlined by lights several miles away. A breeze carried the salty scent of the Chesapeake Bay, and he could hear the hum of distant traffic. It seemed that he had been dropped off in the middle of nowhere.

"Where the hell is everybody?" he said into the emptiness.

"Right here, sir." One of the bushes stood up, a Marine in a full ghillie suit with a long rifle in his hands. "Staff Sergeant Gonzales, USMC scout sniper, sir. May I see your identification, please?"

Sims was aware that several other bushes were also moving around behind him as he handed over his laminated military identification card. The staff sergeant checked it in the briefly seen red beam of a flashlight. "Right. Thank you, sir." He turned and called into the darkness, "Mr. Dillon, you may come forward."

Footsteps in the darkness on the far side of the runway came closer and Sims made out the shape of a small man who extended his hand. "Billy Dillon, colonel, United States Air Force, retired. Glad to meet you." Sims's eyes had adjusted to the night surroundings, and he saw that Dillon was dressed in a ribbed and pressurized black flight suit.

"What's going on, Staff Sergeant? Why is your team out here, and what is Mr. Dillon, a civilian, doing in a restricted area?"

Dillon handed Sims a flight suit like the one he wore. "We will explain while you get dressed. You can't fly with me without it. The boys will tuck your uniform into the Val Pak and we'll carry it in a storage space. Hurry, please, Colonel. Time is of the essence."

Staff Sergeant Gonzales made some hand motions and his men went prone again, facing outward. "We're a Force Recon team, Colonel, out of Camp Lejeune. We're just doing a routine drill here tonight," Gonzales said with a grin of white teeth against his grease-darkened face. "I will say that a couple of unexpected telephone calls had something to do with this assignment. In fact, my Top threatened to feed my ass to the buzzards if I didn't move fast enough to get here before you did."

Sims stripped to his underwear and was struggling into the tight flight suit, which looked like the skin of some prehistoric alligator. "I got a call, too," said Dillon. "Bit of personal history first. I was flying an Air Force F-16 several years ago somewhere that we weren't supposed to be and the bad guys got lucky with a missile. My radar intercept officer was killed, but I got out with just some broken bones. A Marine Special Ops team came and fetched me home, along with the body of my RIO." He helped Sims zip up. "After rehab, I couldn't fly military anymore, so I got another gig. I owe the Force Recon boys big-time, and I always pay my debts."

Gonzales was no longer smiling, and his eyes burned with anger. "All we really know, sir, is that you have something to do with settling the score for what happened over there in Syria. We're here to help. Those were our brothers."

"Let's go," said Dillon, handing Sims a black flight helmet.

"Go where? There's a plane here?"

"Right there. A hundred yards straight in front of us." He started walking and Sims followed.

As they closed in on the spot, Sims saw a ground

crew dressed in black working on a shape beneath a big camouflage net. At a signal from Dillon, they pulled it away.

"And just what the fuck is this, Mr. Dillon?" The plane was almost invisible, with flat black paint, no sharp surfaces, and standing high on a tripod of wheels. He touched the surface, which was as smooth as a mirror.

"Call me Billy, please, Colonel." He led Sims around the strange aircraft and pointed to the small white acronym lettering the tail fin. "Meet the X43-D scramjet, the latest in the Hyper-X series. We're trying to make a reusable space vehicle. You're flying courtesy of NASA tonight, Colonel. I have to get this bird out to Edwards Air Force Base in California before dawn, so we arranged a little side trip to Alaska for you. It will get both of us where we need to be in plenty of time. Up you go into the rear seat." He patted a footstep in the hull.

"You're going to make it from Washington to Alaska and back to southern California in a couple of hours?"

"Yep. The old SR-71 Blackbird used to be the fastest thing in the sky and it only did Mach 3, three times the speed of sound. Tonight, you and I are going to climb about sixty miles up, just under the edge of space, and you'll be able to see stars like you cannot believe. There will be some weightlessness. Then I level off, kick her into high gear, and peg the speedometer at about Mach eight. When we start the descent, we'll be going like a bat out of hell. A ceramic covering more advanced than that on the space shuttle will protect us against the heat of reentry."

"No shit?"

"No shit. It will be the ride of your life. Now let's buckle you in."

"Colonel?"

Sims looked over his shoulder. Gonzales was still standing there. "You have something to say, Staff Sergeant?"

"Get the motherfuckers, sir."

"Bet your ass on that, Staff Sergeant." Sims climbed into the rear seat of a cockpit unlike anything he had ever seen, and ground crewmen reached around him to hook up the hoses and belts.

"Ready back there?" Dillon asked, face-to-face over the televised intercom.

"Let's do it, Billy. I'll see if you're lying about the speed."

The cockpit hummed down and locked into place, the instrument panel glowed green and red, there was the hiss of cool oxygen into the mask, and the radio came to life in his ears. "Hold on, then. We don't call her 'Greased Lightning' for nothing."

37

Kyle Swanson dropped his pack as softly as a mouse's footstep, and moved to the side of the bed. His night-vision glasses gave a clear, green view of the bearded man sound asleep beneath a cotton sheet, and Swanson brought his big pistol down hard on the crown of the man's head. He needed a few moments to set up, so the guy had to stay asleep.

He ripped off a strip of duct tape and pasted it across the man's mouth. A broom leaning against a corner went behind the shoulders, and he secured the wrists to it with flexicuffs and duct tape. He cinched the ankles and the knees together with more tape. Duct tape had many uses. He wound more of it all the way around the bed and secured the torso and legs. Almost ready. He clicked on a single bedside lamp and covered the shade with a towel to cut down on the glow. It would be important that the Frenchman be able to see what was about to happen.

Moving to the stove, he lit a propane flame and propped the largest spoon he could find to roast over it.

Back at the bed, Kyle hauled the sheet up to the man's neck and straddled the chest, his weight pinning the edges of the sheet to the bed like a giant sleeve. With one hand, he poured a cup of cold water on the man's face, while the other hand kept the pistol right between the eyes. Hell of a way to wake up.

The eyes flew wide open in surprise. Kyle said nothing. He knew the value of silence to an interrogator and wanted to establish the parameters of the session before the man even started to think he might have a vote in what was happening to him.

Kyle returned the pistol to the shoulder rig and withdrew his long, sharp knife. He grabbed the left hand secured to the broomstick, and took his time sawing off the thumb. The victim yowled behind the tape as blood spurted out in a dark stream. Swanson got off the guy and brought over the large spoon from the kitchen, holding it up so the Frenchman could see it glowing with heat. Tears of pain and shock and fear spilled from the eyes. Then the spoon went against the bleeding stump, where it sizzled, and the muzzled man screamed again.

When he calmed down, Kyle said, "*Bonjour*, asshole."

He pulled up a chair and looked the man in the face. "That was just to save us some time. We're both professionals, so let's make this as painless for you as possible." He wiped the blood from the knife on the man's hair, pressing the flat of the blade against the skull. "Still going to hurt, though. You decide how much."

Swanson held up the small photograph he had received during the premission briefing. "Recognize this dude? Oh my god, it's you! How about that for a coincidence? Your name is Pierre Dominique Falais, an ex-Legionnaire who is now an intelligence snitch for whoever will pay you. You speak Arabic, French,

English, and German, so don't insult me by saying you do not understand what I am saying." It was easier to break a prisoner early in the interrogation if he thought the questioner already knew everything. Falais had no idea that the French had given up his entire record.

He mumbled.

"Ummmm," said Kyle, sniffing. "Smell that? The unmistakable odor of burning flesh. I smelled it only a few hours ago when I got out of that fucking helicopter. A lot of Marines who were my friends were killed out there, and were burned worse than you." He leaned across and laid the razor-sharp knife blade on the pinkie of the mutilated left hand and cut that off, too, then took his time reheating the spoon before stanching the flow of blood with it. Another scream.

"Okay. You have eight fingers left, ten toes, a nose, two ears, two eyes, lips, legs, arms, and of course your dick and balls, which will go into your mouth or up your ass, I haven't made up my mind yet. But that would be a lot of work, and you would experience some discomfort. So you answer my questions and I won't chop you up like frog legs. I'm going to remove the gag now, and if you try to shout, I will ram this big knife through your cheeks and knock out a few teeth. Then the questioning will resume. Understood?" The man nodded a vigorous yes. Kyle tore the tape off so that it clung to one cheek in case he needed it in a hurry.

The Frenchman sucked in some deep breaths. "Who are you?"

"I ask the questions. Where is General Middleton?"

"You're an American," he protested. "Americans don't torture prisoners."

Kyle felt a wave of revulsion when he decided to hurt the man to get the information, but steeled himself for the job by reasoning that it would take hours to make him talk any other way. He did not have hours to spare, so he slapped the tape across the mouth again. "I can do whatever the fuck I want, Pierre. Not because international laws might be bent enough to allow it, but because, thanks to you, I'm dead. I don't exist." The knife flashed and he sliced deeply through the left ear. The ear is a bleeder, and a crimson pool spread out beneath the man's head, the warm wetness scaring him more than the cut.

After the expected scream, Swanson tore off the tape again and let it dangle.

"The next 'procedure' is something you will recognize, because I learned it while I was on assignment with the Foreign Legion myself. A deep cut down the underside length of a finger all the way to the palm, severing all those nerves on the way." He leaned forward, almost nose to nose. "So once again, asshole. Where the fuck is General Middleton?"

Falais gave up and answered through gritted teeth, "In the house of the Americans."

The mercs! "Well done, Pierre. Now, who are they?"

"There are two of them. Victor Logan is the biggest, and he is crazy dangerous, a former SEAL in your navy. The other man is Collins, ex-army, but really just an extra set of hands for Victor. They work for Gates Global, which also hired me."

When Kyle did not reply, Falais panicked. "Wait! I have money. Lots of money! I will give it to you!"

"No. I'm not in this for cash." Kyle jammed his left

forearm into Falais's mouth hard and slapped him on the wounded ear.

The scream was muffled. *"Merde!"* The Frenchman groaned with the searing pain. "Look. I can help. *I can help you!* I will take you to them."

"Where is the general kept in their house?"

"A small room in the right rear corner, handcuffed to a bed. They have not harmed him greatly, although Victor really wants to. Victor is a killer." The dark eyes studied Kyle's face, seeing if a deal was possible. "You will have to hurry because the jihadists are to behead your general in the morning."

"What kind of security do the Americans keep?"

"None. Everybody here is afraid of Victor, and they have plenty of guns. No one bothers them. Again, let me help."

"How?"

Pierre Falais detected a faint opening, a chance. "I will take you over there and distract the Americans while you attack. We kill them, get the general, and I will guide you safely to Israel. People in the villages know me and will help. I'm the one person around here who can get you out." He was breathing heavily.

"What do you want in return?"

"You let me live," the Frenchman said. "Then I am sure the American government would be generous with a reward. We will not mention what you have done here."

Kyle nodded. "Not bad. I guess you might have some value after all, Pierre. I promise not to filet you anymore." He took a rolled-up towel and pressed it against the bleeding ear, then suddenly reached over with his knife and cut off the small finger of the other hand. "Do you think I'm a fool?" he hissed. "I told you I'm not playing around and I am damned sure not going to let you walk me into an ambush. Tell me what else you know. Tell me everything. Right now, or I cut you some more!"

The French spy broke and started to cry. "That's all I know! What else do you want? I won't ambush you. I'll tell you whatever you want! Just tell me what you need!"

Swanson stepped back, wiped off the knife, and put it away as he looked hard at the bleeding man strapped on the bed. The guy was not holding back now, and further mutilation would be counterproductive. The prisoner had reached the point where he would say whatever he could guess the interrogator wanted him to say. True or false didn't matter, because he only wanted to stop the pain.

"Okay. I believe you." He opened a little box from his medical kit. "I'm going to give you a shot of morphine now to take away the pain. While you sleep for another hour, I'll patch you up, and when you come around, we'll have something to eat and think this over." He injected the fluid into the Frenchman's left arm, and within a couple of heartbeats Falais's eyes fluttered and rolled back.

When the Frenchman was unconscious, Kyle undressed, put on the Arab clothes he had stolen, and doused the light. He put on his night-vision goggles again, checked outside, and quietly loaded his pack, web gear, and rifles into the bed of the pickup truck.

Back in the house, he reduced the single burner of the little propane gas stove to low, blew out the flame, then placed a block of C-4 beside the stove, armed with a ticking detonator that would go off thirty minutes after the other house exploded, causing yet another diversion.

The Frenchman would not feel a thing. Swanson had not wanted to torture him, but having done so, he would allow the man a quiet, easy death. Falais was still asleep when Kyle injected him with two more full syrettes of morphine, and with each heartbeat, the narcotic overwhelmed his system. The man would never awaken. When the detonator ignited the C-4, the explosion would instantly set off the growing bubble of gas in the enclosed house and the place would blow up taking the body of Pierre Falais with it. "I don't make deals with terrorists, particularly terrorists who have killed Marines," he whispered to the dying man.

Kyle Swanson turned off the bedside lamp, locked the door, went back over the wall, and was approaching the truck when he heard the grumble of heavy engines. He hit the ground and rolled under the Toyota just as a pair of BTR-80 armored personnel carriers of the Syrian Army roared past, their headlights flashing along the walls, seeming to search for him.

How did they get on my trail? Oh, fuck, Murphy's Law has screwed me again.

The huge vehicles continued down the street for a few more blocks and stopped at the house of the Americans. Soldiers jumped from the vehicles and spread into a perimeter around it, facing outward like guards, not inward like attackers.

38

Swanson wiggled from beneath the truck and rolled into the flatbed, unzipped the dragbag, rested Excalibur on the rear gate, and brought the scope to his eye. *Good as fuckin' daylight.*

He recognized the telltale four big wheels on each side of the vehicles, and the BPU-1 turret machine gun mounts. The Russians had been selling these relics all over the world for years, but the old dogs still had a lot of bite. His mind turned up the information on the weapons systems faster than a Google search: each carried a 14.5 mm KPTV heavy machine gun with five hundred rounds and a range of two kilometers, and a smaller 7.62 mm PKT machine gun with 2,000 rounds that could reach one and a half kilometers. Smoke grenade launchers were mounted on either side of the turret, and their beefy engines could shove them along at speeds of up to about 50 miles per hour. The lead vehicle bristled with the antennas that indicated a battalion commander might be leading the mission. *Is a whole damned battalion on the way?*

An officer climbed from the command vehicle, walked directly to the front door, and pounded hard. Lights came on, the door was thrown open, and the hulking

Victor Logan stood there, wearing only a T-shirt and boxer shorts but carrying a pistol in his right hand. The Syrian was about half Logan's size, but had an air of authority that made him immune from threat. They spoke for a few minutes, and Kyle saw Logan nod in agreement, go back into the house, and return moments later, fully dressed. He climbed aboard the lead BTR-80.

The officer waved his hand and sergeants barked orders. Logan climbed awkwardly into the front vehicle with the officer and the other soldiers hustled back aboard. A single man was left behind as a sentry and the BTRs pulled out, heading toward the crash site.

The soldier stood at attention beside the front door of the house, his AK-47 at the ready, as the carriers growled off into the darkness. Swanson held his breath as they went past the Zeus and the apparently dozing guard taped to it, but they did not slow down.

The lights in the house were turned off and the soldier by the door relaxed. He unslung the automatic rifle and rested it against the wall, then sat on a wooden crate, leaned back, and made himself comfortable, arms on knees. Through the scope, Kyle watched the man reach into a chest pocket and get a cigarette. A match flared.

As the soldier inhaled the first puff deeply, Swanson lasered the range, and when the man exhaled, Kyle shot him beneath the left arm. The bullet tore out the heart. There was only a slight twitch of the body on impact; then it toppled from the crate onto the dirt. Kyle put a second bullet through the head to be sure he could not cry out a warning.

*

Swanson had to move fast because those BTRs would be coming back. He returned Excalibur to its bag, climbed from the truck bed, and transferred his primary weapons to the passenger compartment. Then he slid behind the steering wheel and cranked the Toyota, which started with a reliable, deep rumble.

He did not have to disguise it, because that was the essence of this "announced attack." By imitating the previous incident, and with the familiar sound of the Toyota in the neighborhood, people would think that he was either the Frenchman or somehow related to the arrival of the army unit. With any luck, Jimbo Collins would be trying to get back to sleep, not alert.

Kyle stopped in front of the house and, mirroring the actions of the Syrian officer, marched directly to the front door and pounded on it with his left fist as he pulled out his pistol with his right hand. Inside, the lamp snapped on again. He heard Collins curse aloud, "Oh, what the fuck do they want now?"

When the door opened, Kyle extended the big pistol and put one round right in Jimbo Collins's chest, knocking him backward, and fired another into his surprised face. He gave the collapsing body a hard shove so that it fell away from the door and did not block the exit. He stepped fast into the room with his pistol held straight out with both hands to scan for targets. There were none, and he closed the door.

There were two more doors in the rear and he chose the one on the left, stood with his back to the wall, and pushed it open with his left hand, the pistol pointing inward. No reaction, but there was a horrible stench, and enough light for him to see the defiled body of a young girl tied to a bed. *Sick bastards!* He did not have to feel for a pulse.

Swanson spun and kicked in the second door. A man wearing only boxer shorts lay handcuffed to a filthy bunk. He was unshaven, and the room stank. The man blinked in disbelief. All he saw was a silhouette until Kyle flipped a switch that turned on the bulb hanging from the ceiling.

"Hello, General," Swanson said, moving around the room, searching for unseen dangers, the pistol out, ready to shoot.

"What?" The voice was firm but raspy. Only moments ago, Bradley Middleton was thinking about having his head chopped off by lunatics, and now an escape was possible? "Who are you?"

"Take it easy, sir. It's Gunny Swanson."

"Swanson? Two hundred thousand Marines on active duty, and *you* are the first asshole through the door? They sent *you* to rescue *me*?"

The silenced pistol waved loosely between them. "Well, that's not exactly accurate, General," replied Kyle. "Actually, they sent me to kill you. Orders are orders, and a good Marine always follows orders."

39

Foreign governments throw parties, receptions, or formal dinners every night in Washington to promote goodwill and develop Beltway contacts. Tonight the Embassy of the Hashemite Kingdom of Jordan was honoring a young filmmaker who was creating a stir in Hollywood with his latest effort, *The Arab Street*. Some of the invited guests arrived at the embassy's ornate gates at 3504 International Drive, Northwest, in limousines, while others, mostly staff members from Capitol Hill, came by subway or walked, intending to let the Jordanians feed them. Invitations to such parties saved on their food bills.

Shari Towne found a guard at the front gate and asked him to page the head of the public relations department. Within five minutes, a slim and elegant woman walked down a sculpted path toward the guard post. A snowy-soft Chanel blouse contrasted perfectly with the black pantsuit and the full dark hair that was cut to frame her face. A loose scarf of white Belgian lace wrapped her shoulders, and her long legs were accentuated by sharp Roger Vivier heels.

"Shari? Darling!" the woman exclaimed in a burst of surprise, opening her arms and wrapping her in a hug.

"I didn't expect you to come to our vapid little event tonight. Why didn't you call?"

"Hi, Mom," Shari responded, and tightly hugged her mother.

Layla Mahfouz Towne whispered, "This little movie director is simply awful, but he's signed a deal with Paramount, which gives us an excuse to throw another 'We're Not All Terrorists!' party." She detected the strain coursing through Shari. Her daughter seemed to be a brittle piece of glass that was about to shatter. "What?"

"I'm in trouble," Shari whispered back. "Can we go inside?"

Layla lifted an eyebrow, then told the guard, "She's with me." He nodded, looked at Shari's U.S. Navy uniform and identification card, and wrote out a pass. He thought they almost looked like twins. Very attractive twins.

Her mother led the way through the swirl of people who were washing down tiny pieces of food with liquor from an open bar, as a Jordanian-American oud player easily plucked the stringed instrument to provide classical Arabic music in the background. Layla said hello here and patted a shoulder there as she smiled a path through the crowd. Shari, although in a crisp white uniform, felt positively early Banana Republic beside her. Women usually felt frumpy in Layla's manicured presence. They went into her private office on the second floor.

As soon as the door was closed, Shari collapsed onto a big, soft sofa and stared at her mother and tears welled in her eyes. She began to cry, angry at herself for doing so. "I'm sorry, Mom. I'm really sorry for barging in like this."

Her mother kicked off her high heels and put an arm around Shari, rocking her back and forth, smoothing her hair and dabbing at the tears with a tissue. In Arabic, she said, "What's going on, Little One?"

The gestures were as comforting to Shari as they had been years ago when her father died in a plane crash. "Something big and complex and dangerous is going on and Kyle and I somehow got dragged into the middle of it," Shari sobbed. "I have to hide for a while, which is why I rushed over still dressed like this. The embassy, thank God, is foreign soil. This is Jordan. They can't touch me here."

"Who can't?"

"The United States government."

Layla gave her another little squeeze, and then put on her high heels again. "My, oh my, Little One. Just like your father, bless him. You never do things by half-measures, do you? I'd better go get the ambassador," she said. "He's an old Rolling Stones fan, and will welcome the chance to avoid having to listen to any more oud music. You, my dear, don't leave this room until I get back."

40

"How fresh is this material?" National Security Advisor Gerald Buchanan asked as he scanned the computer-generated transcript of the conversation between Shari Towne and Master Sergeant Dawkins.

"Almost real-time," said Sam Shafer. "Thirty minutes max."

"Fast," said Buchanan with a nod of approval. He loved, and *love* was not too strong a word, to see the giant security apparatus of the United States bend to his will like a whipped puppy. The sheets of paper before him proved his reach and his power. He held a big whip.

"It's a pretty easy catch on the intercepts when the NSA has exact names and numbers, like her cell phones. She was near the White House when her call pinged the system. The computers automatically translated the audio into printed text."

Buchanan read the conversation again. Kyle Swanson was alive. The man he had sent to make sure Middleton died had almost been picked out of a damned hat, and not only had he turned on them, he had also had a link into this office! "So now we know what she saw, and the sniper is alive out there. What is this relationship between Towne and Swanson? Why should we care?"

"According to the gals in the secretarial pool, Commander Towne has kept it under wraps because she is an officer and he is an enlisted man. That kind of fraternization is against military regulations, although it is violated all the time."

"Ahhhhh!" Buchanan gave a grim smile. "One and one finally equal two. She had thought him to be dead, but the photos proved that he is not. She calls a mutual friend and realizes she has stepped in shit. Right?" He smiled with tight lips. "You have a chat with the secretaries?"

"Yes, sir. The ones whom we identified as her friends, or worked with her. Took them all to the safe house in Falls Church in a darkened van, had agents perform cavity searches to break their spirit, then put them one by one under the kleig lights, just like in the movies. They were most cooperative once I explained that it was a matter of national security and they would be held incommunicado under the Anti-Terrorism Provisos until we cleared this thing up. I pointed out that Section C states that if a White House employee is found to be an accomplice, that employee would face a secret military tribunal. They gave up everything. We also searched their desks, and the whole thing took less than an hour."

"There's no such Anti-Terrorism Provisos," said Buchanan.

"They didn't know that." Shafer wore a look of satisfaction.

Buchanan grunted a small laugh. "Where are they now? I noticed some new faces out there."

"Still up in Falls Church. Can't let them go until it's done. You know women can't keep secrets, and one of them would most likely confide in their husband, boy-friend, or particularly with a close girlfriend. Actually, I believe they feel kind of important right now, helping catch a possible terrorist. They were already whispering together about Commander Towne when I left. Probably guessing who will play who in the movie."

"So no one was hurt?"

"No. Just threw a scare into them is all. Time is of the essence."

Buchanan made a note. "When they come back to work, I'll put a confidential 'Attagirl' letter into each of their files and have it signed by the director of Homeland Security."

"Yes, sir," replied Shafer. "I pulled the Marine per-sonnel jacket on Gunnery Sergeant Swanson and con-firmed he has no identifying tattoos."

"So she called this other guy, who must be a close friend because they are on a first-name basis, and they agree that Swanson escaped the crash." Buchanan steepled his fingers beneath his chin as he thought out loud. "This Sergeant Dawkins also saw my letter and gave it to his commanding officer, a Colonel Sims." He hunched his fat shoulders and stared hard at his aide. "That is not good. You told me you destroyed the letter, did you not, Sam?"

"Absolutely, sir. After having Swanson open and read it, I then personally read, burned, and flushed it. Some-how while this big guy Dawkins was pulling me around the carrier on a wild goose chase, Swanson must have gotten to a copying machine. He's a resourceful son of a bitch."

"Not good. Not good at all. We must contain this

circle of knowledge to only those four people. Where's Swanson?"

Shafer shook his head. "We don't know. In Syria somewhere, disobeying your order and apparently on a one-man raid to pull out General Middleton. He has shut down all electronic contact."

"And Lieutenant Commander Towne. Why do we not have her in custody?"

"Can't find her. Her apartment was locked, no lights or music on. The cell phone and her beeper were in a garbage can outside Starbucks. The gate log shows she never showed up at Quantico."

"At least the master sergeant is confined to a boat in the middle of the Mediterranean, so I can safely assume that Dawkins is now in the brig?"

Shafer was clearly uncomfortable as Buchanan led him on, pounding with question by question like a criminal prosecutor, knowing the answers before he asked. "No, sir. He's still on the carrier, we think, but the Naval Criminal Investigative Service agents have not found him yet. Dawkins is another one of those Special Ops types, and if he does not want to be found, we won't find him. Plus he has a lot of friends on that ship who probably are helping him stay hidden. And it's a really big boat."

Buchanan doodled on a white legal pad. "Send an instruction to the *Blue Ridge* captain to make a shipwide announcement ordering Dawkins to report to the bridge. He won't disobey a direct order."

"Good idea, sir," Shafer responded. "But I think he will stay hidden if he considers the order to be illegal. Sooner or later, we're bound to find him."

"So that leaves us with Colonel Sims, the one carrying the letter itself."

"Another blank, sir. We have him arriving at Andrews Air Force Base a few hours ago, but then it's like he fell off the planet. The aircraft crew dropped him off at the dark end of the runway, didn't see anything, and assumed it was part of a clandestine operation. No records in the tower of any military or civilian planes taking off from Andrews at that time. The only thing that left was an experimental NASA scramjet headed for California on a test flight. So we can assume Sims is still around Washington trying to contact somebody at the Pentagon. The phone call mentioned that he would deliver the letter to 'someone higher up.'"

"Very well, Sam. Keep pulling out all the stops, on my authority. All four of them are now to be treated as national security risks. I want that letter back before the circle expands." Buchanan waved his hand and Shafer took the hint to leave. "Don't fail me, Sam. Understand?"

"Yes, sir. I'll get them." Shafer left the office feeling small saddlebags of sweat growing in his arm pits. A White House assignment was always a prestigious stop on the career path and usually paid off with a lucrative K Street lobbying position, but his job was falling apart. *Damn that fucking Marine to hell!*

After his aide closed the door, Buchanan went to the wall safe and opened it. A hundred thousand dollars was in a padded envelope along with a valid Canadian passport, birth certificate, international driver's license, and authenticated work history under a false name and several one-way airline tickets abroad with the flight dates left open. After making sure all was in order, he put the big envelope into his briefcase to keep it close for the next few days. He had no intention of letting these four small people ruin his lifetime plan to become the most powerful man in the American government, a strong Caesar needed for troubled times. Lock up Shari Towne, Swanson, Dawkins, and Sims in four prison cells, with no charges or trials or lawyers, and it would all be over. At least Gordon's people still had Middleton and he would be killed and done with. That led him to another idea: *Can I have them all executed, or killed while resisting arrest? Something to look into.* It was comforting to know that his documents and the cash were at hand.

Back at his desk, he punched a button on a red telephone, an encrypted line, and automatically dialed the private number of Gordon Gates. It was time to get some help.

"Yes, Gerald," Gates said in a calm voice, personally picking up the receiver after reading the identification number of the caller.

Without preamble and keeping his own voice as smooth as possible, Buchanan reported, "Gordon, it seems that we might have encountered some difficulty."

41

Swanson continued to scan the dirty room with a careful visual search. Although the space was small enough to be taken in with a single glance, he always assumed the worst in a combat situation. Death could be waiting in a closet or a corner, behind a door or curtain, in a shadow, and he had learned from experience that the little bastard can hide anywhere. Only after he was sure no one else was present did he approach Middleton and said gruffly, "However, as you so often told anybody who would listen, I'm not really a very good Marine. So I'm going to disobey a direct order from the White House and get you out of here." Then he smiled. "Let's go home, General Middleton."

He examined the handcuffs. "One of the Americans put these on you? They're Smith and Wesson."

Middleton nodded, still numb from the sudden appearance of Gunny Kyle Swanson, the man he had considered too much of a weak link to be effective in special ops. True, he was good enough as a scout sniper, but he was not a team player at all, and Middleton had on several occasions witnessed the troubling sight of Swanson almost having a nervous breakdown after a battle. Those post-traumatic stress disorders following intense combat came on like thunderstorms, then disappeared just as fast and he would again be normal. Until the next time. The bottom line for Middleton was that he now had to put his life in the hands of an operator he did not really trust.

Kyle handed his pistol to the general, then rummaged through the butt pack on his web gear to get the survival kit, and from among the fishhooks, water purification tablets, bandages, and other items, he picked out a small plastic bag and opened it. "Standard issue. A Smith and Wesson universal key." He unlocked the handcuff with a single, smooth click. A red, blistered welt had been ground around the general's wrist.

"That feels good," Middleton said in a croaking voice, rubbing his sore arm to restore some feeling and blood flow. He handed the pistol back, levered himself into a sitting position on the bunk and groaned. "They busted at least one of my ribs, Gunny, but I can get around. Let's get out of here."

Kyle held up his palm, then put a finger to his lips. "Keep the noise down, sir. I don't think anybody is around to hear at this time of night, but we can't take the chance. Anyway, it's not quite time to leave yet." Kyle handed Middleton a full bottle of water. "Drink this. All of it, to hydrate." He unscrewed another bottle and drank it himself.

Middleton felt slightly better after the long drink, but when he tried to stand up, he was wobbly. Swanson steadied him until he regained his equilibrium.

"I'll tape your ribs, then get you into these fresh robes." He pulled out the clothes he had stolen and tossed them on the bed.

Every movement seemed to aggravate Middleton's broken rib, as if he were being prodded in his guts by a big needle. "Are you the only one here?" he asked.

"We sent in a Force Recon team to get you, but the helos somehow tangled up and crashed not far from here. I was thrown out through a hatch. Hold your arms out so I can wind this around you." Swanson spun the duct tape tightly around Middleton's stomach and lower chest. "I figured out later that we were flying into an ambush."

"Jesus, that smarts!" Middleton hissed through clenched teeth, wincing in pain as the tape cinched tight. "Yeah, you were. I heard them talking about it."

"Sorry, sir. I'm not a medic and we just need to get you mobile. Broken rib hurts like hell, but it won't kill you." Kyle tore off an end of the tape, then ripped off a smaller piece and untied the strip of cloth binding the broken finger. He tied it more securely with tape. "How'd that happen?"

"I had a disagreement with one of the mercs. He was beating up on a woman in the next room."

"Yeah. I saw her before I came in here. Young teenager. He really worked her over before she died." Swanson shoved the remainder of the roll back into his pack. "You need help getting the clothes on?"

The general cursed Logan. "I figured he had killed her. Poor kid."

Swanson did not want Middleton to dwell on anything but their escape, so he held out the baggy pants and the general worked his legs in and tied them off with a loose belt, and they pulled the long shirt down over his torso. He found a pair of sandals and the general put them on. "Okay. Let's get you out to the front room."

Middleton took a shuffling step, and the next one came easier. By the time he reached a chair beside the table in the outer room, he was feeling stronger, and he sat down while Swanson gathered his gear. Jimbo Collins lay dead nearby, blood caking his face and chest. "The other guy, name of Vic Logan, will be back soon," he said.

"We'll be gone by then, sir. He headed out to the crash site with a bunch of Syrian Army types. We have a small cushion of time, but not much. Do you think you can fire a weapon?"

"Sure. Give me some more water, will you?"

Swanson handed him another bottle, then put some pita bread, orange juice, figs, and a Mars bar on the table. "Eat up, sir. We've got to wait a few more minutes before we take off."

The general did not question why. He gulped down the food and liquid, feeling strength surging back to him. "What did you do, Gunny, stop by Wal-Mart on the way over?"

Kyle had spotted the AK-47 on pegs above the front door when he searched the house, and took it down. Loaded and clean. He laid it on the table. "Something like that. Now here's what is going to happen. I planted bricks of C-4 around a house near here where a bunch of raghead fighters are sleeping. It's timed to go off in about sixty seconds. Right after that, you and I are through the front door and into a white Toyota pickup waiting outside, you in the shotgun seat with the AK. The moving will hurt, but you have to force yourself to get in quickly."

He rummaged through the room as he spoke, and ripped a good map off the wall and rolled it up. With the butt of his pistol, he smashed the satellite telephone, but when he started to wreck the two laptop computers, the general stopped him. "Wait! Take them along," said Middleton. "They are probably loaded with intel and e-mails about this whole operation."

Swanson stuffed the map and the laptops into his bulging pack and put it on. "Okay, here we go. Stand with your back against the wall beside the door. Keep the AK ready. I'll do the same thing over here."

Middleton hesitated, but got to his feet. "Watch your tone, Gunnery Sergeant."

"General Middleton, let's get this straight right now. Until we get out of this shithole, I'm in charge. You're my passenger and you do what you are told. Now get your fucking back up against that wall!"

Middleton moved, but with a frown. It felt good to have a weapon in his hands and no longer be helpless. He thought about the poor dead girl in the other room, and about the Marine and Saudi guards and his aide who were murdered in the ambush. He wished Vic Logan would walk through the door right now.

The explosion came with unexpected violence, and the concussion rocked the area. Swanson and Middleton felt the wall shake with the pounding stress, and the falling debris sounded like a hailstorm as the blast wave rolled over the village.

"NOW!" Swanson barked. "Go, go, go!" He led the way out with his M-16 ready and ran to the driver's side of the truck, throwing his big pack and Excalibur into the bed as he jumped inside. Middleton limped behind him and clawed into the passenger seat. The night had changed to bright, dancing light and shadows as fire mushroomed upward from the destroyed structure, where secondary explosions from ammunition stored inside the house joined the carnage.

Kyle propped the M-16 beside him and turned the key, and the little truck's engine roared to life as people rushed out of their homes and into the streets. "You in?" he called over to the general as he pulled his night-vision goggles into place.

"Yeah. Let's go," replied Middleton. "Floor it."

The figure of a man with a weapon appeared in the road ahead and Swanson knocked him down, gaining speed, heading out of town. Middleton fired several bursts at other figures running toward the truck.

Swanson jammed the transmission into second gear, the four big tires dug hard, and the truck lurched ahead as if it was a racehorse. Kyle blessed the care the Frenchman had lavished on the vehicle, keeping it unremarkable on the outside but with powerful mechanical guts. He could feel the strength of the machine through the steering wheel. This was no standard Toyota engine. As he shifted into third as they swung past the big Zeus, they spotted a man climbing into the gunner's seat. With the accelerator on the floor, he sped away into the world painted green by the NVGs.

"Somebody's on the Zeus!" shouted Middleton, raking the area with an automatic burst.

"He's not a problem. I rigged it to blow up when the trigger is pulled."

Middleton pulled his AK-47 back inside and took some deep breaths. He was free! *Goddam*! "So what's the escape plan, Gunny?" he asked.

"We just did it, general," said Swanson. "From here, I got no fucking idea."

42

Major Yousif al-Shoum walked slowly around the remains of the crashed helicopters saying nothing, his eyes taking inventory. He was a small, quiet man whose frail physique belied his importance. It was his brain, not his physical strength, that had won him attention and respect within the Security Directorate in Damascus. He had graduated at the top of his class from the Military Academy at Homs, had advanced training in the old Soviet Union, and won both the Medal of Military Honor and the Order of Umayyads during his extended work in Lebanon and Iraq. Later, as military attaché at Syrian embassies in London and at the United Nations, he developed flawless English. Al-Shoum was a loner with a secret passion for American mystery stories. He conducted his investigations like a slow, plodding, methodical Los Angeles private detective.

He had been assigned to head a special investigation into the American raid and recommend what his government should do with the captive American general. Damascus had known about the abduction from the start, but never officially sanctioned the kidnapping. By turning a blind eye toward the operation, they gained a favor from the Rebel Sheikh down in Basra and several hundred thousand U.S. dollars in military credits from Gates Global. Now the abduction had become a diplomatic problem and Yousif al-Shoum was to gather the facts and make a recommendation.

He originally planned to drive over to Sa'ahn on his own, but when word came that the Iraqi hotheads were planning to decapitate the American, al-Shoum decided to bring the extra guns. He got them without difficulty because he was not really a major, but a general, and head of operations for the Security Directorate. Al-Shoum had chosen to use a lower rank because ordinary people became nervous around generals, and he might want to ask some important questions of the citizens. His security team knew his true identity because it was made up exclusively of soldiers chosen because they were loyal to him. After examining the attack area, he would take custody of the American Marine general. His country was not willing to get sucked into a war over this incident, which had not gone as smoothly as promised.

"You examined this site carefully, correct? And you determined that someone lived through the crash and escaped on a motorcycle." He spoke softly to the large American trailing him, who seemed elephantine in both body and mind.

"Yeah," said Victor Logan, drawing a sharp look for his discourteous manner. "Whoever it was headed west, toward the Israeli border. That's when he blew through those two idiots at the roadblock."

The little officer stroked his thick mustache and continued his circular stroll. He knelt and let a handful of dirt trickle though his fingers. Easy to leave tracks in this loose sand. *The Case of the Missing Marine.* "And you identified him."

"Not me, but our people did. Absolutely. Pictures and dog tags. Doesn't get any better than that."

"Actually, it can, Mr. Logan. Photographs can lie. Identification tags can be misleading." Al-Shoum turned to face the big man, rocking on his heels, looking up at him and motioning toward the horizon with a slow sweep of his right arm. "This land is filled with the bones of foreign soldiers who were never properly identified." He looked up at Logan. "I think you made a mistake."

"What?" Logan almost laughed in the midget's face. "This was a no-brainer, major."

"Suppose we postulate a new theory, Mr. Logan— that whoever got away wanted you to believe that he was someone else. Would he have had time to switch the dog tags?"

"Hell, no! These birds collided, fell down, and everybody died but one. End of story."

"I understand that. But in the very moments immediately after the accident, time stands still. The normal tendency of spectators to a disaster watching is to freeze where they stand, giving time for brain and body to cooperate, and even more time passed before people approached because the ammunition and fuel were exploding and burning hot. That is the reaction of a normal person, not a highly trained military professional. Several minutes passed, time enough for such a soldier to accomplish any number of things, and smoke and fire covered his escape. Therefore, your conclusion was only an educated guess, not much more than an assumption. Am I correct?"

"Then it was a damned good guess, Major. Sometimes things are exactly as simple as they appear. He was a young guy who took off, looking for safety."

"I disagree. Our helicopters and trucks have thoroughly combed the area between here and the Israeli border. Beyond the assault at the checkpoint, they have not found a trace of the man, nor of his motorcycle. Not even tracks."

"So he got lost in the desert. Big deal. He's dead no matter how you cut it."

They walked back toward the waiting armored personnel carriers. "I should have wanted more proof before reaching such a conclusion myself."

"Yeah. Right. So, then, what's your idea?"

Al-Shoum grimaced. "Bluntly put, Mr. Logan, you fucked up. You were the experienced military advisor on the scene and everything depended on your assessment. I think this Marine wanted everyone to believe he was a youthful radioman so they would consider him rather harmless, just as you have done, and not look too hard for him. I agree that we are facing only one man, but in my judgment, he obviously is a rather formidable opponent who has played you for a fool."

Logan wanted to pound the little Syrian Army officer on the head, grind the little shrimp beneath his boots. But he did nothing because they were surrounded by armed soldiers who were watching him closely. "Then who is he, and where is he?"

Before Logan could answer, a tremendous detonation

rocked the village of Sa'ahn behind them as the house of
the jihadists exploded. A column of fire shot into the
black sky. The concussion rolled across the desert and
shook the heavy BTR carriers on their tires. Everyone
turned to watch, fascinated, frozen in place.

Al-Shoum recovered and sighed aloud. "I do not yet
know the name of the Marine who escaped this crash,
sir, for it is not the one you reported. But I do know
where he is. He is right over there." The major pointed
toward the fire and moved back toward his command
vehicle.

"We will return to the village now, Mr. Logan. Unless
I am gravely mistaken, you will find that your prisoner
is gone. My country has been placed in a quite
uncomfortable diplomatic position due to your stupid-
ity and arrogance. Consider yourself under arrest." He
motioned to his soldiers. "Take his weapons."

Victor Logan knew he was in shit up to his eyeballs. If
he remained in custody, Gates Global would toss him to
the wolves because the kidnapping had gone sideways.
The little Syrian asshole was right; Vic had been in
charge all the way. He and Jimbo would be disappeared,
and he would never touch that pot of gold waiting for
them.

The Syrians searched him thoroughly and stripped off
all of his weapons, including the hidden boot knife.
They had been well trained in that little science, which
indicated that they were not common enlisted men, and
he could expect them to be just as professional in other
things, such as shooting a prisoner who tried to run
away.

The best time to escape would be within the first few minutes, before the captors could lock him up tight and establish total control. But that damned explosion had heightened their alertness. They roughly pushed him aboard the carrier, leaving him untied so he could crawl inside. Which meant his hands would still be free when he got out. He still had a chance. An opportunity popped into his mind.

But even if he escaped from these dudes, where would he go and how would he get there? *One thing at a time, Vic. Get out of this mess first.*

He was jerked back against the small seat as the big vehicle lurched forward and turned around to head to the village. Logan kept his hands clasped in his lap, a picture of cooperation, the temporary victim of a mis-understanding between friends.

"Say there, Major?" he shouted over the sound of the engine.

Yousif al-Shoum looked back at him from a front seat. Said nothing.

"My computer, back at the house. I think you'll be interested in some of the things I can do for you."

"Such as what, Mr. Logan? I can access as many computers as I need."

"But mine can get real-time American satellite imagery. I make a call on my sat phone, we're uplinked in half an hour. How's that?"

The major nodded his head and turned around again. "Hmmm," he said.

Logan did not really have access to those satellites, which were so deep within U.S. government security that they were well beyond even the reach of Gordon Gates.

But the major did not have to know that, and Logan believed that by tossing out the satellite idea as bait, he had bought a few more minutes. The inference was that Logan had to be kept alive in order to obtain this help, thus bringing value to his life. They would keep his hands free if he had to work on the keyboard.

So when they walked through the door of the small house, it would be normal to have his hands raised slightly above his head, as if in surrender. He would grab the loaded AK-47 hidden above the door, spray the guards, and hope that Collins would be able to take down a few. Or they could at least force a standoff, with the soldiers still outside the house but with the little major inside as a hostage, with a rifle in his ear. Then Vic could deal on better terms. It is always better to negotiate from strength.

Then a second huge explosion flashed. The gunner on the Zeus had opened fire on the fleeing white truck, and the booby-trapped big gun blew to pieces when the bullets hit the C-4 explosives Kyle had stuffed down the barrels. Cases of ammunition then detonated around it with mighty stutters and new flames billowed up. Logan did not know what this one was, either, and the surprise was plain on his face. The little major turned again and stared at him with total disgust.

43

"Some difficulty? Gerald, we have quite a bit more than that," Gordon Gates said after Buchanan briefed him. "You have let things go astray. I would have thought better of you."

"It will be brought under control soon, Gordon," Buchanan promised stiffly, feeling the back of his neck redden in embarrassment and anger. "I just wanted to keep you abreast of what was happening." He did not like being insulted, and did not miss the careful wording from Gates that this was a problem created by *Gerald Buchanan*. They were in this together! Was Gates distancing himself and his company from the national security advisor?

Buchanan took a deep breath to keep his voice calm, as if they were talking about the weather in Aspen rather than creating a constitutional crisis. "I think it would be good if you and I and Senator Reed meet and discuss our options."

Gordon Gates laughed, a cold sound that disturbed Buchanan's false calm. "Out of the question. You tell me you have things under control, so I shall accept your statement as fact. When you resolve your little 'problem,' Gerald, then we will get together."

Buchanan rocked back against his chair. "But, Gordon, I need your help!"

"Don't be a stupid ass. You are putting thousands of your Junior G-Men all over this situation and there is no telling what they are going to do or uncover in their zest for carrying out your orders. If some eager beaver government cop stumbles onto the truth, *then* we will have a real problem. Isolate these people, Gerald, and take care of them. You've got Patriot Act IV, that Homeland Security Department, and every imaginable legal power you need. Damn, the attorney general would give you retroactive authority if you ask. You are *above* the law! How much more do you fucking need?"

"You won't help?"

"You do not need to know what I will or will not do." There was another long pause.

Buchanan could almost envision the lean face of Gordon Gates concentrating in thought. It was not the face of a businessman, but that of a killer.

Gates spoke. "You must convince the President to increase the threat level up to Red immediately. Make up some excuse tied to the Syrian situation or better yet, change the conditions of the entire argument. North Korea plans another nuclear test. Iran is gathering forces on the border of Iraq. Maybe a rogue Mexican Army unit plans to tear down part of the border fence. Use your imagination. Something international to make everyone look the other way and give us more cover. I give us no more than twenty-four hours."

"Twenty-four hours?"

"Yes. If that sniper brings General Middleton out of Syria alive, this whole thing will blow up in our faces.

Middleton must be stopped, as well as all four of the other people who know about your order. You *must* get to them. Understand this, Gerald, everything is at risk here. Everything!"

"I can do it. I already have the machinery moving," Buchanan said.

Gates was thinking far ahead of him. "We're almost out of time. Once you get the red alert in full force, and homeland protection is at its maximum, I will signal my Shark Teams to prepare Operation Premier with terrorist attacks on multiplex theaters in Houston, Kansas City, Atlanta, and San Diego. They will be in position for simultaneous strikes within two days. Then some schools will be hit during the following week, and the shopping malls. Every day there will be something new until this country finally wakes up and realizes the military and police services and the civilian leadership, as currently constructed, are unable to protect them. Sad, but true."

"I see. Can we avoid significant casualties?"

Gates exhaled in frustration. "Don't be thick, Gerald. It is only when we sustain major civilian losses that this country will finally turn in the direction it needs to go. It cannot move that way now because of that old piece of paper called the Constitution. When television sets across the land show horrific pictures of thousands of dead Americans—many more than 9/11—including a lot of kids, for hour after hour, day after day, you just make sure you have the Declaration of Martial Law ready, as well as your new draft constitution."

"Very well." Buchanan was sweating.

"Now buck up, Gerald, old boy. Do your job and

you will be running the United States of America in a couple of weeks. The clock is ticking. I look forward to talking with you after you have sewed up these loose ends. Meanwhile, you give me every scrap of information you have on those people. Maybe there are some ways I can help after all." He terminated the call.

Only then did Gordon Gates let his anger show. He threw a delicate bowl of blue glass made in Venice against a wall. It shattered, and he yelled aloud, "Buchanan, you goddam fuckup!" Buchanan didn't have the balls or the smarts to take out those four people, because he had never lived in the dark world of spies and special operators. *I have to clean up your shit! You are weak!* Gates poured a stiff Scotch and took a deep drink as he stared out the window at the lake behind his home. Then he activated a special communications device on his desk and prepared to send encrypted messages to some of the Shark Teams. Some would independently be sent to hunt down the four people who had become threats.

He had come too far, planned too much, and spent too much money to let an incompetent bureaucrat like Buchanan screw things up. Operation Premier would go forward, and faceless terrorists would be blamed for the tragic attacks.

He knew the idea of staging false attacks was not original. The Pentagon had seriously considered the tactic back in the 1960s to whip up a frenzy for an invasion of Cuba—shooting down a moon rocket and an airliner, hitting some civilian targets, and killing important officials, blaming it all on Castro. But President Kennedy intervened and trashed those plans. Gates had studied the scheme in detail at the War College, and thought it might have merit in the modern world. This time, he would run it privately so no governmental leadership could block the attacks.

The United States would cry out for someone who could stop the fighting and erase the fear but still guarantee rights for a free people, within reason. Who better to step in and bring order out of chaos than a decorated war hero, a proven patriot, who was at the helm of the world's largest private security company?

First, he had to clean up Buchanan's mess, including that sniper in Syria.

44

As soon as Kyle Swanson saw the headlights of the troop carriers begin to move away from the crash scene, he swerved the pickup truck off the road to the right and down into a wadi that spread into a cultivated field. He stopped beside a thick stand of trees and brush and turned off the motor. The dust the truck had kicked up settled to the road, leaving no trace of their passing.

General Middleton whispered, "What are you doing? Get the hell out of here."

Swanson held up a finger to silence him. Within thirty seconds, the two big armored personnel carriers roared past, heading back to the village where ammo was still crackling in the two separate fires.

Kyle jumped out, dug through his pack, and grabbed a claymore mine bandoleer. Middleton still wanted to move out. "What are you going to do now? Get back behind the wheel! Let's go!"

"I'm going to plant a claymore out on the road," Swanson said as he swung the bandoleer over his shoulder.

"A claymore won't destroy a BTR-80, Gunnery Sergeant Swanson."

"No shit, Brigadier General Middleton," Swanson

shot back. "But the next vehicle moving down the road will probably be one of those BTRs coming after us. With any luck the claymore can puncture the tires, maybe even the gas tank, and also take out whoever has their heads above the armor. The other BTR will stop because they will be worried about an ambush or another booby trap."

"Think, Swanson! It's a waste of time. The other one will just swing around the wreck and keep going."

"No, dammit, *you* think! It will take me three minutes to plant this thing, with the trip wire. When the first BTR is hit, even if it is not disabled, they will stop to sort things out. That will mean at least a ten-minute delay. Do the math, general. We get a net gain of at least seven extra minutes . . . that is, if you will shut the fuck up and let me get on with my job."

Kyle scrambled up the incline of the wadi and opened the claymore kit bandoleer. He loved these things, and his fingers worked fast as he checked off the familiar equipment—the powerful M18A1 mine, the M57 firing device, the M40 test set, the spool with a hundred feet of firing wire, the electrical blasting cap, insulation tape, and two wooden stakes. The whole deadly thing in a single handy package.

The Germans in World War II had invented the concept of a mine with a concave surface that would be capable of slinging a solid slab of steel through the armor of an enemy tank. By Vietnam, almost every American infantryman carried the modern lightweight version of the claymore, which was an inch and a half thick and packed with C-4 explosive and 700 steel balls that could devastate enemy personnel and take out thin-skinned vehicles. Swanson considered it the perfect ambush and perimeter defense tool. The trick was to remember how to place it correctly. It had not been named the claymore for nothing, because like its namesake, the ancient Scottish broadsword, it could cut both ways. The soldier setting it off with the clacker had to be at least about twenty yards behind it and under cover because of the backblast. Embossed on the lethal side of the olive-drab casing was the reminder, FRONT TOWARD ENEMY.

Swanson braced the mine solidly into the dirt with its built-in spikes, stretched the trip wire low across the road, about four inches above the surface, and tied it off to one of the stakes. He ran a quick circuit test and stacked some brush and twigs over the mine. He was counting on the darkness, and the Syrians not expecting to be hit. When the BTR ran over the trip wire, those hundreds of steel balls would blow out up to a height of six feet and in a 60-degree arc, with a casualty reach of up to 330 feet.

He hurried back to the pickup, restarted it, and threw it into low gear. They crashed through the brush and up the side of the wadi, back to the road on the far side of the mine.

"What if a civilian vehicle comes along first?" asked Middleton.

"Jesus, you're a worrywart," snapped Swanson. "You want me to go back and put up a warning sign? With so much stuff going on, the civilians are staying put. And if it happens, it happens. But it won't." He was already tired of Middleton and they had a hundred miles to go.

They sped along in silence with the lights off, and Kyle eyed the familiar surroundings through his NVGs.

Middleton seemed to relax a bit. "They still call you 'Shake'?"

"Don't start that shit on me now, General. We can argue later. Right now, I'm sort of busy." Swanson removed his foot from the accelerator and let the truck coast to a stop without touching the brake.

"Now what?" Middleton shifted in his seat, picking up the Kalashnikov.

"There's a checkpoint up ahead, about a kilometer."

"How do you know? Can you see it from here?"

"No, but I've already taken it out once," Swanson said. "On the way in." He climbed into the bed of the truck.

"So we're going to do it again?" the general asked through the small window behind the passenger compartment. "How?"

"With Excalibur." He unfastened the protective drag bag and removed the long sniper rifle.

"It's too dark and too far away," Middleton protested. "You can't hit them from here no matter how good you think you are. All you're going to do is alert them and give them time to radio for help."

Kyle adjusted Excalibur and racked a round into the firing chamber, then threw his pack on the cab of the truck and pressed a groove in it to use it as a steady platform. He took off the NVGs and clicked on the scope, dialing it to night vision. The scene lit up almost like daylight as the sensors grabbed every available source of light and heat and amplified them, and then the computer enhanced the forms it saw.

One guard was seated atop the checkpoint shack, smoking a cigarette. The other was standing to one side. Both had rifles and were looking at the glow from the village, watching the distant fiery show instead of looking for intruders. Kyle put the crosshairs on the standing man and let the scope do the math and automatically make the adjustments while he took up slack on the trigger. The blue strip flashed and he squeezed the trigger to complete the shot.

The soldier was caught center mass and the big bullet tore through him as it slammed him back against a pile of sandbags. As Kyle racked in a new round, the other guard, apparently thinking his partner had tripped and fallen, stood and looked over the edge to see what had happened. Only two seconds passed before Kyle got the blue stripe again. He fired. At that last moment, the target moved, and the bullet meant for the chest went in above his ear and took off most of his head.

Swanson returned Excalibur to its sheath, dumped his pack into the bed of the truck, and climbed back into the driver's seat. "There. That was easy, wasn't it?" He put the NVGs on, gunned the engine, and took off.

As they maneuvered through the roadblock, Middleton saw that both guards were dead, and the skull of one had been crushed by the force of the bullet. *Shake made a head shot in the middle of the night, while standing in the back of a pickup truck from a klick away, and thought it was easy?*

"Umph," the general said in reluctant approval. "You hit him in the head."

Swanson just drove.

45

Yousif al-Shoum, standing in the hatch of his BMR, saw the smoking ruin of the quad-barrel Zeus as they entered the village. Clumps of junk littered the street in front of the Americans' house, debris blown over from the demolished building of the jihad fighters, which burned with fury. The door to the Americans' place had been splintered by the force of the blast and was hanging on a single hinge. The body of the soldier he had left on guard was sprawled dead beside the steps. He ordered both vehicles to a stop, and his men formed a perimeter.

"Mr. Logan, you come with me." Logan wiggled from the hatch behind him and a soldier followed with a pistol at Logan's back. "Call out to your friend," al-Shoum ordered.

"Hey, Collins! Jimbo! You in there? It's me, Vic. Put down your weapon. We're coming in." Logan stepped to the doorway, but the officer cut in front of him with his pistol out.

"I will enter first." He stepped around the sagging door and into the room. The body of Jimbo Collins was sprawled in a corner. Al-Shoum moved toward the back of the house.

Logan kept his hands above shoulder level as he went

up the steps with the guard at his heels. It was now or never. Get the AK, spray the guard, and take the smarmy little officer as a hostage. When he cleared the doorway, Logan backkicked the guard and sent him reeling. He reached up to snatch the AK-47 waiting above the door, but his hands closed on thin air and his palms slapped the empty wall. He looked up. The gun was gone. NOTHING! He lowered his hands.

The major spotted the pegs. "A weapon was hidden up there, wasn't it, Mr. Logan? For emergencies . . . like this." Al-Shoum smacked Logan's head with the butt of his pistol and Vic staggered, seeing stars. "You were going to try to escape, and maybe shoot me in the process." Two soldiers ran in, grabbing and punching Logan. "Try something like that again, and you will be as dead as your friend in the corner. Now where is the general?"

"Over there, that room behind that door." Logan pointed. "Handcuffed to the bed."

Al-Shoum opened the door, took a look, and stepped right back out. "No one is there. It seems that you have lost your most prized possession. So what about this magic computer? Where is it?"

Logan looked at the table where the laptop usually rested beside the secure telephone. The phone had been crushed, and both computers were gone. He began walking around the room, looking for a place where Jimbo might have hidden them. "It has to be here somewhere. When I find it, I'll show you what we can do. Gates Global has a fantastic network." He rummaged through the kitchen area and the meager belongings in the living quarters, his mind working fast. The damn things were obviously gone.

"And what is this!" The Syrian officer had opened the door to the second bedroom and seen the naked and tortured body of a young girl exposed on the bed, with flies feasting on the dried blood and cuts. Her wide, lifeless eyes stared toward the door and a wide strip of tape was on her mouth.

Logan pushed past him, ran into the room, and came to a stop beside the body. It was time for the performance of his life, or he was breathing his last breaths. He thought of Charles Bronson, but he needed emotion, some heavy Clint Eastwood. "Ohhh. Nooo! Jimbo, you fucking bastard!" he howled in mock outrage. He stormed back to the body of Jimbo Collins and kicked it hard in the ribs. Again. "You sick fucking bastard! Couldn't keep your hands off her! I hope you rot in hell!"

Logan turned to the officer, panting and trying to appear shocked. "She was our cleaning girl, and Jimbo was always giving her the eye, saying what he wanted to do with the kid. He was a sick fuck with a record of sex crimes that got him thrown out of the army. I made him leave her alone because we were here to run an operation, not get involved with his sex fantasies. The sick asshole probably raped her this afternoon, and I didn't know because I came in late. I didn't even know she was in there!"

"A young Muslim woman has been defiled and murdered by you infidels," the major said with stone in his voice. "You tried to find a hidden weapon, your computer has apparently been taken along with the missing general, and somebody is waging a one-man war out there." He buried the barrel of his pistol into Victor

Logan's stomach, then pushed it up his chest and beneath his chin. "I have run out of reasons to keep you alive, Mr. Logan, other than to let the villagers kill you slowly for the death of that child. I'm sure they would be quite imaginative in the punishment. I will suggest that long knives play a part."

For one of the few times in his life, Victor Logan felt fear. "I didn't have anything to do with the girl!" he protested, now Charlie Sheen earnest, like in the movie when he was pitching for the Cleveland Indians. "I didn't touch her. I swear, Major. Jimbo wanted her!"

"Stop lying!" The major cracked him with the pistol butt again. "We can smell the body rotting from out here. You did it yourself, or you let it happen. You are nothing but a piece of filthy trash. Either way, under our laws, you will be put to death. I can give you a bullet in the head right now, but I would prefer that you be gutted in public."

Logan was sweating hard. "Come on, man. Don't even think like that. You know that through Gates Global, I got a lot of resources. Let's just get another computer and I can try to link up with my passwords. I'll give you anything you want to know." He was bartering for time again. Having both computers suddenly go missing had worked to his advantage because he did not have to deliver on his promise yet. And he didn't think the officer was really all that upset over the whore. He had seen how Arabs treated women.

"That will take some time," the Syrian replied. "There probably are no more computers in the entire village."

"Yes, there is. I know of one," Logan said, a desperate

idea bouncing into his head. "There's a Frenchman who was helping us. He lives just a few blocks away. I know that he uses a laptop for his business, and has wireless reception. Maybe I can rig that up to do the job." He could always make it *not* work, and blame it on sand or poor construction, or some other problem. Anything to stop this little shit from killing him for a few more minutes.

"Really? In my opinion, we are wasting time. I want to go find your escaped general now."

"Look, Major, I know you think I'm a fuckup, but there are other ways that I can still help you get him. Really, I can. The Marine who snatched the general has to be some sort of special ops dude, which means that he and I went through all of the same schools and training in the States, because I used to be a Navy SEAL. *I can think like him!* I know his limitations and his strengths and what his choices will be. I can help you find them." Logan was just treading water now, grabbing at straws to stay afloat, to stay alive.

"We have plenty of people trained in special forces techniques. I don't need you."

"Are they right here? Right now? How many of them went to U.S. spec ops courses? I guarantee this guy would run rings around any of them."

"Like in the mystery books, Logan? It takes a thief to catch a thief?"

"You got it. And I want this guy as badly as you do. I know that you will pop me if I don't catch him. He's my ticket out of here, right?"

"Maybe." Al-Shoum told a couple of soldiers to go

to the Frenchman's house and fetch his computer. He had known Pierre Falais for a number of years and considered him one of the better sources of information from the outlying territories, although he played all sides of the street. But Falais obviously had not reported everything he knew about the kidnapping of the American. He made a mental note to have a talk with him a little later.

Al-Shoum dialed a number on his cell phone and got his office in command in Damascus, reporting in rapid Arabic that the Marine general had escaped, apparently with the assistance of a skilled American special forces operator. He paused, listening, and wrote in a notebook. He replied with some questions and listened to the answer with a frown, then closed the telephone.

"Our intelligence sources have come up with the name of the man behind all this," he told Logan. "He is a U.S. Marine sniper named Kyle Swanson. Apparently he is very good, and sometimes does special work for the CIA. The bad news is that Damascus is pressing me to decide what our government should do."

"You get to make that kind of decision?" Logan asked.

"I work in the Security Directorate as the director of operations, and rank is meaningless, because I have the authority to do anything I need to do. That means that I can have you killed at any time and no one will question it. Are we clear?"

Victor Logan nodded vigorously. *Jesus H. Christ! Their top spook!*

Al-Shoum turned on his heel, heading for the door.

"I'm going to let you live a while longer, Logan. You will be my hound going after this fox. And you had better prove that you are very, very good at the job."

Logan kept his face iron-straight. "Not to worry, General. I'll get 'em back."

Another thunderous roar shook the village when the booby-trapped home of the Frenchman blew up three blocks away. Al-Shoum was flung against a wall, and a sharp piece of flying glass sliced the arm he threw up over his face to protect his eyes. Logan was tumbled to the floor and the table collapsed on top of him. Dirt poured from the ceiling, and windowpanes crinkled the floor with glass shards. The men looked at each other.

"Let me guess. The Marine visited the Frenchman's house, too." Al-Shoum got up and brushed himself off, casually pulling the fragment of glass from his arm, then stomped outside and watched the latest fire. A soldier rushed up to bandage the wound. "You are one pathetic operator, Logan."

Behind him, Victor Logan suppressed a grin. There went that computer, too.

46

Ambassador Samir Abu-Adwan of Jordan picked at his dark mustache as Shari Towne told her story. Her mother, his good friend Layla Mahfouz Towne, sat beside Shari, gently holding her hands. Layla had given him a synopsis, and he now listened to Shari himself with growing shock and indignation. Abu-Adwan knew the President of the United States would never order the assassination of a kidnapped Marine general. If such an order came from the White House, it certainly had not come from the President. Shari Towne's superior was running amok and creating an international crisis.

"You do not have a copy of this letter yourself, Shari?" he asked in a smooth baritone voice that showed sincere sympathy. As a veteran diplomat, he had many voices for different situations, but he knew that if he tried any disguise now, Layla would see right through it. Better to be honest.

"No, Mr. Ambassador. I don't."

"And you have never even seen a copy of it, either, am I correct?"

"That's right."

The ambassador entwined his fingers and rested his chin on them. "Gerald Buchanan is a shifty weasel," he said. "Such a thing is not beyond him. I sincerely doubt that the President knows anything about this. Your information adds significantly to the new situation."

Layla blinked. "What situation?"

"One reason that I am being such a bad host and ignoring my guests is that something urgent has come up. The Department of Homeland Security has increased the terror alert status to Red, the highest level, and television networks are reporting that American intelligence agencies have picked up credible evidence of a possible terrorist strike against the United States. I think our party downstairs will be breaking up very soon as people learn that. From what you have told me, this alert also bears Buchanan's fingerprints."

"There was no such terrorist chatter mentioned just a few hours ago when I was at the National Security Council meeting," Shari said, shredding the tissue clutched in her hands. "In fact, everything was focused on Syria and General Middleton. Usually these things take time to build up enough to get our attention. Since the Middle East was my desk, I certainly would have heard something, and I haven't."

"That brings me to the other matter," said Abu-Adwan. "We have received notification from the State Department that U.S. military action is now being contemplated against Syria."

"But why?" Shari was on her feet now, pacing the elaborate burgundy carpet, the tears gone and her mind again at work, picking at the puzzle. "We have no true evidence of Syrian involvement, at least officially. The general was kidnapped in Saudi Arabia, not Syria! Why would they take him back to their country and make a big announcement about it, then allow some terrorist group to threaten a public beheading, which would be a hostile act guaranteed to inflame the United States, just as it is happening right now?"

"Why indeed?" replied the ambassador. "That is why you and I and your mother are going over to State right now to ask these same questions. Before I came to see you, based on Layla's comments, I made some telephone calls and arranged a meeting with Undersecretary James Dalton and the ambassadors from Syria, Israel, and Lebanon to try to make sense of what is going on. Amman has advised me to relay the great concern of King Abdullah and our government about this situation. I asked to include you in our meeting. Mr. Dalton told me that you are a fugitive from justice."

That hit Shari hard, and she took a deep breath. "It's not a good feeling to be considered a traitor to my country."

"I know, Shari. You've done the right thing, and we will smooth it all over after we douse this crisis. For your information, our Syrian neighbors disclaim any active participation in the kidnapping. Didn't even know it had happened until General Middleton showed up in their backyard. They also are distancing themselves from the Rebel Sheikh in Iraq, who is getting too strong and influential for the tastes of many of us. They think that despite what he claims, the sheikh arranged to place Middleton in Syria to embarrass Damascus and cover his own involvement."

"Can we believe the Syrians?" Shari looked at him hard.

The ambassador nodded. "They don't mind plucking

a tail feather out of the American eagle every once in a while, but this incident is spinning far beyond anything they had bargained for. They definitely do not want to bring a hail of cruise missiles down on their heads." He stood up and adjusted his impeccable suit.

"Now, Shari, I think I have a bit of good news for you. There are some reliable reports from Syria that General Middleton is no longer in captivity, and that he escaped with the help of an American Marine who survived the tragic helicopter crash. It seems like your friend Kyle Swanson and General Middleton are on the loose."

Shari sat down beside her mother. "Thank God! They're both safe?"

"Apparently for the moment, but Syrian army units are in pursuit. Let's hope we can settle this mess diplomatically before there is a confrontation," the ambassador responded. "Shall we go?"

Shari balked. "They will arrest me."

"Shari, you must turn yourself in. I will deliver you personally to the undersecretary at the Department of State, and you will tell him your story. There is a high probability that you will never be taken into custody. In addition, the presence of your mother, myself, and the other ambassadors will guarantee an unpleasant diplomatic incident if Mr. Buchanan tries to take any hasty action."

"You don't know Buchanan, Mr. Ambassador. He can do anything he wants to do. If I give myself up, I may be spending the next few years in some dark prison in the middle of nowhere."

The ambassador lowered his voice. "I do not intend

to let you out of my sight until this matter is resolved. I promise that you won't get lost in the system. Under-secretary Dalton is an old friend and an honorable man, and the information you possess is of such value that you were right to seek our protection. Turning yourself in will demonstrate that you were simply trying to stay alive long enough to get the truth out. In fact, I think your government will probably want you to be a witness against Mr. Buchanan in a courtroom. They also will be very appreciative that you did not go to the media with this."

Ten minutes later, Shari was in the front seat of a black Mercedes, beside a handsome Jordanian soldier who served as a combination driver and bodyguard. Her mother sat in back with the ambassador, who was talking on his cell phone.

The ambassador had been correct, and the embassy party had emptied quickly as word spread of the unex-pected increase in the terror alert, everyone forsaking the food and drink tables to rush back to their offices to cope with whatever was happening. Taxis sailed about and traffic was heavier than normal for the hour.

The Mercedes with diplomatic license plates drove easily through the streets of Embassy Row and Shari drew comfort from the familiar monuments and squares of Washington, which was aglow in the early night. People had gotten off work and were packed into the bars and restaurants, and the nightlife was beginning to throb. The driver edged around a bicycle messenger with a flashing taillight. Even at night, those bikers were an effective way to get important documents from one federal department to another, or to bureaucrats from the K Street lobbyists, and the government never really slept.

The car stopped at a red traffic signal, third in line, and Shari knew the State Department was only about five blocks away. Maybe they could stop this madness. And she could not help but be happy that Kyle was alive. If he had Middleton and they were escaping, Kyle was in his element and would use every trick in the book to elude pursuit. Soon they would be together again.

She was startled by a tap on her window, and the bike messenger smiled and made a hand motion to roll the glass down. Beneath the visor of his black helmet, she saw that he had a lean face, with a neat beard and bright teeth. He probably wanted directions. As the driver looked over at the noise, another bike rolled up on his side, and its rider slammed a small sledgehammer into the window, stuck a Sig Sauer pistol into the jagged hole, and fired four bullets into the distracted young driver. Shari screamed and covered her face with her hands as the man's blood and brain matter splattered her. Restrained by her seat belt, she could barely move.

The biker on her side then used a hammer of his own to smash through her window, and Shari felt glass shards cut into her, sharp pins and knifelike slashes chewing at her skin. In the back seat, Layla screamed, and leaned forward to try and reach Shari while Ambassador Abu-Adwan scrambled to grab a pistol secreted in the armrest. Both bikers now had their pistols inside the car and sprayed full clips at all of the passengers while shouting *"Allahu Akbar,"* the familiar "God is great" war cry often used by terrorists.

They remounted the bikes and sped away through a

park, lights off, cutting sharp corners and disappearing into the darkness in moments. Two hand grenades they left behind detonated inside the Mercedes, setting the big car afire as stunned pedestrians and other drivers who had moved forward quickly backed away.

The bikers rode up a platform into the rear of a waiting panel truck bearing the logo of a plumbing company that was parked in a loading zone outside a restaurant. The doors were shut behind them and the blue truck moved out into traffic, heading for a garage in a rundown area of suburban Maryland.

In Alexandria, Virginia, Gordon Gates watched the entire attack unfold on a television screen through streaming video transmitted live by small cameras mounted on the bike helmets of the Shark Team. Buchanan had fed him the information intercepted from the Jordanian Embassy after the NSA computers picked up the name of Shari Towne. Gates assigned the job to his closest sharks, and they did well, he thought. One down.

47

"Are you going to have one of your little mental earthquakes now?" General Bradley Middleton did not take his hand from the AK-47 or stop scanning the darkness moving around the truck.

"You better hope I don't." Swanson kept his eyes on the road, watching a landscape painted green and black in his NVGs. He maneuvered around potholes, driving as fast as he dared without lights. "You know what I like best about being a sniper?"

"What?"

"I get to pick my partner, so at least I'm with someone I like. Unlike now."

The two men settled into an uncomfortable silence as Swanson drove due west. Every kilometer they covered added to what he considered a growing debt of good luck that would not last forever. They were about six klicks out of Sa'ahn, had seen no other vehicles, and the truck was running smooth.

"There's a McDonald's up the road a couple of miles," he told the general. Swanson was extending an olive branch because they had to work together. In this kind of situation, there should be only one enemy. "We can stop and get coffee and a Big Mac."

Middleton actually grunted what might have been a laugh under other circumstances. He wanted to back off, too. "I prefer Burger King. Double Whopper with cheese. Flame-broiled."

"Of course you would. You argue about everything?" Kyle asked.

"Yep. I'm what they call a contrarian." Middleton sucked in a sharp breath, and his words were hoarse.

"I was lying about the Mickey D's." He handed the general a canteen of water. "We'll be able to eat in a little while. How you feeling?"

"Been better. Been worse." Middleton paused, and seemed lost in thought and more focused. He said, "Who sent you to kill me?"

Swanson slowed and steered off the road to avoid a ragged, deep hole. A sharp bump like that might make the broken rib puncture Middleton's lung. "Gerald Buchanan, the national security advisor, wrote the order directly to me on official White House stationery. He didn't give a reason, just the assignment. If the mission to rescue you failed, I was to shoot you."

"He can't do that."

"Well, he did." Kyle pushed the accelerator back down to regain his speed, and another kilometer passed beneath their wheels. "He bypassed the military chain of command by handling it through the CIA, which has used me once in a while. It was handed to me by a guy from his office."

"Why would he want me killed?" Middleton asked.

"Beats the hell out of me, General. But you do tend to piss people off. Why were those American mercs involved?"

"They worked for Gates Global. That's who organized the kidnapping, I think, because of my opposition to the military privatization bill. They were going to let the damned jihadists chop off my head anyway, so why would Buchanan send you out to do the same job, other than as an insurance policy in case that plan failed? There must be a direct link between Gates and Buchanan." He sucked in another breath with a grimace.

Kyle removed his night-vision goggles. The black sky was showing the first signs of the new day, and he could make out shapes along the road. "General, keep in mind that our whole rescue mission was a setup. We were flying into an ambush. We were never supposed to succeed. I might not have even gotten through. Only somebody pretty high up could have gotten that information to the mercs. Buchanan would have been in the loop somewhere."

"Damn. I need to think about this for a while." Middleton fell silent.

Pinpoints of headlights crossing the road far ahead were easily visible in the remaining night. "Those have to be trucks on the main highway between Damascus and Amman," Kyle said. "End of the road for us."

Middleton watched the busy traffic, drivers hurrying with their loads to reach their destination before the sun rose and the heat of the day baked the roadways. "So we wait for a break and just scoot across. The Golan Heights are what, about thirty or forty klicks straight west?"

"We're not going that way," Swanson answered.

"But the Israeli army is all over those hills," Middleton shot back. "It's the quickest way out of here, and solid protection when we reach them."

"There are just as many Syrian soldiers on this side of the border, General, and they all will be looking for us. Hold on." Kyle found a narrow, paved frontage road that paralleled the main distant highway and skidded onto it with a sharp right turn that took them off the pavement. He intentionally clipped a traffic sign, crushed roadside brush, and shifted into a lower gear to dig deep ruts, leaving a clear trail before entering the northbound road.

The general was shoved against the door by the force of the turn and yelped in pain. "You're going north? Toward Damascus?"

"Of course not." Kyle stopped the truck and did a three-point turn to head back the way they had come, careful to stay on the pavement. He jumped out and used a small bush as a broom to erase marks of his reversed turn. The bush went into the truck bed and he headed east again.

"We'll double back for a couple of klicks. The stuff I did back in the village and the claymore ambush worked better than we thought. It slowed them down so much that I haven't seen the BTRs or anybody else on our tail. There are no headlights coming this way, so I think they stopped to regroup and call for help." He mashed the accelerator, tearing along the quiet road.

"There's a little road back here that heads south. We'll get on it for a little while, then hole up for the day. They're going to have a lot more choppers up as soon as daylight comes, so we can't run in the morning hours. Both of us need rest, too. I haven't slept in two days and you're hurt."

Middleton leaned back against the seat. "Not the way I'd do it, Gunny."

"I know. It's hard to stay still when the natural inclination is to haul ass, but this is how to best exfiltrate enemy territory and get out of here alive. Right now, they don't know where we are, and probably will conclude that we are heading straight for Israel. So we have to do something else, and going north to Lebanon isn't an option."

The countryside rolled by as the sky lightened to a warm gray, and as the very edge of the fiery sun showed above the horizon and into his eyes, he found the road and turned right. The Syrians would try to cordon off all of the escape possibilities. Swanson felt exposed and vulnerable with morning coming on so rapidly, the sun seeming to point at him, giving away their position. There was nowhere to hide.

48

"Hello, Ralph. Aren't you supposed to be on the other side of the world?" General Hank Turner returned Colonel Ralph Sims's salute and shook his hand. Turner introduced Sims to a three-star Air Force general with short silver hair who sat behind a huge desk in a spacious office where pictures of airplanes covered the walls.

Lieutenant General Peter Brady, commander of the 11th Air Force, also shook Sims's hand, and his dark eyes examined the disheveled appearance of the commander of the 33rd Marine Expeditionary Unit. "You look a little worse for wear, Colonel. Have a chair. Coffee."

"Thank you, sir, I will. I just came in on a meteor, that NASA X43-D scramjet." Sims was wearing a borrowed Air Force jacket over his short-sleeved summer uniform. What was appropriate wear in the warmth of the Med offered little comfort at Elmendorf Air Force Base outside Anchorage, Alaska. Only a few hours earlier, his uniform had been crisp and starched, and now it was a mass of deep wrinkles.

General Brady's eyes narrowed. "Colonel, there is no such aircraft, but I would like to know how the hell you were riding in it."

"Yes, sir, I understand. I've never heard of such a

plane either, and I'm not quite sure how I ended up in the back seat. The pilot told me to get in, and I did." He sat down, wrapping his palms around a warm mug. "Forgive my appearance. I barely had time to change out of the flight suit before your command sergeant major hustled me over here."

General Turner refilled his own cup. "I heard you were on the way with something special, so I sat here while my plane kept being repaired over and over. I heard that the Sergeants' Network has been busy, so a lot of pretty smart people must think your news is important enough to hold the chairman of the Joint Chiefs on the ground. I am curious." He sat in a big leather chair and crossed his legs. "Let's have it, Ralph."

Sims took a long drink of coffee and felt the warmth go all the way to his stomach. "No disrespect to General Brady, sir, but I believe you should have this on an 'ears only' basis."

Turner waved his hand. "Pete Brady and I go back more than twenty years. I value his counsel. He can listen to whatever you have. Proceed."

"Yes, sir. I'll give you the short version, then answer any questions that I can." He handed the plastic-enclosed envelope and note to Turner and stood by silently while the two generals passed the order between them.

"This was delivered personally to Gunnery Sergeant Kyle Swanson by the senior military aide of National Security Advisor Buchanan," the colonel told them. "It was to be destroyed as per instructions from Buchanan, but the Gunny managed to sneak a copy, which was what the aide unknowingly burned. This is the original,"

Sims explained. "Then Swanson went in with the Force Recon team on the Middleton mission as scheduled, but did not plan to obey the order. When the choppers crashed and it was assumed Swanson was dead, my Top brought that letter to me. Swanson had planned to bring General Middleton out of there safely."

Brady slid the letter back into its envelope. "So you flew halfway around the world to hand-deliver this to Hank?"

"Yes, sir. It was too hot for a messenger and I intentionally bypassed a couple of layers in the chain of command. This is way above my pay grade, General, but I think it has to be illegal for a civilian bureaucrat who has never been elected to anything to use the clout of the White House to order the assassination of a kidnapped American general."

Turner had uncapped an elegant old-style fountain pen and made some notes in a little book. "Bet your ass it is. Does Buchanan know that you were coming to see me?"

"I don't see how, sir," said Sims, taking another sip of coffee. "The only people who knew about the letter, other than Buchanan and his aide, were Swanson, Top Dawkins, and me. Now Swanson is dead. Since Buchanan believes the letter was destroyed, he would see no loose ends."

General Pete Brady glanced out of the window. It was dark outside. Rain scratched at the glass. "He figured it out, Colonel."

"Sir?" Sims asked.

"About an hour ago, Homeland Security jacked the terrorist warning level all the way up to Red, and an

attack in Washington killed the Jordanian ambassador."
He handed Sims a news story downloaded from the
Internet. "Not that we have much to worry about up
here in Alaska, but it certainly got our attention."

"I received a separate message, ultra-encrypted, from
the National Command Center, authorized by none
other than Gerald Buchanan," said General Turner,
beginning to pace around the office. "You are to be
arrested on sight, on a charge of treason, no less. You
are to be held here until Homeland Security personnel
can pick you up for questioning. There's a cheery
thought. How do you reckon he knew to send that
message about you, who are supposed to be in the Med,
to me, who is stuck up here in Alaska?"

Ralph Sims bit his lip. Arrested?

General Brady reread the order. "We couldn't figure
why he would want you in custody so bad. Now we
know. The alert level should have nothing to do with
you being tagged as a bad guy, nor with the strange
message direct to Hank, but I don't believe in coin-
cidences."

"Our question now becomes whether Buchanan is
acting on his own." Turner moved to a wall map. "The
President was on the campaign trail tonight out in San
Diego, one of those thousand-bucks-a-plate things. He
was glad-handing the faithful when he got word of the
attack in Washington and authorized raising the alert
level. He skipped the speech and got back aboard Air
Force One. They're already in the air." He tapped the
map. "We're up here outside of Anchorage, and before
the sergeants intervened, I was en route to Beijing for a
meeting that has been six months in the planning. Nat-

urally, I've cancelled the China trip. Instead, I'm going to rendezvous with Air Force One when it lands at Andrews. You're coming with me, Ralph."

"I just left there," Sims said with a groan.

"Quit whining, Colonel. I hate Air Force weenies to see a Special Ops CO whimper like a little girl. Anyway, you can sleep on the way back, and I've got some good news for you. Seems that your Gunny Swanson lived through the crash after all, and that General Middleton has gone missing from his captives in Syria. Swanson apparently busted him free and has been raising holy hell in the town where he was held. They're on the run, with the Syrians hot on their tails. Things are getting interestinger and interestinger."

Brady turned to his computer terminal and called up a program to show the weather. "This rain squall is just passing through, and the sergeants have assured me that all of our aircraft are suddenly ready to fly again. They're warming up my Gulfstream II/SP even as we speak. I say let's go meet the Boss." The 11th Air Force commander went to a closet, took out a flight suit, stripped to his underwear, and pulled it on.

"We'll go back with Pete aboard his Gulfstream," said Turner. "I could use my own bigass plane that was going to haul me over the Pole to China, but Pete's toy is a lot more comfortable," Turner said. He looked at a big clock on the wall. "Matter of fact, the big bird will be taking off in a few minutes. Bet we beat them to Washington."

"Am I under arrest?" asked Sims.

"Oh, hell, no," snapped Turner. "We don't take orders from that overblown asshole. Buchanan's up to no good, it has something to do with our Marines getting killed, and I'm going to get to the bottom of it."

Sims read the news report about the terrorist attack in Washington while the two generals finished getting ready. "Oh, shit!" he exclaimed.

"What 'Oh, shit'?" asked Turner.

"This story, sir! The four people killed by the terrorists in Washington: the ambassador, his driver, another embassy official, and a U.S. Navy officer, Lieutenant Commander Shari Towne." Sims's face had gone red with anger.

"Come on, Colonel. Talk to me."

"General Turner, it's an open secret that Lieutenant Commander Towne and our sniper, Gunny Swanson, have been together for a long time. One of those don't ask, don't tell things, so nobody officially knew about it. They're almost engaged, from what I hear. That direct link between her and Swanson is only point one. Point two is that she ran the Middle East desk on Buchanan's staff in the White House."

The generals looked at each other. "Goddam, Hank. Those bastards weren't after the ambassador at all!" said Brady. "They were after the girl!"

Turner, Brady, and Sims walked outside toward the flight line, where the beautiful Gulfstream was warming up in a circle of bright light. Plumes of jet exhaust streamed away in the cold air, and the light rain glistened on its polished skin. Brady asked Sims, "Do you think this Gunny Swanson can get Middleton out of there alive?"

Sims nodded his head in the affirmative. "Sir, I'm

beginning to believe that Gunny Swanson can walk on water. Don't bet against him."

A great bellow of noise rolled across from the main runway as a Boeing 707 painted in the distinctive sky-blue-and-white pattern of a VIP of the U.S. government raced past them and gathered speed for takeoff. "There goes my plane. Sort of a shame it's flying empty," said Turner.

Brady added, "The crew is happier to be going home than to China."

They watched it lift smoothly into the air. A spark of bright light flashed on the ground in the distance, and a bright dot streaked higher and higher, gaining momentum and altitude at a dizzying rate. The Stinger shoulder-fired missile rammed into one of the hot engines on the Boeing and detonated, and in a fraction of a second the dark sky seemed filled by a ball of fire that consumed the plane even before it hit the ground.

Ralph Sims grabbed both generals and threw them to the paved runway, sprawling across them. "Jesus Christ, General Turner, you were supposed to be on that plane!"

"Go to Alert One! Scramble the fighters!" Brady yelled to a nearby security guard, who grabbed his radio and relayed the order to the Elmendorf command center. Sirens wailed as ambulances and fire trucks burst from their garages and raced down the runway.

A whine buzzed in the sky, and an explosion shook the ground when a mortar round arced in from the darkness beyond the wire. A second round was on the way before the first one struck and landed closer to a big hangar; then a third mortar round landed right on the building that was filled with volatile fluids and ammunition. It erupted like a volcano. Three fighter-bombers undergoing maintenance inside, out of the weather, were blown apart, and the maintenance crews were incinerated. When Sims saw that the mortars were not coming their way, he got the generals to their feet and they all ran for cover.

Air Force security police surged toward the wire as three more mortar rounds rained down, two of them chewing holes into the main runway. The last one grazed the big control tower and exploded on a parked truck, which set fire to everything around it.

The Shark Team was gone by the time police found the empty launching tubes. Both men had been members of the Security Police and nearing retirement when they were corrupted by the big bucks offered by Gordon Gates to join the Sharks. Weapons had been stashed in an off-base apartment for months just in case they were needed. They also had new identities, new passports, and thick bank accounts and were flying first class to Seattle before it was even discovered that they were missing.

When ground troops had cleared the flight path beyond the fenceline, the Gulfstream piloted by General Brady zipped from the runway, with Turner and Sims strapped into the leather seats. Rolling next were a pair of F-16 escorts, armed to the teeth, which took station off the wingtips.

In the calm skies above the Arizona desert, the President of the United States was briefed about the deadly strike at Elmendorf. Four more F-16s sped out to sandwich over and around Air Force One. The President had no doubt that the terror alert was right at the level it should be. His country was once again under attack.

49

Gordon Gates brought up a secure e-mail from the Sharks who had hit Elmendorf, read it, and then electronically shredded the message through the Magneto program. It vanished as if it had never been sent. They had done an extraordinary amount of damage and gotten away clean. Gates had long ago discovered the truth of the old question, "Who guards the guards?" and had spent a lot of time and money penetrating the security forces of many military bases. Surprisingly, it was not difficult at all to find otherwise good soldiers ready to sell their services to a high bidder.

Buchanan's security net had tracked Colonel Sims to Elmendorf, where he was likely to link up with General Turner, the chairman of the Joint Chiefs, who had been delayed there on a trip to China. Sims would have given Turner the message. So bringing down the Boeing with a Stinger missile meant that Turner and Sims were dead, and the assassination letter would have burned in the crash. Perfect. The mortar rounds were thrown in as icing on the cake to embellish the terrorist possibilities.

Gates considered the situation at this new point. Shari Towne had been taken out in the attack on the Jordanian ambassador's car. He would like to have had visual confirmation on Sims and Turner, but he had seen a lot of plane crashes and the odds were overwhelming that they were both cooked. Nothing had been heard from them since the shootdown. So three of the people who had learned about the letter were dead, which left three elusive Marines—Swanson, Dawkins, and Middleton.

The master sergeant aboard the ship was proving to be invisible, which won an approving smile from Gates for the Spec Ops veteran. It would take some luck to dig him out, particularly if he had the assistance of other people on the boat, but sooner or later he would be discovered. Gates just had to leave that in the hands of the NCIS people for the time being. Dawkins had no proof of whatever he might claim, so he was relatively harmless and totally isolated at sea.

He turned to the problem of General Middleton and Gunnery Sergeant Kyle Swanson, who apparently had been on a rampage in Syria. The stakes for catching those two were enormous. The whole plan hung on finding them. One of his Sharks in Syria was dead, and the second was in the custody of the Syrian army, but alive and helping track Swanson. That didn't worry Gates, because all Sharks were expendable. The risk was part of the big pay and benefits package.

But Swanson had freed General Middleton and had so far eluded the Sharks and the Syrian army. Gates had sent a message to the Rebel Sheikh requesting more jihadists to augment the search, because the more eyes they had looking, the better. It was best not to count too heavily on the Basra cleric, however. He was a slippery devil.

Gates went to a bar built into a wall of his office,

where he kept a bottle of Absolut vodka in the freezer. He poured some into a tall glass and added ice cubes, club soda, and a slice of lime. He stirred and drank, letting his thoughts roam.

Google Earth was an excellent map program that could be used without pinging the military system. He called up the image of lower Syria and projected it on a large plasma screen. The southern area of the country jumped into view and he worked the mouse to increase magnification and tilt the image.

Not much there, he thought. Mostly flat and brown, with some stretches of cultivation. He put his mind in Spec Ops mode, placed the cursor on the village of Sa'ahn, and used the pointer tool to trace and measure possible routes of evasion. He had plenty of time, because the sniper and the general would be hiding in the daylight hours.

Swanson would avoid populated areas. The Syrians had helos in the air, but they had to cover a search area of several hundred square miles and probably would not see him. With so many helicopters searching, Swanson and Middleton had to keep their heads down during the day. If Gates was in the sniper's boots, he would head south tonight and make a dash to the Jordanian border tomorrow at first light.

He sipped his icy vodka and tonic. Then he minimized the Google Earth map and brought up the digitalized copy of Swanson's military jacket. Quite the package: a real war fighter and a gold-plated pain in the ass. Buchanan had screwed up by picking him for the job. Gates thought the man would be a terrific Shark Team leader, but would never flip for money.

He had to be stopped. Both Swanson and Middleton had to be killed. First they had to be found, and who better to look for Spec Ops types than Shark Teams who knew all of the tricks of that dark art? Victor Logan, a violent cretin in many ways, was one of the best, but Gates decided to lend the Syrians some more specialized assistance.

He tapped into his private database to see what was available. There was an unmanned aerial vehicle, a pilotless UAV with a video link, on the ground in Jordan, and he sent instructions to get it into the air. It would be one more thing from which Swanson would have to hide. Gates added the Shark Team that was helping to train Hezbollah fighters in a remote part of Lebanon. That team had a serviceable UH-1E Huey helicopter with miniguns slung on the sides. He also sent in another team from Israel, where the two Sharks were acting as counterinsurgency advisors with the Israelis on how to trap Hezbollah guerrillas. They would drive over in their armored Humvee. He sent a coded message through a Syrian contact to the search team in the desert. Five well-trained Sharks brought a lot of expertise to the operation. Plus the new Iraqi jihadists. A lot of eyes.

Gates studied the Marine's personnel jacket some more, looking for anything that might help. This sniper had already proven to be very aggressive, so Middleton and Swanson would be watching for the watchers. Middleton probably would have the strong binos, while Swanson would use the powerful Unertl telescope on his SASR, the big .50-caliber M82 Special Applications Scope Rifle. That was a hog of a weapon, a real bonebreaker that Gates knew well from lugging one himself.

That would slow Swanson down even more when it came time to run.

Every pound Swanson carried would weigh him down a fraction, and the SASR was 37 pounds even before adding the ammo. The sniper had to be carrying a big pack, more weapons, and maybe some other gear, too. He would start to shed the unneeded items, but in the current time frame, he was losing the speed contest. This was the moment to catch them, while they were at rest and before they could start moving again.

Gordon Gates slammed his drink down onto the thick glass top of his desk. *The rifle!* Of course! He scrolled down through Swanson's jacket to read about Swanson's recent assignment to Sir Jeff Cornwell's company, advising in the development of a new generation of sniper rifle. Vague stories had been carried in the gun magazines about the experimental weapon with the magical, highly computerized scope, and Cornwell had garnered the venture money needed to take it into production. Gates did a web search for the rifle through "sniper" Web sites until he found the name of the weapon: the Excalibur. He waded through a bunch of sites about King Arthur's sword before coming up with some of the specs on Cornwell's futuristic gizmo. It was lighter than the SASR by far, so maybe Swanson had this thing along, the Excalibur, and if he did, he might save on weight, but there was a potential weakness. *Gotcha!*

Gates opened his private electronic Rolodex and found an overseas telephone number. London. A quiet British voice answered.

50

Yousif al-Shoum was biding his time. Logan had been correct, that the sniper would go to ground during the daylight hours, so moving fast was neither necessary nor wise. Al-Shoum rested in a large tent that had been set up beside the road near the village and watched his soldiers probe up the road for more mines and booby traps. Not far from the tent was the burned and blackened hulk of the BTR-80 troop carrier that had triggered the mine. The two men whose heads were above the armor were decapitated by the blast, and the fuel tank ruptured and exploded, which took out three more men. Al-Shoum was alive only because he had stayed behind with the second BTR to communicate with Damascus. Otherwise his own head would have been sticking out of the forward hatch of the lead vehicle.

The Syrian intelligence officer had had his fill of surprises for one day. Five of his men had died in the BTR ambush. Another was killed at the front door of the house in the village, along with one of the American mercenaries. The house with eleven jihadist fighters from Iraq was blown to pieces and they were all dead. Parts of the Frenchman who was everybody's intelligence contact were found in the smoking ruins of his demolished home. The guard who was taped to the Zeus and the gunner who tried to fire it were dead. Two pairs of sentries at the checkpoint down the road had been slain. Two pair! The Marine general was gone. Enough was enough.

Al-Shoum would coordinate the search from this tent and be the spider at the center of the search web. While he waited for more troops and helicopters, he sent a squad back into the village to conduct a house-to-house search to be sure the American troublemaker had not taken shelter back there where he was least expected.

A big map was spread on a table before him, along with two radio sets, a Thermos of tea, water, and some food on clean white plates. Al-Shoum munched bread and cheese. "Well, Mr. Logan. Where did he go?"

Victor Logan had been impressed by the wreckage of the BTR, which still wore big stripes of dried blood and guts. The undamaged armored personnel carrier remained parked nearby, almost as if cowering until the minesweepers pronounced the area clear. This sniper knew what he was doing. Logan wiped his palm across the lower half of the map. "South. Toward Jordan."

"Our scouts report some damage to a road sign at an intersection to the west, several kilometers from here, big truck tires digging around a sharp corner that would lead them north, toward Lebanon."

Logan shook his head, a statue with his beefy arms crossed across his chest, thinking hard. "It's a bullshit play to draw you that way. He's not going there."

"I agree," said al-Shoum. Still, he had to devote some search assets to the area, because from what this American Marine had done so far, he was not beyond leaving a false trail, doubling back on it and then doubling back still again. The Syrian remembered reading about that trick in a detective story about how a serial killer trapped a never-give-up New York cop and his beautiful FBI partner . . . he snapped his mind back to the present. "One would think he would take the general due west, as fast as possible, toward Israel." He glanced at Logan. "Why not?"

"He's made the same deductions that we are doing now. Getting to Israel would be the most logical and quickest route to safety, so he knows your troops will flood the area. Therefore he won't use it, and he cannot head the opposite direction, to the east, into territory that is just as dangerous. To the south is Jordan, which is friendly with the United States. That's where I would go. It's where he will go."

Again al-Shoum agreed, and scratched his head. Logan could afford to guess, but he had to cover all possibilities, and there were many. He could not rule out the dash to Israel, and he had sent search teams toward the Zionist border, further depleting his force.

Then there was the problem of the vehicle itself. The Marine had stolen an old white Toyota pickup truck, which was the most common vehicle in Syria, if not in the entire region. There were hundreds of white Toyota pickups on the roads, going in every direction, in and out of every population center, all day long. The escapees could be in any of them.

In a professional sense, al-Shoum held a grudging respect for his opponent for sticking with his job after the helicopter crash, coming into the village and rekidnapping the general. It did not matter. His job was now to catch them both, and that was what he would do. Afterward, he looked forward to dealing with Victor Logan for the murder of that girl.

He stood and turned when a soldier called out to him and pointed. A dark blue Land Rover came sailing toward them from the village, the tinted windows sealing in the air conditioning as the tires threw plumes of dust into the air behind it. A man with a gray beard and thick eyelashes, wearing clean white robes and head covering, got out of the back seat when the vehicle stopped beside the tent.

"General al-Shoum," the visitor said. "My dear friend."

Al-Shoum bowed with respect, then embraced the senior imam from a mosque in Damascus. He helped the cleric to a chair at the table, and poured tea. A guard moved Logan out of earshot.

"I am always delighted to see you, my friend, for you have the peace of Allah with you. But what brings you to this desolate place?" al-Shoum asked. "A man of the Book need not trouble himself in this routine business."

The old man sipped his tea and spent about five minutes exchanging pleasantries. The children, of course, and the crops and the animals, and also the wife. Al-Shoum grew more impatient by the minute. This imam did not leave his mosque to drop by as a curious tourist. He might have been sent from the government to report on al-Shoum's work.

"Please forgive me for keeping my radios tuned so loudly," he said. "I am conducting a wide search for the missing Americans." *Take the hint, old man.*

"That is part of why I am here, beyond learning the joyous news of your family. I am doing a favor for my fellow cleric and our important ally, Sheikh Ali Shalal Rassad in Iraq, a very respected man in the service of the Prophet, whose name be praised."

"Praise be the name," al-Shoum parroted. "Anything I can do to assist your mission, I shall do." The Rebel Sheikh was sending a message through a messenger of such high pedigree that there could be no doubt about its validity and importance.

"Our friend is most disturbed. He dispatched an airplane early this morning to transfer the American general safely to his hospitality in Iraq. He knows our own nation had nothing to do with the kidnapping, and it appears that many things have changed since the man was taken. Matters have gone to the highest levels."

Al-Shoum said, "Which is why I am present here."

The imam continued without pause. "Our friend, of course, was unaware that you had been sent by Damascus, and offers his most sincere apologies for the misunderstanding. He meant no offense to you or to your abilities. He was only attempting to salvage the situation and help our nation."

Al-Shoum put his hands flat on the table, eyes downcast, humble, obedient as a sheep. *And what's your damned point?*

"But you can only imagine our friend's surprise when he learned that not only has the American general escaped with the help of another American, but that all of the Sheikh's holy warriors who had been guarding him have been martyred. All of them!"

"That is true. His Iraqis apparently were too careless in posting guards." Al-Shoum's tone was a sneer at their carelessness.

The old man stroked his beard, the dark eyes stronger than the frail body. "Something insulting has happened. The American infidel Gordon Gates actually ordered our friend to dispatch even more fighters, a large number of them, up here to join your search. *He ordered a man of the Book to do so!* It is an outrage! So our brother has decided to do what is best for us all."

"Of course. And what was his decision?"

"Naturally, he would never intrude into your operation, brother. He expresses full confidence that you will resolve this situation, and his attention is demanded elsewhere, on more fruitful things." Having delivered his message, the old man rose and gave the Syrian intelligence officer a final hug. "*Inshallah*, the will of Allah be done," said the imam. He bestowed blessings for al-Shoum's sons to grow strong in the service of the Prophet, got back into the Land Rover, and was driven serenely away.

Al-Shoum watched the blue SUV vanish back the way it had come. *Shit!* First that Iraqi pig had tried to sneak in and steal the American general right from under al-Shoum's nose, and now he was abandoning the search. That would leave al-Shoum alone to take any blame if they escaped.

"What was that all about?" asked Logan, ducking back beneath the tent.

"Nothing," said al-Shoum. "An old friend who happened to be in the area and wondered what was going on." Ali Shalal Rassad, who had already lied to the world that his organization, the Holy Scimitar of Allah, was not involved, was washing his hands of the whole mess. The old imam who brought the message was often employed as an unofficial emissary by the Syrian government, which would now be considering doing the same thing to ease international tensions. While al-Shoum sat beneath this tent in the middle of nowhere, the distance from Damascus hung around his neck like an albatross, for he realized that being stuck out here meant that he would not be privy to the final decision-making. Damascus had changed his mission. Instead of making a decision himself, he had been sent off running after a couple of Marines. If a scapegoat was needed, he might be chosen as the sacrifice.

He looked at the sky, where the sun had risen higher. No helicopters in the area. He increased the volume on the radio net. The sooner he captured those Americans, the better, because then he would be on the next chopper back to Damascus, possibly entering the city as a hero. He spun to face the American mercenary, whose help he now needed much more than he had only ten minutes ago. "We are wasting time, Logan."

51

The desolate road led back into a countryside that was green with agriculture rather than the normal desert brown, with ditches on each side to help with the irrigation of crops in a dry climate. Small canals with gates separated the larger tracts of land in a crossing pattern, to feed water from one area to another in a rotating schedule. As the sun crested totally above the horizon, a shining torch that removed the protecting darkness, Swanson found a major canal that apparently spilled into much of the region, with a low level of water. He dropped the truck into four-wheel drive, cut onto a cart path, and bounced down into the big trench.

Middleton grimaced in agony as he was tossed around in the cab, but Kyle kept going until all four wheels were in the water. He plunged ahead into a large concrete culvert that served both as a waterway and an opening through which farm machinery could transit from crops on one side of the road to the other. With a high clearance and only about a foot of water, the truck fit easily beneath the shelter, with both ends deep in shadow. He stopped and turned off the engine, and silence engulfed them. "This is it for the day. No choice."

Middleton adjusted himself in the seat, eyeing the broad openings in front and behind them. "Pretty exposed." Kyle started to respond, but Middleton added, "You're right. Nothing else was around."

Swanson opened his door and stepped into stale water. "The truck sits up high enough for the water not to be a problem. I'll go brush over our tracks." He waded away, back into the daylight, and spent ten minutes covering their tracks from the road into the culvert ditch, then used his binos to examine the fields all around them. Quiet, with no workers, even in relatively cool morning. He returned to the truck and climbed into the back.

Middleton was standing there cradling the AK-47. "Anything out there?"

"Nope. We're okay for now. If they are not working the crops at this time of day, maybe these fields are just being watered. We might get lucky and not have to deal with any farmers coming through. Let's look at the map."

They unrolled it on the roof of the cab, each holding down an edge. "The place where you were being held is called Sa'ahn, over here." Kyle pointed to a small symbol that denoted a village of less than a thousand people, and dragged his finger along a dark line. "We drove all the way over here to where that big highway goes up to Damascus, and then doubled back. I estimate that we are about right here, close to midway between these two big population centers, As Suwayda to the east and Dar'a to our west."

He stopped talking and both grabbed their weapons when they heard a truck engine. Kyle motioned for the general to watch one end of the culvert while he covered the other. The truck came closer and closer, then rumbled across the bridged culvert and pushed on down the road. "We'll probably be getting more of that during the day. Farm traffic."

"So how far are we from anywhere?" Middleton squinted at the map.

Swanson found a scale of kilometers printed on the bottom and measured with his finger. "This road runs into As Suwayda in about forty-four kilometers. About a mile away from where we are now is another small road that goes due south for, let's see, about seventeen klicks."

"Doesn't reach all the way to the Jordanian border," Middleton observed. "Dead-ends at the next crossing. But it looks like a straight shot from there."

"I figure that we are about twenty-one miles, more or less, from Jordan," Kyle estimated. "We can drive closer and hump it tonight if we have to. Just have to get close."

"Should we get rid of the truck?"

"No. It's a hard worker and blends right in. Anyway, if we take another one, we alert more people."

Middleton looked over at Swanson. "What do you mean that we only have to get close?"

Kyle dug into his pack and pulled out the battery-powered satellite telephone he had taken from the dead pilot in the crash. "In a few hours, about noon, we break radio silence and call our guys in the fleet for help. They might not risk coming in just to get me, but they sure as hell will come in to get you!"

"Rank has its privileges, Gunny. Why not call right now and get it over with?"

Kyle sat down and propped his weapon beside him. "When we light up that phone, we expose our position. The Syrians and Washington will be listening, so we want to burn off a few daylight hours to cut into the available search time, but still give the MEU enough of a window to execute a pickup."

Middleton eased himself into a sitting position, holding his ribs. "You mentioned Washington. Made me think of something. Did anything really unusual or important happen while I was being held?"

"No, sir. I don't think so," said Kyle. "I was out of the country and wasn't watching the news before things started happening pretty fast."

"Think hard, Gunny. Anything that impacted the military services?"

Swanson laid down, resting his head on his pack. "Nothing comes to mind. I got to get some zs, General, so let's take two-hour shifts. You wake me up and then you get some sleep. I'm about to fall over." He pulled his boonie cap over his eyes, then lifted it again. "Yeah, wait. There was this one thing. Senator Miller, the old airborne guy, died of a heart attack while campaigning."

"Miller? The head of the Senate Armed Services Committee?"

"Yes, sir. Apparently keeled over in his hotel room after a speech."

"Be damned!" Middleton let out a low whistle, feeling the pieces click together. "Tom Miller was the one person in the government who was more opposed than me to privatizing the U.S. military. We had been working together so that my testimony before his committee next week would block the legislation by turning a bright light on its ugly side."

"So with Senator Miller dead and you held captive and maybe also dead, what would happen?" Kyle pushed back his hat.

"Not good, Gunny. Not good at all. The hearing would probably go forward as scheduled, only with Senator Ruth Hazel Reed succeeding Miller as head of the committee."

"Does that change things?" Kyle cocked his ear and sat back up.

"Yeah. In a big way. Rambo Reed was the one who wrote the damned privatization bill. If major parts of the military are given to the lowest bidder, it will still involve billions of dollars and an immense amount of political power. Worse, it will set the pattern for other parts of the federal government to be sold off." The general rubbed his eyes with the heels of his hands. "I kid you not, Gunny, this thing threatens America as much as any terrorist group. So Gates has some of his mercs kidnap me. They plan an ambush to create a military fiasco, but the choppers crash, doing the job for them. Buchanan has sent you in to make absolutely sure I don't come back. Rambo Reed takes over the committee and pushes the bill through. They're all in this together. Jesus, Gunny, I've got to get back there."

"Listen!"

The thump of helicopter blades was heard in the distance, but coming nearer.

52

Each time Yousif al-Shoum received another report of a white pickup truck being spotted, the position was plotted on the plastic overlay of his map with a red thumbtack pushed into the corkboard backing. After a few hours, the map was littered with the little pins, each a sharp point of failure in his massive search. Several dozen white Toyota trucks had been stopped at checkpoints or by search teams, but all were legitimate, except for one fool who had been trying to steal the vehicle when he was apprehended. It was almost noon when he decided to abandon all efforts to the north and toward Lebanon, peel away some of the strength watching the routes to the Israeli border, and take Victor Logan's advice. He would saturate the southern region all the way down to Jordan.

With a black marker, he slashed a boundary line from the southernmost point of the border with Israel, curving over to Dar'a, then northeast to As Suwayda and back down through El Adnata to Jordan. It was a kill box that had the look of an inverted cup. They had to be in there somewhere, and he would construct a net of roving search parties and scour the area like a broom.

Members of his staff had arrived from Damascus and

he told them what he wanted, leaving it up to them to draw up the grids and issue the necessary orders. One by one, the helicopters and the road units would be reassigned and move into southern Syria. Al-Shoum had never failed, and was absolutely determined to find the elusive sniper. The chase had become a challenge to his pride and his ability, while back in the capital, competitors probably were already measuring his office for their own desks. If the Marines got away, they might be taking his career along with them. That could not be allowed to happen.

The heat was growing. Even beneath the tent, the air was thick and stale and unmoving. He put on his beret and sunglasses and stepped into the sun to have a word with Victor Logan and two mercenaries who had come down from Lebanon aboard a Huey that was parked in the distance with its rotors pegged tight. Logan had told him in advance that the tall man with the dark tan was from South Africa, and that the pilot was a former Russian Spetsnaz commando with big arms that bulged from a skintight muscle shirt.

Al-Shoum paid no attention to their names when Logan introduced them. The mercenary added, "We have two more men driving over from Israel. They should be arriving in about an hour."

"Good," said al-Shoum. "Will you be in charge, or do I have to talk to someone else?"

"Anything doing with Gates Global still comes through me," Logan said, careful not to appear impolite. He had not forgotten to whom he was speaking, and had warned the new men to watch their mouths or they would all end up in a Syrian jail.

Al-Shoum explained the changing search patterns. "There is no need for you to be out flying without a target. It would only waste your fuel and time, for your expertise will be needed soon enough. Brief your team and be ready to move as soon as somebody spots the Americans. When they start to run, as I anticipate, you will go get them."

Logan shifted the strap of his rifle. "Good plan, sir. We'll be ready."

"Very well," al-Shoum said. "I'll call you when something turns up." He turned on his heel and went back to the tent, where more pins had been stuck in the map overlay. He issued a new order: Every Toyota pickup in the new search area would be halted and immobilized until the Marines were found. There was no use counting the same ones twice. The pins seemed to mock him.

"Sir! I've got something here!" A sailor at a communications console inside the Combat Command Center of the *Blue Ridge* remained calm, although it took everything he had to keep from standing up and shouting. The chief petty officer in charge and the CCC officer of the watch moved to the console and plugged in their headsets.

"What's up, Armstrong?" asked the lieutenant.

"We're picking up a repeater sat phone signal, sir. Call sign is Long Rifle."

The bosun tapped a computer to scroll a list of recent call signs. "That's Gunny Swanson from the rescue mission!"

"I've got it." Lieutenant David Garvey immediately

depressed his TALK key. "Long Rifle . . . *Blue Ridge* . . . Do you copy?"

Kyle Swanson gave a thumbs-up sign to General Middleton. "Loud and clear," he responded. "I have a package and need a FedEx pickup."

"What is your address, Long Rifle?" The call was encrypted but was still over an open frequency, which required both parties to use code whenever possible.

"Simple Shackle," Swanson said, then read off a line of numbers in an encoded format specified in the operational orders. The Simple Shackle was a 1-to-10 box grid, horizontal and vertical, that could be interpreted only if the recipient had a similar code sheet. The little code in 100 squares repeats hashed versions of the alphabet. Any specific letter might appear in three or four different boxes that are used at random. "THE" might read 1–12–16 on first use, but 36–98–53 the next time. As an added safeguard, it would change at specified times. Even computers as powerful as those at the National Security Agency would have to put in some time to break it.

"How long can our driver expect you to remain at that address?"

"No more than a few hours, then we are going to see *March of the Penguins*." The brevity code, also from the original ops order, specified that "penguins" meant south.

"Roger on the *March*. Come back in sixty mikes to confirm pickup time." Garvey unplugged. "Chief, I'm going up to see the captain. Keep two men on that frequency at all times."

"Aye, aye, sir." Chief Petty Officer Dwight Marshall

made the personnel arrangements. When Garvey was gone, he switched to a private internal net.

A wall telephone rang deep in the stern of the ship. "Yes?" answered a deep voice.

"Double-Oh. We just picked up traffic from your boy Gunny Swanson. He's coming out with a package. I think you need to be in on this. I'll pass the word for a five-man protective detail to bring you up to meet with the MEU XO." Marshall clicked off, found a Marine, and passed along the instructions. A team saddled up in full combat gear, locked and loaded, and headed down the ladders to escort Dawkins to the CCC. The executive officer of the Marine Expeditionary United would want his top hand in on planning whatever happened next, and no NCIS civilian investigators would be allowed to interfere.

Dawkins pulled on his boots. He had been comfortably whiling away the hours in a secluded area carved out deep belowdecks by creative sailors. It had a locked door, a television set with a lot of interesting videos, access to a nearby head with a toilet and a shower, a comfortable bunk, a tattered easy chair, a bunch of books and magazines ranging from *Playboy* to *Sports Illustrated* to *Vogue*, and shelves holding clean sheets. On a table was a bowl with fruit and candy bars gathered from the mess tables and the ship's store. He had taken refuge in perhaps the most pleasant place on the entire ship, a hidden love nest to which boy and girl sailors could retreat, grossly violate naval regulations, and fuck like rabbits.

53

Jack Shepherd of CNN was having an early pint of beer in a Fleet Street pub with a leggy intern from the London office of the Cable News Network. Chrissie Rogers was blond and busty, a twenty-two-year-old journalism school graduate from Nebraska, and she was enchanted with every word the rugged, veteran foreign correspondent bestowed on her in the privacy of a small booth. He was wondering whether to get her in bed before or after an expense-account dinner. The cell phone clipped to his belt chimed and vibrated. He reluctantly answered: "Shepherd."

"Ah, my friend Jack Shepherd of CNN. This is your friend from Basra." The unmistakable voice of the Rebel Sheikh was smooth. Jack slid out of the booth and walked outside for privacy.

"Good afternoon, sir. How may I help you?" No use wasting time with idle chatter. If the Rebel Sheikh called, it was for a reason.

"I am sorry to interrupt your afternoon, but I have something for you." There was a pause. "This is on deep background, of course. My name and position cannot be used."

"No problem, sir, and you're not interrupting. I'm always on duty. What are we talking about?"

A gentle laugh. "Impatient Americans. Well, the kidnapped General Middleton of the Marine Corps has escaped his captors, with the assistance of a Marine sniper who survived the crash of the helicopters, a man named Kyle Swanson. The Syrian Army and intelligence forces have launched a wide search to find both of them."

"Can I go with this, sir?"

"Oh, absolutely, Jack, providing you leave me out of your report. I just received a briefing from Syria. The manhunt is going on even as we are speaking, so you should hurry and get this on the air. Come see me again sometime, Jack." The Rebel Sheikh gave that little laugh again. "And I really do apologize for interrupting your meeting with the lovely Ms. Rogers."

By using Chrissie's name, the Rebel Sheikh was telling the correspondent that he was being watched. Jack Shepherd didn't care. He wasn't in the television news business to be invisible. He returned to the table, tossed down the rest of his pint, and laid down some money for the drinks. "Come on, Chrissie. Back to the office. Time to do some work."

A woman in Amman, Jordan, was calling a similar alert to the al Jazeera correspondent in his hotel room office.

It took the networks about an hour to prepare the story in their home offices, Atlanta for CNN and Doha for al Jazeera. Both slammed *Special Report* logos on their screens and broadcast the reports to millions of viewers. The twenty-four-hour cable news shows, already awash with Red Alert terrorism stories, would soon launch squadrons of talking-head commentators to argue with each other about just how soon war would break out between the United States and Syria.

The tent outside of Sa'ahn was an oven, and steamy mirages wiggled in the distance. Al-Shoum was sweaty, tired, and irritable from having been up all night. A folding cot was set up in one corner, and he lay down to catch a nap, with strict orders to be awakened if anything happened. He was not the one out there doing the searching, and his staff was running the map and radios, so there was nothing else he could do but wait. He could do that while sleeping. He checked for Logan and saw all three of the mercenaries lounging in the open bay of the helicopter, listening to music. Logan was smoking a cigarette. They were men bred for battle, dogs of war relaxing without a care while waiting to be unleashed. He looked at his wristwatch. Two o'clock. He would sleep no more than two hours.

General Hank Turner and Colonel Ralph Sims were asleep in the comfortable cabin of the little Gulfstream II-SP as it swept above the snowy peaks of the Rocky Mountains on its long flight from Alaska. Turner was dreaming of the moment when his big Boeing disappeared in a blast of flame. General Pete Brady turned the Gulfstream's controls over to his copilot and made his way down the aisle.

"Wake up, boys," he said, standing straight and stretching. "Shit's hitting the fan." He plopped down across from them as the two Marines blinked themselves awake and straightened in their seats.

Turner was instantly awake, but gave a shake of the head to clear it. *I should have been on that plane!* "What's going on, Pete?" Turner wanted to know. "Another attack?"

"Nope. Pentagon just relayed a call to you. Gunny Swanson contacted your *Blue Ridge* boat over a sat link. Apparently Middleton is with him. Swanson gave coordinates not too far from the Jordanian-Syrian border, so the wheels are turning to find some way to get them out of there."

"What do we have out there that can be deployed in a hurry, Ralph?" Turner stared hard at the MEU colonel. Sims had seen that battle stare from Hank Turner before. The man was getting ready for a fight.

"The Force Recon TRAP team is off the board because of the accident in the desert, but we wouldn't want to be stealthy this time anyway. I recommend sending in two full platoons, aboard several helicopters, with Cobra attack helicopters on guard and appropriate cover by fast-movers up top. Lay a secure box all around Middleton and the gunny, with nothing going in or out except us."

"How long would it take?"

Sims recalled the premission briefing and did some silent calculations. "Depending on where the ships are, sir, they should be able to launch within an hour of getting the green light, since they know the coordinates. Less than an hour flying time in, no more than fifteen minutes on the ground, and then get back home."

Turner took out his fountain pen again and scribbled a note. He turned to Pete Brady. "Is Air Force One back in Washington yet?"

"No, sir. I just checked. They are over Arkansas."

"Okay. I need to talk to the President directly and divert Air Force One back toward us. Find me a secure air force base where they can put down with tight security and we can meet them as soon as possible."

"Got it," said Brady. "What else?"

Turner handed him the note he had written. "Transmit this to the Fleet and the MEU, with a confidential copy to the President, encrypted and for his eyes only. Launch the rescue immediately!"

Brady whistled. "Wow. Hank, you're taking a big chance here. You need some big-league paperwork to do this."

"Fuck it. We don't have the time. I'm sending the team in VOCO, on the Verbal Orders of the Commander. This comes straight from me, damn it. After you send it, have my staff alert the other chiefs."

Colonel Sims waited for Brady to step into the Gulfstream's communications suite. "Good on ya, sir."

"Tired of all this fucking around, Ralph. I'm not going to lose those two brave men. When you wear four stars, sometimes you have to remember that you're a war-fighter, not a politician. Despite their bluster, the Syrians don't want a piece of us. So we kick ass first and beg forgiveness later."

The Vice President was unhappy. All of the important players on the National Security Council were present for the emergency meeting except for three. "The President is flying back from California and should be landing momentarily, and I will brief him when he arrives at the White House," he told the others. "General Turner is also flying back. That leaves us with an unexplained empty chair. Mr. Shafer, where is Mr. Buchanan?"

Sam Shafer rose and tugged at the hem of his jacket. "I don't know, sir. He is not in his office."

The Vice President's eyes seemed to smolder behind his rimless glasses. "Have you seen him at all today? Is he not aware that we're dealing with terrorist attacks on American soil, a major international crisis, and a hostile media that is going berserk with war talk?"

"Yes, sir. I spoke briefly with Mr. Buchanan at his desk at five o'clock this morning. As usual, he was going through the briefing papers. When I checked at six, he was gone, and I assumed he was having some breakfast in the mess or at a meeting. I haven't seen him since."

The Vice President growled, "Then go find him! I want him in that chair in five minutes. Do I make myself clear?"

"Yes, sir." Sam Shafer gulped, then hurried from the room.

"We will continue without Buchanan," said the Vice President. "State, you said you have something?"

The Secretary of State pulled her briefing folder close. "The Syrians are panicking. With the media carrying the story around the world, they apparently realize the error of their ways. Our Red Alert, the assassination of the Jordanian ambassador, the attack in Alaska, and the kidnapping of General Middleton probably was not the way they hoped things were going to come down. It's a major embarrassment, even for a state that sponsors terrorism. With our military ramping up for a hard response, Damascus wants to cut a deal and get out of trouble."

"What do they have in mind?"

"They will direct their military to help find and protect Middleton and the Marine who rescued him, and allow us to come pick them up without incident. They blame the whole episode on what they call foreign rogue extremists."

"What do they get in return?"

"No war, and a public statement of appreciation for their assistance."

The Vice President jotted the terms on his legal pad. "Sounds good to me. Any objections?" No one opposed the idea. "I will pass our recommendation along to the President. State, you tell the Syrians that if our men are harmed in any way, if this is a trap, the price for such treachery will be very steep indeed."

Murmurs of agreement around the table. "That's it, then. Get back to work." As he walked back to his office, he put his hand on the elbow of the chief of his Secret Service protective detail and drew him close. "Jim. I want you boys to find Gerald Buchanan and fetch him to me as soon as possible."

"Sorry, sir, that's not our job description."

"Oh, hell, Jim, I know that," said the Vice President. "You're a bright boy. You'll think of something. Just get his fat butt in here."

If Buchanan thinks I'm going to stick around and take this rap by myself, he's crazy. Sam Shafer went to the front hall, the thick soles of his polished shoes beating a tattoo on the marble, and signed out at the Secret Service desk. Then he walked down the long driveway and out the front gate of the White House, trying not to run, and cut across the open plaza into downtown Washington. Within two blocks, he hailed a taxi. "Reagan National," he told the driver.

As the cab crossed the Potomac, Shafer dialed his cell phone and Gordon Gates answered on the first ring. "He's gone," Shafer said.

"I expected it. Buchanan has the balls of a hamster," Gates replied. "You get on up to New York like we talked about and someone will meet your plane. Welcome to the Sharks, Sam."

54

An armed perimeter of guards surrounded Air Force One as it stood alone on the tarmac of Minot Air Force Base in North Dakota at five o'clock in the morning. The President of the United States was as safe there as if he had been in a reinforced bunker two hundred feet underground. The base was isolated ten miles from the town of Minot, not far from the Canadian border, and even under normal conditions, security was always tight there. A hundred and fifty Minuteman ICBM missiles were buried in silos around the home base of the 5th Bomb Wing and the 91st Space Wing. Many of Minot's B52H bombers carrying Air Launched Cruise Missiles were in the air. They were just drops in the bucket of what the President could throw at Syria if he decided to do so.

He was a quiet, thoughtful man, but during his three years in office, his dark hair had gone gray because of situations just like this. He read the note that General Henry Turner, the chairman of the Joint Chiefs of Staff, had given him. The words THE WHITE HOUSE were printed in blue across the top. Turner and a marine colonel who looked like he had been up all night sat in big chairs across from the desk in the plane's spacious office. "I did not order this," the President said. "This is the first time I have seen this extraordinary piece of paper."

"Never thought you did order it, Mr. President," answered Turner. "That's why I interrupted your itinerary to personally bring it to you. That is, however, Gerald Buchanan's name scrawled on the bottom."

The President passed the note to several other key people in the cabin. His chief of staff asked, "Why would he do this, General?"

Turner rubbed his hands together in thought. "Colonel Sims and I have been pondering the same thing. The kidnapping of General Middleton had to have some motive, and the most obvious one was probably to trigger a confrontation between us and Syria, which happened. This note indicates a deeper motive, so the confrontation might just have been cover. He says plain as day that if Middleton cannot be rescued, he should be killed. Why? We had no reason to think that the Force Recon team would not be successful. They ran into bad luck, that's all, or otherwise Middleton would be out of Syria by now. So why send one of the best snipers in the Marine Corps to make sure the general was dead? My conclusion is that Mr. Buchanan knew the rescue was doomed to failure anyway. Why . . . and how?"

The President tilted far back in his chair and crossed his arms. "Colonel Sims, do you think our rescue attempt was compromised?"

"Yes, sir. We had a good plan, we had good men, and the odds were overwhelmingly in our favor to be successful. We practice it all the time and use the same package to pick up downed pilots. I agree with

General Turner. It looks like Mr. Buchanan had advance information that the mission was going to run into trouble."

"It's difficult to swallow. I've known Gerry Buchanan for years. He has always been rock-solid in giving me accurate advice. This just makes no sense."

The chief of staff spoke again: "Gerry is the only person who can answer these questions, Mr. President. Personal friendships aside, I suggest that we have him detained and questioned."

"The Vice President told me a little while ago that he has given a similar order. Buchanan did not show up for the National Security Council meeting." The President, who had been a university president before going into the Senate and then into the White House, was known for his logical and scholarly mind, and always seemed a half-step ahead of everybody else. "Let's put it into context. Buchanan told me to ratchet up the alert status, and now I can no longer believe his counsel, nor his actions. Although we have had attacks on our soil, they have not been traced to any terrorists. I think the red alert was a diversion, part of some larger plan. The first thing we need do is loosen the tension beyond our borders. And we take the Syrian deal to help get Middleton released unharmed."

Turner looked surprised. He had not heard of any deal.

"That offer came in a little while ago, Hank. I got the call about the time you were landing. Good news on that, at least. State is working out the details. Now your rescue team can go in without guns blazing. I think the Syrian crisis has passed, thank the Lord. Now we are going to find out what, and who, is behind all of this."

"Awwright!" drawled Turner. Colonel Sims relaxed for the first time since the original mission briefing. It was almost over.

There was only one woman in the cabin, and the President locked his eyes on Senator Ruth Hazel Reed. "Well, Senator, it looks like General Middleton will be back in time for your committee hearing on the military privatization bill next week after all."

She had flown by corporate jet to her hometown of San Diego to bask in the President's popularity there and gather campaign donations, then joined him on Air Force One for the return trip to Washington. "Yes, Mr. President," she said. "I did not want to be without his expertise. This is wonderful news. He will need time to recover from his terrible ordeal, so I will postpone that hearing for a while." She glanced at General Turner, who smirked.

The President stood up and extended his hand to Ralph Sims. "Colonel, you did a courageous thing to get this out in the open. You are not under arrest or suspicion of any wrongdoing whatsoever. Go over to the visiting officers' quarters and get some sleep, and a plane will be waiting to take you back to the MEU tomorrow. Good job."

Then he shook the hand of General Turner. "Hank, see if you can still make that meeting in Beijing. We can handle the rest of this thing from here." He looked around the room. "Thank you all very much for your help during this crisis. Now if you will excuse us, I would like a private moment with Senator Reed."

Ten minutes later, Ruth Hazel Reed hurried down the stairs of Air Force One. The master sergeant guarding the bottom of the stairway saw that her cheeks were bright red. As she ducked into a waiting staff car, she was dabbing her eyes with a tissue.

55

It was a little before four o'clock in the afternoon when an aide awakened Yousif al-Shoum with a tap on his shoulder. "General, you have a call from Damascus," he said. Al-Shoum blinked himself awake, feeling that the late-afternoon heat had grown intense. "I'm coming," he responded, pouring some bottled water into a cupped palm and rubbing it across his face. The aide handed him a headset with a microphone.

"This is al-Shoum," he said, and a distant voice replied, quiet, pleasant, diplomatic. The aide watched al-Shoum's jaw tighten and the dark eyes burn. "This is official?" he asked with sharpness. "Where does the order come from?" The aide did not dare move closer. "This is insane! At least let me continue the search until nightfall. We're sure to capture them!" Another pause, and deep breathing, al-Shoum's hands clasping both muffs of the headset hard, pressing them close to his head. "Yes. Of course. Very well. I acknowledge the order."

Al-Shoum slipped off the headset and tossed it to the radio operator, then looked at the map on the table. Still more red pins that signified ... *Nothing!* Damascus had decided without his advice to cooperate with the

Americans! The general and the sniper were not to be harmed! American military troops were to be allowed into Syria to pick them up! The map showed him nothing with which he could call back and demand that the orders be changed. He stalked from the tent without a word.

Putting on his sunglasses, he marched to the helicopter and noticed that two more mercenaries had arrived, a German and an Asian who had been one of the famous Nepalese Gurkha soldiers. Of the four men who were surrounding Logan, al-Shoum judged the small Asian fighter with the scarred face and the grim mouth and the huge curved *khukuri* knife hanging from his belt to be the most dangerous. Logan turned to meet him, holding a boxy object in one hand.

"A significant change of plan, I fear, Mr. Logan," said al-Shoum. "Radical, really. My government has been in direct diplomatic contact with the United States, and once again the diplomats have reached an agreement without consulting the soldiers in the field. My new orders are still to find the missing American Marines, but they are to be treated as guests and provided with protection until they can be evacuated." He spread his hands, palms up. "Nothing I could do."

An odd, twisting smile creased Logan's weathered face. The two men walked away from the others. "That's the government line. Do *you* still want these guys?"

"Yes, Mr. Logan, I want to kill them both. That sniper has made me look like a fool, and I cannot forgive that. This failure may cost me my career." He thrust his chin out toward the endless flat countryside. "We have spent a fruitless day on the hunt, with hundreds of men and dozens of helicopters and vehicles. They are obviously out there somewhere, but time has run out for me. My personal desires must now take second place to direct orders from my government. Even if I find them, I cannot kill them."

Logan understood the undercurrent of the conversation. "Right. You can't kill them. But did your orders say anything about *us* doing it? I want them, too. Real bad." He pointed a thumb over to where the other mercenaries were loading into the helicopter and getting it ready for liftoff.

"Let me show you something," said al-Shoum, and brought Logan under the tent. After clearing everyone else out, he had the mercenary look at the map littered with red stick pins. "Each of those is a white Toyota truck. We have no idea where the men are."

"Okay. From that, I see only that you have a bunch of Toyota trucks in Syria." Logan handed him a piece of paper. "Now look up these coordinates: north 32 degrees, 45 minutes, and east 36 degrees, 25 minutes." Al-Shoum traced the map grid with his finger and drew a circle with a black marker at a point midway between Dar'a and As Suwayda.

"Why this particular location?"

"That's them, General! That's exactly where they are! These boys who came over from Israel brought a GPS locator, and our home office in the States gave them the frequency for a signal being used by the sniper. So right now, they are sitting quiet in that little circle, waiting for night to fall. Or waiting for someone to show up and blow them away. So can we go get 'em?"

"I will not disobey my orders," said al-Shoum, hands

on hips, staring at the American, loud enough for most of his staff to overhear. Then, much more quietly, he said, "I will shift my searchers away from those coordinates. If my people actually see the Marines, I will have no choice but to protect them."

"So you have no problem if I fire up the helo and haul ass down there and do what needs to be done, then go away so your boys can come in and make the big discovery of the dead bodies?"

"The two Americans are indeed in hostile territory, and perhaps might die at the hands of villagers who are outraged by the sudden appearance of Crusader forces in their midst. Just be aware that the Americans will soon be sending in another rescue team, this time with my government's permission and, of course, my utmost personal cooperation."

Al-Shoum had another idea flash into his head. "Wait just another moment. Perhaps all is not lost," he told Logan, and scribbled a note in Arabic. He gave it to the mercenary. "Plant this on the bodies. It will be evidence that the deaths were the work of the Holy Scimitar of Allah, the militia group of the Rebel Sheikh. I need to settle a score with that scoundrel in Basra, so let us kill several birds with a single rock. He will have to answer for the slayings of the two Marines, and I will appear as a hero who did everything possible to save them. Damascus will be pleased."

Logan tucked the note into a pocket. "How long before the rescue team arrives?"

"I don't know exactly, but I'm giving you a one-hour head start, Mr. Logan. You must do it within that time, before anyone notices that I am keeping search parties out of the area. Then you and your men must vanish. I never want to see or hear from you again, and if I do, you will pay in full for killing that child in Sa'ahn."

He raised his voice for the benefit of his staff, pointed toward the helicopter, and barked at Logan, "I am through with you worthless dogs. Get out of my country!"

"Color me gone," Logan said, turning and trotting toward the helicopter. He circled an index finger to the pilot to get the rotor turning.

56

General Bradley Middleton was testy. He and Swanson were free! The Gunny had been in intermittent communication via the satellite phone with the MEU, and had learned that the manhunt was over. Syria had agreed to settle things peacefully rather than have the United States bear down on them over something that Damascus had not been too keen about in the first place. The pickup was going to be unopposed, and Swanson had worked out a landing zone about ten kilometers to the south. Then the sniper went back to sleep, leaving the general on watch and ignoring Middleton's demand to move out.

"We go when I say go, General," Swanson had told him. "There's no guarantee that every Syrian soldier in this region has gotten the word not to open fire on us. I want to arrive at the LZ just before our choppers get there so we're not standing out in the open with our thumbs up our asses, just asking to be shot."

At least it wasn't very hot in the small tunnel in which they were parked, since it was shielded by the sun and cooler because of the foot of barely moving water. Middleton shifted the AK-47, sloshed from one end of the culvert to the other, and crouched behind some of the bushes Swanson had stacked on the left side as a makeshift hide. Traffic had been sporadic along the road, and they had grown familiar with the sounds of an occasional car, truck, or tractor passing overhead. Several helicopters had buzzed in the distance, but there had been no other military presence. A farmer driving a mule cart had taken forever to clatter by.

Middleton took a drink of fresh water and sloshed back toward the other end of the culvert.

"Stop!" Kyle Swanson reached out from the back of the truck and put a hand on Middleton's shoulder. He was sitting up, wide awake. "Hear that?" The sniper leaped from the truck bed with Excalibur in his right hand. "Incoming Huey."

Middleton had not heard anything at all, but now picked up the signature *whomp-whomp* of a Huey helicopter's blades. "Probably just following the road to see if he can spot any signs."

Kyle was already at the far end of the culvert, kneeling behind the bushes. "No, sir. He's too low and has been flying straight for the last few minutes, not running a grid search or following the turns in the road or checking any intersections. That's bad news."

"So what? Maybe he's just supposed to give us a ride to the pickup LZ." Middleton regretted saying that the moment the words left his mouth, and Swanson ignored him. "Yeah. That was stupid."

Victor Logan was leaning forward between the two men flying the Huey, calling out the GPS coordinates as the helicopter ran through the sky about a hundred feet above the deck. A strong wind whipped through the open side doors. He saw nothing moving down on the ground.

"Okay," he said into his microphone when the coordinates were exact. "Cut your speed and start making wide circles to the left. Look sharp." The clattering helicopter bent into a left turn as Logan made a final check of the controls he would use to fire the minigun pods mounted on each side of the chopper.

Relying on the GPS coordinates were helpful only to a point. Ten-digit coordinates were precise to within about a meter, but from an unsteady and moving airborne platform like the Huey, identifying that specific meter was virtually impossible. The most they could hope to pinpoint was a distance that would be about two football fields square. If they saw something, the chopper would have to stop, turn around, and go back to find the point where the crew might have spotted something suspicious. Lining up a shot was easy; finding the target was hard.

The terrain was flat and cut into rectangles of irrigated green fields, which told Logan there were a lot of ditches down there in which a Special Forces operator could hide. But Middleton was not an operator, was out of shape, and was injured. That should provide an edge that would allow Logan to find them.

"Hey, Logan," called out the Russky co-pilot. "We're here. Where are they? You sure you plugged in the right numbers?"

"Yeah, asshole, I'm sure I plugged in the right numbers. Just fly this crate and keep looking." *Where the fuck are you, Sniper?*

After completing two wide circles, Logan decided to

look into some of the bigger ditch lines. "There's a culvert at about two o'clock. Let's check it out."

As soon as he heard the pitch change in the blades, Swanson called over his shoulder, "Get in the truck and start it up, General. We're going to have to move fast."

Middleton argued, "I can help you. I'll spot for you. The two of us would put out more firepower."

"No! Damn it! Get in the goddam truck! You're just one more thing I have to think about!"

Swanson ducked deeper behind the brush hide. Stealth was his best weapon, being able to spot the enemy before being seen. The pitch of the rotor blades changed again, to a *THUD-THUD-THUD* sound that indicated that the helo was coming to a hover. If it was going to just hang up there, edging lower and lower, whoever was inside eventually would see the truck.

Kyle was feeling the hard downdraft as the blades pushed churning air against the ground and the ditch funneled the wind into the tunnel. He kept one hand on some of the bushes, but the others blew away, and he was partially exposed.

The helicopter was about thirty yards away from the mouth of the culvert, and about seventy yards in the air, in a hover and beginning a slow 360-degree spin to scan the entire area. The right side was toward him, and he saw the miniguns. *If they open up with those, we're cooked.*

Swanson let go of the other bush and brought Excalibur to his shoulder as he leaned his left side against the concrete curve of the underpass to steady himself. The scope was at his eye by the time the canopy of the helicopter swung around to face him, the chopper spinning to its left. He saw the pilot in the left seat and the co-pilot on the right and someone else between them, probably to fire the machine guns.

"Look!" the Russian yelled over the radio and pointed his finger. "There they are!"

Victor Logan leaned forward a bit more and could see one man in a tunnel beneath the road. It was the sniper, and he already had his long rifle up and pointed at the helicopter. "Shit!" he said, reaching out to fire the miniguns, knowing it was too late.

Kyle waited to squeeze the trigger until the last possible moment in a contest of nerves, speed, and physics. The co-pilot was clear and large in Excalibur's scope, which already had glowed with the blue firing stripe, but he wanted the armor-piercing .50-caliber bullet to do more than just take out one guy. When the angle was just right, he finished the shot.

The big bullet smashed through the Plexiglas canopy, caught the Russian under the chin, and tore off the back of his head. Then it continued upward through the roof of the helicopter and into the complex housing of gears and rods that controlled the rotors.

Kyle held the scope on the helo, jacked in another round, and fired again, punching out another chunk of the canopy. The bullet ricocheted through the control panel. He managed to fire a third round before the pilot was able to snatch the nose back around to the right and break away, trying to get out of the line of fire and gain some altitude. Kyle emptied the rest of the clip at the retreating, wobbling bird.

"I'm losing rotor control!" shouted the South African pilot as the helo coughed and the controls stiffened. A loud ripping noise came from overhead, where the rotor gears were grinding themselves apart, and fire broke out in the cockpit.

He wrestled with the aircraft, trying to push it from hover to full power and then bleed off speed for landing. The Huey wasn't responding, and began tilting on its own.

"We're going in!" he screamed, and covered his face with his arms.

Victor Logan, strapped into a harness that had allowed him free movement, was sprawled on his back. He grabbed the metal struts of seats along the back of the cabin, pushing his feet hard against the bulkhead separating the front compartment just as the helicopter smashed nose-first into a green and soggy field. He blacked out.

Swanson was running to the truck before the helicopter crashed 400 yards away. Middleton had cranked it, left it in neutral, opened the driver's door, and slid across to the passenger side, where he buckled his seat belt and pointed his Kalashnikov out the window.

The sniper piled in behind the wheel, pushed Excalibur over to the general, and tossed him a packet of ammo from his web gear. "Reload!"

Kyle jammed the truck into low gear and mashed the accelerator to the floor. The Toyota's powerful engine roared, the truck skidded a bit in the muck of the culvert and then the big tires took hold, and they crashed out into the daylight, throwing up a wave of water on each side. A curtain of spray coated the windshield. Swanson saw the downed chopper, but that was no longer a threat, so he twisted the steering wheel violently to the right and the truck growled up the embankment and skidded onto the paved road.

"Where are we going?" yelled the general as he pushed five .50-caliber bullets into a magazine and loaded one more into the raceway.

"Away from here! Toward the LZ." He brought the truck under control and looked back in the mirror. Two figures had crawled from the wreckage of the helicopter. "They had us dead to rights back there, General. Bastards knew exactly where we were."

Middleton propped Excalibur between them. "An old chopper like that with no markings. Must have been mercs."

Kyle left the truck in four-wheel drive as they sped along the pavement because he might have to go off-road again at any time. He agreed with Middleton. "Yeah, I'd bet on the Frankensteins, too. And I'll also bet there are more of them converging toward us."

"Want me to call the Fleet and get some fast-movers in here?" Middleton reached for the sat phone.

"No, don't do that. We would have to give a precise location, and it could be picked up by the bad guys. Not much time before the scheduled pickup anyway, so we have to play hide and seek until then."

"Where?"

"Beats me, pardner," Swanson said with a cowboy twang. "I'm a stranger in these parts."

Middleton threw back his head and laughed.

57

"The plan is not yet finished, Ruth Hazel. There are still things we can do." Gordon Gates IV had lost none of his silkiness, none of his controlled modulation. He might well have been discussing a high school football game.

Senator Reed did not see it that way. "It is for me, Gordon. It is not every day that I, me, myself, personally am threatened by the President of the United States of America. It was not pleasant."

They were in the privacy of the manicured flower garden behind Gates's holiday home in Aspen, Colorado. He talked while scraping the honed blade of a fighting knife back and forth across a sharpening stone. "He's bluffing. If he had anything, you would be in custody by now and not making this visit."

"Why do you think the game isn't over?"

"You don't need to know that." Stroke, stroke the blade, a comforting feel in the routine for a man very familiar with how to use a knife. "Just remember that Middleton and the sniper have not yet been rescued. A fatal accident may befall them before they are."

"What do I do, then? Gerald Buchanan will name both of us as accomplices when he is subpoenaed, just to save his own skin. He is a stupid man and we were mistaken to bring him in on this."

"Leave Gerald up to me. He poses neither of us any threat, although he may think otherwise. He really was stupid, wasn't he? An arrogant and stupid man. We should have found someone else."

Reed's voice had a quaver in it as she recalled the chewing-out on Air Force One. "The President was absolutely thunderous. He *yelled* at me! I never saw him show anger like that."

"What did he say?"

"The short version is that there will be a full investigation by the attorney general, and the President does not care who gets taken down. Also, the privatization bill is dead because they figure the Middleton kidnapping was part of a plan to keep him from testifying. The President swore that he would hold a national press conference to veto it should the bill come before him."

That stopped Gates in his tracks. "Interesting." He sharpened his knife and decided to abort Operation Premier. The kiddies could go safely to the latest animated blockbuster this weekend. No use pissing off the Prez even more by blowing up a couple of multiplexes. The guy had brains, but he would also leave office someday, and Gates Global would still be around, bigger than ever. "Well, that just means we put it off for a couple of years and try again. Try to get someone in the Oval Office who will be friendlier to the business community and private enterprise. Someone like you, Senator. It's the job you wanted, isn't it?"

Ruth Hazel closed her political career in that beautiful yard filled with blooming flowers. "No longer. I'll leave at the end of the year when my term is up, go home to California, and undertake a very low-profile life. The choice between my house in Del Mar and prison is a pretty easy one."

"Have you left any loose ends, anything with my name attached?"

"Not a one, Gordon. There is nothing in my files or notes or on my computer that mentions you in any questionable fashion whatsoever. I never had a whispered conversation with a lover, nor a private chat with an aide about our plans." She looked him directly in the eyes. "Even if I have to go on trial for something, I would never mention you. I've always understood that you would have me killed by a Shark Team if I put you in jeopardy."

"Now that's where you are wrong, my dear." Gates grinned at her, then whirled and threw the knife with force; it spun, end over end, and the point stuck deep into the trunk of a tree ten feet away. "It would not be a Shark Team. I would do it myself." He walked to the tree, pulled the blade free, and resumed sharpening it. "We do understand each other, then?"

"Oh, yes. Quite," she said. She reached into her shoulder bag for a tissue, and let her hand brush against the 9 mm pistol she had begun to carry. *I'll be waiting.*

58

They sped south down the highway, to the point where it intersected with a major east–west road. An unfenced area of tired old cars, wrecks, and abandoned mechanical devices and farming equipment was off to one side, a mechanical graveyard that had probably begun many years ago with someone's car breaking down on the road and being pushed to the side and abandoned. It had become a tangle of junk that spread over about ten acres, and Swanson steered into it, driving around until he found a crumbled old Mercedes cargo van that had rolled over in an accident and been hauled to the junk pile to rust in the punishing sun and wind.

Swanson stopped the Toyota next to the wrecked vehicle. "End of the line, General," he said. "We hump the rest of the way to the LZ, a few more kilometers."

"Why not just drive?" Middleton was out of the truck.

Swanson emptied his pack and picked out only a few things for them to carry. Water, more ammo, a few grenades, smoke grenades, and the sat phone. Each of them had a rifle, and he kept Excalibur over his shoulder and gave Middleton the pistol. It was time to lighten the load for the final dash, and if something would not fit on his web gear, he would leave it behind. When the pack was empty, he reloaded the computers in it, along with the sat phone, and gave it to the general to carry. "They will be looking for the truck now in a pretty narrow area, so we have to dump it and stay off the road."

Kyle had a drink of water and moved out, heading into the fields, and General Middleton followed. Swanson figured they were only about three kilometers from the landing zone, but could not go directly to it. He was considering how to circle wide around and come in from the side or the rear while keeping the sun behind him, when he found a small footpath that had been pounded out by generations of goats, sheep, and other animals and their keepers. *Probably leads to water.* "We're pretty near a population center now, so keep a sharp eye out for people moving about. We don't want to be seen."

One step at a time, he led them into the field and moved parallel to the path so as to leave no bootprints. The monotony of taking the slow steps helped him consider how the helicopter knew where to find them. There had been a Syrian army search going on, but that chopper flew in straight and was carrying mercs, and the more he thought about it, the more Kyle believed the Frankensteins knew where he was. He had to assume that someone had sold them out, just as the Force Recon rescue mission had been compromised.

He stopped, and Middleton stepped closer. They had walked about two miles from the junkyard, first through the fields and then tracking near the dirt path, which had narrowed as it went upward into irregular terrain when the cultivated area gave way to wrinkles of land that folded into distant hills. "We'll set up over there," he said, pointing to the first low rise.

A few minutes later, they reached the crest of the initial slope and Kyle got busy digging a hole for them while Middleton gathered bushes and stuck them into the ground in front of the hide. Swanson left Middleton laying there with the binos while he explored higher up the hill. Right behind their position, the little path ducked into a flat pocket of land that skirted a slightly higher hill. Kyle climbed it in five long steps, liked what he saw, and did some more digging, arranging a little wall of rocks and some brushwork, then came back down. He was careful this time to leave plenty of bootprints leading to the hide.

Then he went back off the trail and explored both sides of a small canyon that opened before him, and found a field of large rocks and boulders. He established a third hide there.

He trotted back to the original position. Both he and Middleton drank some more water, then lay side by side while they scanned the country they had crossed, Middleton with the binocs and Swanson with the scope of Excalibur, while Kyle explained the next step of the escape and evasion plan.

They saw it about the same time: a triangular dust trail rising from the road, kicked up by a fast-moving vehicle they recognized as the familiar shape of a Humvee. "Here they come," said Middleton. "With any luck, they'll stop and search the junkyard, or go highballing right on by us."

"Not a chance," Swanson replied. "Get on the horn and tell the MEU to come get us right now."

Victor Logan was in the passenger seat of the Humvee, with a map on his lap and the GPS locator box between his knees. He was sore all over from the crash, and his spine flared with so much pain that he believed he must have cracked something. At least he was better off than that Russky, who was shot in the face, and the pilot, who had two broken arms. The mercenary ignored his body and studied the readout. The numbers had been flashing steadily when the sniper was on the move, but had remained still now for more than a minute. Logan put a checkpoint on the map.

The big German was expertly handling the Humvee and the Gurkha was in the back seat, relaxed. Neither said anything. Logan saw that the road was flat and empty and straight, with some sort of clutter that looked like a stack of junk coming up on the right side in about a mile at an intersection. He located the crossroads on the map, then drew a line from his position on the road to the coordinates on the GPS. "Turn here," he told the German, and pointed off to the left at about a forty-five-degree angle.

The driver did not remove his foot from the gas pedal and the Humvee went slashing into the field, the big wheels crushing a path through the cultivated plants.

"Damn!" Middleton exclaimed as the Humvee peeled away from the road. It had not even gotten to the junkyard, much less searched it. Instead, the vehicle was speeding straight for them.

"Yup," Kyle said. "Be ready to move out." He banished everything from his mind except the oncoming Humvee, and let time slow down on his internal clock as he took slow, deep breaths, never taking his eye from the scope. He let Excalibur do the math for a higher-to-lower elevation at two hundred yards.

The Humvee closed to three hundred yards, then two-fifty, and stopped.

Swanson released the scope to automatic range-finding. "That's fuckin' far enough," he said.

The German got out of the driver's side, and reached back inside to get a weapon. He had pale skin and a shaved head, wore narrow sunglasses, and apparently was chewing gum. The blue stripe flashed and Kyle took him out, the bullet crashing into his exposed left side beneath the arm and rupturing the heart and lungs. The big man was thrown sideways by the impact, dead before he hit the ground.

Middleton opened up with his AK-47 and Victor Logan dove from the other side and rolled into a drainage ditch, while the Gurkha went out the back and jumped to the opposite side of the vehicle. Both disappeared into the thick tangle of cotton plants.

Swanson put two more rounds into the engine block of the Humvee, and his shots were answered by searching, controlled, three-round bursts that pecked around their position. For several minutes, the firefight banged sporadically. Logan and the Gurkha were firing and crawling closer, trying to flank the hide.

A dark speck rose from the field and bounced toward

them. "Grenade!" Kyle yelled and pushed Middleton down hard. The explosion shook the ground, sprayed a cloud of shrapnel, and blew up a cloud of dust and debris. Both attackers were up and running when the detonation occurred, then went back into cover and resumed firing.

"Go now," Kyle said. "You first."

Middleton pushed himself up enough to crawl backward out of the hole, turned, and sprinted up the trail. When he reached the curve, he knelt and called to Swanson. "Come on!" He fired short volleys into the fields.

Logan watched the readout when he saw the figure retreat, and the numbers had stayed steady. That was the general running. The sniper would be next. He took careful aim at a spot halfway between where the grenade had gone off and the spot where he saw the general disappear.

Swanson, with Excalibur in one hand and his M-16 in the other, took off, running low under the general's covering fire. Logan's bullets cracked around him, but he slid safely headfirst into the bushes beside Middleton. Both paused long enough to put more lead into the likely approaches to their old position.

"Drop the pack, take the sat phone, get back to the rocks, and pop a smoke," Swanson said. Middleton did as he was told while Kyle fired a few shots to keep the bad guys' heads down. He did not wait for Middleton to reach the new position. He ran forward, taking a couple of long strides up the little hill to where he had built the other hide, and lobbed the pack into it, then gripped Excalibur around the barrel and flung it into the hole, too. He sprinted back ten meters, dove prone behind some scrub brush, and began to crawl to his ambush point.

The Gurkha and Logan arrived at the original hide about the same time, and were moving fast. The American read the GPS numbers again and saw they were slightly different, but once again still, which indicated the sniper was in a new hide. While the Asian guy covered him, Logan crawled to the curve in the path and snuggled into some rocks and brush. He spotted the position: a hurriedly built hide bordered with rocks and bushes, with bootprints clear in the dirt.

He heard a pop and saw a stream of smoke rising from further up the trail. They had sent up a red smoke grenade, which meant that a rescue team was inbound and was to consider the LZ to be hot. Logan could not worry about that right now. Al-Shoum would be sending helicopters to the smoke, too, and the Marines and the Syrians could figure out what to do when they all arrived about the same time. Should be interesting, Logan thought, but he had to be gone by then.

He used hand signals to communicate with the Gurkha, who was on the ground about twenty feet away, and for the first time saw the man smile. Born in the Himalayas and growing up in the icy shadow of Mount Everest, the small commando felt more comfortable as the fight left the flat land and moved into some hills. His people had lived for centuries among the highest mountains in the world, and the spirit of these little hills spoke to him. He thought he could probably walk to the highest peak without breaking a sweat. Instead of moving directly up the path, the Gurkha crawled around to the left while Logan pumped shots up there to keep the Americans busy. He slung his rifle across his back and unsheathed his long knife with the thick curved blade. By custom, he could not put the *khukuri* away again until it tasted human blood, and he wanted it to taste Marine blood today.

It took him no more than a minute to come around a boulder and be within reach of the sniper's position. The Gurkha flipped a grenade into the secluded hole, ducked away to avoid the explosion, and was immediately up and charging, giving a chilling attack scream and slashing with his *khukuri*. There were no bodies, just the ruins of a long rifle and a backpack that had been shredded by shrapnel. The Gurkha realized his mistake just as Kyle Swanson came over the top, through the smoke, firing his M-16 at point-blank range.

Swanson was exposed during the attack for only a moment, but in that second, Victor Logan fired a quick burst at the shadow he saw moving through the dust of the explosion. Kyle felt bullets punch him in the stomach, and he was spun around, knocked over atop the dead Ghurka.

"*Hoo-ah!*" shouted Logan. "I got you, you bastard! I'm better than you!"

The mercenary felt cold steel at the back of his head. Before he could react, Brad Middleton pulled the trigger of the big pistol, and three shots pulverized the skull and the brains of Victor Logan. "No. You're not," said the general. "You're not even close to being as good as Shake."

Behind him, the sky seemed alive with approaching helicopters.

59

Crisp flight attendants welcomed Gerald Buchanan aboard the American Airlines passenger jet at Miami International and escorted him to a first-class seat aboard Flight 107 to Puerto Rico. After the dankness of Washington, he had been pleasantly blinded by the brilliant sun and the blue Florida skies. *Get used to it.* There were a lot of islands in the Caribbean and he planned to settle on one. He already had a new identity and a list of officials to bribe to avoid arrest and extradition. Marge and the kids would come down in a few months, and they would reestablish a home on a beach somewhere.

He was leaving behind his dream of being the behind-the-scenes king of New America, but felt excitement at moving toward a new dream, one of a long and comfortable life with plenty of money and a big sailboat on the Italian Riviera. He thanked the attendant, gave her a drink request, settled into the soft blue aisle seat, and buckled in. Another attendant was there immediately with an Absolut on ice with a twist of lime.

He looked over at the passenger in the next seat. His luck was already changing for the better, for next to him was an attractive woman in jeans and a loose T-shirt that showed a band of skin around her waist. Dark brown hair was pulled back in a ponytail, and she had kicked off her tennis sneakers to curl up in the spacious seat, working on a laptop computer balanced on the tray table. Graphs and charts and multipage reports danced on the screen as she clicked through whatever her project was. She was drinking a glass of white wine.

"Hi there," he said, taking a sip of his drink. Delicious. "May I ask what you're working on? It seems complicated."

"Oh, just some stuff about fish," she responded with a shy look. Not much makeup, and big wire-rimmed glasses. Intelligent blue eyes looked at him curiously. "Do I know you from somewhere? I mean, aren't you somebody famous on TV?"

Buchanan wanted to tell her everything, to impress her with his name and his title and his extraordinary reach and power. But that was all gone. According to his new passport, he was somebody else, moving toward a tomorrow to find new challenges to test his intellect. "No. Sorry." He extended his hand. "My name is Bob Walsh. I do oil exploration. And who are you?"

"Trish Campbell. Nice to meet you." She sipped her wine and pointed to the computer screen. "I'm a marine biologist up at Woods Hole in Massachusetts, and I've got to get out to the islands to tag some fish we believe are about ready to come off the endangered species list."

He noticed the huge wristwatch, a diver's chronograph with all sorts of dials. "Do you actually go swimming to find them?"

"All the time," she said and brought out a little tube

of lotion, rubbing a dab on her cheeks. "That salt water and hot sun does a job on a girl's skin."

The doors closed, the pilot made his announcements, and she put away her laptop and removed the earplugs to the iPod that hung around her neck and dangled between her full breasts. The diving would explain the tightness of her body. He had no trouble imagining her in a clinging wetsuit with a scuba tank. Flight AA 107 was in the clouds a few minutes later. The seatmates chatted through the first drink, and Buchanan ordered another round.

"Are you going to hunt for oil down here?" asked Trish Campbell.

"No. Just burning off some accumulated holiday time, then I'm off to some other dismal place in the oil patch, possibly up in the North Sea to freeze my ass off," he said. "My family can't be with me for a while. Could I persuade you to have dinner with me tonight?"

She let the question hang as she studied his face, then she gave a warm smile and said, "Maybe."

Buchanan was regaining his confidence, which had been sorely tried by the setbacks of recent days. *That damned Sniper! I hope Gordon takes care of him in a most horrible way.* Of course Trish Campbell would dine with him. By the end of the evening, she would do anything he wanted. They always did.

The announcement came over the loudspeaker that it was permitted to use electronic equipment again, and Trish dug out her laptop and plugged in the iPod. A few clicks of the keyboard and she had MTV rocking, but only she could hear it. On the screen, a sexy girl was humping a boy wearing an oversize basketball jersey and a baseball cap turned to the side.

"What kind of fish are you going to tag?" he asked.

She glanced over and turned down the volume. "What?"

"Sorry. I asked about your job. What kind of fish will you be tagging?"

"Wrong question to ask a marine biologist," Trish laughed. She clicked off MTV and called up a program of big fish swimming slowly too and fro. "Sharks," she replied. "I'm into sharks. I don't want to bore you, but would you like to see something really hot?"

"Sure. I'm really interested." It was always a good play to pretend to be fascinated by a woman's work.

Trish slid the laptop onto his tray table and leaned across to insert the iPod buttons in his ears. He felt the weight of her breast against his forearm, and the clean smell of her perfume. He would gladly put up with MTV and fish for a roll in the hay with her.

"This is really good. You ready? Can you hear it okay?" When he nodded, she said, "Okay, watch and listen very closely," punched in a five-digit sequence, and clicked ENTER.

The fish dissolved slowly into a slide show. Buchanan was stunned as the pictures flipped past. The first was a full view of himself in the front yard of his home. Then came that picture of Marge that they always kept on the baby grand, and a photo of her playing with their dog, Rio. An action photo of fourteen-year-old Lester playing soccer. One of Missy studying in the library at Princeton, followed by a semi-nude picture of Missy on a bed, smiling sleepily at the camera. Photos of his cousin

Florence and her kids, his brother and his family, and his bedridden mother in the assisted living facility.

The last picture was a live camera shot. Gordon Gates sitting at his desk, looking directly at Buchanan.

"Hello, Gerald," he said. "Going somewhere? Don't say anything out loud, just type your replies and look into the little camera button on the side of the computer screen. We will make this quick."

"Gordon? What is this!" he said aloud, but was pinched painfully under the arm by Trish, who pointed at the keyboard. "Type!" she said, and he did. WHAT IS THIS?

"That was a little photo album that we gathered of your entire family." Gates's voice in his ear was cold. "Did you like the one of Missy on the bed? Looks like your little princess just got laid, but never mind that for now. The young woman seated next to you and the big guy across the aisle, who happens to be the air marshal for this flight, are a Shark Team, ole buddy. They are there to make sure you do what you are told."

WHY ARE YOU DOING THIS?

"You bugged out on me, Gerald. Abandoned me to my fate, so to speak. That kind of made me angry, so you have to make things right between us."

I AM NOT GOING TO TELL ANYONE.

"That's for damned sure. By now, Trish should have a typed letter resting on her briefcase. It is a full confession that you were responsible for the entire Middleton kidnapping affair because you wanted to start a war as cover for a political coup in Washington. You realize now that you were wrong, that lives were wasted, that you misused your position and the power of the White

House and besmirched the reputation of the United States. Noble shit like that. It's a good letter: says a lot in two pages. Your new Constitution will also be in the envelope. Sign it."

WE WERE IN THIS TOGETHER.

"After you sign, Trish will give you two little white pills. You will go into the bathroom at the front of the plane and swallow them. Within twenty seconds you will simply go to sleep, feeling no pain, and be dead."

HELL NO FUCK YOU GORDON.

"One second, Gerald, while I rearrange the screen." There was a scramble of the signal and a smaller picture popped into the lower right-hand corner. "There's dear old Mommy, Gerald, sleeping in that fancy old folks' home in Palm Beach. You just visited her about four hours ago, remember? Anyway, I have a nurse standing there taking this picture. You don't sign the paper, Mumsy is going to be put down like a dog with a needle filled with a medicine that will make her last moments hell. She will feel like she is on fire on the inside, and it will take her five long minutes to die. Next on the list will be your little soccer star, Lester, who will fall from a window in a tall building. How could you name a kid Lester, anyway? One by one, until they are all gone. Then the Sharks will kill you anyway."

DON'T PLEASE DON'T DO THIS.

"Sign the fucking letter. Take the fucking pills. Trish will let me know when it's over. You have three minutes before the nurse gives your mother the injection. Terrible way for the old woman to go. Goodbye, Gerald. Do the right thing."

NONONONONONONONO.

The screen returned to the fish show and Trish pulled away the laptop and jerked the iPod buds from his ears. She slapped a letter on the plastic tray and put a pen on top of it. She made a show of clicking a button on her big diver's watch. "Two minutes and fifty-nine seconds . . . two minutes and fifty-eight seconds."

Gerald Buchanan felt a tear come to his eye as he scanned the letter. He would go down in history not as the savior of his country, but as its biggest traitor since Benedict Arnold. No! It was too much of a sacrifice! His reputation through the ages!

"Two minutes and thirty seconds," Trish said, now with a mocking smile on her face. She held up a small plastic bag containing two white pills.

He closed his eyes and put his head against the backrest for a moment, folding his fingers together tightly to keep from taking up the pen. *Everybody has to die sometime, including every member of my family. They are only mortal, after all. Death comes to us all eventually.* He could run to the flight attendant, but the passenger they believed to be the air marshal was actually one of the Sharks! He leafed through the alternatives. They couldn't kill him in the open cabin if he stood up and made a scene! Sure they could. They were professional killers. He was already a dead man. It was only a matter of choosing how he would go.

"Two minutes, darling," Trish whispered in his ear, and her breath was hot. "I'm afraid you won't be around for dinner tonight."

Buchanan looked at her. "Bitch," he said.

"Big Lenny over there and I will do Missy this weekend," she replied with a cold smile. "But your little whore will give us a good time first. An all-nighter. You only have one minute, fifty seconds. Your mutt gets poisoned tomorrow morning. Marge will be raped and then die when the house burns down around her. Cousin Flo and her family are going to have a tragic automobile accident . . . one forty-five."

Buchanan scrawled his name just to stop her awful recitation. Trish snatched the letter away and placed the two pills on the tray. He picked them up without a further word and made his way to the clean bathroom, filled a cup of water, and quickly swallowed the pills before the man in the mirror lost his nerve. Gates had lied. It was not painless. Buchanan went into spasms and convulsions and screamed in agony as fire coursed through his veins and he thrashed about the small toilet enclosure. When the alarmed attendants forced the door open, they found the bulky body of Gerald Buchanan curled into the fetal position. A soapy foam oozed from his mouth.

Trish looked across the aisle at her partner. "Fifteen seconds to spare," she said. She sent the confirmation signal to Gates.

60

Sir Geoffrey Cornwell, Major General Bradley Middleton, and Master Gunnery Sergeant O. O. Dawkins were around a small table, watching the sun settle into the Pacific Ocean. The La Fonda restaurant, perched on a cliff, was almost empty at this time of day in the middle of the week. It was about two kilometers outside the Mexican town of Puerto Nuevo, and subsisted primarily on the weekend exodus of Americans who came down from California like clockwork to play along the coastline of the Baja Peninsula. Steep stairs chipped into the cliff face covered a vertical drop of some eighty feet to a white sandy beach, and beyond that, out on the water, a few surfers were still on their boards, waiting to catch a final wave before the sun set. They knew it was not safe to be on a surfboard after dark, for sharks like to feed at night.

The *Vagabond* was lodged securely in a nearby marina, and Cornwell took Lady Pat and his guests out for an early dinner of lobster tacos and cold Pacifico cerveza. Mariachi bands were playing in some other restaurants, and the songs drifted on the salty air. Lady Pat went shopping with Middleton's wife, Janice, and the three men stayed to drink beer. They raised their bottles in a salute. "To Gunnery Sergeant Kyle Swanson, USMC," said Sir Jeff, and the others said in unison, "Semper fi." Middleton added, "May he rest in peace."

They had all been at the funeral six months ago, and since Swanson had no family, the flag draped over the coffin was folded and given to Lady Pat, whose teary eyes were hidden by dark sunglasses. An honor guard fired a farewell salute, and the chairman of the Joint Chiefs of Staff, General Henry Turner, gave a brief speech before yielding the microphone to the President of the United States, who read the proclamation for a posthumously awarded Congressional Medal of Honor. The service was solemn and proper and very vague on details.

Now, with so much time having passed, Middleton took a long drink and gave a little laugh. "Shake treated me like a new recruit," he recalled of the Syrian fiasco. "I thought a couple of times we might shoot each other before anybody else got the chance."

"It was indeed a merry chase," said Sir Jeff, who had been briefed privately on the details of the mission weeks earlier to help solve the final mystery.

"Not so fucking merry at times," said Double-Oh. "When we came into the LZ it looked like a helicopter air show. The Syrians were facing us, and we were facing them, soldiers spreading out on both sides. Two lines and everybody was locked and loaded. Then those two Harriers came screaming in right overhead, no more than a hundred feet off the deck, and gave the Syrians an attitude adjustment. After that, we all got along just skippy."

The Englishman called for another round of beer. "I

cannot tell you chaps how sorry I am about Excalibur. We have mended the problem, of course."

"I almost crapped my pants when I saw Shake throw the rifle and the pack with the computers into that hole. The grenade tore apart the most likely source of hard evidence against Gates. That's how the bastard skated free of charges."

"General," said Dawkins, "Kyle wasn't there to collect evidence like a cop."

"Of course. He knew that we were bugged, and the only three things that could be giving off a signal were his long gun or the laptops. He didn't have a chance to figure out which, so all of them had to go. It worked. The Frankensteins bit, and went after the GPS position instead of us."

Jeff rolled a chunk of lobster into a warm flour tortilla and covered it with hot sauce. He took a bite, and it was a slice of heaven. After a drink of cold beer, he shrugged. "When we designed the GPS system for Excalibur, none of us even considered that it could be used against whoever was carrying the rifle. It was strictly to help with the computations and to help the shooter know his position, but we did not guess that it might be pirated. Only three of us knew about that capability anyway. Two of them are now dead. My number-one man, a delightfully solid former para named Timothy Gladden, sold us out to Gates."

It was getting dim outside and only three surfers were left, and the waves continued to slope in irregular and small. "My own security team, making a scrub of our telecommunications systems, picked up that someone in our shop had called Gates. I was thinking it was just some industrial espionage going on, not unheard of in our business, until you told me about the GPS tracking device you found on the body of that mercenary. Excalibur's one flaw almost brought about an armed conflict."

"But it didn't," said Middleton. "And it won't again in the future."

"Right-o!" said Sir Jeff. "Unfortunately, Tim Gladden had a terrible accident on our trip across the Atlantic a few weeks ago. He fell overboard during some heavy weather and was never seen again. Tragic."

Only one surfer was left in the fading light, a bearded fellow with shaggy blond hair who seemed in no hurry to come back in. "Look at that lad," said Cornwell. "Sitting out there like he doesn't have a care in the world."

The surfer sat easily on his board, facing sideways between the setting sun and the cliff, waiting for a set of waves. Being dead wasn't all that bad. He could live with it. Anyway, without Shari, what was the point? He unconsciously rubbed the gnarly scars on the left side of his abdomen where the doctors had dug out the two bullets, and then had to go back in later to stop a raging infection caused by tiny threads of dirty cloth taken inside by one of the rounds. He had lost a chunk of his large intestine and his spleen, and a bullet fragment had ripped down far enough to crack a bone in his hip. That was only physical. Losing Shari was what really hurt.

His friends were waiting for him up in the little restaurant overlooking the K-54 beach, but his attention was on the patterns of the incoming waves. His recovery had been very slow, but he had recovered from wounds before. What would not heal was the part of his heart that was missing. Nothing would make that ache go away, but he knew of some medicine that would make it easier to bear.

A shadow curled below the horizon, a set coming in steep and flowing toward the beach with intense purpose. He saw them building and getting higher, and turned the board toward the beach and started to paddle. Then the first wave caught up and pulled the long board into its powerful center. He was riding with the break when he pushed up against his fifteen-year-old board, planted his feet, and stood, relaxed and perfectly balanced, and rode all the way in, wrapped in the pure essence and freedom of surfing.

The man who was no longer Kyle Swanson waded from the water and hauled the board up the worn stairs, bumping it a couple of times on the stones, as always happened at the K-54. It wore its scars with honor, just like its owner.

The following day, the *Vagabond* had snugged into a berth in San Diego after passing more naval ships at rest than most nations had in their entire fleets. Coming in from the sea instead of across by land at the San Ysidro crossing meant no border inspection. Two aircraft carriers were in port, Marine recruits were going through boot camp, and SEALs were training on a Coronado beach. Two-star general Brad Middleton examined the gathered vessels for a while with Sir Jeff, then went belowdecks and knocked on a stateroom door. Master Gunnery Sergeant Dawkins opened it, and Middleton stepped inside.

"You about ready?" Middleton asked. He and Double-Oh were on a unique shopping tour of elite units within the Navy and Marine Corps, looking to steal some hard-bodied warrior types for the general's new command. After the congressional hearings and subsequent investigations, Middleton "went black" and took Double-Oh with him as operations chief.

It had been decided that if Kyle Swanson remained dead and buried, a special unit would be built around the sniper, just as a professional football team could build a championship around a franchise quarterback. They could surround him with support players who were similar masters of their own specialties, and they would have a unit that could go anywhere and do anything, because the people on it did not exist.

Kyle had agreed, on one condition, and his wish had been granted. Now he was at a mirror on the far side of the stateroom with a splattered towel around his shoulders, the result of dyeing his long hair black. "I look like fucking Charlie Manson," he said.

"Naw, you don't have that little swastika thingie on your forehead," said Double-Oh. "You look like some heavy-metal freak."

"You ready for this?" asked Middleton, taking a seat on the bed. "Once it starts, you're on your own."

"More than ready, General. Jeff wants me to field-test Excalibur II. I'll be back in a few days and then we can get to work."

"Okay, Shake. I'll see you back here on the boat in five days." Middleton walked out.

Double-Oh popped Swanson on the shoulder with a balled fist and waved as he shut the door. "Later."

Kyle looked at the photograph on the California driver's license of James K. Polk. A Social Security card and two credit cards in the same name were on a night table, along with a thousand dollars. The dark hair of the man in the picture was pulled back in a ponytail, and the facial hair was neatly trimmed. He picked up the scissors and began to shape the beard.

Taped to the mirror were stories he had clipped from the society pages of *The Denver Post* and the *Rocky Mountain News*. After dinner with Jeff and Pat, he put Excalibur II into the trunk of a silver SUV and drove east. A stack of new CDs kept the music flowing, and he actually felt comfortable for the first time in six months.

EPILOGUE

ASPEN, Colorado (UNP)—The body of missing billionaire industrialist Gordon Gates IV was found late yesterday in the rugged Rocky Mountains, police announced.

Law enforcement sources said that Gates had been killed by a single bullet to the head in an apparent hunting accident.

Gates, a decorated military veteran and avid hunter, was last seen Saturday night when he hosted his annual Christmas season fund-raising gala at his elegant home in this elite mountain resort. Some of the guests said he left about midnight in hopes of reaching a secluded canyon in which a rogue mountain lion recently killed two campers and mauled another.

"Gordon really wanted that big cat," said his attorney, Wilford Stanton, at Gates Global headquarters in Washington, D.C. "He spent a small fortune on guides and employed military-style detection equipment to track it to this particular location. He felt the lion was a danger to everyone in the area, and wanted to be the one to bring it down."

Sheriff Matt Randall said other hunters frequently had also been seen in the area stalking the mountain lion. "Mr. Gates was wearing a brush camouflage outfit, but not a brightly colored warning vest. Somebody apparently saw him move and took a hasty shot. The victim took a large-caliber round in the left temple and was dead by the time he hit the dirt."

A police search for other hunters was unsuccessful. "We are asking anyone with information about this unfortunate accident to come forward."

Gates Global, the multinational holding company, posted a reward of a million dollars leading to the arrest and conviction of the shooter.

Gates had recently been under intense government scrutiny for alleged corruption involving government contracts, and his firm sustained substantial public relations damage last year over alleged involvement in the kidnapping of Marine Brigadier General Bradley Middleton and the Syrian situation. The company insisted it had no knowledge of any involvement, and Gates invited the FBI to search its files and databases. Nothing was discovered that would link the giant corporation to the abduction.

DEAD
SHOT

For Cassie, Ashley, and Karrin

1

THE GREEN ZONE
BAGHDAD, IRAQ

It was just a matter of waiting. Juba was good at waiting. Patience was an important tool for him, as it is for all snipers. The Iraqi desert sun baked and parched him, but his soul remained calm, soothed by the instructions of his two fathers and the sure knowledge that the hunt was on. Once again, he was the sword of the Prophet. *God is great!* he whispered, feeling guilty for breaking his oath and speaking the words of praise.

He had been in the hole for three days, shaded only by a few bushes during the hottest part of the blistering afternoons. He let his face and neck become sunburned and measured his rations carefully, eating and drinking only enough to survive. The last chocolates from his field rations had been eaten, and he had intentionally drained the last water from his canteens the previous day. He was hungry, and thirst clawed at his throat. Good.

Throughout the time in the hide, he had heard sporadic traffic passing unseen only fifty meters away and the occasional boom of an explosion somewhere down the track. Each morning an American patrol rolled past, clouds of dust following the big vehicles. He could have gotten help anytime he wanted it. Didn't want it.

On the fourth morning, the sun was up and the temperature was climbing when he saw the faraway dust clouds kicked up by the oncoming patrol. No wonder they were so easy to ambush. He crawled from the hide, brushed away the signs of his stay by brooming the area with a bush, and staggered to the road. The vehicles now could be seen with the naked eye, which meant they could see him, too, a wobbling soldier alone in the desert.

He held up his hands as if in surrender to the first Bradley Fighting Vehicle that approached, with its .50 caliber machine gun trained on him. Then he collapsed. A lieutenant of the U.S. 1st Cavalry Division instantly recognized the disruptive pattern camouflage uniform and weathered beret worn by the British soldier and jumped down to help. They pulled him into the shade of the big vehicle.

Sweat caked the dusty face and dirt clung to the filthy uniform, and when they started pouring some water into his mouth, he greedily grabbed for the canteen. The American pulled it back. 'Easy, pal. Just a little bit at a time. You're gonna be okay.' He offered another sip. A medic smoothed a wet salve on the sunburned face, neck, and hands.

Juba slowly responded in a British accent, haltingly explaining that his sniper team had been discovered a week ago and his spotter killed in the ensuing fight. The Englishman had evaded the searching insurgents, found this road before dawn today, and walked next to it since then, hoping that a friendly force would spot him before the insurgents did. The Americans were unaware that his uniform and the rifle hanging from his shoulder had been stripped from a British soldier he had killed outside of Basra.

Juba was able to stand unaided by the time a helicopter arrived, and he thanked the American soldiers and climbed into the bird. Within thirty minutes, it delivered him to the landing pad of a military hospital inside the Green Zone of Baghdad. A stretcher team met him, but he waved them off, and they led him into a cool corridor, then into a big room where other soldiers lay on cots. A nurse helped him remove his tunic and stuck a needle into his arm to start a slow drip of hydrating fluids. He had been outside in the heat for so long that the fresh liquid going directly into his veins, plus the air-conditioning, caused a deep and instant chill, and he began to shake as if he were freezing. The nurse recognized the reaction as normal and wrapped a blanket around his shoulders as a doctor came over to check him. Exhaustion, sunburn, and dehydration, but no wounds. Juba lay back on the cot, enjoying the brief rest and the air-conditioning.

As the IV drip was finishing, a courteous U.S. intelligence captain came to his cot, having already notified British commanders that their man had been rescued. 'They thought you were dead,' said the captain, settling into a chair. He thought the guy looked like hell. 'So what happened out there, Sergeant?'

The officer took a few notes as Juba repeated his tale of a mission gone wrong. 'Sorry about your buddy,' the American said and put away the notebook. 'Bad shit.'

'Part of the job, mate.' Juba sighed and leaned back on the green sheet of the metal-framed cot.

'Your instructions are to rest up and then return to

your unit as soon as medically fit,' said the captain.

The busy doctor in uniform came by just long enough to look him over for a final time and remove the needle. 'I've signed your discharge slip, Sergeant. You're going to be fine except for a few aches and pains and that sunburn. Drink a lot of water and have some chow. Here's some ointment for the burn, and if you need more, just come by the pharmacy. You want something to help you sleep tonight?'

'No, sir. I've dealt with worse than this.'

'Okay, then. You're free to leave. Good luck.'

The intel officer was still there. 'Come on with me, soldier, and I'll take you over to the mess hall, then give you a chit for a bed tonight in the guest quarters. Your orders from British HQ are to rest up and then report back to your unit. Meanwhile, you're a guest of Uncle Sam.'

Juba pushed himself from the cot, acting wobbly, then drew himself erect and stretched, turning side to side. The body was lean and muscular. He put on his tunic. 'Thank you, sir, but I plan something a little more upscale. I'm going to get a hotel room, raid the minibar, take a long shower, get some decent food, and then sleep for two days.'

'I hear ya,' said the officer. 'I've got everything I need. Stay safe.' He waved Juba through the door. The sniper ducked into a bathroom, locked himself into a stall, dropped his trousers to retrieve some documents from a plastic bag that had been tucked just above his right boot, and put them in his shirt pocket. He came out, signed for his rifle at the makeshift armory, and left the hospital. Back on the hunt. Closer than before.

*

4

He took his time crossing the military areas of the Green Zone as he made his way over to the new Nineveh Hotel, a five-star, four-hundred-room edifice that offered safety, opulence, an indoor Olympic-sized swimming pool, a gourmet restaurant, and other luxury conveniences to foreign visitors, diplomats, and business executives. The gleaming signature spire and a communication array on the roof made it the tallest building in Baghdad.

Despite the outward appearances of commerce, Baghdad remained a military town, and it was not thought strange at all when Juba unfolded the papers that he had carried in the plastic bag and handed them to the concierge of the Nineveh. The documents allowed him to commandeer the corner suite on the twelfth floor for an unspecified 'military necessity,' the code that unlocked any door in the city. The civilian led him to the suite and joked during the elevator ride about how things were improving. Soft music played in the background.

Juba thanked him, locked the door, and dumped his gear and clothes. He showered, shaved, cleaned his uniform, and put it back on. He snatched three pillows from the bed, piled them on the small dining table in the center of the suite, and stacked his pack atop them to provide a solid support for the long rifle. Crawling on his knees, then his stomach, he moved to the sliding glass door that led onto the balcony and pushed it open by a narrow six inches. Then he wiggled back about seven feet and stood in the shadows of the room, overlooking the neat front garden with lawns of grass that was irrigated to a deep lush green.

Juba lifted his L115A1 long-range rifle, made by Accuracy International UK, the standard weapon of a British sniper. It fired a .338 Lapua Magnum round that was accurate up to 1,100 meters, and it had a Killflash silencer on the muzzle and a bipod. He had zeroed the weapon two days ago and was confident it would hold enough for the task today. From his position, he could see the outside world, but no one on the ground could see him.

Juba had exchanged the standard Schmidt & Bender PM II telescopic sight for the better Zeiss version used by the Germans, and he peered through it to examine the foot traffic along the pathways. A wolf eyeing a flock of sheep. The people below seemed startlingly close through the clear optics. The first potential target to stroll through his kill zone was a civilian wearing a loud Hawaiian shirt and tan trousers. Too easy: a foreign contractor who meant nothing, and killing Americans was not his mission today. It had to be the man with the secret. Sooner or later, he would come along, if the intelligence was correct. Juba would wait. He knew how to wait.

He put down the rifle, sat in a soft chair, and flipped through the English-language newspaper that had been delivered free to the hotel room and checked the football scores to see if Manchester United had won.

He sipped chilled water from a plastic bottle. Scorching outside air oozed through the slightly opened door and did battle with the room's buzzing air conditioner. The flat-screen color television set mounted in the wall was on, and he adjusted the volume slightly to the loud side. News readers rattled on about next week's royal wedding in London, elevating the event steadily so that by Tuesday, the marriage of the prince and his girlfriend would be considered the most important thing in the world. Millions of people would watch. As a British subject, he vividly remembered the legends of the glory days of the monarchy, lessons that had been pounded into him as a student and later as a soldier defending the Crown. He planned to be there for the wedding.

Juba was slightly under six feet in height and slender at 170 pounds, with the fair hair of his British mother and the dark eyes of his Arab father. His skin was several shades darker than the normal Briton, more of a nice California tan that had been darkened even more by his work in the desert. It helped him move with ease in the twilight gulf between Christians and Muslims. Juba could be anybody he wanted to be, and for the past few days, he had again chosen the familiar role of a British Army sniper. It was his best disguise, because he once had been awarded the coveted sniper's patch of two crossed rifles with an *S* between the barrels.

After reading the sports in the newspaper, he put his eye back to the scope and considered the next possible target, an approaching soldier who, despite the midday heat, wore a helmet and a flak jacket. This had once been the safest place in Iraq, the International Zone, home of the giant U.S. Embassy. It once had been known as the Green Zone, and although bureaucrats changed the name to better claim that the war was the effort of many nations, the Green Zone name stuck. Juba was tempted by the soldier, for he always enjoyed the challenge of placing a bullet in the small gaps of the armored vests or between the ceramic plates. Not the mission: Let him pass.

An hour before sundown, four soldiers in full armor appeared, moving in a box formation as they escorted a smaller man toward the Coalition Headquarters building where the first formal interrogation was to take place. The soldier on the left front corner was talking and making sharp, descriptive motions with one hand, probably an officer directing the prisoner transfer. Except that the man was not a prisoner, more a valuable guest of the Coalition. He had arrived yesterday in Baghdad, with the secret locked in his head. The Iraqi physicist planned to hand the information to the Americans and the British officials, but he had made too many mistakes in escaping from the laboratory in Iran. The biggest error was in trusting his coworkers, who were able to provide almost a minute-by-minute schedule for the defector. Then Juba had been summoned.

The traitor could not be allowed to reach the interrogation room alive. Juba pressed his cheek into the cool stock, his fingers roving with familiarity over the rifle to make sure it was ready. They were three hundred yards away, and he checked the flags on the government building. He estimated the wind at seven to ten miles per hour full value, right to left, which would move the fired round two inches to the left at two hundred yards. He adjusted the scope to compensate. Humidity was zero.

He settled the scope on the officer and looked for a weakness. The waving arm! The officer was describing something, and his right arm windmilled to make his point. Juba exhaled and let his heartbeat slow almost to nothing. Under the arm, that's the place.

At two hundred yards, almost point-blank range, he squeezed the trigger back, slow and steady and straight, just as the American raised his arm above shoulder level. The big rifle fired, and the Killflash ate up the noise as the bullet entered beneath the right armpit of the officer, smashed down through the rib cage and exited out of his lower left side, crushing bones and shredding every organ in its path. The officer died before anyone could reach out to help him.

Juba accepted the light recoil and cycled another round into the chamber as the startled group stopped in its tracks. He brought his scope to the small man in the middle. They had heard nothing, but the colonel had just been shot! The soldiers spun around, looking for the threat but leaving the target uncovered. The Iraqi automatically bent down, turning to aid the fallen American. That exposed the left rear side of his neck, and Juba centered the crosshairs right there and pulled the trigger again. He was able to see the vapor trail of the bullet, which impacted right below the base of the skull and ripped out the throat when it came out the other side. Two catastrophic kills.

Juba put aside the rifle, ducked down to the floor, crawled forward, and reached up to slowly close the door to the outside patio. He went back, retrieved his kit and the rifle, tossed the pillows back onto the bed, and left the room.

He increased his pace through the lobby and hurried outside with other armed soldiers and civilian private security company guards who were moving into the attack area. A Quick Reaction Force would arrive within minutes, and uniformed men would be all over the place, with all sorts of weapons pointing everywhere, and Juba would be just another soldier with a gun. He made his way through the crowd and walked out of the Green Zone unmolested.

That evening, a small Royal Jordanian Airlines Fokker plane took off on schedule from the Baghdad International Airport. On its manifest was a quiet Canadian civilian engineer with fair hair and dark eyes. Juba was going to London.

The secret that Saddam Hussein had taken to his grave remained safe. The Palace of Death was secure.

2

Jack Coughlin with Donald A. Davis

Captain Sybelle Summers of the U.S. Marine Corps walked purposefully into a secure briefing room at Incirlik Air Force Base in southeastern Turkey. Many of the combat-ready Marines who were to conduct the mission recognized her immediately, and the others knew her reputation as operations officer of a special operations unit known as Task Force Trident.

'Oh, oh. It's the Queen of the Night,' muttered a lance corporal. 'We've stepped in it. They don't use the Bride of Dracula on small jobs.'

'Count Dracula divorced her for spousal abuse,' whispered the man next to him.

'Shhh. Summers will kick your ass if she hears you.'

The experienced warriors of the Marine Special Operations Command (MARSOC) normally shied away from taking orders from women, but Summers was different. She wore a black jumpsuit with the silver railroad tracks insignia of her rank glinting on the collar of a turtleneck sweater and projected a maximum 'don't give me any shit' attitude as she walked to the podium and flipped open a file folder. Her short black hair, dark blue eyes, and lithe figure disguised the fact that she was the only woman ever to make it through Force Recon training.

'Settle down,' she snapped, and the MARSOC team quieted. 'We are going after a High Value Target tonight in Iraq, and I don't want any of you jarheads to screw this up. Mustapha Ahmed al-Masri has surfaced again, stirring up the Kurds in northern Iraq, and the intelligence pukes have pinpointed his location. They list him as the number two for al Qaeda in the region, which is why he has been designated an HVT and we have been assigned to stop him.'

She walked around the podium to the front and nodded to her left. A door opened and a man stepped in, also wearing a black jumpsuit and with his face covered by a pull-down mask. A long rifle of a sort they did not recognize was slung over his shoulder. Sniper.

'Batman?' whispered the lance corporal.

'Maybe a holdup,' joked his partner.

'CIA spook. Definitely.'

Summers spoke. 'You guys will assault the house at 0500, and I'll leave it to the other briefers to give you the details. By the time you arrive, this gentleman and I will already be on the ground, closing the back door. He is masked simply because you do not need to know who he is. The two of us have been attached as special operators for this mission. Far as you are concerned, we aren't here, and we will go in and extract on our own.'

As she finished, other briefing officers came forward with their maps and timetables. The lights started to dim. 'If you see al-Masri, kill him. The best bet is that he will haul ass once the attack starts, and we will be waiting. You absolutely must remember that this is friendly territory and be sure not to have civilian casualties. If you screw up and shoot at us, even by mistake, he will shoot back, and I guarantee that you don't want that to happen. Be very careful when you pull the trigger. Know your targets. That's it. Good luck and good hunting. Captain Barnes will continue your brief.' She spun on her heel and disappeared out the door with the masked man.

Once they were in the Humvee and driving to the helicopter pad beside the ten-thousand-foot runway, Kyle Swanson rolled up the mask, changing it into a watch cap. His face itched. 'Damn, Sybelle, you are a woman of few words.' He changed his voice to imitate her grim briefing cadence. ' "Shoot at us and he will shoot back!" Way to inspire confidence in the troops.'

They both laughed. 'I had to get their attention. We don't want any mistakes out there.'

'I knew about half the guys in that room,' Swanson said. 'Worked with some of them. It's always strange not letting friends know who you really are.' In special ops, he had a million aliases but no real name at all because he was officially dead.

The Turkish night was crisp and starlit, with a slice of a coasting moon. A giant Air Force cargo plane roared overhead on its landing approach, hauling more material from the States into Incirlik, a major supply dump that fed the war in Iraq. Adana, a modern city of a million people, was less than ten miles away, and the Mediterranean washed onto beaches within easy access. For special operations types, it was a good location. You could get a decent hamburger and a cold beer, jump on a bird and fly off on a quick combat mission, and be back in time for a hot shower and a movie.

Swanson brought the Humvee to a halt beside a hangar, and they both got out and suited up with their web gear. Summers removed her shiny captain's bars because they were entering the world of hiding, blending, and deceiving, a dark place where nothing must reflect light. She had assigned herself to this mission for several reasons, one being that she still spoke the language of her childhood, although her Kurdish last name had disappeared when her father had died and her mother remarried an American. It was a welcome asset.

A U.S. Air Force lieutenant approached, saluted, and introduced himself as their command pilot. He would not be going with them, however, and behind him sat a tiny HTX-I helicopter, the rotors already turning lazily on battery power. Commonly called a TAXI, it would be controlled by pilots far away from the action, with this lieutenant in charge of getting them launched and then handing the flight over to another controller cruising far overhead in an electronics warfare plane.

The TAXI had been perfected by the U.S. Special Operations Command as a revolutionary tactical delivery system for particular missions and could deliver up to four operators to an exact point, then speed away to some nearby isolated site and shut down, roosting there patiently for days if need be, while solar panels recharged the batteries. When summoned, it would zip back in to pick them up. Except for the reconfigured overhead rotor, it hardly even looked like a helicopter. With no pilot, co-pilot, or loadmaster and with the giant internal combustion engines gone, weaponless and without armor, the unique helicopter was a blend of ultralight, stealth, and modern fuel cell and electronic technologies. It possessed extraordinary range and was virtually invisible to searching radar while its passengers sat in pairs, side by side, encased in

a sleek aerodynamic bubble. The HTX-I wore the X desig-
nation to indicate it was still in the experimental stage,
nothing more than an idea on the drawing boards. The
media had never even picked up a scent that it was already
operational.

Swanson and Summers climbed in, checked their gear,
buckled up, and put on their headsets as the flight engineer closed the hatches and backed away, speaking into
a radio to the controller. The reaction was immediate, and
they heard no roar of engines as the TAXI rose from the
landing strip like a quiet elevator, with only a slight whip-
ping sound from the rotors, then flitted away on its run
to the border. Swanson watched the lights of Adana disappear behind them. It was like sailing on a quiet lake.

At an exact GPS location, the TAXI slowed to a crawl
and went close to the ground and then into a motionless
hover. They jumped out, boots crunching desert sand, and
ran to some nearby clusters of trees. The contact who had
alerted the Americans about the presence of Mustapha
Ahmed al-Masri was waiting, and Sybelle spoke to him
in Kurdish, apologetically explaining to him that she was
just a mere translator for the man with her.

Satisfied that as a woman, she was still an underling,
the man guided them into the village and pointed them
to a flat place in a ditch. The road beside them ran straight
for a while, then bent right, and at the curve was the house
that was to be attacked.

Sybelle and Kyle slid into the dry gully, and Swanson
unlimbered some of his gear, setting up shop. Sybelle
thanked the guide profusely and told him he was now
free to go and wait for the main force that would be

coming in on the other end of town. The guide disappeared into the night.

'Let's move,' she said.

Kyle was already packing. They had no intention of staying in a place known to a local. Trust went only so far. 'That house on the left. We go over the wall and get some protection, and I can brace the rifle on top of it.'

They moved out quietly, and Sybelle spider-dropped over the wall and landed without a sound on the far side. Swanson turned the knob on the gate, opened it, and walked through. Sybelle raised her middle finger in response.

During the next hour, they created a hide by using material found around the yard, and Kyle placed his personal space-age sniper rifle, the Excalibur, on a solid rest. Sybelle set up a spotter's scope. Both had a clear view of the target building. They created a range card by measuring distances to points in the target area as they waited in the early morning chill.

At five o'clock, dawn was only an hour away, and parts of the village stirred as men and women prepared for the coming day. Kyle and Sybelle received a radio alert that the assault team was on its final approach, and almost immediately, the attack began with the buzzing approach of two big troop-carrying helicopters. Lights began snapping on throughout town by the time the birds landed on a soccer field a block east of the target. As the other Marines charged for the house, one of their snipers found a high position and took out the al Qaeda guard in front. Swanson and Summers, in the rear of the house, never took their eyes off of the target area.

'I have movement at the door,' whispered Sybelle. 'Tall man. Must be al-Masri's huge bodyguard.'

'I see him,' responded Kyle. In the scope of the Excalibur, strings of numbers scrolled in constant movement as the computer measured the distance and figured the trajectory. So close, wind would not be a factor. Swanson held his fire.

'Second target. I identify him as al-Masri.'

Kyle studied the figure. 'I confirm. Target in sight.'

As gunfire snapped in the house, the two men ducked into a small automobile, with the bodyguard driving, and the vehicle charged into the street with its lights off. Once again, the foot soldiers of al Qaeda were left behind to become martyrs while the leader escaped.

'Not this time,' whispered Kyle. He pulled the trigger. The .50 caliber weapon fired with a jarring *BOOM*, and the recoil kicked his shoulder as the big bullet slammed into the engine block hard enough to make the vehicle jump. A second round then went through the windshield and shattered the head of the bodyguard as the out-of-control car swerved sharply and slammed into a parked truck with the crunch of metal and glass.

'Target down. Other one getting out.' Sybelle's voice was perfectly calm, a monotone devoid of emotion.

'Confirm the other one is getting out.' Kyle took his time racking in a third round, giving the man a moment to open the door. Al-Masri was alone in the empty street. His men were all dead or captured, and he knew that an American sniper had him in plain view. It was time to quit. He dropped to his knees and held his hands high over his head.

Kyle shot him through the chest, and the al Qaeda

officer flopped over on his side. A final shot went into his head.

'Both targets down,' said Sybelle.

Kyle grabbed his rifle and pack, and Sybelle picked up her scope and gear and called out the signal for the controller to send in the TAXI for pickup. They hustled out through the gate and back to the landing zone, where the little bird arrived two minutes later. They jumped in and were gone.

The fighting was over in the house. The nest of terrorists had been wiped out to the last man, and the Marines would secure the area.

'Was he trying to surrender?' Sybelle asked, wiping some camouflage greasepaint from her face. 'Might have given up some intelligence.'

'I saw a weapon,' Kyle said.

'Yeah,' she said. 'Me, too.'

3

They arrived back at Incirlik with plenty of time to shower, change clothes, and have breakfast before their next flights. With the special op done, they could mix anonymously with the crowd. Lines of soldiers and airmen and Marines talked in a garble of background noise, and silverware and china clinked a tinny chorus. The aroma of cooking eggs, sausage, and bacon rose like a cloud from the grills as cooks in stained whites kept the food moving to the steam tables. Air Force chow halls were the best, so although the flyboys wore bus driver uniforms, Kyle was always happy to share their food. He stacked a tray full of the good stuff, while Sybelle settled for bran flakes and fruit. Plenty of black coffee. They found a small table off to one side and put down their trays.

'What are you going to do on your R-and-R, Kyle? Two weeks is a long time.'

'Rack time. Sleep. Wake up and then go back to sleep. I'm tired.' He drank some coffee and thought back over the last few months, during which he had been constantly on the go. The two weeks spent stalking a terrorist in Chechnya had been exhausting, and before that he was looking for a drug operation buried deep in Brazil's giant rain forests. Leading a Filipino marine unit against an island hideout of Islamic terrorists ended in a screwed-up firefight. Last night's raid into Kurd country seemed like just another routine day at the office for Swanson, but even professional hunters get tired.

Sybelle studied him as they ate. Kyle Swanson: the legend himself, the ghost arisen. He was not a big man, 5'9" and 175 pounds, with muscles that were sinewy rather than bulging. The kind of guy with remarkable endurance who could fight all day, long after the bigger guys gave out. Gray-green eyes and sandy brown hair that was longer than normal, even by civilian standards, around an angular face. He was neither handsome nor unattractive, just unremarkable, which was exactly what he needed to be.

On paper and in all government computer banks, Swanson was dead, and he had a tombstone in Arlington National Cemetery to prove it. Two years ago, Kyle was the best scout-sniper in the Marines, a veteran shooter who was often tabbed for special ops work by other agencies. Then General Bradley Middleton had been kidnapped as part of a plot to topple the United States government and put the Pentagon beneath the thumb of a private military contractor. Kyle was on the rescue team sent into Syria, and although the rest of the force had been wiped out, Swanson pulled Middleton to safety while most of the Syrian army hunted them. He was badly wounded in a final firefight, and his fiancée, Shari Towne, was murdered by the plotters in the United States.

Important people realized the value of a single operator in the modern-day climate of terrorism, and it was decided that Kyle Swanson, with no living relatives, should cease to exist. He accepted the deal, with one condition. After recovering from his wounds, the billionaire maniac responsible for killing Shari Towne was soon thereafter found dead on a Colorado mountain, shot through the head in what was ruled to be a hunting accident.

With the fake burial at Arlington, and Kyle's entire identity and fingerprints wiped away, Task Force Trident was created around him, with General Middleton in charge and Sybelle Summers as the operations officer. Swanson was virtually the invisible man, free to take on any assignment. He could kill anybody, anywhere, and walk away untouched by law.

But he had never fully recovered from the death of Shari, his bride-to-be, and one of the reasons that Sybelle had come out from Washington for this otherwise routine operation in Iraq was to evaluate his physical and mental condition. She found that he still had his normal cold edge and the hard shell that made sure nothing got inside. Swanson simply did not care about much. Kyle's problem was not about being dead but about continuing to live with himself.

'Middleton wants me to report back on how you're doing, Kyle.' She held the warm mug of coffee in both hands. 'I know you can still shoot straight, but how's your head?'

'You mean, am I crazy?'

'Are you?'

'Of course. I have to be crazy to do this job!' He grinned. 'No. At times, I get tired of being dead. It can be a pain in the ass. I mean, having to wear a black mask in that room with other Marines? I knew half of those guys but couldn't even say hello. I have to check my latest fake passport every morning to remember my name for the day. They even gave me a set of Dutch identification papers a while back. Do I look Dutch to you?'

'Got to be tough,' she agreed. The ultimate loner. 'Tell you what. You're obviously exhausted and running on battery power alone. So take your R-and-R and rest up, get drunk, get laid, and sweat out a hard physical conditioning program. Then come back to Washington and let's figure out how to slow down the workload. They can't expect you to cover the whole world by yourself.'

'Is the general complaining about me again?' Swanson and Middleton had not gotten along for years, dating back to their first encounter during the First Gulf War. Middleton had come across Swanson after a particularly vicious firefight and saw the sniper trembling as he reflected on the carnage he had caused during the battle. Swanson always had found a few moments alone after a fight to bring himself back to normal, but Middleton had mistaken the reaction as evidence of incompetence. Not only had he tried to get Swanson kicked out of the Marines, but he also used the term 'shaky' in the official report. The attempt failed, but the ironic nickname of 'Shake' stuck, for his friends knew that Kyle Swanson was anything but unreliable in battle. It had taken the rescue in Syria to start Middleton and Swanson on a path of mutual respect and friendship.

'No. He's just concerned. We all are. Without you, there is no Task Force Trident.'

Kyle finished a final slice of toast and pushed away his plate. 'Well, Captain Summers, tell the folks back home that I am just skippy. I still believe in our mission. I still hate terrorists, and I'm still willing to kill whoever the president decides needs a good killing.'

Within a few hours, Summers left for Washington aboard a military transport, and Kyle climbed into a Sikorsky S-76 helicopter. It was shining white except for two narrow bands of dark blue stripes and a gold corporate symbol on each side marking it as part of Excalibur Enterprises Ltd., the holding company for the many businesses of British tycoon Sir Geoffrey Cornwell. The sleek bird was a combination executive passenger vehicle and all-around workhorse, and Kyle was the only passenger in its spacious and soundproof cabin. The aircraft had no ties to anything military, and its flight log for the day recorded just a routine trip for a company executive, but in the world of clandestine operations, Sir Jeff was known to occasionally lend a hand for off-the-book operations. Kyle strapped into a comfortable leather seat as the powerful Turbomeca Arriel 2S2 engines revved up, and in minutes the Sikorsky was up and heading toward the Mediterranean Sea. The steady low throb of the engines helped him fall asleep almost instantly.

'We're landing, sir.' The pilot's voice on the intercom aroused him after what seemed only a few minutes, but when he checked his watch, Swanson saw they had been in the air for more than an hour. The blades were slapping hard, and from the cabin window, he could see the square landing deck of a luxurious yacht with the same color scheme as the helicopter. The sparkling *Vagabond* seemed to rise from the waters to meet the wheels of the descending bird, which touched down lightly on the landing deck.

'Home, sweet home,' said Kyle Swanson as a crewman pulled open the door from the outside. 'Thanks for the lift, guys.'

He stepped to the deck while the chopper was still shutting down its engines and ducked away from the powerful downdraft of the rotor blades. A woman moved toward him from the cabin area. She was Lady Patricia Cornwell, in a blouse of blue silk and dark slacks, with a silver necklace and earrings. 'Welcome back, stranger,' she said, giving him a tight hug and handing over a cold beer. Her eyes took in everything: the weary movement, the sun-reddened skin, a slight limp. He had been gone for almost two weeks. No questions. 'Jeff is on his way back from a NATO meeting and should be aboard before the storm arrives.'

'Good to be here, Pat. Lord, I'm tired.' Clouds were gathering on the horizon, and crewmen in crisp uniforms hurried about, coiling rope and lashing canvas to get the big yacht ready for the approaching heavy weather.

Pat gently touched a small bandage taped on his chin. 'Did you forget to duck?'

'Cut myself shaving,' Swanson answered with a laugh.

'You seem to do that a lot these days.' She punched him lightly on the shoulder. 'Why don't you go take a nap before you fall asleep on your feet, Kyle? We will call you for dinner at seven.'

'Yes, m'lady.' He walked away across the teak deck and disappeared into an open hatch, heading for his own cabin as the yacht shifted beneath his feet on the rolling waves.

Pat stared out to where the black waters met the

graying sky. An unhappy soul, she thought as the breeze pulled at her hair and clothing. She knew that he would fall asleep fully clothed and that they would not see him at dinner.

Swanson heard a soft bump against the hull and immediately smelled rot and decay. He knew who it was before he shrugged out of bed and went on deck to peer over the rail. Below, bobbing in a long, low craft that rode easily on the churning water, was the Boatman, grinning up at him. Dead people sat erect on the benches, three to a side.

'You've been busy,' Kyle observed.

'Wars. Revolution.' The Boatman shrugged with a low cackle. 'I always have many waiting to go over.' He pointed a finger of ivory bone toward a narrow ridge of fire in the north, a glowing rim between the black of the night and the black of the sea. When the Boatman pulled on a long oar to steady the craft, the wind pushed the soiled black robe around his thin figure, and his skeletal face flashed an evil smile of broken teeth.

'So what do you want? You already have a full boat, and I ain't planning to go with you.'

'Not yet. But very soon.'

'Fuck you.'

'I have retrieved the two souls you just killed.'

'Good. They thought they were going to paradise and each would collect his six dozen virgins.'

The Boatman cackled. 'They were wrong.' There was a long pause. 'You are a good and reliable supplier.'

Kyle spat overboard. 'And you are nothing but a bad dream. I'm going to wake up soon and you will be gone.'

The Boatman placed his hand against the white hull

of the Vagabond and gave a push, then leaned onto his oar, and the little boat swung away. A few more sweeps put some distance between them before the specter turned and spoke again. 'Yes? That is true, but I am never too far from you, awake or asleep. I will be back when you finally decide to put a pistol in your mouth and finish self-destructing. It will be a special trip, and you can have the whole boat to yourself.'

The shuttle craft paddled away with its cargo of corpses, the Boatman disappearing into the storm, trailing a croak of laughter.

When Kyle awoke, he was standing outside on the rolling deck of the *Vagabond* in his bare feet with wind-driven rain sluicing over him, drenching the clothes in which he had fallen asleep. Lightning sizzled off the water and thunder rumbled through the night sky as he held the rail in a death grip. Just a dream. Just the damned dream again.

Swanson had been trained for years to keep his emotions in check while on a mission, when precision and control frequently marked the difference between success and failure. It was after the shooting, when he was alone, that he allowed his thoughts to deal with what had happened, and the process was not always pretty. Now, the Boatman had become an unwanted part of that procedure.

All of the storms in the world could not wash away what really troubled him, so he staggered into the main cabin, pulled a bottle of tequila from the bar, and went back outside. Rain didn't bother him. Cold didn't bother him. Killing people didn't bother him.

What gnawed at his brain was the simple equation that Shari was dead and he was still alive. He upended the bottle and took a large swallow, feeling the tequila bite in his throat, then he sought shelter from the thundering gale in the corner of the superstructure and drank himself back to sleep. About four o'clock in the morning, a pair of *Vagabond* crew members found him curled up there, wedged between a locker and a lifeboat, and they hauled him back to his cabin, stripped off the wet clothes, roughly toweled him down, and left him on the bunk beneath blankets.

'We've got a new mission.' Major General Bradley Middleton made himself comfortable in his Pentagon office by opening the lower right-hand drawer of his desk and propping a spit-shined shoe on it, loosening his tie, and unbuttoning his collar.

Master Gunnery Sergeant O. O. Dawkins, one of only forty-five men in the Marine Corps to hold that highest enlisted rank, occupied most of the sofa. Double-Oh had helped write the book on special operations. Next to him sat Sybelle Summers, who had just flown in from Turkey.

In a chair of burgundy leather sat U.S. Navy Lieutenant Commander Benton Freedman, whose hair was always tousled, as if he had just gotten out of bed. He was a brilliant computer geek, engineer, and master of all things technical. At the Naval Academy, he was given the nickname of 'Wizard' because he seemed to perform witchcraft with electronics and possessed an astonishing memory. Middleton yanked the Navy guy into what was essentially a Marine operation when Trident began, where his nickname became 'the Lizard.'

The other member of the team, Swanson, the Dead Guy, was missing, starting an R-and-R.

Middleton pointed at Freedman, whose busy brain had been sucking information from the folder in front of him. 'Lizard, summarize it, with anything you have picked up from other sources.'

'Yes, sir,' Freedman said, not looking up. 'An Iraqi physicist who we thought had disappeared in 1992 showed up two weeks ago in Baghdad. He arranged a surrender to an Army intel officer and claimed to have vital information about a new weapon of mass destruction at a place he called the Palace of Death.'

Sybelle, studying her red fingernails, interrupted. 'A WMD? I thought we killed that old horse and buried it a long time ago. Everybody looked everywhere and nobody found anything.'

'Save the questions and comments,' said Middleton. 'Go ahead, Lizard.'

'Other than saying it was a chemical-biological agent, he was reluctant to give much real information until he was formally given immunity from prosecution and protection for himself and his family. He was kept under wraps until yesterday, when a meeting was set up at Coalition Headquarters for the first formal interrogation, and he was being delivered by an armed escort of four soldiers. A sniper picked him off before he got there and also killed the officer in charge of the escort detail.'

'Talk to me, Double-Oh,' said Middleton.

'A good piece of shooting,' said Master Gunny Dawkins as he went through the photographs of the corpses. 'The first bullet hit the officer by going through the unarmored point beneath the armpit of his vest and

28

took out the internal organs right to left, including the heart. Then the Iraqi was hit in the jugular vein along the neck, just above the collar of his armored vest, left to right. Exit through his throat.' He closed the folder. 'One of those might be a lucky shot. Not two. This sniper hit what he was aiming at, and both victims bled out on the spot. My conclusion is that this was another attack by Juba.'

The general closed the drawer with his foot and slid the chair forward so he could rest his arms on the desk. 'What's your take, Captain Summers?'

'I agree with Double-Oh. It's got to be Juba, sir. Shoots, kills, and disappears. We don't know whether he is just one man or several different snipers, whether he is even real or just some Arabian fairy tale to pump up the spirits of the jihadists. Whatever, he's the best they've got, and pulling off an assassination like this in the Green Zone enhances his reputation.'

Freedman did some calculations in his head. 'I figure the shooter had a target area of no more than an inch. The unprotected opening between the vest and the sleeve of the first victim was only about an inch wide, and the sniper squeezed a bullet in there. The second shot was exact enough to hit the vein, an even smaller target. I can work up the ballistics, angles, and all that if you want.'

'Not necessary,' said Middleton. 'The people in Baghdad are doing that, and we will have their data when it comes in. What is interesting is that he knew exactly who to shoot and when the target was going to appear in a certain place at a certain time. Total inside information.'

'Liz, did the informant say anything else worthwhile

before he got popped?' Double-Oh crossed his right leg over his left knee, taking up even more space. Sybelle pushed him.

'An intel report arrived just before we came in here for the meeting,' interjected Middleton. 'The scientist said he had escaped from a laboratory in Iran, and he gave a general location near the Iraq border.'

'He used that particular word, sir? Escaped?'

'Right. So, people, that's our mission. We are going to do a little snoop and poop and find that mysterious lab.'

Middleton stood and stretched, throwing his arms wide, then put his hands on his hips. 'So we're going in. Sybelle, you will stay here this time and oversee the operation. Spin up an infiltration team and get them over to Doha. Double-Oh, you will lead the team on the ground. On your way over, detour out to Sir Geoffrey's boat and pick up Swanson. Give them a briefing, and then you two hustle down to Kuwait. Order anything you need through Lieutenant Commander Freedman.'

The Lizard blew out a short breath of relief. He did not like to travel far from his desk. 'Sir, is it wise to use Gunny Swanson on this? According to Captain Summers, he really needs some down time.'

Double-Oh answered. 'Liz, if there is any fucking chance at all that we might bump into Juba while we run this job, I want our best shooter along to cover my ass. I'll put my money on Kyle, tired or not.'

'Then he can sleep on the plane to Kuwait,' said General Middleton. 'Get to it, people. Go get me some pictures of this Palace of Death.'

4

EDINBURGH, SCOTLAND

The royal wedding of Prince William and the beautiful Barbara Seldingham, the future king and queen of England, was a plum for the press. A billion people would gather around television sets from Africa to Australia to watch the splendid event. *A billion!* Maybe more.

Television stations wanting to personalize the coverage could send a reporter and crew to London but could not transport their own mobile rigs overseas and had to lease the needed technical equipment. Every such company in the region had been booked for months in advance, and others were created just for that purpose.

Edinburgh All-Media Ltd., in Scotland, was one of the small companies founded to serve the huge demand. It had filed papers for a business permit, found a storefront office, then bought and reconfigured two vans especially for commercial television use, including external generators to power computers and editing gear inside the cargo areas. One was immediately rented by a television station in Little Rock, Arkansas, and the other was leased to a cable company in Italy. The two trucks were given distinctive purple and white paint schemes.

Juba wore a jumpsuit that matched those colors as he drove the lead van away from the city center and onto the City of Edinburgh Bypass, the A720. He slipped on dark sunglasses as he turned east, directly into the morning sun, and drove on until the A720 merged with the A1 at Old Craighall Junction. The second van followed, and they crossed the border at Lamberton.

They made the journey of a twisting 420 miles to London in a single day, entered the city, and maneuvered to the cordoned-off far end of Kensington Park that had been reserved for the regiment of production trucks that would support the television horde. There was a short line of trucks waiting to get in, and the two vans from Edinburgh All-Media slid into position at the rear. A policeman told them to stay with the vehicles until the security teams cleared them. For thirty minutes, they followed as the line grew shorter until Juba drove onto a special parking pad caked with detection sensors, where a four-man squad and their bomb-sniffing dog thoroughly combed the vehicle and found nothing. Once cleared to be inside the quarantine area, a van could not leave until after the wedding.

Juba was given a map with a specific parking slot highlighted with a yellow marking pen: the very back row, against the Cyclone fence. The other purple and white van had a slightly better spot, one row in front and about fifty yards away, to the left. The Italians had more clout than the station from Arkansas.

The driver of the second van caught a late train back to Scotland, where he would dismantle the little office of Edinburgh All-Media Ltd. Juba did not have far to go: he was spending a few days with his mother and father at their small place in the West Midlands, the home of his boyhood.

In the Med, a streak of sunshine as bright as a spotlight came through the slightly parted curtains over the port-hole and hammered the face of Kyle Swanson until he woke up. It was almost noon. Everyone passing in the corridor outside had been content not to awaken him and had tiptoed around his cabin door. After stretching, he took a shower and shaved. By the time he put on fresh jeans and a golf shirt and running shoes, he almost felt human. His head hurt.

Stepping outside, he found that the storm had passed on and had been replaced by a calm green sea and a sunlit sky, and the *Vagabond* was heading east at about twenty knots, churning into the deep water. No land was visible. A squadron of seagulls followed the white wake, and the temperature was warm.

Up one deck, he entered the main cabin of the yacht, a spacious lounge with a full bar in one corner and a comfortable arrangement of sofas, soft chairs, and heavy antique Chinese tables. A giant flat-screen television set and an electronic entertainment center were built into one bulkhead. Sir Geoffrey Cornwell was hunched forward and reading news reports flashing on the screen of a lap-top computer. A retired colonel from the British Special Air Services, Jeff had built a fortune making and selling state-of-the-art weapons systems. He seldom got excited and was very aware that warriors handled stress in different ways. It was not exactly a secret that they got drunk on occasion to deal with the stress.

Jeff raised his shaggy eyebrows. 'Rough night?'

A carafe of chilled orange juice was on the buffet, and Kyle poured a glass and drank it before answering. He filled a thick ceramic mug with coffee and picked up a small bowl of fruit at the buffet. 'Was drunk. Now sober.' No apologies.

Lady Patricia was reading a magazine beside a large window that provided a panoramic view of the passing sea. She looked up, took an elegant pull on a small, thin cigar, and blew away the smoke. 'You are our wayward boy, Kyle. You were quite naughty last night, but we've seen you worse. Do it again, however, and I shall spank you.'

'Is that an offer, m'lady?' He smiled. Conversation made his head hurt.

'Don't act the little pervert now. Ask Dr. Russell to give you something for your hangover.'

'I'm fine,' said Kyle.

'Spoken like a true warrior. You are truly a hard man, Kyle Swanson,' Sir Jeff said without looking away from the screen.

They sat in silence for a while, comfortable, and Kyle let his eyes close. In two minutes he was asleep again, with his head back against the sofa. Pat looked over at Jeff, who gestured that she should keep quiet. 'Let him be,' he said. Jeff had just checked one of his e-mail accounts and found an encoded message from Washington. Trouble was on the way, and Kyle was going to need all the sleep he could get.

Captain Rick Newman was in a garage on a military base in North Carolina, up to his armpits in grease as he worked on his latest automotive restoration project, a

34

1955 Chevy Bel Air two-door hardtop with fender skirts. The outside skin of the old car was in decent shape, not much rust; the original baby blue and cream paint scheme was still visible, the chrome running trim undented. The interior needed major renovation, but it would just take some time and money to make it cherry again. The engine, though, a rare 350 V8, was for shit, and the deeper he dug into its guts, the shittier things got. It would cost a fortune to replace the whole thing, which was against the rules for a serious hobbyist and car trader like Newman. He had bought the car for nine thousand dollars at an Alabama estate sale and planned to restore it personally and sell it on the upside of $50K. It would take years. 'Hey, Cap'n! You got a phone call over here,' shouted a motor pool Marine.

Rick wiped the grease from his hands and picked up the receiver. 'Captain Newman,' he said.

'Hey, Rick. This is Sybelle Summers calling from Trident in Washington.' The voice was some hybrid of a normal tone, authoritative sandpaper, and a purr.

'Hi, Sybelle. Long time,' he said, suddenly alert. 'What's up?'

'We've got a job for you, my friend. Get back to your office right away and call me back on a secure line. Top Secret.'

'On my way,' he said. 'Fifteen minutes.' He hung up, closed the Chevy's hood, and hurried away to clean up and get to his desk. The Bel Air would have to wait. Newman was part of a Marine Special Operations Company that comprised four platoons. The rotation had one platoon in Iraq, one in Afghanistan, one in training at this secret base in North Carolina, and the fourth on ready alert, sitting on a short leash, ready to go anywhere in four hours.

When he spoke to Sybelle Summers on the secure link, her orders were quite simple and explicit. He was to choose five more designated operators for a black mission, get over to Camp Doha, in Kuwait, and link up there with Master Gunnery Sergeant O. O. Dawkins, who would give them a full briefing. Eight men would be going in, and Newman's group would provide the guns in case something went wrong.

She gave him only a brief overview to help pick the specialists he would take and said he could plus up with scouts, snipers, or anyone else he needed. Trident would chop them from their current assignments and arrange the temporary duty. To Newman, it sounded like he was going to need shooters to provide firepower for a special op. He had plenty of good ones from which to choose. He would rather work with people from his own team, highly disciplined and well trained, who already knew each other. His group would click together like a well-oiled military machine. Hughes, Tipp, and Rawls for certain. Two more and himself. The addition was easy. His group was six. Double-Oh made seven. Who was the eighth?

Newman began making calls of his own.

Darren Rawls faked a move to the right, pulled back, and went up and up and up. Rawls, with a thirty-one-inch vertical leap, seemed to levitate in slow motion as he flicked his wrist and delivered a jump shot from the top of the key. His sneakers hit the concrete court as the ball finished its arc to the basket with nothing but net. 'Game over, Rabbit. Pay me the money,' he told Joe Tipp, a lanky white boy who was better at football than hoops. Both were sweating hard in the North Carolina sun that baked the hidden, off-limits military installation. They were the lead instructors in an escape and evasion training mission and had started the young members of the platoon through the assigned exercise at dawn. The first and fastest would be approaching the finish well after dark. At sundown, when the trainees were exhausted but feeling confident about having made the distance, Rawls and Tipp would hunt them down, one by one, and capture them. Then the fun would begin in the interrogation hut. Until then, they might as well play ball or take a nap. Their beepers sang out at the same moment.

Travis Hughes was out pillaging and terrorizing the countryside on his Suzuki Hayabusa GSX1300R. The speed limit was 65 mph, but Hughes had not pimped out his bright red rice-burner to go 65. The Marine staff sergeant, a sniper team leader, wore a blue bandanna around his head, dark sunglasses, creased black leathers with an Outlaws patch, and biker boots. Long red hair flew behind him as he stormed back toward the base. The blonde at the bar had been with Marines before, and when the beeper stuttered on his belt, she knew he was gone. She walked with him outside and gave him a long wet kiss when he powered up his machine. She nibbled his ear and said, 'Stay out of trouble this time, Travis.' Hughes revved up the bike. 'Don't think I can do that, darlin',' he said and launched the motorcycle out onto the road, laughing into the sharp wind that whipped around him. He bent low over the handlebars and cranked it up to a comfortable 110, hauling butt back to the base.

LONDON

Television reporter Kimberly Drake was only two years out of journalism school and still a little fish, even within her Arkansas station. She wanted to be considered a serious journalist, not just a talking head, and sometimes felt that her good looks were no advantage whatsoever. Every station had a beautiful anchor or weathergirl, and she could no longer even imagine an unattractive woman hosting a television newscast. To break out of Little Rock, Kim needed some big stories, and once she had earned her spurs and boosted her reputation, she could jump to a bigger station or at least a cable network.

Then, out of nowhere, the station management decided to send its own correspondent to the royal wedding, just like its big competitors, as part of the continuing battle for advertising dollars. Kimberly would have happily either screwed or killed her news director to get the assignment but did not have to do either. Since the rest of the reporting staff was male and the female anchor was too pregnant to travel, nobody else even wanted the assignment! To the guys, it was just a wedding. Fluff, not like a Super Bowl or a war.

The station gave Kim the job but put very little money behind the trip. Tom Lester, a veteran cameraman, accompanied her, along with a young engineer who would work as a soundman for the stand-ups. The shoestring budget meant they operated out of a small purple and white production van that the station had hired at bargain basement rates.

Kimberly did not care. As she left the Royal Wedding

Command Center Press Office in London with her new laminated credentials on a chain around her neck and walked toward the media production area in Kensington Park, she felt like a real reporter for the first time in her life.

It was not until late that night that reality sank in. Because of her low status, Kim's truck had been assigned a space far away from the parade route, on the very back row. From the camera position atop the van, she could overlook the vast media lot that had been cordoned off, and she was jealous that another purple and white van from the same company, rented by an Italian cable operator, had been given a slightly better spot about fifty yards away.

She had never seen so many media types. British journalists were as aggressive as pit bulls, and reporters and television people from dozens of other countries were arriving, also wearing press credentials for the big event. There were hundreds of them around, many of whom she recognized, although they did not know her. The network people were right at the front! Media money was everywhere. Private residents had fled the city and rented out their apartments and homes at exorbitant rates. Restaurant prices doubled around the heart of the press operations because the reporters were on expense accounts.

Kim Drake stood atop her van and sipped a cup of coffee and stared out over the media throng. She had to admit she was a little fish over here, too. A guppy swimming with sharks. *I'll show them. I'll show them all.*

5

THE MEDITERRANEAN SEA

Master Gunnery Sergeant Dawkins set foot on the spotless deck of the *Vagabond* with supreme confidence, for he, too, was a creature of the sea, having spent much of his life on boats and ships, beneath the water in submarines or flying over it in planes and helicopters. It was good to be back in his element and out of Washington on this sunny Monday morning, ready to take his best bud, Kyle Swanson, on another hunting trip. He left his luggage aboard the bird, since they would be leaving again soon.

Swanson, Lady Pat, and Sir Jeff were waiting at the edge of the helo deck, and they took him to the stern, where a table beside the swimming pool had been set with china and silver utensils and white napkins. The chef had started the eggs when the helicopter was five minutes out, and now an enormous selection of delicious food was rolled out by a female crew member dressed in whites.

Double-Oh plunged into the meal, hardly aware that the others were only nibbling at the feast since they had already had breakfast. The conversation was mild chatter, waiting for him to finish eating before getting down to business. The four of them were family in many ways, except by blood. The brotherhood of spec ops warriors was tight, and the men had known each other for years. Lady Pat was their den mother.

Swanson had joined the Marines while still a teenager, and it was Dawkins, then a staff sergeant, who first discovered that the awkward boy had a remarkable ability in the unique craft of long-distance precision firing and was also a natural in combat. Over the years, as they both rose in rank, Dawkins remained Kyle's mentor and eventually spun him off for use in special operations work by nonmilitary government agencies.

One of Kyle's more interesting assignments had not involved combat at all but was serving as a special Pentagon adviser to Sir Jeff Cornwell in the development of a new-generation sniper rifle that they called the Excalibur. It took several years of off-and-on work by Swanson, and although he always kept people at an emotional distance, he was drawn in by the magnetic friendship Jeff and Pat offered. When he had introduced them to Shari Towne as the girl he planned to marry, she also was taken under the protective wings of the Cornwells. Family. Kyle had thought for a while there that he really had one. Then Shari was murdered, and Kyle almost came apart. Pat, Jeff, and Double-Oh had been helping piece him back together slowly over time. Keeping him busy was important.

Dawkins finally finished eating and filled his coffee cup again. Lady Pat motioned for the crew member to clear the table, and the four of them were soon left alone on the deck as a soft Mediterranean breeze blew across the stern of the *Vagabond*. Pat pulled a soft shawl of Scottish wool around her shoulders to stay warm.

'I am leaving for London tonight to attend a reception for the royal wedding and then spend a lot of Jeff's money on new clothes,' she declared, looking at Swanson. 'But before I leave you boys to talk about whatever the new mission may be, I have something serious to say to you, Kyle.'

He smiled. 'What's on your mind?'

'You are still grieving for our dear girl Shari. Her death left a hole in your heart, a deep hole that you think can never heal, and you think that withdrawing into all of this black ops work will protect you,' she said. 'I did not like how you got so stupefied drunk that you didn't have sense enough to come in out of the rain. You're acting like some dumb ostrich sticking its head into the sand and thinking it cannot be seen. It isn't working, is it?'

'Instant psychobabble from Dr. Pat? You know everything?' He was instantly defensive.

She stood, and he saw tears in her eyes just before she slapped him so hard that his ears rang. 'Don't you dare speak like that to me, Kyle Swanson! Do you believe that you are the only one who loved Shari? That your heart was the only one broken when she died? I still cry when I think of her. I am thankful that she was in our lives at all.'

'So how did you get over her, Pat? What's the secret?' He was growing angry. He did not like to talk about Shari, even with Jeff and Pat and Double-Oh.

She had a hand on each hip and glared at him. 'You think that Jeff and I got over her? How wrong you are. You *never* get over that kind of loss. You just . . . eventually . . . come to accept it as something you cannot change. The sun comes up in the morning, the clock ticks, and Shari will still be dead. You cannot climb into the coffin with her.' Pat pulled her wrap tight around her shoulders. 'Wake up, Kyle. Shari's been gone for more than a year, and you are condemned to live with the rest of us now. I want you back, the real Kyle Swanson, not some war junkie who is on his way to becoming an otherwise useless alcoholic.' She turned, shook her head, and walked away to the main cabin.

Swanson fell back in his chair. *Jesus Christ. She just beat the crap out of me.* Kyle had been disturbed for months when he could no longer mentally recall every detail of Shari's beautiful face, nor smell her fragrance, although he could still imagine her touch and her laugh. He was losing her. She was fading over time. 'What's your opinion, Jeff?' he asked.

'What she said.' He drank some coffee and unblinkingly returned Kyle's stare.

'And you?'

Master Gunny Dawkins picked up his briefcase and pulled out a folded map. 'I'm your friend, not your confessor. Whatever it takes, as long as it takes. But if you get fucked up on booze or dope and get me killed, I shall be very unhappy. Now can we please move past this Oprah moment and talk about the fucking mission?'

Double-Oh laid out the map, pointing at a grid location close to the southwestern tip of Iran. 'This is where the defector said the so-called Palace of Death was located, almost within rock-throwing distance of the border. We know from the satellites that there's nothing important down there except the port town of Khorramshahr. Beyond that is just a lot of dirt, which is why the boss wants to put some boots down and take a look.'

'Could the walk-in just have been looking for a quick cash payment with his allegedly secret information?' Kyle asked. 'Peddling bogus information to Americans is not exactly new in Iraq.'

'Not bloody likely if someone went to the trouble to assassinate him in the Green Zone. There was a reason.' Jeff sat back and folded his hands over a growing belly, the price of success. He was no longer young and jumping out of airplanes.

'That was a perfect stalk and shoot,' Double-Oh looked over at Kyle. 'We're sure it was Juba. The description from the hotel people matches what we know about him, and he did everything but leave his autograph. So somehow he's involved, too.'

'Lots of loose ends,' said Kyle. 'But why Iran? It would be a lot more credible if an Iraqi scientist emerged from Syria, since that's where Saddam stashed his big weapons, up around al-Baida, and in the Bekaa Valley in Lebanon. Iran and Iraq hated each other after eight years of war and a million casualties. I cannot see this level of co-operation, even so many years later.'

Sir Jeff picked up the map and studied it. 'Unless . . .' They could almost see the wheels turning in the man's brain. 'At the end of that war, there were months of negotiations before the two sides agreed to the solution brokered by the United Nations. Very little was changed in the long run, but some deals were made concerning captured territory and the shared use of the Shatt al-Arab waterway.'

'History lesson number 42,' said Kyle. 'What is your point?'

'What if this Palace of Death thing was one of the

backchannel agreements, something even the UN people did not know about? Hussein and the ayatollahs overlooked their differences long enough to make a deal for the future.'

Double-Oh was interested. 'Meaning us?'

'I'll get to that. What was the major thing people remember about the Iran-Iraq War? The use of chemical weapons by Iraq to blunt Iranian frontal assaults. Later came the biochem attacks in the Kurdistan region. You certainly remember the Arab saying that "the enemy of my enemy is my friend." Both sides consider America to be the Great Satan, and both sides anticipated that sooner or later, one or both of them would be facing us in combat.'

Kyle finished his coffee. 'So these crazies, the mullahs and Saddam's thugs, start planning something way back in the 1980s? A jointly owned and operated bioweapons factory? Then they never used the product?'

'If they were trying to come up with something really new and effective and deadly, perhaps it just wasn't ready in time for the Gulf War, and things tightened up quickly during the current war. The United States sold weapons to both sides during the Iran-Iraq fighting, and so much matériel and cash has been lost or stolen during the current war that it cannot even be counted. Throw in the massive support the United States supplied to the Afghan rebels that fought the Soviet Union and it is reasonable to believe they had access to plenty of raw materials and plenty of time for development.'

'So you think there really may be something to this Palace of Death idea?'

'The name is just a name, like Saddam's "Mother of

45

All Battles," but they have to call it something. Whatever is out there needs to be uncovered.'

'That's the job. Kyle and I are heading down to Doha to pick up a MARSOC team, then go in early tomorrow morning.' Double-Oh stood and put away his map. 'Give my apologies to Pat for my not being able to stay longer. I still have some money she hasn't stolen from me at poker.'

Kyle shook hands with Jeff. 'Tell m'lady I'll be thinking about what she said . . . and for her to have a good time in London. I'll be back in a few days.'

Sir Jeff slapped him on the shoulder. 'Right. Only wish I was going with you.' He walked them to the helipad and waved as the helicopter lifted away.

The Marine assault team arrived at Camp Doha in Kuwait as fast as it could be assembled and flown out of North Carolina. They boarded a plane on a sunny afternoon, flew most of the night, and got off to find themselves in the desert sun of Kuwait. A waiting helicopter ferried them to a secure barracks in the special operations sector of the sprawling American base at Camp Doha, north of Kuwait City.

Every member of the team had been to Doha before, during previous tours in Iraq. It was Little America. Uncle Frosty's Oasis, the Marble Palace, the beach, and great Mexican food downtown at the La Palma. Pizza, camel races, ice cream. Doha was not a hardship post.

They knew, however, that this was not going to be vacation time, for the first thing they saw in their barracks was a stack of hazmat suits on a table by the door. They pawed through the stack and picked out correct sizes, tossed the suits onto the bunks, and followed Captain Newman over to a private room in a mess hall for chow. Afterward, he disappeared for a briefing, and the rest of them ambled back to their small barracks. Special operators do not linger in the daylight when starting a mission, and they were glad the sun was going down.

The lights were off, and Travis Hughes was the first one through the door, feeling for the switch. He was snatched from his feet by a big, meaty arm and thrown to the floor, where someone jammed a knee into his chest and pressed a knife to his neck.

Darren Rawls, the next through the door, thought Hughes had tripped and fallen. Then he felt a pistol barrel being jammed under his chin so hard that his head was forced back.

The lights snapped on. Master Gunny Dawkins removed the pistol he held on Rawls and looked furious. A guy with a black mask had Travis Hughes pinned to the floor.

'You people get in here!' Dawkins bawled in a parade ground voice. 'You're supposed to be hot shit MARSOC troops, and you are bumbling around like a bunch of Girl Scouts. Walked right into an ambush! You are on a mission, goddammit, and a lot of you would be dead by now if we were a couple of terrorists. There is no safe place over here, not even in Doha. So pull your heads out of your asses, right now!'

The other Marines sheepishly filed into the room and gathered around Double-Oh. The man in the mask sheathed his knife and held out a hand to Hughes. 'Get up, Trav,' he said. The voice was familiar. The masked guy sat on a bunk, and Captain Newman entered, locked the door, and joined Double-Oh at the front. The attention of the men was totally in focus now because they had been professionally embarrassed by letting down their guard.

'Here's the drill,' Newman said. He explained the snoop-and-poop mission and told them they would be providing fire support, if necessary, for Master Gunny Dawkins and the other man, who would be principal investigators.

Dawkins then took over. 'I know that you do not like going into a possible firefight with someone you don't know covering your back, so we have to break a rule here tonight. You all have clearance for Top Secret material, and you will never speak of what we are about to tell you to anyone, ever. Understood?' He looked around and received nods from each of the six men. Then he nodded, and Kyle removed his mask.

'This is Gunnery Sergeant Kyle Swanson. Because of special ops purposes, he was declared dead back after the Syrian mess. We both now work for Task Force Trident, which you don't need to know much about.'

'Haaaayyy! Shake!' hooted Travis Hughes, while others shouted 'Dude!' and 'Muthafucka!' and 'Awrite!' They clapped, and a few gave him high fives. Everyone knew Swanson, or knew of him. 'Quiet down,' barked Double-Oh. 'Save the happy horseshit reunion crap for later. Right now, everybody get a couple of hours sleep. We leave at 0200 hours. Be ready.'

LONDON

Juba showed his pass and walked without incident into the media grounds in Kensington Park, carrying his bag of tools. A small army of technicians was laying down rivers of cable, lighting specialists were clamping big, glaring bulbs into position, soundmen were rigging microphones, and makeup artists flung powder puffs and eyeliner on the TV news readers while writers pounded out copy and producers pulled their hair in frustration. Juba was just another tech and made his way effortlessly through the dozens of production trucks and the forest of satellite dishes atop thin poles. He spotted the distinctive Edinburgh vans and went toward them.

A pretty young woman was seated on the steps of the truck, working on a laptop computer that was balanced on her knees. She looked up with a start when she realized someone was standing in front of her. He wore a technician's purple and white jumpsuit with a belt of tools hung around his narrow waist. Even in the dark, he looked as if he had a deep tan. 'May I help you?' she asked.

The man referred to a scrap of paper. 'Are you Miss Drake?'

'Yes.'

'I'm from Edinburgh All-Media. They sent me down to give the vans a last-minute look to be sure you don't have any problems tomorrow. Is your engineer around?'

'Sure. He's inside.' She led him into the cargo bay. 'Harold? This tech is from the rental service and wants to see if anything is wrong.'

Juba followed her in, shook the hand of the engineer, and turned back to Kim. 'Nothing is wrong, Miss Drake. Just a precaution, mind you. We want everything to go smoothly for you tomorrow. So, have you encountered any problems?' he asked Harold.

'Nope, but glad you came around to check.' The engineer had on a headset and was working a bank of lighted dials. 'I'm setting the uplink to go live. Let me know if you need me.'

'Right. Won't be a minute.' Juba studied the desktop area, dropped to the floor to look at the underneath wiring, and clicked a flashlight to see into small places. He opened the engine and played around in the compartment, climbed to the top and back down, then crawled beneath the truck, where he removed two cans of aerosol spray from his toolbox. Each was labeled as a commercial product that was widely used to blow blasts of clean air onto delicate computer components. Juba twisted the exterior coverings and pulled out the canisters within, then carefully attached them to small clamps above the exhaust pipe from the muffler. Tiny bits of explosive plastique were on the tips of the canisters, and he joined them with a common wire to a small detonator. It would go off when a certain cell phone number was dialed, and the contents of the canisters would be released.

While he worked, Kim Drake continued preparing for her upcoming live shot for the six o'clock evening news back home. She had managed to snare a good report, standing in front of the palace with one of those tall soldiers in the red coat and funny-looking fur hat. When she was done filming, she stepped away from the spot, and a press officer ushered in another reporter to do the same thing. The news director back home loved it and set the report for the evening news.

Juba finished just as Kim was doing her makeup at a mirror in the van. 'Pardon, Miss Drake, if you don't mind. May I snap a few photos of you and Harold and your cameraman? Hate to be such a bother, but the company wants some pictures for its adverts after you lot are gone. Drum up more business for us in the lean times, you know.' The request was so polite that they all agreed, and Juba took out a digital camera.

'Just wait until I finish my hair,' Kim called. 'I look horrible.' He shot a series of pictures of Harold at the controls while he waited.

Kim snapped off the light and stepped forward. 'Any time you're ready.'

'Are you famous, Miss Drake?' He clicked two pictures.

'No, not yet. Working on it.' Broad smile, hands on hips, blond hair in helmet hairspray mode. American Idol.

'I find that difficult to believe. Obviously you're talented, or you would not be here.' Two more pictures. 'Very good. My thanks to all of you. The company will be pleased up to get these. You are okay here, so I'll just be off now to check the other van. Some Italian chaps.'

He repeated the drill with the Italian van, where only a technician was on duty. There was one big difference. Inside the truck, Juba tilted the driver's seat forward and unscrewed a panel door, and the aroma of fresh coffee filled the interior. 'That smells good. Are you brewing a pot of coffee down there?' asked the man at the console.

Juba explained over his shoulder that they packed coffee around some of the more sensitive avionic components to absorb excess moisture because the damp climates of Scotland and England played havoc with the delicate equipment. In reality, the strong coffee smell masked the scent of the large brick of C-4 explosive attached to a small lead-lined box. Sniffing dogs had moved right over it during the final security inspections. Juba fished out his camera and took a few pictures, then reached inside the lead-shielded compartment and clicked a metal switch attached to the explosive, which lay beside a large aerosol canister. The weapon was armed. He set the timer on a backup detonator, poured in some fresh coffee beans to cover it, screwed the panel back in place, and lowered the seat.

'There. That's it, now. I will be going along. Good luck.' The technician paid no attention as he left.

Kimberly Drake was in a pool of bright light, facing a TV camera on a tripod and smoothing her navy blue jacket over the pink button-down shirt. Her hair and the top half of her outfit were perfect, but since she would only be shown from the waist up, she also wore jeans and white sneakers. She held a microphone in one hand.

She seemed to be talking to herself, muttering as she rehearsed her report. As Juba passed, she glanced up. 'Thanks for coming by,' Kim said. 'Keep watching TV and maybe you'll see me someday, rich and famous.'

Juba returned the smile. 'I have no doubt of that at all, Miss Drake. I am sure that after tomorrow, the entire world will know your name.'

'One can always hope,' she said. ' 'Night.'

6

The dull black special ops helicopter sliced high above the border between Iran and Iraq in the cold early morning hours at 175 miles per hour, and wind howled through the open cabin. Three heavily clad men stood attached to safety harnesses behind the 7.62 miniguns mounted at the side door and the port side escape hatch and a .50 caliber machine gun on the lowered rear deck. The U.S. Air Force pilots had engaged the stealth capabilities of the big MH-53J Pave Low III Enhanced helicopter, such as the infrared engine exhaust suppressors, and the sensor package in the craft's bulbous nose sniffed for danger signals.

The Pave Low had gone across the border at a high altitude but then swooped down like a hawk through the night, the pilots trusting the terrain-following radar as they hurtled the machine forward only a hundred feet off the deck. The biggest helicopter the Air Force had, the versatile Pave Low, a direct descendant of the Vietnam-era Super Jolly Green Giant, was the platform of choice for covert insertions and extractions deep in enemy territory. Two large General Electric engines fed the huge single rotor that allowed extra armor plating, and it could fly in any sort of weather. The eight Marines aboard were an extremely light cargo for the helicopter, for thirty more could have fit into the cavernous cargo space. That absence of weight allowed the Pave Low to perform even more niftily than usual.

Kyle Swanson hunched against the icy blast, protected somewhat by the extra insulation and activated charcoal lining in his bulky hazmat suit. The Mission Oriented Protective Posture (MOPP) outfits were to protect them against chemical, biological, and aerosol agents, but the heavy rubber gloves, masks, and booties made Kyle feel as if he were wading through syrup. On top of the suits, they carried full combat loads, including double water, ammo, and chow for three days.

Swanson breathed steadily, easily. The goal was reconnaissance only, so they would not be going into a hot LZ. It was to be hide-and-seek and not a combat engagement. In fact, Kyle would regard it as a failure if the lightly armed Marine team made any contact at all with Iranian armed forces.

The crew chief's voice cut through the communications link into Swanson's black flight helmet, telling them to get ready. Kyle signaled: two minutes out.

The Marines wobbled to their feet and grabbed handholds as the chopper flared into a hover and lowered. Double-Oh was at the head of one stick of Marines, and Captain Newman led the other, and through the open hatch they could begin making out some details of the land below. Kyle was in the rear to make sure everybody got off. At a motion from the crewman, they all scrambled down the rear ramp and had to hop only about a foot to hit the dirt. Swanson watched them all go, gave a signal to the crew chief, and leaped from the lip of the ramp himself as the Pave Low tilted nose down and soared into a two-thousand-feet-per-minute climbing turn for the return to Camp Doha.

The team sprinted into a perimeter position and hit the dirt with weapons covering all 360 degrees. It was dark out there and also very quiet, an almost tangible feeling of solitude after the racket of the helicopter insertion. Swanson unpacked the chemical and biological detection devices and scanned the area. To give themselves plenty of distance from the suspect site and minimize contamination danger, they had landed four kilometers away. There was nothing dangerous on the breeze. He peeled off his hood and the rebreathing mask and motioned for the others to do the same. They had to do a fast march to find an observation point, and the Marines quickly shed the MOPP suits, which prevented anyone from doing anything quickly.

Newman did a map check with Double-Oh through the red lens of a flashlight and a GPS locator and determined they were just where they were supposed to be. Had they come in by parachute, they would have been scattered all over the terrain, but instead they had landed and could move as a cohesive unit. 'Rawls,' whispered the captain. 'Lead out.' Newman pointed in a specific direction, and Darren Rawls stepped away, flipping down his night vision goggles and going over a rise. One by one, the others followed him, weapons at the ready and moving deeper into hostile Iran with every step.

The quietness was eerie and unsettling. Even in the middle of the night, *something* should be moving about, but there were no birds, no small predators, no night-foraging animals at all. A few empty shacks. There were some sickly-looking trees, and the fields over which they walked were just dirt, with no growing crops, nor evidence of a harvested one. Nothing. An agricultural dead zone near a major waterway.

Kyle kept a close read on the dials of his instruments, but they remained steady and in the neutral zone. 'Some wicked shit,' he said to Double-Oh. Whatever had killed everything was no longer around, but its evil sign was everywhere. He spoke to Captain Newman. 'Palace of Death should be only a half mile now. Let's set up a security position here and then patrol out to find an observation point.'

They were exposed on a plain, and daylight was not far away, but they could not hide in a gulley or a low wadi. Chemicals and biologicals were heavier than air and tended to settle into the lowest points around, and the dirt in a hole might still grip some of the deadly material. The team would have to make a home on high ground, but there was little of that available. While everyone else took a break and filled up with water, Joe Tipp and Travis Hughes ventured closer to the designated area and came back within thirty minutes, puzzled.

'There's nothing much out there,' Hughes reported. 'Didn't see anything but a small bunker complex inside a fenced area. Apparently deserted.'

'No palace?' asked Swanson.

'None,' Hughes said. 'I thought we would find something like Cinderella's castle. This thing looks like a small parking garage on the bad side of Detroit.'

'Huh,' Kyle grunted.

'And get this: The fence is about ten feet high and topped with razor wire, but the gate is hanging unlocked and open.'

Joe Tipp said they had found a decent overwatch site to the south about four hundred meters away, along the single road leading into the site from the nearest population center, Khorramshahr.

'Okay, then, Captain Newman. That's our OP,' Kyle said.

'Roger that. You, Double-Oh, and Tipp set up there, and the rest of us will establish a good support position here. Let's go,' Newman said. Tipp took point, and Swanson fell in behind him, reading the dials, while Double-Oh walked at the tail end. The rest of the MARSOC team began building hide sites and gathering bushes for camouflage.

The OP was in an area where a washboard of ridges began and expanded higher and higher into the distance, so it did not stand out like a pimple on the flatlands. Once at the crest, the three Marines had a clear view of both the road and the target site, so they made themselves a hide among low, decaying trees and thin weeds. In a few minutes, a powerful spotter scope, a pair of binos, and the scope of the sniper rifle were examining the structure, inch by inch, parsing it in every way possible. The clouds had parted, and illumination was good. Not so much as a dog barked.

'Ain't nobody home down there, Shake,' said Double-Oh after watching for a half hour. 'Place is run-down and empty.' Wind had covered up most vehicle tracks, which indicated nothing had been driving around recently, and they could see no footprints.

'Yeah,' said Kyle. 'I don't think we're going to need to watch this for three days. It *feels* empty.'

'Spooky,' said Tipp. 'So we stay here all day and go in tonight? Why not go in right now and be done with it?'

Swanson shook his head. 'We only have a good hour left before daybreak. We need to take our time in there. Remember, slow is smooth, smooth is fast.'

'Too risky right now,' added Double-Oh. 'I don't think anyone is down there, but there may be some activity in the area. We'll watch it all day, then go in as a four-man team tonight. The other four guys will set up a firing position here while we make a thorough snoop.' He found the keypad on his digital communications terminal and typed a message that flashed up on Captain Newman's DCT. *Send Rawls.*

Darren Rawls, carrying a heavy machine gun, appeared at the OP in a few minutes as the other three wiggled around to make room for him. He smoothly set up the weapon, which gave the OP more firepower. Then they began a rotation of two men on watch while the other two slept for a few hours. It was going to be a long day in Iran.

With the sun up, they had a clearer view of the surrounding area. A main highway led out of the city, heading northeast, and the road the Marines were watching seemed to be an isolated track that led only to the site. It was about ten miles long. Two guard posts, one a mile from the site and the other near the wire, were abandoned. Not a vehicle came up the road all day.

Rick Newman crawled to the OP as the sun started to set and found all four of the men there already wearing their heavy MOPP suits, except for the hoods and masks. He agreed to accelerate the mission by a day and went back to bring forward his other Marines and do a communications update. The helicopter was scheduled for 0400.

Swanson, Double-Oh, Joe Tipp, and Rawls hurried through the open gate and stacked beside the gaping entrance to the building, then plunged through as a group. They did a hasty search and clear of the small layout, and Kyle read the dials: nothing dangerous. Their flashlights, however, scanned the walls in four bright circles, and the evidence of a recent fire was clearly visible. Kyle reached out a finger and swiped a path through a deep layer of soot.

A freight elevator was in one corner at the edge of an exterior loading dock, and a broad staircase led down into darkness. The Marines descended in pairs on each side, and Double-Oh kicked the door at the bottom. It burst open to reveal another empty room, which must have been an office before it was destroyed by fire. Through another door at the rear, and down another staircase, they found the tangled debris of what once had been a laboratory.

While the others stood in protective positions, Kyle waved his wands and sensors throughout the room. Whatever the monster that caused so much destruction was, this was where it was born and probably also was where it died. There was no sign of an accident, so the fire was likely deliberate. Apparently the occupants had thrown in some thermite-style grenades after soaking the place in flammable liquids. Fire is the best way to destroy chemical and biological agents, which vanish in the flash of intense heat. The blackness of the soot was even thicker in the ruined laboratory, and the MOPP booties were almost ankle deep in the stuff. The dials remained steady and harmless.

One more door, one more staircase.

They were far underground now, and since fire burns up, not down, the damage was not as great as on the lower level. Kyle found a bilingual sign at the top of the staircase with Arabic script and Korean lettering. Just as in Syria, the underground bunker complex had been built by North Korean engineers.

A central square room was the hub of six separate corridors, and a pair of Marines went down each of them.

'Jesus Christ!' muttered Double-Oh as he and Kyle came to a stop outside a barred cell door. The walls were also scorched back here, but the fire had cooked hotter above, and it would have required some time to reach back along the concrete fingers, where there was a minimum of oxygen. The scorched bones of a human being lay beside the door inside the cell, as if he had been trying to pull the bars apart in his last minutes during the process of suffocation and incineration. Apparently the flammable liquid also had been splashed inside the cages prior to the fire. The poor inmates had been doomed to burn alive.

Every cell held the same gory story. A dead person in each. Swanson scanned them, and there was some light ticking on one of the meters. He backed away.

'Okay, guys. Rawls, you take a position at the top of the stairs by the entranceway while the rest of us break out our cameras and document all of this for the intelligence people to figure out.' He wanted to take the contaminated body out with them, but there was no way to secure it to prevent whatever infection it carried from spreading. He would have to settle for cutting a few samples from the corpses, sealing them in double plastic ziplock bags, and wrapping those tightly with duct tape.

The three Marines removed their hoods and masks, then put them back on because it was so hard to breathe deep inside the bunker complex. It was like standing inside a giant fireplace. They worked as fast as possible, wanting to clear out of this building, go home, and take a shower. 'Palace of Death is right,' said Joe Tipp. 'Not much to look at, but the name is sure accurate down here.'

Captain Newman's voice sounded suddenly in their earpieces. 'Get out now! Somebody's coming fast!'

They were on the bottom floor, documenting the tiny cells and their inhabitants, when the call came in. Racing up three floors on slippery stairs while wearing MOPP booties was pointless. There was no way to make it in time, and when they cleared the final doorway into the upstairs office area, Rawls was motioning for them to take cover. Two vehicles raced through the open gates and braked to hard halts with the headlights shining on the building.

One was an old Range Rover, and in it were a young man who was driving and a woman as a passenger. The second was a military truck with a squad of armed men wearing Iranian Revolutionary Guard uniforms, chasing the people in the Range Rover and not hunting for U.S. Marines.

'Hold fire,' Captain Newman said over the intercom.

The Marines on the overwatch and inside the building observed what was happening with their fingers on their triggers. Swanson had left the sniper rifle behind for the building search. He brought his small M-4 carbine to bear on the group and focused the scope.

The soldiers had surrounded the front vehicle and were yelling for those inside to get out. The doors opened, and the driver exited and was immediately pummeled to the ground and dragged a short distance away, still in the pool of bright light. The woman got out slowly, but she, too, was smashed to the ground and hauled over beside the prone driver. She struggled to her knees, pleading; 'I am just looking for my brother!'

A soldier in a beret, possibly an officer, shouted at her. 'You are a traitor and a spy! You were told to stay away from this place. Your infidel brother has run away.'

'No,' said the woman. 'He would not do that. He is only a student and loyal to our country.'

'Another traitor.' The soldier pulled out his pistol and kicked the driver in the ribs. The man groaned. 'And I know who you are, too, only too well. The president of the university student council. A man who speaks loudly against our government. You did not come out here just to find her brother.'

The driver said nothing, and the soldier gave a signal for several of his men to move in and begin savagely beating the young man, who curled into a fetal position. The woman screamed and was grabbed when she tried to protect him.

'Call in the helicopter, Captain,' Kyle said on his radio. 'We're going to stop this.'

'Negative, Swanson. Our mission does not include contact. As long as they stay outside, we sit tight. Just in case, I'll put the bird on standby.'

There was laughter as the beating and kicking continued until the driver stopped moaning in pain and went silent, unconscious.

'Traitor,' said the officer. He walked over to the still figure on the dirt, raised his pistol, and fired two shots into the head. He turned to the woman. 'You were warned several times. You disobeyed our instructions. A worthless woman troublemaker.' He balled up his fist and hit her in the head, and she fell over.

The soldiers put aside their weapons and moved closer, keeping her in the full light of the vehicles. One reached out and tore away her headcover, revealing the terrified face of a beautiful young woman with long black hair. They began to grab at her clothing, laughing and calling insults.

Kyle said to Double-Oh, 'I think we need to take her back for interrogation.'

'Good idea,' Dawkins replied.

'Are you sure of that?' came the voice of Captain Newman.

Kyle replied, 'My mission, my call.' They were all under his command, there only to support him.

'Roger that. Pave Low inbound.'

Swanson said, 'All members listen up. I'll take the first shot, and my target is the officer with the pistol. Double-Oh, take the target to his immediate left. Rawls, you have the target to his right, and Tipp takes the guy next to the vehicle.' He paused while he scanned the area again.

'Captain Newman, your four men take the two targets behind the vehicle. Ambush commences on my shot.'

The officer was only twenty-five meters away. Kyle pulled the crosshairs of his scope on the man's head, steadied his own breathing, and pressed the trigger. There was a single crisp retort of gunfire, and the officer's body stood still for a moment, then fell backward with half of the skull and all of its contents missing.

The other Marines opened on their targets, and the IRGs were caught in a cross-fire from the observation point and from inside the building. It was almost impossible to miss, and the Iranians had stacked their weapons prior to assaulting the woman.

'Cease fire, we're coming out!' yelled Double-Oh, and the four Marines charged from the building into the remaining IRG troops, moving forward in a line and with their weapons tight on their shoulders. In ten seconds, the entire Iranian squad had been wiped out, and the shooting stopped.

'Let's go,' Kyle said as he plucked a grenade from his web gear to throw into the army truck. Tipp popped one free for the Range Rover.

Double-Oh slung his weapon, leaned over, and easily scooped up the terrified woman in his huge arms. 'Don't worry. You're safe now. We won't let anything happen to you.' He began trotting back to the observation post. Then there was a burst of automatic weapons fire. The big master gunnery sergeant grunted in surprise, paused for a moment, and then resumed his run, staggering the last few feet until he collapsed facedown among the Marines.

'Goddamn! Blow that fucking truck away!' Kyle yelled

as he lobbed the grenade. Some soldiers had stayed behind with the truck and remained unseen in the firefight. A hurricane of bullets now shredded the vehicle, which lurched hard under the impact until the grenade exploded and the truck detonated in a ball of flame.

Kyle scrambled up the incline and dropped to his knees beside Double-Oh, looking at the bullet hole. 'Oh, fuck,' he said.

7

Jeremy Mark Osmand – Juba – awoke from a disturbed sleep into an unsettling moment during which he did not know where he was. The former British paratrooper was drenched in sweat. *Why does it still bother me?* Familiar and terrible memories flooded up during long nights and sat on his chest so heavily that he could hardly breathe. Palestinian kids blown apart by Jew rockets and Russians doing the same thing to Muslim children in Chechnya. A baby dead on its dead mother's breasts in Afghanistan, flies on their open eyes. Pakistan, the Balkans, Colombia, Ecuador, and, for too many months, Iraq.

Then he realized that he was not in some war zone but safe at his family's home in England, awakening to the smell of cooking eggs and sausage. His mother had gotten up before dawn because she knew he had to leave again. He showered and dressed in a blue Armani suit and a D&G Bengal stripe shirt with a solid blue tie, with soft black Cole Haan shoes, and a Fortis watch on his wrist. The upscale clothes were just another uniform, one that said 'successful business executive.' He looked around his old room. Soccer trophies, club flags, ribbons, and photographs of the young striker scoring goals. His old prep school jacket with the golden crest on the pocket still hung in the closet. Yesterday's hero.

He went downstairs. The house was small and immaculate, everything in exactly the same place it always was. A photograph taken ten years earlier would show the same furniture in the same spots, the time difference marked only by the changes in the faces of the people in the pictures. They were all younger then. He lifted his mother from the floor and twirled her in a circle in the tiny kitchen.

'Stop that this minute, Jeremy,' she commanded with a giggle. 'I am cooking! The toast will burn.' As if that were important. He loved her without reservation.

Martha Goodling Osmand thought her son traveled too much, although she had put in more than a few miles herself as a young firebrand human rights attorney when she went out to the hellholes and recorded what the devils were doing. An Israeli bullet shattered her knee during a raid on a Palestinian refugee camp on the West Bank and clipped her traveling wings but not her spirit. Now she worked from home, hosting a Web site to help Muslim refugees.

His father, Dr. Allen Osmand, came into the kitchen and gave his wife an affectionate good-morning peck on the cheek. A thin man with a neat beard, he, too, was impeccably dressed for work, The doctor sat across from his son at the table.

'How long do you intend to keep up this schedule, Jeremy?' his mother scolded as she poured hot tea. 'When are you going to get your company to assign you to the home office here in England? I want to be able to play with the toes of my grandchild before I am too old.'

'Look who's talking.' He laughed. 'You two hauled me all over the world as a kid, taught me languages, how to travel and to get along with people. Now you complain because I'm taking advantage of that training to make a living.' He sipped the tea and cut his toast into triangles, dipping them into the egg yolk. 'I am just a poor salesman, forced to hustle for my next meal at some five-star restaurant in Berlin or Paris, and it's your fault.' He looked at the clock. Almost time to go. 'Are you going to watch the wedding today, Mum? Not going down there, are you?'

'Oh, wouldn't dream of getting mixed up in that crowd. Barbara is quite lovely, and a fine match for Prince William, but my leg tells me to stay here and watch it on the telly. A volunteer from Amnesty International is dropping by to help me catch up on some work on the site.'

His father spoke. 'We expect things to be quiet around the hospital today because of the wedding, so Professor Grosvenor and I should have the lab almost to ourselves.' Jeremy nodded. Good. Perfect alibis, if ever needed.

Father and son finished their tea, and after hugging his mother, Jeremy went to the car and tossed his travel case into the back seat. As his father drove, the son wrote a note and handed it over: 'You *must* stay out of London today.' The father read it and gave it back, with a slight nod of understanding. The son tore it into little pieces and fed it out the window, bit by bit, along the morning highway.

Jeremy leaned back and studied his father, who held the steering wheel lightly with the gentle, sure hands of a talented surgeon, a man who had worked hard his whole life only to see his dreams crushed. He deserved better.

The young medical student had fallen in love with England the moment he set foot in the country from his battered homeland of Lebanon. The golden history of the British Empire enthralled him, and he trekked all over the country, wanting to become part of it but knowing that he could never really be a true Englishman because of his deep skin color, his dark eyes and hair, and the accent; a foreigner forever. To close the distance between him and the society of which he so desperately wanted to be a part, he committed the greatest shame of his life, abandoning his country of birth to become a British citizen.

Aziz Osman gained a reputation as a brilliant young doctor who healed patients of high social status. That was until the old and cancer-riddled Lady Wallendar died beneath his knife. It mattered not that the obese woman was in her eighties, and an extraordinarly poor candidate for any sort of surgery. When Osman opened her up, he found the liver, stomach, kidneys, and heart almost destroyed. Then she had a myocardial infarction while on the operating table, and it was all over in twenty minutes. Lord Wallendar had wanted a miracle and, by God, had paid handsomely to get one. He blamed Osman, and from that moment the surgeon was tainted as just another worthless wog sawbones. The big door of class slammed shut, with Osman on the wrong side, and his practice and dreams evaporated. *Wog!* The acronym for 'worthy Oriental gentleman' was the ultimate sneer.

The doctor determined that his children should not have to face that same barrier, and after taking the advice of friends, Aziz Osman went to court and formally anglicized his name. Aziz became Allen; Dr. Osman added a single letter and became Dr. Osmand. The next year, his son was born, and Jeremy Osmand grew up about as English as a boy could be.

The car pulled up at the new St. Pancras International train station in King's Cross, and Jeremy removed his bag and went inside. Since he would be traveling to the Continent, he ran the magnetically encoded card through a reading device and passed smoothly through customs and an X-ray tunnel, for he had nothing to hide. Once in the sterilized zone for departures, he would not have to go through customs on the other end of his journey, the Bruxelles-Midi station in Belgium. The high-speed Eurostar departed at 6:10 A.M., with Jeremy resting comfortably in seat 55 on the aisle of the first-class, non-smoking car number 9, reading an *International Herald Tribune*.

The Eurostar sped into the mouth of the thirty-one-mile Channel Tunnel, dashed through the Chunnel, and popped up in Europe. Two and a half hours after leaving London, he was in Brussels. He took a cab to the Silken Berlaymont Hotel on the Boulevard Charlemagne, asked for and got early check-in, and went directly to his room. With the wink of a tiny green light above the handle, the electronic coded card opened the door.

Jeremy Osmand turned on the television and placed his cell phone on a small, polished table beside the soft chair facing the set, then hung up his jacket and brewed a pot of tea in the little kitchenette. He checked his watch again and transformed himself, the genial personality of the pleasant Englishman sliding away like the discarded skin of a snake. His feelings shut down. He became Juba.

*

Security agencies were in overdrive, for nothing could be allowed to mar the wedding or threaten the royals. The streets around Buckingham Palace and St. Paul's Cathedral were searched a dozen times, and officers were posted in every building along the route. Security cameras were everywhere, their little eyes probing and curious. Uniformed policemen from the boroughs were brought in for duty, and Scotland Yard's Special Branch detectives threaded through the throng. British soldiers in combat gear were stationed in plain view.

Tuesday was a national holiday in Great Britain, and about seven hundred thousand people were jammed into the parks near the palace – Kensington, Hyde, Green, and St. James's. Each person had been searched before being allowed through the security cordon. The Royal Wedding Command Center in the Palace Gardens had been going nonstop for seventy-two hours before the ceremony and was not to stand down until William and Barbara left for their honeymoon at a private place unknown to the general public.

Every cop in England was looking the wrong way.

The wedding went off without a problem, and the royal couple signed the register after the ceremony and walked back down the red carpet, with Barbara needing help from her bridesmaids to maneuver the twenty-five-foot train of her antique lace and ivory silk gown. The prince and his smiling, radiantly beautiful bride stepped into sunshine amid nonstop cheers and hurrahs and got into a special open landau drawn by a matched team for the trip back to the palace, escorted by the glittering Horse Guards.

Juba, in Belgium, watched the carriage depart and gave it a three-minute start through the adoring crowd. He held his cell phone in both hands. When he finally dialed a number, the call bounced off a satellite and into London. It caused a dart of electricity to pulse across the microscopic gap between two strips of copper, closing the circuit in the small bomb beneath the floorboard in the purple and white press van rented by the Italians. It was a crude device, but all he needed to generate an explosion from the C-4 to rupture the lead container.

The explosion detonated the gas tank and caused a secondary eruption. The Edinburgh van tore apart as the blast peeled away its sides and knocked over the antennas of several nearby trucks. Flying pieces of metal became deadly shrapnel, and all four members of the European technical crew and three passersby were killed. Although the unruffled BBC commentators, far from the scene, continued describing the parade, the explosion was clearly heard by thousands on the ground, and the plume of smoke in the rear of the media headquarters in Kensington Park was seen by millions of television viewers before the camera intentionally swung away.

The horses pulling the landau of the prince and his new princess broke into a fast trot, and the mounted guard closed around them, sheathing their ceremonial swords and pulling free the carbines attached to their saddles.

Kimberly Drake was stunned. The unexpected explosion had smashed her against another truck, and she toppled to the ground, out of breath and dazed. She shook her head to clear the cobwebs just as the strong hands of Tom Lester, her cameraman, scooped her up.

Tom Lester, a photojournalist for more than twenty years, had stepped over a lot of bodies in a couple of wars. Any explosion that did not kill him was someone else's problem, but he had not seen one in London since the IRA had quieted down. He looked at his reporter and saw no blood. Just shock. He poured water into a cupped hand, wiped her face, and gave her a drink. That was enough tender loving care, and he shook her by the shoulder. Hard. 'Wake the fuck up, Kim! Pull yourself together! A monster story just fell right on your lucky little head!' He turned to see the young engineer looking out of the doorway of their van. 'Get back inside, Harold. Get us up live to Little Rock right now. Move, kid! We're not here as sightseers.' He snatched his camera and looked it over, wiped the lens, then hoisted it to his shoulder and adjusted the eyepiece to frame the fire, the debris, and the dead.

Kim was pegged to the spot by indecision over whether to cover the story or help the bleeding victims around her. Lester shouted, 'Get with it, Drake! This story is all ours for the time being, but others are going to be coming. It's your moment, girl. Grab it with both hands.'

'But these people, Tom . . .'

'Fuck 'em,' he snarled. 'We all take our chances in this game. They caught it, we didn't. Shit happens. The medics will be here in a few minutes for them anyway, and our job is to cover the goddam story! You make up your mind right now whether you want to be a reporter or Florence Nightingale. You stop to help those poor bastards and you can kiss your career good-bye.' He had to keep her focused, keep her mind busy, or she would falter. Fucking newbie.

Harold ran up and rigged them with collar microphones and earpieces. 'We've got the station. Go!'

'Kim? What's happening over there?' The familiar
voice of the news director back home in Arkansas com-
forted her.

'There was some kind of explosion in one of the TV
vans,' she said. 'It was not close to the parade route and
probably has nothing to do with the wedding. Maybe an
overheated generator or something.'

Lester broke into the conversation through his own
microphone. 'Fuck that! The goddam thing blew up
almost right next to us! I've got some great fucking shots
here, dude. Bodies and fires and all kinds of good shit.
Kim and I are alone with it right now, but it won't last
long. Get us on air!'

The voice in her ear told her to stand by and be ready
to go live. The news director took a few moments to
confer with the station management. Fire and destruction
always made good television, even better when media
people were involved, but this was frontline action and a
royal wedding at the same time, and their reporter had
it! 'Get your thoughts together, Kim. We're going live in
about one minute, as soon as we offer you to the network
and cables.' The additional revenue from such an exclu-
sive report could cover the budget for Kim's entire trip.

Her heart flopped, but Tom flashed a thumbs-up and
gave a smile of encouragement. The network was going
to carry her report! No other reporters were at the smoldering site yet because they had been out of position,
trying to get close to the parade route. Kim pulled out her
hairbrush and a small mirror, but Tom Lester slapped
them from her hands, saying the unkempt look of the

blond hair dangling over her forehead and the dirt on her face and jacket added authenticity. He did not want her to see the trickle of blood working a crimson path down her dirty cheek. A button had torn from her blouse, enough to give a glimpse of a lacy black bra. Sexy as hell. The voice in her earphone started a nineteen-second countdown. Then she heard the godlike tones of the network anchorman saying, '. . . and here is reporter Kimberly Drake at the site of the explosion. Kimberly?'

In his hotel room in Belgium, Juba smiled as he recognized Kim Drake. She had her opportunity, just as he had predicted. He dialed another number, and this time a soft pop no louder than a firecracker went off unheard beneath the van rented by the Arkansas station. The contents of the canisters bled invisibly into the air, crawled out from beneath the van, rose, and spread.

Kim's mike was live. Her dream was coming true. She was on live network TV! Once she started to talk, her nerves calmed and the training kicked in. Nothing fancy. *Let the pictures speak while you give the who, what, when, where, why, and how.* The network news directors were impressed with the kid.

Crew Manager William Warner of the London Fire Brigade was chewing a chocolate and peanut energy bar when the first explosion detonated less than a hundred meters from his truck. He had kept his team on full alert during the wedding, so they were already in their bulky coats, overtrousers, and fire boots. The truck was rolling in seconds, its lights flashing, the horn honking and the siren shrilling to push a path through the crowd as the crew slapped on helmets and pulled on gloves.

There were some casualties but only a small area of actual damage, and his firefighters were on it immediately with suppressant chemicals, then waded into the charred debris with their tools. Some cleared a circle for emergency medical personnel. Walker found himself bumping against a small American news reporter with a microphone in her hand.

Kim had finished her first report, but the appearance of the fire truck and its flashing lights gave her more material. Tom had them in his eyepiece as they dove into work. *Let the pictures talk!* Her throat was very dry; her eyes started to mist, and her skin itched. Probably the smoke, she thought, and plunged ahead with her work.

She had expected to be shoved aside by the big firefighter because that is what would have happened in the States, but this was England, where people valued courtesy. William Warner let her stand her ground because nothing important was happening anyway and his people had the work in hand. He coughed.

Warner had listened to the reporter and agreed with her quick conclusion that this had the look of an accident, maybe an undetected electrical fire inside the truck that set off a gas tank leak. Only an off-the-cuff hypothesis by an untrained observer, but a pretty good guess. Arson investigators would sort it out soon enough. He had already given basically the same report to the Command Center; the situation was under control. He felt a tug on his sleeve. The disheveled young reporter thrust the microphone at him, and Warner leaned down to answer the question. The telly camera was pointed at him.

Kim cleared her throat, then had to do it again before speaking. Exposed portions of her skin were stinging as if she had been attacked by a swarm of bees, and she felt woozy. She wouldn't let that sideline her. 'I am standing with an official of the London Fire Brigade,' she said. 'Sir, what can you tell us about this explosion?'

Warner was about to answer that all was quite well, that it was an accident, when he actually looked at her. The girl's face was flushing bright red, and she was rubbing her forearm, where a gelatin-like substance was clinging. Then a sharp chirp squealed from a rectangular device attached to the thick collar of his coat. He jerked his head up. More chirps were coming from the crew's uniforms, and his firefighters turned to him with alarm and shock on their faces. They were in the midst of thousands of people, and their hazardous materials detectors were singing like mad canaries.

'Get your rebreathers on and button up!' he yelled. The reporter was collapsing at his feet, clawing at her skin as she sucked in air, having trouble breathing. Her eyes rolled back. The cameraman was falling to his knees.

'Oh, dear God,' Warner said, slapping down his own face shield as he grabbed the radio that was on the frequency of the Royal Command Center. 'Red Alert! Crew Chief Warner in Sector Kensington Three. Red Alert! Dirty bomb! I repeat: *Dirty bomb!*'

8

Dawkins was a big, strong man who had more muscle tissue than an ordinary person to protect his organs, and the adrenaline coursing through his system gave him the extra burst of strength he needed to reach the Marine position while still carrying the woman. Then his eyes closed and he toppled hard to the ground.

Marines do not have medics, but they have a brotherhood relationship with combat-trained Navy corpsmen. Corpsman Rick Suarez trained alongside the MARSOC Marines, even having the mission specialty of being a demolitions expert. Suarez jumped to the side of the wounded Double-Oh even before Kyle scrambled to them.

They used knives and surgical scissors to slice away the thick gear harness, then tore open the MOPP suit and the T-shirt to get to the wound. A lot of blood was spilling from a small entry hole on the right side of the muscled back.

'Help me turn him over to see if there is an exit wound,' Suarez said. There was none, but Kyle could hear oxygen gurgling from the bullet hole, and air flowed out like bubbles in water. They had him propped in a sitting position.

Double-Oh was in the Golden Hour, the vital sixty minutes between the instant a man is hit and the time a field hospital gets him on the table. Keep him alive back to Camp Doha and his chances of recovery improved considerably. Each minute was a treasure.

Captain Newman was on his radio. 'Whiskey One-Niner, this is Hotel Seven. I have one emergency evac. Forty-year-old male. Gunshot wound to the back.'

'Roger, Hotel Seven,' said the smooth voice of the helo pilot. 'We are inbound and will meet you at designated pickup zone. Three minutes. We have a PJ aboard.' A PJ was an Air Force pararescue specialist trained in emergency medical procedures.

'Roger that,' said Newman.

'Alert the PJ that it's probably a collapsed lung with internal bleeding. Vital signs appear shallow,' Suarez called over his shoulder. Newman repeated the information.

'Help me here, Shake. We have to dress the wound and help his breathing,' Suarez said. He rummaged around in his first aid kit, found morphine, and tossed it aside because he could not administer it to an unconscious man. Then his hand closed around a thin plastic card about the size of a driver's license. He pushed it against the bleeding wound. Above that he secured a pressure bandage with medical tape.

Kyle kept holding the unconscious man in a sitting position, talking to him with a stream of vulgarity and insults, just as they usually spoke to one another. Maybe Double-Oh could hear him and maybe he couldn't, but if Kyle spoke normally, then his friend might recognize the voice and believe the wound was not serious. That would inspire hope. Getting all sappy and sorry would have the opposite effect.

'I ain't got time for your crap tonight. Patch up your fat ass and haul it to the hospital, then wait around to see if you bleed out. Probably have to dig your grave by myself and then put up with a bunch of Pentagon pukes at your funeral. You stand up out there like a fucking carnival target and get shot by that amateur? Jesus Christ, Dawkins, you are supposed to be some kind of Superman black ops dude, and I swear you would trip over a crack in the sidewalk if somebody wasn't around to lead you around like a blind mutt. You did this on purpose, didn't you? Just to get some attention and another medal and polish your résumé before retiring. Anyway, what did you leave me in your will? You ain't really got nothing I want but maybe that Ford truck, so I'll take that. Dammit, don't you die until you buy some better stuff, you hear me?'

The time for stealth was long past, so Captain Newman had designated their current overwatch position as the pickup zone for the Pave Low extraction. There was no indication of any more vehicles on the road from the city, but that would not last long if the Iranian patrol was supposed to report in at regular intervals. The roar of the approaching helicopter grew louder, and as soon as it touched down, Marines grabbed the legs and arms of Double-Oh and got him into the open door.

Swanson came next, with his hand tight around the wrist of the girl to help her aboard and strap her in. She took a last look around at the carnage of the ambush, knowing she had escaped certain death, and did not resist. Whatever lay ahead was better than being another corpse for the Palace of Death. Then the Pave Low was gone, leaving no trace that it had ever been in Iranian airspace.

The twin engines strained as the helicopter grabbed for altitude. The PJ wrapped a blood pressure cuff on Double-Oh, leaned in close to use his stethoscope, then reported to the pilot. 'Breathing is ragged, heartbeat still strong. Vital signs weak but steady, so he's holding his own. We can keep him stable until we land. Notify the docs to prepare for a serious gunshot wound in the back. The lung is punctured.' The corpsman cleared an IV needle, found a vein in the arm for a hydrating solution, and then adjusted an oxygen mask over Double-Oh's pale face. He cut away the field bandage, cleaned the wound, administered some medication to the opening, and recovered it with a thick, large sterile bandage.

Kyle could do nothing to help and snapped his mind back to the mission. 'Captain Newman, we got everybody?'

'Roger that. I counted them coming on. All plus one.'

Plus one. The woman. Swanson, seated beside her, was suddenly aware of how they must look to her eyes, a group of large foreign men with faces greased with camo warpaint, laden with weapons and helmets and packs. The attempted rape, followed by the unexpected ambush, followed again by being snatched aboard a helicopter – her senses were overwhelmed, and she sat staring straight ahead, her arms clutched about her. He removed his cap, laid aside his weapon, and pulled a box of baby wipes from an onboard pouch, using the soft papers to wipe away some of the grime and grease on his face. Then he handed her the box. The small gesture was an icebreaker, forcing her to act, to make a minor decision.

After a moment, she pulled out a few papers and wiped her own face, with a small smile of appreciation and a nod.

'Don't worry,' Kyle said in Arabic. 'You are safe with us.'

'They killed my friend,' she whispered.

'I'm sorry we couldn't save him, too.'

The woman sniffled and pulled away her scarf to dab at some tears. Lustrous brown eyes, firm cheekbones, a pretty face. She asked in English, 'You are Americans?'

'Yes. U.S. Marines,' Kyle said, then changed the subject and handed her an unopened bottle of water. 'What were you two doing out at that place so early in the morning?'

'We went out looking for my brother, a student. He was taken prisoner last week because of his political views, and we learned yesterday that he was being held in the forbidden zone. We wanted to help him escape.' She spoke with a slight British accent.

'But it was some kind of secret military installation,' Kyle said. 'You had to know that.'

The woman nodded. 'The site was being evacuated because the work, some government project, apparently has been completed. People were leaving, trucks hauling away equipment. We felt we could be safe if we moved in a hurry.' She began to weep, a nervous shudder shaking her body. 'My brother was just a headstrong boy.'

Kyle recognized that physical shock was setting in, but he would not touch her, for in her country, no physical contact whatsoever was allowed between unmarried and unrelated men and women.

'Did you see anyone in the building?' she asked softly.

'I'm sorry. There was no one alive in there when we arrived,' he said.

As she sobbed, her shoulders heaved, and finally she leaned against Kyle's shoulder for support as the helicopter jarred through the sky. 'He was just a child. Only sixteen.'

He let her lean against him but remained silent. The girl had just broken a huge religious and cultural taboo, and Swanson knew she had reached some momentous conclusion about her life. He would not tell her that her brother was probably one of the six unfortunate inmates who were found dead and locked in individual cells. Instead, he said, 'Try to relax. We'll be in Kuwait soon and sort things out. You'll be okay.'

Travis Hughes watched the interplay between Swanson and the woman carefully, again observing the duality of the complex man. The Marines had expected Shake to remain the coldhearted son-of-a-bitch leader who was perfectly capable of standing in the shadows and letting those Iranian assholes rape the girl rather than take the chance of compromising his mission. With him, the mission always came first.

Nevertheless, no plan ever worked perfectly. Sooner or later, you had to face something unexpected, and Swanson had made an instant decision based on factors that Hughes was only now adding up. It wasn't really the rape at all that triggered him.

If they allowed the IRGs to kill her, the fuckheads probably would have thrown the bodies into the building anyway. Then again, if they were any sort of soldiers at all, they probably would have at least taken a quick look inside the building. Chances of exposure in either case were almost certain, so the mission was already compromised.

That meant that the Marines were going to have to smoke the Iranian troops anyway, so Swanson decided to take them down hard and fast to prevent any information from being radioed back to their headquarters. The woman obviously was not with the soldiers, therefore she was against them, which made her a good possible source of intelligence, but only if she was alive. Kyle had decided all that in the space of a few seconds and triggered a rescue.

It was not a heroic act. Swanson had just figured that was the best way to salvage the mission and at the same time gain a bonus of intelligence. Now he sat over there talking quietly to her and letting her cry on his shoulder, as if this whole effort had been mounted just to save her.

Travis was impressed. He leaned close to Joe Tipp and motioned at Swanson. 'I think ol' Shake has a girlfriend,' he whispered.

Two clusters of people were waiting at the hospital helipad when the Pave Low came to rest at Camp Doha. They were standing apart, grouped by their specialties, as if on different teams. Just because everyone wore the same uniform did not mean they were friends.

The first small group was comprised of medical personnel, and even before the helicopter cut its engines, they hurried forward with a rolling stretcher. The team of medics helped maneuver Double-Oh onto the gurney, and the entire group ran off toward the emergency room of the base hospital, a young triage doctor trotting along behind calling instructions ahead into a handheld radio. Swanson checked his watch. Double-Oh had made it with time to spare in the Golden Hour, and now the professionals could get to work.

The second group was more rigid and moved with serious purpose: four grim soldiers wearing armored vests and carrying weapons. They approached as the MARSOC Marines climbed out of the helicopter and gathered their gear.

'Captain Newman?' called a tall man. 'I'm Lieutenant Zahn, sir. Military Police. We've been sent to collect your enemy combatant for interrogation.'

Rick Newman was surprised. 'What?'

'Your prisoner, sir. We'll take her now.'

Newman looked over at Kyle Swanson and shrugged his shoulders. His brief situation report during the helicopter ride had somehow been read as the team bringing home a valuable enemy prisoner. Swanson had his face turned away from the soldiers but shook his head slightly. *No.*

'Afraid there has been a mistake, Lieutenant. We rescued a civilian who got caught in the middle of a firefight, that's all. You can stand down. We will turn her over during our debriefing.'

The woman understood every word and pushed closer to Kyle as fear grew inside of her. She had heard how Americans interrogated prisoners.

'Sorry, Captain. I don't know anything about that, but our orders are to bring her in immediately because she is a suspected terrorist.' The lieutenant waved his hand, and three MPs, two male and one female, moved forward.

While the officers had talked, Kyle had helped the

Iranian girl from the helicopter and moved her in behind the MARSOC Marines, who appeared to be lounging about watching the episode with disinterest. When the MPs stepped forward, however, they were met by a solid wall of special ops warriors. Darren Rawls, Joe Tipp, and Travis Hughes stood between the MPs and their target. Kyle was close behind but did not want them to see his face.

'Okay, fellows, move aside,' ordered the lieutenant. 'Your part of the mission is done, and now we have to deal with the captive.'

'Sorry. Can't help you,' said Travis Hughes. 'Sir.'

'Lieutenant, you can lead us to the debriefing room if you wish, but that is all,' snapped Rick Newman.

Lieutenant Zahn was not used to having his orders disobeyed. He squared up before Newman and sharpened his voice. 'Captain! I am giving you a final warning. You and your men will stand aside and give us the enemy combatant or you will be placed under arrest.'

Darren Rawls grabbed the lieutenant and leaned into his face. 'You want her? Well, you will have to come and take her. Sir.' The rest of the team formed a knot around the woman and Kyle. Then Rawls pushed the lieutenant so hard that the man sprawled on the helipad.

Newman stepped forward and extended his hand to the fallen officer and pulled him up. 'Be careful there, Lieutenant. Easy to trip and fall around here. How about taking us over to the debriefing room now. You can't have her because we won't give her up. The woman is already in the custody of the CIA, and you don't know shit about what is going on, so let's cut the crap and get on with things before somebody gets hurt.'

Zahn brushed himself off. He made a mental note

about that big black guy who shoved him and would settle that score later. 'Yes, sir. This way, sir.'

The MARSOC team moved as a group toward a convoy of waiting vehicles that would take them over to another part of the base. The MPs posted themselves in a square at the front, back, and sides of that formation, as if taking the whole group to the brig.

'You are CIA?' the woman asked Kyle softly as they walked to the Humvees.

'No,' he said quietly. 'But those people don't need to know that. And don't worry. You will be treated well here.'

'So who are you, then?'

'Me? I'm nobody.'

Major Jim Riley, a surgeon, was ready, scrubbed, and gowned as he pushed open a swinging door with his elbow and stepped into a bright, cool operating room of the 856th Combat Support Hospital. Sterilized implements gleamed on a steel tray, and everyone around him was also gloved and masked.

Before them lay a huge soldier with a bullet hole in the back. The patient had been stripped, cleaned, put to sleep, and thoroughly prepped. There was an IV of blood and another of a hydrating solution. The vital signs were being constantly measured and displayed on monitors.

Dr. Riley had been working in the hospital too long to be shocked by the condition of any patient, since there was a never-ending river of them. He studied the X-rays on the light board and moved over to the table. 'Very well now. Everybody ready? Let's save this guy's life today.'

'My name is Delara Tabrizi, and I teach at a girls' school in Khorramshahr.' She sat at a small table in a well-lighted room with a cup of tea. Across the table were two intelligence officers who had been alerted about the unique circumstances and acted with respect and politeness. Adding to her comfort were Darren Rawls and Travis Hughes, still in combat gear and face paint, sitting beside the door to prevent a recurrence of the incident with the MPs at the helicopter. There was always somebody who did not get the word, and Captain Newman had ordered them to stay with her until final arrangements could be made. Delara was already considering them to be 'her' Marines; she believed they would protect her against any rough interrogation and was ready to answer the questions of the officers.

She had already made up her mind. 'I am now the only remaining member of my family,' she said. 'Everyone has been murdered by the government and its brutes, because we were part of the educated, moderate class. I will tell you everything I can in exchange for political asylum. I know that if I return to Iran, I may be killed, but we must go back.'

'Why?' asked an interrogator.

'I know of another facility, such as the one from last night, and my brother may still be alive there.'

'Just tell us where and we will send in another team.'

She shook her head negatively. 'No. It is near my home village in the north, and I can lead you there. You cannot find it on your own.'

The officer gave her a slight smile. 'Believe me, Miss Tabrizi, when I say that our technology and satellites can find almost anything, anywhere.'

Delara returned the mirthless smile. 'So, have you found it yet? No. You didn't even know it existed until I just told you.'

The officer studied the young woman. Stubborn. Determined. Knows that if she is caught by the Iranians, she will be killed, and yet she is willing to lead a raid back into the country. 'Let me discuss it with my bosses and see if they want to put together a mission. Meanwhile, we will put you up in a safe location and let you rest and clean up while we work this out.'

Delara said, 'I want the same team that was used before.'

'We may not be able to do that. A fully capable and fresh team probably will be chosen.'

'No substitutes,' she insisted and turned to look at Rawls and Hughes, both of whom were nodding agreement. She remembered not only the rescue in Iran but also the confrontation at the helicopter. 'I trust these men to bring me back alive.'

In another room in the same building, Kyle Swanson and Rick Newman were being debriefed, going over the mission step by step. Swanson handed in the bag of flesh samples he had cut from the dead body, and it was transferred to a secure biohazard container. The digital cameras with their documentation were sent off to be copied and analyzed.

'The place was burned to a crisp,' he told the intel officers. He described the construction of the underground laboratory complex. 'Everything was destroyed. Looked as if they flooded it with gasoline or something, then popped some thermite grenades to set it all off. The heat would have been tremendous, certainly enough to burn off any evidence of chemicals or biologicals being produced there.'

'You found prisoners in there?'

'What remained of them. Way back in individual cells at the end of the tunnels. The poor bastards were probably guinea pigs for experiments and were disposed of like everything else.'

Newman described the sudden arrival of soldiers at the site and the ensuing ambush, and how Master Gunny Dawkins had been wounded. Swanson gave his version of the same subjects. The intelligence officers were running out of questions when one asked, 'Why do you think the scientist who was assassinated in Baghdad gave up this site?'

Kyle gathered his gear. 'That's for you intel guys to figure out. Maybe the girl that we brought in can shed some light on it. My wild guess is that the scientist figured that everything connected with the place was going to be eliminated, including him. So he ran. He just didn't run fast enough.'

9

PARIS

Leafy vines tangled like thick ropes around the bars of a big wrought-iron gate that had stood open day and night for almost ten years on a quiet street in the Nineteenth Arrondissement. The property owner had tired of having to open and close it. Thieves came over the walls, despite embedded shards of sharp glass and alarm systems, so what was the point? Then a new owner had arrived and there still was no need to close the gate, for hard-eyed men stood guard, and word spread among the footpads of Paris that it was better to prey on targets that would not cost them their lives. The house now belonged to al Qaeda.

The neighborhood in the northeast section of Paris was in an inevitable transition toward a gentrified future, but pockets of the past still existed in its multiethnic heritage. The mixed aromas of foreign food and spices wafted from the restaurants, and people of all nationalities moved through the streets. Juba was just another face.

Shadowed by the foliage of the gate, he entered the old courtyard and smelled the combined scent of flowers and rot. The concrete slabs of the parking area were uneven, buckled by a century of shifting earth, and a creamy white Mercedes was parked in the center. Juba brushed his hand across the hood as he walked by. Warm to the touch, so the vehicle was recently used, probably to deliver Saladin to the meeting at the three-story home.

A nervous young man with a ragged haircut over a thin hyena face stepped from the shade of the doorway and motioned Juba to stop. The visitor was expected but would be searched nevertheless. Juba obediently raised both arms, then very slowly lowered his left hand to open his Prada sport coat wide enough to show the guard the holstered pistol that rested on his left hip. The young man's eyes went to the gun, which would have to be removed before the visitor could go inside. Juba helpfully opened the coat a bit more, using the diversion to keep the man's attention away from his right arm, which was slowly extending all the way up. When the elbow locked straight, a mechanism strapped to the inside of his forearm was tripped and a small Ruger pistol and silencer slapped into Juba's palm. He shot the approaching guard twice in the head at a distance of only three feet, the blood and brain matter spraying backward onto the paving stones. Juba grabbed the bleeding corpse by the shirt and hauled it into the cool, dark space beneath the stairwell.

He checked his clothes to make sure no blood had spattered on him and then trotted up the steep, curving stone staircase, making plenty of noise so the second bodyguard knew he was coming. His feet slapped with a steady rhythm against the old stones that a scrubwoman had washed by hand that morning. As he neared the top, the gun was hidden at his side. He huffed a bit, as if panting, and called to the guard. 'Long way up,' he said in French.

This man was larger, standing with his hands crossed in front of him. He had a lot of bulk that was more fat than muscle. A thick unibrow stretched in a line across both eyes, and a few gold teeth glinted on the left side of a frowning mouth. A ragged scar ran down his forehead. He was not alert because the visitor had been cleared by the entryway guard. Juba came up the final few steps, raised the Ruger, and fired his last three bullets. The scowling man collapsed where he stood.

Juba put the little gun away and gave the fallen man a look of utter contempt. *They still do not train them well.* The bodyguards chosen to protect the head of the entire al Qaeda operation in France should have been the best combat veterans available instead of a couple of water-front thugs hired because they looked mean and could handle themselves in a barroom brawl. Both died because they were stupid. He stepped inside the house.

The door opened into an area between a neat kitchen that was the color of buttermilk and a living room where tall windows gave a view of other courtyards and buildings on this crowded edge of the city. The fading sunlight was orange and bright. He blinked. As his eyes adjusted, two silhouettes in the living room became a pair of middle-aged men seated in comfortable chairs directly across from each other, separated by a low table.

'My son! Welcome, welcome,' said one, rising and coming to greet him with hugs and traditional cheek kisses.

Juba bowed his head. 'Father. It is good to see you again.' He had not seen his spiritual father, the man known as Saladin, in six weeks and was pleased to find him smiling with a warm greeting, particularly under the circumstances. Al Qaeda was demanding that he hand over the formula, and that Juba deliver it in person. Both of them realized their lives would be worthless the moment that the details of the new and virulent nerve agent were out of their possession, so that could not be allowed to happen.

Saladin appeared undisturbed. He had a handsome face with a well-trimmed beard and sharp black eyes that flashed intelligence, and he was dressed in a dark business suit and a subdued pearl gray tie. Actually taller than Juba, he weighed less and was thin. 'You look well, and you have done well,' he said as he squeezed Juba affectionately on the shoulder. 'I am so proud. Come, please, and meet our host.'

The second man stood. In contrast to Saladin, he wore a cheap suit that could not be buttoned over his stomach, and his belly overlapped the creased belt. The collar tips of his brown shirt flared like dirty wings, and a clump of chest hair had wiggled out above the second button.

'Let me introduce our new friend, Youcef Aseer, a very important leader among our al Qaeda comrades,' said Saladin with some deference. The fat man's tiny eyes did not leave Juba's face.

'I am honored,' said Juba and gave a slight bow. He was not about to embrace this unclean fat man who carried the smell of shallots and sweat.

'No, it is I who enjoy meeting you, the famous Juba. Your work in London has left the infidels in panic. God is great! Well done, young man.' The voice was oddly small for such a large man.

They took seats, and Saladin got straight to business.

'I know you were surprised by this summons, Juba, but something very important has happened to change our plans. Since the London episode, Youcef Aseer has been designated by al Qaeda to see that we all should henceforth work together. It is a great opportunity for us. Al Qaeda offers a generous sum of money and also manpower – dedicated foot soldiers, street demonstrators, and willing martyrs – that we can use in certain situations. In turn, we supply the formula and our field leadership. They want a strike in France, to subdue this wicked nation like a whipped puppy.'

Youcef Aseer chuckled. 'We are closer here than in any other Western nation. One good push is all we need! Imagine an Islamic government in France!'

Saladin clapped his hands. 'Exactly, my friend.' He turned to Juba. 'Our friend Youcef here is now within our small circle of trust. You are to do as he says, Juba. Do you understand that?'

'Yes, Father.' Juba understood very clearly: Al Qaeda was taking over.

'Good. See, Youcef! I told you there would be no difficulty. It will be good to work with al Qaeda again,' said Saladin. 'Let Juba see your list.'

The al Qaeda chieftain handed over a small envelope. The small move was peremptory, the sort of wave of a hand that a master gives an underling. This was his home, and his bodyguards were skillful. Unless these two renegades cooperated, he would have them killed.

Juba rose from his chair, and since he could not go between the two because of the table, he circled behind the al Qaeda leader. 'Excuse me. The light is better by the window.' He looked out at the fading sunlight playing with shadows on the rooftops and ran his thumb beneath the gummed flap of the envelope, pulled out the paper, and read three names, three addresses, all in the southern part of the country. Of course. The port of Marseille had been the initial arrival point for the first waves of immigrants from North Africa.

Aseer grinned. 'The first is a judge who has sentenced our brothers to long terms in prison, the second an undercover detective with a particular skill for infiltrating our group, and the third simply a worthless traitor. Juba, I want you to kill them all to show that our enemies cannot escape the Prophet's justice.'

'And the attack in France?'

'You leave that to us. We will have our own chemists and physicists construct the weapon under your supervision.'

'It is not yet ready. The London experiment showed the dispersal rate remains too high.'

'Another batch just like that will be more than enough for our purposes,' said Aseer. 'We will finish the refining process as time allows.'

Juba nodded and turned to Saladin. 'When do you wish me to start, Father?'

'Immediately, my son. The sooner you complete this, the sooner we can move on.'

They both knew that they would not be moving at all if they remained in the grip of al Qaeda.

'Very well.' Juba slid the note into his jacket's right pocket. The light was dim and purple in the room as he walked back toward his chair. When his hand emerged from the pocket, there was something in it, invisible in the dying, gloomy light. Passing directly behind Aseer, he moved in a blur and looped the strand of piano wire around the neck of the al Qaeda man and yanked hard on the wooden handle in each hand. The wire sliced into the throat like a razor, and the fat man grabbed at the tightening garrote until his eyes bulged and his tongue hung out.

Juba's hatred of al Qaeda pulsed through his strong biceps and forearms and hands and into the killing wire as he slowly lifted his victim all the way over the back of the chair while the struggling man clawed to hold on to the life draining away from him. He could have finished it quickly but did not want death to come easily to this piece of al Qaeda filth. He tightened the wire more, strangling the man as he twisted the body out of the chair and let it fall onto a burgundy rug that was almost the same color as the blood oozing from the deep neck wound. Aseer urinated in his pants as he died.

Saladin remained calm. What a macabre pleasure it was to watch his son at work. The moves were so clean and economical and perfect, like a ballet dancer's, and there was a cold passion to his mastery of so many skills. A maestro of death. 'Imagine, Juba, this fool actually believed we were frightened.' He spat on the body.

'They will come after us again.'

'No, I think they will simply become a customer. This death signals that the formula still belongs to Unit 999 and no one else. It took us twenty years to develop, and we have repeatedly had to defend our ownership. Now that we are so close to success, no one can be allowed to stop us.'

Juba washed his hands in the kitchen sink. 'I will take care of this one, and our men will remove the two guards.'

'Very good, my son.' Saladin refilled his cup of strong coffee. 'The London task was flawless, but of course I expected nothing less from you. I assume the announcement is ready for distribution?'

'Yes. I downloaded the pictures I took in London onto discs and posted them, along with your message, by FedEx, to North Korea, China, Brunei, and Tehran. The packages will arrive at any time and someone will have to sign for them, which guarantees delivery.'

'Then it is done. The word will spread from those seeds. Now we wait.'

'You can wait, my father. I have no time to waste. I will relax when it is all done.'

'Would you rather be back in Iraq, taking target practice?' Saladin teased his assassin.

'No. Paris is better. It is too bad that I cannot stay longer. I long for a few days in which I can just be a pure Muslim and sit at your feet again and study the Koran. Physically I am fine, but spiritually I am an empty vessel. My role is difficult.'

'Which is why you are the only one who can do it,' replied Saladin. 'I promise plenty of time in the future for you to walk openly as one of the faithful and even go on a hajj to Mecca and Medina. For now, you must remain who you are. The Prophet bestowed special gifts upon you, Juba. I know your inner struggle and intercede with prayers for you every day. Until the right time comes, you must carry on. You know that.'

'Yes. I am but an instrument of the Prophet. Show me the path and I will follow. But tonight I leave for Iran again to observe one final test. The director of our remaining laboratory there thinks the formula will be complete after a final adjustment improves the staying power of the gel. The gas in London still spread too fast.'

Saladin laughed to break the serious tone. 'Good. We are finally so very close to the end. After you dispose of this trash, we can go out and have time for a nice dinner before you leave.'

Juba opened the door and summoned two more men to help with the corpses as the slow sun set and the lights of Paris illuminated the night. Saladin stood at the window, feeling the rhythm of the city alter from a daytime center of commerce to a nightscape dedicated to personal pleasures. He liked this house and decided to stay here for a while.

He heard the men removing the body behind him but did not turn to watch. The al Qaeda fool actually believed an Islamic government could be seated in Paris. It was true that France had more Muslims than any other Western European nation, but that was still less than 10 percent of the overall sixty-four million Frenchmen. Aseer must have thought he commanded some German army. Al Qaeda thought in such small terms.

If Saladin had any real problem that evening, it was the knowledge that he must devote considerably more energy to his protégé. Anyone who did not think twice about setting off a device that condemned unknown hundreds of people to painful deaths obviously required careful handling.

He wondered if Juba ever looked deeply into a mirror or thought about the deadly paradox that he had become. The sniper felt betrayed by his home country, England, and most recently by al Qaeda, which had recruited him so many years ago. He had lost *faith*! Saladin had long listened to Juba's spoken outward devotion to Islam and his dream of cutting himself off from the outside world and living like a penniless peasant in the service of the Prophet. The true dedication, however, was not there, and the dream was so unrealistic that it could never be fulfilled.

For while he was a skilled assassin and soldier, Juba's motives were muddled and corrupt. He lived in the moment and was never more alive than when in combat, where his senses tingled with anticipation. He was a perfect fit for the sniper hides and the combat holes, but those assignments did not last forever. In between, in the down time, he had learned to live the good life. He had been ordered to do so and had been declared exempt from violating the Koran! Years of five-star hotels, luxury cars, exquisite tailoring, top-shelf whiskey, and the company of beautiful women in trendy clubs was the lubrication that kept the deadly machine running and ready to strike. The adopted and addictive Western lifestyle cost a great deal of money, and that was the rub: the final rivulet of water needed to bring down his stone bridge back to Islam. Juba had lost his religion, and probably everything else, and didn't really know it. He had learned to like money more than the stern lifestyle preached by the fanatics.

Saladin played along, keeping him on a leash, just as a snake charmer must carefully play a cobra in a basket. Cobras do not care who they bite, and Juba no longer truly killed for any cause, not even vengeance; he killed because he enjoyed killing.

*

**LEBANON
2002**

Saladin remembered his own coming to terms with the future, sweating on the day he stood before Saddam Hussein. At the time, he was just an anonymous lieutenant colonel in the Iraqi army, second in command of the United States Battalion of Unit 999, Saddam's elite terrorism force. The unit was charged with developing what the Iraqi leader called 'special ammunition for special circumstances,' meaning terrible weapons of mass destruction. There were nine battalions in all, up to five hundred men each, based in various regions and countries with orders to strike within those areas if war came to Iraq. Regardless of such a conflict actually on the horizon after the 9/11 attack on America, the crazy dictator was shipping the materials from Iraqi military stores into Syria and Lebanon and even Iran!

Saladin and his commanding officer had been called to one of Saddam's many palaces to report the status of the United States Battalion's mission to develop a virulent biochem nerve agent that could be deployed within the United States. The work had been going on since the 1980s, slowly and steadily, but with the many starts and stops of any major scientific research program. Much of the research had even been done within the United States itself, under the noses of the FBI and sometimes with the willing assistance of the CIA. In the years in which Iraq was fighting Iran, and Afghanistan was fighting the Soviets, the United States had been quite helpful.

They snapped to rigid attention before Saddam, who

was smoking a cigar as he stared at them. Flanking the dictator were Uday and Qusay, his two murderous sons, and at the end of the table was Ali Hassan al-Majid, the man known as Chemical Ali. Those four had created Unit 999 and kept its terrible objective as a secret among themselves.

When Saddam quietly asked if the weapon was ready, Saladin knew his life rode on the dictator's reaction to the answer. Not quite, replied the commander of the United States Battalion. Perhaps one more year of research and development would be required. Maybe even two years. Uday and Qusay exchanged glances and grinned. Saddam tapped his cigar ash and nodded his head, as if in understanding of the difficulties involved.

A burly bodyguard stepped forward without a sound and crushed a long iron bar onto the right shoulder of Saladin's superior officer, who crumpled in agony when the bone broke. Two more bodyguards joined in the pounding as Saladin struggled to remain at rigid attention while his friend and colleague was beaten to death by his side. He could still recall the crunching of the bones, the spreading pool of blood, and the screams, with the uncaring eyes of Saddam Hussein watching him, not the man being beaten to death. When it was done, Saddam leaned forward and said, 'You are now a full colonel and the new commander of the United States Battalion of Unit 999. You have three months to finish the work. You may go.'

Saladin saluted, turned on his heel and marched out of the palace, found a quiet place, and threw up.

Saddam Hussein was crazy, the plan was crazy, and if he stayed in this job, he was crazy, too.

The new colonel was required to stay around Baghdad for a while to help transfer much of the technology and equipment comprising the Iraqi stock of weapons of mass destruction onto railroad cars and refitted Boeing planes to shift the components out of Iraq. He consigned some of it to go to America, through a front company in Jordan.

It had been at dinner in a quiet Baghdad café one night during that time that he was introduced to a unique young warrior called Juba, who, it was said, had been waging a one-man sniper campaign in Afghanistan and was a superb killer of infidels. The man was quiet, with a sense of spiritual loneliness, and Saladin, who was a scholar as well as a soldier, decided to exploit that missing piece. This could be his way out of the disaster that was surely coming toward Saddam Hussein's army.

At nights and in the mosques, he guided his new friend deeper into the Book, behind the words of the Koran and into the concepts of what it truly meant to be a Muslim. He steered the conversations easily toward the approaching war, and Juba agreed totally that Iraq would lose.

Since Juba was so bitter about his experiences in Afghanistan, it was not difficult to convince him that Muslims needed a goal higher than squandering their lives to achieve another round of fourteenth-century squalor.

'There will never be a rebirth of any united nation of Islam, unbound by colonialist borders and not ruled by worthless kings,' he said. 'But that does not mean the struggle should cease.'

Juba snorted and sipped some tea. 'We will lose. Iraq is doomed.'

'What would you say, my friend, if I told you there is a better way that you and I can serve the Prophet?'

'I've heard that promise before, and it was worthless.'

There were only the two of them in the room, studying the Koran. Saladin spread his fingers and laid his hand on the Book. 'I tell you now, and take an oath on the Book, that we can carry on the battle no matter what happens to Saddam Hussein. I am building a weapon that will make the Crusaders weep for their children,' Saladin said. 'I need a strong man I can trust, you, to protect me while I finish the work.'

'So we will not change the world?' the warrior asked.

'No. That is impossible,' the scholar said. 'While Saddam will be defeated, we will continue our work in secret. The project will belong to us then, and together we will unleash Allah's vengeance and fury upon the infidels' own homelands.'

Then the Iraqi colonel inducted Juba into the secrets of Unit 999 and chose to assume a secret identity of his own, the name of the famous warrior-king of ancient times – Saladin.

10

After the debrief, Kyle Swanson dropped by the hospital to check on Double-Oh, who was still in surgery, then went over to the private quarters maintained for special operations, checked in, and took a shower. The television set in the small room was reporting on the London attack, and he punched up some pillows and lay back on the bunk to watch for a while, then catch some sleep. A pounding on the door ended the brief period of relaxation.

Captain Rick Newman and Sergeant Travis Hughes were there, still dressed in their cammies and covered with dirt from the mission. As they described the odd interrogation of Dalara Tabrizi, Kyle realized that by sharing her idea for another cross-border operation with the intelligence officers, she had unintentionally kicked down the first of a long row of dominoes.

The intel pukes would report up their chain of command, then planners would be brought in to examine the possibilities and would kick it to Washington for debate and approval, and then somebody would have to make a decision to send a U.S. patrol deep into Iran because some woman wanted to find her brother. Since the first raid had turned up so little in the way of hard evidence that a chemical device was being built, there would be great reluctance among the higher pay grades to sign off on a risky new mission on the word of a stranger. If any Americans were caught, the international repercussions would be severe. With every hour that passed, the attack in the UK was going to be viewed more as an investigative matter for police, and the military would be sidelined. Maybe a satellite could take pictures of the suspected site, or perhaps a spy plane could do some flyovers, but without having to put boots on the ground. Was it worth the risk?

'What's your opinion, Trav?' asked Kyle.

'She's telling the truth,' he answered. 'Every minute she was being questioned, she just kept getting stronger. Rawls is with her right now over at the mess hall, and she is cool and focused.'

Swanson looked at Rick Newman. 'I doubt if another mission will be authorized,' the young captain said. 'Too much potential fallout.'

Kyle was already putting on his uniform, his mind whirring with possibilities while they watched the latest horrific televised report from London. 'We have to do it, even if there is only an outside chance to get to the bottom of this whole thing. So I am thinking that my authorization for the original mission into Iran is still in force and we returned to Doha just to drop off our wounded man. We have to get out of here because this place is just too damned big and has too many competing interests.'

Travis Hughes gnawed a fingernail. 'The village she mentioned is in the west of Iran, about halfway up the border with Iraq and out where the agriculture gives way to the mountains. We could stage out of Camp Baharia, which is on about the same level in Iraq.'

'Good,' said Swanson. 'Once we are among just Marines, things will get easier. Rick, you get us a plane to take the team up to Fallujah and run the support side of the show from Baharia. I'll get Captain Summers over here, and we can slide it out of the military chain of command entirely and put it under Trident and General Middleton. By the time Sybelle lands, we want to have this thing already moving. If we keep the momentum going, the paper-shufflers will never catch up.'

WASHINGTON, D.C.

Sybelle Summers arrived for work at six o'clock in the morning. Like thousands of other commuters, she rode the Washington Metro to the Pentagon station, patiently took the long escalator ride up to the main entrance, and signed in. As she walked the wide, polished hallway, the place seemed like a giant tomb, and there was an overwhelming feeling of barely restrained excitement as the men and women of the United States military services were preparing to face what quite possibly was a new attack against the homeland. She went directly to the Trident offices.

Major General Middleton and Lieutenant Commander Freedman were watching television, with the general switching from channel to channel as each network devoted its entire programming to the news from England. No cheery and smiling wake-up morning show hosts today, just macabre news reports.

'How is Double-Oh?' she asked.

'The docs in Kuwait say that old warhorse is going to live to fight another day,' said Middleton and immediately changed the subject. 'You up to date on this London attack?'

'Yes, sir. Watched some at home and read the *Post* and the *Times*.' Sybelle dropped her purse on a desk. 'How do the news reports match up with our intel sources?'

'Got no fuckin' intel,' snorted Middleton. 'Once again, billions of dollars thrown at them, few laws to confine them anymore, and the spooks still come up short. How come TV cameras can always be there when the intel professionals can't?'

General Middleton turned the sound down and made a quick telephone call to the Pentagon central command post that was monitoring the emergency in England. He asked for the casualty count, grunted, and hung up. 'Less than a hundred and fifty dead so far, from the dirty bomb explosion to the stampede of people trying to get away, but a bunch of people are hurt. The royals were safely evacuated up to Balmoral Castle in Scotland. Lizard, show her what you're working on.'

Freeman pulled a chair up to a small computer terminal and clicked some keys, and a chart replaced the news report on the television screen. He folded his arms and rocked back. An oval-shaped blob of red designated the most saturated area of the attack, then faded into bands of orange and yellow that followed the wind pattern. 'The initial public panic kept things in gridlock for a while, and the authorities were prompt in swinging the emergency units into action. Traffic control, quarantines and showers, getting people into clean zones. Thanks to the warning from that fire chief, the first responders were in protective gear when they moved in, and they probably will have saved hundreds of lives when all is said and done.'

'The Brits' 9/11,' said Sybelle. 'Worse than the World War II bombings.'

Middleton was grim. 'They picked on the wrong country. Not only are we their big brother and will kick the crap out of whoever did this, but the Brits are a tough bunch. They won't knuckle under. Ask Hitler.'

The Lizard was out of his chair, moving nervously about the room as he spoke. 'I did some statistical analysis to get a grip on what kind of biochem agent was used in the attack and found something I did not expect. Look.' He pointed a finger at the scarlet oval of maximum devastation. 'Look at the very defined edges of this red zone. The material is very concentrated here, as would be expected.' Then he fanned his entire hand out over the other colors. 'But the other bands of contamination are extremely narrow.'

Sybelle caught it, for like all Force Recon Marines, she had been schooled in biological, chemical, and nuclear warfare. The weak point of any chem attack is atmospheric dispersion, for the moment the toxin goes into the air, it begins to dissipate and grows weaker until it is of no significance whatever. That is why prime targets for such attacks are normally underground or very confined areas, such as in subways, where the effects can be contained and multiplied. 'The wind didn't carry it far!'

The Lizard stood and looked at her with a smile, a teacher gazing on a prize pupil. 'Exactly.' He slapped the top of the television set. 'This looks like something new, a heavier-than-air gas that somehow morphs into a sticky liquid on contact with the air. The contamination readings at the center of the attack are still strong right now, many hours after the explosion. This stuff preserves its lethality even in open air.'

'In other words, it stays at home and does what it's made to do.'

Middleton nodded agreement. 'Yep. And that is why we have to be worried. I think this attack was just a field trial. Imagine if huge containers of this stuff went off in the middle of a big city. The death toll could be enormous.'

Sybelle went to a sideboard and poured a cup of coffee, then cocked her head toward Middleton. 'Every intel service in the world has to be working on this, and the Brits have to be going all out. Has anybody come up with anything?'

'Nobody has claimed credit yet. No demands have been made. All of the usual idiots are cheering, but none are raising their hands as being responsible because if they do, they get wiped out.' Lieutenant Commander Freedman read some notes on his computer. 'The explosion came from a truck in the press area, and the chemical canisters were attached to a second truck. The police identified both as belonging to a rental company out of Scotland called Edinburgh All-Media.'

Middleton was bending a paper clip into different shapes, and it popped apart as he pulled on it. He tossed it aside. 'Damned media again. That girl stuck a microphone in the fireman's mouth just as he realized what was really happening.'

Sybelle wouldn't buy his anger. 'Wasn't her fault, sir.

The terrorists wanted this to be as public as possible, which is why they picked the press that was covering the wedding. It sent a warning straight into the living rooms of millions of viewers. Poor Kimberly Drake will always be the face of this disaster.' She felt a shudder as she recalled the horrible death of the reporter on live TV.

The general stood and looked out the window. 'Okay. You're right. I'm just trying to add it all up in my head. Get your stuff together, because we have to be at the White House in thirty minutes for a national security briefing on this attack and whether it may be related to what we are doing in Iran.'

Sybelle asked, 'And exactly what are we doing in Iran, sir?'

'You will find out soon enough. Swanson's taking another team in, and he wants you over there to ramrod the operation from Camp Baharia. The Lizard is setting up a flight, and you are out of here in a few hours.'

'Aye, aye, sir,' she replied, thinking: *Wake up in my apartment in Maryland this morning, go to work at the Pentagon in Virginia, visit the White House for a conference, do a drop-by at the CIA over in Langley for a final situation report, then out to Andrews Air Force Base and into the back seat of a screaming fast military fighter-bomber for a few hours, and sleep tonight in Iraq. Got to love this job.*

KINGDOM OF BRUNEI DARUSSALAM

Ambassador Richard Taffe was a professional diplomat who had been entrusted by the United States government with the crucial position of ambassador to one of the smallest, richest, and most strategic countries in the world. It was not a gift position awarded to some political party loyalist or to the friend of a friend of the president. Instead, whoever held the post had earned his spurs through years of experience in the diplomatic world. Taffe peeled off his sweaty orange shirt after a morning round at the Royal Brunei Golf and Country Club in Jerudong Park and concluded once again that the years spent in Nigeria and Bangladesh and Jordan had paid off handsomely for him. What was there to dislike about Brunei?

A Malay club boy in pressed black shorts and a white tunic buttoned at the collar brought him a stack of fresh towels. The ambassador wiped his face and chest, rolled the towel into a ball, and tossed it into a hamper ten feet away.

'He shoots! He scores!' called his playing partner for the day, Zul Jock Matali, a senior officer in the Ministry of Foreign Affairs and Trade. 'Nothing but net.' It had been a good day, and the ambassador had beaten Matali three-and-two in match play. Now they would shower and dress and have lunch in one of the club restaurants and talk about oil.

Brunei was attached by land to Malaysia but floated on a sea of proven oil reserves rated at about 1.35 billion barrels. The country shipped 206,000 barrels every day, and a great deal of it sailed across the Pacific Ocean to the United States. Taffe's primary job was to keep that black gold flowing.

Taffe took a sip of chilled water from a bottle that had almost magically appeared at his side. There was only one thing to really worry about in this little land where, true, nobody voted, but nobody paid taxes and the country had zero external debt. Oil money did that. The problem was not the human trafficking that masqueraded as migrant labor from other Asian countries, because who really gave a shit? Even human rights groups couldn't keep track of it. Just don't call attention to what was, in reality, a booming slave trade. Neither was there any problem with the mandatory death penalty for drug smugglers, which Taffe's people handled quietly when some stupid American kid got nailed trying to bring in dope in a backpack. There was no official arrest, so there was no trial or death sentence, and the tourist was just turned over to the U.S. Embassy, which sent him home on the next plane. At all costs, keep the black oil flowing.

The real diplomatic problem in Brunei was that the nation's religion was Muslim. The common law could be overruled in some cases by sharia law, and the sultan himself was the official defender of the faith. The same royal family had run the little country for six centuries, even after it was spun off as an independent nation by the British Empire. They displayed some enlightened leadership in spending great wads of cash on improvements and allowing at least the appearance of listening to the will of the population of 375,000 people, almost all of whom were literate. Things were politically quiet, and Ambassador Taffe wanted to keep it that way.

Still, there was discomfort about the overall anti-Muslim zeal that seemed to be sweeping through American politicians, whose words were studied by the Brunei policy makers. There was always the possibility, too, that al Qaeda would jump over from nearby Indonesia, make militant inroads here, and turn this fabulously rich nation into a powder keg of trouble. So far, nothing serious had happened. It was so quiet that a citizen of Brunei still did not even need a visa to fly to America.

After their showers, the two officials went upstairs to an elite restaurant and were escorted to a private table beside the huge windows, with a ring of empty tables around them. Matali was much more than just an official in the Ministry of Trade, for the graduate of Stanford University and the Kennedy School of Government at Harvard also held the rank of brigadier general in the Royal Brunei Land Forces. Part of his portfolio was counterterrorism.

They made small talk as the waiters hovered around to take their orders.

'Are you and Maggie going to the Japanese Embassy reception tonight?' asked Matali.

'Yeah, maybe we should sneak away to McDonald's and get some real food instead of sushi.'

'I can't eat a Big Mac! It is unclean food.'

'So put curry sauce on the chicken nuggets and french fries.'

Jock Matali looked up as a waiter approached and handed him a large cream-colored envelope. 'A gentleman at the front desk asked that you personally receive this, General.'

He opened it. 'Strange,' he said and shook out a letter and some photographs. The dark eyes became serious and scanned the restaurant, which was almost empty. No one was watching.

Taffe also peered around. 'So, what's up?'

Matali lowered his voice. 'It's a contact about London. Someone calling himself Saladin has claimed responsibility and is setting terms.'

'Oh, no, not another Saladin. Let me guess,' said Taffe. 'This latest savior of the downtrodden Middle East wants direct discussions with the president of the United States. Same answer as always, Jock: We don't negotiate with terrorists.'

Matali shook his head, reached over, and put a strong hand on Taffe's forearm. 'No, my friend. That is not it at all. This is an invitation for the finance ministers of Muslim nations, terrorist organizations, and countries that oppose the United States to participate in an auction for the formula of the weapon used in England.'

Taffe rocked back hard in his chair. Matali let him have the note while he looked through a set of photographs. As he read, Taffe's blood chilled.

The London attack was part of an experiment, the note said. A true demonstration of the weapon, which had been years in development, would be unleashed soon in a very public and well-known place, which was not identified.

Parties interested in bidding were to send a buy-in fee of ten million dollars to a Swiss bank account, all but one million of it refundable by the bank escrow officers if the potential bidder did not agree after the demonstration that the weapon was worthwhile. After all, for a measly million, they would be helping sponsor a huge attack against the infidels at no risk to themselves.

If they chose to bid, then the rest of the ten million dollars locked in as the final entry fee, and bids could be submitted. Details would be worked out with the winner to exchange the formula for the cash.

The United States and its major allies in Europe, Asia, and the Middle East would not be allowed to participate.

11

Juba caught a British Airways Boeing 727 out of Charles de Gaulle International Airport in Paris for the long jump to Tehran, more than 2,600 weary miles. He slept much of the way in the darkened first-class cabin, having learned as a soldier to grab sleep whenever it was available, but questions kept pestering him. The director of the site promised that the formula would finally be complete, but so many earlier pledges had been made, then something always went wrong and more tests, time, and money were needed. Unit 999 had labored for years in various places to piece together the extraordinarily lethal mix, something stable enough to transport to a target zone, then able to lock into the area and not blow away with the first puff of air. London had been good, but not quite good enough. Could this really be the time?

The BA plane landed at Mehrabad Airport, and Juba took a taxi to a four-star hotel. He could have pushed things and made the one-hour hop over to Sanandaj on the only Iran Aseman Airlines domestic flight of the day but chose not to. A long drive to the west of Sanandaj also was needed to reach the site and he would be exhausted by the time he arrived. Staying in Tehran also was much better than remaining among the Kurds over there any longer than he had to. They were a dangerous people and would be even more so when they found out what he had been cooking in their back yard.

The test was to be performed tomorrow afternoon. Tonight he would have dinner with three men who would make the trip with him. He would go to the site, watch it, make the decision, and get out, never to return.

THE WHITE HOUSE

Brunei was thirteen hours ahead of Washington, so it was late at night in Washington, D.C., as the president of the United States was climbing into bed in the White House. Every day was a long day in his job; he welcomed the down time, and his staff tried to protect it.

Secretary of State Kenneth Waring knew that, but after receiving the flash traffic from the ambassador in Brunei, he had no choice. Waring telephoned the president's chief of staff, Steve Hanson, and within twenty minutes, all three had gathered in the Oval Office for an emergency meeting.

The president slowly read the message. Smoothed the edges with his hands. Said nothing.

Steve Hanson had known the president for years, and part of his job was to be outspoken on any topic. The Boss wanted it that way. 'Secretary Waring and I believe this to be authentic, Mr. President.'

'A classic backchannel communication from Saladin, whoever he is,' said Waring. 'The police over in Brunei are questioning everyone who was in the hotel at the time, trying to find who delivered it. Nothing yet.'

Chief of Staff Hanson moved to a different point. 'Why an auction? Why not keep this thing as his own little devastating secret, like the formula for Coca-Cola? Or sell a batch once in a while to al Qaeda and the other fanatics?'

The president crossed the spotless carpet, a giant depiction of the Great Seal of the United States, and leaned an elbow against the fireplace mantel. 'Production, Steve. Think back to when we were earning an honest dollar out in the business world. We could have made some of our gadgets in the garage, but constructing them one at a time would never bring real success. We needed manufacturing plants, which is exactly what we eventually had.'

Hanson agreed. 'So this psychopath claims to have the magic formula for a super-deadly biochem weapon but can only churn it out in limited quantities. If he sells it to a nation, say, North Korea or Iran, then the state can produce any amount it wants to brew.'

'Scary thought,' said Secretary of State Waring. He closed his eyes and rubbed them. 'What's next?'

Hanson had been thinking about that. 'Standard policy would be to get the entire cabinet in for an emergency meeting and turn loose the military and CIA.'

The president studied him. 'You don't think that's the way to go? This is among the most important things we have ever handled.'

The secretary of state said, arms crossed, 'It will be impossible to keep it a secret for long if he is reaching out to bidders.'

Hanson was excited. 'It's already out there, Mr. Secretary, but we don't have to throw fuel onto the fire. The president can remain in the background for a while, and all press queries will be directed to you at the State Department. Your statement can be something along the lines that we have heard about some strange new terrorist demands but we have not been contacted directly. Although we take all terrorist threats seriously, we remain confident that our security forces are up to any new challenge, and we pledge again to do whatever is needed to protect this nation.'

The president had been analyzing the information while the others talked, just as he had done when he ran one of the biggest electronic and computer companies in the world. Finally he said, 'I think this Saladin fellow made a mistake. He gives no deadline for responses to the auction idea because he knew that any potential bidders will need time to get their acts together.'

The secretary of state interrupted. 'True. But what do we do with the extra time?'

'Find him. Kill him. Bury him.' Steve Hanson pulled himself erect, all five foot six of him, and shoved his hands in his pockets.

'We don't assassinate heads of state,' huffed Waring.

'He isn't a head of state, Ken!' Hanson said. 'He's a fucking terrorist who has already attacked London and is now coming after us! Anyway, we won't be the only ones after him. Al Qaeda and other big players are going to try to take that formula for free. They don't want some bit actor like Saladin grabbing power away from them.'

The president waved a hand. 'Okay. Go easy, Steve. The secretary of state is correct: The United States does not assassinate people. You guys get things moving while I go upstairs and shave and put on fresh clothes. I want an

NSC briefing in an hour.' He shook hands with the secretary of state and thanked him for bringing the bad news.

Once Waring left the Oval Office, the president turned to his chief of staff. 'Get General Middleton over here right away, Steve. I think we're going to need Kyle Swanson very soon.'

CAMP BAHARIA
IRAQ

Swanson had to smile at the astonishment on the face of Delara Tabrizi when he walked into the special ops briefing room with Travis Hughes and Joe Tipp. They had collected new clothing on the way over and now, instead of American soldiers, they looked like Iranian farmers: baggy pants, long tunics, and wrapped head coverings. Each carried a heavy sheepskin coat. He went over to her. 'Thank you for this new information, Miss Tabrizi. However, you really don't have to go in with us. In fact, it would be better if you stayed here.'

Her gaze was steady. 'No. I must go.'

'We can find your brother, if he's there, and bring him out.'

'You don't know that country,' she said and walked over to a map hanging from the wall. She spread her hand over an area circled in red. 'This is my home village of Kamveh, and I grew up roaming those mountains, tending our sheep and goats. I know the general location of this other horrible place where Iranian people are being tortured and murdered, and I know pathways that can get you there.'

'It will be dangerous.'

She shrugged her shoulders. 'For us, every day we live is dangerous. I am going with you.'

'Just try to keep up.'

Delara Tabrizi bristled at the condescending tone.

She looked up at him with determination in her dark eyes, her face framed by wisps of black hair that escaped from the edges of the emerald green scarf covering her head. Kyle realized that she was beautiful. Less than thirty years old, she stood only about five-five and could not have weighed more than 115 pounds, but she carried a sense of self-assuredness that had been honed by being a woman with a will of her own living in a country run by men and religious police.

The previous year she had been ordered by police to attend classes on respecting the proper attire for Islamic women. Like many of her generation, she still bent the rules concerning the *shalwar kameez,* a boxy full-length coverall that fell from shoulder pads to ankles. Delara's coat was in a muted beige design, fell only to her knees, and was somewhat fitted, although it was still loose and had sleeves to her wrists. Instead of droopy pantaloons beneath it, she wore a pair of jeans and a rust-colored T-shirt.

'I just need a pair of good boots and I'm ready to go. Give me a pistol, something small like a Makarov, and you won't have to rescue me again,' she said.

'We can do that,' laughed Travis Hughes, enjoying the exchange of barbs between Shake and Delara. 'You know how to shoot?'

'I grew up in the mountains. Everybody has to know how to shoot to protect our herds.'

'Girl knows her guns. Cool,' said Darren Rawls, stepping up beside Kyle. 'Gunny, I want to go, too.'

'You can't. You're black, remember? Ain't no brothers up in those mountains,' said Joe Tipp.

'Shit,' said Rawls.

'You and Rawls go by the armory and get us all weaponed up. In case we have to use them, we don't want to leave an American signature with the shell casing. I'll take an AK-47 and a Dragunov sniper rifle. Grab an RPK light machine gun and some RPGs. Get plenty of explosives, water, binos, and rations for three days. Travis, you outfit Miss Tabrizi with whatever she wants. I will make a final comm and logistics check with Captain Newman. Rendezvous at the helo pad in thirty minutes. We are going to have to push it to get into position before daylight.'

A few lights from Baghdad illuminated the bottom of the cloud cover far to the south as the Pave Low raced through the night, each mile seeming to Swanson to take forever. If they could not find a good position by the time the sun came up, they would just have to burrow in somewhere and wait all day long, and he believed that they could not afford the luxury of just staying put for twelve hours. The first site had been totally destroyed, and he wanted to see this second one before it suffered the same fate. He felt in his gut that the time was close. Whoever was running that operation was cleaning up loose ends, and somehow the entire thing was wrapped up with the attack in London. He fought the nervousness and settled into the racket of the Pave Low helicopter. He could not make this bird go any faster.

A crackle came on the radio in his ear. 'Bounty Hunter, Bounty Hunter, this is Slider Base. Come in.' Sybelle's voice!

'Slider Base, this is Bounty Hunter.'

There was a comforting sense of crisp professionalism in her voice. 'Confirming Trident on deck here. Mission is yours.'

Excellent! The spur-of-the-moment special operation to return to Iran had clicked into place, with Rick Newman holding the fort until Sybelle Summers had arrived at Baharia to take over. Now Kyle could stop worrying that some colonel might find out about what he was up to and order a stop to it all or, worse, start meddling to change the mission. He now would report to Sybelle, who reported to Middleton, who reported to the president of the United States. That simplified things.

'Slider Base. Roger on Trident. Out.'

He didn't need to go into any further explanation. Between Newman and Sybelle, all of the support elements would be in place, and whatever they did not have on hand, they could whistle up in a hurry. The best offense was still total secrecy, but it was nice to know that a pair of Marine Harrier jump jets might just happen to be flying near the border soon, along with a few Cobra gunships to protect the helicopter during extraction.

The Zagros mountain range in northwestern Iran was a natural geographical barrier that discouraged visits deep into its saddles and peaks. People only went into the stark and barren reaches if they had a purpose, and population centers were few. Adding to the isolation were roving patrols of the Iranian Revolutionary Guard, who were absolutely vicious in protecting an area that the government had designated to be off-limits because of its importance. Some people who wandered into the area were never seen again.

The mountains could be an advantage for interlopers, since it was impossible for the Iranian military to tightly control the entire rugged area. Roads petered out to paths, communications were difficult, and the villagers were sullen, even hostile, doing what they were told to do only under the threat of force. The mountains also were a resting place for small packs of bandits who enjoyed ambushing a patrol to ransack its supplies. As a result, the Iranian troops stuck close to their small bases during the night.

Because resupply was always a problem, the villagers of Kamveh paid scant attention to the brief clatter of a passing helicopter in the night. The low-flying craft were frequently in the area to transport goods to the soldiers, although the farmers still preferred their slower but more reliable pack mules. A mule did not need radar to get where it was going.

The Pave Low moved fast and close to the undulating terrain to reach its designated landing zone, the bald knob of a hilltop about three kilometers each way between the suspected biochemical site and the village of Kamveh. It flared to a halt and dropped down only long enough to let the three Marines and Delara Tabrizi jump out, two from each side, and then it spun out of the area and let the satellite mapping system carry it safely out of harm's way, dashing back across the border with Iraq, where a refueling plane was loitering to top it off for a slower trip back to Baharia. The special operations crew breathed easier.

Everybody on the ground hunched over and stayed put

for a minute to assess whether any threats were in the immediate area, and then Travis Hughes led the way north, into the treeline. Kyle Swanson followed, followed by Delara, with Joe Tipp trailing. Once they were deep into the trees, they stopped to get their bearings, and Swanson opened a plastic-shielded map. He pulled a red-lens flashlight from his web gear, only to feel a light touch on his arm. 'I remember this place,' Delara said softly. 'There is a shallow stream over to the left and a meadow to the right. We can stay hidden in the trees all the way around the field, but then there is a road to cross.'

Too easy, Swanson thought, but he pointed for Hughes to check out the landmarks, and he was back in five minutes, moving unheard through the foliage. He nodded and took them to the edge of the calm and moonlit meadow. Judging by the height of the grass, it was a grazing area, and although all of the animals had been herded back to the village for the night, the smell of wet wool and sheep dung still permeated the air. Maybe this girl was the real deal with her directions.

Going downhill gave them a vantage point on what was below, and they came to the crest of the little road and paused again. Travis went one way and Tipp the other, slithering through a rocky ditch that ran alongside the dirt passageway. Again the two scouts with night vision goggles returned without seeing or hearing anything, and they all moved on. 'We can follow the road for about half a kilometer north, then we have to cross it and continue down to the valley floor,' said Delara. Her voice was excited, but quiet, as she guided them with certainty through the rugged area she had roamed as a girl. Passing decades did not bring much change to such places, and she was sure-footed and steady as she pointed them onward, recognizing outcroppings of rock and sharp curves in a narrow path as familiar landmarks.

Kyle kept them all at a steady pace, not allowing Delara's unerring directions to hurry them into making a mistake. Security was as important as speed, but she had come up with a route that bypassed all activity except for the noise of an occasional night animal. They reached the valley floor without incident, caught their breath, drank some water, and started up the next mountain.

Going up was harder than coming down, but Travis Hughes set a brutal pace, aware that the darkness had changed with the passing of time. He looked behind him and saw that the others were thirty meters back, unable to keep up with his rate of climb because Delara was a civilian, a schoolteacher, not a trained warrior in peak physical condition. The other three could go only as fast as the slowest member. Hughes held up his right hand in a fist, and everyone stopped as he scrambled back to the group.

'What do you want me to do, Shake?' he asked.

'Get going, and be quick about it. Get up to the ridge-line and be able to give us cover if we need it, and look around for a hide.'

Small and energetic, Hughes turned back and went into what would be considered an uphill sprint, his powerful legs pumping like pistons as he attacked the mountain, moving silently through the foliage.

Kyle, Delara, and Joe Tipp kept their distance, working through heavy underbrush beside a gulley, searching for firm footing with their boots and grabbing roots, pawing at rocks, and huffing for breath. Delara Tabrizi never asked for a rest, although her lungs were aching and her muscles burned with the strain. Once she stopped, and the big hand of Joe Tipp pushed hard on her behind as he whispered, 'Go, dammit!' She went.

Ten minutes after Hughes had reached a position just below the summit, the three others crawled up beside him, gulping deep breaths. 'This is the right place,' he said and then pointed toward a group of boulders about fifty meters away that bumped out from the run of thick trees and undergrowth. They went toward it on their bellies, anxious to clear a place in which the four of them could hide during the coming daylight hours as the morning sun began turning the sky into a definite gray. Delara rolled onto her back, sucking in deep breaths, fighting exhaustion.

Swanson pulled out his binos and crawled to the crest, looked down, and said, 'Oh, damn.'

Below was the site, where frightened groups of people were being herded into small, barbed-wire cages.

Juba drove a Russian-made UAZ-469 jeep directly up to a military roadblock in a mountain pass, stopping slowly at a safe distance from the Rakhsh armored personnel carrier that blocked the road, with its 12.77mm machine gun pointing toward the visitors. Another jeep halted right behind him, and all four of the men in the vehicles dismounted with their hands held high.

'We are expected,' Juba told the young sergeant who approached, then handed over his identification papers. The soldier took the ID back to a guard shack and radioed the site, two miles away. When he received clearance, he ordered the big Rakhsh off the road and returned the papers to Juba with a crisp salute. The other guards snapped to attention, and the UAZ-469s were soon on their way.

'Are we going to have trouble with those boys on the way out?' asked the big man who was riding in the passenger seat beside Juba.

Juba laughed and shook his head. 'No. The Iranians are in on it but have the erroneous idea that they control the situation. They have been excellent hosts and sponsors, but the time has come to say good-bye. We can fly out using a little helicopter that is kept at the site.' The helicopter could not be used to bring them in because the jeeps were loaded with special equipment that might have been questioned by the crew or by people at the site.

All three of the men with Juba were mercenaries, tough guns from the old Soviet Union. Even so, this was dangerous. 'The MOIS is going to be very upset if they are screwed,' said the man. The Iranian Ministry of Intelligence and Security was so notorious and ruthless that its handpicked agents had to prove they could kill and torture before being admitted to the ranks. International boundaries meant nothing to the secret police, and the well-paid mercenaries understood that the MOIS would try to track them down.

'That already has been arranged. We bribed the minister.' Juba saw the building when he came around a final curve. He drove past a series of tall cages, each holding a cluster of three people, men and women, with haunted looks on their faces. The small administration office structure was the only other thing aboveground, and a man in a white coat was walking out to meet the jeeps.

'Leave the weapons and the gear in the vehicles for the time being. I will tell you when.' He got out and went to shake the hand of the site director.

12

Joe Tipp and Travis Hughes lay side by side, sketching the site below and building a range card. Tipp would focus an MLR-40 handheld laser rangefinder on a specific point and describe it, and Hughes would note the digital readout and write it onto their map. The rangefinder was a product of OIP Sensor Systems in Belgium and was used by military forces around the world. Swanson considered it to be a dinosaur in comparison to the rangefinding computer built into his favorite sniper rifle, but he had left Excalibur behind on this mission.

A line of small motion detectors, Sentinels out of a plant in China, had been arranged behind and to the sides of their hide site to prevent anyone from creeping up unnoticed. And a small box was rigged in a safe location nearby, with a small directional antenna pointed down at the site. It was a Swiss-made Grabber V401 listening device that would record up to twenty channels of voice and electronic data traffic. Anything that was said down below for the next fourteen hours would be on a tiny computer disk for later analysis.

Delara Tabrizi had the binos on the cages, shifting her study from person to person, hoping to recognize her brother. So far, she had not recognized anyone.

Swanson was down behind the crest, his back against a tree and the map spread before him, talking by encrypted telephone with Sybelle Summers back at Camp Baharia. 'The site is very active. Something is going to happen soon. A pair of Russky jeeps carrying four guys pulled in a few minutes ago, and a man in a white doctor's coat is leading them around.'

'Can you get to the building?'

'No way. We're in a good hide about seven hundred meters away and uphill, but there is a big clearing around the site, the same kind of discoloration and dead foliage that we found at the first one. Too much ground to cover undetected in broad daylight, and we don't know how many people are in there. Some IRG are also in the area.'

'How is your passenger?'

'Holding up good. We're all watching to be sure she doesn't get too weirded out and do anything stupid if she actually sees her brother down there.'

'Okay. Call if you need me. Slider Base out.'

As soon as he terminated the call, Travis Hughes was at his side. 'We need you up there, Shake. The white coat dude is pointing at us.'

'The wind normally comes from that wooded high ground to the north and pushes on down through the valley,' explained Director Ali Kahzahee, sweeping his hand toward the range of foothills that led down to the plain on which the site was located. 'Our weather forecast today is ideal, with some rain moving in this afternoon. You can already feel the breeze building up, and it will increase, coming from that way. Obviously, we have placed the experimental stations downwind.'

Juba was not interested in a weather report. 'Is this the final test?' He had left his men at the jeeps while the director gave him a tour.

'I believe so,' replied Kahzahee, lifting his chin in the direction of the cages. 'It worked perfectly in animal trials, and I have a high level of confidence that it will work down there today.'

They strolled casually, discussing details, to the first cage, a six-by-six wire enclosure crowned by circles of concertina wire. Three men were inside, all emaciated and fearful of what the day would bring. Two had been arrested during crackdowns on government dissidents and the third was a common criminal, but it made no difference now. They knew they had left the category of human beings and were now just expendable laboratory rats, listening in horror to the explanation Director Kahzahee gave to Juba.

'At this station, there will be a one hundred percent fatality rate within five minutes. First will come an icy feeling as the liquid goes into their pores and attacks their pulmonary systems, which will make them strangle and suffocate. When they attempt to wipe it away from their skin, they spread it to uninfected areas. The effects are irreversible and very painful. Our autopsies have shown significant damage to the major organs as the oxygen supply is terminated.'

Juba looked at the terrified dark eyes. They were scared, yes, but still there was a spark of defiance. Stubborn people, but it no longer mattered.

Another fifty meters and they came to the second cage, this time with a man, a teenaged boy, and a middle-aged woman with long gray hair as the experimental subjects.

Juba had a faint recognition. She was a famous writer who had been heavily critical of the government. Once he placed her face, he ignored her. 'This group will have the same reactions as the first. I anticipate complete success.'

'They will all die within a few minutes?'

'Yes.' The director made the same predictions at the next two cages, still spaced fifty meters apart, then they approached the next to the last enclosure, which was 250 meters from the first one. 'This is where things change sharply. Even with the prevailing breeze today, all of the subjects in the final enclosure will survive for much longer and may recover entirely with proper medical help.'

Juba liked what he had heard. 'Well, Director Kahzahee, it sounds good. Let's get on with the test and see if you have earned your money.'

They returned to the jeeps, where the rest of the scientists had gathered with their measuring equipment and a metal container the size of an oxygen tank. Everyone put on hazmat suits. They were upwind, but none wanted to take a chance with the deadly genie that was about to be set free.

'There he is! I see Mahmoud!' Delara Tabrizi grabbed Kyle Swanson's arm. 'There in the second cage with the woman with gray hair. He's alive.'

Swanson shifted his own binos over and saw the three people clustered together behind the wire. 'It's impossible to get to them right now,' he said. 'We have to wait.'

'I can go by myself. They will not suspect a woman, and then you can shoot them all from up here and call in airplanes.' She started to stand, and Swanson pulled her down hard.

'Listen to me! I'm in charge here and you are a free rider. You don't do anything at all, *nothing*, unless I tell you to. You understand me? I thought that we made that perfectly clear before you even got on the helicopter.' His eyes were fierce and the whispered command thunderous with his anger.

'I cannot just let them kill my brother!'

'You will not be allowed to compromise this mission, Miss Tabrizi,' he warned. 'Our job is to see what is in that building and what they are doing. We will save the boy if we can, but right now, we all stay put. Travis, sit on this woman if she tries to go anywhere.'

Swanson turned back to the scene below. There was nothing they could do now but watch. When he saw the men below donning their biochem protective gear, he turned and softly said, 'Everybody get the MOPP suits on. Right now.'

All four of the watchers slid out of sight below the ridgeline and struggled into their protective gear, with Hughes helping Delara figure out the bulky outfit. Even the smallest size was too big for her and hung around her in folds.

Kyle ignored her. He needed a plan. Something.

Mahmoud Tabrizi knew he was going to die today. He had not really expected to live very long anyway after his awakening to the ideas passed along by some of his friends, subversive talk about establishing some other form of government in Tehran, a loosening of the police state tactics, and profound questions about the teachings of the mullahs. That was treason, and he knew it and didn't care, and he had become known in places where revolution was discussed. Three weeks short of his seventeenth birthday, as he sat on the dirt in a barbed wire cage, he believed that although his contribution had not been much, he had made a difference among the coming generation of students in Iran.

He thought about his sister, Delara, the only other surviving member of their family, and prayed that Allah would bestow many blessings upon her. Mahmoud never believed that religious nonsense that women were lesser than men, nor that he was going to live in some fairy-tale paradise once he died. What counted was what one did while one lived.

The teenager reached out and took the hand of the woman in the cage with him. She had made a difference in the struggle, and he felt honored that they would be together at the end. Although her clothes were now shabby and she was very weak, she had wielded the power of written words. Her poems and stories had bounded across international borders, and the government had been unable to stop them, so they arrested and tortured her. 'Do not be afraid, Mother,' Mahmoud said. 'No matter what these dogs have done to you, or will do to us, you will always be one of our true warriors.'

The woman looked at the boy with her watery eyes and tightened her grip on his hand. 'Freedom, my young friend Mahmoud. Let us cry out for freedom, even with our final breaths.'

A technician in a white hazmat suit drove a four-wheeled ATV to the first cage, pulling a cart with a pair of large containers strapped inside. He parked just beyond the reach of the prisoners and unhitched the trailing cart. He secured the canisters so they pointed in the correct direction, then adjusted a nozzle that would diffuse the gas inside when the valve was opened. When one was empty, the other would begin to unleash its deadly contents. The three men trapped inside the cage had lost their fear and were resigned to their fates and glared at the suited figure and cursed him.

The man had a radio headset inside the helmet and told Director Kahzahee that all was ready. The men at consoles inside the building gave other confirmations. A pause, then Kahzahee's steady voice ordered, 'Begin the experiment.'

An extremely loud signal horn groaned into a wailing siren that blasted through the valley and over the hills, warning the Iranian soldiers to stay away from the area until the siren was heard a second time. At the roadblocks and on the patrols, soldiers looked nervously at each other and ran for shelter.

The technician twisted the knob atop the nozzle counterclockwise three full turns, jumped back onto the ATV, and raced away from the area. Over the barking whine of the little engine, he heard people yelling, calling out, and chanting.

The prisoners who were about to die in agony were standing at the wire, chanting at the top of their voices – FREEDOM!

The hissing gas moved unseen into the air, then spread as it was pushed by the flow of more compressed gas coming behind it. The slight breeze helped it stay airborne, spread apart, and rise higher for a while, but the heavy individual molecules began to chemically weld together and, yielding to gravity, slowly arced back toward earth as spots of liquid. The prisoners in the first cage felt cold droplets, as if a rain shower were passing. They covered their mouths and noses with the rags of their clothing and closed their eyes, but the droplets clung to their skin and coagulated into a sheen of clear gel that seeped into their pores. Two removed the cloths from their faces and tried to brush away the liquid on their skin, but it would not rub off, only spread out in a viscous covering over a wider surface area. The third man kept the rag over his face, watching as the others began to cough loudly; then he could take it no longer, feeling as if his skin were being penetrated by a million tiny drills of heat. He immediately had trouble breathing, as if he had swallowed a large piece of meat that was stuck in his throat.

The first scream was heartrending, but after that there were just too many to tell one from another. All three men in the cage were flailing in torment, grabbing their throats and chests as the poison sped through their bloodstreams and into their hearts, lungs, and brains. Mucus membranes expanded and ruptured, and a clear liquid leaked from their mouths and noses. They were gasping for air, sucking loudly, but their lungs and air passages had filled to overflowing with the mucus discharge, and the fading hearts kept pumping the contaminated blood throughout their bodies. *No air. No air!* It was impossible to breathe.

The expanding bubble of gas moved on. By the time all three of the men in the first cage were thrashing on the ground, Mahmoud and the writer felt the first wet drops and their cries for freedom stopped. 'Inhale it deeply, Mother! Gulp it all in and we can beat them by shortening the pain,' he said, opening his mouth wide and turning his face upward. When the gel formed on his tongue, he lapped at the liquid eagerly, like a kitten at a bowl of milk, then toppled, coughing and gagging, but still holding the hand of the woman.

All three men in the first pen had ceased thrashing, and the bodies entered the final stages of destruction. The final conscious thought of each was sheer pain and the feeling that he had been eaten alive.

The gas moved on, the bubble expanding, and swept up the next three victims in the third cage and then the fourth. The people in the hazmat suits watched with clinical detachment as the ground in the pens was littered with moaning and thrashing human wreckage.

'Now this is where it gets interesting,' said Director Kahzahee. As if it had hit a wall, the sticky gas stopped spreading after causing total destruction for two hundred meters. The three men in the final enclosure had stared at the certain death that had been marching steadily toward them and were wailing in anticipation of the grinding end awaiting them. Then minutes passed and nothing happened. They could still breathe. They were still alive.

'Wonderful,' exclaimed Kahzahee. 'Absolutely perfect. Total lethality in an exact space, with the contaminant lingering there in heavy doses. It could remain potent for up to twenty-four hours.'

The director motioned to several of the workers in the hazmat suits, who moved forward and pulled one of the bodies from the fourth cage and hauled it to the final enclosure, which had not been infected. They dropped it inside, then used clubs to knock each of the final three prisoners to the ground and rub their hands and arms into the gel and mucus on the dead man.

'After an attack, the so-called first responders will show up, the police and medical people. With the poison being clear, there will be no pools of blood to warn them of danger, and they probably would not even be wearing gloves. Anyone without protective shielding who touches one of those people or that clothing will transfer the gel to themselves and can spread it to others. The entire zone becomes a death trap.'

Juba was impressed. The weapon would not weaken quickly in a wind because it had been designed to create a specific cone of death and hold its position for a long period of time. He imagined driving a truck through a major American city, spewing the toxin into the air, and knowing that everybody for two hundred yards on each side of the street would be killed, all along his route. Or rigging a spray from a plane over a metropolitan area. The first responders entering the scene to help would be slain by the lingering, sticky gas, and they would spread it to the hospitals and emergency shelters. On the battle-field, the gas would be a targeted weapon with a specific kill zone that would devastate an enemy but not harm your own troops. Scientists and military tinkerers would dream up even more uses.

'That's it, then. Congratulations on your achievement,' he told the director. 'How will you clear it out down there?'

'We will just have to burn it all where it stands. It's the only way.'

'Then let's go back into your office while your men take care of it. I need to report your success.'

13

The four people in the snipers' hide had felt helpless and were horrified as they watched the experiment unfold, for there was nothing they could do to stop the murders of the innocents in the cages. Delara covered her ears and buried her face in the carpet of leaves beneath her when she saw her brother fall. Mahmoud was dying in great pain, and she was powerless to help.

Kyle Swanson's brain had kept churning, figuring out a plan. The mission had never been to rescue hostages but to get inside the building and its web of tunnels to document what was in there. When he saw how the experiment developed, he got the idea to turn the deadly weapon against its creators.

He gathered the others and explained what they were to do. Aggressive action was the best antidote for the useless feeling that had engulfed them all. Swanson, Tipp, and Hughes would execute a long-range ambush to kill as many of those cold-blooded bastards as possible and then steal their work.

There was no urgency at the site as the workers went about their jobs as if this were a normal day. Perhaps it was, for them. The man with the ATV, still in a white hazmat suit, zipped out to the first pen and turned off the valve to stop the escaping gas. Without looking at the bodies, he reattached the cart and brought the narrow tanks back to the site and returned them to a small fenced area near the building, the loading zone in which the canisters were filled. Another worker waited there with a water hose, buckets, and a scrubbing brush to wash down the driver, the ATV and cart, and the canisters.

The three Chechnyan mercenaries lounged around the jeeps, smoking cigarettes and watching, waiting for Juba to give the signal for them to grab their weapons and kill the scientists, their assistants, and then any leftover prisoners. After that, the boxes of explosives and incendiaries they had packed along would be placed at vital points and the structure would be destroyed. Juba had not yet given the signal. They waited, three hardcore fighters loyal only to the big paychecks, half already paid up front, half on completion. It was more than a fair deal as far as they were concerned. There were no threats among the busy men in the white coats, other than that extraordinary and lethal gas. The mercs were happy the wind was at their backs, blowing away the remains of the spray, and the sprinkle of rain had begun.

Director Ali Kahzahee was in his private office. He had spent many months coming in and out of the site and was glad to be leaving for the final time, the complicated work done. A number of laboratories scattered around the world had worked on various parts of the project, but it was Kahzahee and his team who had brought it all together and made it work.

His personal knowledge was invaluable, and Kahzahee

knew that once the project was completed, his usefulness to the Iranian regime would be at an end. The soldiers who had been guarding the site would probably sweep up the entire team and demand the formula, particularly since Tehran thought they were part owners of the project. Juba and his guards would protect them on the swift journey into Europe, where Saladin had promised to help them all build new lives.

The director folded up his laptop computer, which contained his research, and stuffed it into a black brief-case along with his detailed notes. He then took a final turn around the office, checking every drawer and file cabinet. There were no mementos or reminders. A pile of discarded notes and reams of results was scattered in the middle of the floor, where it would be soaked with gasoline. Everything was to be burned.

The soldiers at the roadblocks might be curious about the smoke, but Kahzahee had not sounded the all-clear siren, and the military would not enter the area until they heard it. He picked up a pair of pliers from his desk and snipped the curling red, black, and green wires to the alarm. The all clear would not sound today.

There was no concern about the people he had killed in the experiment, just a sense of scientific satisfaction. The director grabbed his briefcase and headed for the door.

Juba was in the communications room, where he had placed a call to a number in Paris. Saladin had answered.

'It is ready,' said Juba. 'The test was impressive.'

'Excellent. Do we have the material in hand?

'The director gave me an envelope with a complete disk

and matching set of printouts. I will bring them out.'

'What about backup copies? Does Kahzahee have a set?'

'I would imagine so. The material is too valuable to entrust to anyone working for him.'

Saladin paused. 'Are you somewhere that you might be overheard?'

'Yes,' said Juba.

'Very well. Make sure to destroy any backup material after you dispose of the staff.'

Juba saw Director Kahzahee come into the communications area and smiled at him. 'We will all be leaving soon,' Juba said. 'Yes, sir. I will tell him you said so.' He terminated the conversation. 'Saladin sends his personal congratulations, Director, and says there will be a bonus waiting for you in Paris.'

There would be nothing sexy about the ambush, just total surprise by an unexpected enemy with overwhelming firepower shooting from a secure position on high ground only seven hundred meters away. 'Kill everybody on site so we can get inside. You saw what they did to the prisoners,' Swanson told the others, his voice low and determined. 'They deserve to die. Take down all those fuckers.' Then he laid out the targets and the firing sequence. 'I'll take the bodyguards, and Tipp, rake the area for any targets you see. Hughes, you put some RPG rounds into the container storage area and we will see how they like a little of their own shit on them. Everyone engage on my first shot.'

Kyle considered the Russian-made SVD Dragunov sniper rifle to be a serviceable weapon, but not in the same class as its American counterparts, and certainly far behind his personal Excalibur. The synthetic buttstock fit comfortably against his shoulder, and his right hand eased around the pistol grip. The canvas sling seemed archaic, but the magazine could hold ten rounds of SVD 7.62 × 54 mm ammunition. It was semiautomatic, not a bolt action, and was almost fifty inches in length, upgraded to a POSP 8 × 42 sniping scope that worked well in harsh environments. It was an old hog, dating back to before the Vietnam era, but it would do what needed to be done on this day in Iran. He slowly pushed the barrel through the foliage and scanned for his first target.

He chose one of the bodyguards who had come in this morning and was now sitting on the hood of a jeep, facing away from Kyle. He looked like he was trained as a fighter and therefore presented a primary threat. For a sniper, a back shot is a golden opportunity, since it gives the target no chance to notice that he is taking his last breaths. Kyle had already checked the range card and had done the other calculations in his head for windage and the bullet drop going downhill. He put the reticle just below the man's neck, exhaled, let his heartbeat slow, and squeezed the trigger straight back until the Dragunov barked and the bullet hurtled toward the unsuspecting man at 2,700 feet per second.

The Chechnyan fighter jerked forward as if he had been slugged in the back by a big hammer, his eyes opening wide with surprise as he fell facedown in the dirt. The bullet severed his spine and exploded within him, tearing his organs to pieces before pushing a mass of tissue and blood out through a big exit wound in his chest.

Kyle shifted his aim to another Chechnyan who was spinning around at the familiar sound of a shot being fired. Swanson was cold and smooth, not hurrying. This guy was just reacting, he wasn't going anywhere. Kyle aimed for center mass, and the Dragunov spat out another powerful bullet, which took the second man in the chest. The victim remained still for a moment, then slumped to his knees, grabbing at the fatal wound as blood poured between his fingers. He fell over dead.

Off to Kyle's right, Joe Tipp opened up with his RPK light machine gun, with the long barrel braced on its folding bipod, slapping out three-round bursts throughout the general area ... *Clack-clack-clack* ... *Clack-clack-clack*. Several men were sent sprawling. Tipp had two spare big banana clips for the gun nearby so he could reload quickly. He was not going for any random fire to keep their heads down. As a trained sniper, Joe Tipp was taking enough time to aim and kill people. The gunpowder smell of burned cordite rose in the hide.

To Kyle's left, Travis Hughes came into a kneeling position with an RPG-7 launcher on his shoulder and fired a grenade that burst from the tube with a loud *whoosh!* Four sharp fins popped out to stabilize the flight, and ten meters away, the grenade armed itself. Sizzling at the tip of a hot red exhaust tail, the high-explosive round zoomed into the storage area and exploded hard when it hit metal, setting loose a spray of the poison gas.

The crashing symphony of the ambush was fully under way, and none of the people at the site had yet fired a shot in return. In fact, none had yet even reached a weapon.

Watching through binoculars from beside Kyle, Delara

Tabrizi viewed the destruction with a burning fury on her face. 'Kill them,' she said through gritted teeth. 'Kill them all!'

Inside the building, Juba heard the shots, and three seconds later the RPG explosion shook the concrete structure, blowing around a layer of dirt and debris. An attack was the last thing he had expected, and he instantly recognized that his situation had totally changed.

'What's happening?' Director Kahzahee, who had been heading for the door, stopped in midstride and turned back.

Juba stepped closer, looking through the door and then glancing out a side window. Men were running around trying to find shelter, and smoke was spreading along the ground while a misty haze rose into the air. 'Either the Iranians are coming to take over this place, or some dissident bandits are making a raid. Either way, it is not good for us.'

'The fools are shooting at the container loading area! Some of those canisters are still filled with the gas!' The director dropped his briefcase and grabbed for a fresh biohazard suit hanging on a wall hook as another RPG grenade whumped into the containers and rattled the building.

Gas! Juba was beginning to feel a pull of panic and forced himself to slow down enough to think and act. There was no time to go through the complicated procedure of getting a full biosuit back on, and to just stand where he was would be a death sentence. He had to get out!

In one motion, he pulled a Heckler & Koch 9 mm

pistol from his belt holster and fired two bullets into the skull of Director Kahzahee, picked up the fallen briefcase, and dove through the side window in the wall across the room from the exploding storage area.

He tucked his head and shoulders and hit the ground with a roll, in a shower of splinters and glass that sliced at him. *This wasn't the Iranian government,* he thought. *It was dissidents who were determined to capture the site and expose its secrets to the world, making the government in Tehran be viewed around the world as monsters.*

Juba rose, bent at the waist, and ran toward a little gulley in order to put terrain between himself and the shooters while hoping he was moving faster than the spreading and invisible cloud of gas. The wind was on his right cheek, not directly behind him, so that improved his chances of escaping. Wet droplets splashed on his arms and face.

The sustained chatter of an AK-47 being fired on full automatic broke the rhythm of the incoming rounds. One of his Chechnyans was returning fire, taking the attention of the attackers and buying Juba a few more steps. The hired gunman was covering the escape in an effort to protect his own paycheck and called out, 'Juba! Start the helicopter!'

Juba was standing completely up now, panting and sprinting hard toward the field where an old UH-1 Huey helicopter was stationed, his heels pounding hard. The droplets continued to splash on him. The chopper's rotors were sluggishly beginning to turn, and the engine was coughing. Almost out of breath, he reached the bird and jumped into the cargo area, rolling flat on his back, his fist tight around the briefcase handle. 'Go!' he yelled. 'The gas is escaping.'

The Americans had sold a lot of aging Hueys to the old shah before he was deposed, and the helicopters were a common sight around Iran. The pilot had been running his checklist even before the shooting started. He wasn't worried about some stray bullets, because the Hueys had proven in Vietnam that they could soak up gunfire and keep flying. Bullets were not the threat, but there might be a veil of deadly gas outside his cockpit.

Juba slammed the big side doors shut, found a dry towel, and wiped his face and arms and hands hard, staring straight ahead at the big drops hitting the broad front windows, some of them coalescing into pools. *Rain or gas?* He didn't know.

The pilot made an emergency takeoff, kicking the helicopter to full throttle to let the powerful downdraft of the overhead blades dissipate any gathering fumes. They had to get out of the zone. The tail of the Huey rose sharply up and the heavy nose was almost pointed at the ground; then the lift began as the skids came off the ground. The bird, slowly at first and then more rapidly, sailed along the meadow and then made a sudden jump into the sky, climbing high and fast away from the burning site. No one else had made it out to the field, and the pilot didn't really care.

Kyle saw the third bodyguard hiding behind a Jeep and spraying wildly with an AK-47. The man did not know what he was shooting at and was just throwing out a hail of bullets in hopes of making the attackers duck, or at least pause. Above the racket, Swanson had clearly heard the man shout the name of Juba, but he could not take time to analyze who he was calling to. Swanson pinned the scope on him and saw something happening to his target that made him pause before squeezing the trigger.

The Chechnyan not only stopped firing but dropped his weapon and slapped at his skin. His face was twisted in surprise and then in pain. The bubble of poison gas released by the attack had crawled over the bodyguard, and he was trying to rub it away. Then he began to breathe it, and he stood and ran, as if there were some shelter, grabbing at his throat as if strangling. Kyle understood that the man was trying to reach the water hose and maybe scrub away the lethal drops that were congealing into a gel on his body.

Not going to happen, Skippy. Swanson adjusted the scope, following the movement, and fired. The bullet dropped the bodyguard in his tracks, hitting low on the back, just below the kidneys, and the man crashed and bounced on the dirt. Kyle had not wanted to make a kill shot, just to bring him down. In the view of the sniper, the bastard was not a candidate for an easy death. The man tried to crawl but gave up and rolled on the ground as the gas went into his lungs. He lay there with his chest heaving, turning purple in the face as he choked to death on his own fluids.

'Cease fire. Cease fire,' Swanson called to Tipp and Hughes. 'The gas has them now. Let their little miracle finish them off.'

'Shoot them!' demanded Delara.

'No need,' Kyle replied. 'What those men did to your brother is now happening to them. I will kill any who might survive.'

'One got away on the helicopter,' noted Joe Tipp. 'I tried to nail him, but he was low and moving fast.'

'Yeah. I took a shot at the Huey, but it was too far away for the Dragunov.' *Juba? Now that would be an interesting twist to things.* Kyle stood up. Fire raged in the container area but was not spreading to the building. A dozen bodies lay on the ground, three still twitching in the embrace of the poison in their bodies. 'Anyway, the site is open. We'll wait for a little while to let that shit burn off or blow away before going in.'

A slow thirty minutes passed and an uneasy stillness came to the area, as if nature were eager to take back the dead zone. Things someday would grow here again. No curious soldiers came looking for the source of the shooting and explosions because the all-clear siren had never sounded.

The light rain began falling heavier, which would help dampen the traces of the gas.

'I want to bury my brother,' said Delara.

Kyle was eating an MRE ration. 'I don't think we can do that. The body is contaminated now, and we don't know what the stuff is. In fact, you probably should not even look at it, and you definitely cannot touch him.'

She was also standing. 'I don't care. He was my brother. I cannot just leave him out there.'

'As much as I hate it, we have to leave them all out there. We are taking a huge risk just going into the building for a few minutes.' He stuffed the half-eaten ration back into his pack. 'Look, Miss Tabrizi. Whatever was being concocted down there obviously is one of the greatest weapons-grade poison gases ever created. A real terrorists' cocktail, and we don't know its properties – sarin, ricin, anthrax, whatever. We have seen how it kills without conscience, and the bad guys have it, which means thousands of people are now in jeopardy. Your brother gave his life fighting these maniacs, so don't you think he would want you to do everything you can to bring them down?'

She was near him. Delara knew what he said was true, but . . . 'He is my brother,' she whispered softly.

She looked so small, and there were tears in her eyes. Kyle stepped close and wrapped his arms around her. 'I know. I am so very sorry.'

'Our chopper will be here in ten minutes, Shake. Let's do it.' Travis Hughes had his MOPP suit on.

'Right. Tipp, you cover us from up here with the RPK, then take Miss Tabrizi over to the field where that other helo was. Make that the designated landing zone.'

'I want to go with you!' Delara's response was immediate.

'No. You really don't,' Kyle answered, but with a gentle tone instead of that of a combat commander. 'You will want to remember your brother as who he was. You don't want your last memory of him to be a close view of what they did. Please, Delara, I'm asking that you stay here with Joe. Travis and I are doing a quick search and then we're out of there. Speed is necessary, and you would slow us down . . . maybe put us all in danger.'

He and Hughes were already moving, leaving no time for discussion. Delara watched them go and turned to Joe Tipp, who was scanning the area with his binos. 'He's right. Let's finish this and get out of here,' said Tipp. 'Kyle is good at this stuff. Trust him.'

'Kyle? That is his name?'

'Oh, shit,' Tipp said. 'Forget I said that.'

*

Swanson and Hughes moved as cautiously as if skating on frozen glass, determined to touch nothing unless absolutely necessary. They ignored the bodies and the exterior destruction and, wading through a thin film of lingering smoke, moved into the building. The mist was gone, but rain was coming down harder.

The body of the man they recognized as the leader of the scientists was on the floor, killed not by the gas but by two bullets to the back of the head at close range. Hughes had his camera running and took pictures as Kyle probed deeper into the office area, his weapon at the ready. A pile of papers had been thrown onto the floor. File drawers hung open. Desks were empty.

The door at the far end of the room stood open, and the two Marines started downstairs. The lights were still on, and they entered a spacious area of several rooms crammed with laboratory equipment and electronics gear. Every computer had been destroyed, the screens smashed and the hard drives removed and crushed. Shelves were lined with covered containers, and at one end was a sterile room that could be entered only through an airlock. It was empty except for more counters and scientific gear.

The place seemed to Kyle to mirror the one they had been in earlier in southern Iran, only this one was still intact. He shuddered to think of the experiments that went on in this place. Through another door and down more stairs. A storehouse of material, and smaller areas that indicated mess and health care facilities. The place was like an underground pyramid, with plenty of space at the bottom and narrowing to that single administrative area on the top. Down low was where the really dirty work was done, and Kyle, followed by Travis, went carefully to the bottom floor and finally into the individual spokes and tunnels. He breathed easier when they found that the dungeon cages were empty. All of the prisoners had been taken out and executed this morning. On the side of one of the cells, they found someone had used a rock to scratch numbers into the concrete wall – 999. Hughes took pictures.

'Nothing more down here, Trav. Let's go back up and gather those papers, then get out of here.' Kyle led the way back into sunlight, almost feeling the dark shadows pulling at him from down below, trying to take him into a cell and lock the door. He shook it off.

Travis stepped to the front door and waved up to Joe Tipp. It was time to get moving. 'All clear,' Tipp acknowledged on the radio. 'Bird inbound.'

Kyle took down a pair of white biohazard suits hanging on the wall and tossed one to Travis, and they both stuffed the papers on the floor into the garments. Scientific records, notebooks, computer disks and office documents, letters and notes, but they did not know if it was treasure or trash. Finally, Kyle searched the body of the director and found a cell phone and a wallet. He threw both into the makeshift sack. 'Let's go,' he said.

They trotted through the rain, letting the water wash off anything that might have clung to their suits. Joe Tipp was in the open, guiding the helicopter down, while Delara Tabrizi stood to the side.

Kyle and Travis stopped just outside the radius of the powerful rotor blast and peeled out of their biosuits, leaving them on the ground before they climbed into the Pave Low.

'What did you find?' Tipp asked, pointing to the two bulging white biosuits on the floor. The sleeves and arms were folded tight, but loose papers stuck from the neck openings.

'Don't know. I'm not a scientist,' said Travis, 'but whatever it is, I think the intel pukes will be having wet dreams for the next month or so.'

14

PARIS

Juba had never been so scared. Not in his entire life. In the first twenty-four hours after escaping from the contaminated biochemical weapons site, he took five showers and still was almost mad with worry that he would never be truly cleansed.

His helicopter had landed at a small airport, where he showered and found fresh clothes, then abandoned the aircraft. The helicopter pilot was killed and the body hidden in the equipment shed; then Juba hired a small plane and flew back to Tehran. He was out of Iran on the first available international flight.

Only when he checked into the Four Seasons Hotel in Qatar did he begin to breathe easier, and immediately after being shown into the suite, he got into a shower with water as hot as he could stand, imagining that some of the deadly gel particles were sticking to him even then, burrowing beneath his skin, reaching for his guts and his brain.

He repeatedly coated himself with soap and shampoo, working the suds hard beneath the downpour of scalding water until his skin was red and raw. He turned his face into the falling stream and felt it cook. He vigorously scrubbed between his toes, the bottoms of his feet, deeply into his ears, beneath his crotch, fingernails, nostrils, everywhere. Shampoo the eyebrows and under the armpits, and even the pubic hair and the crevice of his butt.

Steam rose from his body when he turned off the water and stepped from the stall onto the cool tiles and wrapped himself in thick white towels. Wait – what if he had swallowed some of it? He brushed his teeth until the gums bled and gargled with antiseptic mouthwash. He studied the blood on the toothbrush and threw it away.

Moving into the bedroom, he noticed the full-length mirror. He dropped the towels and stood before it for a long time, examining his entire body, turning slowly, looking for rashes and lesions. Then he climbed beneath the covers, only to be seized again by unreasoning panic and break into a sweat. He rushed to the bathroom for another shower, his thoughts anchored on the memory reef of the prisoners dying, trapped in the small cages as the gas ate at them. Every itch he felt was magnified a thousand times, the lingering fear intensified by the knowledge that he had helped make the monster that was trying to devour him. Juba was new to fear, for he had never been frightened by any enemy. This invisible slayer was different, hungry and uncaring about who was right or who was wrong, nor obedient to its creator.

After a few hours and another shower, he calmed enough to have the concierge send someone to purchase new clothes from the nearby mall, and later had a nice dinner at a table overlooking the expanse of the Arabian Gulf. When he returned to his room, he called for a massage, then lay still in bed between clean sheets while the masseur pounded the twisted muscles, loosening the knots with pressure and pain. Afterward, Juba turned out the light, and to avoid thinking about the invisible gas and the wet drops that brought certain death, he concentrated on the long and tangled journey that had brought him to this place on this day.

As a boy, back when he was Jeremy Mark Osmand, he was teased at school in England for having a foreign father and for being a Muslim, although that stopped as he grew taller and stronger and fought anyone who belittled his family. Despite his superior abilities in rugby and soccer, he still heard the ridicule that swam just below the surface of many of his classmates' polite geniality.

In the summer of 1988, his parents took him to Peshawar, in the North-West Frontier Province of Pakistan, where his father joined the surgical staff at a Red Crescent hospital while his mother helped at the refugee center. They lived in a house among the eucalyptus trees of University Town, and from there, Jeremy set out each day to explore the boomtown spawned by the Russian invasion of neighboring Afghanistan. Spies and journalists, Russian planes overhead, distant explosions, the hubbub of the Smugglers' Market and a crush of people, animals, and vehicles of all sorts and every color. Weapons and ammunition were strapped to the backs of trains of mules headed for the border.

The war was an awakening of an Islamic spirit within the boy, and in mosques and youth meetings, Jeremy discovered that London was not the center of the universe after all!

He learned much more about the Prophet and the holy

places and was astonished to discover that the mighty Ottoman Empire was not an ancient myth. Although it had begun back in 1300, it lasted until 1924. Its creation was led by the venerable Osman I! His family's original last name was the same as that great caliph, and Jeremy questioned his father's decision to bastardize and anglicize it. 'Come with me to the hospital today and I will give you the answer,' his father said one morning as they sipped strong black coffee. 'One of my fellow physicians wants to meet you.'

Within the hour, Jeremy was at a small table in the rear of a coffee house near the hospital, deep in conversation, in English, with Dr. Ayman al-Zawahiri, the Muslim firebrand who had been jailed and tortured following the assassination of Egyptian president Anwar Sadat. He had come to Peshawar to help the mujahideen freedom fighters, and Jeremy was spellbound by the intense man with the large eyeglasses, who made sense with his stern and unforgiving religious and political views.

Then someone else joined their group, a tall and slender man who wore common robes although he possessed great wealth. Osama bin Laden was from Saudi Arabia and was famed for lectures that painted a dark vision of Islam and reasoned that it was not only permissible to kill infidels: Under the Koran, it was a Muslim duty. Bin Laden extended a hand and uttered a soft greeting, then encouraged the boy to speak, and Jeremy's new dreams of revenge and hatred spilled forth. Jeremy promised that he was a true Muslim and ready to die, today if necessary, for Islam.

The tall Saudi touched the boy's forearm. 'No, not today. Not for a long time.' He glanced at Dr. Osmand.

'Were you aware that your father has long been one of us?'

Jeremy blinked as his father bowed at the compliment.

'It was at our request that he has endured such shame among the infidels, and the Prophet will reward him.'

'Father? I don't understand. What is he talking about?'

'Our name, Jeremy,' the father replied. 'You believe I changed our name for mere advancement in English society. That is not what happened.'

Al-Zawahiri interrupted. 'Many years ago, I formed the Muslim Brotherhood in Egypt and brought it forward into the Islamic Jihad, and now into al Qaeda. Part of our early work was to create what intelligence services call "moles" who would infiltrate foreign countries and be ready to strike when needed. Your father volunteered to help in this cause and was asked to eradicate the automatic Muslim link of his name so that you, Jeremy Osmand, would have a true British name, speak like a native of England, and act British. Your father has been a loyal soldier.' The dark eyes burned into Jeremy. 'Now it is your turn.'

'So, young man, you will not become a martyr today,' added Osama bin Laden. 'Praise be unto Allah, we have plenty of recruits ready to do that vital work. Yours is a special task that will require years to accomplish.'

Jeremy stared at the two leaders of the most violent sector of militant Islam. They wanted him!

Al-Zawahiri's tone changed. No more polite chitchat or explanations, just a stream of orders. Jeremy was to become as English as he could be, join the British Army and become skilled in its ways, let the army give him as much specialized training as possible.

Osama bin Laden said, 'You must shed any trace of

Islam. Your present knowledge of the Koran must sustain you, for you must not read it again for many years, nor even have a copy. You will eat the flesh of the filthy animal, drink alcohol, walk without a beard, be profane, and fornicate with their women. At times, you may even have to fight against Muslims, and you will do so with your utmost ability, for there must be no question as to your loyalty. When the time is right, we will call you.'

'Turn away from Islam? I don't know if I can do that, sir.'

'That is the answer we expected from you, Jeremy. To satisfy that disturbing thought, a council of holy men has granted a special absolution to excuse the many sins you must commit in the future.' Bin Laden leaned close. 'Follow us, young man. We have heavy hearts in requiring someone to abandon the Prophet here on earth in order to sit with him in paradise. Sadly, you will pretend – and live – as if we are your enemies. The forces of the Prophet are already defeating the atheist Russians in Afghanistan, but we must plan ahead. Great wars will come against the Jews and Crusaders before our final victory. Will you help us protect Islam?'

'Yes. Of course I will,' Jeremy replied, and his father squeezed the shoulder of his sixteen-year-old son.

'Then we will give you a new name. To everyone else, you will continue to be Jeremy. But when we summon you, you will become Juba, named for a village created by fierce warriors many years ago along the White Nile in Africa. You will be our own fierce warrior.'

Jeremy graduated from school the very next year and joined the British Royal Marines. When the shooting instructors saw his skill with a rifle, he was sent to sniper school and then moved to advanced training for special operations, including workouts and instruction at the U.S. Marines Scout Sniper School at Camp Pendleton over in America. Every fitness report glowed with praise, and senior sergeants said they had never worked with anyone so dedicated. He rose in rank to color sergeant ahead of his peers and earned the badge of a master sniper, along with other gongs and citations.

Just a natural, said the other bootnecks. Best stalker and shooter in the game, and in a firefight, I want to see the green lid and Lovats of Color Osmand from 42 Commando at my side.

Early in the spring of 2001, Dr. al-Zawahiri sent the message: It was time for Juba. He resigned from the Royal Marines, dropped out of sight, and was in Peshawar on the first day of September.

It was there that he watched the attacks on the World Trade Center and the Pentagon, which were shown continuously on television. Thousands of Muslims took to the streets in mad celebration. *Enjoy it while you can,* Juba thought. The Taliban was only a mob of thugs, not a real army, and had never even been able to defeat the ragtag Northern Alliance. He knew the oncoming international force of professionals would have no trouble rolling over them. *You're going to take it right up the bum, mates, and there's really not a damned thing you can do about it.*

He was standing ready, finely tuned and bred for battle, but he was dispatched instead to set up training camps in Afghanistan and Pakistan. Volunteers were pouring in to fight the expected invasion, but there was going to be no time to train them. Anyway, they did not want to be trained: They just wanted to blow themselves up in the faces of their enemy and become martyrs. Juba tried to convince them they probably would never even get close enough to an American soldier to do that. No discipline, organization, tactics, or marksmanship, just the wild firing of bullets. He even killed several of the fools as punishment, but even that made no impression on the others. When he asked for new assignments elsewhere, he was ordered to do the job assigned to him.

The air campaign smashed in like a thunderstorm and slashed the Taliban with everything from superb man-hunting Apache helicopters to F/A-18 Hornet fighter-bombers to Daisy Cutter bombs that weighed seven and one-half tons to AC-130 gunships that spewed bullets in incredible swaths. Not a single plane was lost, but the Taliban front line peeled open like a tin can.

Incredibly, in the face of the disaster, a Taliban leader patiently explained to Juba that things were really going well. The strategy was just to draw in the American army and bleed it slowly over the years, not defeat it. Eventually, Washington would give up, just as they did in Vietnam and the Russians had done in Afghanistan.

Juba argued that it might not happen that way and pleaded to be allowed to create a special strike unit that could exploit the Americans' vulnerabilities. He knew this enemy! He was ignored.

The Afghan capital of Kabul fell only two months after the 9/11 attacks, and the developing ground campaign then destroyed Taliban units all through the country, until they found safe refuge in the defensive positions of Tora Bora and the White Mountains along the Pakistan border.

Juba at last was allowed to form a guerrilla group to

attack supply lines and targets of opportunity, but his small team was soon swept back into the overall force, and Juba found himself in charge of troops who had no stomach for real warfare and retreated under the slightest pressure. There were many caves in which they could hide.

In frustration, Juba cursed the day he had met Osama bin Laden and Dr. al-Zawahiri. Their whole grand plan was a bust. He believed there should have been an entire series of attacks and responses ready to follow up on September 11, while the United States was almost totally unprotected, unsure, and reeling. Why weren't bombs going off in cities across America and around the world to keep the enemy off balance? Attack! They should never have allowed the U.S. military to catch its breath. Lies. Al Qaeda had fed him lies. He believed in continuing violence to accomplish military goals, while bin Laden and al-Zawahiri believed in . . . what?

He had no desire to spend a bitter Afghan winter holed up in some freezing Tora Bora cave, waiting for a cruise missile to fall on his head. The war had evolved into a gigantic game of hide-and-shoot, and that was something that ex-Color Sergeant Jeremy Osmand, a master sniper of the Royal Marines, could do better by himself. He did not want, nor need, to be around this mob. He decided to carve a personal, ruthless, and bloody path into the heart of the enemy.

After the disaster at the biochem site in Iran, Juba spent two days luxuriating at the Four Seasons in Qatar, pampering himself and letting the fear of the deadly gel recede from the forefront of his consciousness. To his surprise, he did not die.

He booked a Lufthansa flight to Paris, with a brief layover in Frankfurt, Germany, and took a cab straight to the house in the Nineteenth Arrondissement.

Saladin was concerned the moment he laid eyes on Juba. He looked like a man who was crawling out of a pit of despair. 'Talk to me, my son,' he said. 'What has happened?'

Juba handed over the briefcase. 'The experiment was successful, and I confess it was difficult to watch. Afterward, we were attacked and the canisters of the gas exploded. I barely made it out alive.'

'Who did this?'

'I don't know. Maybe some politicals trying to free some of the test subjects.' He rubbed his palms over his eyes. 'No one survived except me and the helicopter pilot. It was too dangerous to allow him to live.'

Saladin walked to the windows and looked out. It was a bright and pleasant day. 'Can you continue?'

'Of course,' Juba said. 'I was just shaken by the thought that the gas had gotten to me. I am ready.'

Saladin opened the briefcase. 'This is everything about the formula?'

Juba nodded. 'Yes. The site was almost empty, and the rest of the computers and paperwork were destroyed during the attack. We should go ahead and transmit this data to the facility in Mexico. Prepare enough of the gas for the demonstration.'

'And you are certain that you will be able to continue on schedule?'

'Without a doubt,' Juba replied. 'I can be in the United States by the end of the week.'

That brought a smile to Saladin. His man was still

strong. Anyone can stumble at some time. 'There is no urgency about that, so I would like for you to stay here for a while. We will study and talk and let you prepare for the mission ahead. I will send the formula today, but our lab in Mexico will still need some time to produce the gas and transport it.'

'Thank you, Father.'

'And you look as if you could use some good news, my son, so let me give you some: We already have six entries for the auction. That's sixty million dollars before the real bidding even begins, and I expect more.'

'They will all come after us.'

'They can try.' Saladin laughed. 'They can certainly try, but with you running our security, they will certainly fail. We will leave this house together and return to America in a few days, so if our enemies want us, they will have to first enter the U.S., which will be on very high alert. Then, after we collect the money, you and I shall just disappear.'

15

CAMP BAHARIA
IRAQ

On arrival back at the Marine base outside of Fallujah, Swanson turned over the captured material to an intelligence officer who had been awaiting the helicopter. Sybelle Summers was also at the pad, wearing a dark green sweater and black jeans, a small pistol tucked into a black leather waist holster. She looked over the Marines as they hopped from the bird. They seemed okay. Her first look at Delara Tabrizi made her smile, for the small woman seemed like a child among the heavily armed special ops team, but her walk was steady and confident. For a woman who had been a civilian schoolteacher only a few hours ago, and had since endured two major raids and had seen her friend and her brother slain, she had done okay, Sybelle decided. A sister.

Swanson, Tipp, and Hughes brought Delara over, and Sybelle led them to a small office she had used in supporting the mission. 'Not that I care, but the brass is raising hell about this unauthorized job,' she said, plopping into the chair behind the desk and putting her boots on the top. 'We didn't get enough papers stamped and authorized and all that bullshit.'

Kyle dropped his gear on the floor. 'Doesn't matter. What we found and brought back will more than shut up the critics. Loads of recordings of voices, papers and records, some computer disks, pictures. And eyewitness accounts of how this new poison gas works.'

'Can Tipp and Travis do the debrief by themselves?'

'Sure. They saw everything I did, and Trav took the pictures.'

'Good,' said Sybelle, 'because you and I are out of here.'

Kyle agreed. He needed to keep his cover intact, and that would be hard on a base filled with Marines. 'Then I want to take Miss Tabrizi along with us. I don't want her falling into the system. Once she is debriefed, the intel pukes will hand her to the political types, and God only knows where she will end up. She helped us a lot. We owe her.'

Delara was seated, watching the exchange. The woman was obviously an important person and spoke to the Marine like an equal, but they were talking about her fate. 'I cannot return to Iran!' she said. 'I want to kill these people who made this poison!'

Sybelle laughed quietly and looked over at Kyle. 'So let's take her out to the boat with us and let Jeff figure it out. He has a ton of diplomatic contacts and is good at that sort of thing.'

'Who is this Jeff?' Delara asked. 'What are you going to do with me?'

Kyle touched her shoulder, and she immediately relaxed. 'Jeff is a good friend, and by the time he finishes working his magic, you will pretty much have anything you want. A new country and a new future. A new you.'

Sybelle was on her feet. 'Joe and Travis, we'll leave you here. Good job, guys. Thanks for the help.'

'Sure, Captain,' said Tipp. 'Anytime.'

'Y'all take good care of our girl Delara,' called Travis Hughes. 'I already taught her how to say Semper Fi!'

A Humvee was parked outside, and the three of them got into it, with Sybelle at the wheel. 'I didn't want to mention it in there, but there's another reason we have to get back on board the *Vagabond*.' She glanced back at Delara, whose eyes were already closed.

'The Lizard has flown out from Washington to meet us there. You have a Green Light package.'

'I would like to get some sleep first.'

'And I would like to be thinner,' Sybelle said. 'Neither is likely.'

The Lizard had everything ready when Swanson, Sybelle, and Delara flew out to the *Vagabond*. Delara was turned over to Lady Pat for the time being, while Sybelle and Kyle met in Sir Jeff's private office with Lieutenant Commander Freedman. A big pile of documents was at the Lizard's side, and his computer was already running on secure circuits.

'This is the voice of Ahmad Hikmat Aseer, a known al Qaeda operative, in conversation with another al Qaeda leader. The NSA Big Ears picked it up. The caller is so furious that he ignored normal security precautions and made contact from his home telephone.' The Lizard tapped his keyboard and turned up the volume. A torrent of French sprang from the speakers in an angry and threatening tone, so fast that Kyle could not follow the words. It sounded like the guy was spitting on himself in his rage.

The Lizard handed transcripts to Sybelle and Kyle. 'It seems that Ahmad had a brother named Youcef, who happened to be the head of al Qaeda operations in France. Youcef's body was found floating in a Paris canal several days ago. That's when Ahmad made this call.'

Kyle read carefully. Ahmad said that his brother was last seen alive before an important meeting at his home in Paris with the outcasts Saladin and his bodyguard Juba. 'They killed him and his own guards in his own house!' Ahmad Hikmat Aseer sputtered. 'Not only that, the arrogant pigs have confiscated the house as their own!'

He demanded revenge, insisting that al Qaeda send in an execution team, and that was when the other man realized the danger of the call and challenged Ahmad about making it. He hung up.

'By then it was too late; the Big Ears had it. NSA gave it to the CIA, and they turned up an address in Paris for the deceased Youcef Aseer.'

'So why give us a Green Light? Let the CIA handle it.' Sybelle skimmed the transcript again.

'I don't know that. Too far above my pay grade. I could guess that if the CIA mucks up the arrest of Saladin, there would be an embarrassing trail back to Washington. Anyway, General Middleton gave me the assignment to brief you and get you on your way. I have a military jet standing by on shore. You're going to Paris.'

'What about me?' asked Sybelle.

'We go, but to a support point in a separate location. Kyle comes back there when he finishes.'

'When do we leave?'

'Now,' the Lizard said.

*

PARIS

The Lizard had reserved him a businessman's suite at a nondescript and out-of-the-way hotel that catered to executives of companies that did not allow lavish expense accounts. Paris on the cheap. Kyle checked in without any problem. He called down to room service for a steak and salad and a bottle of water. The sun would be setting soon and he could move. Then he stripped down and got under a shower, alternating hot and cold water.

He let it cascade over him for five minutes. Drying off afterward, Swanson stared into the brightly lit bathroom mirror and did not particularly like the man he saw looking back. Bleary-eyed, tired, the mouth a grim line, and blue-gray eyes as hard as stones. The tanned body was nicked with scars and the puckered skin of healed bullet holes. His hair had returned to its normal shade of brown from streaky surfer blond. He splashed more water on his face and went back to bed, with the Glock 17 pistol handy on the night table. *Are the weapons still just tools, an extension of me, or have I become an extension of them and what the fuck kind of question is that, anyway?* He laced his fingers behind his head on the fluffy pillow. A psychiatrist would have said he was undergoing severe depression. Swanson believed this was deeper than any shrink's diagnosis. *I think I am about one step away from going nuts. One small step for man, one giant leap for me.*

There was a knock on the door, and he put on a robe, picked up his Glock, and answered. A waiter pushed in the food cart. Kyle unwrapped his hand from around the

Glock in the pocket of the robe and signed the check with a generous tip. He pushed the plastic DO NOT DISTURB card into the exterior electronic key slot and closed the door.

He surfed the television channels while he ate the steak, watching British newscasters, CNN and Fox, and American sitcoms translated into French. Nothing. Kyle pushed away the food cart, washed his hands again, and then smoothed a white towel over the tufted bedspread. He spread out his personal weapons, which he had been able to keep in his possession because they had come in on a military flight and did not have to go through customs.

Glock, Ruger, Gerber. Marine armorers had given both pistols Limited Technical and Procedural Firing Inspections before he had left for the Middle East, but they needed a good cleaning after the raids into Iran. He opened a small gun-cleaning kit and arranged the toothbrush, the bore brush, cotton swabs, the vial of oil, and a soft rag.

The push of a lever in front of the trigger took off the slide of the Glock, leaving the pistol in two pieces, the barrel assembly and the butt. With the slide out, he removed the spring and began a careful examination to see that nothing was frayed or chipped. A look down the barrel confirmed it was neither dented nor warped. He only wiped down the butt section, because doing a proper job on an intricate trigger assembly was the task of a gunsmith. Swanson spent five minutes cleaning it, then reassembled the Glock and did an ops check to make sure it worked. He pointed it at the mirror on the back of the door. The trigger clicked on empty.

He had four magazines with fifteen rounds in each clip, and Kyle thumbed out the bullets one by one to personally examine them for any defect. The shiny brass cartridges were laid out side by side on the white towel, gleaming in the overhead light, each a marvelous little piece of engineering built precisely by Beretta to fit the barrel of the 9 mm pistol. They were all soft-tipped rounds designed to avoid a ricochet indoors. The bullet would create an entry wound as small as a dime, but once it slammed into bone, the soft nose would splinter with the impact of a small grenade and shred everything around it. It was not supposed to exit the body. Swanson always enjoyed watching movies in which shooters used their knives to carve an X on the tip of a bullet to make it open up. Fantasy. The rounds were already designed to do that. Start screwing around with your rounds and you will screw up the barrel and the accuracy of the weapon; then you are the one who is screwed. He reloaded the magazines.

The little Ruger five-shot revolver was even easier, but the maintenance was performed with the same amount of care. Open the cylinder, visually inspect it, clean it, load it, and bingo, it was ready. The Gerber knife was easier still. Just wipe down the blade, which gleamed along the cutting edge that had been honed in the armorer's shop. Field strip and op check on all weapons. Good to go.

Comfortable with his personal arsenal, he slipped into his night outfit: black jeans, black sneakers and socks, long-sleeved black turtleneck T-shirt, and black windbreaker. A woolen balaclava mask was rolled up into a watch cap and adjusted for a firm fit and so his eyes could see out of the openings. The Gerber went into one pocket; the Ruger was on his ankle and the Glock snug in the shoulder rig. He turned out the lights and lay on the bed to let his eyes adjust to the gathering darkness.

Swanson closed his eyes and lay there for thirty minutes, breathing slowly, trying not to fall asleep because he had work to do tonight. Thoughts of Shari Towne flitted at the edge of his consciousness. As a lieutenant commander in the Navy, she had been given a hero's funeral at Arlington, her coffin rolled to the gravesite on a horse-drawn carriage. The box was virtually empty because she had been riddled by gunfire and blown apart by two satchels of explosives. There was no family present at the funeral. Shari's father had died years before, and her beautiful mother died in the same attack that stole Shari's life. Shari was the end of the family line.

Kyle wasn't there for the ceremony because he had been stashed in a secret medical clinic abroad recovering from bullet wounds of his own. He now considered it ironic that he and Shari were both officially buried at Arlington, yet neither was really in that hallowed dirt. He felt that they were still together, and she occasionally visited him in dreams that were so vivid he could describe exactly what she was wearing. They could not speak to each other, they could not touch, but they could be together for an almost tangible moment, no more than a heartbeat, and she always had that glorious smile. Now another face was also showing up, unbidden, in his thoughts, that of Delara Tabrizi.

Stop it, he commanded himself. *This is getting me nowhere. Keep on the mission, and the other stuff will sort itself out. God, I need some rest.*

Green Light. That order came straight from the top. Finding out so unexpectedly where the man known as Saladin was provided a very narrow window of opportunity. This was the person responsible for the poison gas attack on London, and he was now blackmailing the world. The decision was made to take him off the board while there was a chance and to seize the formula and plans for the weapon. The president was absolutely right that the United States did not assassinate people. But the dead man who used to be Kyle Swanson did.

Darkness had fallen, and it was raining when he opened the window, a nice French rain that alternated between a fine mist and a wet mop in the face. Anyone watching would avoid looking upward, and amateurs would seek shelter. Since he had turned off the lights, the assumption would be that he was sleeping. Three floors below, an alley stretched along the back of the hotel. Empty. No darker shadows huddled within the other shadows.

Kyle stuffed a hotel towel into his jacket, stepped through the window onto a ledge, faced the wall, and closed the window behind him.

The Lizard had provided maps and layouts from satellite imagery and building blueprints, and the room had been chosen because of its proximity to steel latticework erected for some outside renovation. The Lizard had measured it to be exactly eleven feet from the window. Kyle scooted carefully along the wet ledge, grabbed the scaffolding, and was down in the alley in seconds. He went into the shadows of a garbage bin, dried off with the towel, and tossed it.

Turning his back to the street and cupping his hand to shield the light, he pushed a button and the dial of his watch illuminated with a soft blue glow. It was almost 2200 on the dot, two hours before midnight, and Paris was open for business.

Swanson used a combination of taxis and the subway system, frequently doubling back and walking through stores to check for followers, and only when he was convinced that he was alone did he edge to the northeast and into the Nineteenth Arrondissement.

The first time past the house, he had a cab drive aimlessly around for ten minutes, and they passed the small compound without slowing. He got out of the taxi four blocks away at a small restaurant, where he went in, ordered a glass of red wine, and made a cell phone call.

Sybelle arrived within twenty minutes, dry and playing the part of a girlfriend. 'Hi,' she said and touched his hand. She sat down at his table and also ordered a glass of wine, and Kyle explained what they needed to do. Urban warfare is a sniper's specialty because all windows and buildings and fences offer places to set up a hide. He had no intention of allowing the coming fight to be fair, and he and Sybelle could check out the place as a couple on the street without arousing suspicion. They would look for ways to tilt the playing field in Kyle's favor.

Swanson put some money on the table, and the two of them left, squeezing beneath Sybelle's small black umbrella. They approached the house from the north, walking slowly along the old sidewalk, with Kyle's arm around her waist. She snuggled closer and giggled, working on the cover as both of them swept the area with their eyes and ears.

Saladin had strong security. Two sentries stood in the courtyard, and newly mounted cameras were at all corners to watch the surrounding streets and the interior grounds. Guard on the roof. A street person stumbled past them, drinking from a bottle. External surveillance. Plus whoever was inside. Probably an alarm system. Not just good security, Kyle thought, but too much. Like they were expecting someone. *Me?*

Sybelle and Kyle walked back to the restaurant, and she pulled a pair of night vision goggles and small binoculars from her purse and handed them to Swanson. He would go back out onto the rain-slick streets now for a deeper recon from the shadows. 'I'll have some coffee so I can be close by if you need backup,' she said.

'I assume you saw everything that I did,' Kyle said. He had a puzzled look. 'But did you feel that something seemed out of place back there?'

She crossed her arms. 'That flicker of light at the window of the corner building. Somebody else is watching that place.'

'Yeah,' said Kyle. 'We're not the only game in town.'

16

Kyle Swanson did not try to intellectualize the assassination. He had been ordered to do the job and given free rein to carry it out. Besides, he believed that the bastard had earned this as the price for organizing the London attack on a crowd of innocent people and for slaughtering prisoners in awful experiments. The only question that Swanson had was how soon he could pull the trigger, then go into the madman's lair and get the data on the poison gas. It had eluded him in Iran, and he did not want to miss again.

The morning after his scouting mission, he had decided on a plan of attack and needed some things. After a quiet breakfast of coffee, a warm croissant, and fresh fruit, he went downtown to find a good sporting goods store that specialized in alpine equipment. Explaining that he was heading off to do some climbing, Swanson bought a mountaineering axe, some good gloves, a pocket set of Zeiss binoculars, a puffy down jacket, and a black hard hat with a battery lamp attached.

He returned to the area near Saladin's house and scouted for a small quiet street, finding just what he needed only three blocks away. Two warehouses backed against each other, and their windowless rear walls were separated by a shade-filled alley. Using the sharp, curved end of the new mountain axe, he quickly pulled up a sewer lid, climbed down and slid the lid back into position, and put on the hard hat with the bright lamp. With the beam of light boring a hole in the darkness, Swanson began to walk.

Paris had 1,400 miles of sewers, and compared to some places he had hidden during his military career, they were almost comfortable. The sewers were usually as wide as the streets above them, and a channel of water carried the waste down the middle. The walls and ceilings held an orderly array of cables and pipes for electrical circuits and drinking water. Street signs in the caverns were the same as the street signs above.

He easily found his way through the tunnels for a few blocks and stopped at the grate on the curb directly across from the courtyard of Saladin's place. He stepped up on a ledge and brought the Zeiss binos to his eyes, settling in to watch the place and build a range card.

Promptly at 11:30 A.M., two burly guards entered the courtyard, looked around, and unlocked the parked sedan only after searching beneath it for explosives by using a mirror on a pole. One got into the driver's seat, and the second returned to the house and returned beside a slim, well-dressed, dark-skinned man. *Saladin?* The man was heading for lunch. Kyle watched throughout the day and about midafternoon chowed on a baguette with some cheese and an apple. Only when night fell did he return to the hotel and wash off the stink. He needed some help for the next step and went over to meet Sybelle and the Lizard. They had to work fast.

*

Lieutenant Commander Freedman stretched in his chair before the all-seeing eye of his laptop computer. 'Interpol came up with the sketch of the guy they believe is Saladin, based on several sources, including the two al Qaeda operatives who were on the telephone. They were arrested yesterday.'

Kyle only had to look at it for a moment. 'That's the guy I saw in the courtyard,' he confirmed. 'The thin face and well-trimmed beard are pretty unique. That's him.'

'Are the French cops going to hit the place?'

'Not yet,' said the Lizard. 'Everybody is still standing around creating elaborate plans. Being the French, I don't think they really want to make the arrest. They just want him to leave because he is a political embarrassment.'

'Yeah.' Time was ticking faster if others were getting ready to move. He had to be done before the authorities were in place to figure out what happened. Swanson finished a sketch of his plan, using maps that the Lizard had printed out, and gave them their assignments. 'We're doing them a favor. When Saladin sticks his head out for lunch tomorrow, they won't have to worry about him anymore. Lizard, you find us a little SUV?'

'Waiting downstairs in the lot. A gray Peugeot 4007.'

'Okay. Sybelle, give me a ride back to my hotel, then you do your thing and come back here. I should see you both tomorrow about noon at the front of the Air Museum, and we're gone.'

Kyle returned to his room, showered, and took some time to clean the Dragunov sniper rifle he had brought along from Iraq. As soon as he had heard it was a Green Light mission, he had wanted a disposable and untraceable weapon. Then he lay down to sleep, telling his mind to awaken him two hours later, before dawn came.

Sybelle Summers telephoned an all-night mechanic and spoke in angry French. A neighbor had parked his blue BMW Mini in her assigned space again, after many requests not to do so, and she wanted to teach him a lesson by having the car towed and dumped in a vacant lot somewhere.

The mechanic said he was not interested and mentioned that it also was illegal. He was not a car thief, he said. She offered a hundred euros with no paper transaction that might lead back to him, and he wavered. At two hundred euros, he changed his mind. Business was slow this late at night.

Soon the tow truck arrived at the intersection the woman had designated, and she waved him down. Still angry, the driver thought, taking the money and watching as she pointed out the little car that was causing her troubles. Neighbors, he shrugged. He went to work, and within a few minutes, the tow truck vanished down the street with the little Mini hanging from its big hook. Sybelle slipped the rented Peugeot SUV into the spot, got out, locked the door, and walked away. The SUV was parked with its rear wheels just beyond the sewer grate and the high rear end shielding the opening from view, directly across from the gate to the courtyard of Saladin's house. A long, dark ribbon was tied to the rear bumper and moved in rhythm with the passing breeze.

Just before the sun came up, Kyle had disappeared again beneath another sewer lid, clicked on the light of his hard hat, and found his way back to the proper grate, this time with the Dragunov across his back. He snapped off the light before looking out of the grate, keeping the darkness as a guard against being spotted. He was satisfied with the protected and clear view of the courtyard.

The problem was going to be with the timing, for the target would be exposed for only a few seconds, while walking from the house to the automobile. Based on what he observed the previous day, there would be some warning when the bodyguards came into the courtyard first to be sure the area was clear. At that point, Kyle could bring up the rifle, but not before then. Sticking the barrel of a sniper rifle out of the opening of a hide was done only in movies, for it was almost as good as waving a flag. It would be seen, even as well concealed as he was.

The range could hardly be better, close enough to do the job even over the iron sights of an ordinary rifle. The target would appear huge and close in the Dragunov scope. He rolled up the big jacket he had bought and placed it along the ledge just inside the grate opening to provide a more stable shooting platform. He could keep an eye on the windage by watching the ribbon fluttering from the bumper of the Peugeot.

Swanson did not really want to think about how the task would change if Saladin did not go out for lunch today. Then he would have to use the rifle to pick off any outside guards and fight his way into the house, which was as strong as a fort. Too much noise, effort, and danger. But who could resist a nice lunch at a Paris café on a beautiful day such as this?

He drank some fruit juice, picked up his binos, and stood back in the shadows. He glassed the courtyard with intense concentration, for he knew the moment he let fatigue or boredom pull away his attention, the target would appear and then vanish before he could act. Cars and trucks rolled by, the wheels blowing trails of dirt and rocks behind them. The occasional pedestrian hurried along the sidewalk, and the cameras on the corner posts followed. Swanson stood motionless back in the darkness of the wide sewer, his center perfect over slightly spread legs, a position he could hold for incredible lengths of time. He emptied his mind as the minutes went by. For two hours, he remained immobile, except for an occasional stretching of his muscles. Then he changed position, moving closer to the narrow rectangular opening, leaning on the little shelf of molded concrete with his elbows, and continued to watch.

The first guard came out at 11:28 A.M., a muscular young man in pressed jeans, a white shirt, and an open sport coat. He walked out to the street, looked around, and searched the car. Unlocked it and got inside. Turned on the ignition.

Kyle put down the binos and raised the Dragunov, putting the end of the barrel onto the soft, rolled jacket at the inner edge of the sewer grate, with the Peugeot 4007 overhead hiding the opening. The ribbon moved only sluggishly, telling him the wind was not enough to change the scope. He let his breathing slow, and his heart rate, feeling the strap of the rifle dig into his left arm.

The second guard appeared, a large man in a cheap suit, also with no tie. His hand was at his back, beneath his jacket, probably grasping a pistol. This one stepped out of the courtyard and checked the street both ways.

He went back to the front door and said something Kyle could not hear.

Saladin stepped into the open for the short walk to the automobile, no more than ten steps. The bodyguard moving ahead of him opened the door. Only forty meters separated Kyle from Saladin, who was talking on a cell phone as he walked, and the shot, when Swanson took it, was simple. Five steps, six steps, squeeze the trigger, and Saladin never made the seventh step. He was hurled upward by the force of the rising bullet and was tossed backward like a puppet whose strings had been cut, dead before he hit the ground. The bodyguard stared in surprise long enough for Kyle to shift the scope onto him and make a head shot.

The driver threw open his door and rolled out, with his pistol drawn but unable to see a target. Everything beyond the gate looked normal, and the tendency was to look up to find a sniper on a rooftop or in a high window. Kyle had him centered in the scope as the man searched for somebody to shoot at, and Swanson once again smoothly pulled the trigger. Since they were almost on the same level, the flat trajectory sent the bullet ripping into the guard's shoulder, then down through the chest and rib cage before exiting at the hip. He bucked under the impact, and the round wrecked his heart and lungs.

There was no time to waste now, and Kyle pulled the Dragunov back inside and dropped it into the deep sewage channel flowing behind him. A manhole cover was just above him, and he pushed it aside, grabbed the edges, and hoisted himself up and out, staying low behind the Peugeot. He pulled the silenced Glock from his waist and ran across the street, through the gates, and into the sun-dappled courtyard. Three shots, one into the head of each of his targets, and he was on his way inside.

'You see that? Who the hell is that?' asked a big man with binoculars pressed hard against his eyes. 'He just shot our suspect!' Special Agent David Hunt of the Federal Bureau of Investigation was rocked back by the surprise attack and turned in disbelief to Carolyn Walker, an agent with the Department of Homeland Security. She had been seated, watching a small television set that was linked to the adjustable telescopic lens of a camera that had been recording all movements in the courtyard for the past two days. They, along with the CIA, were part of a joint task force assigned to watch the man believed to be Saladin, the person responsible for the London nerve gas assault. When word came from Washington, they would arrest him. The JTF room was on the fourth floor of an apartment building on a corner overlooking Saladin's house, which they believed gave them a total view of the entire area.

But the assassin had come out of nowhere, unseen and with no warning. Nevertheless, Walker now had him on the camera and was recording. She adjusted the focus on Kyle's face, and a USB connection fed the images onto a computer hard drive.

'I got him,' she said. 'What the hell is he up to? Let's go pick him up.'

Dave Hunt threw down his powerful binoculars. A total stranger had barged into their operation and it had all gone to shit, right in the heart of France. 'Can't do that, Carolyn. The French cops are going to be all over this place in ten minutes, and all hell will break loose if they find us up here.'

He stuffed their equipment into large zippered bags, and Walker radioed the joint task force office within the U.S. Embassy to warn them what was happening. As Hunt and Walker ran down the back stairs and got into their dark SUV, more telephone calls were made and agents swung into action, happy to have something to do rather than sit around the office.

Juba was up and moving at the first loud *craaack!* of the Dragunov sniper rifle, knowing exactly what it was. Pistol in hand, he backed against the front wall and peered around the edge of the window, looking down into the courtyard. Saladin was down flat on the stones, in a spreading puddle of dark blood. As Juba watched, there was a second shot and one of the methodical, experienced, and handpicked bodyguards was blasted in the head, the bullet plowing all the way through the skull in a spray of blood and brain matter. Juba looked but could not see the sniper.

There was no time! It might be anybody, even the French, and the house might now be assaulted by counterterrorism agents. It did not matter how they got this address or the name of Saladin. They just had it, and now Juba had to save himself. He stuck his pistol into his waistband and moved across the Persian carpet to the living room table.

He jerked the printer and power cables from the laptop and folded the computer into its black carrying case. All of the information about the deadly weapon was in that little case, and it had to be removed from harm's way. Outside, there was a third *craaack!* and Juba did not have to look to know that the other bodyguard was now dead, too. Neither of the guards had gotten off a shot at the sniper, which meant they never saw him.

The burgundy leather briefcase was beside the table, and he pulled it up and opened it, dumping out the contents except for travel documents and some passports bundled with a rubber band, along with a stack of American hundred-dollar bills that was in one corner. He put the small computer inside and closed the case.

The room was littered with documents and other computer gear that needed to be destroyed, but there was no time to individually shred or burn the items. The entire house would have to go. Juba had spent quite a bit of time planning for just such an emergency, and blocks of explosives were planted at key support points throughout the structure and wired to a detonator connected to a wall switch. He slapped the switch closed without hesitation, which gave him five minutes to leave the house before it blew up.

The noise of three soft, coughing shots came from the courtyard. Juba took the briefcase in his left hand and carried the pistol in his right. He went out, paused at the top of the landing, and snapped off some quick shots downstairs to discourage the intruder.

Juba spun around and headed down the back stairs, putting solid walls between himself and whoever was at the front of the house. In thirty more seconds, he would be clear of the area and in his car that was parked around the corner. With luck, he could make the 5:55 P.M. British Airways flight to Dulles International in Washington. He looked back over his shoulder, up the stairwell.

*

Kyle Swanson pushed his pistol around the corner of the front staircase and fired blindly, twice, then charged up the stairs as he heard the pounding of running feet, retreating in another direction. He took the stairs two at a time, his weapon in front of him, searching for a target.

A door slammed in back and he went that way, noticing the pile of papers in the living room, wondering if the magic formula was among them. Saladin was dead, and that formula was the remaining part of the mission, but he first had to be certain there was no other threat. Whoever was on the run had not continued the suppressing fire, but the footsteps were growing faint. Kyle kicked open the rear door and dove onto the landing of the staircase so the fleeing man below would not have a clear view. He was on his back and then rolled onto his belly with his Glock grasped in both hands as he looked over the top step. The wrought-iron supports for a long railing hindered his view.

Their eyes locked for an instant, and Juba and Shake recognized each other.

'You!' screamed Juba, who was already disappearing around the outer door. He put his back against the concrete wall, reached around and emptied his clip at Kyle.

'Goddamn!' shouted Swanson, off balance and ignoring the bullets as he also started to shoot, although the angles were wrong and his target was out of view.

Bullets whanged against marble and stone, and chips of rock ricocheted in the tight confines of the rear stairwell. Each man knew his opponent's capabilities, so there would be no more headlong charges, for any rash move would be suicide.

Juba dashed through a small gate and disappeared around a corner.

Swanson heard him leaving but edged down the stairs, wary of deception and places that danger might be hiding. He had to suppress his reflex to go after Juba and bring him down. The mission was still unaccomplished. Those papers on the main floor had to be examined, and he had to be gone himself before the cops came. He holstered his weapon with a curse: a golden opportunity missed.

Kyle hurried back into the main room, where papers were strewn wildly across the furniture, the sign of someone who had left in a hurry. They were bound to contain the secrets, and Kyle was about to call for Sybelle and Freedman to come around with the SUV when his peripheral vision caught the blinking of a tiny red light on the wall. He stopped.

The detonator had only two minutes left and was steadily counting down. Any attempt to disarm it would take longer than that, and Kyle knew that Juba had probably rigged it to a booby-trap alternate igniter to protect the explosive sequence.

He ran. The door at the bottom of the stairs seemed a mile away as he rushed toward it, counting seconds as he went. Minute-thirty. In the distance, he heard the dipping whine of sirens that meant the French cops were coming. He jumped over the body of Saladin, went out of the gate, crossed the street, and crawled back into the manhole. A minute. The stinking sewer system was his friend now, for the blast could not reach him belowground, and it would be a while before the police discovered the open manhole cover. Every step he took got him farther from the blast zone. Forty. Thirty.

At fifteen seconds, he found a small side room where workmen could store their tools and used his Glock to shoot the lock. The door wobbled, and he hauled on the heavy wooden panel with all of his strength, pulling it open far enough so he could burrow inside and kneel, opening his mouth so the blast would not rupture his ears. He hoped the cops had not arrived.

It went off with an earthshaking roar in a repeated series of explosions as Juba's booby traps blew up in deadly sequence, one after another, and the big house crumbled and shattered. The blast wave knocked down the old walls of the courtyard, clawed at the nearby brick buildings, and ruptured the neat lines of parked vehicles. The shock wave came pounding down the sewer openings and raced along the main trunk line, tearing down everything in its path, pushing aside debris, causing a small tsunami in the sewer water itself, and slamming the door to the room in which Kyle was crouched. He was knocked to his side and bounced hard against some large equipment.

When it was done, he lay there for a minute, dazed and catching his breath in the darkness. Then he struggled to his feet and opened the door to see a thick cloud of dirt and dust hanging in the tunnel like a curtain. Slapping his handkerchief to his mouth, Kyle was about to leave the little room when he noticed the object he had been thrown against was really the steel rungs of a ladder built into the side of the concrete, leading upward. He climbed and found another door, an entrance to the service tunnel. *Why didn't I find this before?* He moved into the sunshine and looked back over his shoulder at the huge, rising ball of flame and smoke behind him.

Then he walked away, and each stride convinced him that he was uninjured. By the time Swanson arrived at the Fort d'Aubervilliers station, he was walking normally. He would catch the Line 7 train for the five-minute trip north to the next stop at La Courneuve/8 Mai 1945. Nearby, Sybelle and the Lizard would be cruising in a car out in front of the sprawling and popular Air Museum tourist attraction.

They took him at the station when the train rushed up to the platform in a howl of screeching brakes, pushing a blast of air ahead of it. The crowd moved almost as one toward the doors, jostling for position while trying to avoid being touched.

Two needles of a Taser X26 penetrated Swanson's jacket and shirt from the rear, and multiple pulses of electricity totaling thousands of volts hit him with volcanic pain and rendered his motor systems useless. Kyle toppled toward the dirty station floor, aware of a man kneeling beside him, on the left, calling out in English, 'Hey, this guy's had a heart attack!'

As the subway doors closed and the train moved out, two ambulance attendants trotted down the stairs. Kyle was placed on their rolling stretcher, where he was again hit with the Taser to keep him immobile while one of the attendants jammed a needle in his arm.

Commuters parted to let the stretcher bearers exit, carrying some man lashed to the gurney to the ambulance waiting up on the street.

17

Juba was certain that no one was following him because the explosion would have turned all eyes toward the disaster. He hoped Kyle Swanson was buried in that smoking debris. Swanson was supposed to be dead, but there had been no mistaking that angular face that had absolutely no fear on it when they were trading shots in the stairwell. Maybe Shake really was dead now, a thought that made Juba smile. *The only man who ever really beat me.*

Juba used his time well before the flight to America. An executive hotel near the airport rented rooms by the hour for businessmen in transit, and Juba used a Dutch passport to get a room and clean up. Downstairs, he got a close shave, then had a stylist trim his hair to a neatness that would be welcome in a company boardroom. He had her put in a little lighter color, joking that he wanted to look younger because of the competition for a new vice presidential opening at his finance firm. A clothing store furnished new slacks, shirts, underwear, socks, and a blue sport coat with gold buttons. What he did not wear fit snugly into his large briefcase. Unfortunately, he would not be able to take his weapon, but there were plenty of guns waiting on the other end of the flight.

As a final move, he bought a disposable cell phone with plenty of prepaid minutes.

Carrying only the briefcase and the computer bag, he passed through security without a problem and took his seat in the first-class compartment of the British Airways flight to Washington. A hostess brought a glass of chilled water for him while the rest of the plane loaded, and once the plane was moving, gathering speed, and lifting as the wheels left the tarmac, Juba let himself relax. There was no danger now, so he stretched his seat back and ordered himself to catch some sleep. The quiet, steady hum of the engines helped him relax. He dreamed of Scotland.

A special ops team of American Marines had been pitted in a war exercise against a similar team of Royal Marines, and Color Sergeant Osmand was in his element. He had racked up a couple of mock 'kills' and then decided to take the game to a higher level.

For a full day he and a spotter tracked the American Blue Team, then slithered through their sentries and lookouts and set up an invisible hide on a low ridge that overlooked the enemy headquarters and a road the Americans would have to use the following morning. He hoped a general would turn up in his sights. The two of them spent several hours erasing all traces of their passage and improving their hide, then shared a tin of cold meat and drank some water as the night closed around them like a starlit glove.

It was raining, but that meant nothing on a mission in Scotland, where it was always either raining or about to rain. Juba was on watch during the early morning hours while his spotter caught a nap, and it was not only wet but cold, too, and absolutely silent. A fire to warm his hands, of course, was out of the question.

Instead, he remained still, the thistles and weeds sprouting from the slits of his ghillie suit turning him into just another bush on the rugged Scottish landscape. Dawn would come in two hours, and the American Marines would begin moving around. Color Sergeant Osmand intended to slaughter as many as he could and possibly even capture their headquarters, which would give him bragging rights forever over the vaunted United States Marine Corps.

Something even colder than the night, the barrel of a pistol, touched his neck just below his ear, and a quiet voice whispered, 'Bang, asshole. You're dead. So is your partner there, Sleeping Beauty.'

Osmand spun around to see the grinning, blackened face of the sniper they called Shake, Gunnery Sergeant Kyle Swanson. 'I thought you two were never going to get settled. Sounded like a couple of elephants stomping around. You almost stepped on me when you came up,' the American said, casually putting the weapon away. 'Come on. Let's go down there, get warm, and have something to eat.'

On the British Airways plane flying across the Atlantic, a hostess noticed the first-class passenger twitching in his sleep. A dream. She lightly spread a blanket over him.

The dream shifted to what had just happened a few hours before in Paris, when again Swanson had gotten the better of him, ambushing and killing Saladin right under Juba's nose. He vividly recalled hearing the shots and seeing the body of his spiritual father sprawled on the courtyard stones, and that brought sadness and a flare of anger. *What now?* When his mind started tugging at that question, he woke up.

Right now, Juba could disappear. Eight bidders were seeking the formula, at ten million dollars each, nonrefundable. All of that money had already been rerouted to other banks, hidden beneath folds of false accounts in smaller accounts, and he had those account numbers and access codes. His own personal investments were worth about five million dollars and there was still about another ten million in the reserve and operations accounts that Saladin had organized. That meant that Juba could put his hands on almost a hundred million dollars, a life-changing amount.

With so much money, there was no need to continue as a professional killer or as a bringer of death to masses of people. He could go anywhere in the world and buy anything he wanted. With Saladin dead, the entire scheme was compromised and carried much greater risk. The bidders would still want the formula, but now they would be more willing to use guns rather than their checkbooks to get it. They also would want their deposits back.

It would be best to take the money and leave now. The Middle East was afire with Islamic fanatics to carry on the fight against the Crusaders. There was no real reason for him to try to run a one-man reign of terror.

In the end, he decided there were three reasons to continue. The first was that Juba still had the gas, the formula, and several factories in which it could be manufactured. It was he who handpicked the undercover operators to support the attacks, personally distributed the weapons, and communicated with the terrorist cells. Few of the others had ever heard of Saladin before the

London attack and the auction. They answered to Juba and would still obey his orders. Second, he did not really believe Kyle Swanson had died in the explosion, which meant the two of them were on an eventual collision course. If Swanson was after him, the man would never give up the chase. The American was an insufferable pest. Third, Juba knew he would get bored sitting around doing nothing.

Why not use it? The attack on the United States would be spectacular and bloody, and he would expand it for years to come with strikes all over the world. Carrying out the demonstration that had been announced by Saladin would cause the bidders to fall back in line.

That left Swanson, and Juba realized just how badly he wanted to kill the sniper. The threat of the man would always be present, like an unwelcome shadow. No matter where Juba went, he could never relax as long as Swanson was alive. On top of that, the Marine had murdered the one person who really understood Juba, and the death of Saladin could not go unavenged. Kyle Swanson had to die.

He adjusted his seat and brought the laptop from beneath his feet, placing it on the adjacent aisle seat. The first-class cabin was only half full, and the hostess came to ask if he wanted a meal. He ordered vegetarian, put on a headset, and found some classical music, which helped his thoughts roam free. He had an attack to plan. Preparation of the weapon was already under way in Mexico, and he would call later today to make certain the work would continue. All he needed was a target, and he needed to decide quickly.

Las Vegas was a good possibility, a city of sin that tainted the society of the entire world, beckoning to him like the painted harlot she was. Numerous Muslim men had been corrupted by that impure city and its gambling and whores. Juba considered Las Vegas loathsome and cheap, glowing like a carnival in the desert night, and destroying it would have been a personal pleasure. Satisfying but not very effective, for he believed that not many people would truly care. With its flashy girls, card players, and high-rolling rubes, its destruction would not gather much sympathy after the first week of headlines. Hotel entrepreneurs would just bury the dead, then build new casinos right outside the contaminated radiation zone, close enough to let tourists view the destroyed city through powerful telescopes, for a small price.

He would not waste the weapon by killing the wrong people. After all, he remembered, look at New Orleans. A major city was destroyed by a hurricane, and the United States government wrote it off after only a few months. New Orleans was populated by poor residents who did not have political power, so Americans just continued going to the malls and movies as if nothing had happened. The city was still rebuilding.

He finished the meal, placed his computer on the little table, and scrolled through the news sites. Not much yet about Paris, but London was still going on. Kill the right people! He checked the international news, where the lead story was a typhoon pulverizing Bangladesh, and then went to the sports results, for he was still a soccer addict.

Juba read with interest about how violence had broken out at a stadium in Germany during a match, and the idea came to him as the camera panned around to show the thick crowds of fans surging onto the field or fleeing for the exits or just standing around watching. Thousands of people. Thousands of targets.

A sports arena would be an ideal place for the gas attack, for it would bring confusion, destruction, mayhem, and televised horror. It was baseball season in the United States, and he could turn a big game into a nightmare. The Internet let him study the details of every major league baseball stadium in the States and look at the upcoming schedules. Although he did not follow the sport, there were several obvious possibilities. Still using the Internet, he made a flight reservation.

When he arrived in America, Juba lingered at the U.S. Customs portals until he found a place in a line just ahead of a Turk with dark skin and a beard who was wearing a suit with a shirt buttoned at the neck and no tie. The eyes of the authorities were focused on that man, a ceramics trader out of Istanbul, and not the European businessman in front of him. The Turk looked like a possible terrorist. Juba showed a well-used passport, was cordial to the customs officer, and passed through with astonishing ease. A camera recorded his arrival.

Clear of the final barrier, he strolled out into the waiting area, which was crowded with families and friends and business associates welcoming the flood of people who were arriving from abroad. Rental limousine drivers waved hand-printed signs that bore various last names, but he ignored them and made his way all the way to the curb to catch a cab.

He had the cab drop him at a Metro station and used the subway to get out to Reagan National, where he used an American Express card in one of the lobby computers to obtain his e-ticket for a domestic Delta Airlines flight from Washington to Florida. Juba had never seen a major league baseball game and was looking forward to the experience.

OVER THE ATLANTIC OCEAN

Kyle Swanson returned to consciousness slowly as the drugs ran their course. He had no idea how much time had passed, and his last memory was getting ready to ride the subway and then . . . sudden pain, people yelling, followed by an empty nothingness. No dreams. He remained still, eyes closed until his mind cleared enough to suppress the automatic fear of the unknown.

It was not completely dark when he cracked his eyes just a bit. Some light penetrated the area to give shape to objects, but he remained essentially blind, so he allowed his other senses to sort out whatever available information he could gather. He had a slight headache, a hangover from the sleeping drug, but felt no wounds.

The first thing to make itself clear was the steady whining of jet engines and a slight shaking that told him he was in an airplane. He could almost smell the nearby bulkheads, and there was a chill on his skin that matched the hum of air-conditioning. Not a prison cell but a controlled environment. Whoever had him was taking him somewhere in a small, modern jet.

Using his body, he tried to explore further but quickly concluded he was lashed to a small bed. His fingertips told him that he was naked but covered with a blanket. Abnormal. Not the treatment usually given a prisoner in foreign lands. A condom-like device pinched on his penis, a motorman's friend that would let him urinate into a tube. Some thin wires touched his skin. Electrodes for heart and pulse monitors.

For a few moments on first awakening, he had thought terrorists might have snatched him, which would have meant some pretty uncomfortable times ahead. As he lay there on the soft mattress without moving, he could hear muffled voices from a nearby compartment: English. Kyle concluded that he was a prisoner of the United States government. They weren't going to kill him, so there was nothing else he could do at present. There was an almost inaudible click, and another dose of the drug flowed through the IV and into his veins. He controlled his breathing and let it tug him back to sleep.

'This guy is a damned ghost,' said FBI Special Agent David Hunt, the man who had watched Swanson through his binoculars back in Paris. He removed his glasses and rubbed his eyes. DHS Agent Carolyn Walker was seated across from him in the Gulfstream, studying some papers on the table between them. More than four hours had passed since they had grabbed the assassin, and there was still nothing in the way of a solid identification.

The man who was drugged and strapped down in the rear cabin had carried no credit cards in his old black wallet, just some five hundred dollars in cash and an Arizona driver's license that was a phony. There was no Social Security number. Empty pockets. They had photographed the face, full on and both profiles, digitally enhanced it, and transmitted it to Washington along with the fingerprints to be run through the government's entire computer base. So far, the computers were throwing up blanks. Nothing.

Walker spread out the digital photographs that had been taken of the suspect while he slept. 'His body gives us the only real information we have. No tattoos or other identifying marks, but those scars are from bullet holes, knife wounds, and medical operations. Battle wounds.'

'Which means military.' Hunt started pacing. 'Okay. Active or ex? A merc? Damn, Carolyn, we don't even know if he's American.'

She chewed a fingernail. 'My gut feeling is that he's one of ours, because nobody has the ability to scrub an identity from U.S. databases so thoroughly without help from the inside, and that presents the real problem. We have pictures of him shooting Saladin in the head with a pistol, which indicates he also was the one who fired the kill shot with the rifle. He assassinated the man, and that is not sanctioned by our country. That's why we are hauling his ass back home. That's where the answer is.'

'Doesn't make sense,' Hunt said. 'Even if he was on the inside, we should have known about him snooping around in Paris. He is as sterile as they come. That's no accident.'

Another government Gulfstream was also streaking back to Washington that evening, and its only passengers were Captain Sybelle Summers and Lieutenant Commander Benton Freedman. Both were worried. Swanson had not turned up at the designated rally point, and according to protocol, they abandoned the plan after waiting fifteen minutes.

They saw the smoke plume and drove toward it,

viewing the destruction of the house with a fear that Kyle might have been buried inside. The debris was mostly confined inside the grounds, as the building had been brought straight down, one floor pancaking upon another, but damage was visible on surrounding buildings, too. Windows were shattered, and bricks littered the sidewalks.

Sybelle had hopped out of the car and moved to the Peugeot, then dropped into the open manhole. No one in the gathering crowd had paid her any attention because the main attraction was across the street. She walked a hundred meters in each direction down the tunnel. No Kyle.

Their orders were to bail out if the mission was compromised, rather than risk getting caught on foreign soil, which would only make things worse. They hated to obey, but they had no idea where Swanson was or what had happened to him.

The Lizard took them to a military airport, where their Gulfstream was being readied. Once they had taken off, he filed a brief report in code to General Middleton in Washington. There was an acknowledgment that the message had been received, but there was no other reply.

All they could do now was get back home as fast as possible.

18

MARYLAND

An ambulance was waiting at Andrews Air Force Base when the FBI Gulfstream landed and taxied over to a distant hangar. The unconscious patient was transferred to the vehicle, and it drove away at a normal speed, inconspicuous in the morning traffic around Washington. Special Agents Hunt and Walker followed in a black SUV.

The ambulance stayed on the Beltway, then broke away onto less busy highways and finally onto the streets of a town and an even narrower road that led to a Coast Guard station on a rocky promontory that jutted out into the Atlantic Ocean. A storm front was moving in, and rain drummed heavily on the roof of the SUV. Dave Hunt had the wipers on high but still had to lean forward as he drove slowly along a narrow road that was bordered by a mosaic of waist-high walls of rocks.

Both vehicles pulled into the parking area of a weathered old building that was two stories tall, its bare concrete walls dingy from the gravel, grit, and saltwater that had scoured it for half a century. The masts and aerials mounted on the roof were pegged tight on the surrounding rock but strained against the tension of the support wires as the wind whistled around the big masts. The building had been abandoned by the Coast Guard in the 1960s for improved quarters nearby and was now a safe house shared by several government agencies.

Hunt and Walker parked and hurried through the rain into the house, where a team of CIA agents was taking charge of the sleeping man delivered by the medics.

'What do you think, Carolyn? Should we go wake him up and have a talk?'

Agent Walker shook her head. 'Not yet. We're exhausted and need some rest. Let him be for now so he can wake up in there and wonder what has happened to his little life.' She gave instructions to one of the other agents. 'Turn off the air-conditioning and switch on the heater. Have the urine analyzed. In three hours, hit him with the lights and the a/c again, only put it two degrees lower. Alternate that about every hour, and then start the noise about two o'clock, off and on. Give him water only during a dark phase. We want him disoriented, hungry, and thirsty.' She stretched. 'He can sit there and stew while we get some sleep upstairs and come back in, fresh as daisies, and hammer him. By then, the identification will probably have popped out of the computers, and that will make our job a lot easier.'

ST. PETERSBURG, FLORIDA

That afternoon, Juba attended a baseball game between the Tampa Bay Rays and the Toronto Blue Jays at Tropicana Field in St. Petersburg, Florida. The weather was hot, but a breeze from the Gulf of Mexico kept it from being scorching and it was easy to understand why retirees flocked to the place after spending their lives in cold climates. It never snowed in St. Pete, and the locals called the city 'God's waiting room.'

Despite the kind weather, the stadium was an old domed arena that was home to a poor team, and the relatively few fans attending that day's game were mostly older men and women. Most of the seats were empty. Thinking tactically, Juba decided this was not the kind of crowd, nor a suitable place, that would gain the attention he wanted with the attack. In fact, Tropicana would be a waste of time and energy. Don't kill the wrong people.

That evening, he flew out of Florida, and as he crossed the Great Plains Juba's thoughts again turned to Swanson, who was supposed to be dead and buried at Arlington. Juba had been in the military long enough to realize that the entire burial, posthumous Medal of Honor and all, could have been just a charade, a staged black operation event. So, Swanson was actually alive and totally undercover. Was there a possibility that Juba might find a bonus in this situation by having another chance to prove who was superior? After all, Swanson had tarnished the reputation of Color Sergeant Osmand, back in the day. Juba would like to serve a dish of cold revenge to the man. Why not add a one-on-one showdown with Swanson to the agenda, even if it meant leaving a trail of breadcrumbs to help his enemy along? It would be interesting.

His mind was made up by the time his plane began to be buffeted around the sky by the turbulence of the Rocky Mountain air prior to landing at Denver International Airport.

*

Sybelle Summers and the Lizard arrived at the Pentagon only to find that General Middleton was out at Quantico for an emergency conference of Marine leaders. The president had increased the national alert status to orange.

Freedman went to his desk and logged on to his mainframe computer while Summers put on a pot of coffee and checked the unopened mail. They would have a concise report for Middleton by the time he returned.

'Here's some good news,' called Freedman. 'The medical status of Double-Oh has been upgraded to "Good," and he'll be flown back here in a few days.' He went back to the screen. 'And here's an e-mail from Sir Geoffrey saying that Delara Tibrizi is doing okay but is wondering about Kyle.'

'So are we,' Sybelle said and went to her own desk and flipped through copies of the *New York Times* and the *Washington Post.*

'Whoa! Sybelle, would you please come over here?' A pulsing chime was repeating from Freedman's computer, and a small red rectangle flashed in the upper right-hand corner. Something had pinged the automatic warning system he had designed to track any queries about members of Trident.

He clicked some keys and the NCIC/Interpol symbol appeared, along with the expanded data. 'Somebody is checking Kyle's fingerprints in the FBI's National Crime Information Center system! The request lists him as a John Doe and an "unknown suspect."'

'Unknown suspect? That would indicate he's alive and being held prisoner. Does it say who has him, or where?'

The Lizard was frantically scrolling through data, calling up new screens of information. 'No. It doesn't even carry a high priority. Bingo. Look at this link to some photos that are being run through the government's face recognition software. Kyle, for sure.'

'I'm calling Middleton,' Sybelle said, reaching for the encrypted telephone. He was in a car being driven back to the Pentagon and answered on the first ring. 'Gunny Swanson is alive, sir, and someone is checking his fingerprints.'

Middleton paused before answering. 'That fucking Swanson. Where is he and who is checking up on him?' The general could hear the Lizard clack the keyboard, and Sybelle switched them all onto a conference call.

'It looks like the original ping came from the FBI but has since branched out to cover databases around the world, under the flag of the Department of Homeland Security. The ping registered about noon, so we are several hours behind on this.' Freedman tapped a pencil on his desk.

'Stay on it, Liz,' said Middleton. 'Get into the system and sidetrack whatever you can. Do what you can to slow them down. I will be in the office as soon as I pay a visit to the Hoover Building and talk to the Feebs.'

'Yes, sir. Got it.'

Middleton replaced the car's secure telephone in its cradle and stared at the surrounding traffic. Rush hour never ended around Washington, and thousands of cars and trucks were creeping along bumper to bumper. 'Sar'nt Johnson!' he barked at his driver.

'Sir!'

'Turn on your fancy spinning lights and that siren and get us out of this mess and over to the FBI place pronto.' The general buckled his seat belt and was thrown back against his seat as Johnson launched the big sedan across a thick band of traffic and into the lane especially reserved for emergency vehicles. He roared around the cars ahead, tapping bumpers when necessary. Middleton held on, hoped for a safe landing, and repeated to himself, 'That fucking Swanson.'

Carolyn Walker checked the big wall clock in the office that was adjacent to the interrogation room: 5:10 P.M. The clock was a discount store special, and a federal agent precisely adjusted it twice a day to the correct atomic time. Why not just buy a better clock? She blinked and turned her attention back to the man strapped into the chair on the other side of the one-way mirror. 'We've got bupkis. Nada. Diddly-squat. Three damned hours and he hasn't said a word.'

'That's not exactly true, Carolyn. He has told us to go fuck ourselves at least a dozen times, in several different languages,' corrected Dave Hunt.

'He doesn't look like someone who was scared out of his wits after hours alone in that room, buck naked and motionless.'

As if he knew they were watching, Kyle Swanson yawned. Since his head was also strapped to the chair, it was mostly just opening his mouth and flexing his jaw muscles.

'We've got to report in soon. I can't believe that we've caught an assassin red-handed and he's mocking us.'

The urgency they felt to identify him was not shared by everyone in law enforcement, for they were being very cautious about making a splash until they could do so without infuriating the international community. The

French had not even known they were in the country when they made the arrest on a public street. Now safely back home, they had run into a stone wall. Since the national alert level had been raised, traffic had picked up on the computers, and they felt their efforts were falling on deaf ears. They had made a routine blood draw from the suspect to furnish DNA samples but were curtly informed that the backlog was so great that their samples might not get tested for a week. Other requests were being similarly delayed, and their entire system was slowing down, the memory being packed with reams of useless data.

Walker pushed rimless glasses up on her head and fluffed her brown hair in frustration. In her early forties, she was a thorough intelligence professional who had come over to the DHS from the CIA in the big reorganization after 9/11. With a doctorate in psychology and years of interrogation practice, she believed she could get to any suspect. She sighed. 'We still don't even know his name.'

'Nope. Still Mr. X.'

'We have to do more, Dave. If we can't scare him with words, then we must employ some physical stress. I recommend that we use Level Two techniques.'

'I agree. Should we file it up the chain of command?'

'Not yet. Not yet. I can order a Level Two decision on my own authority. Let's crack this guy.'

'Dangerous game, Carolyn,' Hunt warned. 'I can almost hear a special blue-ribbon commission questioning us now. At least let's file a short summary saying our John Doe may be on the terrorist watch list, just to get a time stamp on it and protect our asses.'

'Life was easier when we didn't have so much power,' she said, recalling the time when the agency did not worry about such particulars. 'Okay. They get a synopsis, but I'll keep the particulars vague to buy us more time.'

Agents Evan Brown and Kealoha Kepo'o were large men who had been specially trained in advanced interrogation techniques, ways to intimidate people and make someone hurt like hell without leaving a bruise. Both had played football in college, Brown at Florida State and Kepo'o for Hawaii, and their imposing size was part of the drill, for when they sauntered into an interrogation room, they carried a sense of menace. The subject immediately knew that polite questioning was over.

Everything was choreographed. They were federal agents, not thugs, and their job was to persuade the prisoner to answer questions. Walker and Dave Hunt had briefed them well and let them read the transcript of what had been asked so far. They studied the man through the mirror and decided their next move.

The unidentified subject finally seemed disoriented by the cold, heat, sleep deprivation, bright lights, and hours of questioning. Mixed music, yelling-loud rap lyrics followed by classical melodies so soft that they could barely be heard, had also taken a toll. Walker now shifted the music to a soothing concerto for flute and violin, let the room go dark, and set the temperature just a shade above normal. Comfort. Within five minutes, the man's head sagged to his chest. At that moment, she switched off the cameras and the music and turned on the bright lights, and the two big agents stepped into the interrogation area.

Kyle Swanson had been running through a series of isometric exercises to keep blood flowing to his extremities, muscles, and brain, straining so hard that he had broken into a light sweat.

He had recognized the chair as soon as he had awakened and gotten his bearings, for he had strapped a couple of guys into one just like it in other places, in other times. Stamped into the base of the round metal frame would be a stamp that read PROPERTY OF THE UNITED STATES GOVERNMENT. Kyle had remained still, knowing he was probably being monitored with an infrared camera, and had given the man and woman who questioned him nothing to work with. They weren't going to kill him, so all he had to do was hang on until the cavalry arrived.

He also had been expecting this new tactic, because he was being so uncooperative, and centered his mind on how to deal with it. There would be physical pain, and standard practice was to get the subject out of the chair for a Level Two so the apes could toss him around.

Agent Kepo'o threw a five-gallon bucket filled with cold water onto him, and Kyle did not tense up. He was relaxed and fully alert. Waiting for an opportunity.

Brown stood beside him, hands on hips, and Kyle glanced at the diver's watch on the agent's left wrist. The hands were almost at six o'clock, but a small dial indicated the military time. Almost 1800, which would make it six in the afternoon. Free information. *Thanks, big guy*.

'We are required to ask you one last time to cooperate with the special agents who have been questioning you,' said Brown. 'So I just did that, you little shit.' He slapped Kyle hard with his open palm, and Swanson's head snapped around.

Kepo'o hit him with a return volley, using a fist that seemed the size of a volleyball. The first punch had split Kyle's lip, and blood oozed from it. He shrugged off the pain.

'Now we are going to drag you up out of the chair and kick your skinny ass around this room until you decide to cooperate.' Brown roughly undid the strap around Kyle's right arm and leg while the giant Hawaiian unbuckled the left side. Then Brown released the chest restraint and unsnapped the Velcro head band.

Before the agent could lean back, Kyle grabbed the man's neck in a tie-clinch and jumped up in one fluid move. Brown was instantly off balance, and Swanson pulled down hard on the head while smashing his knee upward. The agent fell, grabbing his shattered nose and fractured eye socket.

Swanson was now able to face Kepo'o, who had recovered from the momentary surprise and moved forward, just close enough for Kyle to lean back and telegraph that a kick was coming. The 275-pound Polynesian saw the slight position change and put his arms down to protect his stomach and groin. Instead, Kyle snapped into a complete fast spin and landed a roundhouse kick that sailed over the lowered arms and slammed against the man's temple so hard that it knocked Kealoha Kepo'o unconscious on the spot and dropped him sprawling to the floor. Swanson stepped forward and kicked the fallen man hard in the unguarded balls. 'That's for the punch,' he said.

Then Swanson grimly faced the mirror and sat back down as Walker, Dave Hunt, and two other agents burst into the room with their guns drawn. Kyle allowed himself to be strapped back into the chair without a struggle.

'Okay, so you're a tough guy. Are you willing to talk to us now?' asked Carolyn Walker.

Kyle stared back. 'No. Fuck all of you. It's almost six o'clock. Can I have some dinner?'

'You're a real bastard, you know that?' Dave Hunt snarled as he turned on his heel and walked out, passing an EMT team coming in to tend the agents. The suspect had taken down Evan Brown and Kealoha Kepo'o as easily as swatting a couple of flies. Hunt said, 'We go to Level Four, Carolyn.'

'No Level Three?'

'It would be idiotic to unstrap him again to make him kneel on a broomstick or hold his arms out with weights attached. We can't take the chance, so we waterboard him instead. Then probably the battery and electrodes, too. Hell, I may even take a baseball bat and a meat cleaver to the son of a bitch! How did he know what time it was?'

'Cool down, Dave. What about getting permission?'

Hunt sighed. This thing was escalating, popping up out of the ordinary run of business and therefore likely to get noticed. The bosses would want to know how two agents had been injured and what was going on, but somebody in Washington would have to sign off on the water-boarding, and few would want their names on such an authorization.

Walker was also disgusted. 'It may take a few hours, but it will be worth the wait. No way should you and I take the fall for this all by ourselves.' She spent some time drafting the request message in careful, legal language, then signed it.

19

General Bradley Middleton was in the spacious office of the director of the Federal Bureau of Investigation. Dark furniture. Framed handshake pictures on the wall. FBI symbols everywhere. It bespoke power, as did the quiet and competent man across the desk from him, who never took off his dark suit coat, even while he was sitting.

'What do you mean, Mr. Director? You've lost one of my people and can't tell me where he is or even if you have him? How does that work?' Middleton cocked an eyebrow.

Director Samuel Banks spread his arms wide, palms up. 'I can only repeat what I just told you, General. As of now, I have no report whatsoever of any unidentified suspects being picked up yesterday.'

'Our alert came straight from your FBI computer system, Mr. Director. Your machine talked to my machine and said one of our hot sets of prints was being examined. The link activates only for that specific reason.'

The director nodded in affirmation. 'And our system shows that indeed a query was made, and that we replied that there were no such prints on record in the NCIC. But our people were not the ones who initiated the inquiry! Anyway, you are military. How can your people not have fingerprints on file?'

'Sorry, Mr. Director. Need-to-know basis on that one.'

'I'm the director of the FBI!'

'I apologize and suggest you take up any questions you have about this with the White House. I do not have authorization to discuss it. Back to business. If the FBI system was pinged last night, where else could it have come from? Can just any hacker or country cop do it? Or could the NSA or a foreign government run something without a trace?'

'No, of course not. There are high-level security protocols and firewalls and passwords that I can't discuss with you. Need-to-know.' The eternal Washington game. My dick is as long as yours.

Middleton smiled, and the director grinned back. 'Mr. Director, I don't care about the inner workings of your computer and databases as long as we continue to have authorized access. I just want my operator back.'

'I understand that, General. Here's my suggestion. I will put a tag on the query. If anything pops up, I will personally give you a call.' He scribbled on the back of a business card and handed it to Middleton. 'Here's my private number in case you need to contact me directly.' The general looked at it. There was no telephone number, just *DHS??*

Middleton put the card in his jacket pocket and rose, shook hands and left, wondering why Banks had chosen such an odd method of communication. Was he concerned that the office of the director of the FBI might be bugged? No, it was simpler than that. Banks *knew* the conversation was recorded, because he was the one recording it. Just in case questions were asked later. *Weird world we live in*, Middleton thought, getting into his waiting car.

'Sar'nt Johnson!'

'Yes, sir!'

'Do you know where to find the Department of Homeland Security offices in this hick town?'

'Yes, sir! The Department of Homeland Security. Uh, down at the far end of the Mall in that really tall, skinny building with the pointy top?'

'That is the Washington Monument, Sergeant, and I have no time for your smart-ass comments this evening.' Middleton noted that it was past six o'clock. He had just wasted hours working his way through the FBI chain of command in order to reach the director for their brief, private conference. He didn't want to repeat that process over at the DHS, starting with some flunky at the front door who would explain that everyone had already gone home for the day. 'Let's just go back across the river to the Pentagon. If I'm going to be sneaky, I want a whole bunch of Marines around. You do know where the Pentagon is, don't you, Sar'nt Johnson?'

'Aye, aye, sir.'

MARYLAND

They had turned the thermostat down again to be sure that Swanson, in the interrogation chair, was thoroughly chilled before beginning the water procedure. They were not about to unstrap him again, because bad things happened the last time they tried that.

As far as Special Agent Carolyn Walker was concerned, the bastard could lie there and freeze to death. She gave a look of disgust through the one-way glass and swiveled her chair around to face Dave Hunt.

'Okay, I'm not waiting any longer. We can't dodge our responsibilities while the bureaucrats argue about conducting a Level Four interrogation on American soil with someone who we think may be an American citizen. An assassin working for a terrorist organization is the most likely scenario.'

'Still a dangerous precedent, Carolyn.'

Walker's eyes were sharp and her mouth a thin line. 'No more waiting, Dave. We can't afford *not* to do this. We have to find out how he is involved. Anyway, screw my goddam career. I want to know what that bastard knows! We will proceed with the first phase while we wait for authorization. I will take full responsibility.'

'I never said I didn't want to do this, Carolyn,' Hunt said quietly, trying to keep her calm. 'I concur, as long as it remains a limited and supervised situation. He has brought it on himself by refusing to talk and putting a couple of our people in the emergency room.'

The room was cold. Both Walker and Hunt wore dark blue windbreakers as they watched other agents set up the procedure. The suspect, shivering from the icy air-conditioning, had been blindfolded; his chair was laid back and a large galvanized tub clattered into place beneath his head. This was just the first phase and would be done with no talking, no questions.

A thick towel was draped across the face. Walker pulled out her stopwatch, nodded to an agent standing beside the chair, and started the timer as he tipped over the first bucket.

Kyle was already shivering, and with his eyes covered, he depended on his other senses to keep track of what was happening. The metallic noise of the tub on the tile floor told him it was probably time for some water, and he sucked in deep, regular breaths. Instead of fighting back when the towel was laid over his nose and mouth, which would have expended both energy and air, he hauled in even deeper breaths. He heard someone pick up one of the heavy buckets, and shoes beside the chair squeaked on the tiles as the agent shifted for better balance. Water sloshed as the bucket came up. Kyle got a final deep breath and heard the click of a stopwatch, and five gallons of water was sloshed onto the towel in a single rushing torrent. He remained perfectly still and let his brain be a clock. At fifteen seconds, he intentionally squirmed, but there was little real discomfort.

Carolyn Walker detested doing what she was doing. Only fifteen seconds had passed and the suspect was already wiggling, showing signs of oxygen deprivation. She pushed her personal reaction aside and pressed on with the procedure, signaling the waiting agent to pour a second bucket over the drenched towel.

Kyle lurched against the straps when the cascade of water washed over him. The towel was thoroughly drenched, and no air would come through, even when the waterfall passed. When his count reached thirty-five seconds, he struggled again, harder, pushing against the straps.

He's drowning under there. Carolyn held up a finger. Still another bucket was dumped on Swanson, and he struggled while the straps dug into his arms and ankles. When her stopwatch hit one minute, Walker held up her fist. Stop. The agent yanked away the towel, and Carolyn looked down at the suspect, who was coughing and sputtering, gasping for air. A full minute underwater. Let him know what was in store if he refused to cooperate. Now give him some time alone to think about it. The chair was elevated to the sitting position to help him catch his breath, and everyone left the room, leaving the suspect alone to fear what might happen next.

Kyle was wet and shivering. He opened his eyes and blinked and allowed his breathing to return to a regular rhythm. Only a minute under the towel? Piece of cake. Any surfer would think so. Cold and wet? He thought about his big surfboard and the frigid waters at the Wedge in Newport Beach, where he usually had to wear a wet suit and booties even on a warm day.

Wet? This was nothing compared to being scrubbed along the sandpaper bottom of the California shoreline after being blown out by a big wave. It could take a minute or so just to get back to the surface. Or being sealed in a fifty-five-gallon drum half-filled with water and rolled down a hillside during a training exercise. Cold? Try trekking over an ice-sheeted mountain during a blizzard with people trying to kill you. In this room, he knew that the water torture was only a mind game to force his cooperation by making him think he was drowning. He would play it out and let them believe they were getting to him. He was, however, cold and hungry, and time was being wasted. *Where's my damned cavalry?*

*

THE PENTAGON

The Lizard, well aware of how the computer age could be made to work against itself, had been jamming useless data down the information superhighway to the unknown computer where the requests about Kyle Swanson were originating. For the past two hours, he had been reprogramming, cutting down that computer's ability to reach out to others without first going through him.

With the help of a friend at the National Security Agency, he eventually narrowed it all down to a half-dozen lines of communication, all of it encrypted on the sender's end but popping back into readable English on his screen.

Sniffing around the U.S. Department of Homeland Security violated a dozen or so laws, but General Middleton had been very clear with his order: 'Find Shake.'

The message for Level Four permission came up. Unidentified terrorist suspect related to Saladin inquiries is in custody at location Delta Two One Sigma. No identification, not even fingerprints. DNA tests were incomplete. Probably ex-military. Subject may have information re poison gas attack. Extremely uncooperative, two DHS agents injured and hospitalized. Urgent request for authorization to conduct a Level Four interrogation. Signed by Special Agent Carolyn Walker of the Department of Homeland Security, with her identification code.

The Lizard didn't know what a Level Four was, but it sounded rather dire. He went to the general's office and knocked on the door. 'I've located Gunny Swanson, sir. He is being held by the Department of Homeland Security at a safe house over on the Maryland coast, used to be a Coast Guard station.'

Middleton was on his feet, walking across his office, and called out, 'Captain Summers!'

Sybelle came in. 'Sir.'

'Round up some Marines and go get our boy,' he said. 'The Lizard will fill you in and arrange a helicopter from here to there.' Middleton was at his private safe, spinning a dial. He opened the door and found an envelope containing a special letter. 'You know our charter, and this is your authorization. Show it to the person in charge, but nobody stands in your way, got it? Bring him home.'

At the safe house, Hunt and Walker let an hour pass, waiting for permission that never came, before they went in to question Swanson again.

'You can end this right now. Just talk to us,' said Special Agent Dave Hunt. 'What's your name?'

Swanson remained silent. He was cold, but he would be warm again, someday. This was only temporary. No matter what they did, it was only temporary. He said nothing.

'Damn you,' Hunt muttered. 'We need answers – now! Do you understand? It is no small matter, and you're not in that chair because of back taxes or some fucking parking ticket. Our national security is at risk.'

Carolyn Walker stepped before him and held up the photograph of a man. 'This is Saladin. You killed him in Paris. Even if you were not the sniper who first brought him down, we have you on video putting a bullet in his head at point-blank range. We were right across the street at the time, and Saladin was under close surveillance.'

She shuffled that picture to the bottom of a small stack and held up another head-and-shoulders photograph. 'Here's your second victim, a bodyguard.' Then she showed him still another. 'Your third was the driver. You massacred three men and then ran inside that house, and that was followed by gunshots and the big explosion.'

She held up a final photograph. 'This was the only other person inside, another bodyguard, and I assume you killed him, too, because you came out and he didn't.' Carolyn Walker stopped talking and stared at Kyle. He had blinked when shown the final photograph. 'What is it? You recognize this man?'

Kyle said nothing. *Oh, yeah. I know him all right.* He had been using the entire time since the last procedure to pump in deep breaths to store up oxygen, because he knew more water was on the way. As a sniper, he had been trained to slow down his life in critical moments, to breathe regularly under stress, and, most of all, to never panic. The picture had thrown off his rhythmic breathing pattern.

'You'll talk,' Walker said. 'Sooner or later, everyone talks.' At her signal, the wet towel was thrown back over his face.

He heard water slosh as a bucket was hoisted and he gobbled air, ordering himself to relax rather than fight it this time. *Temporary. Temporary.* His brain ticked off the seconds as the buckets emptied, pouring over him and into the big tub below. The soaked towel was to simulate the feeling of being smothered but actually helped keep the water moving instead of flooding into his nostrils and lungs. He could hear and sense everything but after the first minute decided to turn off the sound for a while and just lived in his head.

The gnarly pipeline wipeout in Hawaii was one favorite memory. One moment, standing in control on the board with the bright sun overhead and the big wave roaring its protest at being ridden, then the curl catching and dumping him. Down he went into the swirling, powerful wash, and a strong underwater current pushed him beneath a rock. Thought he would never be able to climb out of that hole where the green water was trying to kill him. Two minutes. Chest getting tight, and he let some of the old air bubble in his lungs escape to ease the pressure. Two and a half.

When the towel was removed, he switched on his own lights again. Nothing had changed except his freedom to breathe. Kyle looked up at the agents and brayed a loud and challenging laugh as streams of water streamed down his face. One of his defense mechanisms when he was in a tight spot was to turn it into a game, something that was not so serious. 'Come on, you pussies! Can't you do better than that? Feeling sorry for the prisoner? Damned amateurs.'

Hunt and Walker stormed from the room. 'Did you notice that he didn't even move this time? That first session, he shook like a leaf.' Hunt said.

Walker peeled off her windbreaker and hung it over the back of her chair. 'He was playing with us,' she said. 'I'm bringing the doctor and the crash cart down here to stand by for resuscitation. This time, I'll drown the son of a bitch, if I have to.'

'I just had a thought, Carolyn. We've had him for almost a full day and he has not once asked for a lawyer. Any normal American would be screaming for an attorney by now.'

'Any normal person would have broken by now. He is too well trained to resist pressure and pain. I'm worried that he would rather die than talk.'

'So I will take away that option. If the water fails this time, we resuscitate, then use chemicals to knock him out and push through those defenses.'

'Might be fatal.'

'Might be.'

'Wish that authorization would come through.'

Thirty more minutes passed before they went back into the room, this time with some white coats tagging along with them.

Medical staff, Kyle realized. He no longer gave any pretense of being subtle and started to loudly huff and puff to fill his lungs. One medic filled a syringe with propofol, a white liquid that would erase the last few minutes of Kyle's memory. As soon as he blacked out, the 'milk of amnesia' would be administered, and he would not be able to recall what had happened to him during the drowning moments.

A dry and thinner towel was spread over his face this time. He closed his eyes and relaxed as the water began to pour, this time an almost unbroken stream, bucket after bucket. He raged silently in his mind: *Bring it, you shit-birds! Bring it on!*

A minute. Two minutes. Three. He was paddling off the Baja coast near kilo marker 57, going out several miles and just lingering in the hot sunshine. He was diving without scuba gear along the Australian watery wonderland of the Great Barrier Reef. He was in full rig, practicing planting explosives on the hull of a ship at night. He needed air now, just as he had needed air then. *Running low on fuel here, gang.* Bubbles. Gagging building in his throat. Water winning, seeping into his lungs. Four minutes. *Hold on.* Then an acceptance of death as the body's defenses caved in, the physical machine demanding air. *Temporary.* Five minutes and counting. Nothing left. He gasped and opened his mouth to suck in oxygen and the water poured in. He was drowning.

As he began to black out, he heard sounds, shouting in the room, and the towel was jerked away. *Air!* The chair popped to an upright position, and one of the white coats was there to help him regurgitate the water he had swallowed. His senses returned, blinking on one at a time like a series of switches, as he shivered violently against the straps, vomited water, and sucked in life-giving oxygen.

More people were in the room, heavy boots, yelling, moving like shadows. His eyes focused on a slim figure, a woman with short hair, dressed in black jeans and a black sweater: Sybelle!

She had an envelope in one hand, a pistol in the other, and a wicked gleam in her eyes. The questioners, along with the two agents that he assumed had been the bucket brigade and one of the white coats, were lined up along the far wall with their hands up, covered by four Marines in full combat gear. Sybelle had brought along overwhelming power for backup.

'Hey there, Dead Guy,' she said. 'I have your Get Out

of Jail Free card here, and I'm supposed to give it to some chick named Carolyn Walker. What say we just pop these motherfuckers, get you dressed, and go find her?'

'I'm Agent Walker,' Carolyn said, raising her voice to try to regain control. 'What's going on? Military troops cannot be used in America.'

Sybelle sailed the envelope toward her and told her to pick it up but stay by the wall. She kept her pistol trained on them. 'You medics unbuckle this man and get him warm, right now. Blankets, towels, your own fucking clothes, whatever. Move!' Her voice was steely with anger, and the menace was not lost on the medical team.

Walker's look of surprise was total. 'Dave, it's a direct order from the president and countersigned by the attorney general to give her the full and unconditional interagency support of the U.S. government.'

'Jesus,' said Hunt, reading the letter. He handed it back to Walker. 'Okay, so you are some kind of undercover agent. We still should have been told you were coming onto our turf. And if you have this kind of pull, why didn't you just say so?'

Kyle had a jacket over his naked lap, and a medic was vigorously massaging his shoulders with a towel to get blood circulating again. As his voice returned, he issued orders. 'Give us all documentation – written, video, and audio – of your surveillance operation in Paris and my interrogation. You keep nothing, no copies or backups.' He nodded toward Sybelle. 'We're special forces operators, so I still can't give you my name or reveal any details. It would be best for everyone if you just go back to your other business and pretend you never saw me.'

Sybelle holstered her pistol and had the Marines stand

down and leave. The agents relaxed, but when Dave Hunt started to talk, she snapped, 'No questions. Just gather up that material so we can all get out of here.'

Kyle stood unsteadily as Walker and Hunt left the room. He whispered to Sybelle, 'I know who Juba is.'

DENVER

The taxi spun along mile after mile on the long route between Denver International Airport and the city. The afternoon was clear, and the range of jagged and purple Rocky Mountains, some still topped with snow, commanded his attention. They could be a problem.

After checking into a hotel, he strolled into Lower Downtown, LoDo, which had been a run-down part of the city until the Colorado Rockies were given a major league franchise. Coors Field was dark tonight because the Rockies were playing out of town, but Juba studied how the big stadium had been built right in the heart of the area, near Mile High Stadium, the home of the Denver Broncos football team, and the Elitch Gardens amusement park. Redevelopment flooded in and gentrified the entire former warehouse district. Nightlife now throbbed in fashionable LoDo.

Juba slept late and about noon showed up at Coors Field and joined a group of tourists being given an escorted visit through the ballpark by a charming young woman in a cowgirl hat who was a fountain of information. He watched the flags beyond the outfield, which were stuttering in the steady wind from the mountains, gusts that his sniper's eye judged to be about thirty miles per hour.

The guide said high winds were not unusual around the city.

He considered the situation. Looked west beyond left field to the ridges of mountains. That kind of wind would blow the bubble of poison gas . . . where? Kansas? New Mexico? Empty states. It wouldn't work. He had misjudged this one, too.

Denver was the metropolitan area, but the real population of Colorado lived far out in the suburbs, and commuters thronged the big highways after work, driving seventy-five miles an hour to reach their homes many miles away in bedroom communities.

The West was too spread out for his purpose, big enough to swallow some small nations whole. He could cause severe damage, but even the new and stable gas would dissipate too quickly on those mountain winds. Coors Field was not the answer.

He was looking for more than just a baseball stadium – something that was more of a net, a trap, somewhere with no way out. He checked out of his hotel and headed back to DIA and bought a ticket to California.

20

THE WHITE HOUSE

The president of the United States looked over the top of his rimless reading glasses as his chief of staff, Steve Hanson, came into the Oval Office through the door on the left, which led into the staff offices area. Almost at the same moment, the door on the right opened and Secretary of State Kenneth Waring came through the visitor's entrance. The president tossed his glasses onto the big desk. 'Whatever it is, tell me outside.'

The three moved out the double French doors to the right of the president's desk, across the narrow covered stone walkway, and into the Rose Garden. Secret Service guards shifted their stations accordingly along the columns of the walkway to the living quarters as the president moved down the few steps and onto the perfect rectangle of grass, raising his face to catch some of the bright sun after being indoors all morning. As he stretched his big arms over his head, then bent from side to side, he could see other black-clad agents on the roof of the White House. Sniper teams. Troubled times. 'What's up? Ken, you start.'

Secretary of State Waring's eyes gave away his excitement. His manner remained formal, but his foot was poking at some grass. 'Mr. President, we have good news.'

'Well?'

Waring spoke. 'It looks like the whole Saladin thing has been resolved. Fizzled.' He snapped his fingers like a stage magician. 'Poof and gone.'

'What the hell are you talking about?'

'There was a shooting in Paris a few days ago, and some gang lord took a bullet or two in the head. So did a couple of his bodyguards. Police ran his prints and identified him as an Algerian Muslim leader, a rich guy with a lot of terrorist contacts.'

'Why is that important?'

'It took some time to make the real identification. The dead gangster was Saladin himself!'

The president pumped his fist like Tiger Woods sinking a twenty-foot put for an eagle. 'Awwright!' *Swanson was successful.*

'And the best part is that we didn't have anything to do with it,' Steve Hanson said. 'The French are laying the shooting on al Qaeda. Cops found a sniper's lair in a sewer right across the street, beneath an abandoned car that was rented with a phony credit card and driver's license.'

The secretary of state said, 'The enemy of my enemy is my friend . . . but who really was our enemy on this one?'

'All of them were, and remain, our enemies. We remain at war with terror as a whole, not with a specific name or group.' The president headed back to the Oval Office, taking big, confident strides, and plopped onto a sofa.

The secretary of state took a wingback chair, crossed his legs, and straightened a perfect crease in his trousers. 'This started with an extremely deadly device in the hands of a crazed fanatic,' he said. 'Now the fanatic himself is dead.'

'But where is the poison gas? Has it fallen into the hands of someone or some group we know nothing about?' The president was somber, leaning forward with his elbows on his knees. *Did Swanson find the papers? Why haven't we heard from him?* 'Guys, we have to make sure that monstrous thing does not reach America. If we have won some political leverage in this mess with Mr. Saladin, we need to cash it in now.'

'So go on television with an address to the nation.' Steve Hanson was already arranging the details in his mind. 'No politics at all, no swipes at our critics, just a direct appeal to all Americans to pitch in and help. Better than that, make it a worldwide appeal, because the other nations also remain at risk until that poison threat is nullified.' The secretary of state nodded agreement.

'Pulpit time,' said the president. 'We need to warn the people without unduly alarming them.'

'Yes, sir,' replied Steve Hanson.

'Ken,' he asked, 'what's the international community doing? Anything?'

'They are all keeping their cool right now, Mr. President. The strike in London sobered them all, and none of them want to be on the wrong side of this issue. Until that weapon is located, nobody wants to create problems. They may need the help of their neighbors in a big way if they are picked as the next target.'

'Anything new on the Saladin auction?'

'Apparently that is at a standstill. Any nation or group

that entered the bidding is keeping its actions very private, but who would be around to orchestrate that show now? With Saladin dead, the auction may be dead, too.'

'Hopeful speculation,' said the president. 'There is always a number two man who becomes the number one man. If he has the plans, he can just step in and run the show. How do you rate the chances that somebody else is going to get hit?'

'Honestly, Mr. President, my gut tells me that it is going to happen.'

The president nodded and went back to his desk and sat down. 'Yeah. We'll keep up the pressure. I don't like having the United States of America in the crosshairs.'

'We are doing everything we can, sir. We will lay out all the details at the National Security Council briefing. The news of Saladin's death will be leaking out of France by then. Pressroom will be in an uproar.'

The president put his glasses back on and picked up a pen. As always, paperwork awaited. 'Thanks for coming by, Ken. See you downstairs in a little while.' When the door closed, the president touched the intercom and told his secretary not to let anyone in for the next fifteen minutes and to pass the word along to the Secret Service guards on all the doors.

Hanson stood before the big desk. 'I just finished the debrief with General Middleton. Kyle Swanson got in and did the job, but the house blew up before he could grab any papers. Then he was snatched by our joint task force, brought back here, and worked over a bit, even water-boarded. He kept his mouth shut until Trident got him out. He's okay, and the operation is safe.'

'We tortured our own guy?'

'Swanson is fine. Kyle had a brief firefight with some other guy at the house. He recognized him, but with a bomb ticking down inside the house, Swanson did not have time to pursue. Later, when he was being questioned, he was shown some photos and was able to confirm the identification. Apparently it was Saladin's right-hand man, a British-trained sniper who goes by the name of Juba. Kind of a legend in the dirty warfare trade.'

'He may have the weapon, then?'

'Yes, sir. Or at least control of it.' Hanson paused. 'We're going to have everybody working to find him, so should I keep Trident rolling?'

'Absolutely. And tell them I said they did well in France.'

When the president was alone in the Oval Office, he looked at the paintings on the light vanilla walls: confident Franklin Roosevelt, somber Abraham Lincoln, elegant George Washington. Each had led the nation through times of crisis and into a brighter future. *I'd sure like to talk to those guys,* he thought. *Too bad this job didn't come with a training manual.*

His shoulders slumped; he pushed the papers aside, took off his glasses again and buried his face in his hands. He rubbed his eyes hard.

That weapon of vile poison was coming this way. He could almost feel it vibrating or doing whatever the hell those things did. America was a big place, a gloriously spread-out country with more freedom for individuals to roam than any other nation in the world and a security net that had gaping holes. He thought about how previous administrations had not even been able to stop millions upon millions of poor laborers from sneaking undetected across the southern border, and he understood that the northern border with Canada, although perceived as safer, was much longer and just as unprotected. The coasts and ports were funnels for dangerous men and cargo. So what chance did he really have against a skillful and determined team of terrorists? The tragedy of 9/11 had only proven the seriousness of the problem. The president sat there with the lives of 304 million men, women, and children weighing upon him and knew that he could not guard them all.

America could never be totally protected from those who wished to do her harm. To think she could be was an impossible dream.

SAN FRANCISCO

Juba was enjoying himself in the grandstand at AT&T Park, eating salty peanuts and drinking cold beer as a cool and steady breeze sailed up the bay and spilled over China Basin Park. Canoes and kayaks floated in McCovey Cove to await the splash of home run balls. The San Francisco Giants were playing baseball against the team from Arizona, but that was not the point. He was there to recon a potential target zone.

Almost as soon as he entered the arena and walked past the monstrous, skeletal Coca-Cola bottle tilted at a twenty-five-degree angle next to a huge four-fingered old-style baseball glove, he knew he had found just the place. From the mezzanine level, Juba could see downtown San Francisco and the long bridge across San Francisco Bay. Oakland was only ten miles away. There was a medium crowd that evening, about twenty-five thousand fans, but the New York Yankees were arriving in two days and all of the stadium's 41,503 seats would be filled. The decision made, he used his cell phone to call a number in Nogales, Mexico, and gave the man who answered a brief message.

After the game, Juba wandered down to Chinatown for a hot and spicy meal of garlic chicken before returning to his hotel and tuning in the world news on the thirty-two-inch LCD high-definition television set in his room. The news readers were still carrying on about London and the death of Saladin in Paris. Soon they would have a fresher subject. A better kill zone was being staked out at AT&T Park.

Then he turned to his laptop and transferred a retainer fee to the account of a private detective in Connecticut who was hired occasionally for discreet jobs and background checks. The detective believed the client was a major computer company that required the utmost confidentiality. When the money transfer was confirmed, Juba sent the detective an e-mail telling him to find former U.S. Marine Kyle Swanson.

That night, Xavier Sandoval was in the confessional of a little church in the hills outside of Nogales, Mexico. The religious quandary was nothing new to him, a mysterious puzzle that had haunted him for the past three years. He was not a Muslim, and in fact didn't believe in any organized religion, but the ancient pull of the Roman Catholic Church still tugged at him. It was difficult to give up the teachings of a lifetime.

As a younger man, he had made his way to the United

States to find work only to end up in a bar fight in Texas and be arrested, deported back to Mexico, and slammed into a cell with other failed immigrants. It was shortly after the 9/11 attacks on the United States, and the government in Mexico City was eager to show common cause. Many of the prisoners, including Xavier Sandoval, were declared to be suspected terrorists, and vigorous interrogations followed in locations that were beyond prayer. By the time he was released, he really was a terrorist. He again crossed the border and this time made his way to Michigan, settling into a Muslim area with friends of friends he had known in prison. They were bound by an intractable hatred of the United States.

One day an Englishman appeared and plucked him from the crowd, and Xavier Sandoval went to work for the man everyone respectfully called Juba. He was kind and generous and quite talented at killing.

Still, there was a bit of conscience left inside Xavier, enough so that on the evening of the telephone call from Juba in San Francisco, he bathed, combed his hair, put on his best dark suit with a matching somber tie over a blue oxford-cloth shirt, and went to mass. The deep feelings of the liturgy and tradition and guilt seeped into him and drew him to the next level, staying after the service to give his confession. The priest was puzzled at the vague admissions of carnal and other little sins because it was obvious that the parishioner was greatly troubled, but Xavier knew when to stop talking. He did not expect absolution for his crimes; he had just wanted to hear the calm voice of a priest one last time. Then he walked calmly out into the warmth of the late summer night.

The next morning, he said a final prayer and asked

God, if he was really up there, to grant him courage and forgiveness. It was a lot to ask, since he was about to murder several thousand people. The small man put on khaki pants and a yellow shirt and headed off to his job as a truck driver for the Diablo Gourmet Seasoning Company.

Diablo Gourmet was a *maquiladoras* success story, owned by Americans and operated by Mexicans. Suppliers all over South and Central America cleaned and processed their spices and seasonings and sent them to Nogales, where the company blended and packaged the finished products and sped them on to some of the best restaurants across the American Southwest.

The Diablo operation had been established more than twenty years ago as a false front, a vital part of Saddam Hussein's Unit 999 operations in North America. The only traces of ownership were a lawyer's name and the post office box of a shell corporation in the Cayman Islands. Years of legitimate operations had made the familiar blocky buildings of Diablo Gourmet a welcome money generator in the Nogales area and allowed Unit 999 to smuggle almost anything it wanted to across the border.

About noon, every day of the week, three yellow trucks left the loading docks carrying fresh loads of Mexican spices and herbs. The guards at the international frontier could smell them coming, for the vented cargo holds exuded the powerful odors of sweet cinnamon and ancho chile pods, pungent epazote, overpowering vanilla, chile negro, and the citrusy blast of habaneros, considered the hottest chiles in the world. All were encased in plastic bags, glass bottles, or metal containers and shipped in cardboard boxes, but it was impossible to capture all of the smells. The arrival of the spice trucks reminded the inspectors and guards it was time for lunch, and the veteran drivers regularly left samples for the guards. Everyone loved good Mexican food, and the signature company logo of a little red devil prancing on a background of yellow was synonymous with quality, hot, authentic spices from south of the border.

Three yellow trucks at noon, day after day, year after year.

The trucks were familiar, the drivers known to the inspectors, and the company owned by Americans, so there were never serious delays when the vehicles came to the border, which had every conceivable security device. Big fences, new television cameras, dozens of computers, sniffer dogs, and experienced inspectors worked both sides of the line. The dogs, however, were useless when the small convoy of yellow trucks arrived, because their sensitive noses would twist in agony if they inhaled the scents of peppers and raw chiles. They whimpered, their eyes watered as if they were weeping, and they batted their paws against their muzzles, sneezing. As a courtesy, the lead driver would use his cell phone when the trucks were about a half mile from the border so the handlers could take the dogs for a nice walk away and protect them from the intolerable aromas. Day after day.

Today, one of the vehicles, number 14, had been especially engineered to contain several ranks of high-pressure storage cylinders that stood against the cab wall in the cargo area behind the boxes and containers of spices. Some of the tanks were plugged into small pipes that fed up to and out of the roof of the truck, and at the turn of a dashboard switch by the driver, the contents would flow out of two exhaust fans. Others were sealed for later use. All were filled with the toxic gas that had been perfected in the Iranian lab. From Paris, Juba had transmitted the final formula to a laboratory attached to the Diablo Gourmet factory, and a small production run was assembled.

At noon, all three yellow panel trucks with the dancing devil logos rolled through the checkpoint unmolested. Number 14 was the last truck in the line and was driven by Xavier Sandoval. Three miles from the border, when he passed the Mariposa exit on I-19, Sandoval placed a call to San Francisco and confirmed that he was on his way.

21

BALTIMORE

Sybelle Summers called General Middleton on a secure phone from the safe house and did a quick report to assure him the situation was under control and they would both be back at work tomorrow. Kyle needed rest tonight. Middleton accused him of just being lazy but authorized them to take the rest of the day off. It was already dark outside when one of the government types took them back to civilization, into the swarming normality of Baltimore and the comfort of a large hotel on the waterfront.

After taking showers, they met in the bar. A storm had moved in from the east, and a steady rain whipped by the wind provided entertainment beyond the big window, where pedestrians and traffic did erratic battle at inter-sections and, beyond that, small boats rode the incoming swells.

'What next?' Sybelle asked, tasting a tame scotch and water.

'Try to find Juba again,' Kyle responded. He had already drained a cold pale ale microbrew and was on his second. The water treatment had left him dehydrated.

'That's not what I meant.' She looked hard into his eyes. 'This whole thing has gotten its teeth into me, Kyle. Action, worry, violent ups and downs, and not knowing whether any of us will be alive tomorrow.'

'We'll be alive. At least for tomorrow. Can't guarantee after that.'

'How do you know?'

'If Juba had wanted to set off a demonstration gas attack in Paris, he would have done so by now. Why wait? He's hauling it somewhere else. Probably coming this way.'

'See, that's just what I mean. Tomorrow is going to be just as bad as today until we stop this bastard. Thousands of people are at risk of dying, and you and I are racing to put ourselves right in the middle of the next ground zero in order to stop him.' She reached across the table and grabbed both of his hands in hers. 'Right now I need to stop being a Force Recon Marine and just be a woman for a couple of hours. I want a man's arms around me and some sweet nothings whispered in my ear.'

'I see your point, Sybelle, but I ain't that guy.'

'Oh, I know that. I outrank you anyway, and sleeping with you would almost be like incest. But I don't want you to be concerned if I'm gone for the next few hours. I am going to hit a club or two and look at the lights and dance and have a couple of drinks. Then some smooth-talking and beautiful man is going to pick me up and take me back to his apartment. I suggest you do the same.'

'Pick up some dude?'

'Don't be weird. Call Rent-a-Blonde, or maybe buy a drink for that little brunette at the bar. Just don't be alone tonight.' She squeezed his arm tightly, rose from the booth, and walked out, toward the music that she hoped was waiting for her somewhere uptown. She stood in the doorway to struggle into a raincoat and belt it tight. Kyle wondered what the pickup guy was going to think about the ankle holster and the Gerber knife.

The brunette watched Sybelle leave, then looked over at him. She wore a silk blouse with a subtle Chinese print and a matching brown skirt and shoes, with gold accessories. The triangular face was Midwest pretty, and her hair was shoulder length and layered. The brown eyes were questioning.

He ordered another beer and settled back, letting his mind roam. *We know who Juba is now, so the problem becomes finding him. What is he looking for? How can we put a net over him so I can kill him?* He closed his eyes and ran the mental loop again, everything he could recall about Juba and the earlier Trident discussions about how to nail the enemy sniper back when he was just the scourge of Iraq.

'Do you mind if I join you?' The soft question made him open his eyes.

'Sure. No. I mean not at all,' said Kyle, snapping awake. 'Please. Sit down. Nobody should be alone on a night like this.'

Sybelle dropped her wet coat, slid in beside him, and ordered a drink.

GUILFORD, CONNECTICUT

Christopher Lowry firmly believed that he could find anybody; it was impossible for any American to completely disappear. When the ten-thousand-dollar retainer came in with the request for a location trace, the private detective poured another cup of coffee, put aside the *Courier,* and got to work. He and his wife, their five children, and two dogs lived in an old house on one of the many crooked, twisting roads around Sachem Head Harbor, and he always had bills to pay.

United States Marine Gunnery Sergeant Kyle Swanson. Trying the obvious first, he typed the name into several search engines, looked over the mass of hits, and decided that couldn't be right. He refined the search and got the same result. Then he switched to a restricted military database and again received the same information, along with a personnel jacket that ended with the man's burial at Arlington National Cemetery. The archives of several major newspapers, including the *Post* and the *Times*, contained stories covering the event and awarding the Marine the Medal of Honor. A friend in the state police entered the name into the NCIC database.

This Swanson guy was dead and planted. Lowry drank some more coffee and took the dogs for a walk. They tore around through the thick trees chasing squirrels and went splashing into the shallow water where fields of cattails grew tall, and Lowry let his thoughts go free as he limped along behind them. He had been on the New York Police Department for fifteen years and carried the shield of a detective before a bullet from a crack addict took away much of his left knee and forced him into retirement. Chris Lowry doubted if his client was going to be satisfied with a newspaper report that the man they were thinking about hiring had been dead for some time, buried in Arlington.

Okay, he thought, *so we start at the beginning.* The stories said the man was from South Boston. By noon, he was easing his blue Toyota sedan onto the Connecticut Turnpike, heading for Southie.

BALTIMORE

'Swanson! Where is that asshole and his poison gas?' The voice on the telephone brimmed with authority. Kyle blinked himself awake, shook Sybelle's bare shoulder, and silently mouthed the word 'Middleton.' She threw the bedcovers aside and sprinted, naked, to the open door between their rooms, as if the general could see between Washington and New York. She took nothing for granted, particularly where the Lizard might be involved. He had eyes and ears everywhere.

'General? Jesus, sir, what time is it?'

'Almost 0600. Gimme something that Wolf Blitzer doesn't already know.'

'Can't do it, sir. I've been asleep. Just spent a day getting tortured, you know?'

'Bullshit. You went through stuff worse than that in boot camp. We've got a session at 0900 with the alphabet agencies, and it would take too long for you to drive, so the Lizard has laid on a helicopter to bring you and Summers back here. Where is she, anyway? Tried her room and no answer.'

Kyle took time to yawn and sound sleepy. 'I don't know, General. Probably out for a run. I'm not her keeper.'

'Excellent. I ran three miles before breakfast myself

242

and have been at my desk since five. Go get her and get on that bird.'

'Three miles before breakfast. You are one hell of a Marine, sir,' Kyle said.

'Hoo-ah,' said the general and hung up.

Sybelle leaned against the adjoining door, a white towel around her and her beeper in her hand. 'I have a message to call him.'

'Forget it.' He was leaning on his elbows, looking at her. 'He has a helicopter coming in to fetch us back to the Pentagon.'

'Damn, Kyle. This is what I meant last night when I told you the stress was getting to me. It never ends. Last night was great, but both of us know there is no future for any relationship. There is only room for work, and I almost feel like a traitor for having sex with you.'

'Yeah. It would only complicate things.' It was the first time he had had a serious sexual interlude since the death of Shari Towne. 'But thanks for rescuing me yesterday, in more ways than one.'

She let the towel fall and dropped the beeper on top of it. 'Hoo-ah.'

Precisely at 0845, a shining black government SUV was waiting at the Pentagon and all four members of Task Force Trident climbed aboard. 'Sar'nt Johnson! Take us to the Old Exec and go in through the gate. It's next to the White House. You know where that is, I assume.'

'Excuse the general's abrupt manner, Sergeant,' said Kyle. 'He ran three miles before breakfast and then drank too much coffee.'

The driver managed a smile. They were already out of

the parking lot and into traffic. 'Fast or medium fast, sir?'

'Fast,' replied the general, and the sergeant clicked on the siren and lights and swerved into a hole between two yellow cabs, setting off a round of horn honking.

In the rear, the Lizard looked at Sybelle with a strange smirk.

'What?' she said. *The little fucker knows!*

'Oh, nothing. Just thinking.' He blushed and looked away.

A private and secure conference room had been set aside for them on the second floor of the Old Executive Office Building, and it was empty when Middleton led his team down the checkerboard-tile hallway to an office that was guarded by a uniformed member of the U.S. Secret Service. From the outside, the location seemed no different than any other in the busy office building, but the old wooden door opened into an airlock, and just inside, a step put a visitor above a false floor and into a slightly smaller room that also had a false ceiling and soundproof glass. Sound was imprisoned within the room.

'Send them in, please,' said General Middleton as they entered, and the Trident group went ahead and took chairs around a table. The Secret Service agent opened the door again, and two more people entered.

Agent Carolyn Walker looked refreshed, in a starched white blouse with a crisp collar and tailored gray pin-striped trousers. The night at home had helped her. Dave Hunt of the FBI still appeared disgruntled but was in a different suit. Their eyes took in the four people waiting for them, and puzzlement was written on their faces because they had put one of them through the wringer the previous day and another one had threatened to kill both of them.

'Please, have a seat,' said Middleton, sweeping his hand toward vacant chairs. He smiled. 'Thank you both for coming over on such short notice.'

'General, what is this about?' asked Walker. The urgent summons to attend this meeting had left her in a foul mood. The Old Exec was neutral ground, neither Pentagon military nor government granite. It guaranteed no home field advantage for bickering agencies.

'Simply put, you two are back in the game.' Middleton leveled his gaze at them but did not raise his voice.

'And what game is that, exactly?' asked Hunt.

'Probably the biggest of your careers.' The general opened his file and slid out the picture of Juba. 'You took this in Paris, right? The subject's code name is Juba, and he is a motivated and extremely skillful terrorist operative. We believe he is about to hit the United States with a poison gas weapon much larger than the one that went off in London. We have to stop him.'

Walker nodded but put the picture aside. 'We want to help, believe me, but I don't take orders from you, General.'

'Me either,' said Hunt, his voice not much more than a growl. 'I'm FBI, and she is Department of Homeland Security. We have our own chain of command. I know the letter that woman waved at us yesterday outranked us for the time being, but that was then. Big difference.'

Middleton was unperturbed. 'Earlier this morning, the directors of both of your agencies signed authorizations of temporary duty assignments for you. Now you're mine.' He slid a document to each of them to verify his statement. 'You are veteran and experienced agents, cleared for Top Secret material and beyond, so here it is. Everything I am going to tell you is above top secret.'

'Way above,' agreed the Lizard, pointing a finger toward the ceiling. He had opened his laptop. 'Big way.'

The general glanced over. 'That is Lieutenant Commander Benton Freedman, our do-it-all electronics and communications officer. Next to him is Marine Captain Sybelle Summers, whom you met yesterday. And finally, the man you captured, Gunnery Sergeant Kyle Swanson, also USMC. The four of us make up Task Force Trident, and that is what you are now attached to.'

'So it's a military black op outfit?'

'Is Swanson an assassin? We saw him shoot Saladin.'

'Let's just say he is a specialist,' Middleton replied smoothly. 'And, no, we are not really a military unit at all. We just carry the baggage for Swanson. Now, the reason you could not identify him yesterday is that he is officially dead, with a headstone at Arlington to prove it. Every record was scrubbed clean a couple of years ago. Swanson was the best scout-sniper in the Marine Corps and specialized in black ops. His death was staged to create a unique place in which he could still operate under the deepest of covers. He simply ceased to exist. The Invisible Man.'

'Excuse me, General,' said the Lizard in a quiet voice.

Middleton ignored him, concentrating on the sales pitch. 'Trident was set up to support Swanson. We work for him, because he needs specialized backup, and putting him under the Department of Agriculture didn't seem appropriate. Don't worry, this is totally legitimate, just way off the books.'

Walker rubbed her eyes. 'This is confusing. Why do you want us involved when you have all of the Pentagon resources under your thumb?'

Kyle finally spoke. 'Because you both impressed me. You not only snatched me off the street in France and got away with it, but you also were willing to bend the rules to get the answers you needed. I want that kind of help for this job.'

'General Middleton.' The Lizard again tried and was ignored.

Kyle continued, 'You continue to run your normal operations and use every trick in your books, but cut us in on everything and help push things along with any special needs we might have. Nobody knows about Trident, but everyone jumps when the FBI or DHS shows up on their doorstep. You two bring a lot to the table for this job.'

'You're going to kill this guy? We can't go along with another assassination. That Saladin hit was obviously illegal, but it was done on foreign soil.'

'Of course.' Middleton smiled again. 'If a congressman ever asks, we want to arrest Juba, same as you. I'll back you all the way.'

Dave Hunt grunted. 'I can live with that, but let's look at this from the other side of the line. Even Swanson here admits that we are pretty good at what we do. So why do we need Trident?'

Kyle placed both hands on the wooden tabletop. 'All due respect, Agent Hunt, but you guys are never going to catch Juba if he doesn't want to be caught. He is a master at this sort of thing, and I think he has slipped over a psychotic edge to a point where he doesn't really care who he kills. I want to find him and get his attention enough so that I'll be at the top of his list. The two of us have a bit of a history, so it will be more than a matter of professional pride for him. It's personal. He will want a clean hit and the satisfaction of seeing me fall.'

Walker looked at Swanson. 'You want to set up a duel with this guy? You can make someone that mad?'

Sybelle and Middleton nodded in the affirmative. 'Recall how angry he made you yesterday?' Sybelle said. 'Pissing people off is perhaps what he does best.'

'General!' Freedman interrupted again, his voice urgent, and he would not be refused a third time.

'What is it?' Middleton snapped.

A red warning light was flashing in the corner of Freedman's computer. 'The Connecticut State Police just pinged the NCIC for any and all available information about Swanson.'

BOSTON

Private investigator Chris Lowry spent all afternoon gathering the remarkable life of Kyle Swanson: birth records, family genealogy, education, mentions in wills, Social Security number, job history, a couple of scrapes with the police, driver's license, and then into the Marines. All of it was down in black and white, even with pictures of the young man in the yearbooks of South Boston High. The military file from the Marines was precise, and all of the dates matched. It was odd that the service had been so willing to help when usually there are iron rules against giving a service jacket to a non-family-member. He had listed it all on a yellow legal pad, and everything locked together like a neat puzzle. That was what bothered him. Life was never this neat. Clerks screwed up. Papers were misfiled. Memory played tricks. Information did not always match. This was too clean, as if it had been made that way on purpose. Sanitized.

With the data logged into his laptop, he started hitting the sidewalks, looking for those whose names had been linked along the line with Swanson back in the day. The good thing about a place like South Boston was that many family members stayed in place for generations, and it was easy to track them down. His cover story was that he was a magazine reporter putting together a piece on this true American hero and he needed personal anecdotes. Most were happy to share their memories, and steered him to Kyle's schoolhood chum Michael McLaughlin.

McLaughlin, a short and scrappy man, had been Swanson's best friend in high school and his baseball teammate. Kyle and Michael had been friends for years, and Swanson always felt better when he was pitching to know that McLaughlin was roaming behind him at shortstop. Those nervous, fast feet and incredible reflexes helped Mike make double plays out of hard-hit balls that taller players could not have even reached. Michael also had a remarkable combative streak that went far beyond mere competition. In a day when schools were moving to rubber cleats, Michael stayed with the metal ones, persuading the coaches that they improved his footing. Kyle would often see Michael sitting close to his locker, hands inside and out of sight, sharpening his spikes. Kyle Swanson had always made a point of hitting an opposing batter early in the game, just to set the tone for the day. That tactic would put a runner on first base, who would try to retaliate by taking out the shortstop on the next ground ball, and Michael would grind the runner up like hamburger. Swanson kept score of the players spiked by Mike.

They stayed in touch after high school, when Kyle went into the Marines and Michael tried the minor leagues for a few years before returning home to South Boston. Then Kyle slowly withdrew from the Southie crowd, because when he came back he could not tell them where he had been or what he had been up to. Still, Swanson stayed in distant touch by sending postcards from far-off lands and then birthday and Christmas gifts for his godchild, Mike's daughter, Mary Elizabeth. The nine-year-old girl thought the world of her uncle Kyle and missed him terribly, Mike explained.

The detective thanked McLaughlin for the interview and left. Not much to report after a full day of investigating, using both high-tech and low-tech methods. He found a wi-fi zone at an Internet café and wrote his report, attaching copies of documents and logs of the names, phone numbers, and addresses of the people he talked to and a synopsis of each conversation. He included his own opinion that it seemed someone had made sure that everything pointed to the conclusion that the Marine had been fatally wounded in Syria and buried in Arlington. No further action was possible, the detective wrote, short of going out there and digging up the grave. He sent the e-mail and drove back to Guilford. Traffic was a bear heading out of Boston during rush hour.

A team of FBI agents was waiting in the driveway when he got home.

'I knew this was too easy,' Lowry said to himself as he got out of his car and approached them, holding his hands out from his sides in plain view.

22

WASHINGTON, D.C.

A command center had been established in the Hoover Building, and agents from various national security agencies were working computers and telephones. Printers and faxes churned through reams of paper. Wiring curled around the floor to power the armada of electronics. Maps were pinned on cork boards along one wall, and white greaseboards marched side-by-side down another wall. There was clatter enough to make everyone look busy. All looking for Juba.

Kyle was in an adjacent room with the Trident team, away from the main force of civilians but watching the operation on several television sets. The Lizard complained that the equipment that was being used was practically antique, but Kyle had been impressed by how Dave Hunt and Carolyn Walker had pitched in and mobilized their massive resources so quickly. Things were moving fast now that they were all on the same page and knew who they were looking for.

With Kyle's identification of the man who got away in Paris, British police swooped in and arrested Dr. Allen Osmand and his wife, Martha Goodling Osmand, at their home. A montage of photographs was built of their son, Jeremy, from his sports days at school through the time in the Royal Marines to the fuzzy picture from the house in Paris. A computer smoothed out the details, made comparisons with key points, and created an accurate and up-to-date image.

That was fed into a database of facial recognition software that examined the image against the airport photographs of everyone who had entered the United States in the past few days. The computer did its work at blazing speed, but it still took time to check the digitized photos of tens of thousands of newcomers.

Meanwhile, a nationwide alert was issued for Jeremy Osmand, a known terrorist who was to be considered armed and dangerous. The Department of Homeland Security photograph was given to all of the television networks.

'We've got a hit,' said Agent David Hunt as he entered the Trident enclave and closed the door behind him. 'He came in at Dulles three days ago as a businessman on a Dutch passport. The customs officer and the airplane's crew will be interviewed, but it is doubtful that they will remember him unless he did something to attract attention, which is unlikely.'

The Lizard pulled up the security camera picture of Juba passing through the gate. 'Looks ordinary,' he said.

'That's the point,' said Kyle. 'He disappeared into the background. Nobody would have noticed him.'

'Now we're switching the computer to scan domestic flights to see where he's gone.'

'Good luck with that,' said Kyle.

Hunt took offense. 'We caught you, didn't we?'

'But you got the wrong guy.'

Dave Hunt left the room, muttering beneath his breath.

General Middleton shook his head. 'Play nice, Gunny. What are you thinking?'

Swanson walked around the table and looked out of the only window to the street, where civilians were going about their daily routines in the heart of Washington. Behind him, the image of Juba was still on the three television screens. 'This is all out of some James Bond movie. Those people out there have all the toys, but they still don't know who they are really dealing with. Juba is a damned good sniper. He is not running away to avoid prosecution, he is moving with great speed and deliberation toward a specific objective.'

'He's stalking a target,' Sybelle added.

'And he knows I am coming after him, which is why he had that investigator in Connecticut checking me out.' Kyle picked up the transcript of the exhaustive FBI interview with private detective Chris Lowry, who had been totally cooperative. Discretion was one thing in keeping a client's confidentiality, but a federal subpoena was much different. He gave them everything he had.

'Look down where Lowry reported back to his "client," who has to be Juba using another false front. He listed everyone he spoke with during the day and a brief outline of the conversations. When he was talking with my old high school buddy Mikey McLaughlin, the detective also mentioned that I was godfather to his nine-year-old daughter, Mary Elizabeth. Juba sent an e-mail right back to thank him and added that he would talk with Michael and the girl, Mary Elizabeth, personally.' Kyle dropped the transcript. 'Now why would he do that?'

Carolyn Walker from the DHS had been following the conversation without adding anything, but now she spoke up. 'He did not have to respond at all, and in fact, he did terminate that entire e-mail link after sending that message. The conclusion is that he intends to attack that little girl in order to draw you into the open.'

'And how have you responded to that threat?' Swanson asked.

'Boston is being flooded with extra agents to help secure the area, and some HRT countersniper teams are standing by. He won't get near her.' Walker looked steadily across the table. The routine was in place, concentrating overwhelming manpower on a trouble spot, building a protective web around the target.

'It is a waste of time, money, and resources, Agent Walker,' said Kyle. 'Juba has no plans to go after my goddaughter and couldn't reach her even if he did. What you people aren't mentioning is that you have a file a foot thick on Mikey. His uncle Tim runs some of the healthier criminal enterprises in Boston, everything from gambling and girls to dope and supplying money for what's left of the Irish Republican Army. Mikey is Tim's chief enforcer. No, Mary Elizabeth is quite safe.'

'So why did he send the message, if that is indeed what happened?'

'A diversion. It is a sniper's habit to make pursuers chase their tails instead of him. He took an action with minor risk that caused you people to have a major reaction.'

Dave Hunt came back into the room. 'We now have him in the domestic air system, flying from Washington to Tampa.'

SAN FRANCISCO

Juba's warning antenna was quivering. He had rented a spacious, fully equipped automotive garage in a small industrial park on the outskirts of San Francisco, and while he was working, he kept an eye on a small black-and-white television set perched on a workbench. His picture was on part of the screen, and he walked over, wiping his hands on a greasy rag, to turn up the volume. A colorful SPECIAL ALERT logo was imprinted below the woman news reader giving the report. National security authorities had issued a request for all citizens to watch for this man, Jeremy Osmand, a known terrorist believed to be somewhere in the United States at the moment. Do not approach him by yourself, she said. Call the police.

Juba had purchased a 2004 Ford Excursion, the biggest sport utility vehicle ever produced in the United States, for a 20 percent cash down payment and his signature on a lot of legal papers. It shone dull silver beneath the overhead lights of the garage, where he had been clearing out everything behind the front seats to create a long, flat deck. Now he got in, rolled up the big front door, and drove to his motel, a nice midpriced facility . He parked two blocks away and walked down a narrow alley, with a dirty 49ers cap tilted low on his face. At the corner, he went into a health food store, bought a cup of vanilla chai, and sipped it as he scanned the area.

He had been there for two nights but had only been seen by the night clerk. Had the young man already recognized the picture on the screen and called the authorities? It did not seem that way, because there were no unmarked police cars in the neighborhood, no vans with tinted windows, and no strong young men pretending to do work. No cops, but they would find this place sooner or later. He had to take the chance.

The pistol was snug in the waistband of his jeans, beneath the floppy T-shirt, but he needed the contents of a plastic bag that he had left in the bathroom and the big gun that was hidden in the air-conditioning vent of his room.

It was difficult to buy a good weapon in the People's Republic of San Francisco, but back in the late 1980s, American law enforcement had turned a blind eye toward al Qaeda representatives who had made many open purchases at gun shows around the country. Those guns were believed to be for export to Afghanistan and the war against the Soviets, but a number of them went into secret caches such as the one that had been stored in northern California. He had picked up an Armalite civilian knockoff of the famous .50 caliber Barrett, which had been purchased from a gun show in Sacramento. There was a little .22 Bushmaster, too, but Juba wanted the big kick.

He dumped his drink and circled the block to approach the motel from a direction that could not be seen by the front desk, sauntered up the single flight of stairs, and was quickly into the corner room. The maid had already been by to clean up and prepare the bed, and the room had fresh towels and the smell of pine aerosol. He stole the towels and pushed them into the plastic bag with the box of Clairol Nice'n Easy hair coloring, then unscrewed the wall vent with a tiny screwdriver on his army knife and pulled out the Armalite in its carrying case. Four minutes after entering the room, he was out. Time mattered now, and he still had chores to do.

A hospital located twenty miles from the baseball stadium was commonly known as 'the Saints.' It had been founded by Mormons as a business and charitable venture; the Latter-day Saints sold it to the Catholic Church in 1993, and it was renamed St. Mary's Hospital. Sick people did not care which saints were in charge as long as the doctors and nurses took care of them. The Saints encompassed four floors of a modern building and had earned a reputation as a top-rated trauma center.

The previous day, Juba had picked out an apartment about two hundred yards away from the Saints, and now he drove there and parked in an empty space behind the low building. He went up the inside stairwell and needed only thirty seconds to pick the lock. It was the middle of a sunny afternoon, and the dead bolt had not been engaged by the young mother watching television. She only had time to turn in surprise when she heard the door open; Juba shot her before she could scream. He carefully went through the apartment and found a little boy playing in a bedroom. The kid looked up just before the trigger was pulled. Juba pulled the dead woman into the light blue bathroom that smelled like daisies and dumped her in the white bathtub. Her four-year-old son was placed atop her body. The gunman dipped a washcloth in the boy's blood and wrote his name on the tile: *JUBA*.

In the refrigerator, there was some leftover chicken in a covered bowl, which he heated in the microwave and brought into the living room with a dish of cold potato salad. As he ate lunch, he studied the unobstructed view from the window: a large white sign with EMERGENCY ROOM printed in large blue letters and a concrete ramp that jutted into the driveway to allow ambulance drivers to back right up to it and wheel their gurneys smoothly from the vehicle and straight into the trauma unit.

Then it was back to the garage.

WASHINGTON, D.C.

'About seven hundred and fifty million passengers flew on some eleven million flights from U.S. airports last year,' said Lieutenant Commander Freedman, surging around the Internet. 'That's a lot of faces for the computer to look at, and they won't find anything if he rented a car and drove somewhere.'

'Damn, Liz. Don't even think like that,' said Sybelle Summers. The Trident group was bored. They liked answers crisp and quick. The coffee was stale and so was the air.

'We have people on it down in Florida,' said Carolyn Walker. 'If he's there, we'll find him.'

'That means Juba has split our resources yet again,' Kyle said. 'First Boston and now Tampa–St. Pete.'

'Not much down there,' said Walker.

General Middleton looked up from working the *New York Times* crossword puzzle. 'Right. Nothing at all. Just sunshine and MacDill Air Force Base and the headquarters of the U.S. Central Command, which runs the wars in Iraq and Afghanistan. We've jacked security to the max around them.'

The doorknob turned and Special Agent David Hunt

came in. 'He is still on the move. Flew from Tampa to Denver.'

Middleton swept the newspaper from the table and stood up. 'Oh, fuck,' he growled. 'That's Cheyenne Mountain. Lizard, get me a secure voice link to the Joint Chiefs at the Pentagon so they can lock 'em down.'

Walker knew the incredible importance of the system that was the electronic heart of the nation's defenses. 'That facility is buried two thousand feet underground. It's heavily guarded and can be completely sealed off. Those people are totally safe from any gas attack.'

Kyle Swanson grimaced. 'Their families aren't. Even so, I can't see that as the attack point. Not a big enough crowd, and the security level is always high throughout that area.'

'Then where is he going to hit?' asked Walker. 'What is drawing him to these places?'

'Think about targets,' Kyle answered. 'Juba wants a huge splash, something bigger than London. We don't see it yet, but he does. He is not moving at random.'

SAN FRANCISCO

Xavier Sandoval found the garage address without difficulty, stopped the yellow Diablo Gourmet truck, and honked his horn. Juba pushed a button inside and the main garage door rolled back. Sandoval steered the truck inside and parked beside a huge SUV.

'Welcome, brother,' said Juba, embracing the man as a friend. 'How do you feel after such a long drive?'

'Tired, but not too bad. I have grown to hate talk

radio.' Sandoval laughed. He drank from a cold bottle of water offered by Juba. 'You are aware of the police bulletins that are out with your name and description.'

Juba pointed to the little television set. 'I have been watching most of the day. My parents have been arrested, but the Crusaders still have not figured out what is going to happen. We remain in control, but we must hurry. I hope you have a few more hours of work left in you.'

'That is why I am here, brother.'

They put on coveralls and stacked four fifty-pound sacks of ammonium nitrate fertilizer across the width of the SUV cargo compartment, which could handle up to a ton of payload. A small fork lift was used to hoist a single, heavy fifty-five-gallon drum of liquid nitromethane and carefully nudge it forward against the barrier of bags; then they packed four more sacks of fertilizer along the near side of the drum. Their work was fast and silent, and they moved with determination, climbing inside the Excursion to secure the deadly pyramid of explosive components with strong fabric straps. A blue and white striped awning, common at tailgate parties, was arranged over the stack and anchored by several plastic picnic coolers, lawn chairs, and a folding table. The forty-four-gallon gasoline tanks were topped off with a series of five-gallon cans. Then both took quick showers and washed off the stink and any residue from the dangerous mixture.

Once Juba and Sandoval were clean and dressed in fresh clothing, they pulled a rug from the little office area and spread it out, knelt down facing toward the east, and offered prayers to Allah. Two hours until game time.

*

Juba tested the circuit of a digital detonator, set it for four hours, and plugged it into four bricks of C-4 explosive that were tied together.

'Let's go to the ballpark,' he said. The big door rolled up, and Juba drove away in the Excursion, followed by the Diablo Gourmet truck. The smells inside the SUV were overpowering and forced him to crank up the air conditioner all the way. He sprayed a couple of cans of air freshener back over his shoulder. Even that wasn't enough, and he reluctantly opened the front windows for circulation, but not the blackened rear portals.

At the stadium, he joined one of the lines entering the parking lot, and the nineteen-year-old cash collector twitched her nose at the odor coming from the big SUV. 'Gosh, mister, that's some kinda smell!'

'Uh-huh. I run a lawn service,' said Juba. 'Ordinarily I would have cleaned it, but I wanted to get here early to set up the tailgate. Me and my buddies got seats right by the Yankee dugout.' He smiled at her. 'Hey, you looking for another job? Pay you good wages to muck out this truck every day.'

She took the money and gave him a ticket to put on his dashboard. 'No way. Not with, like, that smell. You ain't got that much money. Enjoy the game.'

He followed the striped lines until he found a parking spot near the edge of AT&T Park, where he got out and closed and locked the door. The truck had an American flag decal on a heavily tinted window, and a green bumper sticker proudly announced: MY DAUGHTER IS AN HONOR STUDENT AT TURNER MIDDLE SCHOOL. Juba considered those signs to be urban camouflage. The Excursion weighed seven thousand pounds, was almost nineteen feet long, and stood six and one-half feet tall but would not draw a second glance in any parking lot.

Still an hour before the first pitch. Beautiful evening. Sellout crowd.

Instead of entering the stadium, Juba walked across the parking lot and found a taxi heading out after dropping off a passenger. He gave directions to go to the apartment building across from the Saints. When he was in position, he called Xavier Sandoval, who was parked about a mile from the ballpark. The game was about to begin.

'Another match! He's hopscotching all over the place,' said Dave Hunt. 'He went out of Denver on a flight to San Francisco. Anything of great military value out there, General?'

'No, not anymore.'

'We are scrambling the West Coast people to check the hotels and motels, and the cops are getting a readout that he might be in their area. Maybe he's just passing through there, too.'

'Could he be going after some other government installation, say, a courthouse, like in Oklahoma City?' Sybelle didn't believe it but was just throwing out ideas.

'Every city has government buildings. He would not have to keep moving around so much to attack one.'

'Maybe a big mall? A theme park.'

'Anywhere in the U.S.A., but none that are unusual or noteworthy in those three cities.'

Kyle Swanson was barely listening. There was nothing he could do but wait and try to think like a sniper stalking a target. He picked up the sports section of the *Times*. The newspaper was great at covering the rest of the world but totally hometown oriented when it came to sports. The lead story was the pitching rivalry for today's game between the Yankees and . . . *Tampa–St. Pete. Denver. San Francisco.* The cities tumbled around in his brain like dice in a cup, and when spilled onto a table, dice always form a pattern.

Stalk the target. Forget a hit on any military installation because the word was out and the guards were alert. *Tampa–St. Pete. Denver. San Francisco.* What do they have in common? No huge conventions going on. No presidential visit. Vacation time in the summer and people in a laid-back mode. Old people in Florida, modern cowtown in Denver, political antiwar nutcakes in San Francisco. Nothing remotely connecting them there. Denver Broncos, San Francisco 49ers, and Tampa Bay Bucs in pro football, but in separate conferences because they were spread across the country. The Devil Rays, the Rockies, and the Giants in major league baseball. Big stadiums. Can't-miss targets. *Yes. That's what I would do.*

Swanson poked his finger onto the newspaper story. 'The game. I'll bet that he's going after the baseball game between the Yankees and the Giants. More than forty thousand people will be there, sitting around peacefully in neat rows, waiting to be killed, with hardly any security to protect them.'

The room went silent for a few heartbeats as they stared at each other. Then Carolyn Walker and David Hunt crashed out of the door and started yelling orders to their people.

The bomb in the Excursion exploded during the third inning, raking the parking lot and shattering the broad edge of the urban ballpark, collapsing part of the wall into a pile of bricks. The first thought for San Francisco residents was that it was an earthquake, a feeling that lasted only a moment, until some people recognized the explosion and started yelling, 'Terrorists!' Ballplayers ran from the field, and fans stormed the exits, leaping over seats, pushing up and down the stairs, and trampling the slow, the infirm, and the small. The stampede steered away from the destroyed side of the stadium, and there was no thought by those in the outfield bleachers of waiting for a slow ferryboat to take them back across the bay. Run! They poured across the green field and out through the concrete tunnels looking for a way out, fighting for a place in the mob to reach a front exit, and adding to the panic.

Police warnings were ignored. Arguments flared, fists and elbows were thrown, and several shots rang out and people fell, ignored by those who were still running. Safety was at the end of the tunnels. Just get out of the stadium and everything would be okay. Screams howled behind them, rising from the stands.

Two minutes after the big car bomb explosion, Xavier Sandoval drove his yellow truck away from the vendors' loading docks at the stadium and stalled it in the path of the fleeing crowd. He ripped out the ignition wires and activated the roof vents and fans, jumped from the cab, and ran for the street. With a hissing sound that could not be heard above the noise, the aerosol spray rose from the poison canisters in the truck bed and spewed into the air, riding the slight breeze into a slow, lazy arc as it settled onto the frightened men, women, and children who were running right into the misty veil that was softly falling across the kill zone.

23

Xavier Sandoval was a nervous man by the time he arrived at the apartment complex. He had run as fast as he could for several blocks, ignoring the chaos creeping behind him, until his breath and limbs began to falter. Traffic had slowed, then stopped as drivers gaped in astonishment at the smoke roiling from the ballpark explosion. He punched one, threw the man out of the way, and jumped behind the steering wheel, hijacking the car. A sharp turn down an alley and Sandoval accelerated from the danger zone, his shirt soaked in sweat.

He parked in the apartment lot and sat still, breathing deeply and trying to convince himself that he had escaped the poison gas. Leaving the keys in the ignition as instructed, he staggered up the concrete stairs and found the door that Juba had designated. When it opened, he almost did not recognize the man.

Juba had showered and changed the color of his hair to midnight black. The hair itself had grown ragged around the edges since he had left Iran, and he had not shaved since entering the United States and had several days' growth of beard, giving him the distinctive look of a foreigner. He wore owlish glasses with round gold frames. If police were profiling suspects to identify suspicious Middle Eastern males, Juba would have fit the image.

Sadoval came inside and locked the door, then sat on a chair and looked up. 'The package was delivered. I will never forget this day.'

'You did a perfect job,' Juba told him with a pat on the shoulder. *The man's courage is slipping.* 'Almost finished now.'

A television set was on in the corner, showing wide shots of the carnage from a helicopter while reporters who were safe within their studios broadcast the warnings for everyone to avoid the area of the ballpark. It was a poison gas attack, and authorities were saying the material was still in the air. Police had established barricades and were evacuating people as fast as possible. The high camera showed the flashing lights of ambulances, police cars, and fire trucks popping bright colors across a multitude of bodies. Among those fallen at odd angles were the uniformed figures of first responders who had tried to help and transferred the poisonous gel to their own skins. The entire rescue effort had slowed to a crawl until the emergency personnel were ordered into their hazmat suits.

In the apartment, Juba heard sirens wailing, coming to the Saints. 'Are you ready?'

Sandoval gulped. 'Yes.'

'I have set up this position carefully for you. The rifle is loaded and ready, and you have a clear line of sight. When the ambulances arrive, open fire on the hospital personnel, the patients, the police, bystanders . . . anyone. We want to create pandemonium in a place that everyone perceives as safe. Keep firing until the clip is empty, then reload and use the second clip, and then the third. Take your time, because no one is going to be coming over here in the face of such hostile action. Then drop the rifle, take the car, and leave.'

'And you, my brother? I do not know about being a sniper, but you do.'

'I'm going to another position higher up and wait until after you shoot. Let them get back to work, thinking the danger is over. That is when I strike. It will be devastating.' He moved to the door as the sirens came closer. 'I will be in contact soon. Good hunting, brother. You have done well.'

Sandoval watched a police car roll up, lights flashing, with a bright green fire truck on its bumper, their sirens gliding to a finishing growl. He was hidden in the shadow of the room. The scene was frightening, as everyone was wearing the bulky hazmat suits, some of different colors but moving like awkward ghosts with no faces, helping injured people they had ferried over from the disaster site. Workers in similar protective gear rushed out of the trauma center, facing the problem of working on horribly injured patients without touching them.

Two ambulances came shrieking in, only to find their way to the ER door narrowed by the emergency vehicles. Everything came to a halt for a moment, and Sandoval had his rifle resting on pillows stacked on a small ledge that separated the kitchen and the living area. His eye was at the scope.

Three nurses, an orderly, and a doctor, all in suits, gathered behind an ambulance, and an attendant swung out to open the rear door. A stretcher was pulled free, the wheels popped down, and the doctor leaned over to make a triage decision on a patient who had been lacerated by the car bomb and was bathed in blood. Another patient was taken out of the back of the vehicle, and a second team moved in on him. Sandoval heard more distant sirens.

He pulled the trigger. The first bullet took a nurse in the back and drilled downward from her shoulder, tearing through her heart on the way out the other side. She bounced against the stretcher and slid to the ground. The second bullet slammed into the temple of the doctor and splattered brain matter and more blood onto the wounded patient.

He stopped for a moment. This was easy. Juba had set it up so that he could hardly miss! He ranged over the stunned first responders and shot a firefighter in the throat and another nurse in the stomach.

Then Juba was beside him, pointing a pistol at his head. Xavier Sandoval never heard the explosion of the gunshot that took his life.

Juba left the rifle where it lay, removed Sandoval's wallet and identification, and walked out the door. The investigating police would find the body, eventually identify it through fingerprints or dental records, and then expend valuable time chasing a false trail toward Mexico.

Juba made his way down to the stolen car. In moments, he was out of the lot, driving north toward Canada.

WASHINGTON, D.C.

The command center was in crisis mode, as if it had personally suffered a body blow even though the attack was on the other side of the nation. The United States had finally been attacked again by terrorists, with horrendous results, and everyone in the big room knew that it had happened on their watch! They would be held responsible! They shuffled around or just stood by their desks with their eyes glued to the television screens. All were trained law enforcement personnel, and their sense was to automatically get to San Francisco, get on the ground, and help the victims and find the bad guy. They were stunned and demoralized, and failure clung to them like sweat.

'I can't believe we let it happen,' said DHS Agent Carolyn Walker, slumped in a chair in the Trident office.

Kyle was at the end of the long table, running his hands back across his head above the ears, frustrated. He could not believe how the civilian professionals were freaking out at the very moment they needed to be at the top of their game. 'We didn't let anything happen, and you cannot undo what has already happened,' he said.

'If we had only moved faster,' Walker said.

'Bullshit,' responded Kyle, growing angry. 'Yes, it is a horrible tragedy, and yes, a lot of people are dying, but there is not a goddam thing you can do about it but stay focused. Our job is to stop it from happening again by getting Juba. That goal has not changed.'

Dave Hunt looked across at him, his hound dog face containing even more lines than usual. 'And I suppose you have a plan?'

'No, of course I don't. All I can try to do is to think like Juba, put myself in his shoes.'

Sybelle got into the conversation to prevent it from getting personal and accusatory. 'We are looking at this attack from a combat point of view, Agent Hunt. The enemy sniper, for that is what Juba is at heart, stalked his target, picked it out, carefully planned his attack, and then struck fast and hard. That is standard sniper doctrine.'

'So what the hell does he do next, this supersniper that nobody can find?'

'He's going to get the hell out of Dodge,' said General Middleton. 'We should consider San Francisco only to be the place that he *used* to be. He is going to exfiltrate that area, and he knows that if he stays in U.S. territory, sooner or later he is going to get caught. Hell, your people were closing in fast, and you know what he looks like.'

Another agent knocked and entered the room, handing a message slip to Carolyn Walker as Dave Hunt asked, 'Then where would you go?'

Kyle had his hands on his hips, looking thoughtful. 'I'd go international again. Run with the purpose of finding a place where I can defend myself.'

Walker passed the message across to General Middleton and told the rest, 'Maybe not. We just got word of a sniper attack on a hospital where patients were being taken. Several more people are dead, but cops found the hiding place and IDed the shooter.'

'This says they got him,' the general announced. 'Juba's dead.'

VANCOUVER, B.C.
CANADA

Juba sat in the international departure terminal at the Vancouver International Airport, trying not to look at his wristwatch, nor the clocks on the wall, nor the digital time reminders above the gates. This was the most dangerous part of the trip, a calculated risk that had to be taken. He would be fine in another 24 hours, but until then, the most hunted man in the world was open and defenseless.

There had been no problem getting through the security procedures leading to the departure lounge on level three of the airport because the description being circulated among police and customs officials concerning Juba was of a Briton who had entered the United States as a Dutch businessman. A white man.

He had not shaved since arriving in the United States, had changed his hair color, wore gold-rimmed spectacles, had visited a tanning salon to darken his skin even more, and had put a rubber lift in one shoe to make him walk with a marked limp, which drew attention to his feet instead of his face. No one paid much attention to him in his new identity as a mild, polite college professor from the faculty of agriculture at a university in Damascus. The passport was in order, as were the university identification card and supporting documents such as a lengthy study of Canadian wheat production methods. It had been in place for more than a year, waiting for the time he might need it. The paper about wheat-growing was important to the disguise because it carried the official seal of the Canadian government on the cover, a tacit acknowledgment that he was a trusted academic and accepted by the government in Ottawa about something, even as minor as making bread. That would register on security agents.

Plus, the 'terrorist syndrome' had automatically kicked into the consciousness of many people in the airport, albeit subconsciously for a number of them, and they cast suspicious glances at all of the dark-skinned passengers gathering to fly to Damascus, a planeload of Middle Eastern people. *Just get them out of here as fast as possible!* None of the passengers looked even remotely like a Dutchman.

So Juba sat quietly, on his own, reading a news magazine, waiting for the morning flight to Damascus.

Complementing the disguise was his recognition that the expected security crackdown had yet to materialize. It would come, but he had learned as a sniper how to bank time by leaving destruction and distraction in his wake, and time was what he needed most.

The Austrian Airlines flight was called, and Juba boarded when the courtesy announcement was made to allow first-class passengers to get on first. He pulled out the news magazine and put his nose back into it, keeping his peripheral vision busy for possible threats. The herd in coach boarded noisily; then the doors closed and the plane began to move. Ten minutes later, they were airborne.

He was safe for the next twenty hours on the one-way flight. Would the enemy figure out his ruse and escape route before then, and if so, would the Syrians be agreeable to the anticipated demand to seize him at the airport? Escape and evasion is a step-by-step process that could not be planned too far in advance. Syria was the next step, and he would concentrate on that when he got there.

He ordered an orange juice from the hostess, and it was presented chilled, with moisture still on the glass. Draining it in sips, he then asked for a bottle of water. He had to hydrate. In all, Juba was satisfied with the way the mission had turned out, but that part was now history.

The San Francisco attack should not only mollify the bidders for the poison gas who might be restless over the death of Saladin, but they would be eager enough again when his next communication was transmitted to resume the actual auction of the formula. Of course, they would not get it, but they did not know that.

It was time for him to turn to the money option while things were falling apart, put the money in safe and accessible places and then vanish. He had years of learning how to become invisible, and this time it would be easy because he had millions of dollars available for the job.

The only real loose end was Kyle Swanson. Shake would never give up, and Juba could not rest comfortably until he killed the Marine. That was the only true option, because no matter what the other authorities might do, say, or decide, Swanson would never let up.

WASHINGTON, D.C.

'I don't fuckin' believe it,' Kyle exclaimed. 'How do they know he's dead?'

'Says here that he wrote his name in blood on the wall of an apartment he turned into a sniper's hide,' replied Middleton, passing the note around. 'Killed a mother and her little boy.'

'Too easy. Another diversion,' Sybelle said as she read it. She handed it to Shake and told Walker, 'No identification on the body itself. We need a picture of the corpse to compare with what we have on Juba.'

Swanson grunted a laugh. 'So somebody, they don't know who, snuck up behind one of the best snipers in the world and put a bullet in his head with a pistol? No way. Run the guy's prints. This stiff ain't our boy.'

Walker rapped her knuckles on the table, a nervous, repeated gesture. 'Yes. I agree. It does seem too convenient. The problem is that with the stadium attack, law enforcement out there is stretched to the limit and snarled beyond belief.'

The Lizard joined in. 'Not only that, the entire comm system is becoming jammed. The time stamps indicate that it had been taking about three minutes for a message to get through. Now it's more, and the delays are climbing fast as people fight for the available cyberspace. Several relay stations are probably going to shut down soon from traffic overload. Even the military channels and backup routes are busy. The governor has called out the National Guard, and the president has declared a state of national emergency. I haven't seen it this jammed up since 9/11.'

Walker said, 'So communications are slow, and everyone with a badge or a crime kit is busy around the stadium. At least two thousand people have been pronounced dead already, and the figure is climbing fast. I will detail a special team to get a firm identification on this body and take over that crime scene and send us a picture, but it's still going to take time.'

'How much time?' asked Middleton.

'Dunno, General. We'll move as fast as possible. Realistically, under the deteriorating conditions out there, it will be a while.'

Swanson ripped a page off of the yellow legal pad before him, balled it up, and flipped it across to a trash can in the corner. It hit the rim and bounced onto the floor. He studied it with resignation and said, 'He's gone.'

24

General Middleton, Captain Summers, Lieutenant Commander Freedman, and Kyle Swanson took a final look at the command center, which was slowly coming back to life. 'We're done here,' said the general.

'Okay,' replied Carolyn Walker. 'Thanks for your cooperation.' Her tone was neither warm nor cold, but she was glad to get rid of the secret military unit. Now things could get back to normal and law enforcement could do its job without second-guessing by people who were not trained as investigators.

'Anytime. Just keep us in the loop if you catch a break and when you identify the corpse they think is Juba.' Handshakes all around, and the Trident team left by a side door. 'Come on. I'll buy us all a big breakfast. There's a good pancake house over in Alexandria.'

They were all tired and frustrated, lost in their own thoughts as they drove over the bridge and into the redbrick section of Old Town, then on west to where the neighborhoods were not as ritzy and there were fewer antique stores, and then to an area that was rather seedy. The sun was bright, and the day was warming as they got out of the car. The restaurant parking lot was half full, mainly pickup trucks among two big rigs, because the eatery was popular among the over-the-road gang. A long wooden trestle table, worn smooth by generations of elbows of hungry working men, was empty in a rear corner by the kitchen, and the Tridents slid onto the benches. Napkins and silverware and a rack of syrup were already on the table. Coffee appeared as if by magic from a passing waitress, followed soon by platters of pancakes, sausage and bacon, warm biscuits, and scrambled eggs, served family style. Everybody ate the same limited, delicious menu here.

'So, none of us believes that Juba is dead, right?' The general stated. 'We unanimous on that?'

Everyone agreed.

'Pass the blueberry syrup, please,' said the Lizard. 'The communications net is absolutely overloaded, there is probably not an investigator to spare in San Francisco, and the disaster is going to be sucking up all of the resources. If the DHS agents don't get to it in a hurry, the other officers won't get around to doing our corpse anytime soon. Juba always seems a couple of steps ahead.'

Kyle refilled his coffee cup. 'He is no longer in the U.S. I'm confident of that. The air system was not shut down, and the West Coast airports dump dozens of international flights into Asia every hour. More to Europe. He needed a disguise and new papers, and he had to move quickly, but I would bet he made one of those planes.'

'Mexico? South America?' asked Middleton.

'He doesn't specialize down there. Maybe he has connections, probably does, but right now he is looking for a comfort zone. As a sniper, he is extracting after completion of his mission. South America would be alien to him.' Sybelle ate a mouthful of eggs while she thought, then continued. 'Same thing with most of Asia, from Japan to New Zealand. The only Muslim safe zones would be in the Philippines or Indonesia, and they would not risk the wrath of the United States by knowingly giving him shelter and protection. Maybe North Korea or Iran might shelter him, but he's a pretty hot potato right now, and they could make points with Washington by turning him in.'

Middleton said, 'Know what? I think the final destination for this crazy, murderous shitheel is Iraq. That's the only place where he can disappear.'

'That's my bet, too, boss. He is going to hide in the war. And that's where I am going to find him.'

'Okay. So go get him. Sybelle will go along to keep everything under the Trident umbrella, and the Lizard will do his keyboard magic from our office here. Take whoever or whatever you need, but remember that there are no orders for anything, there is no paper trail, nobody ever heard nothin' about nothin'. Then be clear on this, Dead Guy: I want Juba's fucking scalp.'

'Aye, aye, sir,' said Kyle Swanson, already feeling the rush. Sniper against sniper. Me and Juba. *Bad shit comin'*.

AUSTRIAN AIRLINES
FLIGHT 512

Ten hours. Halfway. Juba was feeling talons of claustrophobia seizing his flesh, as if the airplane were shrinking in on him. The spacious first-class seat had narrowed and the bulkheads seemed closer, but he had work to do, so he popped open his briefcase and removed the laptop computer and a single condom in its sealed plastic container.

The diagrams, the formula, and the instructions for assembling the weapon were spread over several files, and he had spent some time in Paris putting it all together for future use. It was in several folders, to meet different contingencies. From the briefcase he removed a tiny memory stick, attached it to a USB port, and downloaded the final file, which included the updated material from the Iranian laboratory, the final step in the process. The folder containing the date for the poison weapon used in London was in a file by itself, called File 999, and contained no indication that it was incomplete. The product would kill, but not do what was done in San Francisco. When the ultimate formula file was downloaded, he sighed with resignation and erased it from the hard drive.

Then he spent time transferring the various bank accounts and codes to the tiny memory stick and erased most of them, too. He pulled the memory stick free and he pocketed it, then stashed the computer.

When he got up to go to the bathroom, his head whacked the overhead storage bin. In the narrow bathroom thirty thousand feet in the sky, Juba washed his face and hands and under his arms and stared into the mirror: The disguise was still good.

Stop this nonsense! He stared hard at the reflection, an edge of his mouth slewing downward, angry with himself. He was a professional, and this was all part of the plan. It had been expected, just as a sniper has to remain immobile and idle for hours at a time in a hole. *Sweat it out. Losing personal control is not going to get this big damned airplane to Damascus one second earlier. Turn the glass over and instead of being only ten hours away from North America, you're halfway to freedom!*

Remember that you are no mild little college professor. You are still a sniper, a killer of men. You are still Juba. You can do this. You will do this.

He took a deep breath, allowed his bodily rhythms to settle, and then unbuckled his belt and dropped his trousers. Moving swiftly, he tore open the condom packet and removed the lubricated rubber contraception device and slid the computer memory chip in as far as it would go, folded the condom over, and tied the end. Another deep breath and he bent over the sink, spread his legs, and pushed the condom deep into his anus. Uncomfortable, but not impossible. Drug mules did it all the time, so he could do it, too.

He readjusted his clothing, washed his hands and face again, opened the door, and returned to his seat. A movie was playing on a little screen that he could tilt, so he put on the earphones and tuned it in. A tray of food was presented. Lunch. When the movie was over, he pushed up the covering of the window and watched the blue sky that stretched out forever, but he refused to look at his watch.

Halfway. More than halfway there.

WASHINGTON, D.C.

'Middleton is going to be up to his eyebrows in bitching generals. We can't run this mission as a usual black op because we are going onto other units' battle space and crossing boundary lines. They don't know who we are; they could open fire on us.' Sybelle was at her desk in the Pentagon, and Kyle was across from her.

Operating beyond the shadow of secrecy presented problems, but Swanson figured it was worth the exposure because they were going to need the entire might of the U.S. military establishment to make this work. Iraq was a huge country, and they needed to shrink the number of places where Juba could feel secure, which meant using intelligence assets from satellites to local informants. First chase him across continents, and then across nations, then into a city or town or village, onto a certain street, into a specific house. Make the rabbit run for his burrow.

'We'll work around it. No big deal. How big a package should we field?'

'Do we want mobility or firepower or both?'

Kyle thought about that. 'Mostly mobility. A small team can move faster, and we will have support troops all over the country we can call on. Even get air support in a tight spot. But we will be moving in the cracks, chasing one man, and I just need to get close enough to get a shot.'

'So we have enough to cover your ass and call for help if and when we need it? Ride in on tanks?'

'Use the whole available force, Sybelle. You run the show from a mission command post in real time.'

'Bullshit. I'm going in with you.'

'Bullshit right back at you. You're a damned good operative, you don't have to prove that to anybody, but your real value is in coordinating the show.'

She stared at him, hard. 'I'm no little damsel in distress, Kyle.'

'That's not the point. Juba is dangerous and he can bite. If I have to call for help, I want you on the other end of the horn, not someone without the warrior smarts who might not deliver when the shit hits the fan. Shooters I can get elsewhere.'

She pushed her legal pad aside. 'Getting in some field work is important for me now, Kyle, because I don't want to be tied to a desk for the rest of my career. I've been selected for major . . .'

Kyle interrupted. 'Selected below the zone? That's great, Sybelle. Proves my point. Even the Pentagon thinks you're something special.'

'General Middleton recommends that my next step be a tour as a White House military aide.' Sybelle Summers was clearly displeased that she was obviously being groomed for higher rank, moving up ahead of her peers. 'Very nice, but it's not what I signed up for, or why I went to the Naval Academy, and certainly not why I put up with Force Recon training. When I try to look over the horizon, all I see is desks, desks, and more desks! The men get field commands and I get another glass ceiling.'

Swanson grinned at her. 'Golly. That's really awful. I'm very sorry that your career track is pointing you toward being a general someday. That is not today's problem, however. We are trying to catch this mass-murdering terrorist son of a bitch Juba, remember?'

That made her laugh. She could only talk about that sort of stuff with Kyle. 'Right on, Gunny. I think we should do this with some of the same MARSOC guys that we used in Iran, since they are pretty much up to speed on it. Captain Newman to be the ground commander again.'

'Yeah. Rick is good people. I'd like Travis Hughes along as my spotter, then Darren Rawls and Joe Tipp as shooters. Five of us should be plenty to move fast or hold tight while you bring in backup and blow the hell out of whoever is bothering us.'

'I can do that,' she said with a nod. 'But I'd rather be a shooter.'

'We all got problems.'

DAMASCUS, SYRIA

Juba was buckled in his seat and eagerly looking out of the window of the passenger jet as if he were a first-time flier. After the announcements were made for landing, the plane descended with a professional smoothness; the wheels came down with a hum and locked in place. The wheels kissed the tarmac and the nose came down and the engines roared and the brakes took hold. Normal, normal, normal. His senses were alive, and the bulge in his anal tract seemed enormous. This was the last point of danger, but he was back on friendly turf. Or, if not friendly, at least not unfriendly.

As was his habit, he unbuckled as soon as the plane came to a halt so he could have freedom of movement, although there was really nowhere to go on the big Boeing. It coasted toward the terminal without delay, meeting the printed arrival time. Juba knew the Damascus airport was a hard place for passengers lining up for departure, but the arrivals seldom had much difficulty, and part of what the purchase price of the first-class ticket bought was being allowed to get off of the plane first and gain an advantage in the customs area. Once he cleared customs, he finally would be able to breathe easier.

The crew unlocked and opened the doors, and the covered exit ramp oozed out from the side of the terminal like some great worm. 'Please remain seated until the doors are clear and secure,' came the overhead announcement in three languages. 'Passengers in the first-class cabin will be able to depart and . . .'

Juba never heard the rest of the announcement. Three large men in civilian suits with pistols drawn and two uniformed soldiers with submachine guns came running aboard and into the first-class section as the crew stood aside. They surrounded him. 'You will come with us,' said the leader, with a tone of outright menace. *Mukhabarat*, Juba thought. Secret police.

They placed him in the middle of the guards and picked up four more security operatives on the way out of the airport and into the waiting convoy of husky Land Rovers. Motorcycle police rolled out on their bikes with sirens wailing to lead the way over the eighteen miles into the city, and Juba heard the distant *wocka-wocka* of a helicopter overhead. They were taking no chances.

He settled back in the seat, a guard on each side, and considered the situation. Were they keeping him from escaping, or preventing the Americans or other covert operators from snatching him? The arrest had been abrupt and disappointing but not rough. Damascus International Airport was a known entry point for young men sent from other countries to be martyrs in Iraq, to strap explosives around their bodies or drive car bombs into targets. The arrival of another terrorist would not cause much concern there. But, Juba reminded himself, he was no longer just a terrorist but the most wanted man in the world. Nothing was certain.

The Land Rovers swooped into the city, and he began to pick up familiar landmarks and got his bearings, for he had been to Damascus many times in transit to other places. The convoy pulled to a stop at an ugly gray office building across from an open area with a few palm trees, a tall monument, and a small domed mosque, the Sahat al-Marje, Martyr's Square. Uniformed guards popped the doors and fanned out in a protective cordon while the three civilian agents hustled him inside the Ministry of the Interior, took him up two flights of stairs, and placed him in a nondescript office with orders to sit down and wait. He asked for some water and was ignored.

For almost thirty minutes, he sat still in the chair before a desk, gazing out the window and meditating to keep his heart and pulse under control. If they were going to kill him, they would have done it by now. This being Syria, they still might do so. Wait and see.

Behind him, the door finally opened, and a cheery voice called out, 'Jeremy! It has been a long time since we have talked!'

A man who stood no taller than five foot five came in, white teeth gleaming in a smile beneath a thick mustache but with nothing showing in the dark, intelligent eyes. General Yousif al-Shoum, head of operations for the Syrian Military Security Directorate, came forward and tossed a blue-covered folder onto the desk, then took a seat. A young man in a white tunic followed, carrying a tray of cold drinks and hot tea. He placed it on the table and left.

'Please, have a drink. You must be thirsty after such a long flight.' The English was flawless, thanks to al-Shoum's tours of duty as a diplomat and spy in London and New York.

Juba unsnapped the white cap on a bottle of water and drank. 'General al-Shoum. I did not expect to be seeing you today.'

The small man laughed. 'You were coming to Damascus but would not pay me a courtesy visit? I am shocked.' He flipped open the folder and removed a copy of a message from Interpol. 'The facial recognition program got you boarding in Vancouver, despite the disguise. You almost made it, but close doesn't count.'

'What happens now?'

'Did you notice on the drive in that you passed the Tomb of Saladin? The real Saladin, not your former partner. I really do not want to also have a Tomb of Juba here.'

Juba did not squirm although he knew that al-Shoum would carry out the threat without batting an eye. He was being told to deal or die. 'I had few choices. My plan is to go back into Iraq and kill Americans.'

'Now you see, Juba, that, unfortunately, is not my plan at all.' Al-Shoum backed against the desk and leaned there with his arms crossed. 'Every country in the world will soon know that you have landed in Damascus, dragging along the stink of what you did in San Francisco. The death toll there, by the way, is now at four thousand five hundred people. Amazing. The Americans want you back badly.'

'So you can make points with Washington by giving me up?' Juba cocked an eyebrow. Al-Shoum was a complex man, adept at playing several games at once.

'That is one option.'

'General, let's get on with this. What is your preferred option?'

'You are in such a hurry, Jeremy. Well, first of all, we want our ten million dollars back.'

'Done,' said Juba. 'Plus another million for you personally, because of the inconvenience I have caused.'

'I don't know. There is already immense pressure.'

'Two million, then. Bank account of your choice.' Bribery, *baksheesh*, was the most stable currency in the Middle East.

Al-Shoum went around the desk and took a chair, looking even smaller until he tucked a pillow beneath him. 'Can you do that from here?'

'If your people will bring in my laptop, sure.'

'Then there is another point, the matter of the auction itself. I have decided that we won the bidding, so you turn over the formula to me. That is indeed a mighty weapon that was deployed in California. I want it.'

'Wait a moment, General. I give you all of your money back, plus two million more, and the formula for free?'

'That sums it up very well, Jeremy. Either that or you will be killed trying to escape . . . after we force the information out of you.' The dark eyes were stones now. 'We will get that formula. Voluntarily, chemicals, or skinning knives, it is of no matter to me. The best choice is to remain friendly so you can leave this building alive.'

Juba looked down at his hands for a moment, quiet in his soul, even while negotiating for his life. The secret hidden in his body seemed to be pulsing signals to him. 'I don't have any choice, do I?'

'No, not really.' The little general smiled.

Juba feigned reluctance. 'I hope that your government will use the information to strike the infidels?'

'What we do is not your concern, my friend.'

'But I get to keep the other money that was put up for the action?'

'And your life, Jeremy. I think that's fair,' said al-Shoum. 'Turn it over and you leave this meeting rich and healthy.'

'I still don't like it.'

'I don't care. Give it up. Now.'

Juba stared at the general and let his shoulders slump. 'You win, General. I think it may be best anyway because the project has become too unworkable for one man. You will see what I mean.'

'How will you get it to us?'

'Right here, right now. It's all encrypted on my laptop. I will transfer the money and download the formula so your chemists can check it out.'

Now it was al-Shoum's turn to think hard. This was too simple. Juba was willing to give back the ten million, hand over the formula, and transfer a sizable sum into the general's personal account. It was not in the man's character to give up anything without a fight.

'You have something else, don't you, my friend? Something that prevents me from taking all of the things you offer and then still hanging you from a meat hook in Martyr's Square? What is it?'

Juba showed a hint of a smile, almost flashing fangs with the anger boiling within him. 'Back before the war started in Iraq, Saddam moved many of his special weapons and special ammunition into your country under the supervision of Unit 999. The Americans never found those records, but I know where they are, General al-Shoum, because my boss, the man known as Saladin, helped move them and had me hide the records somewhere in Tikrit – Saddam's home territory. Even if you tortured me to get the information, you still could not retrieve them because of built-in safeguards. That is my insurance policy. Should I not return safely, those documents will automatically find their way to the Americans. Imagine how happy Washington would be to finally know exactly what happened to those WMDs. You let me leave Syria alive and I will destroy them and send you proof.'

Al-Shoum laughed aloud and slapped the desk. 'Excellent! I knew you would not disappoint me. So we have an agreement. The only condition is that you remain here in Damascus as my guest at the Four Seasons Hotel until our chemical experts examine the formula. One day. Then we will help you get back to Iraq to eliminate that WMD data.'

'And kill more Americans.'

'Yes. That, too.'

The computer was brought in for Juba, and he shifted the funds, put the bank material onto a disk, and downloaded File 999, the London poison gas recipe. He slid the computer over to al-Shoum, and the deal was done.

25

DAMASCUS, SYRIA

General al-Shoum kept his end of his bargain with Juba, which might or might not be important in the future. As soon as the government's science experts concluded that the formula provided by the bloodthirsty maniac was as deadly as advertised, the task switched to spiriting the killer out of Syria. Two Land Rovers from the Ministry of the Interior picked Juba up at the hotel the following afternoon and headed out on the long drive from Damascus to the border town of Abu Kamal on the Euphrates River. There were many places along the route where Juba could have been killed and buried, but al-Shoum wanted those WMD papers, although he had doubts as to their existence. He did not bother to say good-bye.

At the border, Juba was given one of the Land Rovers and drove off on his own into the bleak country. Once word was received that he was gone, the shrewd little general triggered the next part of his plan. He had kept his word to Juba, but now he had more to do.

The diplomat was waiting, scarecrow-thin Foreign Minister Rustom Talas, when he entered the conference room. The intelligence chief did not begin with formalities.

Al-Shoum put Juba's laptop computer onto the slick, polished table and shoved it toward the foreign minister. 'Here it is. Everything about how to make that devil bomb.'

Talas asked, 'And the money?'

'The wire transfer has already been made. All ten million is back in the treasury.'

'Your decision on this, General al-Shoum, is most unusual, and I say that with all respect. As a diplomat, I always look for leverage in political negotiations. This information about the weapon could help me pry substantial favors from the United States.'

Al-Shoum switched to English. 'Mr. Foreign Minister, you are a fucking moron! If they find out that we have this formula, the United States of America will come after it. They have lost almost five thousand American lives because of this and want to hold somebody responsible. They would not bargain, they would demand, and we could be the next country invaded! Is that what you want?'

'No, of course not.' The foreign minister coughed. 'I was speaking in the broadest terms.'

'Just listen, you old fool, and stick to the story. We pulled Juba off the plane as soon it arrived, but he killed two security guards and got away. Are you with me so far?'

Minister Talas was almost grinding his teeth over being spoken to like a schoolboy. 'Yes.'

'Then we launched our own search, and a security camera outside the airport showed him getting into a waiting vehicle, a Land Rover. We issued a nationwide alert and discovered that he has crossed the border into Iraq. We deeply regret that this mass murderer slipped through our security net, but he is indeed a formidable opponent, as the Americans know.'

'So what do I tell Washington about the weapon?' Talas said. 'That information is worth its weight in diplomatic gold if we hand it over.'

'Tell them nothing! We don't know about any formula, because Juba got away from us! Understand that? Instead, deal them this information: Our informants tell us that Juba may be headed toward the city of Tikrit in Iraq.' Al-Shoum scribbled a note and handed it to Talas. 'This is the license number of the Land Rover he was driving.'

'Why Tikrit?'

'You don't need to know that, Foreign Minister Talas. Just tell Washington that we hope they find him soon and make him pay the ultimate price for his monstrous deeds.' He leaned forward menacingly. 'And you tell no one, not a soul, about our having the formula. If I hear a whisper that you have revealed this information, you and your family will die.'

Al-Shoum was through with diplomats. They bored him. He turned on his heel and walked from the room, back to his office, humming a little tune, two million dollars richer and in sole possession of one of the most powerful chemical-biological agents ever devised. He would hold on to all of it for a while. Saladin had a good idea about the auction, but he had made it too public, and the time was no longer ripe for such a play. Who knew what deals were to be made in future years?

*

COMBAT OPERATING BASE SPEICHER
IRAQ

The Army briefing officer with the scraped-clean scalp wore spotless and creased camouflage BDUs and had a 9 mm pistol strapped into a leather shoulder holster. Kyle Swanson wondered why everybody wanted to look like a warrior, even the ones whose jobs kept them safely inside the wire at all times. The man flashed aerial photographs on the white wall. 'We have ascertained a suggested target that fulfills the requested parameters to facilitate your mission,' the officer said. Swanson groaned but paid attention rather than interrupt the intel puke. The other members of the Trident team were having the same dual reactions.

'Somewhere along the way, the hajjis came into possession of an M120 heavy mortar. Normally this 120 mm weapon is carried on an M1100 trailer attached to a Humvee, or by truck or tracked vehicle, but the insurgents have developed a suitable alternative method of transport.'

Darren Rawls spoke up, in his Mississippi drawl. 'You mean the ragheads stuff it in the trunk of a car.'

The officer cleared his throat. 'Yes. Anyway, once it is mobile, the mortar can be moved into position to provide high-angle organic indirect fire support across a wide area with high-explosive, illumination, or smoke rounds. It requires a crew of four men.'

Swanson knew the M120 weapon well and respected its ability to lay down good fire support. It was not only able to be put into a car but also could be broken down and man-humped by the four guys on the crew. One would carry the tube, another the base plate, the third took the bipod, and the fourth would have the lightweight sight and the ammo. Even assembled, the thing only weighed a little over three hundred pounds. Once in place, it could fire up to four rounds a minute, then be torn down and moved to a new location before counterbattery fire could find them.

From Swanson's viewpoint on this job, it would be almost ideal because that four-man crew would train and fight together, which meant they would be together during the down time, too. He wanted them all. It was important that he have more than one target in order to get the message to Juba.

Middleton and the Trident team had guessed right that Juba had fled to Iraq; then the net was narrowed even tighter, to the Tikrit area, through a diplomatic communication from Syria. Somebody in Damascus had dropped a dime on Juba, and now Kyle had to draw him out.

'And you have this one located? A solid ID?'

The briefer was back on stride. 'We have a high confidence in the location.' He clicked on a narrow laser pointer and a red dot ran across the photo on the wall. 'There's the car, and there's the house that the crew is in. Humint confirms the photo reconnaissance.'

'Humint' was military-speak for human intelligence, which meant somebody actually saw it. The best kind of intelligence there is. He looked over at Sybelle, who glanced his way and nodded.

'How fresh is this?' she asked the briefer.

'The photograph was taken this morning,' he said. 'We consider it to be actionable intelligence.'

Sure you do, Kyle thought. *You aren't the one that has to get out there and kill them.* 'I'm go with it, then,' he said. 'We need to move fast.'

The area was the hotbed of Iraqi opposition during the opening battles of the war and the violent aftermath, and enemy eyes were still always watching what was happening in and around Combat Operating Base Speicher, only three kilometers outside of Tikrit. Swanson felt that he was always being watched from the other side of the wire, although Task Force Hammer of the U.S. 1st Armored Division kept security tight.

Swanson knew that security and secrecy were two different things, and loyalty to Saddam Hussein ran deep in the dictator's hometown on the Tigris River. Saddam built his biggest presidential palace there, drew the members of his inner circle from his home tribe, and was now buried near there. Tikrit, a hundred miles northwest of Baghdad, was an anchor point of the hostile Sunni Triangle.

Even at one o'clock in the morning, as Swanson led the Trident assault team aboard the helicopter, he felt as if some Iraqi diehard were counting noses and radioing an alert. They all wore loose local clothing and face paint. As a precaution, the helicopter took off in a direction ninety degrees different from the true target area. It would circle back to the attack path only when it was well clear of the base.

They were dropped in an empty area four kilometers from the town that contained the suspect house and automobile, and Travis Hughes took point as they trotted forward in silence. No talking, no metal jangling, no hard breathing, just a half-dozen shadows moving steadily in the dark of a moonless night. A steady wind helped mask their approach, keeping their scent away from the animals.

Few lights flickered in the windows during this dead time of night, and the group steered clear of them, carefully threading through the outlying streets and clinging to the shelter of walls and alleyways. They seldom paused and entered the tangled neighborhood where the suspects were without detection. Joe Tipp snaked forward on his belly, elbows, and knees to scout the house. No one was on guard, and the old white Ford sedan with a rusting roof sat just where it had been shown in the intel photo, right outside the gate of a small wall around the house.

Hughes fell in beside Kyle to be his spotter, and the two of them scurried away to set up a stable firing position while Captain Rick Newman fanned out the others in a protective arc and messaged Sybelle that they were in place.

'You sure you want to do it this way, Shake?' asked Hughes. 'I don't like being so exposed.' They were in prone position in the middle of a street.

'We want to be seen, Travis. This time, I want people to know that a sniper was at work here.'

'Still. Just saying.'

'I know. Come on. Let's build the range card.'

At four o'clock, Kyle clicked his microphone twice, and Newman and Rawls set off at a lope around the front of the house. Swanson nestled his cheek into the custommade stock of his personal sniper rifle, the Excalibur, and brought the scope to rest on the engine of the car. His world began to slow down as the moment of action neared.

Rawls started kicking at the front door, hard and noisily, and Newman smashed his rifle into the glass of a window, shattering it. Voices were heard yelling inside. Newman popped in a red smoke grenade. Neither man had said a word while causing the occupants of the house to head for the back door.

Out they came, some of them coughing and wiping at their eyes as the trails of red smoke followed them. Hughes had his binos on them. 'One, two, another, four. That's all of them. Nobody else coming out.' The mortar crew made straight for the car, and Swanson waited until they were all inside and the doors were slamming. 'Fire. Fire. Fire.'

He let his finger pull back slowly on the trigger and Excalibur roared, snapping a .50 caliber round down the street. It burrowed into the engine block, and the car shook with the impact. Now it was a matter of reloading and shooting fast, but accurately, at men trapped in a ruined car only a hundred meters straight ahead of him. He took out the driver first, before the man released the steering wheel.

'Target down,' reported Hughes. The man seated behind the driver jumped out and filled the sight. Kyle shot him in the chest. 'Target down!'

Swanson shifted to the other side of the vehicle and nailed the man scrambling from the passenger seat. He was part of his rifle, the world a black-and-white place of mechanical action and reaction, and he felt the new bullet reloading as the old brass ejected out. 'Target down.'

There was one more, and he ran. Excalibur roared again and the bullet tore out the Iraqi fighter's heart as the forward momentum propelled him into the courtyard. 'Target down,' Hughes said. 'Let's get out of here, Kyle.'

'Follow the plan, Travis. Stay with the plan.' Swanson watched the Marines form up near him, in the shadows, and Hughes joined them. Rawls and Newman were back.

'Helo inbound,' said Newman.

Kyle Swanson stood up in the street, holding the ominously long Excalibur at his side with his left hand, and moved without hesitation toward the car. Lights were coming on, but no one was yet on the street. Fear and confusion were making them pause. He paced deliberately forward until he was standing beside the body of the man who had been behind the driver.

Swanson propped Excalibur against the car and used his knife to cut off part of the dead man's shirt, which he twisted into a knot. Squatting beside the car, he dipped the shirt in his victim's blood and slowly wrote a single word on the driver's door: *JUBA*. Wherever he found Juba, the secrets to the poison gas would be nearby. The terrorist would never let that information be far from his side, and it was more dangerous than he was. A matched set, and Kyle had to get them both this time.

He picked up his rifle and strode away, a perfect target but also a fearsome figure in the darkness. The neighbors had heard some noise, but no talking, then a volley of five steady shots from a high-velocity rifle. That meant 'sniper,' and while no one wanted to stick a head out the door, they did watch from the windows.

When he reached the Marines in the shadows, Darren Rawls grabbed him by the shirt and pushed him forward, making him run, and Kyle's senses rolled back into normal time. 'You a crazy mutha, you know that?' called Rawls into his ear, running right beside him. 'Now haul your ass!'

26

HARGATT, IRAQ

The city of Tikrit is hemmed in tightly by a dirty neck-lace of small towns and villages, and in one of them, a tangled little place called Hargatt, a tense meeting was under way. Light razored sharply through the window of a bullet-pocked two-story building, illuminating a husky, bearded man who sat in a worn green chair in the main downstairs room. Guards were at every window and on the roof, and one stood directly behind him. The area commander of the Iraqi insurgency asked, 'Why did you do this thing, Juba?'

'I told you. I did not do it. What reason would I have to kill four of your men, who are helping to protect me?' Juba had been staying at the man's spacious and comfort-able home since arriving in Tikrit. He had already secured a new laptop computer and filled it with the data from the disk that al-Shoum had provided in Syria, plus the vital material from the memory stick that he had carried for three days in his rectum. Juba was back in business.

'The townspeople have described in detail that a man wearing our style of garments and carrying a long rifle had the courage to walk down the middle of the street

299

after the murders. He wrote your name in blood – *Why?* – and then walked away again. *Walked*, as if he owned the town! No Shiite dog would take that chance, and certainly no American.'

'One would. His name is Kyle Swanson, he is a Marine sniper, and he wants to personally kill me.'

The commander took a few breaths before speaking again. 'You did noble things in London and the state of California, Juba, and for that, I have granted you sanctuary. But death follows you like a plague.'

Juba motioned toward the guards and the windows. 'How long has this war been going on? You and the people of Tikrit are no strangers to death. I didn't bring it. It was already here.'

'Why would this Swanson Marine do this thing last night? It was foolhardy. He would be aware of what we do to captured snipers, but his audacity stunned and delayed the fighters who might otherwise have swarmed outside and taken him. That was why many of them thought it was you out there.'

'Swanson was, ah, communicating with me. Telling me he was around here and looking.'

Finally a glimmer came into the man's eyes. 'So he will be back?'

'Yes. No doubt.'

'Are you afraid?'

Juba softly laughed. 'No. Of course not. I want him to find me, because I am going to kill him.'

The commander's mind was suddenly busy with ideas. 'Then we shall lure him in close and hope that he brings many friends. You kill him, we kill them.'

'I like that,' said Juba. 'Just be sure to leave him for

me.' Once he cleared away the Swanson obstacle, he would find a safe haven and resume the auction process. General al-Shoum would not be pleased to learn that he had been swindled, but Juba planned to be a long way from Syria by then. Tahiti and Fiji both sounded good.

'First, let us show the Swanson Marine that what he did will not be tolerated.' The commander smiled. 'Go and communicate with him.'

COB SPEICHER

Kyle Swanson was in a bunk, fast asleep after the night's work. The rest of the Trident strike team was doing the same thing, while beyond their separate building, U.S. Army troops were going about their daily routines.

An armored patrol rumbled out through the front gate of the combat base, large warfighting machines clanking in the lead and helicopters zipping ahead to look for threats along the wide road. A short time later, several smaller patrols went out, spreading to different directions and different roads. Iraqi civilians were also on the move, wary when approaching American roadblocks. Unemployed young men and kids congregated on some corners in the towns as American troops moved through on foot. Shops were open. Business as usual.

Swanson snored peacefully. He had made his move, and now, while sleeping without dreams, he was still at work, a sniper lying in wait for his target. Army psychological operations teams were in high gear all around Tikrit, handing out paper flyers with Juba's photograph and broadcasting over the radio and loudspeakers mounted on vehicles, promising a five-million-dollar reward to whoever turned him in.

Kyle had nothing to kill but time. It was Juba's move.

HARGATT

The insurgent commander and Juba stood on the flat roof of the tallest building in town while guards listened for marauding American helicopters that might see them. The advantage of height increased the distance they could see, and they had a good view of the spot where a road crested a small ridge and then came down into a little valley and a bridge under which a canal flowed to the Tigris.

'The Americans always vary their routes of approach, but there are only so many routes they can take. Repetition is inevitable.' The commander pointed toward the ridgeline. 'Before they approach our area, they usually stop at the top of that high ground, as you see, and take time to study what is going on before moving forward.'

Through his binoculars, Juba studied the site. A pair of gigantic M1A2 Abrams tanks were on each side of the road, with their 120 mm cannons and array of machine guns having total command of the area. Other armored vehicles, both tracked and wheeled, rolled arrogantly down the main road, occasionally stopping to let a patrol dismount.

The commander had it all figured out. 'See? When they stop, you can shoot them.'

'All right,' said Juba, shifting his binoculars around the zone. 'See that farmhouse about halfway down the slope? I want your people to clear it out tonight so I can use it tomorrow morning.'

'Of course,' said the commander. 'We all look forward to seeing a display of your skill against the Crusaders.'

Juba gave a slight bow of appreciation but said nothing as they went back downstairs and into another building for some lunch. If he took a shot from that farmhouse, those big Abrams would be on him in a heartbeat with a hurricane of plunging fire, then the Humvees, armored personnel carriers, and troops would run over him, unless they decided to let an Apache helicopter gunship take care of the job. He had no intention of telling anyone, including the commander, where he would set up. Not with that five-million-dollar reward on his head.

During the afternoon, he borrowed a car and went out alone. As the commander said, there were only so many roads that the Americans could take into the area. Out of the bleak terrain and houses, an opportunity rose like a mirage at a little crossroads, and Juba stopped the vehicle beneath a few tall palm trees, got out, and walked around. His eyes studied the isolated area and the single Iraqi government traffic policeman on duty. The deep ruts made by the passing of numerous tracked vehicles spider-webbed the crossing. The Americans came this way often.

Then he restarted the car and drove some more to find the second site he wanted. This was payback for Swanson's daring raid, and the method in which the challenge would be answered had to be special. The scorecard would be kept in human lives not their own.

Back at the safe house before nightfall, he studied a map, ate only a bite of food, and went shopping for the few supplies he needed for the coming hours. He retired to his room about eight o'clock and spent a long time cleaning the weapon he had chosen from the insurgents' stockpile, a beautiful HS .50 Steyr Mannlicher long-range, single-shot, bolt-action, precision-fire sniper rifle that could punch right through the body armor worn by the Americans.

A few hours after midnight, he left the house. He had a small backpack that contained some rations and his compact computer.

COB SPREICHER

'He's out there tonight. I can feel it,' Kyle Swanson told Sybelle Summers as they sat atop a sandbagged bunker and watched a pair of bright flares drift down on small parachutes to the west. A moment later came the chatter of an automatic weapon and the loud booms of a big gun. 'He will hit back soon.'

'I don't know, Kyle. Task Force Hammer has things pretty well buttoned up. Patrols were rolling in and out of the gate all day, and the surrounding bases report nothing unusual.'

Swanson pulled his knees to his chest and wrapped his arms around them, rocking back and forth, feeling the muscles stretch. 'Would all that stop you, if you were him?'

She picked at a rip in one of the bags, and the sand beneath was hard. Been there a long time. 'No. Just slow down and take my time. Pick my spot.'

'Umm. That's what he's doing, too.'

A shadow appeared beside them and Travis Hughes flopped down. 'Hey.'

'Hey,' said Sybelle.

'Let me pick your brains here,' said Swanson. 'Juba is pissed off and wants to get even, right? But what is going to be his target, and can we stop him?'

'Hell, Shake, we can't stop the bastard until we know where he is. As for the target, my bet would be that he is going to want to match your number of kills, if not surpass it.' Hughes spit over the side of the bunker.

'Classless jarhead,' said Sybelle, disgusted. 'Travis is right. He's going to want a nice body count, so he will be looking for somewhere that American troops are bunched together.'

Travis laughed quietly. 'Hell, maybe he's going to come in here. Lots of people gathered at the Subway. They're even giving Latin dance lessons over at the Morale Building. Hell of a war.'

'No. He might be able to get inside the wire, but it's too dangerous. The man is not stupid.'

Darren Rawls crawled up and joined them. 'Just visited a friend for a couple of beers,' he reported. 'Man, the buzz is all about what you did last night. That is interesting, because nobody on our team would say anything, which means informants are spreading the word about the badass snipers in town.'

'We wanted the word to spread,' Sybelle commented. 'Part of the game. What we don't want is for the whole of Task Force Hammer to go charging out, trying to track Juba down, because he will take off and we will have to find him all over again.'

'They won't,' said Kyle. 'Remember, Sybelle, that you and I specifically let Colonel Withrow know during our introductory briefing that Juba and the poison gas formula was our assignment.'

'So where the hell is he, Shake?' Hughes asked.

Kyle laid back on the bunker and stared up at the stars. 'I don't know. He's out there somewhere. I can feel it.'

HARGATT

Juba had no way to really know if an American patrol would come through that crossroads seven hundred yards away from his hide today, but all those track trails and torn berms and crushed vegetation indicated that it was frequently used. Just like animals create paths through a thick jungle by padding along the same route, the steel animals of the American tanks and other vehicles were following a familiar pattern, apparently thinking the lone Iraqi cop directing traffic there was adequate security. After all, it was just a way station; the fighting forces were just passing through.

He had a position in the rubble of a destroyed shop that had collapsed upon itself in a jumble of timbers and stones. Many of the cement blocks were painted white on two sides, the outside and inside walls before it all came crashing down. During his scouting, he had found a narrow entrance that dropped into the shop's storage basement, and by moving aside a few big rocks, he had opened a good view down to the crossroads. He had put the rocks back in place when he left, returning with his gear a few hours ago.

Working in the narrow beam of a flashlight, Juba built a sturdy hide that provided maximum protection on top and to all sides. Stacking stones and wood, he created a firm platform on which to rest the Steyr Mannlicher. The tip of the muzzle would be four feet back in the room. Turning off the light, he practiced his escape route several times, returned, and walked around the devastated shop to rearrange more debris. A dirty piece of blue and white canvas that had once been an awning was spread across the rear opening and anchored in place with loose rocks.

Dawn was coming, and, with luck, so were the Americans. After planning and prayers, luck helped. At first light, Juba slowly removed the loose stones that would create a ragged window facing the crossroads, one by one, inch by inch, until the hole was about two feet wide and two feet high, just behind some scraggly underbrush outside. When a sniper fires, it is an automatic response for the people in his target zone to look up in order to sweep the rooftops, where the attacker may have the height advantage. Juba had chosen a place with a two-story building nearby. That was where he expected them to concentrate during the critical moments that he was firing three shots, no more, following standard doctrine that shooting more than three times from the same place allowed the enemy to pinpoint your position. And kill you. Three and out.

The previous day, during his scouting ride, he had noticed that the children in the neighborhood were eating candy from America, scribbling in notebooks with ball-point pens, and playing with silly plastic toys. Gifts from U.S. soldiers. A relationship was being built. Good.

There was a distant grinding rumble, and as he expected, his juvenile early warning system began to shriek as a dozen kids took off running toward the intersection. A pair of bulky M2 Bradley Infantry Fighting Vehicles surged down the road, raising big roostertails of dust behind them, where three up-armored Humvees trailed. Juba made a mental note that the 25 mm Bushmaster chain guns on the Bradleys were his biggest threat. *Don't give them a chance to engage.*

The kids were running alongside the vehicles, dodging the tracks and the wheels with ease and calling up to the soldiers in broken English. Sure enough, little packages of gaily wrapped candy showered down on them. The convoy pulled into the crossroads and into a line along one axis. The policeman steered traffic around them. Everyone was relaxed, and Juba focused his rifle on the second Bradley, which had a number of aerials sticking up from it, clearly the command track. The turrets were open, but the gunners were at ease, bantering with the kids. Then the soldiers got out, their rifles hanging loosely, some squatting down to the children's level. They came here often to rendezvous with other convoys before heading out on individual missions. Only two troopers took sentry positions, one at each end of the convoy. Iraqi adults stayed away, clustering in doorways or just going about their business.

Luck. Juba let his mind wash itself clean of outside noise. The command track was a tempting and militarily significant target, the place where the officers lurked. Kill the officers, tilt the battlefield. No. That was not what he wanted today. Just take the easy ones and go before they knew what hit them. Give them something to remember, to enrage them, to drive them crazy with rage. He brought the Steyr rifle to him like a lover and remembered his schoolboy Shakespeare, a line from *Julius Caesar*, 'This foul deed shall smell above the earth.'

The scope was on a small boy, about seven years old,

with dark hair and a smiling face, all white teeth and dirt, who stood beside a kneeling American soldier, talking to him. The rifle stilled its movement. The boy turned enough for a back shot, and Juba pressed the trigger with four pounds of pressure. The snap of the gunshot was loud inside the hide but was barely heard on the outside, and the big bullet smashed hard into the child, knocking him in a bloody heap onto the American soldier, who grabbed the boy and fell atop him to shield him from further harm. He was already dead. *One!*

The moment of frozen realization that danger was upon them occurred when Juba squeezed the trigger the second time and brought down an American who had been smoking a cigarette, the bullet ramming through his armored vest and into his vital organs. The man staggered, a look of disbelief on his face, and fell. *Two!*

Now came the chaos of children screaming, soldiers yelling and getting their weapons up, and the ugly Bushmaster cannon looking for somebody to shoot. *Sniper! Where?*

Now he wanted a good shot, a difficult shot, to put his seal on this attack, and he found it with the soldier who had made the mistake of grabbing a telephone handset from a radioman. The officer, calling in for help with this ambush. He was on his belly beside one of the Bradleys, peering out around the track, searching for the threat, just enough for Juba to see his eyes beneath his helmet. Easy, smooth trigger squeeze and the Steyr snapped again. *Three!*

The firing began in his general direction, but there was no target. The bullets were just chewing dirt and rearranging rocks. The soldiers and the Bradleys would be on the move in seconds. Juba wrapped his rifle beneath his loose robe, tore away the old awning, and walked into the morning sun, down the alley and around the corner. No one was on the streets because of the sudden eruption of gunfire. He got into his car and drove away.

Fifteen minutes later, he was snuggled beneath some bushes that lined the top of a hard mud fence some four feet high at the edge of an irrigation ditch. He peered over the berm and saw the crossroads, which had become a beehive of activity as the Americans swept into the neighborhood he had just left. It was hard for them to keep their professionalism, for the murder of a child does something to the American psyche. Snipers have to know about emotions. They were after the shooter who killed the kid, and he was somewhere in that neighborhood. Even their new defense perimeter was oriented toward the original hide, the place of the perceived threat, and not toward his new location behind them.

He had a plain view of the medical personnel working frantically with the three victims, who were laid side by side, trying somehow to keep them alive long enough to get them back to the aid station at COB Baharia. Juba was not depending on luck now but on expected responses. Suppress the threat and evac the wounded. The troops were in the village, and no more shots had been fired, so a medevac chopper was coming in.

He heard it before he saw it. Then the helicopter zoomed in low toward the battle site, flared to a stop in the air, and settled to the ground, the rotor wash throwing up a blizzard of dirt. Red crosses were painted in large white squares on the green chopper. Mercy flight. Juba aimed.

Two soldiers picked up a stretcher that carried one of his earlier victims. A medic leaped from the helicopter to give them a hand, and Juba shot him in the stomach to tear out the liver and a kidney. *One!*

The Bushmaster gunner atop one of the Bradleys was facing toward the village, exposing his back. Juba put the scope on him and fired a bullet that hit center mass. The soldier threw his hands up on impact and fell straight down into the vehicle. *Two!*

The medevac pilot had realized they were under attack and started winding up his bird for an emergency takeoff, but Juba had a clear view through the side window. Tight head shot. The pilot turned his head, and Juba, using the dark sunglasses as his aiming point, once again gently squeezed the trigger. The bullet crashed through the pilot's helmet and destroyed his head. Immediately, the helicopter began to power down while the stunned co-pilot took command. *Three!*

Juba ducked away behind the wall, carried his rifle back to the car, and quickly vanished into the streets again. *I am here, Shake. Come and get me!*

27

Captain Newman had the Trident team in a tight security perimeter while Kyle Swanson and Sybelle Summers probed through the sniper hide behind the mud wall like crime scene specialists on a TV show. As soon as the attack was reported to the base, orders rocketed back to hold in place, and an uneasy silence engulfed everything up to a mile away on every side. Extra troops were dispatched to bolster the available firepower, and the Trident team hustled in aboard a helicopter.

The mud-wall sniper's hide was the closest to the landing zone, so they went there first. A trooper had marked the spot with a yellow cloth tied to a stick, and the slash of bright color was stark against the bland brown surroundings. Kyle went in from one side, Sybelle from the other end, looking for booby traps, but they found nothing. Some bushes had been crushed where the sniper had lain on them, and there was a crease in the wall on which he had braced the weapon. Three hefty .50 caliber brass cartridges were scattered off to the right of the position, flipped out by the weapon during the reloads.

'Excellent field of fire,' Sybelle said, looking over the wall to the bloody crossroads, still the center of activity.

'Particularly if you have the enemy looking the other way,' said Kyle, kneeling in the dirt to study the placement of the attacker's body. He would have had a solid base and fired with an economy of movement. Swanson reached out and touched a dirty piece of cloth that was still in front of where the rifle muzzle had been. Wet, spread there to tamp down the dust, which otherwise would have been thrown up when the weapon fired and given away the position. A thorough pro, taking care of the little things. Boot prints led away from the wall, toes deeper than heels, indicating he was moving fast but not running. Those prints vanished at the small road almost hidden by the wall. A vehicle was waiting for him.

They all walked as a group across the action zone to a destroyed building that had been marked by another yellow flag, and Kyle and Sybelle again went into the sniper's hide. The canvas curtain had been torn down, and three more .50 caliber brass cartridges blinked in the light. Sybelle turned them over in her fingers.

'Same as the others,' she said. 'One punched clean through the armored vest. My guess is it's an M8 armor-piercing incendiary. He was going for a big wallop.'

Swanson agreed. A velocity of 3,050 feet per second and a range of 6,470 yards. It was overkill to use such a weapon from only seven hundred meters. Was the shooter trying to prove a point? There was a makeshift rest for a rifle in the middle of the room, well back from the opening in the far wall. He went closer to the odd window and looked at the sparse vegetation that had been broken and singed by the muzzle blast.

Rick Newman came into the basement hide. 'What do you think, Shake? Was it Juba?'

'No doubt,' Kyle replied. 'He left his shell casings behind, which he does as sort of a signature. Then, this double ambush was the work of a single professional, because not even two average shooters would be able to pull it off with perfect coordination. Three shots maximum, then move, that's standard doctrine.'

Kyle crouched behind the table and aimed along the viewing line that the sniper had. He could almost reach out and touch the men at the crossroads. 'Finally, he waited to attack the first responders who came in to help. He did the same thing in San Francisco because it's such an immense shock to everyone else. For a while, every soldier who comes around here is going to be thinking about snipers, and that will inhibit their freedom of movement.'

'Well, we gotta go. I just had a call from Colonel Withrow. He wants to meet us back at the base pronto,' said Newman.

The three of them walked out into the light, and the entire team went back across the field to a waiting helicopter. 'What are you going to tell the colonel?' asked Sybelle. 'He's not going to like sitting around and having this kind of attack on his men without fighting back.'

'But that's exactly what we have to get him to do, Sybelle. Withrow is no fool, and he realizes that catching this terrorist is the most important mission on his list right now. This mess today was bad, bad shit, but it proves that Juba is right here in this area and is not hiding somewhere in the urban maze. We are getting closer, and the funnel is narrowing. First we tracked him across the United States to Canada, then to Syria and then into Tikrit, which meant we did not have to search the rest of Iraq. Now he is here, for sure. The bottom line is that it is still a fight between the two of us: I called, and he has answered. Now we just have to make a date.'

Army Colonel Neil Withrow, commander of Task Force Hammer, was standing with his executive officer before a large plastic-covered grid map of the town of Hargatt. Black and red marking pens had slashed and stabbed to mark positions and events. 'Two days ago, this area was quiet. Real progress had been made both politically and militarily.' He turned to face Kyle and the flinty blue eyes bore into the sniper. 'Now it looks like World War III outside my front gate again.'

The XO pointed to marks on the maps. 'Here's the ambush site this morning. Since then, we've had two IEDs take out vehicles, with one man KIA, four wounded. An ambush by a militia organization we thought had been tamed left another two of our troopers wounded. Sectarian violence has flared in one part of the town, and a suicide bomber hit a market street. Two mortar rounds came into the camp but caused no damage. All this in broad daylight. It's getting hot.'

The colonel ran a hand flat across his crew-cut hair, then crossed his arms. 'We're going to have to go in there and settle things down, sooner rather than later, if we want to keep a lid on. How much longer do you people think you will need?'

Kyle saw the dilemma facing the colonel. The job of catching Juba was undoing a lot of good work. 'Sir, I have to ask you to hold back for two more days.'

Withrow groaned aloud. 'Look, Mr. Swanson, I have followed the orders in your letter of special authorization and provided your team with maximum cooperation here. Unfortunately, you have ignited a powder keg.' He pointed toward the window of his office. 'My soldiers died out there today, and morale is sinking because we have all of this power at our fingertips but are not responding. Your mission is hampering my ability to protect my force.'

'Yes, sir. I understand that completely and feel just as strongly as you about the loss of life, and that the best defense is a good offense. Unfortunately, our job still remains more important right now. The key to how he pulled off the San Francisco attack is with him, and if you throw a bunch of Abrams tanks and Bradleys into the game, Juba could just fade back into Tikrit or possibly return to Baghdad and we will lose him. I'm sorry, sir, but we need that material, and the only way we get it is to get him. We need two more days before you turn loose Task Force Hammer.'

Withrow looked back at the map. 'This one asshole killed six people out there today in a matter of minutes, but he killed thousands more innocent Americans before he even got here. The most dangerous terrorist in the world is in my sandbox. Do me a big favor when you find him, Mr. Swanson: Don't arrest him.'

'Oh, hell no, sir. I'm going to blow his fucking head off.'

The colonel exchanged glances with his XO. 'Very well. We will keep the troops on a short leash for another two days. Meanwhile, what can we do to help?'

Kyle moved to the map, picked up the red marker, and drew a great circle around Hargatt. 'Close it all off. Roadblocks on all major highways, secondary roads, and cowpaths, and put roving patrols in the open fields. Nobody in or out for the next day, no passes honored for any reason. Iraqi police and troops will work only within the task force perimeter. Juba is somewhere in that circle, and I want to keep him there.'

Withrow said, 'You got it . . . for forty-eight hours, and then we have to reevaluate the battlefield. But our hand may be forced if the violence continues to increase. We may have to start kicking in doors.'

'Yes, sir. Agreed. We will keep each other informed.'

Sybelle and Rick Newman flanked Swanson as they left the headquarters building and walked down the neatly kept road. 'Can we do this in only another two days?' Rick asked.

Kyle Swanson looked up at the sky and adjusted his cap against the hot afternoon sun. 'I don't know. I had to tell him something to give him some hope, and he is right that his task force cannot sit on the sideline forever. We can try. See what happens.'

HARGATT

The commander of the insurgents smelled opportunity. A few minor attacks during the day had drawn some American blood, but they had not responded in force as usual. The presence of Juba made a difference.

Juba, however, just wanted to kill the Swanson Marine, while the commander had a much wider agenda. The big force stationed at the camp three kilometers southeast of Tikrit had enforced the uneasy peace, allowing the time and space needed for the political process to move forward. The residents of the villages and towns in the entire area were feeling safe beneath the umbrella of tanks and helicopters and soldiers. They were imagining what peace might be like, and for the commander, that was the most dangerous thing of all.

'Are those houses ready?' he asked the man in charge of helping plan attacks.

'Almost. The people have been removed, and we have begun the storage.'

'How long?'

'Transporting and placing the gasoline, the explosive plastics, the propane tanks, and artillery shells require caution and skill. We should be finished in a few hours,' said the aide.

'Let me know as soon as you are done. We don't have much time.' This would be a fine operation and should not interfere at all with Juba's own personal vendetta. The commander had a war to fight, and he would ask a favor of Juba tonight.

It was a fine day outside, the temperature holding around one hundred degrees, but dropping as evening approached. He wondered where Juba was.

Juba had carefully cleaned the Styer Mannlicher rifle during the long afternoon hours, caught a power nap during the hottest part of the day, and then went back on the prowl. It was cooling off, and he was ready to work again, far across town from where he had been that morning.

Hargatt was not a large city, but big enough to draw in potential customers from the surrounding area, and many of the buildings remained in surprisingly good condition. He drove down the broad main avenue, an unremarkable presence in the late afternoon crowd of pedestrians, cars, and trucks. There was a tension in the air, and people in the shops were talking about the growing violence. There was some confidence, too, that the Americans and the police would bring things back under control.

The symbol of that confidence stood at the end of the wide boulevard, the blocky new police station that had been built with a $3.4 million grant from the United States government. The location obviously had been chosen carefully to show that the Iraqi police force had come of age as a trained unit and was present, ready to help. It was a point of pride for the emerging new government, and Juba considered it a worthy target. He could crush that rising spirit of safety.

A three-story building was on a corner about a thousand meters away, a place of shops and small offices. He parked around back and jogged up the steps and into the building. The doors were unlocked because the merchants were begging for work and did not want locks to keep customers out.

The door to the sewing shop on the top floor was not only unlocked but slightly open, too, to create a cross-draft through the stuffy rooms. A middle-aged woman with a wrinkled face was at a sewing machine, a round cushion full of needles and pins pushed high on her arm. Juba smiled in greeting, closed the door, turned, and shot her twice in the head with a silenced pistol. He spun the CLOSED sign around, locked the door, dumped the body out of sight, and arranged multicolored bolts of cloth into a crude rifle rest away from the open window. He retrieved the Steyr from his car, settled into the back of the room, and checked the scope; a clear view of the police station. Several American Humvees were parked out front, indicating that there were some discussions going on, probably about him.

He studied the building at the end of the street and sketched a range card while he waited. After an hour, he drank some water, then returned his eye to the scope, watching people go in and out of the ornate main entrance of the station. Some American soldiers, probably the drivers, were talking with some Iraqi policemen. Laughing. Cordial. Friends.

A stir rustled the small crowd. The soldiers shook hands with the cops and climbed behind the steering wheels of the Humvees. Two men were at the door, then at the top of the steps. Juba focused on the Iraqi officer dressed in dark blue trousers and a light blue shirt with rank epaulets on his shoulders. He was squaring away a blue beret on his head. A final check of the range card, eye back to the scope, a squeeze of the trigger, and the explosion of the shot filled the small room as the big gun kicked back against his shoulder.

Without waiting to see the fate of the policeman, Juba worked the bolt smoothly to rack in a second round and shifted his aim to the U.S. Army officer. He was wearing a vest, but that would not matter, and Juba brought the scope to center mass and fired. Two targets down.

The third round was fed into the chamber, and he looked for one more victim. The bodyguard with the sunglasses? The young sentry in the guard post? One of the Americans rushing out of the building with their weapons ready, searching for the sniper? He paused a few seconds to let the scene develop, like the image on a photograph in a darkroom. One American was pulling the fallen officer back inside, his weapon dangling uselessly as he hauled with a hand on each of the man's wrists. A medic? Juba shot him in the heart.

This time, he left the rifle in the room as he walked away. The military and the police would be looking for anyone carrying anything suspicious, and Juba had access to other rifles to use in the future. He disappeared into the crowd that was running away, scurrying for their homes.

28

COB SPEICHER

The Army soldiers were starting to mutter beneath their breaths in the chow lines and in the barracks, feeling that they were losing control of the area. It was no longer a secret that the dangerous terrorist and sniper Juba, once an evil legend down in Baghdad, was out there roaming their turf with a big motherfucking rifle. The fact that everyone now knew his name and background did not detract from the reputation but made it even more ominous. The guy was no raghead shooter popping off rounds from a rooftop but a former master sniper and color sergeant in the British Royal Marines, one of *us,* a real professional, not one of *them.* Could shoot the hairs off a gnat's nuts. He had done Baghdad, he had done London, he had done San Francisco, and now he was doing Task Force Hammer and every soldier venturing beyond the wire felt a target on his back. Count the bodies, button up tight, do your job, and keep an eye peeled for the nearest armor in case Juba comes to play.

Albeit, the Army could not do its mission that way. It had to have men in the gun turrets when they went out because you could not sail blindly into dangerous territory. Then the soldiers eventually would have to dismount and go on foot patrol, out in harm's way with a pucker factor of ten. Snipers cause problems even when they are not around.

In his office at the sprawling camp, Colonel Neil Withrow was in a tense and private meeting with his XO and his top intelligence officer. The blinds were twisted to let in light but keep out the heat, and an air conditioner churned hard to keep the air clean and the temperature in the eighties, which was twenty degrees or more lower than outside. The machine was overmatched.

A new map of Hargatt was spread on the colonel's desk, and the intelligence officer, a major, used a big magnifying glass on a sliding mount to make the images jump out. 'We've been looking for these places a long time, and finally it has all come together,' said the major.

Two square dwellings were colored in bright red, about a half mile apart on the scaled map. 'Each one is a safe house where the new foreign fighters and al Qaeda types are gathered before being sent down into Baghdad. The fighters are usually the young suicide bomber fanatics. Al Qaeda sends in better-trained men to help coordinate and run the show down there.'

The XO, a lieutenant colonel, added, 'Your sources say that both houses are full right now?'

'Sources, as in plural, and not just some joker off the street with a grudge against his neighbor and looking for a quick cash payout?' The colonel stared at the map, his mind running through the options.

'A good source that we have used before, and a separate

backup. Both are locals.' The intel officer had vetted the information carefully before presenting it. The last thing he needed was some turncoat informant giving false information at this point. The backup source not only confirmed the information but added a sense of urgency. It was authentic, and the aerial recon photos showed men moving in and out of the houses.

'Colonel, we estimate maybe twenty-five fighters are in each house. They filter them out a few at a time as more come in. As we have suspected, Hargatt is a major stop on the insurgents' underground railroad to get fresh fighters and arms into Baghdad.'

Withrow remained cautious. The Juba mission was still paramount, but this was a golden opportunity. His overall mission would continue long after the Juba situation was gone, and bringing down these two houses and bagging fifty bad guys would chop a major insurgent resupply line. Still, it might compromise the other thing.

'Okay.' He made a decision. 'Now that we have the informants' material, I want some American eyes on it for confirmation. Send two scout-sniper teams out to recon on both target buildings and report back.'

'Why not use those special ops types who are after Juba? They look pretty competent.'

'This doesn't have anything to do with Juba. If he happens to be in one of those houses, then we take him, too. Task Force Trident doesn't need to know everything we do.'

'Yes, sir.'

The colonel ordered, 'Get your planners busy. The sniper teams go in as soon as it's dark enough. They are not to engage, just scout out the houses and report back.

If the targets are valid, then we roll out and hit both places at 0500.'

The XO was in total agreement. He, too, was tired of getting punched around without striking back. 'What kind of force, sir?'

'A full package on each house. Abrams on the corners, Bradleys bring in the infantry, with Apache choppers overhead. Way up overhead, I want a couple of flyboys with smart bombs targeted to those places in case things go to shit.'

'What about the Tridents? We told Swanson they would be kept in the loop.'

'And they will. They will be notified if and when we are ready to roll. Right now, we are just trying to gather actionable intelligence on some insurgent strongholds. Get to it.'

HARGATT

An M40A1 rifle, the exquisite weapon of U.S. Marine snipers, lay on an unzipped gun bag on a table in the commander's kitchen. Juba picked it up gently and made sure the safety on the right side of the receiver was fully to the rear before handling it further. Satisfied, he observed that a lightweight oil covered the surfaces instead of normal lubricating grease and breakfree, which tended to hold grit in desert climates. Then he disassembled it on a clean cloth.

He depressed the bolt stop in front of the trigger and pulled the bolt straight back to remove it and check the inner surfaces. Clean as a whistle.

'We took it from a Marine sniper who died in a road-side ambush, and we have not disturbed it,' said the commander. 'A gift for you.'

At first glance, it seemed the weapon had been well cared for and protected. That meant it had been cleaned with a .30 cal bore brush from the receiver end, not the muzzle end. No pits in the muzzle or dents or bulges in the twenty-four-inch stainless steel barrel. The chamber, the entire bolt assembly, the receiver, the Winchester modified Model 70 floor plate, the sling swivels, the magazine follower, and the spring, trigger, and trigger guard had been tenderly handled with soft patches and brushes and cotton swabs. The springs were taut, the stock was free of cracks, the bottom of the barrel had been shoe-shined with a cloth, and the Pachmayr recoil pad was new. The bolt slid freely when he put it all back together. He put the safety off and pulled the trigger to check the hammer fall. No trigger creep.

It was almost as if a Marine armorer had handed him the 7.62 mm rifle. Fresh ammunition was plentiful, with each round to be loaded individually. The rifle could hold up to five bullets, but in action, the sniper would put one in the chamber, leave three in the magazine, and then, after three shots, stop and reload. Never let it run dry. A ten-power Unertyl scope crowned the package, and its lens was still pristine although it had been kept in the bag.

The weapon seemed to be asking to be set free of the confining gun case and allowed to kill. It had to have put five rounds within a three-inch shot group at a distance of three hundred yards just to get out of the armorer's shed. Up to a thousand yards, the M40A1 was considered by many to be the best sniper rifle in the world, and this one was aching to do its job of killing people. Juba approved.

'Now I have a task for you and this beautiful new rifle,' said the commander. 'We are finishing a massive trap for the Americans, two entire houses that are filled with explosives that will be triggered by remote control. Earlier, we led a couple of men whom we know to be informants for the Crusaders to believe that the houses are secret rest stops and rendezvous points for jihadist fighters headed toward Baghdad. Those dogs went running to their masters with the news.'

Juba looked puzzled. 'You want me to kill a couple of informants? You can do that with your own men. I do not want to risk exposure for such minor targets.'

The commander chucked. 'Oh, no. No, indeed, my friend. If the Americans operate with their usual thoroughness, they will want to confirm what was said on their own before committing to an attack. We have watched this before. Air reconnaissance will not work, so they most likely will send in scouts to validate the information. These men are invisible and move like ghosts.'

'Scout-sniper teams,' said Juba. 'A spotter and a shooter working together, probably one team for each suspect house, probably tonight.'

'Yes. I want you to find them all. Kill them all. Use this weapon.' The commander put his hand on the M40A1 and gave it a friendly pat.

Juba winced. *Shit, now I have to clean it again.* 'May I suggest an alternative, Commander? It is an old custom in your part of the world to leave one victim alive to carry tales of horror back to his army. Suppose I kill just three, and then you have women desecrate the bodies with long knives. We make the fourth man watch and then throw him out on the road so he can be found by the Americans. They will be absolutely enraged. If your goal is to lure them in to attack those houses, you can bet they will be coming hard. But I will not take part in that fight.'

The commander looked hard at Juba. Brilliant and bloody-minded, extremely proficient and totally mad. He clapped his hands with enthusiasm. 'Yes. We will do it. Darkness will be on us soon.'

COB SPEICHER

Colonel Withrow was waiting four hours later when a Humvee ambulance with the big red crosses painted on the sides rolled up to the hospital. Doctors and nurses were ready to work, but when they loaded the young soldier onto the wheeled gurney to get him into the operating theater, Withrow put out his hand. 'Stop,' he commanded in a soft voice.

The soldier was the spotter for one of the scout-sniper teams sent into the town, the only survivor, and although he was covered in purple and yellow bruises, he had lived through the experience. A lump the size of an orange surrounded his closed right eye from where he had been clobbered. The problems were not physical but mental, and he was in shock. Tears carved paths in the greasepaint on his face. He looked up with his one good eye and recognized Withrow.

'Sir, they butchered them. We never got near that house. The bastards *butchered* them, sir!'

A patrol on the outskirts of Hargatt had found him

wandering on the road, beaten and dazed, wearing only his pants and boots. The colonel saw the circle welts of cigarette burns on his chest. Rope burns around the biceps and wrists. Trigger finger broken.

'Try to tell me what happened, son.'

'It's that fucking Juba, sir. We never saw him coming. He's crazy good.'

'Easy. Details, please.' The colonel looked at a doctor standing there with a syringe of painkiller and shook his head. Not yet. This was too important, and the boy wanted to talk.

The soldier also shook his head at the doctor. He had to report. Had to. 'Jenkins and I were doing our thing, Colonel, and everything went fine from the drop-off from the tank until we were about thirty minutes into the village. We found a drainage ditch and were crawling up the block, with no lights on anywhere. Really, really dark. Then Jenk ducked under a little bridge, had to hold his breath in that crappy water, and when he popped up the other side there was a single shot and Jenk took it in the head. I managed to snake down under the bridge to pull the body back, but somebody came up and coldcocked me. Knocked me out cold.'

The colonel closed his eyes and patted the scout on the shoulder. Fucking Juba. 'Then what?'

'I came to in the street, aw, Jesus, sir, it was awful.'

'Come on. I need to know.'

'Three bodies were piled up, and somebody flashed a light so I could identify the faces. Jenk, Tony White, and Ian Grable, and they all were obviously dead. I saw a lot of shadows milling around them, as if waiting for something. That's when I actually saw Juba! He told me in

British English that everyone had been waiting for me to wake up. They had shoved a gag in my mouth so I couldn't scream, and Juba went behind me and held my head so that I had to watch what happened next. You know that scream that Muslim tribal women do, that quick *la-la-la-la* tongue clicking? Well, that started up and got loud, like it was some kind of celebration, and then a few more lights were turned on.'

The words were pouring out, as if the soldier believed that by telling the story he might force it from his mind. The colonel knew, though, that there was a good chance the boy would see the same scene every night for the rest of his life. Still, despite the horror, his training had kicked in, and he was giving a good, solid report before accepting medical treatment.

'Old women, sir, and young girls and mothers. Just women. They fell on those bodies like a pack of wolves, stripped them naked, and then went to work with big sharp knives, cutting and cutting . . .' The tears started again. 'They cut off Jenk's head and threw it at me. They flayed chunks of skin and meat from all of them and hacked off arms and feet. Men were laughing and encouraging the women. Then somebody hit me hard on the head again and I was zonked, thank God. Next thing I know, I was being helped toward the sound of a Bradley that was idling behind a patrol. The ragheads shoved me into the street and left. Sir, I'm sorry. I fucked up and got them all killed.'

The colonel motioned to the doctor, and the needle punched into the soldier's arm. As the sedative took hold and the eyelids fluttered, Withrow took the boy's hand. 'Bullshit, trooper. None of this was your fault.'

The patient was rolled away, and Withrow stepped back and stood silently for a moment before turning around. The XO was there, as were Kyle Swanson and Sybelle Summers. 'We're going to go get those bodies,' said the colonel. 'Bastards wanted my attention, and now they have it. Nobody does this to my people.'

Swanson had listened to the young soldier talk. He also had reached his limit.

29

The colonel had made his decision and was not going to change it. The escalating violence in Hargatt had nullified the forty-eight-hour deal he had made with Kyle Swanson. Withrow had to plug this bleeding sore before Hargatt, and perhaps Tikrit, fell back into their old, bad ways and the locals lost confidence that the Americans would respond. Another Fallujah was looming out there.

'We can't wait any longer, people,' he told the small group in his office. 'There is no time for collecting and analyzing information. We are going to hit those houses hard with a full company package on each one: tanks, Bradleys, and Apaches. If that fucking sniper opens up, we will send the Abrams tanks after him and crush the son of a bitch into the rubble. Apache gunships will hose down the escape routes.'

'There will be substantial collateral damage, sir,' reminded the XO.

Colonel Withrow's face was an angry shade of red, remembering what the women had done in cutting up the snipers. 'Right now, I don't give a shit. As far as I am concerned, anyone still in the area will be considered to be enemy combatants. Those suspect houses are seeping hatred like spreading cancers and *I ... WANT ...*

THEM . . . DEAD !!'

Kyle Swanson stared at the latest map pinned to the wall of the office and let his thoughts jump ahead to the action planned around the two houses that were circled in red. Four massive M1A2 Abrams tanks would lead the charge through the streets just before dawn and advance to within a hundred yards of each corner of a house, blasting away with their 120 mm smoothbore cannons. A dozen Bradley Fighting Vehicles with Bushmaster chain guns buzzing would then swarm forward and disgorge three platoons of infantrymen, or 'dismounts' in cavalry talk. Support vehicles would zoom into the area on the ground while the Apaches roamed overhead. Brute force.

'Mr. Swanson? You disagree?' The colonel was almost daring Kyle to challenge him.

'No, sir. It's your show. If you get him, we will go in afterward and try to find his information. He doesn't have to be alive for that.' Kyle disagreed a lot, but there was no use butting heads on this one. The sniper deaths and torture had set off a firestorm of reaction. It could not wait any longer.

'Very well. You and your people can go along with us in a support capacity.' Withrow turned to his XO and intelligence staff and planners. 'We launch at 0500 hours. Remember, no man left.'

As Kyle and Sybelle walked back to the special ops area, he looked up at the crescent moon, then at his wristwatch. It was thirty minutes past one in the morning. Not much time. 'You're coming with me,' he said. It wasn't a question.

'Yeah,' she answered. 'Of course.'

*

Sybelle and Kyle spoke with the rest of the team while saddling up to go into Hargatt and finish the recon job and see what else they might turn up. The rest of the team would cover for their absence in case the Army started asking questions. Then Captain Rick Newman would join one of the strike packages for the predawn raid, and Travis Hughes would ride along with the second one.

A blacked-out Humvee driven by Newman pulled up to the camp's front gate fifteen minutes later, with Hughes in the shotgun seat with the radios. Crouched unseen in the back were Kyle and Sybelle, dressed in local clothing, and Rawls and Tipp, whose faces were covered with greasepaint and who wore black combat clothing beneath their web gear.

'It's dangerous out there in the dark, Captain,' warned the corporal who checked them through the gate. 'You guys be careful.'

'Thanks, Corporal. We are just going to do a quick recon of the main road up to the intersection. See what we can see. Be back in about fifteen minutes.'

From the depths of the sprawling camp behind them, everyone could hear the rumble of the big tracked vehicles moving about and getting arranged for the morning's attack. Fuel and ammo were loading.

Newman kept a steady speed up to the intersection, where he made a three-point turn and drove right back the way he had come down the road, at the same speed. During the turn, the four people in the rear tumbled out of the doors and lay still. Joe Tipp and Darren Rawls belly-crawled up to the mud wall that had shielded Juba the previous day and swung into an observation position, ready to go in and support Swanson and Summers if necessary.

Kyle and Sybelle went into the jagged window of Juba's first hide and waited to see if anyone had reacted to the passing of the Humvee. There was no clatter of running men, no shooting, no bright lights, but the air was thick with tension and there was a steady undercurrent of quiet noise. As their senses adjusted to the night, they could make out the sounds of people moving and some low talking. They flipped down the night vision goggles and slid out the front entrance and into the shadows at the edge of the town. Suddenly, it seemed as if some giant had kicked over an anthill and streams of green ants were moving everywhere. Both recognized the familiar prebattle scene. Everyone in the area knew the Americans would be coming in with deadly force soon, and refugees were getting out of the way. Men, women, and children were shuffling along, carrying a few belongings, looking to get into the perceived safety of Tikrit before the American tsunami arrived.

It made the job of Kyle and Sybelle a bit easier, for with so much movement, no one would notice just a little bit more. Things were being kicked, and people were bumping into objects and each other, talking in low tones, but never stopping in their flight. Making a little noise was not a problem for the two snipers, and they removed the goggles, tucked their weapons and gear beneath their flowing clothing, and stepped into the tail end of the sporadic march, allowing the surge of frightened refugees to carry them straight into the middle of town. Sybelle wore a scarf over her head.

Rounding a corner in the thickest part of the village, the line of refugees bent to the right as it approached a couple of armed guards standing in the street and waving the villagers to the side. Kyle and Sybelle did not break stride or look at the men, but when they were about twenty yards beyond the guards, they swerved into a tight alley and pulled out silenced pistols. They had reached the first suspect house and anticipated that it would be bulging with insurgents, but it wasn't. Sticking with the shadows, they split up and circled the structure and still saw only the two guards out front.

Sybelle pointed to her eyes and then the building. *Look inside.*

Swanson went off in a low trot to the rear wall, and she covered him. He crouched and put his night goggles back on and let his eyes adjust to the strange glow before standing up, pressing his back against the wall, and slowly peering around the edge of the open window. He inhaled deeply then waved to Sybelle, who ran to join him.

'The place is empty, but you get that smell?' he whispered.

She took a breath. 'Gasoline fumes. Chemicals.'

Kyle levered himself into the window and balanced on the sill but did not drop inside. There was a nightmare collection of explosives stacked around the walls, ready to blow. Cans of gasoline, boxes of ammunition and grenades, bricks of C-4, and a collection of artillery shells were all ready to obey the spark that would explode it all. Looking at the door, he could see no thin wires stretched taut, awaiting the boot of an American soldier coming in. No wires around the windowsill. The bodies of the three Americans were stacked in the middle of the ground floor.

He dropped back outside. 'No insurgent troops in

there, but a hell of a lot of explosives and it doesn't seem to be booby-trapped,' he told Sybelle. 'Looks like they want to get a bunch of Americans in the middle of the place before setting it off. Let's go check the other one.'

This time it took about a half hour to make their way to the target building because the line of refugees was thinning out and it was dangerous to continue to use the streets. The best way to go house-to-house was out one window and into the window of the home next door. With the buildings standing empty, progress was clumsy and tiring but uneventful, and they got there unseen by any rooftop observers.

Two guards were at the front of the second house, too, and another circled the building at random. Swanson and Summers squeezed into a shadowed alcove, and when the sentry disappeared around the corner, Kyle ran to the building and looked inside. He did not expect to find anyone looking back, and he was back with her in fifteen seconds. 'Same thing,' he said. 'Damn big bomb. Let's back off and call it in.'

They were both sweating by the time they found a safe zone about halfway between the two houses. It was four o'clock when Sybelle got on the Trident secure radio link back to the observation post, where Joe Tipp relayed the message back to Camp Speicher.

Captain Newman was standing beside a Bradley, drinking lukewarm coffee, when his earpiece buzzed. He listened intently, dumped the coffee, and jogged up to the command track, throwing a quick salute to Colonel Withrow.

'Colonel, Captain Summers and Swanson just reported in, sir. They are inside Hargatt and report that both of the suspect buildings are stacked to the rafters with explosives. It's a trap, sir, to draw us in and blow up the buildings right in our faces. The bodies of the three snipers are in the first house, probably booby-trapped.'

'Your people are in the town?' The colonel looked at Newman in surprise. 'You let them go in without telling me first?'

'We had a tip about Juba, sir. They just decided to finish the recon on the houses along the way when they saw an opportunity. Lots of refugees are moving out and covered their approach.' Newman and Withrow both knew that was a lie, but it was a discreet way out of the problem.

'Swanson recommends strongly that you hold off on entering the town for a little while longer but make a big feint at first light, growling about on the outskirts to draw the attention of any fighters who are still there. That will help him and Summers continue snooping.'

The colonel looked at his XO and a smile creased his leathery face. 'Well, I'll be damned. Okay, we'll do it.'

A soft dawn spread over the quiet town. The streets were empty, the shops closed; the last of the refugees had padded away. The insurgent commander and Juba stood atop the distant rooftop of the commander's home, watching the storm build.

'Here they come!' said the commander. 'They are so predictable.'

The ground vibrated as the mighty armored armada waddled down the roads approaching the village, throwing up clouds of sand in its wake. The monstrous Abrams tanks fanned out from single file into one long row and took their time parking wheel to wheel, and the

Bradley Fighting Vehicles maneuvered behind them in V-formations. Overhead, Apache gunships swung around to the west of town, darting close, then withdrawing to a safer and higher distance. Behind the armor came marching columns of infantrymen who wheeled about and spread out, almost in parade formation. A task force was on the move.

'Is this what you wanted?' Juba asked. 'You think you can stop all that?'

'I do not intend to stop it, my friend. Let them come in. I want them to try to retrieve those bodies. We have a few fighters planted around to deliver just enough fire to channel the Americans toward the two houses. When their soldiers fight their way inside, the houses detonate on them. It shall be a great victory, praise Allah.'

Juba's more practiced military eyes saw what the commander did not. All of that armor out there snarling at the gates was not actually doing anything but making a lot of noise. The Abrams normally operated in violent but precise choreography, and their crews were extra-ordinarily well trained with the machines. Now they were having difficulty *parking* the damned things? Not bloody likely. And all that marching, like some old army forming up in a straight line for an attack? The hair on his neck prickled, as if touched by a cold hand. This was, somehow, Swanson at work.

'Bingo,' said Kyle. 'I got the spotter. On the roof of that building five doors down on the diagonal street to our left.'

Sybelle checked the rooftop through the scope on her rifle and caught the sunlight flickering off the lenses of a set of binos. 'Uh-huh. He's got a good view of both places from there and is safe, back out of the attack zone. Has to be the triggerman.'

'Yeah. Let's go get him.'

They squirmed out of their hide in the back of an abandoned house, checked the outside, and went into a cautious lope alongside the walls. The place had the look of a movie set, lots of empty buildings but no activity. Still, they took their time and proceeded with great caution: stop, observe, assess, move.

The building was a three-story affair of concrete blocks, with the third story added much later to the original structure. It leaned slightly to the right, and mortar had oozed out between the bricks before drying. A shop was on the first floor, and residences probably were above it. They stopped for almost ten minutes and waited in silence, watching for movement inside.

'There has to be a guard in there,' whispered Kyle. 'Just can't see him.'

Sybelle handed him her rifle and got her local clothes back in order with the scarf over her hair and a veil pulled across the lower part of her face. 'I got it.' She stood and walked along the side of the building, stepping boldly through the front door.

The guard was seated in a straight chair, leaning against the wall of the shop with his AK-47 balanced on his lap. He looked up at her silhouette in the doorway and barked, 'Woman, what are you . . .'

Sybelle whipped the pistol up from her side and shot him twice in the face, and Kyle came ducking inside at the soft coughs of the silencer. They rotated through the cluttered store, finding no one else, and Swanson pointed to the stairs. Sybelle took a moment to step out of the cumbersome gown and scarf and followed Kyle up.

A closed door was at the head of the short staircase, and Swanson eased it open. He went to the right and Sybelle went left. Nothing. There was only one other room. With Sybelle covering, Kyle pushed hard through the closed door, and it flew open but did not bounce off the wall. He immediately double-tapped two rounds through it, and the guard hiding behind the door gave a little cry of pain and surprise and toppled to the floor, where Kyle shot him in the head.

They moved on. The third floor was empty, and when they crawled up to the roof, they saw the triggerman standing nine feet away, exposed in the morning sunshine, binoculars to his eyes, watching the sideshow being put on by the rumbling beasts of Task Force Steel. Kyle Swanson kicked him behind the knees and jerked back on his head at the same time, forcing a fall. As soon as the surprised man was on the deck and out of sight from the street, Kyle shot him in the eye and dragged the dead man inside. Sybelle jumped over the corpse, swept up two cell phones that lay side by side on the top of the wall, and also hurried back through the door.

Inside, she examined them as gently as if they were diamonds. Normally, a cell phone used as a trigger would be predialed to a number and the operator only had to press the SEND button to complete the circuit. 'Whoa, girl,' she said to herself. 'Easy does it.'

'Look at this, Kyle,' she said, pointing to the \ and ⋎ marks scrawled in black greasepaint on the faces of the phones. 'The Arabic symbols for 'one' and 'two.' Got to be the houses.'

'Good to go,' Swanson said. 'I checked this guy out and he's nobody. Probably a midlevel type who could be trusted with just enough responsibility to carry out this job, but I doubt if he had anything to do with the planning.'

'So how do we get higher up the food chain?' she asked.

Kyle grinned. 'Let's blow some shit up and see who comes calling.'

'Oo-rah,' said Sybelle, picking up the number two phone. She pushed down on the SEND button.

The entire town seemed to jump on its foundations as a bright and blinding flash of light ignited like the wink of a miniature sun and was followed by a deafening, crashing roar. The three outside guards were swallowed in a hell of fireballs that cometed into the sky and rolled out into the street while debris scythed through the air, chopping at everything in its path. Then came the rolling concussion, giant fists slamming across the landscape and splintering windows.

Swanson and Summers were burrowed in the corner against the interior wall when the concussion rolled through with freight-train power. Rafters sagged and plaster cracked. Toys and dishes and furniture tumbled around, and they breathed through open mouths to equalize the pressure pounding at their ears. A flying lamp cracked Sybelle on the head hard enough to make her see stars, and Kyle was punched in the gut by a table leg.

When the initial explosion was done, a secondary series of smaller detonations began cooking off with loud booms, and when Kyle and Sybelle finally crawled outside on the roof, they saw that the target building was utterly gone, leaving behind a blackened hole in the ground from which smoke rose in filthy columns. Destruction ringed it. Dozens of U.S. troops might have been killed in a raid on the place.

Three blocks away, the commander of the insurgents was knocked flat by the explosion and jumped back to his feet with a shout of exasperation and fury. 'He set it off too early! That stupid, ignorant son of a whore! The Americans are not even in the streets yet and now they have been warned! I am going over there and kill him myself!'

Juba laughed. 'You're a fool. If you go out there, the only one who will die is you. Your crude ambush attempt is over.'

The commander spun around in anger. 'Don't call me a fool! You cannot accept the hospitality of my home and then dare to insult me! Do not forget that it is you, Juba, who is under my protection, not the other way around.' The bearded man vaulted down the stairs, grabbed an AK-47, and sprinted toward the triggerman's building, trailed by a bodyguard.

Juba raised his eyes and looked beyond the edge of the village at the armored vehicles bumping about over a couple of miles of ground. Nothing but a feint. *Shake*, he thought. *Getting closer.*

Couple of guys running this way, and they don't look too happy,' said Sybelle, peering around the edge of the door.

'Right.' Swanson dug a finger into each phone and levered out the batteries and then smashed the instruments with hard stomps of his boots. 'Let them come in and we grab them.'

The insurgent commander was the first through the door, and he was allowed to rush into the center of the room, but when the bodyguard crossed the threshold, Sybelle clocked him hard in the mouth with the butt of her M-4. His head snapped back, his feet flew out from beneath him, and he collapsed. At the same time, Swanson launched onto the commander's back and rode him to the floor, rolled him over, and popped him hard on an ear to daze him. By the time the man collected his senses, a strip of duct tape was across his mouth, plastic flexicuffs ensnared his wrists behind his back, and more duct tape had been wound around his ankles. Between the colors and shapes dancing in his eyes, he saw that the bodyguard was sprawled unconscious, also being wrapped like a mummy in black duct tape.

'You speak English?' Kyle asked, peeling back the tape across the mouth just enough to let the man speak.

'Who are you?' The words came out in a garble, as if he were talking around a cigar.

Kyle slapped him hard. 'I ask the questions.'

The commander shook his head. He understood the seriousness of the situation. His attempt to trap the Americans had failed, the town had been penetrated, the remaining explosives would be neutralized, and he had been captured. The plan to bleed the Americans badly and write the name of this village in the annals of resistance had failed. Without his leadership, his fighters would fade to other locations and the village would return to peace.

'I will tell you nothing,' the commander grumbled. 'Nothing.'

'Then you are of no value to me.' Kyle stood, took out his pistol, and fired a shot that ripped away part of the man's ear. The commander jerked at the pain and the impact. 'Last chance,' Swanson said.

Sybelle spoke. 'Kyle. Hold on. No use wasting more time on him. He may have some intel, but the interrogators will wring it out of him. Let's just leave them tied up here while we go find Juba.'

The commander looked strangely at them and shook his head vigorously, grunting for attention. Kyle lifted the tape again.

'Now you suddenly got something to tell me?'

The man bounced his head in understanding. 'The woman just called you by the name of Kyle. Are you the Swanson Marine?'

'Maybe.' Kyle ripped the gag all the way off with a swift pull that yanked out patches of beard.

'If you are, then I can tell you exactly the location of your enemy, my friend Juba. He wants you to find him,

345

Swanson Marine,' said the commander, a slit of a smile on his bloody face. Here was a chance to repay Juba for calling him a fool. Maybe both of them would die. 'He is waiting just down that street.'

Juba was in a mouse hole. Over the past few days, he had used some of the idle hours in the commander's home to create a unique sniper's hide, oriented along the most likely line of approach, and now he crawled into a prone position and made himself comfortable.

The moment was finally approaching, and without realizing it, he had started losing perspective. He was so intent on killing Kyle Swanson that his thoughts rejected anything but that one goal. The smart play was to leave now and fight somewhere else, some other day, but he wanted to finish it here. Never would he have a better opportunity. Swanson had to come up that single road and straight into the crosshairs.

Each decision he made now contained a trade-off, because a defender cannot defend against everything. The situation he had created was imperfect, for a mouse hole opening was so narrow that the shooter could not remain too far back in the darkness. The muzzle of Juba's rifle was no more than a foot behind the opening.

Nevertheless, arranging a battlefield of his choice had been important, for Swanson would have to be the one risking exposure. The biggest advantage was Juba's intimate knowledge of his enemy, the operational concepts of a sniper and the combat habits. He could get inside of Swanson's head and think along with his adversary.

Juba had opened all the windows in the three-story house and pulled the curtains almost closed so they would flap in the air. He chipped out several cinder blocks up high as decoy hides and stacked another dummy emplacement on the roof behind a barricade of loose wood. A sheltered animal pen stood to one side of the house. Swanson would have to be wary of all of them and might make a mistake while doing the recon. Snipers always scan a target house from top to bottom, and the higher the defender's position, the more it stands out and the more likely it is to draw attention. The mouse hole was only on the fourth row of cinder blocks up from the foundation of the house, below eye level. Juba would be watching for a slight movement of a rifle and a scope as Swanson ranged over the possible hides higher in the building, an advantage of a few microseconds.

An added bonus was the spider hole. Almost every house in Iraq had a small pit in which a family could seek shelter if and when bullets started flying outside. Juba's position was right beside the hole that had been constructed below the commander's home, which normally was kept covered by a small door and a rug. Once in the pit, there was a narrow tunnel some twenty feet long that led away to a dry well next door as an emergency escape route.

Juba had rolled away the rug and removed the wooden hatch to leave the hole uncovered. He placed the computer in the backpack and laid it on the far side of the hole. Once again, he had downloaded the important information on the memory stick as a backup, and the small device was in his breast pocket.

It was going to be a one-shot battle, and whoever fired first probably would win – but that shot had to score. Otherwise the advantage, however miniscule, switched to the other sniper. Juba would be patient, take the critical shot, and then grab the backpack, roll into the spider hole, and leave. Shoot and scoot, the American snipers called it.

He racked a round into the chamber of the M40A1 and settled behind his scope to wait.

They wrapped both of the captured men tightly in rings of duct tape. A hand-drawn map of the area had been pulled from the commander's pocket, and Sybelle and Kyle spread it on the floor, compared it with their own maps, and worked out the grid coordinates of the house where Juba was said to wait.

'I don't like this *High Noon*, mano-a-mano bullshit,' Sybelle said. 'The guy is too good.'

'Hey, I never said that I want a quick-draw contest. He's the one fixated on taking my scalp to show he's the baddest sniper around. That ego is forcing him to stay put instead of hauling ass.' Kyle sat on the floor, with his legs crossed and his M40A1 resting in the crook of his right arm. 'I just want to kill the bastard any way we can.'

Sybelle, down on one knee, brushed some hair back from her eyes. She was sweating, and it was still morning. 'You're not going to play fair?'

'Nope. Never happen. As much as I definitely want to personally blow him away, we have a lot of other gadgets in our toolbox.'

When he explained his plan, Sybelle relayed the orders back to the task force.

The big armored force that had been moving awkwardly suddenly fell into exact positions and nosed casually into the village streets, heading in to secure the area, disarm the remaining house lined with explosives, and retrieve the bodies of its dead soldiers. Sporadic small arms fire whanged off the thick armor plate and was answered with booming cannons and machine guns.

Fifty thousand feet overhead, a strange-looking toothpick of an aircraft received new commands from its controller on the ground at Balad Air Base and tipped over to descend to a lower altitude. The MQ-9 Reaper hunter-killer unmanned aerial vehicle had been on station for nine hours and had plenty of fuel left. It wore a pair of GBU-12 Paveway II laser-guided six-hundred-pound smart bombs beneath its wings.

'Let's do it,' Kyle said. 'You go high and paint the building, and I stay down on the dirt to draw his attention.'

Sybelle gave him a long look. 'Take it easy out there, pardner. And remember we have exactly fifteen minutes, not a second more. Do *not* go in that building.' Then she rolled through a side window and was gone.

Kyle gave her a minute's head start and then went out the back door, hooked a left, and ran across the road and into a doorway. The rumble of the approaching tanks and Bradleys shook the stones on the surrounding streets, and Kyle used that to mask the noise of breaking windows and jumping to the adjoining house. Juba's hideout was no more than a thousand yards away, an easy shot for either of them.

As planned, a Bradley Fighting Vehicle suddenly came around a corner on the far side of the building, scraped alongside it in passing, and then screamed down the street at high speed, crunching over an automobile parked in its way. Kyle ran to another building on the right-hand side of the street and dove through the door. Good diversion. Juba had to feel the hard whack of the armored vehicle against the side of his house. *Surprise the enemy. Force him to conform to your plan.*

As soon as the Bradley passed, Sybelle lobbed a smoke grenade down from the roof of a nearby building, and it bounced once in the street before igniting. Kyle let the gray blossom smolder and spread, then sprinted back across and climbed a low wall. He was about eight hundred yards away now. Close enough. He went inside the building and spent time clearing both floors and checking his watch. He had less than ten minutes left.

He pushed an eating table close to the rear wall opposite the window facing up the street and began stacking up a pile of pillows, then fronting it with overturned furniture to break up any regular lines. The sun was on the back side of the building, at an angle that did neither sniper any good, other than keeping them obscured in darkness.

Kyle pulled up a solid wood chair behind the table, sat down, and found a comfortable and firm rest for his sniper rifle, with the muzzle poking through the lattice-work of debris. He pulled the weapon back, checked the load, and pushed it forward again. His eye went to the scope.

Sybelle's progress had been easier. After throwing the smoke grenade, she took a roundabout route over rooftops and through houses, then angled back to the target zone. An Apache gunship hovered a few blocks away, securing her flanks and back. No one shot at her.

She went prone when she reached a rooftop on the left

side of Juba's location, cleared it for safety, and clicked her radio as the helicopter swung into a new protective position.

'Good to go,' she said. A double click meant that Kyle had heard her message and was also in position.

Putting her rifle to her left side and laying her pistol within easy reach on the right, Sybelle removed a small monocular from a rubberized carrying case. Since she had been working as Kyle's spotter, she had packed along the laser rangefinder, which now had another use.

She edged her eyes above the top of the small revetment running along the edge of the roof and had a clear view of the cream-colored target house. Bringing up the monocular, she focused and pushed the switch to activate an invisible laser beam, which bounced off the sturdy target house and came back to the electronics packet with an exact reading. She secured it into a firm position. 'Target is painted,' she reported, and at Balat Air Base, the controller linked the information to the circling Reaper UAV, which then descended another ten thousand feet. From that point on, Sybelle's laser was married to the Reaper's guidance system. Where the point of the laser rested, the bombs would hit.

'Confirming that target is lit and weapon is armed,' came the voice from Balat. 'Three minutes.'

Juba let his breathing slow and felt his heart beating normally in his chest, not thumping with excitement. This was his house. This was his safe zone. And he was Juba! He was the Sword of the Prophet, and he intended to become an even sharper sword by brewing the terrible poison gas! He let the scope run down the street to where the American troops and vehicles surrounded the other house of explosives. They had gone in and nothing had happened, so the trap had not been sprung. Both the triggerman and the commander were probably dead by now, but that was beside the point.

Kyle Swanson might be somewhere in that milling crowd of American soldiers, and while Juba could have shot several of them with ease, the only person he wanted in his crosshairs was his old nemesis, Shake. Since Swanson always liked to be in on the action, maybe he was down there checking out the strange bomb.

Juba's trigger finger tightened momentarily when a figure in black walked across the scope, but it wasn't Swanson. He eased off and kept searching, facing the target zone, in his hide, waiting like a patient spider.

No, Swanson would not be down there. He was stalking, coming closer. The unexpected, noisy passing of the Bradley and then the smoke grenade was enough confirmation. Up in one of those many windows facing him on a street filled with buildings and homes? Low on the ground beneath a bunch of junk? A doorway? A shadow? He moved the scope slowly across the most likely danger zones.

Swanson studied the various openings in the Juba building. The shitbird knew his business and could be in any one of those places except on the roof, where the helicopter would have taken him out. Slow and steady scan, top to bottom, left to right. He couldn't fire without a target because the first shot would give away his position and draw a return bullet in instant retaliation.

The radio spoke to him again. 'One minute.' Out of

time. He could put down the rifle and let the bomb take care of it, but hell, he *did* have some pride invested in this hunt to the death. He cursed himself for even thinking about something that ridiculous. Who is the better sniper? Horseshit. Nobody cares. Whoever walks away is better. Keep the scope moving. Nothing. Nothing.

Juba thought about saying a prayer. No. Stay focused. The butt stock of the rifle was cool against his right cheek. Plenty of time to pray later. *Where would I be hiding if I was Shake?* That window looked a bit curious. The others had ordinary lines in the rooms behind them. The shadows in this one seemed jagged and jumbled, as if a storm had passed through. A hide?

The impersonal voice in Kyle's headset said, 'Weapon free. Weapon released.' The big GBU-12 fell away, and the Reaper jumped higher at the sudden subtraction of weight and then curled back onto its course. There was no pilot getting tired, and the controllers at the base would simply swap off to a fresh shift as soon as this job was done and the UAV would perform some other job, somewhere else.

The bomb was in free fall, with big fins on the rear providing lift and the four smaller fins on the front allowing the guidance unit to steer it. The internal guidance system locked on to the laser beam that Sybelle had affixed to the side of the house and transitioned the control services from simple ballistics into a precise line-of-sight flight path. The bomb twisted into a smooth spiral motion, gaining speed as it plummeted nose down toward the target.

Kyle took up the slack on the trigger and held it so as not to require that extra fraction of a second if he found the target. Then he saw dark against darker in the small hole left by a missing cinder block almost at ground level. *There! A movement!* A rifle muzzle was on him!

Their rifles fired at almost the same moment, but Kyle had been a hair faster.

His 7.62 mm bullet went through the mouse hole opening and struck Juba in the left cheek just as the terrorist pulled the trigger of his own weapon. Kyle's round bored in straight along the jawline, taking out a line of teeth and a chunk of the left side of Juba's face before shattering the jawbone and exiting.

The return shot had been deflected at the moment of firing, and Juba's bullet crashed into the wall just above Kyle's head.

In the mouse hole, Juba rolled away from the jarring pain, feeling as if his head had been torn off. *Kill shot*, he thought. He toppled into the spider hole, fighting to remain conscious to pull the wooden door into position. When it fell into place, he lay back with his hands holding his destroyed face and agony racking his body as blood rushed through his open wound. He could see the light of the tunnel beckoning, and began to crawl.

The heavy, speeding bomb smashed through the roof and penetrated the ceilings before the warhead detonated in the kitchen. Everything in the immediate vicinity was vaporized in a gigantic explosion, and the concussion blew the walls apart. Support beams and interior walls were torn to pieces, and the house collapsed into rubble, with thick layers of wood and dirt and junk piling up over the spider hole, sealing it shut and totally obscuring it from view. At the bottom lay a shredded computer.

Juba, bleeding heavily, was thrown against the walls of the narrow tunnel like a doll by the explosion. His head, already savaged, now felt like it was being kicked from his body, and his eardrums ruptured and began to bleed. His mouth and eyes filled with dirt, and when he cleared his vision, he saw that the frail walls of the tunnel were giving way and the light was disappearing. He put a hand to his breast and felt the slight bump of the memory stick secure in the pocket as the world collapsed about him.

Down the street, Kyle had been rocked from his chair by the explosion but quickly got up and went to the window. Fire had broken out in the wreckage of the house, and flames licked out of the mouse hole as a curtain of smoke climbed out of the rubble. He was satisfied. If he had not killed Juba, then the bomb had obliterated him. And with Juba gone, so was the formula and the overwhelming threat of the poison gas. Probably. He had to believe that.

Kyle put down his rifle and took a deep breath, staring at the scene of destruction. 'Burn in hell, motherfucker,' he said.

EPILOGUE

ABOARD THE VAGABOND

The white yacht was alone on this deep swath of the Atlantic Ocean, churning a lazy wake in the late afternoon. Kyle rested his elbows on the rail and watched with awe as a huge whale broke the surface of the sea, launched a third of its black bulk into the open air, and fell back with an immense force that threw curtains of water high into the air. Then it was gone, burrowing into the depths of the ocean, and the disturbed water on top settled back into a normal rhythm. An instant of action followed by a disappearance. *My kind of whale*, he thought and raised his beer in salute to the beast. A two-week holiday was just starting, and he felt good.

'What are you doing?' Delara Tabrizi joined him at the rail, and the sea breeze stirred her dark hair. The multilingual schoolteacher from Khorramshahr, Iran, was now the beautiful personal secretary of Lady Patricia Cornwell, well on her way to becoming a British citizen. The government was appreciative and discreet about her help on tracking the device that had struck London.

'Did you see that whale leap up a second ago?'

'Yes. We see them frequently out here, far from the shipping lanes.' Her voice was quiet, her British accent thicker. 'Amazing creatures. How can anyone put something like that into a tourist attraction?'

Kyle looked over at her. The brown eyes were devoid of worry, the lines of stress from the mission and her brushes with death were gone, and she wore slacks and a casual white blouse, with minimal makeup. She didn't need makeup, he decided. 'So you're okay?'

'I am fine,' she replied, and her voice was firm with decision. 'I think about my family, my former students, and my country. It's like that part of me is dead, and a new Delara is being created.'

Swanson laughed. 'I know the feeling.'

Delara blushed and also laughed, a hand shading her brown eyes. 'Oh! I forgot that Kyle Swanson is dead, too. You *do* know the feeling.'

'Yeah. Welcome to the club.'

'Lady Pat and Sir Jeff told me the story, Kyle. They swore me to secrecy, but since you are such a frequent visitor, and such an important part of their own lives, they felt that I should know your background. I am very sorry about Shari Towne. She sounds like a wonderful woman.'

'That she was. That she was.' *Such a long time ago,* he thought to himself. *Long time.*

One deck above them, Pat and Jeff were watching, drinks in hand. 'Couple of strong kids, healing,' Jeff said.

'Sir Geoffrey Cornwell, you are a blind old bat,' his wife said. She put a hand on his shoulder and leaned against him. 'Even you should be able to see the sparks flying between those two.'

'What? Patricia, they're not even standing very close together. Just having a friendly conversation.'

She smiled. 'Of course, dear. Right as always.'

BALI, INDONESIA

The dreams were a vivid new form of existence, sustained by strong opiates and undulating waves of soothing incense. Shiva, the destroyer, pursued, his four arms and the third eye and the hair of snakes. Then Shiva would dissolve into the golden-feathered Garuda with the bulging eyes and hooked beak, bringing some calm of the all-knowing Vishnu. A flash of pain, then more and stronger opiates and more horrible dreams. The pattern went on for a very long time as the mystery patient bordered on constant hallucination. The doctors at the special clinic wondered how he was still alive, shrugged, and went about their work.

Then one day, the weeks of massive facial and dental reconstruction were finally over, and the patient, his left eye blinded forever, was allowed to awaken. Only a week later, he was out of bed, walking the clean wooden floors of the clinic, helped by nurses, as bright sunlight played through long, slatted windows. Physical therapists guided the recovery, but the patient seemed to suck up pain and constantly pushed the boundaries of exhaustion, several times passing out from doing too much. Within a month he was walking on the nearby beach, alone, hobbling because of the broken leg, but determined to stride out strongly, and day by day, he got stronger. At night, he fell asleep to the noisy mumbles and chirps of jungle creatures and insects. He fed a curious gecko wall lizard, and it became his friend.

After a few months, he was moved from the clinic to a villa that overlooked a plain of rice paddies and forests that stepped down to the sea, and the medical specialists came to visit. Servants tended him and were amazed at his regimen of sit-ups, push-ups, crunches, running, martial arts exercises, and practice with knives and guns. He ate a perfect diet.

Two men who were not doctors came to the villa one day, wearing thin and decorated short-sleeved shirts over dark trousers. They did not remark on the partial paralysis around the mouth and jaw, or on the latticework of facial scars, or on the black patch over the left eye. 'We have a job,' one said.

'Excellent,' said Juba, who was tired of paradise. 'I'm ready.'

KILL ZONE
&
DEAD SHOT

SNIPER NOVELS

GUNNERY SGT **JACK COUGHLIN**, USMC (Ret.)
WITH **DONALD A. DAVIS**

PAN BOOKS

Kill Zone first published 2007 by St Martin's Press, New York
First published by Pan Books 2008
Dead Shot first published 2009 by St Martin's Press, New York
First published by Pan Books 2010

This omnibus first published 2011 by Pan Books
an imprint of Pan Macmillan, a division of Macmillan Publishers Limited
Pan Macmillan, 20 New Wharf Road, London N1 9RR
Basingstoke and Oxford
Associated companies throughout the world
www.panmacmillan.com

ISBN 978-0-330-54556-3

1 3 5 7 9 9 8 6 4 2

A CIP catalogue record for this book is available
from the British Library.

Printed in the UK by CPI Mackays, Chatham ME5 8TD

KILL
ZONE